W9-BLU-095
PINO

FROM A FRENCH CHATEAU OF INFAMY
Where a wanton noblewoman and her husband teach young André Lafabre the strength of his male beauty and the peril of the passions he arouses . . .

AND A VIETNAMESE PALACE OF INTRIGUE,
where a weak emperor plays into the hands of a sensual sorceress, and Prince Ahn Le, a royal nephew and the one man capable of saving the kingdom, gambles his future on a shocking marriage . . .

COME A HUMAN LEGACY OF POWER AND CORRUPTION
Louis, as handsome and irresistible as he is infinitely evil . . . Felise, enslaved by her need for one faithless man . . . Che Lan, hating his French blood and determined to wipe out its stain in rebellion . . . Paul, torn between East and West, and forced into an agonizing choice. . . .

THE IMMORTAL DRAGON

Never before has so much adventure, passion, intrigue, love, death, bloodshed and sex lit up the pages of a giant epic spellbinder.

THE IMMORTAL DRAGON

Michael Peterson

A SIGNET BOOK
NEW AMERICAN LIBRARY
TIMES MIRROR

PUBLISHER'S NOTE

This novel is a work of fiction. Names, characters, places, and incidents either are the product of the author's imagination or are used fictitiously, and any resemblance to actual persons, living or dead, events, or locales is entirely coincidental.

NAL BOOKS ARE AVAILABLE AT QUANTITY DISCOUNTS WHEN USED TO PROMOTE PRODUCTS OR SERVICES. FOR INFORMATION PLEASE WRITE TO PREMIUM MARKETING DIVISION, THE NEW AMERICAN LIBRARY, INC., 1633 BROADWAY, NEW YORK, NEW YORK 10019.

SIGNET TRADEMARK REG. U.S. PAT. OFF. AND FOREIGN COUNTRIES
REGISTERED TRADEMARK—MARCA REGISTRADA
HECHO EN CHICAGO, U.S.A.

SIGNET, SIGNET CLASSICS, MENTOR, PLUME, MERIDIAN AND NAL BOOKS are published by The New American Library, Inc., 1633 Broadway, New York, New York 10019

First Printing, July, 1983

1 2 3 4 5 6 7 8 9

PRINTED IN THE UNITED STATES OF AMERICA

Author's Note: The Dragon

Of the four symbolic animals which figure prominently in Vietnamese mythology—the dragon, the unicorn, the tortoise, and the phoenix—the dragon is the most important.

Dragons are immortal. They live beneath the earth, in the sea, or in the air, and though there are not many dragons, their number can increase because another fabulous creature—half lizard, half snake—becomes a dragon at the age of a thousand years.

The dragon's appearance is fierce, with horns on its head, protruding demon eyes, scales running down its neck to its flaming tail, eagle claws, and the paws of a tiger, yet it is not a symbol of evil, but rather of power, nobility, and intelligence.

I

It is said that when the first sailing ship from the West appeared in the Orient and the news was rushed to the Imperial Palace, the emperor did not even go to the window to view the harbor scene. Instead, he consulted his books and old texts, and on the basis of the writings and prophecies, determined that it was a dragon, part of the natural order, and therefore nothing to be concerned about.

1

Hue, Vietnam: 1847

ON HIS THRONE ON THE RAISED dais in the vast hall, deep within the maze of the forbidden reaches of the Imperial Palace, the Emperor Tu Duc sat beset with problems. Enemy warships blocked the harbors of two of his great cities, Saigon and Da Nang, and he knew it was only a matter of time before the French intruders sent soldiers to attack the capital itself.

The emperor had spent the last hour alone, contemplating in the gardens and pavilions of the Dai-Noi, the "Great Within" of the immense walled interior of the sacred palace. When he had wandered into the The-Mieu, the temple built in veneration of his great-grandfather, who had unified Vietnam forty-five years ago, the priests had scurried away like water bugs on a pond. He had entered without being announced, his silk robes trailing on the polished floors, making a slight whisking sound as though angered snakes had been set loose, and he had raised his fingers ever so slightly, dismissing the priests.

The temple had been built facing north; thus, though the light and elegant structure blended harmoniously with the surrounding cypresses and sculptured gardens, and its burnished reflection floated serenely on the jade-green pond in front, a darkness, even at the height of day, fell across the building. This cool opacity was especially evident within the temple, where the deep red tiles and cedar panels created shadows of almost mystic heaviness. Although the interior was severely simple, marked only by slender supporting pillars, the dimness and muted shafts of reflected light gave it a somberly ornate appearance.

From time to time a breeze hastened through the temple doors, rustling the flowers and the pale candles which burned at the altar, causing shadows to fall across the emperor's face, flickering and darting like his own restless thoughts.

The scent of incense, usually sweet and comforting to him, today seemed malodorous, the smell of decaying flowers, and he could find no peace here among his ancestors' spirits, so he left, seeking solace in the gardens, his purple robe brushing the pebbles along the paths he walked.

He wore a summer robe, but because of the heavily brocaded gold-dragon motif, it was stiff and heavy, the folds of the robe falling in unbroken lines from the shoulder to the ground, covering the black leather boots of Ming Dynasty origin which he wore. On his head was no crown, but only a mandarin's black steeped bonnet, so today his appearance was of muted elegance and authority, a dark contrast to the vibrant summer gardens into which he passed.

The gardens had been designed to capture the essences of the succeeding seasons, the finely graveled paths and carefully balustraded flowers, the espaliered white and pink tree peonies providing a setting for the soul of each season. To the south and up a gentle rise was a stand of plum trees, older than the imperial dynasty itself, where each spring the delicate perfume of an infinity of white and pink blossoms was carried to the palace on warm breezes. The trees were mirrored in a shallow lake on whose surface floated huge white lotuses, and where, on early-summer mornings, a purple mist rose and drifted across the palace courtyards.

The emperor walked the paths slowly, then stopped under the massive camphor tree in whose branches he had sat for hours as a child, a sad, lonely prince-child, dreaming not of his future kingdom and power, but only of someone to play with.

The air was heavy under a late summer's midday sun, and low clouds hung like rose opals over the spired battlements of the citadel walls.

He would like to be that child again, despite the loneliness; today he didn't want to be an emperor. He was eighteen years old and there was little happiness in his life.

His gaze dropped from the sky to a chrysanthemum bush and he bent to pick a flower, but already the blossom's white perfection was marred—in its brown-edged petals he saw the first hint of autumn's sorrow, and he let it drop to the ground, feeling tainted by death and decay.

He was completely alone. The palace guards had removed everyone, lest the emperor's vision or thoughts be marred by human imperfection, and the entire citadel seemed deserted. For a moment he let his eyes roam his ghostly imperial city, secure within the miles of red walls which encircled it.

Before him was the Thai Hoa, the Palace of Perfect Peace, lavishly decorated in red and gold, with its steep golden roofs on whose overhanging eaves and cornices ceramic dragons prowled watchfully. Across the courtyard was the Dien Tho, the Longevity Palace, the residence of the queen mothers, and he gave thought a moment to visiting his mother, but the disturbance he'd cause would be too great, and it would not be seemly for him to do what he wanted, place his head in her lap and let her comfort him.

Maybe he could find peace in his favorite place of solitude, he thought. He glanced longingly to the east, where there was a large square pond with a miniature island in the middle. On it were a pavilion and a pagoda for contemplation, where he often went.

But he knew he would find no tranquillity today, so he crossed the gardens into the palace, startling the guards and scribes, whose papers fluttered like leaves in a fall wind, and he dropped down unhappily on his throne.

The mandarins in their richly ornate brocades, as soundless and colorful as a coral reef, did not look up when he entered—that was forbidden—but they could tell by his hesitant, shuffling walk that he was troubled.

Only indirect light pervaded the lofty throne room. Neither gloomy nor bright, it seemed caught, like the young emperor himself, between a beginning and an ending.

After the brief stirring his entrance raised, the guards and scribes settled back to their tasks, the guards to indifferent watchfulness, the scribes to recording a history that seemed dusty even as it was being written.

The emperor allowed himself to be lulled by the calm sea of the mandarins' brightly and heavily brocaded robes with their long sleeves and elaborately tied sashes. As they worked, they swayed gracefully, their green, gold, blue, and red silks shimmering and sparkling in the quiet light, their glitter contrasting greatly, and seeming almost frivolous against the dull glow of the emperor's vestment, like the sea's surface to its dark, portentous depths.

Behind him two eunuchs cooled the air with feathered fans, and in his own hand he held a small ivory-handled mirror, behind which he would shield his face in symbolic humility before the spirits of his ancestors.

His fingers softly traced the intricately carved whorls of his gilded throne, at the base of which carved golden temple dogs reposed watchfully, and he contemplated the enemy ships.

Yet were it not for the French, he wouldn't be on the throne at all, for six months ago his father, Emperor Thieu Tri, disgusted and angered at yet another French naval show of force, had sent his war junks out to attack them. The emperor's fleet had been annihilated by the French ships and Thieu Tri had died shortly thereafter, his fatal seizure no doubt hastened by the disgrace.

So now Tu Duc sat on the throne, and the problems of the ships and the French were his. He wouldn't make the mistake his father had, but he was going to have to do something soon, for only five years ago a small French force had landed near Saigon and sent an attacking column through the surrounding province. They'd established a firm hold in the southern part of the kingdom, and Tu Duc knew they were merely biding their time before striking against Da Nang, or even Hue itself, for it was greed which governed these people, the Western disease of avarice, and it knew no bounds.

It was a disease whose carrier was the priests, an infection started over a hundred years ago. Ships had brought the priests too, and these men, dressed in black, had fanned out through the countryside like roaches, seeking to convert everyone to what Tu Duc considered a cruel, uncharitable cult of nonsense. He had sought to understand it, but he wasn't even sure how many gods they worshiped—one, three, or more, what with fathers, and sons, and ghosts, and virgin mothers, and a bewildering retinue of angels and saints. It was as bad as the Hindus, and he had thrown up his hands long ago. Besides, even with their wealth of deities, the only things these severe men in black seemed interested in were money and everybody else's sex life.

The priests were bad enough, but now a plague of soldiers and politicians and merchants was just offshore, clamoring to get into his kingdom. And the French were just the latest arrivals—before them it had been the Portuguese, and the Dutch, and the English.

They had all come for trade, the fulfillment of their quest for the fabled East, but though there were spices, and minerals, and textiles, Vietnam had not proved as lucrative as China, nor the people so pliant, so trade quickly turned to robbery and exploitation, and the priests, coming to save souls and convert the heathen, merely added insult and further suspicion.

Tu Duc and his forebears understood what was happening, certainly were not untutored in wile or exploitation—their own mandarins were surely the match for any white-skinned corrupters from across the waters—and for a while they received them in order to gain from the trade. The Westerners brought remarkable weapons and technology, but they would not leave the trade at that—they wanted more, ports and souls, and in their avaricious eyes could be seen their real desire: dominion. No, it wasn't nutmeg and cloves and cloth they wanted; they wanted the land itself, and the people to serve them. Look at India; look at China.

The Europeans had sent out their little wooden water beetles across the oceans to search for the Indies to break up the trade of the Arabs and Venetians with the Far East, and once having done that, they vied with one another for power and colonies. Each had established its own East India Company, and they waged war with one another for supremacy. For a while the Portuguese had dominated, but then the Dutch and English had supplanted them. Now the French had arrived to extract their measure, afraid of being left out in the carving up of this part of the world. And they brought their own priests, the vanguard of an even more insidious assault, for minds and souls.

Tu Duc's hands smoothed over the throne's gilded armrests, and his eyes narrowed, almost as though searching for his enemies in the dark recesses of the room. No more—the time had come to get rid of them.

Gia Long, his great-grandfather who had founded the Nguyen Dynasty in 1802, had made a mistake by tolerating the Christians. Gia Long was repelled by Christianity, primarily because of its prohibition of ancestor worship, but under his rule there were no persecutions. His son, Minh Mang, however, was violently opposed to Christianity and began persecutions almost immediately. Minh Mang's son, Thieu Tri, pursued a moderate course, and there were no missionaries killed during his reign, though as his hatred for the French grew, so did his animosity for the missionaries, and this hatred was passed to his son, Tu Duc.

One of Tu Duc's first acts was to order a purge of the missionaries; he wanted them out of the country, and he didn't care how many were killed in the process. He had enough problems in the empire without importing new ones on ships. For two thousand years his country had struggled for independence; for a thousand they had suffered the Chinese, and only forty-five years ago had the great Gia Long overcome all resistance and rebellion to unify the empire. And he, Tu Duc, only the fourth emperor in the Nguyen Dynasty, was not going to let everything slip away, especially to these barbarians who knew nothing about the principles of harmony in the universe. He would preserve his kingdom.

Though considerably agitated by his thoughts, Tu Duc exhibited calm; his face was smooth and composed, and he sat in apparent serenity, for it was considered bad form for a man to show emotion.

The emperor was beguilingly soft in appearance, of normal height for a Vietnamese—five feet, four inches tall—fleshy but not fat, with languid movements and extraordinarily delicate hands. The roundness of his face was emphasized by the Chinese fashion in which he wore his hair—pulled back tightly and braided. But his appearance was deceptive; he was an extremely clever young man, a master of intrigue with a labyrinthine mind; moreover, he possessed not just the self-confidence of born rank and a lifetime of being deferred to, he was convinced that the mandate of heaven had been passed to him and that what he decreed was divinely meant to be. Though without any great desire for power, he was a most resolute ruler.

Yet despite the absoluteness of his rule, his manner to all was civil; arrogance would have been an unseemly indulgence, at odds with the code of conduct of a mandarin, and out of character for him personally. He believed foremost in harmony and balance. He was courtly beyond his years, an extremely agreeable and mature youth.

As he sat in thought, a chamberlain prostrated himself before the throne and announced that his cousin, Prince Nguyen Ahn Le, had not appeared for his scheduled audience.

Tu Duc made the slightest motion with his fingers, a rippling dismissal indicating this was not acceptable, though he was not surprised: nothing about his cousin surprised him.

Ahn Le was also the grandson of the Emperor Minh Mang, Thieu Tri's sister's son, and Tu Duc's first cousin, a nineteen-year-old hellion who'd been taught nothing good and learned it well.

Ahn was the prime irritant in Tu Duc's life, a formidable young man who made not even a pretense of proper respect and duty to the emperor.

Tu Duc did not like his cousin, but he was wise enough to know that Ahn could not help being the way he was—his mother had died when he was three, shortly after her husband had been put to death for intriguing against Minh Mang, and Ahn had grown up as an overly indulged child of court, everybody's favorite. He even had the run of the throne room; Minh Mang had felt so badly about having put his father to death that he couldn't have the boy disciplined or restrained, and the child would climb into the emperor's lap and make faces at everyone. Tu Duc had never been so favored, and he resented it. The two youths shared nothing in common except their royal blood, and made little effort to conceal their disdain for each other.

What made matters worse in Tu Duc's mind was that Ahn had the classic features of his mother and the quick mind of his father. As a boy, Tu Duc had been awkward and ungainly, with the unfortunate moon face of so many of the Nguyens, and the dynastic weak chin. Ahn, on the other hand, was five feet, eight inches, tall for a Vietnamese, with a sinewy build of a gymnast, and he carried himself that way, graceful but tense, as though forcibly restraining the energy that seemed ready to burst from within. Also, he had the finer looks of the south, the Malay-Polynesian blend of delicate beauty that was a positive contrast to the bland features of the north, which Tu Duc and most of the Nguyens had.

Tu Duc knew it was jealousy he felt for his cousin, and he had sought hard to overcome it, but burned too deeply into his memory was his own unhappy, solitary childhood, and his shy, tortured adolescence, so different from Ahn's. Ahn had been too handsome, too intelligent, never suffered any doubts, and women had made fools of themselves over him since he was twelve.

Though Tu Duc himself had a large number of concubines and was attended whenever he wished, he knew it was this he resented most, and he still envied Ahn's success with women, his revels, and his outrageous carousing. It pained him most to see even the wives of his ministers flirt shamelessly with his cousin.

Finally, sealing the case against Ahn was that he'd been brought up under the tutelage of Chien Yu-Kuang, in Tu Duc's mind the most bogus Confucian master in that seemingly endless line of court frauds. Chien, now in his early thirties, had studied under Ts Chu, the great master of the Ching court of Peking, and had come to Hue with the master Ku-Yuan. He was declared by both his teachers as their brightest pupil, and when Ku-Yuan died suddenly, Chien had been persuaded to remain in Hue rather than return to Peking.

Chien had come to Hue when he was seventeen. Minh Mang was so impressed with him that he was given charge of the royal children to instruct. The only person not impressed and captivated by the rugged Chinese youth was Tu Duc, who was himself a Confucian scholar in his own right and who since the age of five had been offended by Chien's overpoweringly confident manner. For his part, Chien thought the future emperor dull, and he made little attempt to disguise his feelings, or his favoritism for Ahn.

Tu Duc believed Chien a charlatan, interested only in self-promotion and seduction, and several scandals had put his fortunes on the wane even before Tu Duc was enthroned, one with his aunt, a daughter of the Emperor Minh Mang.

Now Chien's sole patron and benefactor was Ahn, his pupil of fifteen years. The two were inseparable, their relationship having passed from teacher-pupil to that of comrades, and their riotous debauching together was notorious. Tu Duc could barely countenance them, and had sent them off on a meaningless diplomatic mission simply to get rid of them. Their behavior in Saigon had been reported back to Tu Duc, and it was the report of this mission that Ahn was now late in making.

Tu Duc brought his hands together and leaned forward slightly, as though to give the words more force, though they were spoken in an even, calm tone. "Find him."

The chamberlain backed out bowing—no one was permitted to turn his back on the emperor—and once beyond the massive bronze doors of the throne room, he sent the guards racing to find the youth.

Tu Duc leaned back on his throne, as motionless as onyx, his cold eyes seemingly sightless, but regarding everything. From a dark corner of the room came the song of a single lutist. The soft melody was the only sound, wisping around the scarlet limewood pillars which supported the throne room, seeming to come from the open mouths of the carved golden dragons which entwined them.

Ahn was asleep, stretched naked on satin sheets in a back apartment of the palace, in the bed of the lord treasurer's wife.

The woman, many years younger than her husband, but ten years older than the youth in her bed, lay propped on her elbows, staring at his lean body. He slept like a child, sprawled on his stomach, arms and legs outstretched, content, vulnerable. Sunlight from the windows bathed his body, highlighting his golden skin.

Though for hours, since her husband had left that morning, the two had made love, she was not sated. She never was with him; even now she wanted to smother him with her body, crawl upon him like a kitten would on a baby, or pull him entirely into herself, keeping him locked inside.

She ran her hand down his shoulders, over his hairless back and buttocks, to the inner thigh, and she stroked there softly until he moved slightly, opening his legs wider.

Lady Deng had contrived for months to get him into her bed,

and now that she had, she was not about to let him get away, for she knew how many others were eager to have him.

All her life she'd been the desired one, so this role of pursuer was new to her. Lihn Deng was not one of the reticent, thin, hipless women of the court. She was a former courtesan of full and radiant beauty, trained to be whatever a man wanted, as the occasion demanded—earthy or genteel, retiring or engaging. She was so highly esteemed and admired for her talents that no one looked askance when the elderly lord treasurer married her upon the death of his first wife of forty years. But she had grown bored quickly. There was little for a woman to do at court, and none of it interested Lihn, but as the wife of a high minister, she couldn't engage in common dalliances—her husband was understanding, but he wouldn't tolerate her sleeping with the palace guards. An affair with the emperor's cousin was another, acceptable matter.

But starting the affair had been much more difficult than she'd anticipated, and she'd been distressed when none of her coquetry or enticements had worked in interesting the youthful prince. Then she discovered that there were simply so many others with whom he was sleeping that he had no time for her. So she dropped all coyness and decided to confront him directly one afternoon in the gardens of the inner court, blocking his path on his way to the throne room, where she knew he had an audience with the emperor. But he was forty-five minutes late and she'd had to spend that time outside in the hot sun. A lady did not spend time outside at noon, even in the shade, and certainly no courtesan did.

She was wilted and highly annoyed when he approached at last. Her irritation overcame her discretion, and she felt her age and experience entitled her to confront a nineteen-year-old, even if he was a prince.

"You ought to be ashamed of yourself," she said angrily.

He didn't seem surprised to see her, or at her words, and he dropped his head and said contritely, "I am."

That took her aback, for she herself had only a vague idea in her mind of what he should be ashamed about—his tardiness for his audience, of where he'd been (another woman), of making her stand outside in the sun—so she asked in surprise, "For what?"

He looked up sensuously, not a bit contritely. "For having wasted the past hour while you were out here."

"I was not."

His hand touched her hairline by her ear and he showed her

his moist fingertip. "Women who stay within the palace don't perspire."

"Wretch." Then she laughed. "I thought I was going to melt out here. If you'd been much longer, you'd have stepped into a pool of me."

He grinned. "I would have lapped it up."

"That's what I had in mind, without all this discomfort. Do I have to make an appointment? Do you keep regular hours? Is there a long wait?"

"Is your husband at home?"

She shook her head and led him back to her apartment, the emperor forgotten.

For nearly fifteen years she'd practiced as a courtesan, couldn't begin to count the number of men with whom she'd slept, but that day in bed with Ahn was the most memorable she had had. He was the only man who had completely fulfilled all her expectations, desires, and fantasies. They met often after that, but he had been gone the last month to Saigon and this was their first time together since his return.

His smooth face reposed on the pillow. His black hair was perfectly straight, shorter than most men at court wore theirs, and unlike most men, he had neither beard nor mustache. It was as if he knew how good and strong his features were, and wanted nothing to hide them.

She bent forward and kissed his lips, then washed over his face with her tongue, tracing down his slightly flared nose.

Just to touch him excited her. She came to her knees and moved over him, her mouth drifting from his face to his muscled neck, then down his back, licking and nipping at his body. He spread his legs fully and she knelt between them and worked her mouth lower on him, teasing and tantalizing him with her tongue, until finally he rolled over on his back to give her greater access. Her hands caressed his broad chest, palmed his flat stomach, and her fingers entwined in the dense hair of his groin as her cheek stroked up the sides of his shaft. He lay motionless as she ministered to him, but their eyes were open in full erotic delight of each other.

When she rose from between his legs, she crouched above him, then let herself down slowly, sighing as she filled herself with him. His hands went to her breasts, gently pinched the nipples, then traced down to her thighs, stroking inside, and his fingers worked her expertly as she rotated on him, then began driving up and down on him.

Her gentle moans grew louder and sharper until she cried out and he had to bring the pillow from behind his head and she clamped her mouth on it, twisting her head violently as she thrust against him wildly.

Then he rose up and deftly turned her over without withdrawing. She lifted high on her knees as he dug deeply into her, her mouth chewing the pillow.

She was in such abandon that she didn't notice the bamboo screen slide open or see the tall Chinese fill the entrance. The man was as powerfully built as a Manchurian warrior, over six feet tall, with a strong broad face and intensely penetrating eyes.

Ahn didn't cease his movement when he saw the man, but only grinned and worked his hips harder.

Chien brought his hands to the top of his head to form a pointed crown and puffed out his cheeks in imitation of the moon-faced emperor.

Ahn jerked his head back, remembering the audience with his cousin. He brought a hand from the hip of the woman and motioned to Chien that he understood, but Chien didn't leave. Instead, he folded his arms and watched appraisingly. Ahn's movements became even more forceful, driving powerfully into her until finally he shuddered as spasms gripped him.

When he withdrew, Lihn dropped forward, facedown on the bed, her eyes closed, and she didn't notice as Ahn left the bed and dressed quickly. He put on a simple military-style brown robe and crossed to the screen. Without looking back, he closed it behind him and put his hand on Chien's elbow, leading him away.

"I was waiting for a discreet moment," said Chien when they were in the corridor, "but it didn't appear there was going to be one. I thought I would spare you both the embarrassment of the palace guards breaking in to drag you off her."

"He sent the guards?" But before the question was answered, two guards ran up the long hallway toward him. They wore cone-shaped helmets and carried golden spikes; they were barefoot and wore yellow leg wrappings, a color allowed only to the emperor's immediate entourage. Ahn raised his hand and waved them away. The guards pressed back against the walls as he passed, then fell in step behind him.

"How late am I?"

"To an emperor, a minute's wait is the life of a tortoise."

"How did you know where I was?"

Chien reached over to smooth Ahn's hair and straighten his robe. "The sound of lovemaking is like a bird's sweet song in my ears. Surely I could hear the screech-owl calls of Lady Deng."

Ahn laughed. More guards approached, made way, and fell in behind the two.

When they reached the garden that separated the apartments from the inner palace, Ahn dismissed the guards and he and Chien entered together. Though Ahn tried to rush Chien's steps, he would not be hurried, and Ahn had to slow down.

In the middle of the garden, at the base of the camphor tree, Chien stopped and gazed up to the sun, letting it warm his face. Out of respect, Ahn waited for him.

When Chien lowered his head, he saw the dropped chrysanthemum. He knew that only the emperor would dare pick a flower in the garden, and seeing its brown edge, he guessed Tu Duc's disquiet, and why he'd dropped it; he knew well his former pupil's melancholy nature.

Chien held out the flower to Ahn, becoming again his instructor.

Ahn took the flower and contemplated the white petals etched with decay.

"What do you see, young lord?"

"I see the widening ring of mortality, master."

Chien raised his head again to the sun. Ahn studied the flower, then squinted up to the sun, whose rays would now quickly wither and darken the petals, and he saw Chien's meaning. It was his constant reminder to him, the message of the yin and the yang—the completeness of contrasts, the harmony of opposites: what nurtures, kills; in receiving, there is loss; in beauty, decay; in life, death. Above all, it was Chien's reminder to him to savor what is, to slow his impulsiveness.

Together, and serenely now, at Chien's pace, the two continued through the gardens and entered the palace.

In the antechamber of the throne room, Chien dropped down into a chair as the chamberlain went in to announce Ahn's arrival.

"He'll make me wait twice as long as I made him wait," Ahn said as he sprawled in a chair, stretching out his legs.

Chien withdrew an apple from his robe. "You misjudge him. He succeeds against pettiness better than you."

Ahn tapped his fingers on the arm of the chair, the lesson of the chrysanthemum lost already, though he still held it in one hand.

The antechamber was a long, narrow room, austere in the extreme, with nothing to catch the eye or distract the mind. Its barrenness was designed to contrast with and emphasize the ornateness of the throne room, so that when one passed through the simple wood doorway, the massive bronze doors beyond, with their dragon-headed handles, came as a stunning surprise.

Since the day Tu Duc had become emperor, Ahn had badgered him for responsibility, and finally, to get rid of him more than anything else, Tu Duc had sent him to Saigon as his emissary to determine the situation with the French. But the mission was a sham—Tu Duc was not remotely interested in contact with the French, and had already decided to launch an offensive against them as soon as the priests were purged.

Chien sat stoically, munching the apple. He knew the mission had been an empty one, but had said nothing to Ahn because the youth had taken it so seriously.

Ahn had given considerable thought to the problem of the French. He believed liaison should be established because they were too formidable to resist militarily, yet he didn't see them as a threat to the culture or life-style of Vietnam because he believed their influence could be easily absorbed. There were even things to be learned from them, he thought, though he knew his cousin and the ruling mandarins wouldn't be receptive to that idea.

Ahn jumped from the chair and began to pace. He strode up and down the room several times, then stopped before Chien. "Don't you have any advice before I go in?"

Chien didn't look up. "I'd do as well to advise the apple not to be eaten."

Ahn grabbed it away and took a bite. "If you ever practiced the moderation you preach, the apple wouldn't need advice, it'd still be on the tree."

Chien snatched it back, plopped it in his mouth, and smacked loudly. "Now it's part of me and fulfilled of a higher destiny. Call him 'lord,' not 'cousin,' that's the only advice I have."

Ahn laughed and sat down beside him. "But it annoys him so much when I call him 'cousin,' and since I'm not going to tell him anything else he wants to hear, there's no point in making that small concession."

Chien delicately took three seeds from his mouth and placed them on the youth's wrist. "As seeds need proper soil to grow, advice needs a fertile mind in which to root." He slapped his hand down hard, knocking the seeds to the floor. "Call him whatever you want, fool."

Ahn rubbed his hand. The blow had hurt too much to have been in jest, and he looked at Chien quizzically.

"When you're ready to listen, I'll give you advice, but I'm not going to talk to a boy whose vision is only to the end of his penis, and who can't see the danger on the throne in the next room."

Ahn looked down at his feet. "I see it," he sighed, deflated. "And I know he doesn't care what I have to tell him today."

Despite his exuberance and impudence, Ahn was thoughtful and perceptive. He knew his cousin's feelings for him, and knew the vast differences in their natures prevented any reconciliation. He'd been able to get away with as much as he had because of youth, but his behavior couldn't be tolerated much longer; no emperor was going to countenance disrespect and insolence, he knew.

Close male relatives of the emperor were in a tenuous position; there was more than incidental risk in being the brother, nephew, or cousin of a king. Ahn knew that Tu Duc would indulge him only so far, but wouldn't hesitate to eliminate him at the first provocation, for the emperor would always view him as a threat and potential usurper.

Ahn knew that his life would always be lived under a cloud of suspicion. He'd be expected to do nothing, say nothing, think nothing; he'd never be consulted for anything, and no mission of any importance would be entrusted to him. His life would be ornamental and useless, without freedom or dignity.

"You were kind to pretend what I was doing in Saigon was important," he said to Chien. "Thank you."

He began to pace again, his brow furrowing deeply, creating a somewhat comic effect, for he seemed too young and confident to be so troubled. He was no indecisive Hamlet, but now a mournful Romeo. "All right, I'll listen, but I don't want any platitudes—save that nonsense about apples and seeds and banana trees for bed talk with silly girls—I want practical advice."

Chien smiled; he did love the boy, and was pleased with him. Chien put his hands on his knees as he always did when he was about to speak seriously, though this was infrequent, for he was not a solemn man. His eyes fixed on the youth soberly. "Can you live here at court?"

"No."

"Well, then?"

Ahn stopped and faced him, startled at the clarity.

At that moment the door opened and the chamberlain bowed. "His majesty will see you."

Ahn started forward, but when Chien made no move to follow, he stopped and gestured for him.

"My presence provokes him even more than yours does."

"Come with me."

Chien followed reluctantly.

The carved bronze doors swung open. They entered the huge throne room, with Ahn staring straight ahead, the only person who ever looked directly at the emperor, and with Chien trailing three feet behind, his eyes riveted on the youth's heels. The position was annoying and awkward, and when Ahn stopped abruptly, he stumbled into him.

Ahn gazed about the room as he always did before acknowledging his cousin, doing this both out of curiosity at his surroundings and to indicate to the emperor that he wasn't intimidated.

The size of the room was overpowering, its length and height planned to diminish the stature of individuals, except for the emperor, who sat on a massive, ornately gilded throne which dominated the room from its raised position at the far end. Muted sunlight from high, open windows arced the throne, but left the rest of the room in shadows. Mandarins sat like statues in wide semicircles before him, and bent scribes sat at desks below him and to the side. A long, wide area directly in front of the throne was left open for those who approached the emperor.

Ahn finally brought his eyes to him and bowed slightly. "Good morning, cousin," he said, and Chien grimaced to himself.

"Good morning, cousin," Tu Duc answered, without a trace of annoyance at either the impudence or for having been made to wait. He noticed the chrysanthemum in Ahn's hand and in it saw the work of Chien; his cousin would never stop to pick up a flower on his own.

"And good morning to you, Master Chien."

Chien dropped to his knees and lowered his head to the floor.

Ahn turned and put out his hand, indicating that he was to rise, a total breach of etiquette—only the emperor could give such a command.

Tu Duc ignored the gesture and said smoothly, "I'm eager to hear your observations, cousin, though I understand not all you observed in Saigon would be proper subject for discussion in court. Your prodigious energy was reported to me, not without awe."

"I wanted to meet as many of your subjects as I could."

"Most considerate of you, especially since those you visited were not likely otherwise to meet a member of the royal family." Tu Duc's eyes fastened on the chrysanthemum and he had to fight back the disquieting envy rising in him. "But let us confine your report to what I sent you for."

"Yes, cousin. The French want to establish a permanent envoy to you. I think you should accept it, because if we don't accommodate them, they'll simply strike against us, and they're too strong for us to resist."

"How does one accommodate the lion without being eaten, cousin?"

"The French aren't lions, cousin, and they're not interested in devouring us; they're interested only in financial gain. We can negate their military power by working with them." He had planned to use the analogy of quicksand, but he couldn't resist offending his cousin's sensibilities, and he said with offhand, almost sleepy sensuality, "The soft, moist vaginal lips of a woman can absorb and make meek the fiercest and most insistent ram of a man."

Tu Duc's face registered nothing and his response came without hesitation. "And for its acquiescence find itself laden with a very bitter fruit."

Ahn grinned appreciatively; then he shrugged. "There are other ways to disarm the ram. If we invite the French in, they won't need to break down the doors. Besides, we have as much to gain from them as they have from us. The world is changing, cousin; they can teach us much."

Tu Duc inclined his head. "Thank you very much. I shall give careful consideration to your words. Is there anything else?"

Ahn dropped his insouciance, stood straighter, and drew a deep breath. "Yes, there is." He felt Chien shift nervously behind him. "I have two great favors to ask. I would like your permission to leave court and to marry."

His words caused an immediate sensation.

Tu Duc, despite his efforts to affect composure, was obviously taken aback. Chien stepped forward to restrain the youth from saying anything further, and the seated scribes and mandarins stirred noticeably, barely able to keep their heads down.

"I want to marry Le Xuan Huong and take her to live in Ban Me Thuot. The province of Darlac is unstable and I can serve you by bringing those people to greater loyalty and appreciation for your wise rule."

Tu Duc dropped all pretense of equanimity; he looked at his cousin with frank suspicion and was about to dismiss the requests out of hand when Ahn continued rapidly.

"We know that I can't live here. My presence is a constant aggravation to you. I'm sorry for that, but I can't change how I am. My only chance for happiness is to serve you somewhere else. Don't make me become a court lackey. Let me go in peace;

let me marry Xuan Huong, and let me be of some service in life. I promise you fidelity and obedience."

Tu Duc's long fingers softly stroked the arms of the gilded throne, and his agile mind raced over all the possibilities and ramifications of the requests. He wanted time to deliberate, but emperors weren't allowed indecision; he had to respond immediately to such a forthright request. What Ahn said was true. Tu Duc saw that, of course, and he was somewhat disarmed by the apparent sincerity, but he played for time.

"I was not aware of your love for Xuan Huong. Is she?"

"Of course," he lied boldly.

"What with all your other . . . interests, I didn't think you'd have time for a courtship also."

The request to marry Xuan Huong was an even greater surprise to Tu Duc than the request to leave court. Of all the women at court, of all the women in Hue or the entire kingdom, he would have last guessed Xuan Huong to be his cousin's choice; he would have been far less surprised had Ahn chosen the most outrageous whore in Saigon. But Xuan Huong—he was stunned.

She was not the most unattractive woman at court, but near enough to be disconcerting; she was twenty-six, long past marrying age, with no fortune, a convert to Catholicism, and worst of all, making her a pariah, she was the granddaughter of the last emperor of the Le Dynasty, the man overthrown by Gia Long in 1802. She lived at court at the indulgence of the Nguyens, an outcast, and it was unthinkable that any man would marry her.

Tu Duc could see no conceivable benefit to Ahn in this woman, and the fact that Chien was so noticeably appalled confirmed his thoughts. It was an unbelievable stroke of good luck, he thought; almost too good, he suspected, but he decided to take the risk—he might never again have such an opportunity to get rid of his cousin.

"Though we shall be very sorry to see you leave, I wouldn't want to interfere with what you believe is your only chance for happiness. I offer you my blessings and congratulations. Have you decided on a date for the wedding?"

"The day after tomorrow."

Tu Duc's mouth fell open. "You aren't serious? It would take six months to prepare a ceremony worthy of you and Xuan Huong."

"We aren't interested in ceremony, cousin; our love desires immediate fulfillment."

Chien was making such a stir behind him that Ahn turned to him. "Are you all right, Master Chien?"

Chien made a garbled sound and clamped his eyes shut.

"If that is your desire, then it shall be done, cousin. As my wedding gift to you, I decree you overlord of Darlac and entitled to all revenues from the province. We shall prepare for you the finest wedding possible in the short time you've given us."

Ahn bowed. "I'm moved by your generosity, cousin, and I vow I won't ever do anything to make you regret it."

He turned to leave, but had to prod Chien, whose eyes were still tightly shut. Chien shuffled backward, trying to keep up with Ahn, who had turned his back on the emperor and was striding out.

When the doors closed behind them, Ahn dropped down into a chair to await Chien's reaction, but the Chinaman fumbled in his robes for an apple, examined it carefully, then began to eat, studiously oblivious of Ahn.

"Well?"

"Well what?"

"Aren't you going to congratulate me on my forthcoming marriage?"

"Obviously I've been placed in an evil trance; I shall talk with you when the spell is broken." He walked to the portico and looked out on the gardens, talking sotto voce to himself. "Or maybe it was an enchanted apple that I ate. There I was, in the presence of the emperor, and suddenly I hear the voice of a normal, healthy young man asking to marry the ugliest woman in the kingdom, a woman old enough to be his mother, a woman guaranteed to ruin him, a woman I believe he's never met, and he begs to run off with her to live in the jungle."

"Oh, sit down. You know I have to leave; you just told me so. And Xuan Huong will make a fine wife, as far as wives go."

Chien came back to sit beside him. "My young lord, I see a glimmer of rationality in what you've attempted to do, but it is a candlelight in the vast void. If you want to stab yourself in the heart, it isn't necessary to throw yourself off a cliff first. There are ways, and then there are ways not to live at court. Why have you chosen a way with a woman old enough to be your mother?"

The youth said simply, "I want a wife. And I tell you, Xuan Huong will make the best one."

Chien sighed. "If you want a good wife, marry a eunuch—they cause no trouble at all. And besides, you're not marrying just Xuan Huong, but Xuan Huong and that awful man."

"The priest? Father Bergere? He's her mentor, her spiritual adviser, as you are mine."

"He's the most obtuse individual I've ever encountered. And the most boring."

Ahn smiled. "I wonder what he says about you."

Across the gardens, far removed from the imperial household, a handmaiden threw open the door to Xuan Huong's chamber and rushed in.

The apartment was in an older part of the palace, completely isolated, screened away by a heavy growth of bamboo. It was quieter here, with only the occasional splash of carp in an emerald-green pool to break the stillness.

Seated at a simple wooden table across from Father Bergere, taking instruction from the catechism, Xuan was dressed in a white ao dai very unlike the ones other women at court wore. The unadorned garment fitted loosely and the side slit of the dress ran only to her calf, completely utilitarian rather than provocative. She wore no makeup, and her black hair was pulled straight back in a single braid. She looked up in surprise at the unprecedented intrusion.

"Madame!" The chambermaid bowed continuously as she approached, her head bobbing up and down like a pigeon's, and the words rushed from her mouth. "Madame, you're to be married. The emperor said so. A scribe just brought the news. In two days you're going to be married. We're all leaving. We're going to Ban Me Thuot."

The girl reached Xuan; then, seeing the severe look on her face, she dropped to her knees.

There was complete silence in the room. Only a small parrot, startled by the interruption, hopped restlessly in an airy wicker cage. Finally a gentle, bemused look came over Xuan's face. It was not an unattractive face, but a strong one, highly intelligent-looking, with the full, rather rough features of the north. Beauty is often equated with blankness, and because there was nothing vacuous in Xuan's expression—instead, great character—it was this that many found so unattractive and unwomanly about her.

"What are you talking about?" she asked at last.

"Madame, it was just announced that you are to be married. The emperor himself is giving the wedding."

"I see." A slight smile crossed her face. "By chance, did the emperor mention whom I am to marry?"

"His cousin, Prince Ahn Le."

Xuan looked incredulous.

For the first time, Father Bergere moved. He jumped up,

dropping the catechism. "Ahn Le! That's scandalous. Get out of here, you silly girl."

Xuan laughed. "Father, please sit down. This is obviously a joke." She waved her hand to dismiss the girl. The girl began to protest, but Xuan motioned her out.

When she was gone, Xuan bent over for the book and handed it to the priest, but Father Bergere was too agitated to continue with the lesson.

"That's the most shocking thing I've ever heard. That girl must be discharged. It's an outrage even to suggest such a thing. Imagine! That boy's the most wicked creature in the country. Why . . . why, the stories . . . Well!" He wrestled with the book, unable to articulate his feelings. "It's blasphemous," he said at last.

Xuan suppressed a smile. She had heard the stories; everyone knew the stories of the emperor's cousin. They were shocking, and he was outrageous, but the stories were the best entertainment at court. And of course he was a boy, only nineteen as she remembered, so the very idea of such a thing as marriage was ludicrous. She was too old for him. Where in the world could such a thing have come from?

Xuan hadn't thought of marriage in years; when she was very young, before she realized her disfavor and the aversion to her which prevailed, she had dreamed of such a thing—of a handsome prince, of kisses and whispered talk of love. Oh, she'd yearned for it, but then she found it was not to be—she was a leper princess, sealed alone in her colony, as removed from life at court as if she'd lived on the moon. She had no friends, no one with whom to talk or gossip, only her attendants, and her priest, another leper at court.

But she had resigned herself to her fate, becoming what other women at court were not—happy and educated. She had so many interests that now she didn't have time to be unhappy: she knew history, and languages, and mathematics; she did painting and flower arranging, and recently she'd begun writing poetry. What little time remained, she devoted to her religion.

Father Bergere had been with the family for almost twenty years; her mother had been a convert to Catholicism, and he was her priest, and now he was Xuan's, and her sole friend and confidant. He was a Jesuit who'd come to Vietnam as a young man charged with missionary zeal, but now he was isolated and filled with failure, though his faith and idealism were undaunted.

The priest was forty-two years old, but looked older, a man of medium height, gaunt nearly to emaciation, completely gray-haired, and with the most sorrowful countenance. Even his fellow Jesuits believed him exceptionally devout; in the seminary they'd nicknamed him "Saint Bergere." They also called him "Father Pangloss," after Voltaire's optimistic philosopher. He was an ascetic with no vices, except perhaps the studied seriousness with which he took his work—he viewed it as a sacred trust from God, and he didn't discharge it with moderation. His frail appearance belied his tenacity.

Father Bergere opened the catechism, but the intrusion had been too much for him. He could not dislodge the appalling thought from his mind. "You don't think there's any possibility of that being true, do you? I mean, that would simply be . . . Why, he's just . . ."

"Father Bergere, don't you think I would know if I were to be married day after tomorrow?"

"Who knows what could happen in this wretched place?"

Just then the door flew open again and the servant girl rushed in, wilder this time, her slippered feet skating across the polished floor. "He's here. He wants to see you. He's waiting."

Xuan grabbed the girl's hands and made her look up. "I want you to stop this foolish behavior. I don't care what happens in this world, or who's waiting outside, we won't have unseemly and undignified conduct."

The girl bowed her head contritely.

"Now, what is it you want to tell me?"

The girl looked up, trying desperately to suppress her excitement. "The prince. He's waiting to see you. He asked if you'll allow him in." That said, she flushed deeply and said, "Oh, he's so handsome." Then she brought her hands to her mouth, shocked at her own words.

A quizzical, disconcerted look crossed Xuan's face, but she composed herself immediately. "Please have him come in."

Father Bergere was on his feet, more agitated than Xuan had ever seen him. "This is intolerable. You can't see that man. That boy. My dear lady, this is—"

"Father, I'm sure I'll be safe with him; and he is a prince—I can't refuse to see him."

"As you choose." He made his way across the room, but as he was leaving, Ahn entered with his customary vigor, bumping into the priest, almost knocking him down.

Ahn reached out quickly to steady him, then he jostled him upright, shaking him back into position.

The confrontation was profoundly upsetting to Father Bergere. In his mind, the youth represented everything he stood against;

moreover, there was an intense aura of sensuality that exuded from him, a sexuality that struck Father Bergere with almost physical impact, and sex was a subject of great embarrassment to the priest.

Yet the young man was the emperor's first cousin, third in line to the throne, after Tu Ducs eight-year-old brother, so the priest had no recourse but to bow deeply.

To be gracious, and in a sincere gesture of conciliation, Ahn took Father Bergere's trembling hand and shook it vigorously, then said in execrable French, though the priest was fluent in Vietnamese, "Good morning, Master Bergere. How well to see you. I am charming. Is the water here potable?"

The priest looked at him as though he were mad. Then he rushed out, his face deeply distressed, and ran into Chien, who was also frowning in deep agitation.

As soon as the two men saw one another, their expressions instantly smoothed. They nodded tranquilly and took seats across from each other in the antechamber. Father Bergere opened his catechism and began to read serenely. Chien stared straight ahead in calm meditation. The two men looked like moss-covered idols, each consciously oblivious of the other, each contemplating a serene horizon marred only by the other.

Ahn closed the door behind him, turned, and bowed formally. Xuan had risen, and she too bowed.

Though of equal station, both the grandchildren of emperors, Ahn ranked higher, for Xuan was of a dispossessed dynasty. Nevertheless, she was entitled the accord due a princess. The two approached one another as protocol dictated.

"My lady, thank you for seeing me."

"My lord, thank you for your visit." Yet she couldn't resist, and her eyes lit mischievously. "The water is perfectly fine. Would you care for a drink?"

Ahn looked confused. "Why, no. But thank you."

"I was just wondering. As best I could make out from your French, you asked Father Bergere if the water here was drinkable."

"Really?" He laughed, his face breaking into an ingenuous smile. "It was just something I remembered from my studies; I thought it was polite chitchat. Anyway, it doesn't make any difference; nobody pays attention to French."

She motioned for him to sit; he chose a chair but waited until she sat.

They sat with their hands folded in their laps, correctly bland expressions on their faces, though behind these masks they were scrutinizing each other.

His experience was with girls and courtesans, and he felt keenly the formidable nature of the woman before him. This was not a silly, giggly creature, but an obviously intelligent, perceptive woman; yet in their brief exchange he saw that she was both warm and gentle, and playful. He liked her very much, and was pleased that she was nowhere near as unattractive as her reputation. True, she wasn't a great beauty—her features were not fine or delicate enough—but there was about her simple, unadorned elegance that raised her far above the ordinary. She looked, he thought, as an empress should.

To her he was a boy, an extraordinarily handsome one, but she perceived immediately that there was more than appearance to him. He possessed that self-confidence and smooth grace which beauty bestows, but he carried with it the firm assurance of intelligence.

She saw that the stories about him had to be true; he obviously could be devastating with women. His eyes were hypnotic, and across his mouth was a slight sensual grin. Yet what appealed to her was not his looks or boyishness, but a strong sense of refinement and control—incipient majesty, she thought. He was, she realized, exactly what she'd imagined her prince to be when she was a girl.

Finally he leaned forward and said with resolution, "I have come to ask you to marry me. Will you?"

She looked at him forthrightly, then inclined her head gracefully. "My lord, I'm most flattered, and doubtless the envy of every girl at court, but I find this proposal incredible."

He seemed taken aback. "Why?"

His guilelessness disarmed her, and she smiled. "Because you are nineteen and I am twenty-six, because as far as I know, we've never met, because I have neither position nor wealth, because I can think of no reason in this world why you are here this morning making this proposal."

"My lady, of all the women at court, you possess the greatest, perhaps sole, wisdom, intelligence, warmth, ability, and bearing. Why should I want to marry anyone else?"

She laughed. "My lord, I know you're not mocking me, but if I possess any of those qualities, I possess them in no greater measure than a host of others far more suitable and beneficial to you."

"Nonsense, there isn't a girl here who knows a thing. Take my word for it."

"I'm sure your knowledge is extensive, and firsthand, but I must demur nonetheless."

He flushed slightly. Not knowing how to proceed, he stood up and began to pace. He brought his hands together, pressing his fingers against themselves; then he slapped his sides and sat back down on the sofa beside her, his face pressed closely to hers. "Yes, you are older, but what possible difference could that make? I can't marry one of these silly ornaments which decorate the palace. I don't want to spend my life with a twittering bird, live with a feeble woman-child with whom I couldn't even talk, who could only offer momentary amusement, and that no different from what I could find anywhere else. I want to live a full life with a woman I can love and respect. I don't want to decorate my house, I want to share it. I want children of a woman who would be worthy of them, of a woman they must prove themselves to, as I must."

She gazed into his intense eyes, then lowered her head, moved by his words.

He touched her chin and raised her head gently so their eyes met. "I've known for years that I would marry you. I never thought of marrying anyone else."

"We never met, my lord."

"But I knew about you, and observed you secretly. I watched the way you conducted yourself, and after seeing you, I knew I could live with no one else. I just never knew when I'd ask you. I wasn't ready before this." He smiled with genuine and charming self-deprecation. "I'm not sure I'm ready now. Or worthy."

"Why are you asking now?"

"Because I can't live at court any longer. I have neither use nor purpose, nor favor with my cousin; my life here would be meaningless and venial. I would become a decoration too, for I have neither the mind nor the patience you have to dedicate myself to study and abnegation. I'm going to Ban Me Thuot to administer the province of Darlac. I want to rule wisely and well, and I want you to be with me. You are meant to rule too. Let us do it together."

They stared at one another for a full minute; then he repeated the question: "Will you marry me?"

She watched his lips as he spoke, saw each word formed; then she studied his face carefully, so intensely that she saw the pores in his skin and the light stubble that had grown only since he'd shaved that morning. Her senses were so heightened that she detected an odor about him that was not naturally his, a faint scent of a woman's perfume, and suddenly in everything about him, his still slightly mussed hair, the relaxed animal eyes, she knew that he had only recently come from a woman's bed.

The realization did not anger her, but faintly frightened her, yet at the same time stirred a long-suppressed carnal impulse in her. Almost in response to this she felt a sharpened intensity about her; the parrot seemed to hop in agitation, the sunlight streamed more brilliantly through the open windows beyond which the stillness of the garden seemed broken by surfacing carp in the pool.

She listened for a softer, more reassuring sound, a murmuring wind, a lark's gentle call, or for the light to fade as a shadow lengthened. But instead there was only his face magnified, moving closer, inclining slightly, and his lips met hers.

He was the first man to kiss her. His lips pressed gently, and she closed her eyes. She felt the tip of his tongue trace over her mouth, and she shivered. Then he withdrew and she heard him whisper, "Marry me."

She opened her eyes, and in his face she saw exquisite tenderness, but also unruled passion. Yet she saw no threat, only promise and completeness. Could it really be? she wondered. This was a girl's dream, but she was no longer a girl. Her hand went to his face and touched it, as if to test its reality. He didn't move as her fingers stroked his cheek and rounded his jaw.

"Yes," she said.

He took her hand and brought it to his lips. "I hope I never make you unhappy," he said.

"You won't," she answered. "I won't let you."

They sat for a long time holding hands, sounding each other's eyes; then he smiled gently and said they should tell the others. She stood, smoothed her gown, and together they went to make the announcement.

When they walked into the other room, hand in hand, everyone in attendance stood, and by their carriage, both Father Bergere and Chien knew what had happened.

Ahn said simply, "The Lady Le Xuan Huong has consented to be my wife. We shall be married the day after tomorrow."

He withdrew his hand and bowed to her; then he left.

Her head remained lowered until he was gone; then she returned to her chamber and closed the door.

Father Bergere and Chien stood facing one another. For a full minute they were motionless, simply staring, knowing their own lives were now forever entwined; then the priest heaved a great sigh. "God works in strange ways," he said at last.

Chien glared and grumbled darkly, "They certainly do."

2

The Crimea: 1854

ALAIN LAFABRE HAD NO PREMONITIONS about the morning's battle. He had taken part in so many sieges of Sevastopol that he'd lost count of the number. In the beginning he'd had fears and premonitions, had awakened in the middle of the nights in cold sweats, had trembled in wet mornings on the line with the others, eyes darting furtively to one another to see if they could tell who would not return, praying, "Not me, please not me, God," but his visions had come to nothing. For a year now he'd been in the Crimea with the army of the Emperor Napoleon III, a battle-tested veteran who simply went along in the attacking force, moving with the relentless predictability of, and no more thought than, a wave in the morning tide.

Now he had little reason to fear, not since he had been assigned to the personal guard of the Duke of Parnasse, a young nobleman who, Lafabre had observed, was not likely to present himself anywhere on the battlefield that might prove dangerous.

Alain's extraordinarily handsome features clouded at the thought of the duke, and he yelped angrily as he burned his finger on the kettle he'd been stirring over the fire. He allowed himself a stream of profanity, indulged himself long after the finger had ceased to hurt, then turned his oaths on the food.

At least he'd expected better food while serving the duke, if indeed what he was stirring could be termed food, but the true marvel was, for he had not believed it possible, that what he ate here was even worse than what he'd been served on the line. That was because, he knew, his provisions came out of the duke's purse rather than the emperor's, and the duke was not a generous man.

Dear God, Alain thought, what he would give for real food. A baguette. He would kill for a baguette. And for a woman. He pulled his hand quickly from the kettle, for he knew that thinking about a woman, he could burn his hand to the bone and not notice. Indeed, what would he do, or not do, for a woman?

He stirred the kettle absently, intrigued by the paradox which took root in his mind: if he was fighting and killing for the emperor and getting neither food nor women, what would he have to do to get food and women?

Though by no means a profound individual, he saw suddenly that if he'd remained in Paris he'd have both—without having to kill or risk his life or die of boredom sitting alone around a campfire waiting for a cringing duke to stumble back drunk to be put to bed.

The clarity of that insight didn't please him at all; worse, it brought to mind his grandmother's denunciations of war, politics, religion, men, and especially himself. Grandmother had the tongue of an adder, and—he crossed himself quickly for his uncharitable thought—damn her for being right: he *was* a fool. "An imbecile," she'd called him; that and many other things when he'd told her he was joining the army. "You are every bit the fool your father and grandfather were."

Her own husband had been killed at Austerlitz in Bonaparte's army, and her oldest son, Alain's father, had died in service to Louis Philippe during the July revolution that overthrew the Bourbons. She had no doubt that Alain's fate would be the same; she had literally chased him out of the house, screaming at him, "You have a wife. You have a son. You belong here. Imbecile."

She was an old woman of seventy-eight, born in 1775, in the beginning of the reign of Louis XVI, and she said she'd lived through every stupidity and wickedness that God could imagine, and a few He probably hadn't until Robespierre, Napoleon, and the men of France began to confound Him daily.

But Alain had gone off to the army anyway, and his grandmother had moved into the house to stay with his wife, Denise, and help care for their four-year-old child, Andre.

The frown left Alain's face at the thought of his wife and child, and he ladled whatever was in the kettle into his messkit, eating contentedly, not at all tasting; just the thought of Denise filled him with such happiness that it drove away all troubles.

What he felt first when he thought of her was tenderness, and one watching him at such a moment might have thought he was in prayer, for there was a look of perfect peace on his face. He appeared like a very large child. And he was that. He was twenty-three years old, uneducated except for the most rudimentary things, which did not include reading or writing, and his beliefs were those of a child. He accepted everything he'd been told or taught, and his allegiance to his country and God were unquestioning and unbounded—"The peasant of peasants," his grandmother called him.

Though undistinguished in other ways, his appearance set him apart, so much so that his commonness in other regards was a bit of a surprise and a disappointment. "Looks you got from me," his grandmother told him. "Brains, I don't know who you didn't get those from."

His features were his father's, through his grandmother, and they had come via Italy. Her family was from Genoa, all blond, light-skinned, blue-eyed. The descending generations, with the French blood, were a darker mixture, but still mostly blue-eyed and more light-toned than most French. Alain was almost a throwback to the Italian forebears, so fair, tall, and lean, with the particular sensual carriage of the northern Italian, that he stood out in every gathering.

Also from his grandmother came some common sense and a great exuberance for life. He knew he was handsome, and he was good with women, and even his grandmother was not immune to his charm, but then, she'd had a definite weakness for his grandfather, bearing him six children in six years of marriage.

Once Denise had confided to his grandmother that Alain was remarkable in bed, and the old woman had smiled deeply to herself, carried back almost a half-century. She didn't say anything for a long time; then she nodded and sighed. "Yes, damn them for that too." She didn't explain to Denise that it was that memory of life and love and joy for which she had lain awake and wept every night since her husband's death forty years ago.

The look of prayerful tenderness quickly passed from Alain's face; his eyes glinted and his face sharpened, losing its smoothness, and even his body tensed, mirroring the raw sex which flooded his thoughts.

Without a father, he had grown up an unruly child, and the priests had despaired of him early; his mother, not a bright woman, had tired of motherhood and its constrictions, and when he was seven, had run off with another grenadier and was never heard of again. He was passed among the brothers and sisters of his father, but the only anchor was his grandmother, and she recognized right away that he was the reincarnation of his father and grandfather—a hopeless case, yet she went through the motions of discipline and denunciation nevertheless.

"The only difference between you and your grandfather is that your grandfather married an intelligent woman," she told him when he brought poor, pregnant, sixteen-year-old Denise home, a fact that, although true, didn't endear her to Alain's new bride.

Yet he did seem to love her. More surprising, even though only seventeen, he turned out to be a good father. He doted on Andre, and poured the love into that relationship that he himself had never had.

When Alain had appeared with Denise, his grandmother had, she thought, held her tongue admirably. It was obvious to her that the girl had no more sense than a mushroom, and though morals then hadn't contracted to what they later became, and she herself was certainly not a prudish woman, she thought their behavior no better than that of dogs. She had told them that: "Why don't you go out in the street? You don't need a house for the way you carry on." They could literally not keep their hands off one another. Finally the old woman had left her own house, abandoning it to them, and moved in with one of her children, telling them her house had been taken over by savages. But everyone knew she wasn't entirely displeased.

Alain's and Denise's relationship had been physical from the beginning, and it never slackened in their four years together; they never tired of one another.

Alain had worked as a stable boy for a large mercantile firm, then had become a blacksmith, but the Crimean War came, and the lure was too great for him; it was in his blood, and none of Denise's pleadings or his grandmother's excoriations and theatrics (she had stormed out many times and fainted twice) dissuaded him.

But she had been right; he saw that now. He had been a fool.

He realized suddenly he had an empty spoon in his mouth, and when he looked into his messkit he saw that he'd eaten everything. That was good, he thought, for he hadn't tasted a thing, but on the other hand, now he had nothing to do.

After washing out his messkit, he searched about for something to occupy his time and settled on working on the duke's equipment, for the duke was very vain about his appearance, and no matter how well he looked, he was never pleased. But tonight it would make no difference, for he would notice nothing in the morning. Every night before battle he got drunk, so drunk that he had to be helped onto his horse in the morning, at a time when danger was long past.

Alain had been very proud when he'd been pulled from the line regiment to be part of the personal guard of the Duke of Parnasse—a man, much to his surprise, his own age. He had assumed he'd ride in the rear of the army beside an elderly, fat, goutish nobleman; instead he found a young man almost as tall as himself, very dark and lean, with good strong features and remarkably sharp eyes.

The duke was properly distant with Alain, yet not entirely impersonal. And he talked a good fight, dazzling Alain with visions of stunning charges into the midst of the enemy. Alain at first was wildly devoted to the young nobleman, personifying cause and country with him. The night before their first battle together, Alain slaved over their equipment, even going into the duke's private quarters to check on his uniform, a responsibility not his but the valet's, because he wanted everything perfect, with nothing to mar their splendor when they appeared on the battlefield. He didn't even sleep that night, but waited up for the duke's return so he could personally watch over and wake him.

It was a very long, lonely, and cold wait, for the duke didn't return until dawn, carried back by servants of another nobleman and put to bed; he didn't wake until past noon, after the siege had been turned back, and by the time he was dressed and mounted, the army was already straggling back.

Alain passed off the incident: everyone drank too much at times, he reasoned. Yet a pattern developed. In the three months Alain had been with the duke, he'd not yet made it to the battlefield. Alain struggled to keep from believing he was a coward; after all, who was he—a stable boy, blacksmith, grenadier—to question a duke, a chamberlain to the emperor? Still, man to man, he knew there was something wrong.

He decided not to work on the equipment, but to tend the horses and go to bed. The duke probably wouldn't even return tonight—he'd dismissed all his attendants, something he'd never done, so most likely he intended to stay at the camp of the Duke of Saville.

Alain stretched and looked out over the plain below him. He saw a thousand campfires, and the wind carried the voices of the soldiers on the eve of battle. He wished he was among them; here he was a courtier, and he didn't like the role. He belonged with those below, laughing and drinking, boasting and gambling. Perhaps he would ask the duke in the morning to be released back to the line.

Anything would be better than this, he decided. It had been a woeful experience, all of it. He had come to war with visions of glory and grandeur, filled with mission, charged with country and cause—though he wasn't altogether sure what the cause was, something to do with Russia and the Turks and the Holy Land, but how it all fitted together and had anything to do with France and himself, he had no clue—but after a year, glory, grandeur, and mission were all gone, leaving only loyalty. He was tired of the war and wanted to go home, but to whom could he tell that?

Alain drove the thought of home and family from his mind; that was becoming too difficult to bear. He couldn't think about the war because he thought it stupid and futile and it only made him angry, and he didn't want to think about the duke because what entered his mind was disloyal, so there was nothing to do but check the horses and go to bed.

As he moved off, he saw a man approaching. Alain stiffened in preparedness; then he saw the man stumble, and he sighed, knowing it was the duke. But it was too early and he wasn't that drunk, so Alain was mystified. Perhaps he'd lost everything—but no, the duke always won at cards, no matter how drunk he was.

Alain ran to offer whatever assistance he could.

"Good evening, Excellency." He never ventured anything beyond a simple greeting, nor would he have felt it his place to ask a question.

The duke put his arm around his shoulder and dropped a heavy bag of gold coins onto the stones; it was obvious he had won a considerable sum. Alain, supporting the duke, knelt to pick up the bag, and led him off into his tent.

"Where is Costin?" the duke demanded when he entered.

"You told all of them they could leave tonight, Excellency."

Parnasse nodded absently, remembering; then he turned to Alain and waited. The young grenadier stood motionless before him.

"Well? Do you expect me to undress myself?"

Alain stepped forward and began to unfasten the tunic. Actually he *had* expected him to undress himself, but he complied without hesitation, and tried not to mind the offensive alcoholic breath.

Parnasse watched Alain fumble with the tunic and said disdainfully, "I hope you don't undress women so clumsily. Do you undress women, Lafabre?"

"Yes, Excellency. But not recently."

He steadied Alain's hand and guided it to the remainder of the buttons. Alain carefully hung the tunic in the wardrobe. When he came back, the duke was seated, one leg up, presenting his boot. Alain struggled with it, then the other. All the while, the duke's eyes were fixed on him, and he was beginning to feel uncomfortable under the intense gaze.

"Do you like it with me, Lafabre? Better than on the line?"

Alain hesitated; here was his chance to return to his regiment.

"Oh, so you don't like it here. You think I'm a coward."

"No, Excellency. Of course not." He shook his head vigorously.

"I know how you feel, but any soldier down there would trade places with you. How would you like to be the first man on the line tomorrow? Would you like to lead the siege? It would take only a word from me."

Alain said nothing; he didn't understand what had provoked the duke, so he bowed his head. Those who led a charge died, it was that simple, and he knew it was well within the duke's power to have him killed.

Parnasse stood. "You would never see Paris again, Lafabre, if I sent you to the line. Wouldn't you rather stay with me?"

Alain still didn't raise his head.

Parnasse moved closer. "Well?"

Alain looked up timidly; the duke was only inches in front of him.

Parnasse smiled harshly. "You aren't that stupid, Lafabre; you don't want to die tomorrow." He took Alain's hand and placed it on the webwork of buttons that laced his waist and crotch. Alain's fingers didn't move, and he looked curiously into Parnasse's eyes.

"Yes, Lafabre, I want you to finish undressing me."

Alain unfastened the buttons and removed the trousers, slipping them down over his hips. He saw Parnasse was fully aroused, and stood up quickly and folded the garment, then placed it on his bureau.

When he turned, the duke was before him, blocking his movement, so close that his erection pressed into him.

Alain glanced down, then up to Parnasse's eyes, registering confusion rather than hostility.

"Now it's your turn." He reached to Alain's tunic and began undoing the buttons, but the grenadier pulled back.

"I thought you understood me, Lafabre."

Alain stammered, "Excellency, I . . . I don't understand."

Parnasse reached again for Alain's tunic. "Surely you know this is why I took you from your regiment."

Alain was too surprised to resist. This was something he had never conceived. For a man to touch him, or want him sexually, was an idea as remote for him as Euclidean geometry. He stood stock-still as the duke's hands went under his tunic, then slipped down his belly and boldly felt his crotch.

Alain pulled away forcefully. "I shall go now, Excellency. I think you've drunk too much and don't know what you're doing."

Parnasse pressed him again, roughly grabbing his body. "If you don't do what I say, you'll be the first man in the charge tomorrow."

Alain pushed him away. "That's what a soldier's for." He didn't bother to check his disgust. "Not for this. I won't be a woman."

Then Alain made his fatal mistake. He spat at the duke's feet and turned away to leave.

In a fury of rejection and humiliation, Parnasse grabbed his sword and rushed Alain.

The blade slipped easily through the flesh of his back and penetrated his heart.

Alain jerked upward, gasping, sank to his knees, then fell forward on his face.

Parnasse stood over the body, horrified at what he'd done. He'd never intended such a thing. He wasn't a cruel man, only weak, and if he hadn't been drinking and Alain had not degraded him, he wouldn't have attacked him.

He listened a moment, but no one was about. He'd have to explain this, though no matter what he said, his word would be accepted; no one would care about one more dead soldier. But he'd make a hero of Alain, not a villain—he felt too much remorse for that. He went for the sack of gold, sprinkled coins near the body, and left a trail going out the tent; then he tossed the sack beyond, as though it had been discarded by a thief. He'd tell everyone that his grenadier had died defending the life and property of the duke. Then he dressed and went for help.

And that was the explanation Denise received in Paris three months later. She carried on hysterically, far too much, thought Alain's grandmother, who had expected it, and who'd received the same news of her husband and son forty and twenty years ago. "Accept it as God's will," she told Denise. "He works in strange ways, but He's consistent."

A month later an emissary from the duke knocked on the door of their shabby single-room dwelling in an overcrowded, dilapidated building on the Left Bank, not far from the Pantheon. The man had had to pick his way through trash and urchins, his sword at the ready against beggars and thieves, and when he reached the dark, squalid room where they lived, he didn't bother to hide his disdain, but he nevertheless expressed the regret of the duke for Alain's death, who in appreciation for his service wanted his widow to have a gold napoleon. Actually he'd been ordered to deliver ten coins, but he felt one was sufficient. Then he left.

Denise turned over the coin several times and showed it to Alain's grandmother. The old woman, dressed in black, a shawl over her white hair and shoulders, didn't look up from her knitting. "He meant you to have more, of course; but why did he give you any?"

Denise, a remarkably pretty girl with long curly black hair, but a girl despite her six-year-old child, stamped her foot in exasperation. "Because Alain saved the duke's life."

"Nonsense. Anyway, dukes don't give money for that. They do things only for gain or guilt."

Denise rolled her eyes and turned away. She was accustomed to the contrariness of the old woman and suffered it now only because she was a help with the child.

Her husband had died gloriously, saving the life of the Duke of Parnasse. That idea almost canceled out her grief, which indeed was genuine. Each day she told Andre the story of his father's death, each day embellishing it, but now there was concrete proof, a gold napoleon.

"See this, Andre? The duke sent this to us because your father saved his life. He was so grateful that—"

The grandmother knit furiously. "Stop telling the child such foolishness; he'll grow up to be the donkey his father and grandfather were."

"Shame! Alain was a—"

"Donkey. And this poor child, with the most stupid parents in France, is going to end up the same."

"Don't listen to her, Andre. Your father was a hero. Even the emperor said so. Why, on the battlefield there was no one—"

"Bah!" The old woman threw down her needles and left in disgust. Without even packing, she went to one of her sons' houses across the city and stayed two months, but at last she couldn't bear it: the child needed care, and she believed Denise was too stupid to provide even that, let alone food and clothing.

Which was near the truth. Denise had conceived at sixteen, wildly in love with the handsomest boy she'd ever seen, and their years together had been joyous—no matter they didn't have much or that the old woman was almost beyond bearing, or that the child was more trouble and noise than they could have imagined—all that paled before their love and passion.

The war was a terrible thing, and she carried on disconsolately when he left, yet it was a grand adventure, and he looked even more wonderful in uniform, and after all, what were men supposed to do if not fight for emperor and country?

However, his death ended that drama as theater, and she was suddenly faced with harsh reality: she was twenty-two years old, with a child, and no means of support—the widow's pension barely bought bread. She had been perfectly content sweeping out her room and burning meals and going to bed with Alain; she was not prepared for this stroke of bad luck and found life very cruel.

The old woman moved back in and nagged her incessantly, and she was forced to take work as a scullery maid. Times were very hard, and there was no fun anymore, and she knew it would not be long before she turned into another of the wrinkled, bitter old crones who filled the streets of Paris.

All she had to separate her from others was the gold napoleon; she carried it everywhere, both as reminder and as talisman, and it was the coin which finally led her to the duke. One day in the kitchen of the café, which served mostly mule-team drivers, hot and dirty, sweat pouring from her, she reasoned that surely he had more, and surely he would be willing to help her, if only to give her a job. If she was going to be a scullery maid, better at a palace, where no doubt he lived, than here.

In fact the duke was in Paris; Sevastopol had fallen shortly after Alain's death, so Parnasse had returned to France. He discovered that his father had depleted the family fortune, leaving only the château on the Loire, a fine apartment in Paris, and heavy debts. His mother and two sisters were entrenched at the château, so he moved into the apartment, faced with the immediate task of raising capital.

As it turned out, he had no need to worry, for he'd underestimated the value and draw of his title. He was a Bourbon, a nephew of Charles X, the last Bourbon king, restored after the Napoleonic debacle, but purged by the Orleanist Louis Philippe. Though no longer a member of the ruling family, he was surprised to discover the appeal and fascination his nobility had for others.

His youth and handsomeness merely added to his appeal, and he couldn't begin to accept all the invitations sent him upon his return. He was pursued by wealthy widows, lesser titled families in search of a partner for their daughters, and the nouveau riche, drawn like mosquitoes to his royal blood. He was an authentic prince, with the royal blood of kings coursing through his cold veins.

Yet parties became boring, talk drearily repetitious, the sex staged and insincere. Money became critical, so in a haste that he was to rue forever, he struck a bargain with the Faure family.

Catherine Faure was the seventeen-year-old daughter of Henri Faure, one of the wealthiest entrepreneurs in the country, a merchant and munitions supplier to the Emperor Napoleon III, an odious fat man with dreams of grandeur and a fixation on royalty. He fawned obsequiously on Parnasse, but he knew exactly his financial plight.

A contract was made, settling a huge sum in dowry, a fixed and generous annuity for each, and the payment of all of Parnasse's debts.

The wedding was to be in six weeks, and Parnasse was a very happy man, thinking all his problems solved. So when Denise presented herself at his apartment, she couldn't have chosen a more auspicious moment.

Parnasse's luxurious quarters were on the Rue de Rivoli, near the Palais Royal, only a short distance from where Denise worked. She had gone on impulse directly from work, arriving dirty and disheveled, but she had finally persuaded the liveried attendant to bring in the gold napoleon to the duke and ask for an audience.

He did so, announcing that a young woman of low class and great filth desired to see him; the attendant presented him with the coin and said that the woman had a garbled story to tell of her husband in the Crimea.

Parnasse was going over wedding arrangements, and his heart stopped cold for an instant. But he recovered quickly and told the man to dismiss her.

The attendant told Denise the duke would not see her, did not return the coin, and slammed the door on her. Stunned, she withdrew to plan her strategy.

She quit her job without telling Alain's grandmother, but left every morning as before and stationed herself on the Rue de Rivoli, on the corner down from the duke's apartment. On the third afternoon she saw the gates open and his carriage emerge.

She ran and threw herself against the door, holding on so tenaciously that the coachman couldn't dislodge her. Inside, Parnasse pulled back in shock as she shouted at him, "My name is Denise Lafabre, Excellency. My husband served with you in the Crimea. He saved your Honor's life. You sent me a gold napoleon but it was stolen from me. Please help me. Please. Please."

The coachman wrestled with her, but she kicked him savagely.

"I must see you. I must ask you about my husband. My son is dying."

She began to weep, but didn't loosen her hold on the door. Parnasse waved away his driver.

"When I came to your Excellency's house I gave your man the coin, but he never gave it back. I have nothing; I can't even feed my child. Please see me."

Parnasse's eyes narrowed on her. He reached over and drew the curtain. "Come tomorrow at four."

Denise dropped away, overcome with joy. The duke would see her; that alone was enough for her, for a woman of her station had no hope of ever encountering a man of his rank.

When she returned home, she was quivering with excitement, and though she fully intended to keep her own counsel about the matter, she immediately told Alain's grandmother.

To her great surprise, the old woman said nothing, only contemplated her silently for a long time, and almost before Denise's eyes the old woman seemed to age and her body shrink. Because of her vitality and physical presence, Denise frequently forgot how old the woman was, but now, sunk into the chair, her face haggard and her eyes deep, darkly ringed pools, she looked all of her eighty years.

At last she lifted herself heavily from the chair; she walked as though carrying an immense weight and went to Andre and clutched the boy to her. Denise shrugged and went off to prepare for tomorrow.

Neither woman spoke of the matter again, though in the afternoon, as Denise was leaving, the old woman took her hand in hers and held it a moment; then she patted it gently, a sad smile on her lips.

Denise had spent the previous evening and the entire day getting ready, though she had not thought out what she would say. Her preparations were solely physical. She had never felt so clean, having bathed twice, and she was very pleased with her appearance. Her dress was bright red, her bodice so tightly drawn that she seemed to have no waist, and reams of white ruffles circled her neck and cascaded down her front. Her hair was drawn back as severely as a Gypsy's, and piled precariously on top of her head.

Had the doorman not been told to expect her, he would have slammed the door in her face, for she looked exactly like a whore from Pigalle. Denise had never before worn rouge and had spent her last centimes purchasing some. Both cheeks were bright red circles, and in the middle of one she had, thinking it the fashion, boldly pasted a black beauty spot. The effect was that of an archery target.

For a moment the doorman stared openmouthed, then told her to wait outside while he announced her. On his way to inform the duke, he alerted everyone in the household to the sight on the doorstep. They all peeked out windows, and the chambermaids clicked their tongues, too shocked even to titter, and unbelieving that she would be admitted.

But the doorman bowed upon his return and led her in. They walked across the marble foyer, past the magnificent staircase, where, on looking up, Denise thought she saw several figures staring down at her.

Never had Denise seen such opulence, nor even imagined it. Her eyes tried to take it all in, but there was too much—chandeliers, figurines, statuary, tapestries, gilded furniture. She felt smaller and smaller as she approached the massive carved-oak double doors, and her bright red dress seemed less and less impressive.

Without knocking, the attendant swung open the doors. "Madame Lafabre."

The doors closed behind her and Denise stood barely inside the room, unable to take another step. She had been brought to the library, a huge high-ceilinged room with leather chairs and down-cushioned sofas, and more books on the four walls than she knew existed in the world. A blue-and-gold Oriental rug of the most intricate design covered the entire floor.

Across the room, the young duke stood motionless also—he had never seen such a dress, nor more ruffles or rouge, and he squinted to see if perhaps she had a beetle on her cheek. But he recovered quickly and went to her, bowing slightly, his heels clicking, the only aspect of the military he'd mastered.

She did not offer her hand, for which he was grateful, nor did she know what to do, merely stood, mouth slightly open, overwhelmed.

He was in uniform, dazzling in rank and medals. She thought he was beautiful, and she saw for the first time how young he was.

"Madame. I'm delighted you came. Please sit down." He graciously directed her to a sofa and sat two cushions away.

It was just as well that she had not thought of what to say, for she would have forgotten it; she sat paralyzed. Parnasse realized her fright. Though a cold and calculating man, he was not without charm and grace. Yesterday he'd been shocked to see her, fearing she might know something, but he soon realized she couldn't possibly, and only wanted money. He'd give it to her, of course—he wasn't petty—and now he set to putting her at ease.

"Forgive me for not calling on you, but my duties since my return have been very pressing. Yet I should have made time to call upon the widow of such a brave and noble man."

Denise lowered her head, genuinely overcome, and began to weep.

"Your husband died valiantly; his emperor and I are in his debt, and I extend my condolences and gratitude to you."

Denise sobbed.

"There seems to be a misunderstanding. Yesterday when you . . ." He was about to say, "threw yourself on my carriage." ". . . when we met, you mentioned a gold napoleon. I sent you ten. Didn't you receive them?"

She looked up startled, tears gone, and quickly shook her head.

"I see. And you mentioned that the one you sent in was not returned to you. I shall amend that, and see that you receive the others. Is there anything else that I can do for you? You need only ask."

Grief gone, and emboldened by his generosity and her good fortune, she pressed her case quickly, thanking him profusely and telling him her plight, that she had to care for Alain's small child and grandmother. She begged a position in his household.

Parnasse listened sympathetically, and saw that despite her garish costume and makeup, she was a very attractive woman. He said that he would find her a position.

She jumped in excitement and without thinking reached out her hand to thank him, grabbing his arm. He jolted at the touch.

She was about to withdraw her hand, but when her eyes met his, she didn't move. He let the hand rest for a moment; then he put his on her shoulder.

She neither protested nor resisted as he moved to her, nor would it have occurred to her to do so; he was a duke, and she had not the strictures of her husband to deny royalty what it wished. Indeed, that such a man desired her was so gratifying and beyond her hope that it would not have been possible for her to deny him.

Since she wore no undergarments, his hand met no resistance—cloth or modesty—and her daring filled him with uncommon passion and desire for a woman.

Parnasse was definitely responsive to women, and experienced; it was simply that his preference was for men. Given a choice between Alain and Denise, he would have desired both, but would have chosen Alain first.

The women he had slept with had mostly been paid to do so. Like all young noblemen, he'd been attended by expensive courtesans; there was no need for a man of his rank to learn the art of seduction—this scene in his library was as close to a seduction as he had come, and the idea of his own conquest fueled his passion.

And her response was genuine—that he knew. She was a remarkably sexual woman and it had been over two years since she'd been touched by a man; his hand rekindled immediately all the heat that had so long smoldered within her. She gave herself completely to him, her fervor creating even greater lust in him.

He had never had sex with anyone this passionate; the mere stroking of her inner thigh caused her to moan and writhe, and for the first time in his life he discovered the overpowering sensation of satisfying a woman's desire and need. She taught him the force of a woman's response, and the pleasure of fulfilling it. Before, his attention to a woman's body and needs had been cursory; he'd viewed women merely as vessels to satisfy his own physical drive. Now he learned that an equally exquisite pleasure could be gained by tending theirs.

Her movements and sounds increased until finally she threw herself against him, closing her thighs on his hand, pumping against it, and her own hands went to his clothes, pulling at the buttons and lacing.

He was not even able to get his trousers off before she moved astride him. He gasped as she forced herself down him, working him so violently that he exploded inside her almost immediately, but she didn't stop. Her cries and spasms drove him wild and he thrust until he reached a second orgasm, his own head thrashing on the cushions in pleasure. Her movements slowed, yet still she didn't release him, only worked him softly and smoothly within her.

Their eyes opened on each other simultaneously and for a second she seemed shocked at the position she was in, and she eased off him, moving away on the sofa, pulling down her dress. She realized that she had lost control of herself, and the situation, and she was mortified.

Parnasse stood and fixed his trousers, then sat back down—not near her. Neither knew what to say.

At last she stood, smoothed her clothes, and asked shyly, "Am I still to work here?"

He jumped up. "Yes. Of course." He said it quickly, that

taken with her, and that gratified. For the first time he felt like a whole man.

He rang for the chatelaine and explained that Denise would be employed on the household staff.

Madame Vourey had been mistress of the household for fifteen years; she had run the household for the old duke, knew all his follies and weaknesses, and had similarly placed several of his favorites. She had expected a directive such as this some time ago, especially considering her master's age. Her only question was whether Denise was to have her own room. Parnasse nodded, and the two women left.

Thus began Denise's service to the duke.

Because everyone knew of the relationship, Denise was treated with deference by the other servants. She was given a comfortable room and a chambermaid's uniform, but her duties weren't explained to her. Madame Vourey decided to wait until she could determine the extent of the young duke's infatuation, and its length. From her experience, she knew such involvements could last a day or a year, though since the duke was to be married in a few weeks, she couldn't imagine this lasting beyond that: the duchess would toss her out if he didn't have the sense to get rid of her before then.

Denise didn't return home for two days. When she did, all she said was that she had taken a position as a chambermaid with the duke. Alain's grandmother nodded and said nothing. To Andre, Denise explained that she'd be gone a great part of the time. She told him in glowing detail of the duke's apartments and their furnishings, and of the duke himself, the man his father had died for. She thought it imprudent to show the ten gold napoleons, so she hid them; then she brought out a package of fine pastries which she'd taken from the kitchen, and even the old woman overcame her scruples to eat them.

So a routine was established in which Denise spent part of her days and many of her nights away while the old woman saw to the care and teaching of Andre. The boy found nothing amiss, and even the old woman accepted the situation—what was so bad about it? she asked herself. So the silly girl was mistress to a duke? She cared for her child and brought them all fine things—surely they'd never eaten so well, if only table scraps—and she was happy, so where was the harm? If life had taught her anything, it was that you get by the best you can; fine sensibilities were for people who could afford such luxuries. Sin and morals were things to dwell upon in the hushed sanctuary of the cathedral, but not to fret about in the streets.

Alain's grandmother had seen many things in her life, but the sight of Denise gaily tripping back from the duke's chambers wasn't one of the worst. Even Denise's manner changed to her, and the two settled into amicability.

Denise was happy, though her relationship with the duke wasn't what she'd expected; he was certainly not a demanding lover, nothing like Alain. She had no delusions about his feelings for her, but she'd been surprised at the infrequency with which he visited her or called her to him. At first she thought it was out of discretion; then she attributed it to her belief that he had other lovers, but that didn't seem to be the case, so at last she was just perplexed.

He was not an expert lover like Alain, but their sex was satisfactory and he always seemed pleased; she was not demanding and so posed no threat, and he was happy with the arrangement.

Eventually she was firmly established in the household and the others held no rancor for her. They saw that she was a sweet and simple girl, and they even developed sympathy and understanding for her. She received no special treatment from the duke and her wages were no more than the others'; she was given light duties, performed them uncomplainingly, caused no troubles, and wore no airs.

Madame Vourey grew genuinely fond of her and looked out for her interests; moreover, she saw Denise's usefulness. The duke, she had discovered, was not overly interested in women, and this girl, by meeting his undemanding needs, eased what could have become a difficult situation. It was expected and respectable that a young nobleman would have mistresses and sleep with his chambermaids—more respectable than if he didn't.

Her only concern was for the reaction of the duke's new wife.

Some people are simply not meant for one another. Though not wicked or evil by themselves, together they feed each other's weaknesses, turning petty faults into cruelties, and fuel the fires of vanity, jealousy, and greed. The unhappiness they suffer from one another they turn into vindictiveness toward everyone else.

Philippe Parnasse and Catherine Faure were such people. Though born of very different station, their personalities were uncannily alike; they were more siblings than mates.

Catherine was an indulged, willful, extremely intelligent, beautiful girl who had been raised to believe that position and money mattered above all things. She had no sensitivities because she'd been shown none. She was not kind because she had never seen kindness demonstrated. She was raised only to marry well. Love had nothing to do with it; she didn't know what love was, for she hadn't seen that either.

The man she married was just as woefully uninstructed in human feelings. His parents had had no time for him, were interested only in their own amusements and intrigues. Catherine and Philippe were young people who needed help but who couldn't help one another.

Yet all seemed to bode well from the beginning. On first meeting, they were pleasantly surprised. For the amount of money her father had settled on her, Philippe had no great expectations; he'd braced himself for the worst, prepared for an ugly, fat merchant's daughter, but instead she was strikingly beautiful, vibrantly alive with eyes that flamed mercurial green. Her skin glowed with health and spirit, a rose luminosity heightened by her soft silky chestnut hair.

For her part, to become a duchess she'd have been willing to marry a titled troll, so when she saw the tall, handsome young duke, she was delighted.

In addition to their mutual physical attraction, he found her intelligent, clever, and informed, and she found him gracious and without pomposity.

Everyone's expectations for the marriage were high; the marriage of royalty to commerce was commonplace now. The past century had created the nobility of money, and the Bourgeois Monarchy of King Louis Philippe, who had succeeded the last Bourbon king, had sanctified such marriages. It was understood that royalty needed financing, for those who hadn't lost their heads during the Revolution had most surely lost their fortunes.

The marriage of Philippe Vincent Tourney Bourbon de Parnasse and Catherine Faure was the major social event of 1856 in Paris. Balls, parties, and receptions were given for the young, attractive couple, and the emperor himself attended three such functions, an unheard-of honor.

The marriage was performed at Notre Dame, with the cardinal archbishop of Paris officiating.

No one begrudged the couple their moment, nor the extravagance. Even the new victims of society, the industrial workers who labored eighteen hours a day for less than the waste on a single plate of a single dinner, were caught up in the pageantry and pomp. The marriage was seen as a testament to the glory of an older France, and the promise of a new and greater one.

But like most expectations, it fell short immediately.

They honeymooned at Château Parnasse, on the Loire, sixty miles from Paris, and by the third day they knew theirs was not a heavenly match.

Catherine was a virgin of little sexual knowledge but high anticipations. She discovered immediately that Philippe was not the lover she'd fantasized about. The initial intercourse was fundamental and expeditious. That would have been acceptable had not the next been the same; and on the third night she was frankly bored. What made it worse, intolerable, was that the entire setting was geared for romance and sexual extravagance—the private and isolated château, the hushed and attentive servants, meals served in the bedroom, extended baths and toilettes—yet the sex was infrequent, unsatisfying, and uninteresting. She learned that she was a passionate woman but that the man she'd married was not going to be able to fulfill her.

Yet what hope was there? She was beautiful, with silky skin and perfectly formed breasts, a firm young woman's body, but he found her threatening. He knew he wasn't able to satisfy her passion, and knew also her disappointment in him. He didn't want the heavy responsibility of satisfying her sexuality; he would have to perform, and he couldn't manage that.

Had they known better, had more experience, been able to talk, they might have overcome their problems, but instead they withdrew from one another to nurse their grievances and disappointments and in short time they formed a wall of impenetrable hostility. By the time they returned to Paris, the foundation for their resentment was firmly laid; yet perhaps because they realized so soon that they were mismatched, they were able to guard against a mortal blow from the other.

Outwardly there was no strife, for both were too proud to reveal any weakness to the world, yet it was obvious to the household by the hard looks they exchanged, by their silences, by the way they avoided one another.

At first Catherine was content to allow Madame Vourey to run the household, but quickly she took the reins herself. She wanted a strict accounting for everything, and her manner was not at all relaxed. She was a daughter of commerce; she knew everything's price and value, and expected full return for each expenditure.

It was also not long before she began to prod Philippe to do something with his time. Her father and brothers worked hard and turned a profit at their enterprises, and she thought her husband should do the same. They didn't need money, had a title, so she turned her sights to power. She liked movement and action, saw politics as the fulcrum for it, so she urged him in that direction.

He was both willing and competent, and his money and position made it easy. Besides, it was a way to prove himself, since she'd made it clear that he was sexually deficient.

And sex was Philippe's cross to bear. He'd resisted his own inclinations from both shame and fear of exposure, and because he didn't want to be the way he was. He was still haunted by Alain's masculinity and rejection, and that night in the Crimea returned to him with greater frequency.

At first he sought with Denise to overcome the memory of Alain and the reality of Catherine. He turned to her in desperation to prove himself, to vindicate himself with her response. And though surprised with his sudden and unexpected passion and attention, Denise responded. She intuitively felt his desperation and need, and became more than lover to him; she became mother and protector, and he grew more and more dependent upon her, and more devoted.

Madame Vourey watched with increasing foreboding, the frown marks furrowing deeper on her coarse broad face, and she awaited the explosion.

Catherine had never suspected Philippe of infidelity; he seemed so uninterested and unaccomplished in sex that it didn't occur to her that he would be sleeping with anyone else. Her discovery of his liaison with Denise was completely by accident.

She was aware of Denise, but her narcissistic nature was such that it prevented her from dwelling long on another person; moreover, there was nothing exceptional about this chambermaid. She saw that she was attractive, but she was merely a servant, and so much older than Catherine. Some months earlier, when Catherine was thinking of paring the staff, she'd suggested to Madame Vourey that they could do without two of the chambermaids, and why not Denise, who didn't seem to do much of anything. Madame Vourey had rushed to her defense, explaining to the duchess that Denise was a special case—her husband had served with the duke in the Crimea, had saved his life, and he felt obligated to provide for his widow. Moreover, Denise was supporting a child and an old woman, and was very simple.

The explanation mollified Catherine; she gave no more thought to it, but one day when going through the residence, she discovered that Denise had her own room. The other servants lived four to a room, and Catherine didn't understand why this chambermaid had her own, especially one so well appointed, with a huge bed, nightstands and bureaus, and even a rug on the floor.

Madame Vourey's hands fluttered nervously and she stammered an explanation about the duke's gratitude and indebtedness to the widow, but Catherine's suspicions were aroused and she pulled open the drawers to a bureau to find lingerie as fine and expensive as her own.

In another bureau she found clothing of Philippe's.

When Catherine turned, Madame Vourey looked into the most cold and furious eyes she'd ever seen. They flashed emerald green, the eyes of a jealous goddess, and she expected to be physically attacked, but instead Catherine shut the drawers and left the room without saying a word.

Madame Vourey flew to alert the staff and sent Denise from the house immediately, pushing her out the kitchen door, telling her not to return unless the duke himself summoned her.

He never did.

By the time Philippe returned that evening, Catherine had purged the house of everything and everybody. No servant opened the door for him or took his cloak, and he found himself alone with his wife. She performed no hysterics, didn't weep or ask why she had been so wronged, she simply told him that if he ever humiliated her again, she would inform her father and brothers, and he knew what he could expect from them.

Indeed he did; their crudeness and violence were without bounds. He was afraid of them, and of her. She reviled him and isolated him, took away his confidence and comfort, so he turned to work, throwing himself into it, callusing his pain with a hardening exterior and a meaner spirit, all suiting him perfectly for a meteoric rise in the Ministry of Foreign Affairs.

Catherine's wound was just as great; she didn't understand, and saw his actions as a rejection of herself, a humiliation she couldn't bear. She'd been willing to accept a disappointing and unsatisfying sexual life, thinking it her exchange for title and position, that the man she had married was not passionate, but instead she found that her husband was indeed interested in sex, only not with her. She was furious when she realized that so many nights when she'd yearned for his body, he'd been with a chambermaid. Now she was disgusted with the thought of ever sharing a bed with him again.

And she never did.

Yet it was Denise who suffered most, for she had been the happiest, and her fall was the farthest. She fell lower than from vhere she started, for she'd had a taste of a better life, seen into different world, was older, and everyone had known about her nd envied her, and now they rejoiced in her fall.

She took a demeaning job in the kitchens again, with long, rduous hours and little pay, and she felt acutely her poverty and umiliation. Alain's grandmother was too old to work, so Andre, vho had been able to go to school, had to quit and take work ixteen hours a day to earn enough to purchase bread and a little heese.

The years passed with inexorable slowness; hard, joyless years f drudgery and deprivation, and it was only the strong influence f his great-grandmother which prevented Andre from turning nto one of the urchins who roamed and salvaged through the treets of Paris, embittered and resentful of the opulence of the ew Napoleonic order, which favored only the rich.

Grandmother was unrelenting, barraging him with dreams of he future, lacing them with heavy doses of fundamental Catholicism: he would read, he would write, he would learn, he vould be good—that was her message over and over. The readful spell of poverty and ignorance had to be broken, and he vould do it.

She didn't let him out of her sight when he returned from vork, and used every wile to keep him home—fainting spells, eizures, heart attacks—but she also told him marvelous stories, nd he found there was no better entertainment on the street than er performances.

He saw little of his mother, only that she was aging quickly, hat the bright, happy, tittering woman of before was turning into haggard, mournful, middle-aged woman.

Yet there was tranquillity in the house; the two women were at eace, fighting only when Denise would try to tell Andre of his ather and the glory of his army service. Then Grandmother vould launch a scornful diatribe.

The boy was growing into a fine-looking youth, his father all ver again—fair-skinned and blue-eyed, six feet by the age of ixteen, broad-shouldered and muscled, with none of the frailty nd sickliness of other youths of his station. He was bright and uick, and could read and write. Yet, as Grandmother said, "What good is it to be the prize pig in the butcher shop?" He ad to get out of his caste, but she saw no way to raise him.

Andre himself was not worried; he knew exactly what he vas going to do: the day he turned seventeen, he was going to oin the army. The military was all he thought about, and no mount or intensity of his grandmother's vitriol disturbed him in the slightest. He would listen to her ridicule his father's and grandfather's and great-grandfather's service, nod politely, and both he and she knew what he was going to do.

Military fever was again over the land: empire troops were in Mexico and Egypt, France was aiding the Confederacy in the United States, and the Prussian Bismarck had maneuvered Austria into war. Everyone knew it was only a matter of time before there would be a war with Prussia.

The country was swept up in slogans and propaganda; military pomp and the promise of glory incited everyone's dreams, and Andre was caught up in it. He badgered his mother for stories of his father, and she eagerly told him. When he told her of his desire to serve, as his father had, she was pleased, and decided to help him the only way she could. She would appeal to the duke. Surely he couldn't have forgotten her.

Indeed he hadn't. For years he'd suffered without letup for his indiscretion. He and Catherine lived entirely separate, sharing only a superficial social life for appearances, nursing their dissatisfaction and lack of fulfillment on the venom they felt for one another.

Yet Philippe's career in government had been successful; he'd risen high in the Foreign Ministry and earned a reputation for smoothness and control. His future was bright, but his personal life was not rewarding. He'd had numerous, almost obligatory affairs with women, for a man of his position, with title and wealth, charm and attractiveness, was constantly being assailed, but he found the affairs hollow and joyless. The deeper desire he harbored within had only limited outlet—sordid, furtive forays into a darker world with male prostitutes, which made him feel cheap and dirty and which constantly threatened him with exposure and ruin.

Catherine too had affairs, diverting amusements for short periods, but without great passion, and devoid of love—perfunctory affairs with perfunctory men, casual trysts as shallow as and no more meaningful than her social engagements. Love and sex were great disappointments to this passionate woman; she'd expected so much more. She saw that the men with whom she had affairs were no better than her husband—inconsequential, weak men who bored and didn't satisfy her. She still dreamed of love and passion, but it was wistful fantasy now. She was no longer a girl; the illusion of romance had been jaded by reality. She had missed the abandon, the noisy, rollicking fun and gaiety of sex. She'd found that she'd paid a heavy price to become a duchess.

Both Philippe and Catherine had accepted their situations, but suddenly Denise reappeared, altering everything.

Denise's plan was simple. Since it had worked before, she decided to throw herself on the duke's carriage again. Yet she was not as young as before, and gendarmes were posted at both the ministry and his residence. For several days she watched his departures and the route he took; then one morning when his carriage stopped at a busy intersection, she ran to it and jumped in. Her movement had been so quick that the footmen hadn't even noticed.

The duke was too surprised to move. He didn't recognize her at first, but then he looked more carefully. "Denise?"

She knew how badly she looked, what the years had done to her—she was only thirty-four, but poverty and work had trampled her youth and pummeled her body, so that what now sat across from Philippe was not a girl of passion and lightness, but a worn, shapeless, drab, aged woman.

She took his hand, and there were tears in her eyes. "Please help me."

Her plaintiveness, and the memory of their past, so stirred him that he responded immediately, knowing that whatever she wanted was within his means to grant. "Of course."

She wiped her eyes and looked at him shyly. "You are as handsome as ever, Philippe."

He wasn't; the years had taken their toll on him also. He'd grown soft and fleshy; too much work and alcohol had marred his fine features. There was a ring of sadness and dissipation around him, and there was no boyishness left. He called to the coachman to drive through the Bois de Boulogne.

They talked for a long time, circuitously, about the past, and Denise told him about Andre, a strapping seventeen-year-old whose only desire was to serve in the military, as his father had. But she couldn't let him go off as Alain had; he was bright, could read and write, and she wanted him to be an officer. She had come to beseech Philippe for an appointment to the Ecole Militaire for her son.

Parnasse told her that it would be very difficult for a boy of his background and standing to succeed; the factors of his birth would be held against him, and he wouldn't be happy.

"Just the opportunity," she said. "Just give him that. He must have a chance."

The duke nodded and took her hand. "Of course I shall do it." He told her he would arrange the appointment and pay all expenses, but that to remain at the academy, the boy was on his own—he would receive fair treatment, but no favors.

When they said good-bye, they both fought tears for what had been lost, and Philippe hardened even more in his resentment for his wife.

Denise decided not to tell Andre, just in case the appointment didn't come through, though to keep her secret was the most difficult thing she'd ever done.

Finally one night when Denise, Andre, and the old woman were sitting before the fire, there came an authoritative rap at the door.

Andre opened it on a bemedaled, glitteringly uniformed officer of the Royal Guard. "I am looking for Andre Lafabre," he said.

Andre was so overwhelmed at the man's appearance that he simply stared—the Savior at the door wouldn't have been a greater surprise, or as impressive.

The officer, thinking perhaps he was confronting an idiot, eyed him warily. "Does Andre Lafabre live here?"

"Yes," he said at last; then his wits came to him. "I am he."

The officer indicated with his eyes that this was what he'd feared, but he opened his pouch and handed him some papers, asking as an afterthought, "Can you read?"

"Yes, of course."

The officer clicked his heels. "The papers will explain themselves."

For a full minute Andre stared at the empty doorway; then he brought the papers to Grandmother, but she turned to the fire and wouldn't look up.

He read the papers twice before he said in confusion, "It's an appointment to the Ecole Militaire. It must be a mistake."

Then Denise told him what had happened, exaggerating the duke's gratitude to Andre's father and downplaying her own role.

Andre burst with joy. He shouted and ran about the room, hugged and tossed up Denise, and lifted up his grandmother, laughing as she swatted him on the head.

In the following days he was in rapture, and seeing how complete was his happiness, the old woman ceased to castigate him.

He quit work and devoted himself to exercise and study, and perhaps a hundred times a day he reread the letter of appointment.

One day when he was studying mathematics, his face locked

in furious concentration, his grandmother, who had been watching him for many minutes, called to him, "I am an old woman, Andre."

"Unbelievably so," he said, his eyes twinkling, but still on the formulas in the book.

"And I've seen many things, and I'm not stupid, but I don't understand about you. Why don't you have girls?"

He hadn't expected that, and his eyes came up from the book.

"You're seventeen years old, why aren't you sleeping with girls?"

He flushed. "That's a sin, Grandmother."

"Nonsense. But even so, when did sin ever stop anyone from doing anything? Don't you like girls?"

"Of course. I just haven't . . . well, found one."

"They're not like truffles, you know; they're everywhere."

"Grandmother, I don't want a girl like that."

Her old face crinkled like parchment. "Don't you get urges?"

"Of course I do."

"Well, what do you do about them?"

"Grandmother!"

"That's a sin too, you know." She was enjoying his discomfort and her own salaciousness, but then she turned serious. She beckoned him to her and he sat at her feet before the fire.

She stroked his head gently. "You're too idealistic, Andre. Love and purity, God and holiness, country and duty—child, that's all illusion, glittering garb like that silly officer's uniform. It's all for show, Andre; underneath is ugly flesh, be it female, priestly, or royal."

She grabbed the skin on his arm and rolled it. "This is what you are." Then she pinched the wrinkled skin on her own arm. "And this is what you become."

He looked with confusion into her eyes. "What would you have me do, Grandmother?"

She smiled. "Be exactly as you are, but try not to get hurt too badly." Then she sighed and rested her head back. "And try not to become as old as I am."

On the day he was to report to the academy, he rose early and put on his best clothes, ate a quiet breakfast with his mother and grandmother, then kissed them good-bye. His mother wept at his departure, but his grandmother's eyes were dry and disquieted.

His haversack on his back, he walked proudly down the street, but he didn't head for the Ecole.

Promptly at nine in the morning he knocked at the residence of the Duke of Parnasse. When the door was opened, he gave his name and requested permission to see the duke. He said the matter was of great importance but would take only a moment.

The doorman told him the duke and duchess were at breakfast but he would relay the message. He announced to the duke, dining silently with his wife, that a young man, clean, respectable, of high manner but low birth, desired an audience. He had forgotten the name, thinking it unimportant.

Parnasse was about to have him dismissed—he received so many appeals for favors—but Catherine, eager for any diversion, curious at a caller so early, and simply to contradict her husband, directed him to be shown in.

Andre left his haversack in the hall and followed the footman to the dining room.

Had he not been so self-conscious and nervous, he would have noted the sensation his entrance caused. The duke started noticeably, as though confronting a ghost, and Catherine's jaw dropped open.

As he had practiced, Andre clicked his heels and bowed from the waist; then he recited his memorized speech, but neither of them heard a word.

For Parnasse, it was Alain who stood before him. The youth was a duplicate of his father. For Catherine, the youth in the doorway was the handsomest male she'd ever seen.

Both of them merely stared at him, then simultaneously realized that he'd said something and was waiting for a response.

Parnasse recovered first and stood up. He introduced his wife and told her the young man was the son of a man who'd served with him in the Crimea and that he had secured an appointment for him to the Ecole Militaire. He thanked Andre for the thoughtful courtesy of his visit, and he wished him every success at the academy.

Andre bowed gravely to the duchess, again to the duke, then left.

When he was gone, both Philippe and his wife went back to their breakfasts, neither commenting on the intrusion, and both feigning indifference. Yet both of their minds swirled, and almost identical feelings were awakened in each of them.

Philippe was overpowered with memory and desire. A youthful self was recalled, and all the unhappiness of the last eleven years was swept away.

Memory too played heavily in Catherine's thoughts: so this was the boy of that chambermaid who had slept with her husband and ruined her life, she thought. This beautiful boy.

They both looked up at the same time, accidentally catching each other's gaze. Slight smiles, an attempt at nicety, but startlingly carnal and wicked, came to both their lips.

Totally unaware of what had happened, or was about to happen, Andre Lafabre crossed the Seine and headed toward the Invalides and his career.

3

Hue: 1847

LADY DENG SAT BEFORE THE mirror of her dressing table, looking as malevolent as she felt.

Like any actress, she loved makeup and costumes, and often spent time before her mirror creating outlandish masquerades that gave expression to what she felt inside. As a courtesan she'd been able to indulge herself this way, appearing in guises of seduction or of the macabre—they were her release, her only method of true self-expression, because all the rest was artifice and pretense, humbling herself before loathsome men—but in the palace she'd had to be more circumspect. She hadn't been able to give vent to how she really felt, but now she did.

Her nails had been lacquered black, and while she waited for them to dry, she made faces in the glass, her brightly glossed red lips baring and pursing, her deeply shadowed eyes flaring furiously.

Her husband had brought her the news of Ahn's forthcoming marriage. He had borne it with smug satisfaction, but then he hadn't been prudent enough to withdraw immediately, though he well knew the wrath his wife was capable of, and knew he was too old to be a match for it.

Her rage and fiery nature were things he should have anticipated, but he hadn't, despite the warnings of his friends and the counsel of his grown children. Everyone had urged him to beware of this woman, but he had been helpless before her. He had believed that this attentive, charming courtesan could really love him, because he was, he thought foolishly, different.

He had believed he was all the things she had said he was: wise, powerful, kind, handsome, sexually expert. Perhaps he was some of those things, but he was, nonetheless, seventy years old, and she had married him for wealth and position, and having achieved these, she now took great pleasure in reviling him, and made no secret of her liaisons.

She combed her long black hair straight down, letting it cover her face; then she ran her fingers through it, brushing it wildly aside so that the effect, coupled with her anger-twisted face, was that of a madwoman in a Kabuki play. Then she brought her palm slowly across her face, and as it passed, the features magically smoothed, and suddenly there was a simpering courtesan in the glass. But she couldn't sustain it, despite her great prowess and ability, for her anger and hurt were too great. She had never been wronged like this, never been so humiliated, and she could not hide her pain, and the depth of her feelings had made her vulnerable to her husband.

Everyone knew of her affair with Prince Ahn; it was so well known that her husband didn't even suffer public ridicule for her infidelity—his age bestowed a merciful immunity on him. But it hurt him nonetheless, and the only pleasure he received now from his marriage was the rare opportunity he had to inflict unhappiness on her.

Gian Ke Deng had been in court when Ahn had made his spectacular request to marry Le Xuan Huong. Though lord treasurer and privy to all court secrets and gossip, Deng had known nothing in advance of the request, and he'd suffered rebuke for not having been able to prepare Tu Duc. What he'd learned since was of little help, only that Ahn's request seemed genuine and without underlying motive.

Deng had also learned that Ahn had made his request immediately upon leaving the bed of Deng's wife. That too was common knowledge now, passed by the soldiers and the maids, and it provided Deng with one of those infrequent opportunities to hurt his wife.

With mock innocence, his aged, frail body almost quivering with pleasure, he perched birdlike on the edge of a chair in her bedroom, rubbing his bony fingers together gleefully.

"Maybe you'll receive a special invitation to Prince Ahn's wedding," he said. "As an honored guest of the groom. Or perhaps of the bride, who no doubt has you to thank for having mesmerized the prince with your magic ah—"

Though he was not a large target, her aim was precise, and her flung brush hit him alongside the head, knocking him to the floor. She retrieved the brush and stood brandishing it over him.

"You vile, impotent, old, sychophant. I should flog you. I will flog you," and she hit him again. "Like Duyet, that's all you're good for."

She lashed out at him with the brush and screamed, "Duyet, Duyet, Duyet," until he was able to escape, covering his head, tottering out of her bedroom.

She called after him, "I'll have your tomb flattened. I'll make love on it every night. I'll writhe under the bodies of a thousand men while you rot. The smell of real men's semen will mock you."

She shrieked "Duyet!" and the name echoed in the corridor as Deng scurried away.

She was referring to Le Van Duyet, the last powerful eunuch, whose tomb Minh Mang had had leveled and lashed symbolically only a few years ago. Before then, as in China, eunuchs often rose to high positions in the mandarinate. Duyet had been so highly esteemed by the Emperor Gia Long that he'd been made vice-king of Cochin China, but two great mistakes destroyed him: he protected the Christians, and he opposed the ascension of Minh Mang to the throne. His death in 1832 ended the protection of the Christians in the south, and ended forever the power of the eunuchs.

Still in a rage, she ran outside, and seeing her husband crossing the gardens, screamed again, "Duyet!" He covered his ears and continued his rapid shuffle, well aware of the attention drawn to him, and cursing himself for having been so foolish.

Lady Deng then turned on her maid, and it took a full hour before her fury slackened and she was able to plan revenge. Ahn had mocked her. Everyone knew that he'd rushed from her bed to ask the emperor's permission to marry the most unattractive woman at court—a charmless old Catholic woman (Lady Deng forgot that she herself was some years older than Xuan).

Lihn Deng was not a woman to be trifled with under any circumstances, but especially not when her ire was aroused. She was the wife of the lord treasurer, no longer a courtesan to be used and cast off, a whore to be left naked and spent on a bed. He had publicly humiliated her, casting her off with no regard to her feelings or station, and the insult was intolerable.

But it was her feelings which were most hurt. Not only had she liked him, felt for him what she'd felt for no man before, she believed he'd held her in special regard. She thought that she meant something to him. But no, she was to him as all the other men had been to her—nothing.

She brought her fingers up to the mirror, her long black nails clawing the glass, her eyes and mouth grotesque, and she vowed vengeance.

* * *

Across the palace, the emperor listened attentively to his chief adviser, the Lord Chamberlain Huynh Bo Linh.

Even had he not been at the top of the mandarinate, Huynh would have commanded attention and respect. He carried his tall, thin frame with imperial dignity; he was never rushed and there was never a wasted movement or flawed gesture. He was fifty-three years old, yet had served three emperors in the highest capacities for the past twenty-five.

The mandarinate was a democratic system based solely on skill and brilliance, and it handled all administration in the country, down to the smallest detail in the lowest province. There were nine levels of mandarins, each level having two degrees, but only rarely was there a mandarin of the first level, first degree. At Tu Duc's court, only Huynh held this position.

He'd risen from obscure beginnings in the spring of 1822 when he'd journeyed with three thousand other students to take a provincial examination in an open-air camp guarded by soldiers to prevent anyone from receiving outside help. There were four test sessions, each beginning at three A.M., when the student was given paper and sent to his tent to work until the following midnight.

The applicants were tested on philosophy, ethics, poetry, rhetoric, history, and political science, but not on the exact sciences because Confucius had taught that natural phenomena surpassed human understanding.

Finishing so well, Huynh took the regional examination, then was one of fifteen selected to take the national competitive examination, given every three years. The questions were made up by the emperor, and those who passed were eligible to take the court examination, conducted personally by the emperor.

At the age of twenty-eight, Huynh was raised to the second level by Minh Mang, the most scholarly of all the emperors.

So now Tu Duc listened to him with respect and attention, though he didn't like what he was hearing—Huynh was again urging moderation in relations with the French and especially the missionaries. Huynh felt the French could be played off against one another, and didn't want the Christians persecuted because that would force them to ally themselves with the military.

"We have two enemies, not one," he told Tu Duc. "Keep them apart. Their distrust of one another is even greater than it is of us. Deal with them separately."

But Tu Duc and the other mandarins didn't appreciate the temporal and secular differences of the West, and they viewed Huynh with increasing suspicion and distrust because they wanted no dealings whatsoever with the French military or the French Catholics, and they did not share Huynh's enthusiasm for the marriage of Ahn to the dispossessed princess, the Catholic Xuan.

Huynh saw the marriage as an opportunity to merge Christianity into Vietnamese society and diffuse the disruptive power of the missionaries. He felt that if he could find a similar means to link French military and commercial interests to the society, the entire foreign threat could be absorbed. He was convinced that the foreigner and the foreigner's culture would disappear almost without trace into the jungle marsh of Vietnam.

Yet he should have been more cautious in his enthusiasm for the marriage, and it was surprising that he didn't foresee Tu Duc's disquiet, which turned to frank suspicion when he suggested that Ahn take a leading role in a plan to reconcile with the French military. Huynh suggested that instead of banishing Ahn to Ban Me Thuot, he should be made regent of Cochin China in Saigon, with the hope of reaching accord with the French.

Tu Duc could think of nothing less desirable; he was allowing this marriage only with the couple banished to Ban Me Thuot; should they ever show the slightest sign of coveting power, he'd crush them.

Listening to Huynh, Tu Duc inclined his head in a relaxed manner and his eyes were mild, but it was at such moments he was most on guard. It was bad enough that there was a pretender to the throne in the north, near Hanoi, but now his chief adviser wanted him to install an equally dangerous threat in the south. The pretender, a direct descendant of the last Le emperor, was Catholic and, supported by the missionaries, was creating serious unrest. Tu Duc was not about to countenance a similar situation in the south and allow his cousin to form an alliance with the French military.

In his eagerness to combat the French incursion, Huynh didn't see that his solution played upon all of the emperor's fears—of Ahn, of the Le descendants, of the missionaries, of the French military. Huynh was strangely blind to realizing that Tu Duc was threatened by Ahn's marriage to the niece of the Le pretender, fearing that together they might bridge the differences between the Buddhists and Catholics, and the Vietnamese and the French.

And now, Tu Duc saw, with all the problems and difficulties he faced, there was an added one—the unreliability and possible treachery of his chief minister. He found it disturbingly more than coincidental that the chief threat to his throne and his own chief minister shared similar thoughts and goals.

When Huynh finished pressing his case for sending Ahn to

Saigon, Tu Duc said he'd take it under consideration; then he asked Huynh to personally oversee all the arrangements for the wedding, because he wished to attend the Catholic ceremony.

Huynh suggested that this might create particular difficulties because the emperor must always be seated to the front and above all others, but Tu Duc said he'd make his presence unobtrusive, and follow the customs of the ceremony.

Such magnanimity should have sounded a warning within Huynh, but instead he interpreted it as an endorsement of his counsel.

Father Bergere, a man of singular political naiveté, was far less concerned with the heathen emperor's participation in the wedding than he was with Xuan's. She should have refused Ahn when he first proposed, realizing that she couldn't marry a non-Catholic. The situation had gotten completely out of hand; now, suddenly, the ceremony had become a state occasion with the emperor in attendance. How was it going to look, he wondered, when the wedding had to be canceled because the groom was unfit on the grounds of religion—the same religion the emperor professed.

Father Bergere was not particularly mindful of the niceties of diplomacy, but even he could see that the situation was explosive, and insulting to the throne.

Yet it was, the priest felt, a very simple matter: Princess Le Xuan Huong was Catholic, and Prince Ahn was not.

Father Bergere saw none of the political intricacies of the situation, though he was mystified at the emperor's attitude. Rather than being shocked and resentful about the marriage of a member of the royal family to a much-despised Catholic, the emperor was being surprisingly cooperative and supportive. Father Bergere did not understand this.

Though Jesuits were schooled in politics and diplomacy, Father Bergere showed no aptitude for these fields. He was blunt to the point of rudeness and knew little of tact and discretion. The intricacies of the current situation were not beyond his intellect, but they were so removed from his interest that he simply couldn't grasp them.

Father Bergere had come to Vietnam to convert the heathens, charged with zeal, seeing the world in stark blacks and whites, but now, after so many years, the freshness, zeal, and contrasts had all been overcome; it was almost as if the intense heat and brilliant sun had rendered them insignificant. His Western ideas and thoughts had lost all definition in the corona of the Vietnamese sun.

Now, after twenty-five years of toiling in the Lord's rice paddies, as he called it, he saw that he had not been particularly suited to be a missionary, nor were the Vietnamese particularly suited to be Catholics—he thought that perhaps the Lord had intended them to be exactly what they were. He was, he realized, no Xavier. He had no interest in money, politics, or power, and he didn't like the constant interfering of his fellow missionaries in the political affairs of the country; he sympathized with the mandarins who so resented the Jesuits.

He himself had at last found his niche, pastor to a converted, dethroned dynastic family, and he was spared all the exigencies of missionary life—which was fortunate, because he didn't think he could wholeheartedly convert the heathens anymore. What, after all, was wrong with ancestor worship? And how did it significantly differ from the belief in saints and miracles? Why not honor the graves of forebears rather than erect Gothic charnel houses over the bones and relics of martyred saints?

Yet still he had his duty—the sacraments of the Church must remain inviolate; Xuan must not marry Ahn.

But when he went in to see her, his resolve fled. His face was as somber as he could make it, yet when she ran up to him and grabbed his hands, he softened immediately, for he had never seen her like this. The woman was gone, and suddenly there was someone in her place, not the girl of her own youth, because even when younger there had been no occasion for girlishness, but an entirely different person.

Her face was happy, and he'd never really seen happiness there before. Peace, contentment, compassion, understanding, wisdom, looks of maturity and depth—all of these he'd seen, but not simple happiness, not the pure, unadulterated joy that comes to lovers. In her face he saw even more, for the joy and happiness were of expectation; her face shone with the radiance of hope.

She couldn't contain her feelings; she pulled on his hands and led him into her bedroom.

"Oh, Father Bergere, you have to help. What should I wear? And what should I bring? Should I wear jewelry? And my hair—what should I do with my hair?"

The priest hesitated, torn between rebuking her for her foolishness, and tenderness for her plight. She should be allowed this joy, he thought, surrounded by a covey of giggling girlfriends helping her try on dresses and jewelry, sharing whispers and gossip, all under the erotic aegis of youthful sex.

He looked to her spare dressing table and saw on it a variety of brushes and combs and makeups, no doubt lent by her maid, and their disarray demonstrated her bewilderment at their use. Looking at her closely, he saw smudged traces of rouge and mascara, and too that her hair had been brought down in an attempt at some style, then, defeated, gathered back and pinned.

Suddenly she seemed embarrassed; her hands fluttered to her hair and face; then she laughed, not a giggly titter, but a woman's laugh at her own silliness.

"I suppose I should leave bad enough alone," she said. She looked disappointedly toward the mirror. "I thought maybe I could do something with myself." Her voice was resigned but slightly peeved. "I'm so plain. And he's so handsome."

She did giggle at that, then caught herself immediately. "But he's a good man, Father, not the silly boy everyone thinks he is."

"Madame Xuan—"

"And everything is going to be fine. Even if I am plain and he finds—"

"Madame, we must talk."

Just then the maid carried in an infant and brought it to Xuan. When Xuan cradled it close to her breasts, her face broke into a wreath of softness and love.

The child was one of many brought from the Catholic orphanage in the city to receive special care and attention. Father Bergere and Xuan devoted time each week to helping at the mission, which teemed with unwanted, illegitimate, diseased, and retarded children. There was no medical care, so the most pitiful cases died, but a few survived because Xuan brought them back with her to the palace. She kept them until their health stabilized, then returned them because there were so many others who needed special care.

The child she now held had been with her several months, longer than any other she'd kept, and she'd decided that perhaps she would keep this special one.

The baby had been born two months premature and for weeks clung to a thread of life, gaining no weight, hovering at the margin of existence. The baby was baptized Mary and given the last rites of the Church at the same time. Every day Xuan went to the mission to be with her and each day she expected to be told the baby had died, but weeks passed and there was no change.

Finally Xuan took the child with her, and it thrived. She didn't think she could relinquish the baby now.

A slight frown crossed her brow as she stroked the infant, who responded to her touch and voice with a great smile. Xuan laughed and looked up to the priest. "How could I give her back? But what do you think he'll say about her?"

"Madame! Stop it. There will be no marriage. You cannot marry him."

Xuan's face was open and friendly, yet resolved. "I wondered when this was going to come," she said. "But yes, I shall marry him, Father."

"You cannot; he is not a Catholic. Think of your duty to God."

She stroked the baby's cheeks, and her eyes were indulgent on the priest. "I don't think that God is a Jesuit, Father. I wonder sometimes if he's even Catholic."

The priest met her long look, and seeing the determination in it, he sat down in a chair across from her and held out his hands for the baby.

She gave over the child and he held it easily. The infant recognized him and broke into a wide smile, but he didn't smile back; instead he looked deeply into the dark eyes. Then he lifted up the tiny gown and studied the still-fragile and emaciated form.

What did God have to do with any of this? he thought as he gently touched the thin, undeveloped limbs. This child's life, this woman's happiness? Did it all really hinge on such a thing as a young man's faith? No, he didn't think it did, but he didn't know anymore quite what to think, whether he was right or wrong, or even if he knew the difference.

Yet still he had his duty, and his faith, and it was duty and faith which carried one through doubt; it was the bridge across the abyss, and as long as one clung to it, there could be no fall.

"Madame, it is not left to our discretion to change the rules of the Holy Church. You would be committing a grave sin, imperiling your immortal soul by marrying this man."

She looked at the priest with the baby, then about the spare room, almost devoid of personal effects, and there was no sound whatsoever except for the slight brush of the baby's movements within her blanket. Late-afternoon sunlight streamed through the windows, mingling and dancing with the shadow leaves of the fig trees on the gleaming hardwood floors.

"I will marry him, Father. Don't tell God it's wrong. Bring Him to us. Bring Him to Ahn as you brought Him to me."

Their eyes met for a long time; then Father Bergere smiled faintly. "You know," he said, "when I was a child, before I was told otherwise, I thought that God was a woman. Then, after I came here, I thought that God should be a woman. Do you suppose that may be so?"

She shook her head. "No, but He does have a mother. And sometimes it's best to listen to her."

Father Bergere handed back the baby and stood. "I suppose there'll be time for me to bring God to that wretched boy. Maybe this is His way of doing it."

"You will marry us in the Church?"

"Let me talk to the young prince, and I'll see."

"Tell him about the baby. I must bring the child with us; I don't think he'll mind. I think he likes children. I know he will."

The priest bowed and left the two together.

In late afternoons, the imperial gardens were always deserted, and it was this time of day Father Bergere liked best. It was just as well the Vietnamese wouldn't have chosen this hour to sit in the garden, for the priest's presence would have disturbed their contemplation, and his manner would have unnerved them. While a Vietnamese would have sat serenely viewing a single tree, or one flower, the priest entered the gardens briskly, as though with purpose and plan, and he viewed everything, seeming to take inventory and noting the changes from his last tour. His enjoyment was active, not the passive enjoyment a Vietnamese would have derived, but it was just as real.

Dressed in his black cassock, his tall, thin, but very erect form moving quickly down the pebbled paths, his large, severe face led by his sharp and substantial nose, turning rhythmically from side to side, he resembled a large awkward bird. But he missed nothing as he proceeded with directness through one section, then into another, and he saw the startled geckos dart from his path, their shrill warning cries mixed with croaks of outrage for having their lairs disturbed and their insect prey sent into flight.

He was not reflective as he trooped the gardens, but thought strenuously, his mind turning over the ambiguities and annoyances of his present mission. He didn't want to go to Prince Ahn, for he saw no way the situation could be successfully resolved, but he couldn't stand the prospect of having to make an unhappy report to Xuan.

Still, he knew there'd be no unpleasantness with Ahn, for that was not the Oriental way; there'd be no confrontation, rather a bog of evasions and perplexities and equivocations so civilly advanced that the resulting confusion seemed clarity and harmony itself. The method was to submit a policy so vague and ambiguous that one could not possibly disagree with it, and thus by encountering no opposition, the policy became the action, and whatever form that took was therefore, by default, acceptable. The method was, to a Westerner, especially a man of Jesuit training and logic, maddening in the extreme.

Well, not in this situation, he decided firmly; the subject was holy matrimony, one of the sacraments, and there could be no compromise: the prince would have to become a Catholic, and that satanic Chinaman would have to be dismissed.

Father Bergere quickened his pace so that he seemed to be marching at double time toward the end of the garden which led toward the royal apartments.

He had never been in this private part of the palace, but his manner and stride were so assured that he wasn't challenged by any of the guards, though finally in the dark maze of corridors he had to ask where to find the apartment of Prince Ahn.

Suspicion now met him, but he was politely escorted through the labyrinth. It conjured for him the image of a huge honeycomb, and indeed the vast complex encased dozens of royal cells behind whose sliding doors powerless, helpless relatives to the throne, including the survivors of the fifty-one sons of the Emperor Minh Mang, and their children, and so many others, lived lives as useless as any trapped bee beating its wings within its confined chambers. They were fed and pampered within their cells in the event that someday they might be called, yet faced the imperial sting should they venture out.

Finally he was brought to a section where the corridors were wider and the rooms more distantly spaced and the guards more numerous, and led to a detached and more private wing, finally to a massive wood door on which a guard knocked lightly.

It was immediately opened by a barely clad girl of perhaps fifteen.

The guards turned to Father Bergere, waiting for him to announce his mission, but the priest was too flustered to say anything, so instead one of the guards informed the girl that the priest had come to see the prince.

The girl closed the door and Father Bergere waited with the four guards until the door reopened and the girl politely and respectfully asked the priest to come in.

Father Bergere, towering a foot over the girl, riveted his gaze on the top of her head and followed.

He passed through an absolutely bare entrance foyer into a large formal waiting room which contained only three hardback chairs and one low table.

Father Bergere went to one of the chairs, thinking he was to wait, but the girl indicated for him to follow, so he passed into another room, larger and equally bare. The priest, with nothing to look at, finally lowered his gaze to the girl. Her movement was desultory and her hips swayed erotically. Though he was certainly surprised at the severity of the prince's apartment, he saw he'd been right about him: depravity didn't need opulence, it thrived anywhere.

Into yet another stark room they passed. The room was over twenty feet in length and nearly as wide, but in it, before open bamboo screens that led into a rock garden, there were only a desk and a single chair. All the rooms were bright and airy, not at all what he'd expected, and were it not for the overly ripe girl leading him forward, he'd have felt almost at home in these monastic surroundings.

When they reached the bedroom, he was surprised, for in his mind he'd had some vague conception of a dark, incense-smothered room of extravagant bad taste, where salacious silks and velvets were floor to ceiling, and perhaps tethered leopards padded in corners while gaudy parrots squawked at copulating monkeys who hung from trapezes over the bed.

Instead, it was as Spartan as the other rooms, and just as clean and bright. Two teak campaign chests were against one wall, and against another, facing toward the garden, was a pallet bed, large enough for two, he noted, or even more, but made up now in military fashion. A simple flower arrangement was on the floor near the bed, behind which hung a Chinese screen of cranes, and on the bed there was a single faded chrysanthemum. The floors gleamed of polish and a cool breeze swept in from the open sliding screen.

Father Bergere saw in all this an aspect of Ahn's personality he'd not guessed at, and he was comforted by the fact that there was nothing overtly heathen in the surrounding—no idols or altars, not even a family shrine before which every Buddhist placed offerings for ancestors.

The girl, doubtless out of perversity he thought, bent over the bed and needlessly straightened a corner, lingering longer than necessary with her buttocks provocatively raised and spread; then she moved on, but Father Bergere stopped. "Where are we going?" he demanded.

"The prince is in the bath."

The priest frowned severely. "I shall wait here. No"—he turned to leave—"I shall wait out there."

The girl's voice came sharp and direct. "You are to come with me, he said."

Father Bergere did not look back. "I shall wait in the other room."

But before he took three steps, Ahn's voice stopped him. "Master Bergere! Wait. Come back."

The priest turned at the enthusiastic, friendly voice, and he saw the prince standing in the doorway, water dripping from his naked body.

Father Bergere closed his eyes. Ahn crossed quickly and took him by the arm. "What brings you? How is Lady Xuan? Come, we'll talk in the bath."

He did not speak in French and was totally unaware of the priest's discomfort.

"I need to talk with you, my lord, but I can come back later."

"Now is a perfect time," and he pulled the priest toward the doorway.

Father Bergere continued to protest, but Ahn cast it all aside, taking his coif from him and handing it to the girl. "The bath is the best place to talk," he said, virtually yanking him into the changing room.

Father Bergere wasn't sure if he was more embarrassed at Ahn's nakedness, or the prospect of his own, or the presence of the girl standing next to Ahn, awaiting his bidding.

"Is Lady Xuan all right? You haven't come with any bad news, have you?" He said all this so guilelessly, and at the same time tugging at the priest's cassock buttons, that Father Bergere couldn't gather his thoughts.

Ahn tried to lift the crucifix from over Father Bergere's head, and for several seconds they appeared to be wrestling over it, until finally the priest pulled himself away, breathing heavily.

"My lord, I must discuss an important matter with you, but this is not the place. And I cannot have this girl here. And you should have clothes on."

Ahn didn't seem to see the problem, but he gestured for the girl to leave. He looked for something to drape about himself, found nothing, and looking down on his own nudity, merely shrugged, perplexed.

Father Bergere sensed his own foolishness and realized how

near he was to insulting the young man. Remembering his vow to Xuan, he took a deep breath and lifted the crucifix from around his neck and began unfastening his cassock.

Ahn looked reassured, and his friendly manner returned. "I suppose you were surprised when I asked Lady Xuan to marry me." He laughed. "Are you here to see if my intentions are honorable?"

"I'm sure that they are," Father Bergere said as he carefully folded his cassock and looked about before continuing to disrobe. "Are there no towels?"

"You aren't wet yet," Ahn said reasonably.

The priest sighed and continued his undressing under the explictly curious gaze of Ahn.

"You have very white skin," the prince said, reaching out and pinching a fold of buttock flesh between his fingers. "It's very nice," he said with admiration.

"Thank you."

Ahn led him into a large, tiled, steaming bathing room. In the center was a huge sunken bath, and in it, sitting like a lordly toad, was Chien. A young woman, also naked, sat behind him on the tiles, pouring cool water over his head and wiping his brow.

Chien lumbered up and bowed. "Why, Father Bergere, what a curious place to find you." He motioned to the girl to go attend the priest, but Father Bergere literally jumped into the water and waded to a depth up to his chest, his breath coming in deep gasps from the intensely hot water. He felt his face turning red and he had to grit his teeth to keep from crying out.

Chien sank back down expressionlessly.

Before entering the water, Ahn stood on the edge and let the girl sponge him off, her hands moving delicately over his entire body; then he stepped into the bath and sat down in water up to his neck. "Is it too hot?" he asked Father Bergere, genuinely concerned for his comfort.

The priest shook his head, unable to speak or even open his eyes, though he felt his body growing blessedly numb.

Chien felt guilt, for he well knew, unlike Ahn, the modesty and embarrassment of the priest. He gestured for the girl to leave, and he himself brought the ladle and bucket of cold water to Father Bergere. He poured it over the priest's head, and Father Bergere exhaled in grateful relief.

Ahn jumped up. "It is too hot. I'm sorry." He clapped his hands, summoning the girl back. "Perhaps something cool to drink."

Chien glared at him and shook his head. Though not understanding, Ahn waved away the girl and sat back down.

Finally Father Bergere was able to speak. He moved from the deeper water to sit close to Ahn. He would have preferred to be alone with the prince, but he saw no way to politely ask Chien to leave.

"There is a dilemma, my lord, and I must speak to you about the problems that have to be overcome before you and Lady Xuan marry."

"What problems?"

"Princes Xuan is Catholic, my lord."

"Oh, that." Ahn shrugged and said generously, "That's no problem. I don't mind."

"But you are not a Catholic, my lord."

Ahn said nothing for a moment. His expression remained pleasant, but there was an edge of shrewdness in it. "Would there be a problem if I weren't a Catholic?"

"Indeed there would be, my lord; Lady Xuan couldn't marry you."

"I see," said Ahn, and he ladled cold water over his head. "Well, fortunately I am a Catholic, so there is no problem."

Father Bergere stared at him; then he looked to Chien. The Chinaman nodded. "It's true, alas, the boy is Catholic."

"Nonsense! What a sacrilege!"

Chien continued smoothly, "It's quite true. He was baptized years ago. I was there."

"Shameless lie!" The priest jumped up, then realizing his exposure, plopped down again.

Ahn placed his hand on the priest's arm. "Why should there be a problem over this matter?"

"Because a marriage in which the couple do not share the same faith would be doomed to failure."

"Then tell me what she believes and I'll believe it too—surely it can't matter much. She doesn't believe in terrible things, does she?"

"Certainly not. She believes in one God, in Holy Mother Church, and in the divinity of Jesus Christ our Lord."

Ahn considered that; then he nodded easily. "That sounds all right; I'll believe it too."

At first Father Bergere felt outrage; then, because it was advanced so genuinely, he smiled. "My young lord, perhaps you would like to take instruction in the teachings of the Church, but to become a true disciple of Christ and a convert to His faith will take more than a profession in this bath. The teachings of Christ are rigorous and call for denial. I'm afraid there's much to Catholicism that you'd find incompatible in your life."

"Oh I'm sure I could manage it. Probably even Master Chien could. What is it that's so difficult?"

"Faithfulness, my lord. Not just to God, but to your wife."

"Of course I shall be faithful to God and my wife. What kind of man do you think I am?"

"I mean sexual fidelity. You are never to sleep with another woman. Nor should you have slept with any before this marriage."

Ahn was obviously surprised. "Why not?"

Father Bergere turned to Chien to verify the hopelessness of all this, but he saw such a look of incredulity in the Chinese's face that he turned back immediately.

Ahn sat in contemplation for several minutes, then said earnestly, "Master Bergere, there must be much to your religion that I don't understand. I certainly don't see what is wrong with sleeping with women, but I give you my word that I will listen to everything you tell me and I'll try to believe as much as I can. Master Chien has taught me that how one acts is more important than what one believes, but I don't think that's incompatible with what you teach. Let Le Xuan Huong marry me, and I promise to sit at your feet and listen to your teachings."

Chien grumbled darkly, "I've heard about this Church, about popes with children, and ten-year-old robins. Cardinals. And all manner of unspeakable things."

Ahn ignored him and pressed closer to Father Bergere. "I'll have time to learn about the Jesus God, but I must marry Xuan tomorrow. Help me, Master Bergere."

The priest looked deeply into the youth's eyes and he saw there the same sincerity and earnestness which Xuan had seen. "Will you promise in writing that any children of this union shall be raised Catholic?"

"I will."

"Blackmail," mumbled Chien.

"There is one more matter," said Father Bergere.

Chien turned to Ahn. "You must cut off your testicles."

"Lady Xuan has a child she's taken from the mission orphanage, a pathetic little creature she's nursed and cared for and which she now wishes to bring with her in this marriage. She prays that you have no objection. The child must be treated as a legitimate offspring of this marriage, loved and cared for by you, and raised a Catholic."

"I have no objection," said Ahn. "Lady Xuan is her own person and will have her own life. I will never tell her what to do. And if she loves this child and takes it as her own, then so shall I."

Father Bergere studied him for a long minute; then he stood up. "I shall be happy to marry you both."

Ahn jumped up and took his hand. "Thank you," he said, and pumped it energetically.

Even Chien stood up, and the two older men bowed to one another; then Father Bergere waded out of the bath, no longer embarrassed at his nudity, and feeling very good.

After their bath, Ahn and Chien went into the garden.

"Do you still not like the priest?" Ahn asked.

Chien opened his hands noncommittally.

"I like him."

Chien closed his hands.

"I think he's kind."

Chien looked up to the early-evening sky, his face seemingly absorbed in the brilliant horizon.

"You're jealous."

Chien bent down and examined the grass.

"You think I'll become a Catholic, that . . ." He stopped abruptly as he saw Lady Deng bearing down on them.

Chien looked up at the sudden interruption, and when he saw Lady Deng coming furiously upon them, he straightened to his full height. "First the priest in the bath, now Lady Deng in the garden—you've got to start keeping better company, my lord."

"What in the world is she wearing?" Ahn whispered to Chien while she was still out of hearing.

Her face was garishly made up; slashes of mascara and rouge accented her eyes and mouth into slits of cruelty, and her visage was one of terrible hatred. Her dress was a hideous clash of colors, and when she drew near, they could feel her hot breath.

Chien bowed deeply. "Ah, Lady Deng. On your way to temple?"

Her eyes and nails flashed at him. "You leering fake. Hypocrite. Child molester. I know all about you." She turned furiously on Ahn. "Would you like to hear some of the stories about your mentor? This holy man. Ha!"

Ahn motioned him away.

"And you," she screamed, "You disgusting jackal."

Ahn touched her arm to soothe her. "Lihn, you shouldn't appear like this. And you must not speak to me in such a manner."

She slapped at his hand. "Don't talk to me of propriety.

You've ruined me. I'm the mockery of court, a whore whose bed you run from to ask to marry that withered, ugly—''

''My lady, do not speak this way. I command you to be respectful.''

She spat. ''Pah. You horny little monkey, mounting me like that, then running off, with everyone knowing. I'm a laughing-stock. I can't show myself anywhere—ladies turn their backs and men walk away. Everyone is glad, and my husband has his revenge. I served you; I loved you, and you destroyed me. I hate you and that horrible crone you're to marry.''

Ahn took her hand again. ''If I caused you hurt, I'll make it up to you.''

She pulled away. ''How, by mounting me again? Giving me money? Inviting me to your wedding? There's nothing you can do for me. You'll leave here with that relic and I'll become a pariah. All my life I worked—the worst kind of toil, under the gross, sweating bodies of clawing men—and finally I became someone. I had position and attention, and respect. But then, fool that I was, I wanted something more—I wanted love and joy, wanted to laugh, and to be with a man and not feel disgust for myself or for him, so I went with you. And you abused me, and ruined me, and have cast me back to a lowly place from which I can never rise.''

Her black nails dug into his arms and her eyes burned with malice. ''Well, young prince, you won't get away with this. Or that bitch.''

Her nails drew blood, but he didn't flinch; then she spat again and left him, walking through the gardens as regally as a sorceress.

Shaken by the confrontation, he sat down on a bench near the great banyan tree. He had never had an unpleasant exchange with a woman, not even one moment's unhappiness, nor had he witnessed feminine malice. Women were tender and kind, loving and attentive; with their supple flesh and soft mouths, they were for love and play—not to be mistreated or neglected, but not to be hard or demanding, either. He'd not known that a woman could appear in such light as Lady Deng had, and saw that he'd been ignorant of certain aspects of women's character. Yet how could anything as wondrous as a woman, pliant and silky, gentle and delicate—and in his mind now he saw spread cushioned thighs and the moist fleecy sexual lips—turn into a screeching Lady Deng?

Suddenly Chien was at his side, looking down with a faint smile.

''Well, Master Chien, you certainly didn't teach me everything.''

The Chinaman sat beside him on the bench, his hand groping for an apple in his robes. "Oh. Women." He held the apple up to the diminishing light, searching for a worm. "I thought I'd let the priest teach you about them."

"You know, we never have discussed women. You never taught me much about them."

Chien laughed outright, one of the few times Ahn could remember such a thing. "Women are like science, natural phenomena beyond human understanding. Each woman is different and reacts differently with every man—there are no certainties; it is a very confused geometry. Besides, you wouldn't have listened—no young man can believe an older man knows more about women. You put your faith entirely in that divining rod between your legs. You can't help but hit shale sometimes."

Ahn frowned, vexed that for once a situation seemed beyond his ability to control. "She's very unhappy."

"Then you must be very careful. You've made a grave error. Be on your guard."

Ahn shrugged. "What can she do?"

Chien grabbed the youth's chin and jerked it toward him, and his gaze was harsh. "When a woman gives you everything, honor what little she asks in return. You've trampled on the dignity of another and made an enemy forever. You compounded your stupidity by incensing a dangerous woman. What can she do to you? There's nothing she can't and wouldn't do. Your imagination isn't fertile enough to even guess it. You're dealing now in the bowels of human character—what festers there is malignant beyond comprehension."

Chien released him and returned to his apple, munching placidly. "Never underestimate the tenacity or memory of a woman. They may forgive, but they never forget." He finished the apple and let the core drop to the ground. He bent to examine it, and Ahn leaned over also, almost expecting it to take root and blossom. Chien looked over at him. "And I'm not altogether sure they ever forgive."

Ahn kicked at the core and sent it flying. "Why did you never marry, Master Chien?"

The Chinaman made a slight grunt. "I would not have made a good husband; consequently I would not have had a good wife."

"Do you regret it?"

Chien slapped Ahn's leg and stood up. "Wives can be wonderful creatures, and most men should have several, but . . ."—his hand took in the garden—"they mar the landscape, and certainly pierce its solitude. . . ."

"Come," he said, holding out his hand to Ahn. "Though a young man is supposed to drink and revel on the night before his wedding, let us have a spare meal in silence and contemplate the mystery of women." His hand gently touched the youth's forehead. "And the marvel of children."

4

Paris: March 1868

ANDRE LAFABRE SLUMPED AGAINST A wall in the barracks and closed his eyes; every muscle in his body ached and he knew he couldn't finish scrubbing the barrack floor in the thirty minutes he'd been given while the other cadets were in the lecture hall. He was missing a geometry class and would have to beg someone for the notes, which would only begrudgingly be given; then he'd have to sneak into the bathroom in the middle of the night to copy them and try to understand them on his own.

All this was part of a campaign to get rid of him, but he was lasting longer than anyone had expected, though he knew he couldn't go on much longer. The harassment came not only from the officers and faculty but also from the other cadets, who bitterly resented this peasant among them. They felt he demeaned and tainted the Ecole Militaire because he was the only cadet not born to nobility, or position or wealth, or as the son of an officer.

What made matters worse was that he was physically stronger and more agile than the others, and every bit as intelligent. Worst of all, he didn't defer to the others, but acted as though he belonged among them and was their equal. Unfortunately, France in 1868 was not a place for liberty, equality, and fraternity—these ideals had all gone the way of Robespierre's head. It was the time of the Second Empire, not a time for those with visions of equality and democracy, or for those of low birth to mingle with royalists.

France had had two disasterously short-lived republics since Louis XVI had been guillotined, and both ended in Napoleonic empires. Both Napoleons knew that while people mouthed the words of republicanism, they were more comfortable under the rule of royalists; the pomp and brocade of monarchy hold much more fascination than the drab linen of democracy. They knew, as the devil knows: not only is it better to reign in hell than serve in heaven, but many would rather burn below than worship above.

Andre had not expected the hatred and revilement he received. He had thought that his efforts and ability would be rewarded, but he soon discovered that no matter what or how well he did, he ended up in detention, or drilling by himself in the cold and rain, or scrubbing floors and cleaning toilets. He was the butt of all jokes and the particular target of scorn of the royal-born cadets.

The young Comte de Chambrun found his very presence intolerable. Jean Chambrun traced his ancestry not just to the Bourbons, but to Charlemagne, and for him to share living quarters, to have to wash beside the son of a grenadier, was beyond bearing. To be bested in dueling or military history by a peasant was unspeakable, and it was because of his hatred that the harassment against Andre had mounted to the point where Lafabre knew he couldn't go on much longer.

The only free time Andre had was once every two weeks, when the cadets were given a weekend off and all the others went into the city to drink and whore. Of course he was never asked to go, but he had no money in any case, so he had the time alone in the barracks to study and sleep. He would have liked to visit his mother and great-grandmother, but he didn't have the strength to walk that far, and certainly not the money a coach ride would have cost.

Despite the harassment and the realization that he was despised, he still burned to be an officer and serve his country. He was as caught in the fervor of the times as all the others. French troops were in Suez and Mexico, and war against Prussia was just on the horizon; the Prussians were finishing their conquest of Austria and everyone knew it was just a matter of time before the two continental empires faced one another. Someone had to stop this Bismarck and the upstart kaiser, and who but France? Waterloo would at last be avenged.

Not only would he become an officer, he'd prove he was worthier than the others, so he turned aside their ridicule and his humiliations. He wouldn't let down his mother, or the memory of his father, and he'd prove he merited the generosity of the Duke of Parnasse.

This burden of what he had to prove spurred him on, and now, thinking of it, he stripped off his tunic and dropped to the floor with the brush and pail of water and began to scrub.

He had completed half the work when the Comte de Chambrun

walked leisurely into the room. His boots were muddy, and he tracked them over the scrubbed floor and stood mockingly over Andre.

Andre rose, not out of respect, but because he didn't want to be on his knees before the other youth.

"You haven't done a very good job, Lafabre," he said with a sneer, looking back at his muddied tracks.

"What do you want, Chambrun?"

The youth stiffened. "*Count* Chambrun. That's required, and you know it. I'll report you for that."

"Your ears must be full of shit, Chambrun, I always use your title. It's required."

Chambrun would have hit him, except that as strong as he was, he knew he was no match for Lafabre. "You'll pay for that." He turned and walked out casually, scuffing the floor as best he could, but at the door he turned, picking up Andre's tunic and holding it away from him like a filthy rag. "I almost forgot. The commandant ordered you to report to his office. I was told to get you immediately, but I was delayed; I had to piss. You were supposed to be there fifteen minutes ago. You have a visitor. A woman. It must be your mother. Doesn't she usually come Wednesdays to service the garrison?"

Before Andre could get at him, Chambrun ran out with his tunic.

Andre had no time to change, but even to appear bare-chested would be better than to keep the commandant waiting. He raced down the stairs and sprinted across the parade field to the commandant's office, arriving sweating and breathless. He was about to knock at the door when it opened and the commandant himself stepped out. Andre threw himself to attention and braced for the explosion that was to come, but instead the colonel merely grabbed him and pulled him into the office.

"Where's your shirt?"

"Sir, I don't know, sir."

"For God's sake, Lafabre, can't you for once not be a disgrace?"

The commandant appeared more nervous than angry, and he was going to summon a guard to have him give up his jacket, when suddenly the door to the commandant's inner office opened and a black-shrouded woman appeared.

"It's all right, Colonel," she said.

The commandant clicked his heels, bowed, then closed the door behind him as he left.

The Duchess of Parnasse slowly unfastened the silver clasp at the throat of her dove-gray traveling cloak. Then, slightly arching her back and shoulders, she allowed the garment to fall to the floor so that it seemed to swell at her feet like a summer rain cloud. She stood dressed from head to foot in heavy sapphire-blue velvet. Her veil was held by a small oval-shaped riding hat whose only ornament was a pure white egret feather that lay in stark contrast to the intense blue of the hat and the woman's darkly curling hair. The dress too was cut nearly like a riding habit. The long sleeves and bodice were tight and the jacket came to the throat, where only the lace-edged collar of a white blouse showed. Then, from the tightly gathered waist, the great folds of the skirt flowed outward to the floor. The only embellishments were a double row of onyx buttons down the front and a wide bow of the same intense blue tied in back at the waist and blending into the slight train of the skirt.

"Come in, Andre," the woman said, and stepped back into the inner office.

Andre followed.

"Close the door," she said.

When he did, the Duchess of Parnasse lifted her veil and smiled. "Where *is* your shirt, Andre?"

Andre froze and stammered unintelligently.

Her eyes appraised him so intensely that he began to shake with embarrassment.

"Military life seems to suit you very well," she said at last. Her gaze fixed on his gleaming chest, then dropped to his flat stomach, and lower. "Maybe the duke should come back here for a refresher course." She laughed and sank into the cushions of a settee.

Andre didn't know how to act or what to say, so he merely stood in extreme discomfort.

"You mustn't feel so shy, Andre. We'll be seeing a great deal of one another. The duke and I are very interested in your progress. I merely came today to inquire about your welfare."

Andre was awed and overwhelmed and could think of nothing to say except for a mumbled thank-you.

The first time he'd seen her he'd been so nervous he remembered little about her, but now he saw how beautiful she was, and much younger than he'd supposed—she was twenty-eight, but appeared much younger. And now for the first time he realized the position and power of the Duke of Parnasse. Even the Comte of Chambrun was subdued and deferential before the commandant, but this woman could cast the commandant out of his own offices with a wave of her hand. Andre had not followed

Parnasse's career and knew only that he was an adviser to the emperor, but not how highly placed.

Catherine patted the seat beside her. "Come, Cadet Lafabre, I won't hurt you." Her eyes were soft and alluring, a warm green sea of expanse and promise.

He sat stiffly and in mounting agitation. He had not spoken to a woman or even been near one since he'd entered the academy. His experience before that was limited to several fumbling petting sessions and one awkward attempt at intercourse that ended for him even before he got his trousers off. Women were fabled creatures for him, and one with the beauty, poise, and position of Catherine Parnasse filled him with such wonder that he was literally struck deaf and dumb.

Catherine sensed this, of course, and found it both charming and tantalizing—so welcome after the callous and self-admiring men she'd had affairs with. Her own youth had been squandered in her unhappy marriage and she'd never known the wondrous carnality of youth, its hunger and abandon, but now she felt it stirring in her, and more than anything she wanted Andre sexually. He was even handsomer than she'd remembered, and the months at the academy had turned him into a perfect physical specimen: his shoulders were incredibly broad, his body tapered in rippling muscles, his hips and thighs firm.

Her hand went to his chest, her fingers gently stroking down, and they both shuddered. She withdrew her hand immediately.

"Now, tell me," she said. "How are things here for you?"

He merely nodded his head and swallowed. She thought of a stallion. "Come, Andre, say something. I'm not so fearsome, am I? Don't you talk with women? I've heard about cadets and their young girls. Don't you go into the city with the others?"

He shook his head vigorously.

"Why not, for heaven's sake?"

He lowered his head, his eyes fixing on her breasts. "I . . ." he stammered, "I . . . the others don't like me, and I have no money. I must study."

"Are you treated badly here?"

He said nothing, but she perceived what was happening.

"I see," she said. "Well, that will be no problem." She stood up, and he rose instantly, a huge erection pressing noticeably against his leg, which he could do nothing about, and which she stared at explicitly.

She held out her hand. "I think the situation will improve for you. Good day, Andre."

He had never kissed a woman's hand, didn't know how to do

it, so when he reached out for it, he did so too roughly and yanked her off balance, and she fell against him.

She laughed, pulling away. "Goodness, you must learn to be gentler. You could be lethal in bed."

He crimsoned and backed rapidly toward the door; then he bowed quickly and ran out.

In a moment the commandant came into the room. Catherine's manner became that of a duchess and her face was all disdainful reproach.

"Colonel, Andre certainly didn't say anything, but I could tell that he's not happy with his treatment here, and that is not going to please my husband."

The commandant looked puzzled, but wary, for it had been announced only days ago that the duke had moved to the War Ministry and been appointed to the Council of State. It was rumored that he would have direct responsibility for all preparations in the anticipated war against Prussia. No military man would think of jeopardizing his career by displeasing him.

"I see that my husband hasn't spoken to you about Andre."

The colonel shook his head, obviously disturbed now.

"I see. Well, what I tell you must be in the strictest confidence. You must promise never to breathe a word of this to anyone, or indicate to my husband that you know."

"Of course, madame. You have my word. The last thing we would want to do is trouble his Excellency, especially now, with all his added responsibilities."

"Precisely; we don't want him distracted in this period of national peril."

Catherine paused, took a deep breath, and began slowly. "Colonel, the duke, when a young man, was somewhat indiscreet, as I understand is the nature of young men. He had an affair with the mother of Andre Lafabre."

This was not a lie, she reasoned, as she measured the widening eyes of the colonel at her words.

"My husband has never wished to shirk his duties and has remained in communication with the mother. Now he is taking a more personal interest in the boy." Also not a lie, she thought, for Catherine was aware of her husband's proclivities. "You understand, Colonel?"

"Absolutely. His actions are most admirable." The colonel decorously inclined his head. "Though all this must be most painful to you."

"It was when I first learned." She put her hand to her forehead and was silent a moment, the pain of recollection obvious. "But I am resigned. As I am resigned to a greater sorrow." She seemed to struggle for composure, and when she spoke, her lips quivered slightly. "It appears that my husband and I are to be childless."

The colonel moved to comfort her, but she motioned him back. "If this is to be the case, as God wills it, then my husband will no doubt seek to legitimize Andre as the heir to his property and title."

The commandant sucked in his breath.

"Yes. Andre may become the next Duke of Parnasse. So you see, my husband is eager that he be well treated, and would not be pleased if he learned otherwise."

Colonel Laval's gratitude was genuine. "Madame, I can't thank you enough for this information, which of course will never pass my lips, though I want you to be assured that Andre, Cadet Lafabre, has received only the best treatment, and will continue to do so."

"Excellent." She rose to go. "I want to thank you for your graciousness, and I do apologize for this intrusion into your busy schedule, but I felt I must come to see how Andre was doing, as I know the duke is so concerned for his welfare."

She brought the veil down over her face and was escorted out, Colonel Laval himself helping her into her carriage.

As it happened, many cadets witnessed the scene and wondered what could have transpired that would send the commandant racing back into his office the second the carriage disappeared.

All they knew for sure was that something important had happened, and that it had to do with Andre Lafabre and the mysterious woman.

Colonel Laval was as good as his word; he never told anyone exactly what had been said to him, but he summoned his officers and directed them to ensure that Cadet Lafabre receive every attention, ordering that his welfare be the first concern of every officer on the staff.

The change was instantly noted. An officer of the garrison walked into the barracks, and finding Andre on his knees still scrubbing the floor, shouted at another cadet, the Marquis d'Postel, who was lounging on his cot, to relieve Cadet Lafabre.

The marquis was dumbfounded, as were all the others, and there was silent incredulity until the Count of Chambrun stepped forward. "Sir! That's unthinkable."

The officer went up to Chambrun and thrust his face into his, delighted at last to be able to humble him. "Is it, Cadet? Perhaps you're right. Then you relieve him."

Chambrun said indignantly, "I will not."

The officer struck him alongside the head so hard he knocked Chambrun to the floor; then he dug the heel of his boot into the back of his neck. "Disobey another order and I'll have you locked up." Then he took the pail from Andre and emptied it on the floor and dropped the brush in front of Chambrun. "Now, clean up that mess."

The effect was sensational. No one knew what to make of it, but they knew that for some reason Andre had been raised suddenly above everyone else. The knowledge was reinforced by incident after incident as deference to him became patently obvious.

Two days later Andre was summoned again to the commandant's office.

Colonel Laval, legendary for his severity, was solicitous in the extreme for his welfare. Though he properly kept Andre at attention, his manner was almost avuncular.

"It's been brought to my attention, Cadet Lafabre, that you haven't left the barracks on any weekend. That's not good. We give you time off for a reason. All work and no play—why, that makes a German . . . and we don't want that, do we? Now, I want you out of here this afternoon, and I don't want you back before midnight Sunday. And I don't care what you do, but here's something to help you do it with." He tucked several bills into Andre's trousers and dismissed him, waving away the young man's attempt to thank him.

Andre ran behind a pillar and pulled out two fifty-franc notes, a staggering sum, more than what his mother would earn in six months. He knew of course that the money, his sudden prominence, and the deferential treatment were the result of the duchess's intervention, but he had no idea what had prompted it. She'd been friendly, even a bit forward, touching him and staring at him so directly, and at the memory of that his groin swelled, but . . . that was just his own fantasy he knew.

Grandmother had taught him that good luck was like a found coin: you picked it up and didn't ask where it came from, and spent it before the owner came to reclaim it.

He packed his bag and left immediately, not exchanging a word with anyone—the other cadets subdued before him—and he left the school and hired a carriage and gave the address of his home.

When he banged triumphantly on the door and called out, his great-grandmother opened it.

He threw his arms around the old woman and lifted her up and carried her out to see the carriage. "Want to go for a ride?"

"Fool!" she said, hitting him on the head.

He carried her back inside and put her before the fire. Almost begrudgingly she said, "You look good."

"I look wonderful. I *am* wonderful." Then he launched excitedly into stories of his life at the academy, though she interrupted him frequently, calling him fool and imbecile and telling him she didn't want to hear such nonsense. Nevertheless, she listened raptly, but when he got to the part about the duchess's visit and the immediate change in his treatment, she stopped him, throwing her hands up to her ears.

Andre was puzzled. "Why don't you ever talk about the Parnasses? Both of them have been very good to us."

She grew serious, and the frailness of her ninety-two years dropped away, and he saw what a formidable woman she must have been. "Never talk to me of those people, and don't mention the visit of the duchess to your mother . . . and you," she said, pointing a finger at him, "be careful. You might think you're wonderful, driving up in a grand carriage, but all you'll become is a little morsel for such people. It's fine to have big ideas and great designs, but don't begin to think you are one of them."

As always, she deflated him, but as soon as his mother returned, his happiness and excitement came back. They hugged and kissed, and she wept and had him tell her every detail over and over, though he omitted the duchess's visit and downplayed the ill treatment he'd received in the beginning.

The next day he bought presents, exotic fruit, pastries and candy, meat and fresh vegetables, gloves for his mother, a bright shawl for Grandmother, and he still had thirty francs left, which he gave to his mother. He told her the money was what he'd saved, and she believed him, but Grandmother spat in the fire.

He spent the entire weekend eating and sleeping, and when the time came for him to leave, his mother wept, but he told her he would be returning soon and frequently.

When he arrived back at the academy he found that, if anything, the deference increased; he was no longer assigned menial tasks, and when asked something in class, the question was posed with excessive politeness.

Everyone had a different story about Andre's rise: that the woman, a close relative of the emperor, was his mother; that he was her lover; that he was actually a nobleman who had just inherited fortune and title, and the black-shrouded woman had borne the news.

When the other cadets saw that the respectful submission to Lafabre was to continue, they clamored for his attention and friendship, all except the Count of Chambrun, who was too proud for that.

Andre was suddenly asked to join in their activities and amusements, and when they went out to drink, they fought to pay for his. His advice was sought, his stories listened to, his jokes laughed at. He was not just included, he became the focal point.

And of course he succumbed to it, for who is so deaf he cannot hear flattery, so blind he cannot see adulation, so insensitive he cannot respond to stroking? And for those who hear, and see, and feel—what hope do they have to remain humble?

He knew he was being fawned over, but it was so nice he couldn't resist, and when they tried to wheedle out of him who the woman was, he dropped outrageous hints: she could not keep her hands off him in the commandant's office; her husband was so much older . . .

Is that why he would not go with them to the brothels? they wanted to know. And he made it seem so, for how much easier it is to allude to faithfulness than to admit shyness and fear, or, even harder, moral scruples. So they continued to disappear upstairs in the brothels, leaving him to his manly fidelity downstairs.

Soon he was as snobbish as the others; then he was insufferable, taking the deference as his due. His affectations became indistinguishable from the others', and one would have guessed he'd been raised in a château, waited upon by servants, and was merely putting in his time at the academy until he took his rightful place in society.

And the bubble didn't burst, but expanded, for a month before the end of the term, Andre had another visitor.

This time a high-ranking officer of the garrison came to escort him to the commandant's office, and when he arrived, there was no pretense of treating him as a simple cadet; Colonel Laval himself fawned, and ushered him into his inner office and withdrew discreetly.

Andre was hoping to find the duchess, but instead, across the room, was the duke himself.

Andre was not so impressed with himself that he didn't freeze, and the affectations and pretensions fell from him like chipped ice.

But Parnasse immediately set about putting him at his ease. He strode briskly to him, his hand out. "Ah, Andre, my boy, how good to see you. I had to come on an inspection, and I thought, how crude it would be not to inquire about you. I was told such impressive things, I wanted to congratulate you personally."

Andre was too awed to detect the forced manner of Parnasse or to note that he was actually nervous.

Parnasse, in uniform, was bedecked with more medals and ribbons than Andre had ever seen, though of course not once had Parnasse been on the battlefield—the medals were all gratuitously bestowed, but Andre had no way of knowing this; he assumed they were for valor.

Instead of the tailed and rather loose military coat worn on formal occasions, the duke was wearing a field tunic. The jacket, cut to follow the natural taper from shoulder to waist, gave him, he thought, his best appearance. The jacket was dark blue, and ornamental, with a red sash and rows of medals and ribbons. The stiff, straight collar, rising almost to the chin, accentuated the duke's already haughty bearing, but the overall effect was one of tight discipline rather than arrogant snobbery. The buttons on the tunic gave the mute radiance of actual gold and heightened the gleam of the heavily fringed epaulets and the golden scabbard and hilt of the sword he wore. Held by a black leather belt, the sword lightly brushed the duke's tight-white-trousered thigh and reached just below the top of a black riding boot that only a servant with nothing else to do could have brought to such a luster.

So impressed was Andre that he didn't notice the dissipation in Parnasse's features, the white, puffy skin, the soft fleshiness, and the bloodshot eyes—to Andre, the duke was the model of magnificence and nobility. He saw how ridiculous his own posturing had been and how insignificant he was: here before him was a descendant of kings, with blood more royal than the emperor's. He felt that he should fall down before the incredible wealth and power and position that this nobleman represented, a man so gracious and generous. He was utterly humbled before the Duke of Parnasse.

But Parnasse was too nervous to sense this. He had come to the academy expressly to see Andre—the inspection was a mere pretense—and he had spent hours preparing, as flustered as a maiden, changing his uniform, arranging his medals, rouging his face, and fidgeting over his hair. For months he'd wanted to come, but knew it would be unseemly; yet during this period, his fixation and desire for the youth had intensified unbearably.

And now, seeing him, he was anxious and distressed. The

youth was the image of his father, Alain, only younger, more handsome and strapping, better poised, and more intelligent. What the duke felt, he realized, was more than physical desire: he was in love, as he had never been before. It was a crushing feeling because he knew it could not be reciprocated; he loved what could not love him, what would hold him in contempt and revulsion.

But he had to pursue his feelings, his desires, his love; he was helpless, as well as hopeless in what drove him. He wanted to drop down and profess his feelings, but of course he couldn't; he had to play the game, gambit by gambit, sullying his love, reducing it to a cheap trick.

"Well, Andre," he said with mock gusto, "how are things? Are they treating you properly here?"

Andre stood rigidly and shouted the answer. "Yes, Excellency. Cadet Lafabre, your humble servant, can't begin to—"

"Oh, for heaven's sake, stop that nonsense. And for God's sake, stand at ease, this isn't a parade." He grabbed the youth's shoulders and tried to shake him into a relaxed stance, but it was like trying to untense a frightened horse, and he couldn't move him. The touch of solid muscle was electric, and he stepped away quickly.

"Don't call me 'Excellency.' A simple 'sir' will suffice. Sit down."

Andre sat stiffly on the edge of a chair, ramrod straight, his eyes diverted from Parnasse, for he was too shy to look at him directly.

"We never really have met, have we? Just that one time when you came to see me."

"No, Excellency. Sir!"

"Dammit, boy, relax. And look at me. I feel like I'm talking to a statue. That's better. You really do remind me of your father. He was a fine man. Do you remember him at all?"

"No, sir."

"Well, he was a fine man."

"Thank you, sir."

Parnasse fell silent, the image of Alain evoked with searing pain; then he bit his lip and sighed, guilt and remorse sweeping over him.

"Well, well, well," he said at last, and looked intently at Andre. "This won't do at all. We must get to know one another better; we have much to talk about, and I'm very interested in your future. I'd like to have you come visit us. My wife and I are going to our château on the Loire in a few weeks and we'll be there for some time. Why don't you plan to visit with us when the term ends. Would you like that?"

"Sir, I . . . I don't know what to say. You've been so generous to me, I—"

"Then it's settled. I'll have it all arranged."

"Sir, that's too kind. I can—"

"Not another word." Parnasse picked up his cloak. "Well, I must go."

Andre jumped up and ran to the door to hold it open, but Parnasse put his arm around his shoulder and ushered him out first, into the outer office, where the highest-ranking members of the academy stood at attention.

"Well, Colonel Laval, you've done a fine job with our boy."

The commandant bowed respectfully. "On the contrary, Excellency, it is he who has done the fine job. We are merely capitalizing on his potential. We are very grateful you sent him to us."

Parnasse patted Andre on the shoulder. "Well, lad, keep up the good work. Perhaps you'll get a chance soon to employ what you've learned here, and bring honor to us all. Maybe we'll all get a chance soon to teach some manners to those barbarian neighbors of ours. Colonel, I congratulate you on the exemplary work you're doing here. And, Andre, we'll see you at the château in a month or so. Gentlemen, good day to you all."

He left escorted by the commandant and his staff, and Andre returned to his barracks, the entire scene observed by all the cadets, glued to windows.

The impact of the duchess's visit had been dramatic, but the duke's was stunning. A cadet had been in the outer office when Parnasse came out with Andre, and he reported to the others that Parnasse had allowed Andre to precede him, and put his arm around him like a father.

"Father, hell," said the Count of Chambrun. "He might have had his arms around Lafabre, but it wasn't a fatherly hug. Everyone knows about the Duke of Parnasse. And now we know why Lafabre doesn't go to the brothels."

Whether true or not—and some believed it, while others didn't, preferring to believe that Andre was the son of the duke—they all saw that the deference and respect paid to Andre by the entire staff and faculty of the academy bordered on the obsequious.

Such behavior began to rankle not only the other cadets but also many on the faculty who had been there for years and were accustomed to the sons of royalty. Yes, the duke was powerful, and, yes, he might become minister of war, and he was a confidant of the emperor, and, yes, their careers might depend on his favor or whim, but still they found the treatment of this youth distasteful. However, they didn't find it so distasteful as to alter their manner.

And it was not long, of course, before Andre fell victim again to the flattery and servility and syncophancy of the others. His manner became demanding, overbearing, and obnoxious.

One day on the athletic field, matters came to a head. The cadets were training with padded lances in simulated hand-to-hand combat.

Andre had always been the most formidable pugilist, and no one had wanted to go up against him, but this day the Count of Chambrun challenged him to a match.

Smarting under the attention Andre had been receiving, Chambrun had bided his time, avoiding Lafabre whenever possible, and when they were together, extended the coldest civility. He was the only one who had made no overtures to Andre; he also had been practicing secretly with the lances.

Jean Chambrun was not a coward, or unprincipled. He was a powerfully built young man who believed absolutely in his own superiority. He was born to give orders and accepted unquestionably that he was due whatever he desired. Yet he worked and studied hard, believing in the obligations and responsibilities of nobility, as well as their privileges.

He saw his duty now was to put this peasant boy in his place. He knew Andre was not a duke's son; everything about him rang of peasant stock—his features were too broad and solid, with nothing about him to indicate the refinement and gentility of nobility. The others might be taken in, Chambrun thought, but not himself: a descendant of Charlemagne could not be fooled by a pretentious peasant.

As there are no secrets in the rarefied strata of royalty, Chambrun had heard the rumors about the Duke of Parnasse, his discreet yet undue interest in young men, and he was convinced that Lafabre was in the academy as a sexual favorite of the duke. The idea affronted and disgusted him.

The athletic director squared them off and handed each a lance, but he noticed that Chambrun was not wearing his body padding and told him to put it on. Chambrun told him it wouldn't be necessary. "Not against Lafabre," he said disdainfully.

So of course Andre took off his.

"Better be careful, Lafabre. You might lose your means of livelihood."

"What does that mean?"

They moved together to shake hands, as was required. When they were close, Chambrun said, "The duke won't have much interest in you when I knock your balls up into your throat. He'll have to find someone else. But maybe you can be his eunuch instead of his stud."

"You bastard!" Andre swung wildly, but Chambrun was ready and landed a hard blow to his abdomen. He followed with another to his chest, and swung up to his groin. Andre parried but Chambrun hit him against the side of his head and Andre went down.

Chambrun was about to deliver a tremendous blow while Lafabre lay helpless, but the director intervened and stopped it.

"Saved again," said Chambrun. "You whore."

Andre dived at him, but Chambrun kicked him in the head and Andre fell unconscious.

He had to be brought to the dispensary, where his cuts and bruises were treated, but they could do nothing for his pride.

The incident was reported and the two cadets were brought before Colonel Laval, who made them promise they would put aside whatever problems they had while at the academy.

Chambrun and Lafabre, having given their word, stayed away from one another; neither even mentioned the name of the other, but they were spoiling to meet again.

Not only was Andre mortified at being bested, he was outraged at what Chambrun had suggested, and shocked when he realized that Chambrun actually believed it. He himself couldn't even conceive of such a thing, and he was deeply insulted, and insulted for Parnasse, whom he believed the most honorable of men.

Yet he pretended that nothing had happened and, in defense, assumed an even haughtier and more overbearing manner. When the term ended, he was at the head of the class, to no one's surprise.

The week before classes ended he received a message that the duke's carriage would arrive for him on the morning of the last day, and Andre made his only request of the commandant: he asked permission to go home for the weekend to tell his mother that he wouldn't be returning for the vacation period. He had not been home since his one visit months ago.

His visit this time was far different from his other. He was reserved and aloof, and treated his mother like a servant; he offered no help around the house and expected to be waited upon. Denise was confused by his attitude but so glad to see him, and happy for him, that she willingly served him.

He affected great boredom and told her casually that he wouldn't be returning for some time. "I've been invited to the duke's for vacation. I think I'll go."

"Andre! You mean you saw him?"

"Yes, he came to see me. He's very interested in my future."

"Did you hear that, Grandmother? I knew this would happen!" She clasped her hands to her chest, overcome with happiness.

The old woman said nothing; she'd hardly spoken to him since his arrival, though he'd felt her eyes on him uncomfortably. But his mother had told him that his great-grandmother was beginning to slip, her mind weaving in and out of time.

The next morning Denise had to go to work, but she planned a big celebration for their last evening together and said she'd return early.

As soon as she was gone, Andre began to pack his bag. The old woman sat cold and disheveled before the morning fire, wrapped in her shawl.

"I thought you were going to stay for dinner," she said.

"I should be getting back. I have much to do."

"Your mother will be very unhappy."

He shrugged, but glanced away quickly and busied himself with his bag. When he stole a look back at her he saw her eyes were on him fiercely, and he couldn't ignore it.

"I think it's time you learned about life, you little marionette."

He smiled indulgently. "I'm doing all right, Grandmother."

Andre knew the dark side of the old woman, knew the poison of her tongue, but he'd never seen her this angry before, and he knew if she were younger she'd rush at him—he'd heard the stories of her violence, and how she'd physically attacked his great-grandfather, his grandfather, and his father. She'd never struck him, but he saw in her furious eyes what he'd been spared.

She leaned forward and hissed, "You odious, pretentious shit." He'd never heard her use profanity, and he was stung even more than if she had struck him.

"Your father, and grandfather, and great-grandfather would be disgraced."

"Grandmother! I'm not so bad. All right, I'm sorry; I know I've acted badly, but you don't have cause to say these things."

"Disgraced! They were stupid men, all of them, but they worked hard, and were honest, and did the best they could. They never did anything disgraceful. Ever."

"Nor have I. What are you talking about?"

Suddenly, as though her anger had burned out a connection with reality, she seemed lost. She looked at him dazed and confused, the sharp focus in her eyes turning cloudy. Her head dropped slightly and saliva dribbled from the corner of her mouth.

He went to her and stroked her white hair, unwashed and unkempt; then he dropped down on his knees and lifted her face. The fear he saw in her eyes made him look away; he'd never seen her afraid, and it wasn't right, he thought—she's too old and helpless. It isn't fair that she should have to suffer terror too; the physical humiliation should be enough.

"Oh, God," she groaned, as though some horror in the bog of her mind, some awful phantom emerging from the vapor of her subconscious had come to substance, but he saw her struggle against it, and through willpower alone pull out, and she grabbed at his hand. "Alain . . ." she said.

"It's Andre, Grandmother."

"Andre, don't let me get worse. Don't let this happen to me. Please."

"Grandmother . . ."

"Don't. Promise me. Don't let me live in darkness. Promise!"

She was so intense and afraid that he said, "Yes."

Relieved, she settled back, and when he saw she'd recovered, he said gently, "Grandmother, God decides what happens to us."

"Nonsense. God doesn't decide anything. Or if He does, He gets it all wrong. I'm not Catholic anymore."

"Since when?"

"Since I saw how cruel life was—a long, long time ago. If God has anything to do with this, I don't want anything to do with Him."

"But you always told me about the Church, and took me to mass."

She shrugged. "It didn't hurt you. Or me. Besides, it was free and I couldn't afford to go to the opera. And no one ever invited *me* to a château."

He laughed and dropped down before her. "What's so bad about that? Why are you so angry that I'm going to stay at the duke's?"

She studied him carefully, seeming to debate for a long time; then her face set firmly and she leaned forward. "I'm going to tell you about some of the cruelty in this world. And what I tell you, I want you to be a man about, not a fool. Understand and have compassion, and don't think badly about your mother. Just learn."

She sat back and said firmly, "Your mother was once a mistress of the Duke of Parnasse."

"What?" He jumped up. "I don't believe you."

"Sit down."

Reluctantly he sat again before her, and then she told him the story of Denise's and Alain's marriage, their youth and happiness, his death, and all her trials, then finally of Denise's work as a maid for Parnasse and of their relationship, and of how the duchess discovered it and cast her out.

When she finished, Andre was crying. He lowered his head, and his voice was agonized. "Why did you tell me this?"

She was resolute and unflinching. "Because you're going into their house. They'll consume and destroy you, then cast you out as they did your mother. You might even deserve it, for you've been a fool, but your mother doesn't deserve it. Spare her more humiliation. The only good thing that came of your mother's suffering is the happiness of seeing you at the academy. Don't throw that away."

"I'll kill him." He brushed at his tears, and his face turned vicious.

"Yes, that will help. Then you mother can watch you guillotined."

"The bastard. That rotten bastard, and my father saved his life. God damn him! He'll pay for it. I swear he will."

She pulled him down. "I didn't tell you this for you to seek revenge. I told you this to spare your mother. Don't be a fool."

He pulled away. "I can't stand it." He went for his pack and threw clothes in it furiously. Then he stopped and beat the wall with his fists until he slumped down, crying and exhausted.

The old woman hobbled over to him, her bony hand patting his head, and she said sadly, "It's not easy to be a man. Or a woman. Or God, I suppose. We each have to do the best we can. Some do better than others, but none does very well. Just try, Andre. Don't cause more suffering; there's already too much in the world."

He grabbed his bag, still sobbing. "I can't see her now. I couldn't look in my mother's face."

Then he ran out He walked the narrow, trash-littered streets of where he'd been raised, shielding his face, but at each beggar he encountered, every wasted and empty-eyed child he saw, all the poverty and madness, his heart hurt more; then it steeled, and when he headed back toward the Ecole, he was a changed man, and he was ashamed at what he'd let himself become. He'd been a fool, a disgrace, and he could hear his forebears railing at him.

During the final week of the term, he spoke to no one; he was sullen and avoided everyone's company. All he thought about was revenge.

As scheduled, and exactly on time on the morning of his last day, a carriage bearing the crest of the duke appeared for Andre with two deferential coachmen. They loaded his bags and he got in without a word.

He stared out unseeing on the city, for it could no longer stir him, nor nation nor glory, and when the carriage passed the majesty of Versailles and Fontainebleau, his gaze was cold and hateful. What he had once held as august and glorious he now saw as corrupt and destructive. What had his father died for? To have his mother ruined and himself humiliated.

The drive was eight hours, and when it grew dark he was rocked asleep by the swaying carriage. He had still not settled on a plan for revenge and only hoped he would be able to remain enough in control so as not to give himself away. He knew he was going to have to be very careful.

He was shaken awake by one of the coachmen, and rubbing away the sleep from his eyes, he looked out at the imposing Château Parnasse, a massive stone edifice of the seventeenth century, a baroque fantasy of colonnades and balconies and vaulted domes, set ablaze by a thousand candles.

It was the most amazing sight he'd beheld; it was to him the maw of hell.

5

Hue, Vietnam: 1847

THAT NIGHT NEARLY EVERYONE WENT to bed early in expectation of the wedding festivities, yet maybe because of the turmoil surrounding the final arrangements—the frenzy in the kitchen and the whirl of the imperial household staff—no one slept well.

Xuan woke suddenly from a dreamless sleep and felt a presence so keenly that she spoke out, and when she finally settled back and closed her eyes, she couldn't regain her peace. She slept fitfully and her mind was filled with visions of violence and blood.

Ahn retired early but was awakened many times by bad dreams. He got up once and went to the garden, and he thought he saw a tiger, but that could not be possible he knew, so he went back to sleep, yet the tiger persisted in his mind, and he woke feeling the animal's rancid breath on him, and he flinched from the imagined bared teeth.

Chien, who almost never dreamed, was also troubled with strange visions. He saw the imperial gardens desolate and the great banyan tree withered; he was walking alone and saw himself crying, a tattered, deserted old man.

Father Bergere went to bed pleased and filled with accomplishment, his gentle soul at peace, happy at the prospect of the marriage, but he woke in the middle of the night hearing cries; they were so real he got out of bed and went to the door. The sound disappeared, but throughout the night he heard cries and weeping, women and children, and finally in early morning, after intermittent sleep, he had a vivid dream in which he was murdered. A young man, not Vietnamese, with remarkable features and the cruelest eyes, stood over him. It was in a jungle, it seemed, and the man's hands came down on his neck, and Father Bergere woke gasping for breath.

Tu Duc was asleep with one of his concubines, a beautiful and insatiable girl of sixteen who'd already awakened him twice that night. He slept soundly until near dawn; then he began to toss in agitation. The girl woke and saw that the emperor's face was contorted and that he was bathed in sweat. Knowing only one way to ease him, she slid her hand under the covers to caress him, but when her fingers closed sensually around him, he cried out and jerked forward, striking her away. The girl whimpered and cowered at the edge of the bed, and it took several moments before Tu Duc gained full consciousness. He wiped the sweat from his forehead and removed the covers to look down at himself. What was it he'd dreamed? he tried to recall. Something horrible, like castration; yes, he remembered, it was that, and it came back so vividly he shuddered and looked over at the girl with suspicion. She tried to move back to him, on her knees above him, but he told her to leave and for a long time he lay awake. Dreams were portents, he knew, and this one's meaning was all too clear.

In the morning, everything was forgotten in the rush of activity.

Xuan spent the morning in contemplation and prayer. Father Bergere came in several times but saw that she'd rather be alone. Her face was Madonna-like, so happy and tranquil that he bent and kissed her forehead. She dressed in her mother's wedding gown, and wore no makeup.

The gown had lain for many years in a sandalwood chest. A traditional robe of floor length, it was made of rare silk from northern China and had once been the silver white of a winter moon. When Xuan removed it from the chest, however, she saw that time had muted the brilliant white sheen. Now the robe was the color of purest ivory and the simple brocaded flowers that once had shown so clearly now were faded into the lambent background and gave the merest hint of decoration. It is a gown more suitable for a woman like me, Xuan thought, not the urgent white of spring, but the calm ivory of autumn.

As soon as the robe was on, Xuan was ready. She wore no flowers in her hair and carried only a missal. The preparations that usually took a full day, she had accomplished in a few minutes. And thus she spent the remaining time calmly waiting.

The girlish joy that she'd felt before was gone, replaced by a womanly peacefulness, and yet in her mind she knew that sorrow lay ahead. She could feel mortality this day, so tangible that it seemed a silent presence beside her in the garden, a stately, dolorous companion wordlessly imparting sad tidings of the future to her—yes, there would be love and laughter and children . . . but oh, my dear, there is more, so much more. Beware. Beware.

Of course Ahn felt nothing like this. He strode energetically through the morning, overseeing last arrangements and making plans, a self-possessed young man who knew he could overcome all adversity and before whom life was an open vista of promise and fertility. He felt, as young men do, immortal, and no silent sentinel stood at his side.

Ahn's robe, though traditional, gave no hint of time and tradition when he put it on minutes before the ceremony. Only the bottom third of the robe was ornately brocaded, and the weight of thousands of yards of silk thread slightly pulled and tightened the robe so that the gown molded itself to the contours of the man's upper body. The white silk, making a natural foil for the strong golden flesh that showed at the neck and sleeves, seemed iridescent with the joy, strength, and impatience of youth.

Father Bergere and the lord chamberlain had solved the dilemma of the emperor's attendance at the ceremony by excluding everyone else, and certain rituals, such as the giving away of the bride, were omitted.

Certain accommodations were made to Tu Duc's position; as no one could arrive after the emperor, the couple were already at the altar when he entered the small chapel and went to his throne, which was centered and elevated against the opposing wall, equally dominating the room.

On straight-backed chairs against the other two walls sat Chien and the lord chamberlain, and against the far wall, arranged sideways, was the altar.

Tu Duc, in a gesture of true generosity, had had the finest blossoms from the palace gardens cut and used to decorate the small chapel. Banked from floor to ceiling, from the chapel porch to the altar, the full luxury of summer filled all space. Only the whitest chrysanthemums, representing chastity and purity of spirit, were placed on the altar. Nearest to the altar were red poppies representing sacrifice and hope. The other blossoms were then placed wherever space could be found.

Chien grudgingly admired the display, despite its ostentation. Father Bergere simply wondered whether it might not have been easier for everyone concerned to have the ceremony in the palace garden.

The priest raced through the mass and didn't speak after the gospel. He gave communion to Xuan and winced as Ahn opened his mouth also for the host, then chomped down on it, smiling up afterward, seeking approval.

After the final blessing, Father Bergere nodded to the lord chamberlain. Huynh went to Tu Duc and informed him the ceremony was over. Surprised at the brevity, and not having understood a single thing, the emperor clapped politely, then stood up. The others in the room bowed until he'd left; then Father Bergere moved quickly to the couple, clasping their hands.

"You are blessed in the name of Christ, and I hope you will be happy always. Forgive me for having doubted the rightness of this marriage." Then he raised his hand in benediction.

Chien went to the couple and bowed to Xuan. "May ten thousand seasons of joy and love be yours, and may the seven stars lighten any darkness with truth and wisdom."

Then he bowed to Ahn. "May your children and grandchildren and their children sit at your feet and learn your counsel, and may they bring you only honor."

Both Xuan and Ahn bowed in return; then he held out his arm to her and they left the room in stately grace.

Chien and Father Bergere watched after them; then the Chinaman turned to the priest. "Didn't you forget to sacrifice the sheep?"

"We never do that with heathens about, only in secret."

The faintest of smiles pressed both of their lips; then each gestured politely for the other to lead the way out.

The afternoon was set aside as the time for the couple to formally receive congratulations and gifts, and they held court in one of the private chambers of the emperor.

The rituals for courtship and marriage were exact, and the horoscope determined the timing for everything, yet in this marriage all tradition had been cast aside and no regard whatsoever was given to consultations with the horoscopes, nor had even a chiromancer been brought in to read the palms. The marriage was looked upon with skepticism, and no one believed it boded well for the participants. One did not flout the gods in such a manner, and everyone knew the ancestors were restless at such improprieties.

Only the emperor's approval and attendance gave the marriage official sanction; otherwise, its deviation from rigid tradition would have caused it to be completely avoided.

But because Ahn was a prince, and the marriage had the blessing of Tu Duc, everyone of importance made an appearance and brought gifts. Only the lord treasurer's wife, Lady Deng, did not come.

The formal reception was followed by a banquet given by the emperor, the couple as yet having no time whatsoever to be alone.

The banquet seemed an endless feast; already it had gone on for more than two hours, course after course brought about by servant boys in bright red vestments, served in the Chinese fashion, presented on red-and-black lacquered trays to guests seated at low tables, sitting on floor mats, with pauses between servings so that the participants could rest, even nap if they wished.

The meal had started lightly with cha gio, rolls filled with noodles, a variety of meats and chopped vegetables, wrapped in rice paper and deep fried to form a fine crust; then the courses had become heavier and more complex, a piquant and bounteous offering of pork, beef, crab, shrimp, and the freshest fish, each served in a different sauce, mixing slivered bamboo, greens, and nuts, all arranged on the imperial porcelain plates of intricate floral design in order to appeal to the eye as well as the palate. At each table were huge bowls of steamed rice and slender vessels of nuoc mam, the ubiquitous pungent Vietnamese sauce distilled from sun-dried fish. Later would come tea, fruits, and cakes.

No cup was ever allowed to be empty of rice wine, and special plumb brandy from the fruit in the royal gardens was brought around again and again.

Musicians played softly so that a melodious background of lutes and strings wafted throughout the vast hall.

Though it was a formal dinner with Tu Duc in attendance, the mood was relaxed and lively because the emperor himself seemed in such a good mood. At public or state functions he almost never moved from his throne, and no one save his closest advisers ever approached him, but on this occasion he startled everyone by moving about the great hall, even making polite conversation and inquiries.

He chatted amiably with Ahn, then congratulated Xuan. He even spoke with Father Bergere, who had been studiously ignored by everyone but who now gained some measure of respectability.

Tu Duc's manner was so friendly that Huynh, the lord chamberlain, was disarmed, interpreting this change in the emperor's behavior as the result of his own counsel. So pleased was Huynh at this marriage, this link of religions and dynasties, that he was not temperate in his congratulations and effusions, and he doomed his own position. He spent a great deal of time with Ahn, and as Tu Duc watched them together in intense conversation, his suspicions turned to animosity, though his face remained placid.

He sat on this throne, a remarkably composed and wise-looking young man, happy to indulge the revelers below, but his thoughts were not benign. He thought there was too much drinking and he didn't like the demonstrations of enjoyment. He was angered at his lord chamberlain and now convinced that Huynh would conspire with Ahn to subvert imperial policy. He didn't like Xuan, who did not show proper intimidation in his presence; she seemed too regal and indifferent to him. And he was acutely troubled by this religion and this priest of hers. He'd hoped for some barbaric nonsense of a ceremony, something so outrageous that he could safely dismiss the cult as harmless, but this was not the case; the ceremony, though incomprehensible, was dignified, and the mysterious aspects of it, the hushed speech and incense, the bells, all this he knew would merely contribute to its interest and appeal. It was sufficiently decorous, muted, and enigmatic to please his people. But what these priests advocated was dangerous, treasonous—a god supreme to the emperor—, and subversive—ideas about charity and land distribution and curtailing the power of the mandarins. And what made this all so disturbing was the nature of the priests. This Father Bergere was no madman, certainly comported himself more respectably than some of the Buddhist bonzes. None of this boded well for himself or his empire.

The French Catholics, his rivals to the north, his cousin here in this room, his faithless minister—all this played on his mind as he sat in apparent serenity in the huge banquet room. There would be blood, he knew, a great deal of it, and its flow was coming soon, a swollen river washing over the country, and in spite of himself, his visage darkened. Why was there no peace in his kingdom?

At that moment Lady Deng appeared.

A hush fell over the room; everyone stopped eating and drinking, and all eyes except Ahn's and Tu Duc's turned to her entrance.

Then everyone lowered his eyes and pretended to go about his business, chopsticks working furiously, but still no one spoke, all conversation forgotten, as they watched her present herself to the emperor, and waited to see how he would react to this scandalous woman.

No one had believed she would show her face here, certainly not walk directly up to the emperor.

Her attire, only slightly muted from what she'd worn earlier in the day, was shocking, but she felt she no longer had anything to lose; she could fall no further, and in fact had taken a calculated risk that her brazen appearance, her daring, might appeal to the emperor.

Her silk ao dai was scarlet, as were her nails; she wore more jewelry than was proper and her makeup was too garish to present to an emperor—mascara overshadowed her eyes, and her cheeks were circles of rouge.

Lady Deng brought her hands together, then dropped to her knees before the throne.

The lord chamberlain motioned to two guards, who understood that they were to drag her away if the emperor did not acknowledge her presence.

Yet he did turn. His gaze appraised her coolly. The guards closely followed his hands, waiting for a gesture, but to everyone's surprise, and no one's recollection of a similar courtesy, he left his throne and went to her and held out his hand to help her up.

The effect was sensational, though the untrained eye would have detected nothing from the demeanor of those in attendance: heads remained bent, chopsticks stabbed in and out of mouths, quiet conversation resumed.

Lady Deng was not only reinstated but now raised to an invulnerable position, one which only Tu Duc himself could undermine, but which he could with the turn of his head or the droop of his eyes.

Her look was triumphant when she finally backed from the throne and faced those who had previously disdained her, and her eyes gleamed with malice and the prospect of revenge.

Of course Tu Duc knew exactly what he had done, as he had known all the circumstances about Lady Deng, her husband, and Ahn; courtiers were happy to keep him informed of every gossip and intrigue, not just to curry favor but to undermine all others who hovered with hummingbird frenzy about the throne.

Here, Tu Duc realized, was an opportunity to enlist a formidable ally, a ruthless combatant who owed him everything and whose hated enemy was his own. A simple step from his throne would gain him a fierce and devoted supporter, and he was certainly not loath to bestir himself for such a short journey.

He could use her, and he could control her; all he had to do was stay out of her bed, and that wouldn't be hard, for a woman such as she in no way appealed to him.

With a glint in her eyes, Lady Deng approached the wedding couple. As the emperor had stood for her, form now dictated that every male stand, but Ahn remained seated. Xuan nudged him, not understanding this interplay, but he didn't move, and only barely acknowledged her transparently insincere best wishes.

The banquet continued in a subdued state until the emperor left; then the revels grew boisterous.

Ahn moved about the great hall, talking and joking with different groups while Xuan sat quietly at the table. No one approached her, but she was content to watch the proceedings, and took happiness in the enjoyment her husband was having.

Finally, however, Lady Deng approached her. Ahn saw this with some alarm from across the room, but he couldn't disengage himself. He saw Lihn Deng bow with formal politeness, and from his wife's gestures he knew that Xuan was inviting her to sit, but Lady Deng chose to stand, leaning close to talk.

He tried to discern from Xuan's expression what was being said, but there was no expression whatsoever on her face. Finally Lihn bowed and turned away, and Xuan's gaze returned to surveying the others in the room. It seemed as if the mildest and most polite of exchanges had passed between them.

Which was not the case at all.

As her face was hidden from everyone except Xuan, Lady Deng made no effort to disguise her hatred and scorn, and her mouth dripped acid. "I've come to offer personal congratulations, Princess Le."

The use of her maiden name was a shocking breach, even more so because the tone was of deepest mockery, but Lady Deng pushed on before Xuan could say a word. "Though you might need advice more than congratulations. That will be my wedding gift to you, advice. You will have to work hard to keep Ahn interested in your bed. He is accustomed to freedom and variety, and favors certain techniques which you must learn to master. He loves the tongue to caress his long shaft and for lips to suck in his lovely spheres, one at a time. Then—and how he loves this—to have you part his cheeks and lie with your face there, your tongue circling and teasing that sweet chamber."

Her own tongue moved slowly over her own lips, then made darting, viper motions. "But if that is not to your taste, you needn't worry; there are many who'd be happy to serve his needs."

Her face leered wickedly, but all anyone saw was her polite bow as she left.

When he was able to break free, Ahn quickly returned to Xuan, dropping beside her on the mat and taking her hand in his. She responded warmly and patted his hand.

The exchange with Lady Deng hadn't troubled her; she passed it off as the jealousy of a former lover, though she was puzzled with its vitriolic nature, surprised that it came from a woman so graciously received by the emperor. Still, obscenity held no fascination for Xuan, so its calculated insult was lost on her; she was, as her expression reflected accurately, indifferent to it.

Sex was not a squeamish subject for her, and what Lady Deng described didn't offend her in the slightest. Her own imagination was expansive, far surpassing the meager demands of sex, whose boundaries paled to the frontiers of life and love and art over which her mind roamed uninhibited.

After what he considered a disarming period, Ahn said almost absently, "I saw you talking with Lady Deng."

"Yes," she answered, enjoying his quandary and curious to see how he'd proceed, waiting for the revelation of character and behavior which, five hours after their marriage, would expose his basic nature to her, doom him to be understood, and make all his actions predictable—while he of course had not a clue about her.

He waited another transparently calculated period, drinking slowly and nodding to others about the room. "A pleasant talk?"

"Curious," she said.

"Oh." He shifted and rearranged his tunic slightly, avoiding her eyes.

She sat as motionless and tranquil as a porcelain figurine.

He didn't know how to proceed, whether to pursue or withdraw, and lacking the patience for intrigue, and having no interest in the murky shadows of deception, he said exactly what was on his mind, as though he were opening the screens on his thoughts to let in air and light. "I don't like that woman. Be wary of her."

She inclined her head slightly, and had there not been others in the room she would have rested it on his shoulder, so pleased and comforted was she by him, for he seemed so honest, and forthright, and she wanted to tell him she wished to leave, yet it wasn't her place to do so.

But he was ready to leave also. He searched about the room for Chien, wanting to say good night. Ahn had observed him drinking and eating more than usual, for moderation was his nature, but he attributed it to the jollity of the evening, a bacchanal by court standards, and because Chien, who pretended to disdain court life, loved all aspects of it, especially the availability of women, and he knew this was his last evening at court.

He was with a girl young enough to be his daughter. His head lay in her lap and her fingers swirled lightly over his brow.

Ahn excused himself from Xuan and went to them. When he drew near, the girl's eyes lit happily, and Ahn remembered he'd slept with her once, or maybe twice, but he could remember nothing else about her.

The girl was pretty, and fleshy, as was the taste in courtesans. The roundness of her face was accentuated even more by black bangs, which gave her a distinctly Chinese cast, and Ahn wondered whether this might not be part of the reason for Chien's interest and obvious contentment. Too, the pink ao dai the girl wore was not only cut in a more Chinese fashion, the collar being higher and the skirt more loose and less deeply slit, but it was also decorated in red with the Chinese characters for serenity and wisdom. Indeed, the effect of the deep red characters against the warm pink fabric worn by the sensuous young girl doubtless appealed to the sage's sense of irony.

His head lay in the pink lap; he smiled peacefully as the fingers swirled lightly over his brow, wisdom and serenity floating on the breasts above him.

She tried to raise Chien's head, but he was either asleep or pretending to be and didn't respond, yet as it was required that one of lesser rank stand at the approach of a prince, she deftly moved from under him and stood, while Chien's head hit the floor with a bounce.

He squawked loudly and rose with reluctance and difficulty when he saw Ahn standing over him.

"Ah, my lord, how good to see you."

"Master Chien."

They bowed, the girl ignored, for she had no standing whatsoever, was there only to swirl brows and soothe, a comforting backdrop, a piece of the setting.

"I wanted to bid you good night, Master Chien. You've been my teacher and guide, my father and friend, and I wanted to express my love for you on this special night."

The tone was so respectful and sincere, and so unexpected, that for once Chien was without words. He made a genuine gesture of humility, raising both his hands up as though to catch the words; then he brought his hands to his chest, near his heart.

Ahn, moved himself, bowed and left. He had one more mission, and he set on it with resolution.

Father Bergere saw him coming and wondered what prompted this trip across the room and the solemn determination in the youth's eyes.

The priest had been bored to distraction for the past two hours, wondering if Ahn and Xuan would ever leave so that he could also, for no one could leave before the wedding couple, except the emperor. Of course no one had spoken to him, and the conversations he'd overheard were venial beyond bearing. He tried to dissociate himself from his surroundings, raise his mind to loftier thoughts, but it remained mired in the nonsense of the room. He was about to resort to his rosary, at least get his prayers out of the way, so that if he ever did reach his bed this night he could go directly to sleep. But here was Ahn marching toward him.

Father Bergere was on his feet before the prince reached him, and he bowed politely.

"Are you having a nice time, Master Bergere?"

"Lovely. You are kind to inquire."

Ahn noticed that the priest was sitting entirely alone, and there was no evidence about—empty cups, plates, cushions—that anyone had been near him all evening. Ahn frowned slightly, ready to rectify the matter. "Did you not want a girl, Master Bergere?"

The priest sighed to himself, at, and for, his new convert, and said politely, "You are too kind. But not tonight. I'm too tired."

Ahn nodded in understanding. "Well, I came to ask if you would bless the bed now. We are going to retire soon."

"Bless the bed?"

"Yes. And maybe you have a potion to make a boy. Perhaps you could sprinkle some on the sheets."

The priest leaned forward to examine Ahn's face. Was this a joke? Or was the heathen serious? Finally he decided that the prince was not jesting, yet he was too tired for outrage or explanation. "I think it's Master Chien you want for that, not I."

Ahn shook his head. "Oh, no. Chien doesn't believe in such things. He says it's all superstition and nonsense."

Father Bergere couldn't check his anger. "Then what, pray, made you think I would administer such superstition and nonsense?"

Ahn saw that the priest was offended, and he hastened to make amends. "I didn't mean it that way. Never, never would I insult you. I don't know where I got the idea. Please accept my apologies. I told you I didn't know much about your religion. But I shall learn." He looked at the priest with concern. "Did I grievously wrong you?"

The anger ebbed instantly. "Of course not. I shall do better than bless the bed; I shall pray for you both."

"And for a son?"

Father Bergere smiled gently. "I shall leave that for the Lord to determine without prompting."

Ahn started to bow, then changed his stance and reached out for the priest's hand and shook it energetically. "Thank you for all you've done. My wife and I know the trouble you went to, and we are in your debt. I welcome you to my house as an honored guest forever."

Then he turned and strode back to Xuan.

He sat beside her for several minutes trying to think of something tasteful to say indicating his desire to take her to his bed. He was not a coarse individual, but in his brief adulthood there had been no cause for him to demonstrate refinement, delicacy, or restraint. With anyone else at this moment he'd merely stand and indicate for the girl to follow him.

His behavior to Xuan throughout the evening had been so reserved and respectful that if one had not known, one might have thought they had never been introduced before, or one might have guessed they were a married couple of many tired years, but certainly not a wedding couple.

He turned to her and said casually, "I'm bored. Are you?"

"Yes," she said, knowing the difficulty he was having, and again curious to see how he'd handle this.

"Would you like to see my rooms?" he asked.

She laughed outright and immediately brought her hands to her mouth, for a woman never laughed in public; such behavior indicated that the woman was not refined, or worse, that she might be laughing at a man. Though Xuan knew all the social rules and possessed all the graces, she'd had no occasion to put them to public use, and because she'd never lived under the constraints of social mores, her behavior was more natural than that of other women. She herself did not notice that no other woman ate more than a few bites of food and that her own intake, modest as it was, was viewed by the others as gluttonous. Women were not to eat at banquets and staved off starvation by having gorged themselves previously in private. Yet while most women thought that Xuan's behavior was immodest, many saw the sense in it.

Everyone saw her laugh, but she did it so well that again

many women saw that normal expression had its appeal, and even some men were captivated rather than shocked.

"Yes," she said finally, "I would like to see your rooms. Am I not staying there tonight? If not, you're going to have to have my things sent back."

He liked her manner even more than ever, for he loved honesty and directness and humor and these were nonexistent qualities in court women. Suddenly, looking at her, he saw beyond himself and the present, something he had never done before, and he saw a warm, full future, a gray-bearded self, stooped and aged, but he was laughing, and she was beside him, aged and bent also, and they were cloaked with love and affection.

Ahn stood and held out his hand to her, which she took, and rose gracefully.

Immediately there was polite clapping from everyone, a most decorous tribute, which they acknowledged with bows; then he held his palm up and she placed hers on it, and together they walked with unhurried elegance from the hall.

They didn't speak as they walked the corridors of the palace, and when they reached his apartment she waited for him to enter, for men always preceded women, but he moved aside and allowed her to enter first.

A man in his position had no need to please another, and pleasing others is not a characteristic of youth; therefore his behavior both confused and intimidated her.

And his apartment surprised her also; it was even more bare than her own. Like Father Bergere, she had expected opulence and decadence, cushions and pillows from wall to wall, but instead there were polished hardwood floors which reflected the moonlight from the garden, and instead of the rooms being hot and stuffy, they were cool and open to the night air.

"I sent your maid away," he said. "There's no one here."

That pleased her, for she didn't like the idea of ritual, of being undressed and prepared by others, then placed sacrificially on the bed.

He led her to the bedroom, where she saw her nightclothes laid out, but he went directly to the screen and opened it; then he stepped into the garden. She stood alone a moment, then followed him outside.

The garden was larger and better tended than her own, but sparer. There was no pond and no vegetation except for the thick bamboo border. Instead of grass there was sand, raked perfectly smooth, and there were three large rocks around which concentric rings gave the impression of waves on the ocean. But there were lesser stones in the sand, also around which there were circles, so the overall effect was not of peace and harmony, but of turbulence and forbidding austerity.

"I have never seen such a thing," she said.

"Master Chien told me about Japanese gardens, so I made this. Do you like it?"

She studied the garden carefully and saw how intricately it had been planned. The simplicity was deceptive and the mood, she realized, was not austere so much as it was forlorn and mysterious. The moonlight on the rocks and sand created an effect of expanse and isolation.

"This is not a happy garden," she said at last.

"No, it isn't. It's how I feel when I'm alone."

She watched him look out on his garden, and in his faraway gaze she felt saddened and disturbed. Suddenly he appeared very mortal and vulnerable, and he didn't intimidate her any longer. Instead, there welled in her a feeling of immensity and imperishability, that her own being, her womanness, encompassed everything that could be felt, and more, more even than what this garden symbolized, and that he, poor man, was but a mere rock lost in this expanse. The garden overwhelmed him, but not her; it was his futile attempt to capture the inexplicable, but for her it merely represented a part, not totality. She knew that he saw in it hidden meaning, the incomprehensible, what he could not know or guess, or express, but for her it was merely a sand garden with a few rocks arranged in it, neat and beautiful, but small and limited. He'd couched it with significance, like men do everything, but she, as women are wont, saw it for how little it was.

Her husband, she saw, could be melancholy. Oh, dear, she thought, and so young. Yet he was showing her his most personal and meaningful possession, and so she admired it, and commented on its profoundness. But she wondered, as she had so many times, why is it when men seek to be profound they are so mirthless and gloomy. Why is there never profoundness in joy or laughter, in babies or freshly washed hair?

But now he felt full, and rich, and generous, and his melancholy deserted him. He felt vibrant and sexual, and looking at the woman beside him, he felt loving and protective. And he could not have guessed that she felt exactly the same way; it would have surprised him, and perhaps not have pleased him to know that she felt so alive, so warm and full, and protective also.

He leaned close and kissed her fully on the mouth. He thought the moonlight in the garden just perfect, and the breeze magically caressing, and he pulled her to him, pressing his body against her, but she thought the garden too dreary and the wind too cold, so she disengaged and took his hand and led him back into the bedroom. She didn't want to be made love to in the sand, surrounded by rocks, exposed to chill and illumination; she wanted to be made love to on a bed, warm and comfortable.

She didn't feel shy or maidenly; she felt like a woman, and she knew she was every bit the woman Lady Deng was or all the others he'd brought here. She didn't feel embarrassed or nervous, nor did she think that what she felt was wanton or lascivious. She felt sensual, and the desire that was in her seemed to shine lustrously.

The moonlight and shadows in the bedroom warmed and excited her, but for the briefest instant, before gently releasing her own awareness and yielding to Ahn's physical insistence, she looked back at the garden. The wind had blown a few fingerlike clouds across the moon's face. They floated in silence, etched blackly against the bright surface, and almost imperceptibly filtered the light. What formerly had been bathed in a harsh, brilliant white now shimmered in a softer, burnished silver. The hard and resolute lines of the garden were relaxed. The strength and tension and power were still there, the essences of the man, yet now they were muted and passive.

Xuan knew that beyond the heavy bamboo shadows lay evil and unhappiness, but now, for the moment at least, they were held at bay, as the darkness was by the chaste white moon.

He undressed and stood naked before her, his golden body framed by the open screens; she felt tremors of passion moving through her, and she yielded to him when he stepped forward and loosened the stays in her hair so that it fell over her back. He entangled his hands in it, then smoothed it down, almost to her buttocks.

His eyes were smoldering on her, and with his desire for her, her own was stoked even more. His hand went to her gown, but she stepped back and disrobed herself, her eyes never leaving his, an intensity building between them so erotic it became tangible.

When she too was naked, they stood apart for a full minute, eyes searching on each other's, then each other's bodies, and when their eyes met again there was undeniable eagerness, yet still they didn't move together.

Finally he stepped to her, but not close enough for their bodies to touch. She raised her hand to accept him, but he gently pushed it down. Then, lightly with his mouth and tongue, he kissed her lips and eyes, tracing with his tongue down her jaw, washing up her face, then moving like a feather down her neck. She opened her neck to him, and with her eyes closed began to move under the touch of his tongue.

Using only his fingers and lips, he glanced over her shoulders and breasts; then he dropped to his knees and grazed over her abdomen and thighs.

She ran her fingers through his hair, then stroked his face, and lifted his head so that their eyes met, for she wanted the proof of his gaze that this was real. How could it be? she wondered. How could it be so wonderful, and did he really care for her? And his eyes told her yes.

She pulled him closer, hugging him to her, so happy and full, and when his hands went around her hips and he kissed her, his tongue washing over her wet lips, she breathed in sharply and her legs felt weak; then, with the lightest possible touch of his cheeks and hair, he rubbed over her belly, and thighs, and mound, until the sensation became too intense and she couldn't bear it any longer.

She sank to her knees also and they kissed passionately, more deeply and with more desire than she thought possible, and she wanted this consummated now, wanted it more than she had ever wanted anything, for he'd awakened in her a vastness she'd never known existed.

Her mouth sought his hungrily, wanting to engulf it, him, and when he rose, pulling her up with him, feeling his hardness for the first time, she gasped and thrust against it, her hands pulling him to her, her legs spreading to feel him, and rising to meet and take him, and when he slipped into her, she cried out from pain, but it passed so quickly that the cry was lost in her rapid intakes of breath, and she raised up and her arms went around his neck and her legs wrapped around his waist, and she thrust wildly against him.

She was crying when she finally ceased moving, and she felt so limp that she would have fallen from him had he not carried her to the bed and laid her down.

He knelt between her open thighs and gently entered her. His eyes were open on hers and he stroked slowly and deeply, and in a moment an even deeper and more powerful awakening came to her and she thrust back until her entire being was rocked with pleasure, intensified even more by what she knew was his.

He rested inside her long after they lay still, until she felt him grow harder and he began slow, lingering strokes, barely moving his hips, easy, gentle slides deep inside her, until his breathing quickened and he made a final thrust and pressed heavily against her.

But before his weight became uncomfortable, he withdrew and lay beside her, drawing her against him, her head on his chest.

He said nothing and his breathing became slow and rhythmic. She rested on his chest, listening to his heart. It sounded strong and pure, but she knew it couldn't be beating with the strength and purity and satisfaction of her own. She was wide-awake, didn't want to sleep, or close her eyes, or have this minute end. She wanted their hearts to beat together in a single imperishable beat, and she hugged him tightly, trying to press into him, merge their bodies and hearts.

How wonderful is life, she thought. How happy I am. And how good is the world.

Almost unconsciously her gaze went beyond his naked, sleeping body, through the screens, where a patina of soft moonlight had transformed the garden. The tension was gone; the power remained, but it was turned inward on itself and closed in matchless harmony.

She pictured this garden in the daylight: stark, powerful, strong, unyielding. In the day this garden, like the man, would impose its clean, uncompromising edge on all who drew near. Her time was the night: strong and uncompromised in its own way, but calm and still, giving and receiving, and she felt her inner self unfolding as it had so many times in the past, the evening lotus, to reveal and merge with the unity of the universe. Now, this night, his garden relaxed in the still white moonlight to reveal its own unity and calm. She wondered if he'd ever known this other face of his garden, and seen his own strength, undiminished, turn gently inward on itself. This, perhaps, would be her first gift to him: the harmony of night.

She stroked his warm back and kissed his hair, and without her even realizing it, tears fell from her cheeks onto his chest.

Across the palace a screen was thrown open and the quiet air of a room was suddenly charged with turbulence and danger. A sleeping baby woke, not at a sound, but an intensity of malice, woke from a deep sleep so suddenly and so startled that it was struck silent.

Lady Deng entered the room with the violence of a gale, blowing open the windows and doors of a deserted, isolated house, exposing it to the fury of storm and devastation. She stood in what seemed a halo of maleficence, charged with electric force, and she moved with stunning speed to the baby's crib.

As Lady Deng had drunk, her mood blackened. All she'd heard was talk of the charmed couple, for, fickle and capricious as it is, the public taste had settled in favor of Ahn and Xuan—after all, he was young and handsome, a prince, and she was virtuous and kind, a lost princess deserving happiness and reward; it was like a fairy tale. And wasn't it wonderful that she went to the orphanage and tended sick children? Lady Deng's hurt and anger turned to blinding rage; it was bad enough that Xuan would be in Ahn's bed, that what she herself coveted, hungered for, was now another's, but this other woman basked in public esteem. What mattered it to her than an emperor extended his hand when what she wanted was the caress and touch of a young man?

She publicly abused her husband and turned viciously on everyone she encountered, their acquiescence merely fueling her fury until she stormed from the hall. She started in the direction of the royal apartments; she would break in on them, separate them, and drive the other woman out, but the guards who'd decorously disappeared when Ahn and Xuan had walked to his rooms were now back and their eyes were hostile and suspicious. She knew she could not gain entrance to the inner sanctums, so she turned away.

She thought furiously of Ahn and Xuan together; maddened by her imagination and fantasy, she left the palace and crossed the gardens toward Xuan's isolated apartment.

She burst in ready to meet resistance, but there was no one there. When she realized that everyone had been dismissed for the night and that she was alone in the other woman's chambers, her rage turned to controlled and cunning cruelty.

She went quickly to the bedroom, but finding nothing there, she went to the next and threw open the screen.

The room was bare except for the crib and one chair. A screen was slightly open on the garden, allowing the faintest light to bathe the room.

Lady Deng rushed at the crib. Her face, contorted in anger and grotesque with makeup, glared down on the startled infant, too stricken and frightened to cry out. She brought her hands up and the baby's eyes fixed on the long bright nails, gleaming in the moonlight, coming down like blood-drenched blades.

Her hand thrust into the crib and grabbed the child by a leg and jerked it up. Holding it by its foot, she rushed to the screen and cast it open and in an instant was in the garden. Her arm reached back and flung the infant into the middle of the pond, where it made a single splash and sank.

Ahn woke early, uncomfortable with desire, his erection pressed into Xuan's sleeping side. He pushed against her, grinding his hips, and his mouth buried into her neck, nuzzling her awake. He rolled her onto her stomach and moved on top of her, neither gentle nor considerate, simply demanding, and his hardness stabbed between her buttocks and he raised her hips up and entered quickly. His mouth was harsh on her neck and he bit sharply into her flesh.

She didn't like this position, tried to move up on her knees because his body pressed so heavily on her, but he wouldn't let up and kept her pinned beneath him. She was sore from the night and his thrusts were rough and deep. But she endured it, knowing this was an aspect of men which needed release, and she felt no resentment because she knew that force and demand were the other side of tenderness.

She realized that he didn't even care who she was this morning, that she could have been anyone who woke beside him. But that didn't bother her either, and when he shuddered and rolled from her, she merely drew her legs together and closed her eyes to regain her sleep.

Ahn lay in the warm comfort of sexual fulfillment and stretched tiredly; then he snuggled closer to her and fitted his body against hers, and she was right, he gave no thought to who she was, though if one had shaken him alert and asked, he'd have professed deep love and embroidered grandly on the simple animal act.

The baby was found shortly before dawn by the nurse. The crib was empty and the woman looked at it in bewilderment. No sensible solution came to her. No one would take such a pathetic thing, yet it didn't leave on its own. She saw the screen open on the garden, and with curiosity rather than trepidation, she went outside.

She saw the child immediately, floating facedown in the pond, and her mouth opened to scream, but there was no noise and she rushed inside, throwing open Xuan's door, having forgotten she was not there.

In a panic she ran and banged on the door of Father Bergere. When he opened it, standing sleepily in a white gown and nightcap, she babbled at him incoherently.

Sensing something awful, he ran to the child's room, and seeing the empty crib, he walked outside. The sun was on the horizon, the morning cool, and there was utter peacefulness in the garden, the only movement that of the slowly drifting small figure in the pond.

The priest crossed himself, knelt by the edge of the water, and pulled out the infant, laying it on the grass, its bloated features frozen in terror; then he gave it the last rites.

For many minutes he knelt beside the body; then he felt sudden and extreme pain, like a physical blow, and he moaned in anguish and raised his head.

He was not seeking understanding, for he knew this was a human act, and he knew the malice and evil in the human heart, and he was not questioning God or His motives. This was no crisis of faith for him; he raised his head in prayer, for mercy on the soul of the child and for mercy on the soul of whoever did this. He didn't want to know who did it. He wanted to cover it up, hide it away, forget it, because he couldn't bear wickedness; it hurt him like a wound.

And how could he tell Xuan, and on this morning? He crossed himself and rose stiffly, then placed the child in its crib and went back to his room to dress. When he crossed the gardens to inform Xuan, he found Chien sitting in contemplation near the banyan tree. Chien rose every morning before dawn to watch the sunrise, and he sat every morning in the same spot, rain or shine, and he took enjoyment in all he saw, and loved the rain and cold as much as brightness and warmth.

Father Bergere said good morning and was about to pass on when he changed his mind and sat down next to him.

They were in odd contrast, black cassock and white robes, solid, massive form beside frail and thin, looking out on the world so differently—Father Bergere wanting to refashion and change it, Chien never giving a thought to altering a thing.

"The baby is murdered," the priest said. "I must tell Lady Xuan, but it would be better if her husband told her. Would you tell him that the baby was drowned in the pond? Someone threw it in the water during the night. I don't know who."

Chien knew immediately who had done it, but he didn't move for a full minute and made no indication that he'd heard the words.

His thought was visual; he saw things in his mind as in a mural: the dead child was not a simple image, but a depiction in a vast panorama of natural and human complexity, and whatever single emotion might wish to surface in his feelings—anger, lust, even hunger—was immediately washed away in the sweep of his vision and comprehension.

He stood and said simply, "I shall tell him."

He went directly to Ahn's room and sent a servant to wake him. Ahn came out sleepy, tousled, scratching himself. Chien sat, legs spread, hands on his knees in the chair in the antechamber, ignoring the foolish grin on the youth's face.

"You must tell your wife that the baby is dead, murdered last night, tossed in the garden pond."

Ahn looked at him without comprehension.

"Your folly has brought about an awful misfortune."

"My folly?"

"Who would murder a child?"

The words, and understanding, finally registered. Ahn closed his eyes.

"You are her husband. Go tell your wife."

He lowered his head. "I can't."

Chien rose. "Go. You will bear many sad tidings in your life. One day you will become one."

Ahn sat alone for many minutes before he woke Xuan, telling her gently but directly what had happened.

She dressed quickly and ran from the room, crossing the garden, followed by Ahn. They met Chien and Father Bergere and the four went to the baby's room. Xuan cradled the child in her arms and cried. She too knew who had done this, but she said nothing, nor did she hold Ahn responsible in any way.

When she put down the baby, she dried her eyes, then turned to him. "Can we leave? I don't want to stay here any longer."

"Everything is ready," he said. "We can leave as soon as the carriages are brought and loaded."

They separated to make their final preparations, then gathered in the great courtyard, the four of them and their servants. There were seven carriages, five entirely laden with possessions and baggage, and eight guards on horseback.

Though it was only seven in the morning and the palace not yet bestirred with activity, the sun was already high and the heat palpable.

Xuan did not take a last look before entering the carriage, but Ahn, Chien, and Father Bergere did. The walls of the inner palace were forbidding, sealing in an inpenetrable silence.

Just as he was about to enter the carriage, Ahn looked up to the emperor's apartments and saw Tu Duc looking down on him.

Their eyes met, but neither made any sign of recognition, and Ahn got into the coach and the door closed behind him.

The captain of the guards looked up to the emperor's window. Tu Duc nodded and the captain bowed; then he gave the signal and the small procession moved through the gates.

In the first carriage, Ahn took Xuan's hand as they passed through the great walled citadel. He didn't tell her that their survival depended on all the strength and cunning they could summon.

Then the carriages passed over the Perfume River and rumbled in the direction of the jungle, toward Ban Me Thuot.

6

Château Parnasse: 1868

ANDRE LAFABRE WAS SHOWN INTO a glittering reception hall that was dominated by an immense staircase of white Italian marble. To the right and left were the state dining room and the great ballroom.

The staircase led to the more private and personal areas of the château, up fifty flawless white steps, on every tenth of which stood a footman dressed in the duke's emerald-green livery, holding a candelabrum. The light from these blended with the light from the central crystal chandelier and all was reflected a hundred times over by the deeply cut gilt-framed mirrors that lined the walls.

In the midst of this splendor stood the duke and duchess, she on the first step, he on the one above.

The duchess's dress was mint-green satin, deeply scalloped at the hem with satin of slightly darker green. The skirt was not hooped and thus fell by its own weight into a formal train. The duchess, whose neck, shoulders, and arms were completely uncovered, wore but a single piece of jewelry—an emerald necklace. This necklace, with the soft curls of her pulled-back hair, was all that touched her throat.

Parnasse himself was a stunningly elegant study in black. In the sparkling hall, surrounded by gold, crystal, and white marble, only the narrow band of Spanish lace on his shirtfront deferred to the surroundings; all else was apart, and above.

''Welcome,'' he said, ''We're delighted you've come. You remember my wife, don't you?''

Andre clicked his heels and bowed.

Catherine held out her hand. He saw her brace herself, but he took her hand lightly and kissed it.

''Did you have a good journey,'' she asked.

He tried to close out the magnificence about him, straightened, and looked at her directly. "Excellent, madame, thank you."

Parnasse intervened immediately. "You must be exhausted. Henri will show you to your rooms. I'm afraid we weren't able to reproduce the austerity of your barracks, but I hope you'll be comfortable nonetheless. We waited dinner in the hope you'd be able to join us. Would thirty minutes be enough time for you to get ready?"

"Thank you, that's more than enough."

"Excellent. We'll be in the salon."

Andre was led to a separate wing of the château. He'd geared himself for opulence and luxury, but despite his preparations to ward off intimidation, he couldn't remain immune to the incredible wealth about him. All that helped was for him to tell himself that this was plunder from the exploitation of people such as his mother.

He was brought down corridors on whose walls hung mural tapestries chronicling Parnasse history, and shown to a suite of four rooms where an elderly valet attended him as soon as he entered. Andre had never been waited upon before and it made him nervous, especially a man this old who struggled with bags he himself could easily throw over his shoulder. Andre wanted to dismiss him, or ask him to sit down, but he knew he had to play this through exactly.

He'd wanted time to think in solitude, but the old man made him so nervous that he was happy to flee at the end of thirty minutes. He got lost once, taking a wrong turn down a hallway, but at last he was shown into the salon.

"Sherry?" Parnasse asked when Andre entered. "Or would you care for something else?"

Andre flushed. "Sir, I really don't know much of anything. I wouldn't know what to drink, and I don't know what is proper behavior here; I've never seen anything like this, and I've never had anyone wait on me before. I can't even pretend to know what's right. You'll have to be understanding and make allowances. I'd be most grateful if you and the duchess would help me."

They were disarmed completely, captivated by his ingenuousness. He appeared so fresh and eager, so utterly guileless, and so extraordinarily handsome that they both fell over themselves attending him.

"Sherry," said the duke. "That's always proper before dinner."

"Any aperitif," said the duchess. "Try them all until you find one you like."

"Well, actually," said Parnasse, warming expansively, and

taking Andre by the shoulder and leading him to a chair not near his wife, "a man can do anything he wants as long as he does it with authority. The trick is not what you do, but how you do it. Why, I've seen the Baron de Rothschild have a beer *during* dinner. Yet he did it with such flair and authority that it set a trend; for months people swilled beer at dinner parties—some people did, certainly not myself. Then it came out that the doctor had ordered Rothschild to drink nothing stronger because of his gout. The point is that if you act like you know what you're doing, it's acceptable. Don't be timid; let that be your guiding principle."

"That's very true," said Catherine, "but in order to flout rules, one has to know them; otherwise one is merely boorish. We shall teach you the rules, then you can disregard them. That's where the fun comes, in breaking conventions. Isn't that right, my dear?"

"Yes," the duke said, adding cautiously, "within reason and propriety."

"Of course," she murmured, and looked at Andre with startling seductiveness.

And so it continued in this manner, both playing for him, as though wooing him, and at first he felt uncomfortable, but with more alcohol and their increasing suggestiveness, he began to feel more assured. But the assurance fled when they went in to dinner. Andre was again overcome by the magnificence, and his own ineptness; he had never dined like this. On entering the huge room, he was met by a blend of the perfume of flowers, fine linen, and the savor of the food. The flambeaux in the candelabra were mirrored in tongues of light from the silver chafing dishes. Cut glass, silver, the finest china, were at each setting, and on each plate was a napkin folded like a bishop's miter, holding a little oval roll.

Waiters in silk stockings, knee breeches, and green jackets brought him course after course, a lobster bisque, salmon, veal, the most delicate vegetables he'd ever eaten, salad, cheese, dessert, and throughout the meal poured him an endless stream of white and red wines.

Yet despite the opulence and bounty and his own feelings of inferiority, he saw that none of it mattered to the duke and duchess; it was he himself who occupied them.

He finally perceived their relationship was of husband and wife in name only, and that he was the object of both their desires. He saw that Chambrun had been right about the duke, but he hadn't anticipated this, and he saw it placed him in a precarious dilemma. He enjoyed the attentions of Catherine, but those of the duke made him nervous, and he struggled to remain sober so that he could return to his room and sort out these developments.

When he did get back, having gotten lost twice in the corridors, he collapsed on the bed.

Charles, his valet, appeared immediately to help him undress, but Andre roused himself and had the old man sit down.

"There's no need for you to be here. I can get undressed and take my own bath, and I'd prefer to do things for myself. Would it be all right if we just pretended you were my valet, and you just went about your business?"

The old man smiled. "That would be very fine with me, young sir. I wasn't looking forward to fawning over a surly young man."

At the door he turned. "This isn't a happy place. You must be very careful here. Good night, sir."

Andre locked the door after him, then sat in a chair and reviewed the situation, and he decided exactly what he'd do. He'd avenge his mother by making Parnasse's wife his mistress. Yet when he thought about it, the idea seemed ludicrous; he was nineteen years old and had no sexual experience. How could he make a duchess his mistress when he'd been too shy to venture upstairs in a brothel?

But she seemed eager enough; he wasn't so naive he couldn't tell what she was trying to convey with her eyes and movements. All right, then, he decided, he'd think of her as a brothel whore, and treat her like one.

But Parnasse was going to be the difficulty, for the meaning behind his eyes and movements was equally obvious. Merely the idea of such a thing caused Andre to shudder.

As he sat thinking, he heard footsteps in the hallway; then he saw the doorknob turn. He held his breath, too afraid to move. He heard the jingling of keys, but whoever was there didn't have the correct one, and the footsteps went away.

Andre ran to the door and bolted it. He didn't know if it was the duke or the duchess who wanted in, but whoever it was, was persistent, for lying in bed, he heard the key in the lock, pressure against the door, but the bolt held.

In the morning he joined them both for breakfast, but he couldn't tell from their manner who had tried his door; both were utterly at ease and casual, and their eyes revealed nothing.

"Would you like to see the grounds?" Parnasse asked. "It's a beautiful day; we could ride over the property and be back for lunch."

"I'd like that, thank you, sir."

Parnasse turned to his wife. "Would you like to go? You haven't been on horseback this year."

"I think not," she said languidly. "And for heaven's sake, wash before you come in to dine; I hate the smell of horse sweat. Perhaps this afternoon I'll show Andre the gardens, if he has an interest in the more delicate forms of beauty."

"Indeed, madame, I do; I'd be honored."

Parnasse stood. "You'll have to wash after that excursion too. I detest the odor of wisteria and jasmine."

Catherine's eyes lit so lasciviously that Andre felt himself color. "He's certainly going to be well scrubbed, isn't he? Your skin will positively sparkle by the time you leave us, Andre."

Andre saw this was all said for the other's benefit, and that the allusions to horse sweat and jasmine meant the scent of the other on him. This was a rough game they were playing, he saw, and realized his great-grandmother was right: he could be devoured and spat out exactly as his mother had.

But away from his wife, the duke seemed a different man, kinder and nicer, and more vulnerable, and he behaved with absolute propriety. They rode over the entire estate, and Parnasse seemed to take genuine pleasure in pointing out his favorite places, as though he really wanted to share them with Andre. He was so considerate and amiable that Andre had to remind himself continuously what this man had done to his mother, and what he wanted to do with him.

In late morning they stopped in a deep forest to rest the horses and let them drink from a nearby stream. Parnasse sat on a tree stump, staring up at the heavy green cover.

"I'm very glad you came," he said at last.

"Thank you for inviting me."

The duke spoke wistfully, though not with self-pity. "You know, I never had any friends. I missed that. And now, well, a man in my position can't afford to have friends. There's really no one to talk with. Catherine and I, well . . . And now I'm getting old."

"You're not old, sir," said Andre politely, thinking the duke, at thirty-eight, very old indeed.

"Well, I don't feel old. It's as though I'm the same person I've always been, the same as when I was your age, only that some awful wand has been waved over me, or that I've been covered with layers of wrinkling soft skin that has nothing to do with me. I feel as though I've been tricked."

A sudden bitterness rose, but immediately gave way to pensiveness. "It would have been easier if I'd had a son." His eyes sharpened on Andre. "We were both cheated, I suppose." His gaze rested intently on him a moment. "Maybe fate is intervening here."

Andre said nothing, merely waited respectfully.

"I'm the last Parnasse, you know. My sisters are unmarried. This will all go to a cousin of mine someday, unless I have a son."

He let it go at that, but the implication was clear, and suddenly Andre realized the stakes in the game had been raised geometrically. The duke was hinting that he might make him his adoptive son and heir.

"Well," the duke said, standing and going to his horse, "if we race back, we'll get there just in time for lunch."

The duke was a far better horseman and he had his horse stabled by the time Andre returned.

"I wish you'd give me lessons," Andre said sincerely.

"I'd be happy to. I'll teach you fencing also."

"I learned that," Andre said with pride. "I finished first in the class."

The duke laughed. "There's a great deal of difference in the way . . ." He had been about to say "a man and a boy . . ." but he caught himself. "Then perhaps you can teach me," he said politely. "In any case, thank you for your company this morning. I enjoyed it very much."

"Thank you, sir," he said truthfully, his voice betraying some surprise. "I enjoyed it very much also."

Andre was puzzled by the morning; he had almost anticipated having to fight the duke off, but instead Parnasse had intimated that he was thinking of making him his heir. Was he serious, Andre wondered, and had he egregiously misjudged Parnasse, or was the duke merely dangling title and fortune before him as a bribe? Andre wasn't sure, but he saw that old Charles had been right: he was going to have to be very careful.

At lunch Catherine ignored her husband and turned her attentions on Andre. "Did you have a profitable morning?" she asked sweetly, though he detected irony in her voice.

"You have a beautiful estate," he said noncommittally. "I look forward to seeing the gardens this afternoon."

"That should be rewarding," said the duke, slurping his soup so loudly and with such intent that Catherine glared at him, and Andre almost laughed.

After lunch Parnasse excused himself.

"Do you really want to see the gardens?" Catherine asked. "You needn't be polite. I quite understand that flowers might not interest you."

"But they do. I'd very much like to see the garden."

She seemed pleased in a shy, almost childlike manner, and immediately the sharp edge in her manner disappeared.

She jumped up and Andre had to hurry to open the door for her. Once outside, she transformed further; years fell from her, releasing a long-suppressed gaiety. She seemed no longer a duchess, a woman of twenty-eight, but a girl suddenly freed, a child too long kept indoors, now let out to play in the sun.

He was trying to act with decorum, walking stiffly, his hands behind his back, properly commenting on the intricate pattern of hedgerows that formed an entrance maze into the gardens.

It was a warm, sunny day, but not too hot, and the gardens were in full bloom.

Catherine could barely control her exuberance. She threw her bonnet on a bench and took out her hairpins, then shook her hair loose; streaming down, it made her look even younger and her face was flushed with happiness.

Andre saw that away from one another, Parnasse and his wife became entirely different people.

"I never get to show anyone my gardens," she said. "Oh, people come, but they're so stuffy."

Andre looked about him, bent over some roses, and said very stuffily, "It's all quite lovely, madame."

She pushed him as hard as she could, and he fell into the bushes, yelping from the cutting thorns.

She shrieked with delight and picked up her skirt and ran down a path.

Andre extracted himself gingerly from the bushes and pulled thorns from his palms. Blood trickled down his neck, and he wiped his bleeding hands on his trousers.

When he looked up, he saw Catherine at the end of the path. She was laughing; then she called out, "Stuffy ass," and she shrieked again and ran off. She had let her hair down, and she tossed her head gaily. She appeared like a filly, her chestnut hair flowing behind her in the breeze.

He ran after her, but when he reached the end of the path she wasn't there. There were banks of roses and jasmine, and thick vines of wisteria whose scent was overpowering. Then he heard giggling and running feet, and he ran toward the sounds, but when he reached the spot where he knew she'd been, she was gone, and he heard her laughing from somewhere else.

For twenty minutes he sought her; then he hid off a path, crouching silently.

Now she was confused, having lost him, and he heard her tentative steps drawing near.

Finally she stopped directly in front of him, looking about, and when he jumped up and grabbed her from behind, she screamed so loudly that it threw him off balance and together they fell backward, crashing to the path, wildly entangled.

They tried to pull away from each other but only succeeded in drawing closer.

The odor of the garden, the softness of her flesh, the building tension of lying in wait, the bursting need of his youth, all suddenly overcame him and he rolled her onto her back and fell on her, his mouth devouring hers.

She was too surprised to resist, and her own passion was so great that she threw her arms around him and pulled him more crushingly against her.

Their hands clawed at each other's clothes, but the buttons and stays merely frustrated them more, and they thrashed and thrust against each other.

She said over and over, "Oh, my God," and struggled to unfasten his trousers, to pull him into her as he ripped at her undergarments, but he couldn't wait, wasn't interested in her need, only his release, and his hips thrust roughly against her, driven even more furiously by her hands working at his groin, and when her hands grasped him, he spilled out immediately, groaning and driving into her.

He shuddered and ceased moving, and as soon as he did, she cried out and worked herself against him, pulling him harder on top of her, digging into his hips, her mouth still working his, but at last she stopped and he moved off her.

He was acutely embarrassed and he tried to set distance between them, but she wouldn't release him. She kissed him tenderly and ran her hands over his back and hips. He responded by kissing her gently, exploring her mouth as his hands smoothed over her body.

Finally she pushed him away, though when they attempted to stand, they were still kissing and their hands roamed over each other. He tried to bring her down again, but she resisted.

"There are gardeners everywhere," she said.

He wasn't listening, pressed harder against her, and she almost relented, but finally pulled away.

"I'll come to your room tonight," she said.

"Now," he said, and tried to grab her.

She laughed and arranged her dress. "If I can wait, you can. Even if you didn't," she said, and pointed to his trousers and held up her hand, then wiped it against his cheek.

He brushed at his face and looked down at the huge wet stain on his pants.

Then she ran off, laughing.

After a decent interval he went back to the château, trying to cover himself and avoid everyone as he made his way back to his room.

Andre took a bath, changed, and tried to divert himself with a book, but he couldn't concentrate. Nor was he thinking about his plan to seduce Catherine—he didn't care about that anymore, all he wanted to do was see her, touch her, lie with her. There was nothing deliberate in his thoughts, only desire. He didn't want to humiliate anyone. He wanted to possess her, not out of vengeance, but for lust. He wanted her like he'd wanted nothing in his life. He'd gladly have thrown away anything he had, his school, his mother's honor, his life. He was utterly consumed by her.

When informed that the duke and duchess were waiting for him in the drawing room, he didn't think he could maintain the composure to make polite conversation. He knew he'd give himself away to Parnasse.

He was shaking when he entered the room, but he forced himself to bow to them both.

"We debated whether to have you called," said Parnasse. "We thought perhaps you'd be too tired after yesterday's trip and today's activities. Were you asleep?"

Andre affected a yawn. "I thought I was reading, but I think I dozed off. I'm more tired than I realized; I think I'll retire right after dinner."

"I think you should," said Parnasse. "We've kept you too busy. A drink might relax you nicely, though. Would you care for anything?"

"Sherry, please. Thank you."

Andre raised his glass to Catherine. "Thank you for showing me the gardens this afternoon, they were lovely. And thank you, sir, for the ride this morning."

They chatted inconsequentially, then went in to dinner, and the conversation remained light, no one remotely indicating the upheavals of the day.

Andre tried not to wolf down his meal, and he devoted most of his attention to Parnasse.

When dinner ended, the duke invited him into the library for a drink, asking Catherine to join them, but she told him he knew she couldn't bear cigar smoke, and besides, she had a busy day before her and needed to get to sleep. She excused herself, and the two men went into the library.

"Brandy? Port?" Parnasse asked. "Here, let me pour you a little of each, then you can decide which you prefer. Cigar? No, that wouldn't suit you."

Andre said he liked the port better, sat in a leather chair, and politely waited for Parnasse to speak, though he had to rivet his eyes on the duke to keep them from wandering to the door.

Parnasse merely wanted company; he was tired from the morning's exertions and from tending to matters of the estate in the afternoon; all he wanted was someone to relax with. He didn't notice Andre's agitation as the time dragged on, and he grew expansive on politics and the mounting problems with Prussia.

Finally he wound down and yawned, tired and content. He patted Andre on the shoulder as he left. "Sorry to have gone on so long. You were very kind to listen. Good night."

Andre rose when he left, and fought the urge to bolt back to his room. Instead he poured another glass of port and waited a decent interval before making his way casually back.

As soon as he locked his door, Catherine came from the adjoining room. "I didn't think you were ever going to come. I thought I was going to have to send for Charles."

Before he could say anything, she was in his arms, her face upturned, and he didn't bother with explanations.

Their mouths fell to one another's and their hands tore at the other's clothes, but finally she struggled from his grasp and pulled him toward the bedroom. "I don't want you to get too carried away," she said, and slipped from his arms.

The room was brightly lit from candles, but when he went to blow them out, she told him not to.

She stood before the bed and slowly took off her clothes, pushing him back each time he stepped close to touch her. "Just watch," she said, her own arousal building as she saw the effect she had on him. His eyes followed her hands hungrily, and when she was completely naked before him, he was breathing heavily, hardly able to remain apart.

"Now take off your clothes. Slowly," she said as he started to tear at them.

He did, finally stepping out of his trousers to stand naked before her. She was the first woman he'd seen nude and he was overcome with desire, but her hand raised to keep him back while she studied him, her gaze eager on his massive erection.

"Don't move," she said as she stepped closer. Her mouth pressed into his ear and she whispered, "Remain perfectly still."

He clenched his fists and closed his eyes as her mouth moved from his ear and her tongue licked down his jawline. She nibbled at his chin; then her tongue moved to his neck and she chewed gently on his skin. He was moaning when her fingers scratched lightly on his chest, and she rubbed her cheeks against hard muscle. When she kissed his flat belly, he drew in his breath, and as her tongue washed over his abdomen and her fingers softly stroked his tight buttocks, he started to thrust forward.

"No," she said, and held him still; then she dropped to her knees and her hands caressed his long shaft. She stroked between his legs, down his inner thighs, and when she bent forward and took him softly in her mouth, she felt his legs give way slightly. She steadied him and her mouth went over him eagerly, licking up and down, until she knew he couldn't bear any more, and she pulled away.

She went to the bed and lay back, motioning him to come to her. "Slowly," she said. "Don't hurry."

He bent down, and only his tongue touched her lips. When she strained up with her mouth, he pulled back, keeping contact only with his tongue. Then, as she had done to him, he moved his mouth over her. When he reached her nipples, he sucked them gently, circling them with his tongue, his teeth softly pulling.

She began to move under him, her body undulating slowly, then faster as his mouth worked lower, and when he kissed between her legs, she parted them and thrust up. When his tongue entered her, she cried out, and her hips began to thrash. He buried his face between her legs and she grabbed his hair and pulled him even deeper, pushing wildly against him, crying loudly.

Spasms racked her and he struggled free to breathe, but she reached up for him, grabbing him by the shoulders to bring him down, and he fell on her, entering quickly and deeply, and she screamed so loudly that Andre tried to pull away, but she held him tightly, pulling his hips, forcing herself even deeper on him. She thrashed so powerfully under him that he lost all control and thrust into her with all his force, their bodies slamming together,

her cries urging him on until finally he exploded inside her and she screamed out a final time, and they collapsed together.

For a full minute they said nothing, trying to gain their breath; then he rolled off and fell beside her on his back.

"My God," she said, "I was right. You were almost lethal."

"Do you always scream like that?"

"Did I scream? Could anyone have heard?"

He laughed, his eyes closed, uncaring. "Probably everyone in France."

She reached out and grabbed his still-swollen cock. "God, that was wonderful." Then she moved up to straddle him. "Just leave it in me." She moved up and down on him, pulling out to the tip, then pushing down hard, squirming. Their eyes locked on each other's and her mouth opened as her breath came heavier. She worked her hips stronger, deep gasps and sighs coming from her; then she started to thrust uncontrollably, and her cries grew louder, and again she screamed as she climaxed, only this time he put his hand into her mouth and she bit down, so hard that when she finally ceased moving there was blood trickling down his wrist.

Her abandon had aroused him fully, and even the pain from his hand excited him. He threw her off and got behind her, lifting her up slightly on her knees, and he pushed in, ramming his thighs against her hips, savagely mounting her, but again, quickly, she responded and thrust back, and their bodies became one wild motion, and when they climaxed together, he fell on her, crushing her beneath his weight.

When he finally moved off her and rolled to the side, she snuggled into him, and they held each other tightly; then they began to kiss and stroke one another gently, as though they were only now discovering tenderness. They slept intermittently, entwined; twice he woke her, his hands and mouth bringing her from slumber, and in early morning she woke him.

They seemed not able to get enough of one another, as if all their needs and longing had been stored up for this night. And it was not just lust, but the need of each for something deeper, until now withheld or denied—affection and sharing, the simple need of touch.

In early morning, still dark, though the meadowlarks had begun their song, he lay watching her dress. He was sleepy, but not sated, and he reached up to grab her, but she pushed him back on the bed and laughingly stepped away.

"I'm too old to be Juliet," she said. "Besides, it was Romeo who had to sneak out. My God, how can I face anyone today? I feel like I've been ravished by the Prussians."

He came at her again while she was fastening her buttons. She slapped at his hands. "Stop it. For God's sake, I can hardly walk as it is. I'll have to tell everyone I went horseback riding last night."

He jumped out of bed and helped her finish dressing; then he kissed her on the neck. "I had no idea anything could be so good. I think I love you."

"Nonsense." Then she turned and contemplated him a moment. "But that's very nice of you to say. You're a lovely boy."

"I'm not a boy."

She laughed. "No, you're not, but you are very young, and I am the first woman you've slept with, and one can't use the word 'love' in those circumstances."

She seemed a grown woman suddenly, as though she'd put on years and maturity with her clothes, and he saw the incongruity of the situation: he was a cadet, nineteen, and she was a titled woman with husband, wealth, and position, with engagements and responsibilities, a life entirely separate from and irreconcilable with his own.

He stepped back and lowered his head slightly, and she saw she'd hurt him. A frown crossed her features, for there was stirring in her something she'd never felt before, and it disturbed her and felt somewhat painful. My God, she wondered, could I be falling in love?

She kissed him quickly and hurried to the door, stopping to look back at him, and when their eyes met, they both knew they were caught in something beyond them. The frown reappeared on her brow; then she turned and left.

Andre couldn't go back to sleep; he wasn't tired, was far too excited by what had happened to go to bed, and this was the normal hour for rising in the barracks.

Things were not turning out as he'd planned; he'd not expected to feel anything for Catherine, had thought he'd merely use her to humiliate Parnasse, but now he discovered that he didn't want to use her, or humiliate Parnasse either. Everything had become much too complicated. Feelings—that's what caused all the problems. Why did he have to have any? He was betraying his mother and the memory of his father. Dammit, he thought, not only was he finding that passion was not easily governed, it was unpredictable and dangerous.

What was he going to do now? How was he to respond to Parnasse? The man had been kind to him, had helped him and confided in him, and in return he'd slept with his wife. And how was he to treat Catherine? Pretend nothing had happened, maintain a facade of indifference and politeness?

He had no idea what was going to happen, but he knew that matters were beyond his control and that he was walking on a precipice. He washed and dressed, trying to decide what to think and how to act, but he came up with nothing. He didn't want to act at all; he wanted to be natural. Maybe Catherine was right in that he was too young and inexperienced to be in love, but he wanted to be free and uninhibited, to let his feelings and emotions run loose. But he couldn't.

Not wanting to meet either of them because he wasn't sure he could maintain the charade, he decided to go down to breakfast now, before the others, then go out riding.

Yet when he entered the dining room, Parnasse was already seated.

"Good morning, Andre. You're up early."

"Good morning, sir. Habit, I suppose. I hated reveille, but now I hear the bugle even when there isn't one."

"The soldier's curse. One of them, anyway. Sleep well?" His eyes were pleasant, but Andre felt they were too penetrating and watchful. Did he know? Had he heard Catherine's cries, or had he been told? Perhaps he'd seen her returning to her own room. He felt immense guilt and discomfort.

"Very well, sir. And you?"

Parnasse murmured noncommittally, and just then Catherine swept in, seemingly not surprised at finding them both there.

Andre jumped up. "Good morning, madame."

"Good morning, Andre." She nodded at her husband. "Philippe. Are you both going out to ride?"

Parnasse looked at Andre, his eyes clear and commanding. "Yes, I think we'll go out for a while."

So he knows, Andre thought, and he had trouble swallowing the rest of the food in his mouth. What would Parnasse do? Certainly Andre knew that he could forget about returning to the academy. And with sudden force Andre realized what that would mean. He had no place to go, only back to the squalor of where he'd come from, and there would be no hope this time of rising from it, not with an enemy such as the duke.

Catherine finished her coffee and stood. "I've got to go into Orléans; I'll stay the night with Elise."

"I didn't know Robert had opened the château," Parnasse said. He didn't get along with the Duke of Orléans, though their wives were close.

"He hasn't. Elise did." Catherine turned to Andre. "The duchess is much younger than her husband; they find time away from one another therapeutic. She's very amusing. We're like silly girls together."

Andre stood as Catherine left. Trying to conceal his anguish that she'd be gone, he said politely, "I hope you have an enjoyable visit, madame."

He realized that he was staring at the door long after she had disappeared through it, and somewhat embarrassed, he sat down too quickly, feeling the scrutinizing eyes of Parnasse on him.

"My wife and I are not happy together," Parnasse said.

Andre did not raise his eyes. He sat straight, his head bowed, awaiting the blow he knew was to come.

"Are you in love with my wife?" Parnasse asked. His voice was steady, though heavy with sadness and resignation.

Andre looked up in agony, yet when he saw Parnasse's eyes, he realized that the duke did not know. But this made it only worse, for he saw Parnasse's pain and suffering, but also hope, an eagerness, almost desperation to be told no, to be lied to, to hear that Andre did not want his wife, but himself.

And indeed Parnasse did not know what had happened. In his room the previous night he'd drunk a great deal, to help himself sleep and to douse his desire and torment, but sleep had been fitful, though he heard nothing and had no suspicions. This morning he woke tortured with longing for Andre, almost unbalanced with what he knew was love, and in anguish with the realization that it could not be expressed, much less returned. Now, seeing Andre's puppylike look after Catherine, he was suffering, the rejected suitor, and he felt self-loathing and disgust.

"Sir, I . . . I . . ." Andre stammered, unable to lie, yet unable to tell the truth. He struggled with his own emotions; then he pushed himself away from the table and ran from the room, outside toward the stable.

He had saddled a horse and was about to ride away, not knowing where, when Parnasse came in and held the horse's bridle.

"That was wrong of me," the duke said. "Forgive me. I never should have said such a thing. May I go with you?"

Andre couldn't look at him, turned aside, but nodded his head.

They rode out together, Parnasse speaking casually. "I'm sorry I suggested that. I know you're too honorable to even entertain such a thing. She is an attractive woman, and of course you must feel something—what normal man, especially a young one, wouldn't? But I know you would keep something like that buried deeply. I apologize for impugning you."

The more Parnasse said, the worse Andre felt, and now he was consumed with guilt. And yet of course he couldn't wait for Catherine to return.

They rode hard for most of the morning, stopping only briefly to rest the horses, and Andre learned more about riding in these few hours with Parnasse than he had in all his classes at the academy.

The duke was an excellent horseman and a patient instructor. He asked Andre if he'd ever done any steeplechasing, and he said no, it wasn't done at the academy, but he'd like to try, so Parnasse set out a moderately difficult course—fences, hedges, and water jumps—but he cautioned Andre that it was trickier than it appeared because of the control of the horse.

As soon as they began, Andre realized that he was in trouble; his horse barely cleared the first two obstacles, and slipped further out of his control as it sensed the rider's insecurity and inexperience.

At the water jump the horse pulled up and Andre flew out of the saddle, his landing cushioned by the muck on the other side of the obstacle.

Parnasse dismounted quickly and ran to Andre, but by the time he reached him, Andre had pulled himself up and was rubbing his bruised shoulder and side, more embarrassed than hurt, and dripping mud.

"Are you all right?" Parnasse's face was anxious, and he castigated himself for initiating the sport.

"I'm fine, really; I let the horse get away from me."

"Your shoulder. You're hurt."

"No, just sore. Though if I hadn't landed in the mud, I might have broken something." He headed back toward the horse. "Let's try it again."

"Absolutely not."

"I'm fine, really. I want to do it again; I don't want the horse to think it can get away with this."

"I won't allow it. That's a command." Then Parnasse laughed. "Well, I can't command you to do or not-do anything, but I ask you for my sake not to. We'll try another day. We must practice first. Come, let's go back and get you cleaned up."

Andre shook his head. "I'm not going back looking like this. I'd be a laughingstock. There's a lake a mile or so back, I'll clean up there."

By the time they reached the lake, Andre had thought better of the idea and realized the possible implications, but there was no way to change his mind without implied offense to the duke, so when they reached the water he quickly stripped off his clothes and dived into the water. Parnasse threw Andre's clothes in after him to wash, then sat on the bank.

The sun was near its apex and the day was hot. The water felt so good that Andre forgot his hesitancy and lost himself in cool enjoyment. "Come on in," he shouted at Parnasse.

The duke smiled and shook his head. He watched Andre swim and dive, musing on the pastoral beauty of the scene, and he said fondly, "I used to swim here when I was a boy. The last time was when I was your age, maybe a little older, just before I went to the Crimea."

And that of course conjured up Alain for him; the memory jarred him so that he had to look away, but Andre was emerging from the water, coming directly toward him, dripping water, his body gleaming in the sun.

Completely casual about his nudity, Andre carefully spread out his clothes to dry; then he dropped down near Parnasse and closed his eyes, luxuriating in the warmth of the sun and his own happy exhaustion.

Parnasse stole glances at him, wanting to stare at the youth unashamedly, and as the moment lengthened he felt such intense longing that he began to shake. Twice he raised his hand to reach out for Andre, but brought it back at the last second.

He was in acute pain. He loved the boy, and it went far deeper than physical desire. For the first time he truly loved another, and he couldn't bear having to withhold it.

"Andre . . ." he said softly, and though the youth had been dozing, the tone of the voice brought him awake instantly. His eyes jerked open and his body stiffened, and when he realized his exposure, he sat up to cover himself unobtrusively.

In this Parnasse saw that while the youth was naive, he understood enough, and was wary.

"I think we'd better talk," the duke said.

"Yes, sir," Andre said, and got up to put on his clothes, though they were still damp.

"Don't." Their eyes met and Parnasse said evenly, "I like to look at your body; it's beautiful. Don't worry, I'm not going to touch you, unless you let me."

Andre's face was expressionless; then he sat back down, slightly out of Parnasse's reach.

"You know, don't you," Parnasse asked.

Andre nodded.

"And?"

Andre said nothing, but kept his eyes steady on Parnasse.

"The time has come, Andre, to get this out in the open, for I can't keep it inside me any longer. I'm attracted to you, very much so. Physically, but in other ways. I've never felt this for anyone else, and I know it must be difficult for you to understand. Does it offend you?"

Andre considered the word. "Offend? No sir, but I . . ."

"Does the idea of male love disgust you?"

Andre shifted uncomfortably, and he tried to be polite. "I think that . . . well, if people are interested in that, then it's all right for them."

"But you are not interested."

He said quickly, "No, sir, I'm not."

The way he said it reminded Parnasse of Andre's father; there was the same firmness, the same unyielding manner, though Andre seemed more understanding and tolerant. But remembering the violent consequences with Alain, Parnasse proceeded with caution.

"You are a grown man and I suppose you understand how the world works, that one receives by giving, that one pays for what one gets—one way or another."

Andre said with considerable maturity, "I understand that, if one is not discussing love or friendship."

"Ah," Parnasse murmured. "You are making this very difficult, because I cannot separate out love and friendship. I feel both of these for you. Alas, I feel much more. I want you to understand that. Can you? Can you keep in mind that I feel deep concern, kindness, affection for you, that in one sense I love you as I would a son, and in another sense as I would a close friend?"

"Yes, sir, I think so."

"But in another sense what I feel is strictly sexual."

The word jarred Andre and he stirred uneasily.

Parnasse pressed on quickly, "So let's forget love and friendship; let's discuss the practical aspect of this. I've done a great deal for you. You are at the academy because of me; if I notified them that you were to be dismissed, you of course would be dismissed. You will become an officer only if I remain your patron. You understand that?"

"Of course."

"You want to become an officer?"

"I did."

"Would you like to become much more? Let there be no misunderstanding—I'm offering you not only my continued support but also wealth and position, and I'm willing to make a formal agreement in writing to this effect. I'm offering you an opportunity in life which you'll never have again. I'm offering you your future. And you understand what refusal will entail?"

Andre took a deep breath. So here it was, crystallized, brought to the surface with brutal speed and directness. Not even for a second was he temped or did he vacillate. So, he thought, it was all over, he was to be cast back into the gutter. Suddenly he relaxed, for the idea didn't perturb him. There was no disgrace in returning to his home, not if his honor was inviolate—disgrace came from losing honor, never from upholding it. He smiled unconsciously, thinking of the word "disgrace" and of his grandmother.

But Parnasse misinterpreted the smile, and in the youth's now calm features he saw resignation and acceptance, and he didn't want to ruin it by pressing him or by gloating. He thought he would make it easy on Andre now that he felt he'd won. "Give it some thought," he said. "I want you to weigh this all carefully. We'll discuss this later. Perhaps tonight." He stood up. "Your clothes are probably dry now."

They rode back in silence, stabled the horses, and went in to lunch, but as soon as they entered the house, Parnasse was informed that an emissary from the emperor was waiting for him in the library. He excused himself, and Andre, gratefully, dined alone.

Just as Andre was finishing, the duke came into the dining room, greatly angered. "I've got to leave," he said. "I've been summoned back to Paris. The Spanish throne is about to fall and there's fear of an alliance between the new government and the Prussians. That could be disastrous for us."

Andre jumped up, the prospect of war exhilarating him. "Queen Isabella has been overthrown?"

"It's imminent. And Moltke, the chief of the German general staff, has moved his army from the Austrian front to our borders." Parnasse sat down to eat and said disdainfully, "The emperor is disturbed."

Andre couldn't hide his eagerness. "Will there be war?"

Parnasse put down his knife and fork and contemplated him. "You had better hope not, young man. War is not like the games you play on the Champ de Mars."

"Sir, we will destroy the Prussians!"

Parnasse went back to his roast. "I think not. In any case, Bismarck is not yet ready to engage us. He knows what our fine officers, and you, don't seem to grasp: fervor is no match for practicality, nor passion a substitute for competence."

Andre was astonished, and he said with reproach bordering on contempt, "You don't think we could defeat the Huns?"

Parnasse's smile was sagacious and cunning. "I think you had better study the sky carefully some night, Andre. What appear to be stars are sometimes only short-lived meteors, and the brightest star in the sky is merely a planet more drab than our own. Primitive people often mistook a fire for a rising sun, and there are among us many who will discover that what they believe is their sun is in fact only a brief bonfire in a long night."

He stood and patted Andre on the shoulder. "You'd better make provision for the darkness. I myself plan to be around for the new dawn. I'd hate to see you left shivering in the cold night of failed glory."

He went to the door and turned before going out. "By the way, I'm not speaking cryptically, but literally. Please give thought to our talk this afternoon, and I'll see you when I return in a few days."

Andre could hardly believe what he'd heard. The duke spoke treason: he was talking about the defeat of France and the fall of the emperor. A chief adviser, a minister for war, a supposedly close friend of the emperor, was planning for the defeat of his own country and the collapse of the throne. He was probably plotting against the emperor, Andre thought, secretly working with the Prussians.

Not only was he a homosexual, but a traitor and a coward. Andre was overcome with fury. He had to tell someone, had to warn the emperor.

He hated Parnasse, and his rage mounted so that had the duke been in the room, he'd have attacked him. He was disgusting, attempting to bribe him for sexual perversion, now working against his own emperor and country. Andre shook with anger. He had to do something; but who would listen, let alone believe him? The only person of any consequence who'd even receive him would be Colonel Laval, and he could imagine what would happen as soon as he spoke against the duke.

Yet he couldn't just stand by. Parnasse was responsible for the defense of France, and he was a traitor.

In extreme agitation, Andre went outside, just as the duke's carriage disappeared. He debated whether to leave immediately, to ride into Paris and attempt to convince someone, or to remain and work out a plan. Realizing it would be futile to try to convince anyone, he set about devising a strategy.

Perhaps Parnasse had incriminating papers, correspondence with the Prussians, maybe even secret defense plans he was going to give them. Andre's imagination took hold and he saw insidious plots against his country and emperor, and he saw himself as the only foil; he'd expose Parnasse and save his country. All he needed were documents to prove the duke's treason.

Andre affected nonchalance around the household staff and in late afternoon announced that he was going to take a nap and that he wasn't to be disturbed for any reason; but instead of going to his own room, he went into the private apartment of the Duke.

But there, surrounded by huge mahogany chests, several massive desks, campaign chests, and wardrobes, he saw the impossibility of the task before him: he didn't know where to begin to look, even if he knew exactly what he was looking for and could recognize it.

Perfunctorily he opened a few drawers in a desk and lifted up some papers, but he gave up soon, both because of the size of the undertaking and because he found it so distasteful. He didn't like going through another's belongings, no matter the cause.

Yet he had to find the evidence. He took a deep breath and started again. For two hours he sorted through papers but found nothing which even remotely looked like war plans, and no communications with the German general staff. All he found were old letters and receipts, and a mountain of papers dealing with the estate.

He closed the last drawer in the last chest, then halfheartedly went to a wardrobe and looked through it. It was filled with old uniforms and military paraphernalia, but Andre found it interesting, and he brought out several uniforms to view more carefully. Then he noticed they didn't belong to the duke; they were the still-soiled uniforms of a grenadier, and judging by the insignias, they dated from the Crimean War.

Andre held up the uniforms; they were almost exactly his size, and suddenly, with a sickening feeling, he realized they were his father's. He searched inside and found penned in a childlike scrawl, "Lafabre." On the floor he found his father's boots, and way in the back, hidden, he found his father's sword. He got everything out and laid it on the bed. What did this mean, his father's belongings here?

He'd never seen anything of his father's; nothing had been sent back, and the body had been buried in the Crimea. Now, here was his father vividly conjured up for him—sweat stains on the uniforms, caked mud on the boots, a wooden box of pathetic mementos: a deck of cards; a lock of hair, probably his mother's; a few coins; and a tiny infant's bracelet.

Andre brought his hand up and began to cry, and he couldn't stop. Why did the duke have his father's belongings?

He didn't want to contemplate it, so he gathered everything up and stumbled back to his room with it all, blinded by tears.

He put everything in a closet, then fell on the bed and cried himself to sleep.

He woke in the dark to caressing hands. Jerking forward, he struck out viciously.

Catherine screamed and fell away, and when he jumped from the bed, she cowered on the floor, whimpering.

He grabbed her around the neck and squeezed. "Tell me about my father."

She tried to scream, but he shook her roughly and tightened his hold. "I want to know about my father. Tell me."

She gasped out, "I don't know anything."

"Yes you do. You threw my mother out."

Her hands went up to him, pleading, and in the dimness he could see her terror.

"Andre, Andre, it's not how you think. Oh, my God. Please." She took deep gasping breaths and struggled up, though he still held her, and his voice was cold and demanding. "Tell me."

"I don't know anything about your father, except that he was a soldier for Philippe."

"What about the duke and my father? What happened?"

She shook her head in confusion and fear because she saw that he was beyond control. His eyes were murderous. He threw her back on the bed and went to the wardrobe. "These are my father's uniforms. Why are they here? Why does he have them?"

She drew back on the bed, truly afraid, but all she could do was shake her head and whimper, "I don't know, I don't know anything."

He went to her and stood threateningly. "All right, tell me about my mother."

Catherine began to cry, turning her head away, burying it in the pillows, but he grabbed her by the hair and yanked her up. "Tell me!"

She screamed and he yanked harder, almost pulling her from the bed by her hair. "I'll tell you. Don't hurt me. Please."

He let go, and her words rushed out between choked sobs. "I married Philippe when I was sixteen. I didn't know anything. My father made me marry him. I was only sixteen. And he was terrible to me. And he never slept with me. He was sleeping with your mother. She was a maid in the house. I didn't know anything about her. I never even spoke to her. But she was sleeping with my husband, and I was humiliated, and I didn't understand. It hurt me, and yes, I threw her out. My life was ruined."

She collapsed, overcome by deep, racking sobs. "It wasn't your mother's fault. But it wasn't mine, either. I was just a girl, and I found out about my husband, and . . . I didn't mean to harm your mother. And I know she didn't mean to hurt me."

Gaining control of herself, she sat up. "Andre, neither one of us was to blame. Please understand that I never meant to hurt your mother, but what else could I do after I found out?"

"Why did the duke help me?"

She said softly, "Don't you know?"

He lowered his head. "Yes." Then he brought his hands up to his face. "Oh, Jesus. Oh, God. I can't stand it. My father, and my mother . . . and . . ."

He began to cry, and she pulled him down on the bed and put her arm around his shoulders to comfort him.

"What am I going to do?"

"I'll help you. I won't let him hurt you. He's done enough, to all of us." She turned his face to hers. "I love you. I came back to be with you. I left this morning so that I could sneak back in the night . . . then I found out Philippe was gone."

She dug her nails into his neck as she pulled him toward her, and he responded, his hurt and anger welling up and bursting out in aggressive sexuality. He tore at her clothes, maybe even trying to hurt her, he didn't know, but she matched his savagery, and they fell on one another, hands and mouths trying to consume the other, their passion desperate, hurling against the other's, and their bodies were wild, feeding on each other's, and when they both climaxed, they were in tears, gasping for breath, exhausted, and they collapsed in each other's arms and slept.

She spent the night, and in the morning they went down to breakfast together, making no attempt to hide their feelings from the servants. That day and for the next two they spent every minute together. Andre almost forgot everything that had happened; she filled him entirely, and he realized that he was in love with her. She was passionate and gentle, funny and tender, and so open in her feelings for him that he couldn't bear to be out of her presence.

They rode, walked in the garden, went on picnics, and made love wherever they could.

"What's going to happen?" he asked one morning when they were lying in bed. "He's going to come back anytime."

"I don't care. I hate him. He's vicious and cruel and . . . I don't want to talk about him."

"Is he a traitor?"

"Philippe? What a curious thing to ask. He's many things, but he's not that. Why do you ask?"

"He was talking about war with Prussia. He said we'd lose."

She snuggled against him. "Don't underestimate Philippe. He's the smartest man advising the emperor, and if he said we'd have a war against the Prussians, he's right. He's disgusting, but he's shrewd."

She brought her hand to her mouth. "Oh, my God. Don't go to war. What would happen if you were killed?" She grabbed between his legs and squeezed. "Or worse."

"What if he finds out about us?"

"Let him. What can he do? I won't let him hurt you. I know enough about him so that he can't do anything. Besides, all the money's mine, not his."

"Well, tomorrow we'd better plan on what to do."

"Tomorrow. Not now. Now just lie back."

That night they had a special dinner in her apartment. She made it as romantic as she could, and she fed him on the chaise while she sat at his feet, and he felt like an Oriental potentate, or that she was Salome, and when she led him to bed, she was more passionate than ever, acting as though this was their last night together, and she dominated him, and her cries filled the rooms.

She was on top of him, both naked, she driving down on him, moaning with pleasure, when the door flew open on Parnasse, towering in fury.

"You slut! Whore!"

She didn't even move off Andre, only turned, her eyes and mouth lascivious, her body riding the youth's. "Who are you jealous of, Philippe, him or me?"

"Bitch!" He ran at the bed and struck her. Andre jumped up, but Parnasse hit him brutally across the face, knocking him to the floor. "You bastard. You little nothing. I'll see you guillotined."

Andre scrambled up, but Parnasse was on him, raining blows and kicks. "You're nothing, like your father. Nothing!"

Andre dived at him, crying out, "What did you do to him? What did you do to my father?"

Parnasse drew his sword. In a fury he thrust it at Andre. "I killed him. Like I will you."

Catherine screamed.

Andre dodged, and his arm caught Parnasse's, but the tip of the blade sliced deeply along his cheek.

Parnasse raised the sword again. Andre grabbed a cane-back chair and swung it with all his might, catching Parnasse on the side of the head, and the duke dropped instantly.

Andre stood over him, reached for the sword, but Catherine rushed to his side. "Run. Get away. There may be others downstairs. Hurry."

Andre hesitated; then he yielded to Catherine's pushes. "Hurry. Run. Oh, Andre, quickly."

He struggled into his clothes, looked a final time on Parnasse's motionless body, and ran to the door. Catherine pulled on his arm, thrust what he knew was money into his hand, then threw her arms around him and cried. He let her head rest on his chest for a moment before gently easing her back. They kissed tenderly, sorrowfully; then he opened the door cautiously and stepped out.

There were many voices downstairs; he heard laughing and drinking and assumed that Parnasse had come back unexpectedly with friends. It would only be a matter of minutes before suspicion about Parnasse's absence was raised and his body discovered—Andre had no doubt that he'd killed him with the blow against his temple.

He crept stealthily down the back stairs and made his way outside. It was a beautifully clear night, warm and star-bright, and circling around the château, he heard raucous laughter and clinking glasses. Eight horses were reined in front; he chose the strongest-looking, led it halfway down the path, then jumped on and was gone.

He couldn't go back to Paris, he knew, so he took the road south. He had to leave France, for if caught, he'd be guillotined for the murder of the duke. He could never return to see his mother, or Catherine. His only hope was to get away before the murder was known throughout the country. But where could he go? Parnasse was a high minister of state, an adviser to the emperor, and his murderer would be pursued throughout Europe. He wouldn't be safe anywhere.

All his hopes and dreams were now nothing. He had no life in his country anymore; he was a fugitive. He couldn't serve his country, would never be an officer, would never fight against the Prussians.

He whipped the horse on, galloping along the dusty road

under the near-full moon. He rode all night, pushing the horse too hard, but by morning he'd reached Lyon, where he traded horses, arousing suspicion by accepting a much lesser horse in trade, but the horse dealer was so pleased by the exchange that he said nothing.

Andre was exhausted, drenched with sweat, and every muscle ached, but he knew he had to press on, so he saddled up and took the road to Marseille.

By the time he reached the huge port city, he'd decided on a plan. With the money Catherine had given him and with the money he'd get from the sale of the horse, he'd book passage to Suez. There he'd enlist in the army under an assumed name, or find work on the construction of the canal. He'd rather have gone to Mexico to fight with the French forces, but the Emperor Maximilian had been overthrown and executed the year before. The only other alternative was America, but that would mean cutting all ties with France, and he couldn't bear that thought. Besides, America was too imposing, and their Civil War was long over, and the prospect of fighting savage Indians didn't appeal to him. He was determined to be a soldier. If worse came to worst, he could join the Foreign Legion. They didn't inquire into an enlistee's background and their ranks were open to all. He knew they were in Algeria, and in his simple geography, he believed Algeria only a short jaunt from Egypt.

When he reached Marseille he sold the horse and tried to find anonymity in the bustling harbor area, thinking he'd blend in easily with the soldiers and sailors, so naive he didn't realize how his appearance contrasted with these seasoned men. He looked too intelligent, too clean despite his ride, and his bearing was too genteel; he looked exactly what he was—a young man running from the authorities, trying to lose himself.

If his speech and manner hadn't given him away, reading the newspapers to find out if his crime had been reported yet would have—no one else where he was could read.

He picked one of the worst and roughest sections for lodging, and was instantly spotted as any easy mark.

On his first night, several sailors made friends with him, promised him sights and wonders he'd never seen, got him very drunk, stole his money, and when he came to, he found himself on board a ship steaming out of the harbor of Marseille.

A petty officer toppled him out of his sling bunk and told him to get topside for a crew's manifest.

He staggered up, having no idea where he was, attempting to explain that a mistake had been made, but the petty officer boxed his ears and informed him there was no mistake. He'd signed on that morning, and the officer produced the paper, pointed to his signature and the witnessing marks.

Then the officer grabbed him by the neck and forced him toward the gangway.

All Andre managed to ask was where the ship was going.

"Vietnam," the officer said curtly.

He'd never heard of it.

7
Ban Me Thuot: 1866

FROM A SHORT DISTANCE, HIS eyesight diminishing with age, Father Bergere saw the garden pavilions of the palatial estate of Prince Ahn. The sixty-year-old priest was exhausted, but he quickened his strange shuffle-step—he had to warn Ahn.

Coming nearer, he could make out the outline of the vast complex—a sprawling network of wood buildings and annexes with both tiled and thatched roofs, steep in the Japanese style, surrounded by a resplendent garden, and set back deeply in a clearing within the jungle.

The complex was of remarkable design, a blend of styles which nevertheless created an effect of simplicity and harmony, an architectural metaphor for the compatible diversity which lived within. Indeed, the Jade Palace, as it was called, for a palace of jade it appeared to be amid the shimmering jungle, was the result of the plans of the four vastly different personalities who'd arrived unexpectedly and without fanfare nineteen years ago: a royal prince, cousin of the emperor; his new wife, herself a princess and granddaughter of an emperor; a Chinese sage, huge and lordly; and a thin and ascetic French priest.

At first the people had resented the young prince, for he was not of them, had come from a life of ease in Hue, and was a representative of a throne they didn't like, yet he'd won them over effortlessly. The people, elders, and mandarins were confounded by his reign, benevolent, compassionate, and scrupulously just, unlike anything they'd ever witnessed—a combination of Vietnamese tenacity, feminine understanding, Chinese wisdom, and French logic. It was a rule like his strange and labyrinthine palace—the product of four minds—and the results were always a curious blend of intuition, intellect, force, and reason.

So successful was his rule that the Emperor Tu Duc came to

view it with increasing unease, for he saw it as one more thing undermining his throne.

In stark contrast to Ahn, the years had not been good to the emperor or his country; the rule of the Nguyen Dynasty and the independence of the nation were precarious.

Four years earlier, in 1862, Tu Duc had signed a treaty granting France control of Saigon and three surrounding provinces in order to enlist French support against a new Le pretender who'd staged a rebellion in the north. Tu Duc couldn't fight both the French in the south and a pretender to his throne in the north, so he'd made peace with the French and concentrated his military in the north, reconquering the provinces he'd lost to the rebels near Hanoi.

But now, in 1866, the French, not happy with the territory already ceded them, were making an all-out assault for the entire southern part of Vietnam.

Tu Duc felt besieged from all sides—the French to the south, rebels to the north, Ahn in Ban Me Thuot, and the missionaries everywhere. For years Tu Duc had waged unsuccessful war against the priests, beginning their executions and explusions in 1851, but the missionaries had retaliated by forcing the government in Paris to protect them with military power which culminated in the conquest of Saigon in 1861.

Yet after the Treaty of Saigon in June 1862, which promised religious freedom for Vietnamese Christians, Tu Duc ordered their persecution, and thousands of Vietnamese Catholics were slaughtered.

To the shock of the missionaries, the French military allowed the persecutions, and they came to realize that they'd been used only as a pretext for military intervention in Vietnam. Paris didn't care about the missionaries or the souls of the Vietnamese; they had sent their military for economic and political gain. Tu Duc's chief adviser, Huynh Bo Linh, had been right fifteen years earlier—unfortunately, his advice had gone unheeded, and he'd been purged, a victim of court intrigue, his fall coming immediately upon that of the former lord treasurer, Gian Ke Deng. Lady Deng, violently anti-Catholic, especially after Ahn's marriage to Xuan, had prevailed, and the Lizard Woman, as she was now called, exercised vast influence at court.

No matter what he did, Tu Duc seemed unable to stem the tide running against him. Making matters worse were the corruption, arrogance, and inefficiency of his mandarins, which made his own rule so unpopular and created a wall of hatred between Tu Duc and his people. The emperor could no longer count on his people to side with him against the French or against the pretender and his rebels in the north.

The only bright spot in the country was at Ban Me Thuot, where there was peace and efficient administration, but in this Tu Duc saw a threat, for he knew there was talk in the kingdom of a revolution to replace him with his cousin, Prince Ahn.

But if Ahn knew of this talk or of such a movement, he didn't indicate it. He was preoccupied with his own responsibilities and his family, and these in fact took all of his time—the wise rule of a household being no less difficult or demanding than the wise rule of a kingdom, especially a household of three daughters.

His eldest, Gia Minh, at eighteen was a unique blend of her father and mother; she was willful and clever, loving and warm, without Xuan's sense of artistry and with no interest in painting or music, but with her father's interest in politics and history and religion, and she challenged him frequently, and debated endlessly with Chien and Father Bergere. She exasperated them all, possessing her mother's self-confidence and mind, but asserting herself with none of Xuan's subtlety.

Ahn grumbled about her frequently these days. She was not feminine enough, he said, and she talked too much. No one will ever marry her, he said to his wife. "She's eighteen and has no prospects, and she won't let me arrange anything, refuses even to meet anyone," he said.

"I was twenty-six before I married," Xuan reminded him.

"She'll frighten away every boy," he said.

"I didn't frighten you."

"No, but how many mes are there?"

Xuan laughed. "She'll settle for what she thinks is the best she can do."

"Can't you talk with her? She doesn't listen to me."

"Oh, yes she does, she just doesn't want you to know it."

Which was true; she played her father masterfully, her feminine intuition capitalizing on his vulnerability for women.

At thirty-nine, Ahn was not much changed from when he was at court; he was merely an older youth, possessing the same vitality and sexuality of twenty years ago—well, not quite, he allowed, but enough to make him extraordinarily attracted to and by women. He was not a faithful husband, nor had he been from the beginning of his marriage, but Xuan was not bothered by this, for she knew that he loved her and realized that for him other women were a matter of compulsion and necessity, but limited involvement. She knew that in his mind fidelity was of such little significance that she couldn't hold him culpable;

besides, she'd known before her marriage what he was like. She loved him, now more than ever, and their life together was happy in all ways.

The household was filled with talk, and art, and laughter, and fights, and passions, and much theater, and the three daughters were unsparing in their tricks and jokes on the three men who had raised and tutored them. They knew the weaknesses of all three and teased them accordingly.

It was this richness of life and gaiety, and the three daughters especially, which Father Bergere was rushing back to. But anything would be welcome after the drudgery of the past week. Father Bergere had returned to missionary work, though not with the zeal he'd had forty years ago. Yet what he lacked in fervor he made up for in industry and efficiency: he'd built nine schools, three orphanages, and two hospitals, all in addition to his priestly duties and tutoring Ahn's three girls. His only failure had been with Ahn, who'd listened carefully over the years to all he'd said and taught, yet who'd let every single word bounce off him.

The toll of his labors was telling on the priest; he looked old and frail, especially now after a week's travel and work through the province.

When he reached a gazebo in the garden, he stopped to rest, knowing he'd be welcomed back in the house with exuberance, and forced to relate all that had happened and all he'd seen.

He dropped down on the wooden bench inside the gazebo, closed his eyes, and drew deep breaths. The cool stillness of the evening and the heavy fragrance of the garden were immensely relieving, reaffirming for him the goodness of God and life.

His eyesight had become so bad, and his tiredness so complete, that he didn't notice Chien sitting in the shadows across from him. The Chinaman sat like a huge Buddha, and as still as stone. He waited until Father Bergere was almost asleep; then he spoke, his voice low and serious. "You'd better hurry if you're going to catch that heathen I saw running through the garden a short time ago. You'll never save any of us if you spend afternoons sleeping in gazebos."

Father Bergere didn't open his eyes, but smiled happily at the sound of the voice.

"You're looking tired, Father. The Lord's business seems very demanding—he must not manage his affairs very well."

Father Bergere had learned long ago to brush aside Chien's comments. "How is everyone, Master Chien?"

"Exceedingly sinful. You're back just in time. How is the world beyond the garden?"

"Exceedingly sinful. I was just in time."

Chien smiled. The two had grown comfortable with one another over the years, and though neither would have admitted it, each enjoyed the other's company. While they ridiculed each other and never had anything good to say about one another in the presence of others, they felt respect and solicitude for each other.

For Chien the years since Hue had been mixed happiness and sorrow; he was not the same man who'd come nineteen years ago, and his appearance reflected the transformation. At fifty-three, he seemed older, and the muscular bulk that he'd once had was now soft fleshiness.

Though not happy to have left court at Hue, he'd adjusted well. His learning and wisdom were esteemed in the province and he was frequently consulted by the elders and mandarins. He tutored, went for long walks and contemplated, did calligraphy, and kept busy; then, ten years ago, to everyone's surprise, he married a girl of seventeen. Ahn knew that Chien was bored by Ban Me Thuot's provincial, rustic life, so he supposed the marriage was a result of loneliness, for the girl was, to Ahn, just that, pleasing to look at and attentive, but not what he'd have expected Chien to choose as a wife.

He knew that Chien had little respect for the thoughts of women—Xuan was a singular exception—and he felt his knowledge was wasted on Ahn's daughters, whom he tutored. Nevertheless, Ahn had expected Chien to choose a wife of some learning and mental agility. Such was not the case; Luu was a beautiful but simple girl.

Yet the marriage was extraordinarily happy, and he seemed as devoted to her as she to him. Moreover, he changed, becoming felicitous and playful. He had never been a somber man, but before Luu, there had been an edge to his humor, a pointedness too sharp, a cynicism too pronounced for a sage. This all disappeared when he married Luu. He laughed openly, and the three daughters took to calling him "Jolly Uncle."

When Luu became pregnant, Chien was as solicitous as a hen. He grew superstitious and found omens and signs in everything.

But he had not seen tragedy in the signs, so when his wife died in childbirth and the baby was stillborn, Chien was devastated. He allowed no one to comfort him, and he left, disappearing after the burial, simply walking away.

He was gone six months, examining himself, he said, and it was a different man who returned, not bitter or unhappy, but older, no longer playful, and the girls changed his name to "Grandfather."

The role of grandfather seemed the most appropriate to him; he thickened around the middle, let his beard grow, and paid little attention to his appearance. On seeing him, one might have expected a doddering mind, but though the rest of him might have softened, his thoughts hadn't in the slightest.

Chien studied the priest's drawn and haggard features and said seriously, though it was not a question, "Why do you bother?"

He was a man of contemplation and moderation who believed the world was as it should be and that change was not good—the order of the universe should not be disturbed; restraint was wisdom, and knowledge was power. Human nature was basically good, and evil was the result of excess and intemperance. He liked quiet. Noise, quick movement, emotions, disturbed and unsettled him. There was mischief in haste and innovation, and a restless spirit was an evil one. One strove for knowledge above all things, and knowledge was an existing quantity of historical fact and philosophical truth which the learned mind could gain only by study and contemplation.

Father Bergere kept his eyes closed and said, though it was not an answer, "Because."

The priest's thought was not passive or contemplative: man's nature was not good and the world was to be reshaped and refashioned; knowledge was not a storehouse of past thought, but an ever-changing quantity to which men added by innovation and invention. Darkness was to be pushed back, heathens were to be saved, technology was to be advanced, poverty was to be eradicated. Father Bergere's thought was active and aggressive, and he despaired the stagnant Oriental mind.

And yet as different as their thought was, each made allowances for the other's, for they were both wise and experienced enough to realize that maybe, just maybe, there was something valid in the other's thinking.

"You're too old to chase over the countryside, trying to uproot trees," Chien said. "Nothing is going to change."

Father Bergere opened his eyes, and despite his exhaustion, they lit with passion and conviction. "Things are changing. You should see what I saw—children learning in schools, orphans cared for, the sick and old nursed, farming improved. The whole province is improving and prospering."

Chien folded his hands around his stomach. He drew a deep breath of fragrant air and his eyes moved from Father Bergere to beyond, serenely taking in the cool evening, the garden and house, the lush rain forest gradually being swallowed by the encroaching darkness, and in this panorama he saw the insignificance of man's work, a presumptuous and momentary clearing in the jungle, a sand citadel on the beach—an orphanage, a school, a hospital indeed!

He could not understand Father Bergere's obsession with buildings, as if one could construct peace and harmony, build understanding and serenity—by throwing up enough brick and mortar, erect wisdom. These foolish Westerners didn't seem to know that all they sought came from within and could be achieved only through quiet meditation. All this rushing about, this action and striving, were doomed to failure—one might as well attempt to nail down the horizon to prevent the sun from rising as to try to remake the world in one's own image.

Poor Father Bergere, he thought, roaming the land, trying to change things, not knowing that as soon as he was gone, maybe even before, all he sought to accomplish would be absorbed like spring rain. Useless, he thought. Ego and pretension. Flood waters—swirling and powerful, whose fate was the burning sun and the unquenchable earth. In his mind Chien saw all this, a vast canvas of kaleidoscopic color and scope, a gigantic whirlpool in whose swirling vortex was Father Bergere, about to be dragged down into oblivion.

But he said nothing and brought his eyes back to the priest. The man looked unwell. Chien stood and held out his hand. "Come, Father, help me get back to the house."

Su, the youngest daughter, saw them coming; she called to her sisters and the three ran to meet them, chattering and asking questions. They wanted to hear everything, and demanded stories.

But Xuan, who met them at the door, saw Father Bergere's exhaustion, shooed the girls away, and called for Ahn.

Ahn himself put the priest to bed, scolding him for neglecting his health.

The priest settled under the covers, sighing in contentment, but he wouldn't let Ahn go. "I have to tell you something. That's why I rushed back."

"It can wait. Just get some sleep."

"The priest shook his head. "You're in great danger."

"I? From whom?"

"The emperor has sent spies out to question people. He's building a case of treason against you, and if that doesn't work, he's going to send assassins."

"Why? And how did you learn this?"

"People tell me things. Because I'm a foreigner, they confide in me; also they know that what they say will get back to you, and they want to help you. There's great unrest in the country. People know about the invasion in the south and Tu Duc's inability to stop it, and they know about the unfavorable treaties. They also know about the rebellion in the north. Surely you know your cousin is not a popular ruler."

Ahn said reasonably, "Times are difficult; he has many problems."

"Most of his and his advisers' own making. Do you know about the secret societies? That's why the spies are here. The societies are against both the French and Tu Duc, and he thinks you're behind them; he's trying to get evidence of your involvement so he can move against you. He fears you because you're popular and many want you on the throne."

"But that's all nonsense."

"Not to Tu Duc. Believe me, you're in grave danger. I do you no good, both as a Catholic and French—it certainly wouldn't take much to convince people that I'm a spy, or your liaison to the French. And Xuan, with her ties to the pretender—a case could easily be made of her sympathy with the rebels."

Ahn smiled at the priest, scrunched down in the bed, blankets pulled up to his neck, his eyes intense and his voice a whisper. "I can remember, Master Bergere, when you cared nothing for politics and intrigue."

"I know," the priest said. "I was very dreary. The true nature of the priesthood came late to me. In any case, Tu Duc has spies all over the province; it's only a matter of time before he takes action against you, and you know it's not just you who are in danger—he wouldn't hesitate to seize your wife and daughters."

Ahn patted his arm. "We'll talk later."

Ahn stayed until the priest fell asleep. Father Bergere's face eased into peaceful repose and he began to snore, but almost immediately his face darkened and twitched, revealing his concern and agitation.

At dinner everyone was disappointed that Father Bergere didn't appear, and was surprised when Ahn casually mentioned that he was going to Hue in the morning.

"I thought I'd go see how things are," he said, trying to bluff his way past his family's suspicious looks. He turned to Gia Minh. "Would you like to go with me?"

"Just tag along, and maybe find a husband?" she said with scorn. "Father, you're so transparent."

"Well, it's not a bad idea," Su said. "We'll never any of us get married as long as you won't even look at a man." Though only fifteen, she was already worried that she'd never marry, because she couldn't take a husband until her older sisters had.

"If she doesn't want to go, I do," said Ke. "I'll find husbands for both of us." Ahn's second daughter was a vivacious girl of quick mind and quicker tongue whose interest in art and learning had recently faded as her awakening sexuality took greater hold. She was going to be a problem, Ahn thought. He'd have to have Xuan talk with her. He couldn't bring himself to discuss sex with his daughters; he knew, correctly, that they'd laugh at him.

Xuan said diplomatically to Gia Minh, "I think it would be lovely for you to go with your father. It's time you were presented at court. Don't you want to meet the emperor?"

Gia Minh wanted very much to meet the emperor, and observe firsthand life and intrigue there, but about being presented at court she had no interest whatsoever; that she placed on the same crass level as searching for a husband. She wanted to see the people, and especially the notorious Lizard Woman, Lihn Deng.

"All right," she said, "but I'm not going like a pig to market for you to auction off to the highest bidder."

"Good thing," said Chien without missing a spoonful. "A pig brings only its own value—no one looks to the worth of its master. As they do daughters. Fortunately for you." Then he looked to Ahn. "What time should I be ready to leave?"

Ahn laughed. "How do you always manage to read my mind, Master Chien? I was just about to ask if you'd like to go."

And so the journey was arranged, all thinking that Ahn's motive was to find a suitable husband for his daughter, though that night, preparing for bed, Xuan asked him what it was that Father Bergere had said which prompted the hasty departure.

"Don't try to mollify me with lies," she said. "I'm sure I'll imagine worse things than the truth."

He told her, and she readily agreed with his decision to speak directly with Tu Duc. "Tell him that all we wish to do is live here in peace."

"Peace," murmured Ahn. "I don't think our country is destined to have that."

He was staring out an open screen to the dark jungle, normally a soothing sight for him, but now the night seemed quickened with dangerous portent, and the noise of the cicadas was an ominous warning. Xuan put her arms around him and rested her head on his chest.

"I don't like to think about the future," he said softly; then he kissed her hair, its freshness bringing him such happy memories, but then he had to squeeze his eyes shut to stop welling tears, because her hair was now streaked with gray, and what was left of youth was memory.

Ahn sent no word ahead that he was coming, for he didn't want Tu Duc to have time to prepare for him, and he wanted to see court life exactly as it was. To ensure surprise, he traveled day and night, with only the lightest guard to provide safety. Travel had become dangerous throughout the country, as armed bands from different factions, including those of the emperor, stopped travelers and took what they had, and common bandits raided caravans and killed whomever they encountered. This tempo of violence had dramatically increased in recent years—one more sign that Tu Duc was no longer capable of ruling his country.

The party arrived unexpectedly and without fanfare, but they were admitted without hesitation to the walled citadel.

Ahn's appearance caused a sensation. He, followed by Gia Minh and Chien, entered the palace with great confidence, striding through the corridors, radiating health and assurance.

Though his pace was rapid, he noted the changes in the palace. Everything was grander and more opulent, as though the imperial decay, the corruption, the weakening authority, could be hidden by ornate splendor. It reminded Ahn of rotting fruit, pungent and soft; everywhere were gilt and brocade, and even the walls were adorned with filigreed silver and inlaid enamel.

Chien saw all this too, but for Gia Minh the most impressive thing was the obsequious deference rendered her father—she'd had no idea he was this important, and she wondered why he'd given up this to live in obscurity in Ban Me Thuot. She trailed behind him, feeling regal for the first time in her life, and loving it.

When the party reached the antechamber to the throne room, Ahn bade the lord chamberlain, nervous and distraught, to ask the emperor if he would see his cousin and if it would please him to receive his daughter Gia Minh, named after their grandfather, Minh Mang.

The lord chamberlain scurried off, returning in minutes to usher them in.

Ahn instructed his daughter to show deference and respect, but to meet the emperor's eyes.

Ahn entered the throne room with more reserve and respect than he had as a youth, not out of fear, but to make a point of homage and veneration for imperial authority.

Tu Duc, sitting as he had nineteen years ago, remarkably

unchanged in appearance, sensed this immediately, and was relieved and grateful. He had not feared a confrontation, he knew Ahn would not risk that, but he'd been anxious that Ahn would create an impression of disrespect.

When he reached the designated position before the throne, Ahn bowed deeply; then he raised his eyes as of old, the only person to look upon the emperor, and he said with a slight smile which only Tu Duc could see, making sure that Tu Duc knew that he was consciously dispensing with the familiar greeting, "Thank you for seeing me. I bring you the greetings, best wishes, and loyalty of your subjects in Darlac."

Tu Duc's eyes were mild, even kind. "It is you we thank for this happy visit. Many times we have thought of you, and wished for your wise counsel. Had we known you possessed such a lovely daughter, we would have ordered you here."

Gia Minh dropped to her knees, so awed in the presence of the emperor that she forgot her father's words, and could not raise her eyes.

"We understand that you are thrice blessed, Prince Ahn. We hope to see them all here soon. But what is it we can do for you on this trip to compensate you for the joy you've given us?"

"I would like a personal audience."

"That would be our pleasure, not a compensation. You will be our guest this evening. We will send word for dinner."

Ahn bowed in gratitude, thanked Tu Duc for his graciousness, and withdrew.

Both Ahn's and Tu Duc's faces were without expression, but behind stoic masks, each wondered what it was the other was up to.

In the antechamber, Gia Minh rushed up to Chien. "He's wonderful," she said, "the most polite and graceful person I've ever seen. Father's going to have dinner with him, alone." She turned to him. "Aren't you excited?"

Ahn felt slighted by his daughter's wonder, and grumbled, "Well, he is my first cousin, you know."

Just then a side door opened, and preceded by two eunuchs, in came Lady Deng, aflame with makeup and laden with jewels, overweight and without a trace of softness, exuding raw sexuality, her eyes rapacious, her entire manner triumphant.

Gia Minh's eyes widened as the woman who'd made herself indispensable to the emperor approached. Lady Deng was Tu Duc's filter, through which everyone passed before seeing him. Her judgments were harsh, but always correct, for no one was able to deceive her. She was utterly loyal to Tu Duc, realizing that her power rested solely on his authority.

Trailing linen, waving aside her eunuchs, she stopped directly in front of Ahn, who, having seen her out of the corner of his eye, only now turned casually to acknowledge her.

She inclined her head, a quick nod, perfunctory, almost contemptuous for his rank. "We heard you were here."

"We?" questioned Ahn mildly. "Does everyone at court now use the royal pronoun?"

Her eyes flashed; she was not accustomed to having anyone stand up to her. She turned to Gia Minh, her hand reaching out to her face, long nails trailing down her cheek. "What a pretty child. I don't see much of her mother in her."

Ahn looked away, affecting boredom. "I'm told she looks like her great-grandmother, Empress Liu, Minh Mang's wife. You remember her; weren't you schoolgirls together?"

Lady Deng smiled, pleased to have a worthy opponent. "And Master Chien, how you've changed. You look like a fat old frog."

Chien bowed and said with mock sadness, "I know. I may have to start painting myself like you to hide time's ravages."

"At least time hasn't ravaged you," she said to Ahn. "You look unchanged, perhaps even more handsome." She turned to Gia Minh. "We were all in love with your father years ago. He broke many hearts. Have you heard the stories about him?"

Gia Minh shook her head, fascinated, not daring to speak.

"Perhaps you're too young to hear them. A country upbringing wouldn't prepare you for such stories. Ah, but you've been missed," she said, turning back to Ahn. "Now all we have are eunuchs and very ill-equipped men." She sighed, her eyes and mouth lascivious. "Even the guards aren't what they used to be." Her eyes fixed on him. "How long will you be here?"

"A few days. I thought it was time to introduce my daughter to court."

"Then let's start things off properly. You must all be my guests this evening." She took Gia Minh's hand. "I'll introduce you to everyone you need know. Is it settled?"

Gia Minh said with genuine disappointment, "Father's dining with the emperor tonight. We can't come."

Lady Deng turned to Ahn, a smug smile on her lips. "Well, we'll dine without him, just the two of us. There's much I can tell you, much only I can tell."

Ahn nodded. "That would be kind of you. Gia Minh considers you a heroine. I can't think of a better way for her to be introduced to life at court. I hope I'll be able to thank you properly."

Lady Deng's mouth moistened. "I hope so too." Then she swept unannounced into the throne room.

Gia Minh was dazzled. She turned to her father, a wicked look on her face. "I think she'd much rather dine with you."

"Your mother wouldn't approve."

"Since when did that matter?" she sniffed.

Chien smoothed his robes. "You're adapting to court life very quickly, child. Lady Deng will be surprised how little she has to teach you."

Gia Minh, despite the country upbringing, was not a woman to be trifled with. She turned sweetly to Chien imitating a frog, and said, "Ribbet."

"Enough," said Ahn, and led them to their apartment, luxuriously laid out and attended by many servants.

That night before he left, Ahn kissed his daughter and told her to exercise caution because Lady Deng did not like her mother and could not be trusted.

"You were her lover once, weren't you?"

"Before I knew your mother, yes."

"She still wants you."

Ahn shook his head. "She's more interested in power. She uses people. Please be careful."

When Ahn reached the imperial apartment, he was shown in immediately. Here the opulence was even greater, and though such richness and ornamentation were not to his personal taste, he found it regally elegant and artistic, not gaudy, and it reflected the discrimination of the emperor's subtle eye.

The private rooms were laid with thick Oriental carpets, Chinese and Persian. Carved openwork grilles framed room sections, hung with the finest screened landscapes from China. On mahogany and rosewood tables lay a profusion of priceless celadons of Sung period, their simplicity of shape and restrained decoration focusing attention on their superb willow-green glazes. Cobalt-blue Ming vases, nearly waist-high, were scattered throughout the rooms, as were, almost haphazardly it seemed, ceramics and porcelains in a variety of shapes and colors.

As a footstool before the gilded couchlike throne where the emperor sat or reclined was a Ting-ware pillow, a Sung Dynasty porcelain in the form of a slumbering baby floating above a green lotus pond.

The decoration of enamels and lacquers was too much for Ahn

to take in at once, yet the overall effect of such splendor was of burnished richness and soft harmony.

A screen noiselessly opened and the emperor entered. He had discarded his intricately formal robes and was wearing a simple brown robe without decoration. His head was bare and he bore no accoutrements of power. His feet were slippered in silk and his walk was measured and sure.

He returned Ahn's bow, his manner relaxed and informal, and he motioned for Ahn to sit across from him. A servant instantly appeared, offering tea and rice wine. Both chose wine, lifting their cups to the other before drinking.

"I'm glad you came," said Tu Duc. "There have been many problems," he said delicately.

"I think you haven't always been best served by your advisers, or received the most accurate information. That's what brings me now."

Without preliminaries he told Tu Duc what had been reported to him by Father Bergere. "I gave you my word nineteen years ago that I'd never give you cause for regret in having been so generous to me. I've been scrupulously loyal to you. You could not have a more faithful servant. Even your spies must have told you that. Undermine me, and you bring down yourself."

Tu Duc made no comment. After the second cup of wine and a brief discussion about their families, Tu Duc asked Ahn's opinion of how to deal with the French.

Ahn said that it was now too late to accommodate them; the beast had been blooded, and liked the taste. "They are going to have to understand that we'll fight them," Ahn said. He went on to tell him that the people would support Tu Duc against the French, but that if they saw he was going to become a French puppet, they'd desert him. "Our people will never be subjugated," Ahn said. "A thousand years of the Chinese proved that, and these silly pale people from afar have no hope of dominating us. They don't bring us anything better than what we have, only greed and a foolish religion."

Tu Duc told him of the insurrections in the north, but Ahn waved that aside.

"They're caused by the corruption of the mandarins. The people are not happy with the way they're ruled. If the people are well treated, there will be no problems in the kingdom. End the corruption and the people will help you cast out the pretender and the foreigners. But do nothing and they will stand aside and watch you fall, and no amount of fear, no number of spies, no terror can prevent that."

Ahn leaned forward and said with fervor, "Our country is on a precipice; we face generations of war and misery. The dynasty will collapse, the foreigner will rule, and our children's children and their children, and theirs, will have to fight for the freedom that we lose." He reached out and touched his cousin, the first time he'd ever done that. "Tu Duc, be strong and resolute. Be good to your people and lead them against the French. Better for us to fight and maybe die than for our children to live in misery. I will help you," Ahn said. "I will do anything. Don't doubt me, don't fear me. I'm not your enemy."

Tu Duc took his hand and patted it gently; then he looked away, seemingly lost in his troubles. "I get so lonely. There are so many problems. I don't understand it, the intrigue, the rebellions, the French—it's too much. I never have any peace. I go into the gardens and the birds are shrill and insistent; I seek solitude in the temples and I'm pursued by the unhappy spirits of our ancestors; I sit on my throne and I hear whispers of unrest; I lie in my bed and I'm plagued by dreams of ruin.

"I want to rule wisely," the emperor said. "I want my people happy; I want peace in the land; I want the foreigner out. I don't want to fight; I want to be left alone and have my people left alone."

He smiled ironically. "It's not easy to be an emperor, Ahn. Perhaps you would have been a better one than I."

Ahn shook his head. "No. Master Chien said long ago that you were better suited to rule. I don't envy you at all."

They talked until very late; it was a rare and happy time for Tu Duc, and he was sorry to see the evening end, but Ahn said he had to check on his daughter, who'd spent the evening with Lady Deng.

At the mention of her name, Tu Duc tensed. "I wouldn't let my daughter spend any time with her," he said, and pointedly added, "I certainly wouldn't myself."

"That was long ago; I was very young. And my daughter must learn to take care of herself."

"She is a wicked woman," Tu Duc said. "But useful."

Ahn stood to go. "Wickedness has the bad habit of exceeding its usefulness. Master Chien told us that." Ahn laughed. "You should see him here; the poor lecher is beside himself, trying to make up for all the time he's lost. You'll have to put extra guards on the concubines."

Tu Duc smiled, asked graciously if Ahn were interested in one, recommending a particularly nubile girl, but Ahn declined.

When he returned to the apartment, Ahn found Gia Minh in

bed, reading. He sat beside her. She looked up without warmth, then went back to her book.

"Did you enjoy yourself?" he asked.

She didn't respond, continued reading.

Ahn waited a moment, then struck the book from her hand with such force that it hit the opposite wall. "When I speak to you, answer me."

Her eyes leveled on him without fear and her voice was cold. "What did you ever see in that crude, coarse woman? She told me all about how you were together."

"That was twenty years ago. I was the same age as you, and no wiser, though perhaps more tolerant."

"Is she what men want? Tell me, is she what attracts men—leering and panting?"

"I married your mother, didn't I?"

"Well, I want to go home! I don't want to stay here. You shouldn't either. That woman wants you; you're all she talked about. She was disgusting."

"I have friends here I want you to meet. And you should meet the empress; she's a fine woman. And the dowager empress, Thieu Tri's widow, a lovely person. They're your relatives. You're a member of the royal family and belong here; not everyone is like Lady Deng. Didn't you like the emperor?"

"Yes," she allowed, softening slightly. "But I was too in awe of him. I learned things about him too."

"From Lady Deng."

"Yes. And that's another reason you shouldn't stay here; he's weak and afraid of you. He'll turn against you."

Ahn smiled. "The first thing to learn about life at court is not to believe everything you hear."

"I don't plan to stay long enough to learn the tricks. I might even learn to leer and pant," and she leaned forward on the bed toward Ahn, blinking her eyes seductively and breathing heavily.

He laughed and stood, kissing her on the forehead. "Think about staying a few days. You wouldn't want to spoil Master Chien's good time, would you?"

"He's disgusting too; I learned all about him. I think all men are disgusting."

"Not all. Maybe you'll find the perfect one."

"Not here I won't."

For three days they remained at court, feted and entertained, and Ahn presented his daughter formally and brought her to pay her respects to the dowager empress, a small but lively woman of seventy who told Ahn that Gia Minh was the only interesting woman she'd seen at court in forty years, a period which pointedly encompassed the life of the present empress, her daughter-in-law.

"Send her to me for a while," the dowager empress said. "I'll make an empress of her."

During this time Ahn learned that things were worse than he'd suspected. Corruption was pervasive and Tu Duc was heavily influenced by advisers who were conducting secret liaisons with the French. Tu Duc was heavily in debt to the French for their support against the pretender, but as much as he loathed them, he could not shake their growing power and control.

Yet the visit passed well and Tu Duc himself gave a banquet on the eve of their departure. Lady Deng was conspicuous by her absence, brooding because Ahn had so obviously avoided her.

Chien told him that he would have been wise to court her. "You haven't played her right yet," he said. "Remember the last time you crossed her."

But the mere thought of currying favor with her turned Ahn's stomach.

Ahn's departure this time was far different from the one nineteen years ago—too different, for from his window Tu Duc observed his entire court paying homage to his cousin. He found the enthusiasm and affection too demonstrative, and his suspicions and fears were rekindled even before the carriage passed through the gates, suspicions and fears masterfully fueled by Lady Deng and others seeking to ingratiate themselves with the emperor.

In the carriage, settling back for the long journey, Ahn said, "It was a great success."

"But I didn't find a husband," said Gia Minh with mock anguish.

"The idea," said Chien, "is to trail the bait in the water, causing ripples, not to stun the fish by slapping the surface."

"Exactly," said Ahn. "We'll have nibbles soon enough."

Gia Minh was disgusted. She sank back in the carriage belligerently. "Let my sisters have them, all those puffy girl-boys and those ridiculous peacock boys. And dear Lord, why are there so many eunuchs about? What a perfectly foolish place. No wonder the country is a shambles. I could rule it much better." She turned to her father. "And don't think for a moment I'm going to settle for one of those silly boys you kept presenting to me. Bait indeed! Besides, there's nothing to be caught in that stagnant pond. Everyone knows that the best fishing is in the ocean."

Ahn raised his eyes. Dear Lord, he thought, wherever will I find anyone to take her from me?

Almost answering his thought, Chien said, settling himself comfortably, extracting an apple from his robes, "True. Remarkable creatures do jump out of the ocean—dragons and the like—and never when you expect them."

8

WHAT ANDRE DISCOVERED FIRST AFTER learning the destination of the ship was that he didn't like being a sailor at all; it was so distasteful that it cast doubts in his mind about his previous desire to be a soldier: if one branch of the military could be so bad, could another be that much better?

Being treated like a common seaman was for him only a small part of the problem. In the beginning he'd been seasick continuously; he could not adjust to the roll and pitch of the ship, but of course no one sympathized with that problem. He had no room, a sling hammock for a bed, no privacy, no decent food, no good company, and no women. He could not understand why anyone would seek such deprivation and degradation.

The only good thing he saw in his situation was anonymity—no one cared who he was, where he came from, what he'd done, or why he was here. He could easily have changed his name and assumed a different history, but he realized it made no difference to anyone, so he kept his name. He realized that when he left the shores of France he'd entered a different world, one not necessarily less civilized, but one of different rules and expectations, a harsher world to be sure, but a freer one also.

Though he hadn't been impressed into the navy, and was carried on the rolls as a voluntary citizen seaman, he might as well have been in the navy, for *L'Orient*, a two-masted merchant-marine cargo ship only recently converted to steam, had been placed under the command and service of the Imperial Navy because of the impending war with Prussia.

Gradually his seasickness abated and he learned to be a competent seaman, not a difficult task, and he found his companions amiable, though more loutish than he'd have chosen for friends, but they liked him and sought him out to listen to their never-before-expressed ideas, and asked him to write letters home for them.

Several of the men had been to Vietnam before—Cochin China, as the southern, French-occupied part was called—and they spoke of a jungle paradise with bone-white beaches, of water so clear one could see fathoms down, of fruit which fell from trees into one's hands, of a sun which never burned and a moon which stayed full, and of beautiful women who knew only about love.

Altogether it sounded attractive enough, Andre thought, yet he reasoned that after months at sea a man might even find America attractive, a place where everyone knew savages ran loose and scalped women, and the people ate corn.

What he could not learn, and did not understand, was why the ship was going to Vietnam, or why any Frenchman had gone there in the first place. He heard that they had a king, a fierce warrior over nine feet tall, with a harem of ten thousand women, who ruled over a country with a history even older than France's, a well-defined empire with nothing to interest a European.

Why his own country had sent a military force there to colonize it was a mystery to him. Orientals were strange people—that he knew, of course—but not barbarians, not like Africans, who ate one another, or people who wore grass clothes and lived in places like Bongo Bongo. Orientals were civilized, and they did have a religion, bizarre as it was, but they could never become Frenchmen, so why not let them be what they were?

Andre believed himself as patriotic as anyone, and was willing to lay down his life for his country, but he reasoned that other men in other countries surely felt the same way about their homes. He understood war—that was in the nature of things, a respectable endeavor, honorable and manly—but the rationale behind colonization escaped him, and it didn't sound like it would work: it was one thing to beat a man in combat, to teach him a lesson and have him accept your superiority, but it was something else to make him a slave. If he were a slave, he'd never rest until he was free. Wouldn't everyone else react the same way?

When he saw his first Vietnamese, this belief was reaffirmed.

On the ship was a large contingent of Vietnamese men, kept in the hold for the most part and made to perform the most menial tasks, but periodically they were brought up for sun and air. They were all young, several inches shorter than the average Frenchman, but remarkably lithe and muscular, and they exercised the entire time they were topside.

Andre studied them carefully and saw intelligence and cleverness in their features; their eyes never rested, and while they spoke little to one another, their behavior was cohesive and brotherly. These were not people to be colonized, he saw; their manner was in no way docile. From a distance he formed sympathy and respect for them; in a sense, their situations were similar, forced into service they didn't understand or like.

Their guards treated them with contempt, but they bore it stoically, though Andre could see smoldering resentment and hatred.

For the first time in his life he felt guilt for being French, and shame for his countrymen, and to compensate for what was being done to the Vietnamese, he made it a point one day to be on deck when they were brought up for exercise. He'd saved some fruit, and picked up what his shipmates hadn't eaten, and he left it unobtrusively near a group of Vietnamese; then he engaged the nearest guard in conversation to distract him.

The Vietnamese gathered up the fruit and hid it, and thus began a ritual: Andre stored leftover food and fruit in his seabag, and on those days he knew the Vietnamese were to be brought up for air and exercise, he left it where they could find it.

As well as giving him something to do to help the Vietnamese, it provided him with his only diversion on board.

At first Andre hadn't known if he could bear life on ship; it was tedious beyond belief, but gradually he found himself content to watch the rolling sea and ever-changing sky. He saw the sea was never the same even hour to hour, but constantly shifting colors and hues and shapes, placid or threatening within a few moments' time.

He worked strenuously in the boiler room, which was hot, but he liked being kept on the edge of exhaustion, for it made the idle hours more bearable, and he liked the coarse humor of the men he worked with, though they seemed interested only in women and liberty at the next port.

And finally the ship made its way around Cape Horn to its first port, Fort Dauphin, a small French settlement on the southern tip of the island of Madagascar.

Andre went on liberty with his shipmates, drank far too much, but when they dragged him into the long line going into a brothel, he broke away—there were forty-two men in the line.

When he staggered back to the ship and up the gangplank, he felt so dizzy and sick that he had to lean against the railing.

It was a beautiful star-filled night. Andre stared at the southern sky and tried to pick out the constellations, swaying with the slow undulation of the ship, lulled by its gentle rocking, and he almost fell asleep, but a sudden dip jarred him. He pulled himself up to make his way down to his bunk, but crossing the deck, he stopped suddenly. There were figures in the shadows.

Startled, he looked about for security, but there was only an officer on the bridge above him. He thought of calling out, then changed his mind and moved closer.

There were five men, Vietnamese, standing perfectly still. He hesitated; then, because of all he'd had to drink and because they didn't appear hostile, he stepped directly up to them. For a moment they stared at one another; then one said simply in French, "Thank you."

At first he didn't understand; then he realized they were thanking him for the food. He shifted his shoulders in embarrassment and wanted to say something, but he didn't know how to begin, or even if they would understand him.

He whispered to the one who'd thanked him, "Do you speak French?"

The man nodded.

Just then the officer on the bridge shouted out, nervous and demanding, "Who's there?"

Andre stepped out of the shadows. "Seaman Lafabre, sir, reporting back to the ship."

"What are you doing? Who else is there? Step out so I can see you. Master of arms! Topside!"

The Vietnamese man whispered, "Tomorrow night," and Andre heard rustling behind him as the men disappeared.

Andre waited until an armed guard approached, and he identified himself, telling him that he'd come back early from town.

The guard gestured to the bridge and told Andre that the officer on duty was a young ensign afraid of everything. The guard asked him how the town was and if he'd seen any of the women. They chatted a few minutes; then Andre went down to his bunk.

The next day Andre offered to take the guard duty of another sailor in exchange for a future favor.

As part of the guard detachment he had access to the entire ship, so he went below to the hold, where the Vietnamese were quartered, in hope of finding the man he'd spoken with the night before, but what he found was unimaginable squalor—an airless, fetid, stifling hold without water or sanitation, a hundred men cramped into space meant for a dozen.

He stepped over bodies lying in their own vomit and excrement, and he thought he was going to gag. He searched about for a recognizable face, but not finding one, he left, holding on to the bulkhead for support.

As he was going up the ladder, there was a tug on his trousers, and gazing down, he saw the man he'd been looking for. Andre motioned for him to follow him up, but the man was too afraid. Andre grabbed his arm and tried to pull him, and finally the man relented and went up with him to the next deck, still a deck below the ship's water line.

Andre felt sick and drew deep breaths as the man watched him cautiously from several feet away, his hands on the ladder railings, ready to drop back down into the hold.

"How do you stand it down there?" Andre asked, trying not to gag.

The man gave a harsh laugh, as though asking what alternative he had. Jumping overboard? Dying?

"I want to help," Andre said.

The man stared at him curiously. "Why?"

Andre could only look at him blankly. "Why?" He pointed toward the hold helplessly. "Because." Because it was inhuman. Because no one should live like that. Because he felt anguish and outrage. Sympathy and brotherhood. How could he tell the man that? "Come up tonight. I'll get you food. After midnight."

"Water," the man said.

"Yes. I'll get water."

The man stepped closer to Andre, his face only inches away, and he seemed to study every pore on Andre's face; then finally he nodded and stepped back. At the top of the ladder he tapped his chest and said, "Che Lan."

Andre didn't understand, had never heard a word of Vietnamese, and he cocked his head in perplexity.

The man smiled. "My name. Che Lan." He said it again slowly.

Andre repeated it; then he pointed to himself. "Andre."

The man nodded solemnly. "Andre," he said, then disappeared into the hold.

That afternoon Andre gathered up all the food and supplies he could safely get away with, and while making the rounds of the ship, he brought it piecemeal to the top deck and hid it under canvas tarps.

The junior ensign again had the night watch, and Andre went out of his way to display respect and competence, hoping to allay his anxieties, but the officer never left the bridge. He prowled it continuously, gazing down on the top deck at every creak and groan of the ship.

Shortly after midnight Andre heard movement, faint rustlings from the cargo hold, and he stationed himself at the opening. He saw Che Lan staring up at him and he motioned for him to come up. Che Lan crept out of the hold and hid in the shadows. Andre went to the tarp under which he'd stashed the food and supplies, and raised it for Che Lan to see.

"It's too dangerous tonight," he whispered, and gestured toward the officer above. "Tomorrow night. But get the food when you hear a splash." With that Andre disappeared.

He went to the starboard side, facing the water, and loosened a bale that had been lashed to the deck. Struggling with it, he lifted it to the railing, then pushed it over.

As soon as the bale splashed into the water, he heard the officer running, and immediately came the shout, "Master of arms! Starboard!"

Andre came out of the shadows and at the railing made a great production of looking for what had caused the splash, asking the officer to direct his lantern over the side.

"Sir, I don't see anything. There's nothing over the side."

The officer was not appeased and stared for a long while, scanning the surface for a swimmer. In port there was always the danger of someone boarding the ship from the water side, and it was not uncommon to find stowaways after each harbor visit. But, too, the ocean was never still or silent, and no man who had ever been to sea would presume to explain its unaccounted-for motions and noises.

Finally, long after the Vietnamese had had time to carry down the supplies, the duty officer returned to his watch.

The next day Andre went into port and bought all the fresh fruit he could afford, having arranged again to have the night watch. No one was suspicious; in fact, they began to think he was smart for volunteering for duty in this port, ensuring he'd have liberty when they reached what had to be more exotic ones.

The officer that night was an older, more experienced man who spent little time on the bridge, instead stayed inside writing letters. Andre reported to him every hour, and each time, the officer was pleasant and offered him coffee.

Che Lan brought up all the Vietnamese and they stayed topside for Andre's entire watch.

Andre kept his distance, not wanting to disturb them. They whispered among themselves and pointed to the stars, and every now and then he heard deep sighs and lungs filling with clean air.

Toward the end of his watch, Andre gave Che Lan the fruit and told him they would have to go down.

"Tomorrow?" Che Lan asked.

Andre shook his head. "We sail. I'll tell you when."

When he went in to make his final report, the officer posted his replacement, then told Andre to sit down, and again offered coffee. No one had treated him kindly since he'd been on ship, and he sat stiffly and ill-at-ease.

"So nothing unusual at all happened during your watch?"

"No, sir."

The officer smiled. He was old enough to be Andre's father, and though his features were grizzled from years of exposure to the elements and his heavy beard cast a harsh ring around his face, his eyes and voice were kind. "Nothing unusual in a thousand savages trooping the deck, taking in the night air?"

Andre jumped as if shot.

"Be curious to see what you'd think was unusual, lad."

"Sir! I . . . I . . . I mean . . ."

The officer leaned back in his chair and placed his feet up on the desk before him, his hands folded in his lap. "Lad, an ensign could walk the bridge all night and miss the Battle of Trafalgar; but an old salt like myself can feel a gull perching at the top of the mast. Besides, no sailor volunteers for the night watch twice in a row. Though you're no sailor, of course. What is it you're up to? Tell me. I'm not going to have you keelhauled, just want to know what's going on."

So Andre told him, and in the process the officer drew out from him his history. He listened carefully but made no comment, and finally dismissed Andre, telling him that he was going to think about it all.

Badly shaken, Andre returned to his bunk, knowing that what he'd done could get him court-martialed, put in the brig, or worst of all, sent back to France. He thought of jumping ship, but realized he'd be easily caught on the island; moreover, he couldn't leave the Vietnamese to suffer for something that was his fault.

The next afternoon he was summoned to the wardroom, where he found Lieutenant Gambier, and to his horror, Captain Massena.

The ship's captain was feared and disliked by the entire crew, a thin, aristocratic-looking man of fifty who in no one's memory had uttered a pleasant word, and whose eyes now rested on Andre with piercing concentration.

Truly afraid, for he knew well the absolute power of a ship's captain, a dictatorial authority with no equivalent on land, Andre reported in with the military crispness he'd been taught at the Ecole; then, mustering all his courage, he said to Lieutenant Gambier, "Sir! I would like to add one thing to what I said last night. Permission to speak, sir!"

Gambier turned to the captain, standing several feet behind. Massena nodded curtly.

"Sir, I encouraged the Vietnamese to come topside. They should not be judged at fault. I assume all responsibility for the incident. I insist upon it."

Captain Massena leaned forward slightly, his eyes like an eagle's, searching Andre's face, and he repeated the word as if he'd never heard it before. "Insist?"

Andre braced himself for what he knew was to come.

Lieutenant Gambier cleared his throat. "Seaman Lafabre, I was going to have you repeat to the captain what you told me, but in light of your words, I don't think that'll be necessary." He turned to Massena. "Do you see what I mean now, sir?"

There was silence for what seemed an eternity to Andre. Sunlight streamed through the portholes, and the ship rocked gently at anchor; from the dock Andre could hear the shouts and activities of the final loading. Everything was calm, but he awaited the crash.

Finally Captain Massena's voice came, utterly impersonal, almost bored. "How was it again that you killed the Duke of Parnasse?"

"I hit him with a chair, sir."

Lieutenant Gambier snickered, then diverted his face immediately.

The captain nodded. "Yes. Formidable weapon. And the reason once again?"

"I am not at liberty to divulge that, sir."

"Ummm," said Captain Massena; then he walked past Andre to the door, and said without turning, "Carry on, Lieutenant."

When he had gone, Lieutenant Gambier told Andre to stand at ease. "I told the captain everything because there can be no secrets on a ship from its master; that could prove fatal to all hands in a crisis. Now, what you did, allowing the Vietnamese to come topside, was wrong, meriting severe punishment. You understand that, don't you?"

"Yes, sir, I know it was wrong."

"There are procedures to be followed if you have suggestions, or are dissatisfied. On ship we are a society with rules rigidly enforced. Henceforth, do not disobey them."

Andre jumped. "Henceforth"—that meant in the future, and he realized with surging joy and gratitude that he was not going to be punished. Could that be, after what he'd done and admitted? Was Captain Massena actually going to let him go free?

"The captain's making certain changes on ship. The Vietnamese will be allowed to come topside for exercise every day, and a larger area of the hold will be cleared for them, and their rations will be improved."

Andre's mouth opened in incredulity.

"Though not pleased with the manner in which you brought this to his attention, Captain Massena was grateful to learn of the situation of the Vietnamese. You see, Lafabre, the Vietnamese were under contract to the private owners of this ship, in no way associated with the French Navy. We've limited our presence and interference with the commercial aspects of the ship as much as possible—too much, it seems. We weren't even aware of the number of Vietnamese on board. We were told there were fifty men; in fact there are one hundred and eighteen. Consequently, Captain Massena has placed them directly under his authority—they've been impressed into naval service and are no longer bound to the commercial firm."

He smiled faintly. "You've been impressed also. You're now a seaman, third rate, in His Imperial Majesty's Navy. Report first to the purser, then to the master of arms. You're dismissed."

Andre was too stunned to speak or react.

"You understand what I've told you?"

Andre finally gathered his senses. "Yes, sir!" He saluted, did an about-face, and went to the door, but then he turned. "Sir, thank you. And please thank the captain."

Gambier nodded, trying to suppress a smile, and thinking, as Andre left, that the army's loss was the navy's gain.

So overwhelmed was Andre that he forgot that nothing had been said of his murder of the Duke of Parnasse.

The Vietnamese only partly understood what had happened, but knew they had the young seaman to thank for their improved conditions.

For Andre, now one of the guard overseeing the Vietnamese, the best part was that he had an opportunity to mingle freely with them. He had their trust and gratitude, and they accepted him.

Many of the Vietnamese knew French, but he spoke mostly with Che Lan, who said he was from a place called Ban Me Thuot, a small village surrounded by lush countryside and mountains in the middle of Vietnam. There he'd learned French, taught by an old missionary. He said his family had sent him to Saigon to take his examinations for the mandarinate, but he was so alarmed by what the French were doing to his people that he'd joined with others to stop the intruders.

He told Andre that if necessary he'd fight the rest of his life to cast them out. He said the emperor, out of weakness, had given Saigon and the control of the south to the French; it was a humiliation, and he and the others would never rest until Vietnam was free.

Andre said that he understood; then he asked Che Lan how he and the others had come to be on the ship. Che Lan told him that they'd been seized by the French and forced to work on the harbor. They were slave labor for a construction firm; then they were sent to France, where the company had contracts, but the company had been forced to send them back because the workers couldn't adjust, were constantly sick, and didn't respond to punishment. Of three hundred Vietnamese sent to France, only one-third were returning.

Che Lan spoke without bitterness. His manner was calm and polite, but resolute. He was a few years older than Andre, and said that as soon as he returned to Vietnam, he was going to continue the struggle against the French, and the emperor too if he wouldn't lead his countrymen against them. "We will be free," he said, "though it may take longer than my life."

Andre was immensely impressed with his fervor, knowing that he'd do the same thing—if only he had a worthy cause for which to fight.

From these men, mostly his own age, he formed an appreciation and understanding for Vietnam; these men weren't savages, were more learned and cultured than his comrades, and he saw they behaved the same way: they laughed and joked, quarreled and fought among themselves, shared and coveted, helped and harmed.

For them he was an anomaly. Their hatred of the French had been long established, yet here was an individual who treated them with kindness and respect. The revelation that all Frenchmen weren't cruel or barbaric came as an unpleasant one: it's much easier to fight an enemy lacking any redeeming quality.

The remainder of the voyage was uneventful, and the weather remained good. On several occasions Andre asked the officers on the bridge to explain the maps and charts to him, but what he learned was disconcerting. The other European powers had staked out huge territories in this part of the world. India, Malaya, Singapore, Hong Kong, Burma, and parts of Borneo were claimed by the British, while the Dutch claimed the remainder of Borneo, Sumatra, Java, Indonesia, and numerous islands. The Spanish controlled the Philippines, and Portugal exercised power over many islands, but his own country had only tenuous ties with Cambodia, and controlled only a few provinces in the southern part of Vietnam.

The naval officers explained to him how dangerous this was for France, how this part of the world was being carved up without France, and the balance of power was shifting away from his country. Surely, they said, he could see the need for extending the French empire into Indochina. Looking at the maps, he was convinced of their arguments, until he talked again with Che Lan. When he tried to explain about the English and Dutch, Che Lan said no nation had the right to seize another, and how could their actions justify what France was doing?

By the time the ship entered the waters of Cochin China, Andre didn't know what to think.

His first impression of the land, however, was of a paradise exactly as described—crystalline waters, gleaming white beaches, and beyond, a lush jungle ripe and full, whose haunting calls reached and stirred a primeval spirit in him, as it did the Vietnamese on board, who stood at the ship's railings and stared for hours as *L'Orient* made its slow progress past Vung Tau on the tip of the Mekong Delta upriver toward Saigon.

It seemed as if a magic spell had been cast over the Vietnamese and that they were responding to a haunting call from within the jungle. They were hushed and reverent, their faces registering overwhelming relief and joy.

Yet as with all ports, the beauty was man-marred long before the ship reached harbor: bilge and oil floated on the surface of the water, and wreckage and shanties and the attendant litter of maritime enterprise formed a gateway into Saigon.

Yet still Andre could see the beauty, and the sun shone down brilliantly on what appeared to be a peaceful Eden.

Andre had given no thought to what he would do once the ship docked, but even before *L'Orient* reached its berth he knew that he would stay. When he was given the option of remaining with the naval garrison or returning to the ship's crew, he elected without hesitation to become part of the garrison.

He was paid by the purser, collected his gear, reported in to the post and was given a billet, and was immediately granted seven days' liberty.

Several others had chosen to remain with the garrison, and together they went into the city.

Andre immediately discovered the reasons for a long-at-sea sailor's reputation in port, and he fell easily into the time-honored tradition of drunken disorderliness, joining that joyful sailing brotherhood of back alleys and broken chairs and weeping friends forever, becoming stupidly, hopelessly, gloriously drunk for days and nights.

At the end of his liberty, stumbling back with the others, he had only the haziest recollection of what had happened, but he knew it had been wonderful—no matter that his entire body hurt and each step seemed to dislodge his head further from his shoulders. His clothes were ripped and he smelled awful, an odious combination of sweat, sex, beer, dirt, cheap perfume, and vomit.

Of the women, his memory could not focus sharply. He remembered beds and brothels, small, golden writhing girls with long black hair, and the envelopment of soft flesh and soothing words, and the mere thought of it stirred his groin, but only fragments of what had happened came back to him clearly.

Uppermost in his mind was the desire to do it again, but that would be no sooner than a month, until he was paid again, for he had not a penny in his pockets.

What he learned next was what every sailor and soldier before him had learned, that the mouth of the cannon and the maw of the sea are easier to bear than life in garrison.

Gone was the luxury of being left in peace, of action and diversion, of laxity; the garrison was demanding and boring beyond bearing, a life of inspections and spit and polish, of drill and parades, of attention to the minutest detail, and discipline and punishment for the slightest infraction.

Andre found nothing redeeming in such a life; the Ecole had been demand and discipline, but he'd learned something; here was endless routine and repetition, regimentation and boredom to try the patience of the dullest man.

One lived only for liberty, and liberty became nothing more than stupors of drunken brawls and bedlamic whoring which barely compensated for the boredom in between, and finally liberty itself became boring.

He saw nothing of the country and learned nothing of the people, only that they were as willing and adept as all others in taking his money. The girls chattered and giggled and enticingly stroked his crotch while cadging drinks in the bars, then relieved him of his money and anxieties, and at the end of the month he went back into the bars again tight and frustrated.

All this he could have borne had he found any significance in garrison life. He was part of the security detachment, but the province was completely secure.

The only time there was any relief from the tedium was when another ship came to port. Then they learned news from France, perhaps had a few prisoners to guard, formed a new friendship or so, and were sent into Saigon as the shore patrol to protect the new arrivals and the city from one another.

Andre spent four months with the garrison before he was mercifully transferred to a small outpost in Cho Lon, the Chinese section, a self-contained, prosperous district recently experiencing unrest. Thc Chinese had been the first to welcome and cooperate with the French, seeing political stability and mercantile advantage in their arrival. They worked closely with the French authorities, and paid handsomely for the protection and favor they received.

This alliance, however, was deeply resented by the Vietnamese, whose hatred of the French was exceeded only by their hatred for the Chinese. Isolated attacks and violence increased until it was obvious to the Chinese and French that a full-scale campaign of harassment and terror was under way. The Chinese demanded the protection their bribery had bought, and the French were forced to increase the Cho Lon garrison.

It was difficult for the French troops to muster enthusiasm to safeguard the Chinese, who treated them contemptuously and cheated them in all their dealings; however, soon the French were the targets of the Vietnamese attacks, and they turned their resentments and frustrations against them.

Of course, not speaking the language, or understanding the culture, or being educated to begin with, it was impossible for the troops to distinguish the Vietnamese who meant them no harm from those who did, let alone for them to understand what prompted the hostility.

Though many of the troops saw no sense in protecting one set of foreigners from another, and felt a glimmer of impropriety in persecuting a people whose country they were in, Andre was the only one who truly sympathized with the Vietnamese, and with increasing reluctance went out on the patrols that always ended in the seizure and beating of some Vietnamese youths.

Of course these actions only provoked deeper hostility and brought on more attacks against the French, who responded with more patrols, seizures, and beatings, and thus the violence escalated until soon Cho Lon became a center of unrest and conflict.

Tensions became so exacerbated that any meeting of French and Vietnamese turned into confrontation, and bloodshed became commonplace.

Though Tu Duc had granted authority over the provinces surrounding Saigon to the French, this authority was openly flouted and the emperor himself publicly denounced. Seeing matters seriously deteriorate, the French increased their military presence and intensified their actions against what they now called "the insurgents."

As the attacks and counterattacks increased in number and degree, all perspective was lost; men saw their comrades wounded or killed, their own hatreds were fueled, and they in turn sought to inflict greater harm on the other side.

Andre watched with despair as the situation worsened. He could not reason with his comrades, yet he suffered with and for them, and he couldn't go against them, yet he couldn't share their feelings against the Vietnamese or bring himself to join in the assaults on them.

Because the others knew his feelings, they became more suspicious and hostile as time wore on. Matters culminated one evening on a routine patrol down the crowded back streets of Cho Lon. Six men, including Andre, went from the garrison. The troops were nervous, but primed to fight, ready to avenge an attack earlier in the week in which two grenadiers had been seriously wounded.

As the patrol wore on without encountering resistance, only hostile faces, the troops began to look for provocations. A barking dog was bayoneted, and when a child rushed out to comfort it, she was pushed away roughly with a rifle butt. The mother screamed and ran out to help her, then threw herself on the grenadier who'd struck the girl.

The soldier knocked her to the ground. The child shrieked to see her mother hurt, and the street filled with Vietnamese rushing to help, brandishing sticks, calling out furiously.

Confronted by the angry crowd, the troops panicked, drew bayonets, and assumed an assault position. The crowd formed around the girl and mother, then began to move on the soldiers.

Had the soldiers, shielded by their bayonets, stood their ground, the situation might have been saved and bloodshed averted, but a young grenadier in the front rank, faced with angry screams and taunts, sticks and rocks waved threateningly at him, buckled under the pressure. He stabbed out with his bayonet and caught a man in the shoulder.

The man shrieked as blood gushed from the wound. The crowd recoiled, then surged back in fury.

The troops immediately formed a firing position, the front rank dropping to their knees, the back standing, rifles at their shoulders.

Andre was in back. He had not raised his rifle, and now, knowing that the troops were going to fire into the crowd, he made his decision: he knocked the rifles from the shoulders of the men beside him, then pushed forward against the men in front of him, knocking them off balance, sending them face forward in the street.

The other two soldiers were so surprised that they merely turned to him in incredulity, and in that moment he threw himself against them, knocking them backward.

By then the Vietnamese were upon them, but they too were so surprised by what they'd seen that amazement replaced fury. They quickly seized the rifles, but only halfheartedly hit and kicked the soldiers on the ground.

Scrambling up, the troops fought furiously and the crowd began to withdraw, but they saw one soldier break away and run, and they recognized him as the one who'd prevented the shots.

The other soldiers shouted at him, then gave chase, forgetting both their rifles and the Vietnamese.

The crowd hesitated a moment, then also ran.

Andre had no idea where he was or where he was going, merely ran on impulse, blindly down back alleys, knowing that if the soldiers didn't kill him, they'd drag him back to the garrison, where he'd be shot for insurrection. Since his sympathies for the Vietnamese were known, he knew he could expect no leniency.

He crashed through patchwork backyards, jumped fences, knocked over garbage, sent chickens and pigs scurrying, but he couldn't shake his pursuers, who finally cornered him in an alley.

He faced about, prepared to fight as they came at him slowly, trying to catch their breaths and regain their strengths.

"You'll never get out alive, Lafabre," one shouted at him.

Another picked up a large piece of wood with nails in it, and two others found broken glass lying in the alley.

"You're going to have a bad accident, you bastard."

"Too bad, Lafabre. We'll tell everyone we did everything we could, but the slant-eyes dragged you off and cut you up."

Just as they were about to fall on him, there were shouts from behind, and turning, they saw the alley blocked off by many Vietnamese, the ones in front pointing rifles at them.

The Vietnamese closed in, took away the glass and boards from the soldiers; then several grabbed Andre and pulled him away while the others held the soldiers at bay.

He was hustled down a maze of streets, out of Cho Lon, into the center of Saigon. No one spoke until they reached their destination, a wooden hut pressed indistinguishably among hundreds just alike in a crowded, busy section in the middle of the city.

Inside the hut he was shown a place to sit and within minutes was brought water to drink, then tea and a strange mixture of batter-fried vegetables and fish. This he was offered politely, and he accepted gratefully; then he was left alone, though the many men in the room watched him with intense curiosity.

For almost two hours he sat on the floor, trying self-consciously to be relaxed and unobtrusive, and mindful of their searching looks and whispered talk.

Finally several men entered to great commotion. One approached him, stood over him a minute, then repeated the words said to him long ago: "How do you stand it down there?"

Andre was so startled that it took him several seconds to recognize the man; then he scrambled up and grabbed him. "Che Lan!"

They hugged each other, oblivious of everyone else's amazement. "When I was told what had happened," Che Lan said, "that a French soldier had helped our people and turned against his own comrades, I said that I know that man. And look, here you are."

"But why did they tell you? And who are these people?"

"I told you that we'd fight until we were free. Did you think we'd forget, or let your people do whatever they wanted to our country? All of these men feel as I do, and there are many others. We'll fight as long as necessary, and teach our children and grandchildren. It is only beginning."

They talked for a long time about what had happened since they'd last seen each other; then Che Lan became practical. "What are you going to do? You can't go back to the garrison."

"I don't know," Andre said. "I can't go anywhere."

"Don't look like that. I'll help you. So will the others. They know what you did for us on the ship, and saw what you did today, but the young ones are confused—they didn't think there was such a thing as a good Frenchman. Now they're faced with the unhappy reality that your people are like ours—some good, some bad."

"Are you their leader?"

"Several of us more or less guide things," he said modestly. "But the problem is that you can't stay here; it's too dangerous. Someone might inform. It's only a matter of time before your soldiers find you, so we have to get you out of Saigon."

Che Lan thought a moment. "I will take you to the home of my parents; they will care for you. You'll like it there, it's a beautiful place."

"I remember you telling me about it, but I forgot the name."

"Ban Me Thuot."

And so Andre left Saigon, traveling by cart, on foot, by donkey, at first only by night, then, once beyond the French-controlled territory, in daylight for the one hundred fifty miles.

It truly was a paradise, Andre thought, and he was so taken with the beauty of the journey that he forgot the reasons behind it and gave no thought to what might lie at its destination.

Time seemed to run like grains of sand in an hourglass under the intense heat and brilliant sun; all his problems and all meaning dissolved. What came to matter was the call of birds and the cry of the gibbons in the virgin forests and dense jungle they passed through.

He had entered a new world, an emerald-green realm of tall banana and mango trees, of bamboo, and banyan trees whose aerial roots wound like giant snakes around the trunks of other trees. Lianas as thick as his arm hung from branches, and the heavy fragrance of a thousand different blossoms cast a sleepy spell over him. Civet cats and deer, foxes and boar, crossed his path, and overhead, brightly plumed birds screeched and called.

There was no time and no fear in the jungle, and it was never completely dark at night; he discovered to his surprise that tropic nights were radiantly blue; the moon gave more light than in France, and stars shone like tiny suns. And it was never quiet; rustling foliage, the soft beat of wings, startled cries of prey, mating calls, the hum of geckos, and the buzz of insects formed a symphony in the dark.

His eyes could not take in all the color, nor his ears the sounds, nor his mind the rapturous tranquillity. It was the calm in the midst of this vibrancy which most struck him, a calm he saw reflected in the faces of all the Vietnamese he encountered.

Toiling in the fields, chatting among themselves, or merely sitting alongside the road, everyone he saw registered repose and impassivity. There was stoicism in all eyes, as though the viewer had an understanding of his insignificance, and was calmly waiting out his time in a world in which he would return again and again until he finally overcame desire—life itself—and merged into the dispassionate nothingness, and until that time, in this short span of suffering existence, his life was not one of action and striving, but of dreams and meditation, of small griefs and small joys. Each seemed content in what he did, content to sit on the side of the road as others traveled down it.

As he himself walked, Andre found comfort and strength in their demeanors, and he felt peace and calm as he never had before.

The journey took two weeks, and by its end he felt close to Che Lan, a kinship he'd never had with anyone else. He spoke in French with Che Lan about the grander subjects—life, religion, politics—but in Vietnamese he learned the names of birds and animals, and the phrases of politeness and civility.

His uniform had been discarded for loose-fitting peasant garb, and his skin tanned golden: walking with Che Lan among the people, he resembled a tall, healthy bronze being dropped from another planet.

As they drew near Ban Me Thuot, a rural capital, less commercial, pastoral, Che Lan became even more placid. Both his body and mind were affected by the land, as though soothing waters washed over him. He took deeper breaths, and every now and then sighed with satisfaction. Andre saw the profound significance of home to a Vietnamese; it defined him and gave sustenance to his soul.

Che Lan had spoken of it with reverence, a place not just where he was born and where his family lived, but of something elemental; home was a place of spirits and ancestors, a temple, hallowed yet alive.

Andre felt deeply about his own country, but it was not like this; what a Vietnamese felt, because of religion and ancestor worship, was deeper and more personal, and Andre felt more convinced that this land should be inviolate. Who was he, who was anyone to transgress and desecrate the shrine of another's belief and existence?

The land was mostly jungle and rain forest, but the careful cultivation of the fields indicated greater prosperity than in the south, and to Andre the people looked healthier and more animated.

Che Lan seemed to know everyone. To each he bowed and smiled; around some he threw his arms, and to each he introduced Andre. He didn't stop long to talk, but waved a farewell and promised a visit.

Che Lan's family were farmers who owned a sizable tract on the edge of Ban Me Thuot.

The two arrived in early evening, just before dinner. At first Andre was ignored in the shouts and tears and laughter, but as soon as Che Lan made the formal introductions and told his family the story of their association and of the help Andre had given on ship, he was treated with a respect and deference which embarrassed him. That night, after word was spread of Che Lan's return, family members from everywhere came to the house, and all night the huge gathering listened to his adventures over and over, and they were interpreted by the elders, and everyone had a comment to make.

They talked of the French and the emperor, and for the first time Andre heard of the powerful prince who ruled the province, and everyone wondered what he would say to the arrival of this young Frenchman.

Both men and women, old and young, came up to Andre and ran their hands along his skin and examined his features carefully, an old aunt opening his mouth to check his teeth as one would a horse. They were all immeasurably impressed with Andre, nodding at him constantly and patting him in approval each time he passed or they passed him. For all of them he was the first European they'd seen, except for Father Bergere, but the priest seemed ethereal in comparison with this youth.

For two days the house was filled with relatives and friends who came to hear firsthand the stories and see the tall stranger whose color they debated endlessly—some favoring pink or rose, some white, some gold—and they all ran their fingers through his blond hair, and the more bold ones pulled on the remarkable hairs growing on his chest, and the old aunt, who kept returning for yet another look, pulled down his trousers and exposed white buttocks, to her absolute amazement. She wondered if he had white blood, and thereafter Andre watched her carefully, lest she stab him to find out for sure.

On the third day, to everyone's surprise, Che Lan announced that he was returning to Saigon, saying that though he wanted to remain, the cause of his country's freedom was more important. He asked his family to accept Andre as their own and to treat him as they would himself.

Che Lan shook Andre's hand, wished him well, kissed every member of his family, and departed immediately, leaving so suddenly that no one had time to react; only when he was gone, with Andre and the family staring at one another, did the significance sink in.

The next several days were a study in politeness and artful dodging. Andre tried to make himself as unobtrusive as possible and spent most of the day walking over the countryside, trying to come to grips with the situation. Finally he confronted Che Lan's father, who himself had spent long hours in his fields wondering what to do with this stranger in his house.

The elderly man gathered his entire family about him, and a comedy of gestures and charades ensued in which eventually Andre was able to convey that he wanted to learn to become a farmer, and wanted a small parcel of land to tenant farm.

This was considered reasonable, and an agreement was struck: Andre would work for the family four days a week, for which he'd receive land of his own, given outright, seed, and materials with which to build his hut.

So began Andre's tenancy, and people managed to come from all over to see this strapping white, rose, or gold young foreigner work in the fields of Che Lan's father, and once a week they contrived to pass by Andre's land to see his progress.

Andre worked hard, and everyone was impressed. He was friendly and always smiled, and though they laughed behind his back at the way he spoke, they respected that he was trying to learn their language, and among themselves they spoke approvingly of him.

Every now and then, Andre woke to find food on his steps, and on occasion there would be small gifts—a tool, some cloth. He knew that he was gradually being accepted, but still he was very lonely, and wondered what future he had in this strange place.

Then one day, working his own land, stripped to the waist and sweating heavily, he knew that he was being watched, and when he looked around he saw a strange sight, a black-cassocked priest standing on the edge of the fields, arms folded, staring at him.

Andre was so surprised he didn't know what to do; a priest was the last person he'd expected to encounter in this blazing land. Moreover, the man was almost as tall as Andre, thin and angular, and under his hat, his skin was white, gleamingly so, as though it had never been exposed to the sun.

The priest raised his hand in greeting, and automatically Andre's came up in response; then he dropped his plow and started toward the stranger, slapping dirt from his hands against his legs and wiping away sweat.

Coming closer, Andre saw the priest was not a young man, despite his ramrod carriage, but perhaps sixty, and he looked haggard and worn, though his eyes were bright and friendly.

"Good day," said Father Bergere. "How are you?" he asked in French.

Andre beamed to hear his native tongue. "Very well. And you, Father?"

"Old, tired, hot, and thirsty."

They shook hands warmly, as though they'd been seeking each other for years; then they stepped back to see one another better, and they started to speak at the same time, saying together, "What are you doing here?"

9

ANDRE OFFERED FATHER BERGERE WATER, and invited him inside the hut for something to eat, but the priest declined, and pressed him immediately for his story, saying that he'd heard such strange tales about him from the villagers that he'd had to come out to see firsthand.

Andre related his story, omitting the details of the murder, Catherine, and touching only lightly on what had happened in Saigon.

At the end, having listened carefully and politely, Father Bergere asked, "You are a fugitive from France. And a deserter from the navy?"

Andre nodded.

Father Bergere was thoughtful a moment, then said, "Only one man can help you, and you're going to need help, because it won't be long before the French hear about you or the emperor sends troops to arrest you."

"Is this the prince I've heard about?"

"Yes. Prince Nguyen Ahn Le, cousin of the emperor and overlord of this province. Would you like to meet him?"

"He would see me?"

"He would. He might even speak to you in French, though it won't make any sense. But the princess speaks beautiful French, and so do his daughters. Oh, dear," he said, suddenly thinking of them, and anticipating their response to this extraordinarily handsome, exotic youth.

Then Father Bergere told his story, and the story of Ahn and his family.

The two talked all afternoon, exchanging information and news of France and Vietnam, squatting in the front yard, brushing aside flies, and ignoring the heat. Finally, in early evening,

Father Bergere rose creakily and said he had to get back, but he'd return in three days and bring him to see Prince Ahn.

The priest returned too late that night to discuss the matter with Ahn, and he debated the entire next day how best to broach the subject, knowing it was going to require some delicacy, for Ahn was not disposed to the French, and he might be reluctant to harbor a fugitive who could cause stress and difficulties with the emperor or the French.

He decided the best time to bring up the matter was at dinner with the entire family in attendance, realizing that everyone's curiosity would force Ahn to receive Andre, and once that happened, Ahn could not help but extend protection.

And so in the middle of the meal Father Bergere casually mentioned that he'd encountered a foreigner living only a few miles away, a young Frenchman with a most unusual history.

The girls pounced on the news and demanded a full accounting, but Ahn sat back, a faint smile on his lips, knowing exactly what the priest was up to, and knowing too of course of Andre's presence in the province.

"Is he handsome?" asked Su insolently.

Chien chewed meat complacently. "Stupid girl. How can he be? He just told you that he's French."

"He must be very poor," said Ke, the second daughter.

"Very," said Father Bergere.

"What about his family?" asked Gia Minh.

"A sad story," said the priest. "His father was killed in the army many years ago, and his mother had to take work as a scullery maid. She's not well and he hated to leave her, but he had to flee France for his life. There is an old great-grandmother near death. It's very sad."

There was a chorus of sympathy.

Finally Ahn said, "Enough. When did you tell this poor, pathetic youth you'd bring him here, Master Bergere?"

"The day after tomorrow."

Ahn turned to his daughters. "Can you wait that long? All right, Master Bergere, bring him to us; I'll see him afternoon after next."

Xuan said gently, "Tell him we welcome him to our land."

"Will he eat with us?" asked Su.

"We'll see," said Ahn firmly, ending the discussion.

Andre carefully mended and washed his clothes, and was waiting expectantly when Father Bergere appeared in late morning.

"Will he see me?" he asked.

Father Bergere was so struck by the youth's eagerness and innocence that he wanted to pat him reassuringly, but instead he said solemnly, "The entire family wants to meet you. I'm sure you'll make a good impression.

"What should I say to the prince?"

"Be polite and gracious. Answer his questions, and tell him that you wish to live in his province peacefully."

As they were leaving, Father Bergere said, "It is customary to bring a gift when one is received by the prince."

Andre lowered his head. "I have nothing to give a prince."

The priest smiled. "Have you forgotten your catechism, my son? The gift which pleases most is always the humblest one."

Andre went back to the hut and unwrapped the leather packet of his father's that he'd taken from the duke. He chose a medal which he thought was gold, and he put it in his pocket, then wrapped the packet up and put it away under his pallet.

Though the distance was but five miles, the trip took over two hours because of Father Bergere's tortured pace. "I'm afraid I'm going to have to use a carriage soon," he said, "though I'll look like a spoiled bishop, and Chien will never let me live it down." He stopped abruptly and raised his hand in warning. "Now, there's someone you'll have to watch out for. Awful man. Worst possible influence."

"In what way?" asked Andre.

"In all ways." He shook his head and continued on. "Fortunately he's almost as old as I am and can't get into too much mischief anymore. But there was a time when he was a terrible influence on the prince."

"What religion is the prince?"

Father Bergere snorted. "It lacks definition, but it isn't Catholicism. And you, my son?"

Andre flushed, trapped, for he'd carefully avoided any conversational opening which might lead to religion. "I was raised a Catholic," he said at last.

"But you haven't lived like one, is that what you're trying to say?"

"I haven't been to mass in a long time," he said noncommittally.

"Nor confession, I take it?"

Andre said nothing, and Father Bergere let it pass, though he set his jaw tighter and said sternly, "Watch out for that damn Chinaman."

Inside the palatial house, the three daughters had grown unbearably restless. They stalked the corridors, pressed against the windows, and even went to the door several times to scan the horizon. Though Gia Minh affected indifference to the appearance of the young Frenchman, nevertheless she managed to be near a window every ten minutes.

Finally Su saw the two men enter the back gardens. For a moment Gia Minh forgot herself and pressed against the window with her sisters for a better look, but then Xuan, hearing her daughter shriek, came into the room and chased them out, admonishing them for their behavior. The three went serenely to their separate rooms, where they rushed to push chairs to their windows in order to crane their necks to see out.

From the garden gate Andre stopped to view the palace. Though not on the grand scale of Parnasse's château on the Loire, it conveyed a magnificence and majesty surpassing it. Understated and muted, yet regal and sovereign, it was obviously a lair of power, not a playhouse, even though there was nothing ostentatious about it, and there was not even a sentry on guard.

"I have to rest a moment," said Father Bergere when he reached the gazebo. He dropped down thankfully on a bench. "I need my strength to enter that house; it's bedlam, with never a chance to catch your breath."

Gazing at the graceful, serene beauty of the house, seeming to have grown out of the clearing in the jungle rather than having been placed in it, Andre could not imagine anything hurried, discordant, or unmannered within. He saw only calm and quiet in the view, and not for a moment did he feel the tension and suspense of those watching him from windows, nor did he hear the impatient stamping feet of annoyed girls.

"Is he very powerful?" Andre asked.

Father Bergere closed his eyes, exhausted from the walk, and luxuriated in the respite before he had to enter the house. "Yes. But he's a good man, and wise, and many would like to see him on the throne rather than his cousin."

Andre wanted to ask questions, about the prince, about politics, about the daughters, but he restrained himself out of politeness, and attempted to achieve the calm that seemed so pervasive in this country.

But he failed, and was very relieved, almost as much so as those watching, when Father Bergere finally stood up.

From the way the priest had talked, Andre wasn't sure what to expect when he entered the house, but it was absolutely quiet, as dignified and tranquil within as it appeared from without. Yet he noted that Father Bergere seemed surprised at their hushed reception, looking around as though expecting someone to rush out.

Two servants met them with cool water; then a dark-robed scribe informed Father Bergere that Prince Ahn would see them at any time—after they ate and refreshed themselves, if they desired that first.

The priest asked the scribe to convey their appreciation to the prince for his thoughtfulness, but they preferred to see him directly.

The scribe disappeared, and Andre had a moment to take in his surroundings. The palace was cool and airy, gleaming with highly polished dark-wood floors and walls, and lightly furnished with intricately carved teak; yet the interior was not somber, for there was almost a gaiety in the rich brocades and Chinese rugs, and all the sliding screens were open, creating an expanse of unobstructed space. Moreover, the vestibule in which they stood, like all the rooms, opened onto an interior garden around which the entire structure had been built.

Andre had removed his boots upon entering and was provided with slippers. He slid them cautiously before him, testing them, so he wouldn't slip when he had to walk.

The scribe returned to lead them down a corridor, then another, until they came to an open screened room, and he stepped aside to let them enter unannounced.

Andre was amazed that the man they were to see did not keep them waiting, and made no pretense of busyness or interruption.

Instead the prince, for there was no mistaking this man's position, stood just inside the entrance, attentive and expectant.

The man was much younger than Andre had anticipated, taller and leaner, beardless, and dressed in a simple tan robe. His face was remarkably sharp, and though his eyes were intense and penetrating, his countenance was pleasant and reassuring.

Andre was immediately at a loss, for he had given no thought as to how he would present himself, whether he should bow, kneel, or offer his hand, but before he had a chance to flounder, the prince stepped forward and extended his hand, greeting him in good French.

"I've heard intriguing things about you, Mr. Lafabre, all of which did not lead me to expect such a young man. Please sit down. Would you care for tea? Or perhaps coffee?" He clapped his hand to summon a servant.

Father Bergere's eyes widened in amazement and he forgot himself entirely. "Wait a minute! I've known you for twenty years and never heard you speak an understandable word of French. What's happening here, and where is everyone?"

Ahn laughed happily and said to Andre, "He taught everyone in this house to speak French. All their lives, when they didn't want me to understand something, my children have spoken French. Fifteen years ago I realized that if I wanted to know what was going on in my house, I'd have to learn French. Master Chien and I have been practicing on each other for years. And as to where everyone is, I'm sure no one has missed a thing. Knowing my daughters, they're hiding, watching you both. Now, tea? Coffee?"

"That's deplorable!" said Father Bergere. "And deceitful! Pretending you couldn't understand. I would have expected something like that from Chien, but not from you. You should be ashamed of yourself."

Andre was openmouthed at the exchange. He had expected great formality, yet here were intimate things revealed in his presence, and the prince was treating him like a confidant. Suddenly he realized that both men were staring at him.

"Tea or coffee?" Ahn repeated gently, and when Andre stammered a "Thank you, no," the prince dismissed the servant. "Now," he said, his gaze intense and trenchant on Andre, "tell me why you're here, and what I can do for you."

Andre shifted nervously, then felt for the package in his pocket and brought it out carefully, feeling it was such a woefully inept gift, and almost too ashamed to give it, but finally he pressed it to the prince. "I . . . I wanted you to have it . . . for . . . your kindness to me."

Ahn took it somberly. From its age and the way the youth held it, he knew it was a gift of great personal meaning. He opened it and saw the small medal. He guessed it was all the youth had, even guessed it had belonged to his father, and he knew the great value it had for the boy.

"Ah," he said admiringly. "It is a war medal. For valor." He handled it appreciatively for a moment, then handed it back. "But I cannot accept such a thing. It is another man's valor. Honor is not transferable. Your gesture is magnanimous, and I am in your debt. Thank you for the generous gesture." He bowed slightly, impressing Andre even more. "Now, tell me why you are here."

Andre looked to Father Bergere, who nodded; then he leaned forward and said earnestly, "Sir, Excellency, I am here because I am a deserter from my country's navy and if they find me they might execute me. For certain they would put me in prison. I don't want to go to prison. I want to start a new life here."

"A deserter? Does that mean you ran away?"

"Yes, Excellency."

Ahn waited for excuse or explanation, but none was forthcoming. "I understand you had to flee your country. Why is that?"

Andre lowered his head. "I killed a man, sir. I was running away."

Father Bergere sucked in his breath sharply. "You killed a man! Who? Why did you kill him?" He crossed himself furiously.

Andre's hands wrestled with one another and he twisted on the chair in obvious agony; then he took a deep breath and looked directly at Ahn. "Sir, I killed the Duke of Parnasse, a man of high position in my country. I killed him because he found me in bed with his wife. I didn't mean to kill him, but I'm glad that I did."

Ahn nodded evenly, but when he looked over at Father Bergere, he thought the priest was going to have a heart attack. "Quite a busy young man you've brought to us, Master Bergere."

The priest pointed at Andre accusingly, his face purple and choked. "You never told me a word of this. You should get down on your knees and beg God's forgiveness." He jumped up, truly angry. "And you should go to prison!"

"I think there's more to this story," said Ahn. "I want to hear it, and I want Master Chien to hear it too." He clapped his hands and sent a servant for Chien, then all three waited until he arrived.

Ahn introduced them. Chien bowed formally, and hearing Ahn speak in French, he smiled innocently at Father Bergere and took a seat.

"Master Chien, this young man has just told me he deserted from the French Navy, and previously fled his homeland because he killed a man who found him in bed with his wife. We are now going to hear the entire story; then we must decide what to do with this young man who wants to settle in our country and begin a new life."

Ahn turned to Andre, indicating for him to start his story.

Andre spoke for an hour without interruption, relating everything he could remember that he thought relevant. He spoke forcefully and without any attempt to curry sympathy or favor. When he spoke of helping the Vietnamese on shipboard and in Saigon, he did so without false modesty or self-congratulation. He ended by saying that he was sorry that everything had happened as it had. He was a Frenchman, had a mother and grandmother who needed him, and he wished he could return to his country, but since that was impossible, he asked to live in peace in Ban Me Thuot.

When he finished, no one spoke for a long time. Finally Ahn said, "Since you were so honest, I think it's only right that we discuss this with you present. Father Bergere, what do you think should be done?"

The priest's outrage had long subsided, but as a Western thinker he could not put aside the rules of law, especially those of his own country. He spoke with care and deliberation directly to Andre. "I believe you must answer to the laws which you've violated. The laws of France are just and moral. Moreover, behind the laws are justice and mercy, and I believe you'd receive both."

Father Bergere turned to Ahn and Chien. "He is a citizen of France and must be returned to French authority. His case would be heard with understanding and sympathy; our laws and justice are not barbaric." To Andre he said, "You will never be happy as a fugitive and deserter, nor as an outcast from your country." He sat back, a slight frown on his face. "I think we should plead your case to the French authorities."

Andre bowed his head, seeing that the priest was right: he was a citizen of France and must accept her laws and justice.

Ahn too saw this. How could this youth be happy outside his country? Could he himself? He didn't know French law, but surely it could not be so harsh. But then, he thought, the crimes were murder and desertion. He turned to his right. "Master Chien?"

The Chinaman looked into the distance and his words seemed extracted from the horizon. "Law is an arbitrary line drawn by men—a transitory demarcation in the jungle, or desert, or beach, or even France. If you choose to live in the jungle or desert or beach, or even France, then you must stay on the accepted side of that line, and be willing to accept punishment for transgressing it."

Andre bowed his head, but Chien waved his hand. "But we must not have any delusions about the permanence or hallowedness of those lines."

He turned to Father Bergere. "Unlike law, justice—good and evil—is not clearly demarcated. We know when one crosses the line of law, but the territories of justice and injustice, good and evil, have no defined borders. They fit together like the yin and yang, merging and complementing, not clashing."

Chien opened his hands to Ahn. "That man killed this youth's father and sought to pollute him, and this youth slept with that man's wife and then killed the man. I see no point in seeking justice, good or evil, in these depths. This youth has come to us in good faith, and in good faith we must accept him; to do otherwise would be a breach of brotherhood. We must welcome him among us."

He turned to Andre and smiled ever so slightly. "And teach him where we have drawn *our* lines."

Ahn sat for many minutes in deep concentration, weighing and judging. Finally he put his hands on his knees, a mandarin delivering a verdict. "It is not in my authority to enforce the rules of France. If the French come to me for you . . . I'll consider the request. Until then, you're welcome to live among us, with my permission and under my auspices. That will take care of the present. I myself am uninterested in the past. The future will require careful consideration and planning, but at least there'll be time for that."

He looked benignly at Andre. "Is there anything else you wish to bring up or have us consider?"

Andre stood, grateful and moved. "No, Excellency. All I want to do is thank you. I'll never give you cause for regretting your kindness and generosity."

Ahn smiled at the words, almost the same ones he'd used himself when Andre's age. "I'm sure you won't."

Andre bowed deeply to the three of them and was about to leave when Ahn stopped him. "I'm afraid you're going to have to do me a favor before leaving."

Andre stood in his best military manner. "Anything, Excellency."

"I shall never hear the end of it from my children if you don't dine with us; they're probably apoplectic as it is, wondering what's taken so long. They're very foolish girls, but I'm afraid you're going to have to suffer their company for dinner."

Andre flushed. "I'd be deeply honored."

The three men all stared at him a rather embarrassing length of time, for each was thinking nearly the same thing—of the disquieting encounter between this youth and Ahn's three daughters. Andre blushed deeper at their scrutiny, until finally Ahn realized his discomfort and their rudeness.

He stood. "Let me introduce you. They can show you the grounds, then we can eat."

They didn't have far to walk before they encountered the girls, who, fearing that the young Frenchman would get away before they met him, had posted themselves at the end of the corridor. Even Gia Minh had given up all pretense of uninterest and was there with her sisters.

Ahn made the introductions, wincing but saying nothing at his two youngest daughters' giggling deportment; then he sent a servant for Xuan, and he excused himself, suggesting they all have tea, then show Andre the gardens before dinner.

Chien and Father Bergere also excused themselves, and the four young people stood awkwardly in the corridor until Gia Minh finally took charge and led them into a room which she took great care in referring to as the salon.

None of the girls had the slightest experience with a man, and Andre was far too intimidated and shy to say a word, so the four sat perched on separate chairs, the girls staring at him as they would at a giraffe that had walked in, while Andre seemed intent on counting all his fingers.

Finally Xuan entered. Andre jumped up, realizing that he didn't know how to address her, either. He knew she was a princess, but he didn't know what form dictated in meeting Vietnamese royalty.

Xuan sensed this of course and went directly to him and extended her hand. She meant for him to shake it, but he assumed it was to be kissed, which he promptly did, to the shock and gasps of the three girls, who had heard Frenchmen did such things, but never expected to witness it, least of all to their mother. They buzzed excitedly at this display of daring and worldliness, but Xuan silenced them with a glance.

Xuan, herself surprised at the kiss, but charmed, sat down across from Andre, gesturing for him to be seated also.

Though her manner and thought had not changed over the years, Xuan's appearance had. She had aged, but in the most graceful manner. The years had softened her, had seemed to caress her and smooth her features; gone entirely were the shyness and awkwardness, the faintly sharp edge of her keen intellect. Instead, emanating from her was an overpowering sense of kindness and understanding, a gracious elegance that radiated confidence and compassion.

She was slender and beautiful in carriage, moving with stately grace, and when she withdrew her hand from him, her eyes bestowed on him the most warm welcome, yet too only the slightest hint of appreciative amusement, as though she understood everything and everybody, and granted all their folly through her benevolence.

To Andre, whose knowledge and experience with women was

limited to his mother, his great-grandmother, Catherine, and prostitutes, she was the embodiment of feminine gentleness and kindness, and he fell promptly in filial love with her.

She turned to her daughters in soft admonition. "Haven't you sent for tea? Where are your manners?" She clapped her hands, and when the servant appeared, directed refreshments be brought in.

"We're going to put you on the spot," she said to Andre. "We want to know everything about you. Except for Father Bergere, we've never seen a Westerner. All we know of France is what we've read, so please don't take offense at our inquisitiveness. Just tell us everything."

Andre flushed at this command to speak, and captivated them all. "I wouldn't know what to say, or where to begin, madame."

Su giggled and brought her hand to her mouth. "First tell us if all Frenchmen are as handsome as you, then tell us what French girls are like."

Andre crimsoned, but Xuan interjected smoothly. "I am sure most Frenchmen are not as handsome, and I am sure that all French girls, no matter what they look like, are better behaved and nowhere near as silly as you . . . and please get your hand out of your mouth and sit up straight."

She turned to Andre as though nothing had happened. "Why don't you tell us about your family."

"Yes, madame." He started as if giving a recitation, but the memories of his mother and home were so real and longing that soon he was speaking with fervor. "I was born in 1849 in Paris. My father was a soldier who died in the Crimea when I was five years old. I was raised by my mother and grandmother. We were poor. My mother was a maid and she worked in the house of a duke. I spent most of my time with my great-grandmother; she taught me to read and write, and she used to yell at me all the time, but she told me wonderful stories. She's very old now, and I miss her a great deal. My mother too."

He spoke for a long time, leaving out far more than he told, but they hung on every word, and no one gave a thought to the garden walk.

Finally, after nearly two hours, Ahn entered the room. He chastised his family for having held Andre captive all this time, and they were so mesmerized by what they'd heard that no one even noticed that Ahn spoke French. He sent them off to get ready for dinner and directed a servant to attend Andre.

Only at dinner was it brought up that Ahn and Chien were speaking a language they supposedly didn't know, and the meal turned into a light affair of teasing and joking, though not until later in the evening, after Andre had left, did Ahn realize that Gia Minh hadn't spoken a word.

Andre departed enthralled by everything and everyone, and with no awareness of the remarkable impression he'd made. He was pressed to return in two days, and he walked home whistling and singing to himself, happier than he could ever remember. He loved the air, the jungle, the birds, the moon and the stars, this country, and he forgot there was any sadness in his life, or the possibility for sorrow in the future.

In their separate rooms that night, the three girls had similar, if somewhat undefined thoughts and dreams about the young Frenchman. Surely he was the most attractive and exciting person they'd ever met, and each entertained a mild and discreet fantasy.

"He's a very charming young man," said Xuan to her husband as they prepared for bed.

Ahn murmured noncommittally. He caught his reflection in a full-length mirror and contemplated himself. For a reason he didn't understand, Andre's presence was disturbing to him. There was of course the unhappy reminder of age, and the stirring of memories, but there was more to his perturbation—faint jealousy, he supposed, or perhaps a natural territorial impulse, a man on guard for his property and daughters. Whatever it was, he examined himself carefully in the mirror, frowning slightly at the evidence of years, a bit more flesh than he should have, the muscle tone beginning to sag, his face creasing with wrinkles, his hair graying.

He sighed unhappily. His wife understood better than he what was wrong. She moved behind him and placed her arms around his waist, resting her head on his back.

It was dangerous and unproductive for a man to think about himself, she knew. Men were not good at contemplation and introspection—it led to melancholy and despair and self-pity, and was called philosophy.

And for them to think of younger men led to jealousy and bitterness and competition, which came to be called war.

She kissed his back and her hands moved from his waist to soft stroking of his lower abdomen and thighs, then through his pubic hair, and finally she gently caressed his genitals.

He watched in the mirror, intrigued by the arms and hands coming around him like a multilimbed Hindu god, and he watched his own arousal. The image was highly erotic, and his own hands moved over his body, and he forgot everything in the pleasure of touch, and when they moved to the bed, their love-making was more intense and passionate than it had been in a long time, and he went to sleep peacefully, untroubled and without dreams, as a young man might.

Andre returned in two days, an interminable length for him and the girls, and thereafter a pattern was established in which he visited every Sunday, attending morning mass offered by Father Bergere, then dining with the family at noon, then spending the afternoon talking and taking walks with the three daughters, Xuan, and frequently with Chien and Father Bergere. Only rarely did Ahn and Andre see each other, and never alone together.

The Sunday visits were the highlight of the week for him and the others, and he became a permanent and welcome fixture, though his relationship with the family remained strictly formal.

He worked extremely hard but his labors paid off handsomely in the esteem and goodwill he received from his neighbors, and in the cultivation and development of his property. He found that he liked being a farmer and enjoyed toiling in his fields, and never gave a thought to becoming a soldier again.

His only frustration was in not being able to penetrate the hard shell of formality that separated him from a more personal relationship with anyone in Ahn's family. He wanted very much to develop individual relationships, especially with Ahn and Gia Minh. Ahn remained distant because of time and responsibilities, but with Gia Minh he sensed aloofness; she seemed to take little interest in what he said, and rarely spoke to him. At first he'd hoped this was merely a pose, or perhaps shyness, but he came to believe unhappily that she simply wasn't interested in him, a view reinforced by her sisters, who frequently teased her about how she thought she was too good for any man and doubtless would remain a spinster. He noticed that she had no difficulty talking and arguing with Chien and Father Bergere, and engaged them both in what he considered were learned discussions, but she never talked politics or religion or philosophy with him, much as he'd have liked that, and he decided it was because she didn't think he was smart enough. When he talked with her sisters or told about life in France, she bore a slightly amused and patronizing look on her face.

However, he did discuss religion and politics with Father Bergere and Chien, and through them learned a great deal about the thought and customs of Vietnam.

He learned that despite the outward tranquillity, the country was roiling in discord, that just beneath the surface were riptides of unrest and dissension, and that the peaceful house he visited every Sunday figured prominently in every political consideration.

One morning in the middle of the rice harvest, when Andre went to the fields of Che Lan's father to help, the old man was not there, and when he didn't appear by noon, Andre went to his house to see if he was ailing.

Che Lan's youngest brother, Nha, met him stonily at the door but didn't invite him in. Andre asked him if his father was ill. Nha told him curtly that the family was in mourning. They'd just received news that Che Lán had been caught and executed by the French.

Before Andre could register his shock or express sorrow, Nha told him that he was no longer welcome at their house and his assistance in the fields no longer desired. He was relieved of all obligations of the contract, though the land was his to keep and he was asked never again to visit; then the door was shut in his face.

Andre returned to his fields, and didn't leave his land for a full month, too hurt and ashamed to see anyone, and there was no one to whom he could express his sorrow and regret. He felt completely alone and isolated in this strange country, and his unhappiness grew almost to despair. He dreamed of France, of his mother and great-grandmother, and he wished more than anything to go home.

Though he worked his fields hard, he let his appearance go, not bothering to shave or wash, and he took no care for his food.

Finally one day he saw a bizarre sight, the huge, snowy-robed Chien disdainfully picking his way through the muck and mud of the fields toward him. Andre was so happy to see him, anyone, that he ran to greet him.

When he reached him, Chien's garb was splattered and his look anything but benign.

Andre bowed joyously. "Seeking enlightment, Master Chien?"

The Chinese returned the bow. "I found it long ago; it was not in the shit and stink of rice paddies." Then he assumed his mock-sage serenity and opened his hands. "Though a man may find enlightenment wherever his eyes and ears are truly open, and the scent that wafts his spirit need not be that of the rose."

Andre laughed and grabbed his sleeve. "Come inside. I have food and water, and you can rest. Are you just passing by?"

"No. I came to see you." He gazed forthrightly at Andre, taking in the deterioration of the past month. At the door of the hut he peered in curiously before entering, saw the disarray and dirt, frowned in distaste, but went in.

"Father Bergere would be disappointed," he said at last. "There's no sign of a woman's hand here at all. That's why he hasn't come to visit, you know—he's been afraid of what he'd find; that dreadful Jesuit has entertained visions of licentiousness and outrage." Chien smiled. "Concerns not without basis, from what I understand of your past life."

"I've lived the life of a monk since I've been here," Andre said.

Chien's eyes traveled the youth and the room. "Monks, even the Jesuit ones, are clean." He dropped down and looked to Andre expectantly; finally Andre realized he was waiting to be served, and when he went to bring something, Chien called after him, "Why haven't you come to see us? What's wrong with you?"

Andre stopped, startled by the directness.

"I came to see why a young man, befriended and welcomed by a generous family, would rudely turn on that family. I came to see why a young man would stop paying visits to young girls."

When Andre lowered his head, Chien said, "I also came for something to eat."

Andre looked at him anxiously. "I didn't mean to be rude. I didn't think they'd want to see me."

"And why would young girls not want to be visited by a young man anymore?"

So Andre explained to him about Che Lan. "I don't feel that I belong here," he said at last.

"You don't," said Chien. "Neither do I. Neither does Father Bergere, but that doesn't stop him from meddling everywhere he can. We all shall be foreigners, never accepted, but that doesn't mean we can't live here in peace and harmony. If you are honest, treat all alike, and are faithful to your word, you'll be honored and esteemed. Virtue is without class, or color, or nationality." He smiled at Andre. "Virtue is a universal coin. Almost as good as cash. Or food."

Andre laughed and brought a plate and set it before Chien. "Then the family would not object if I came to visit?"

"I think they're perplexed and unhappy that you haven't. The girls are in despair, thinking that you find them unattractive and uninteresting."

"But that isn't true!"

Chien stood, looked about casually for something else to eat.

"All the more reason for them to believe it. Though Father Bergere is always quoting 'The truth shall make you free,' I've found it seldom has such a happy result. Deception is like a chameleon—harmless, sometimes quite lovely, and better suited for jungle survival."

"But it's they who don't seem to find me attractive or interesting. Especially Gia Minh."

He said it so plaintively that Chien could not help but smile. The Chinaman's face creased in mirth, but then there crept across it flickers of sadness—perhaps nostalgia—and he patted Andre's cheek. "What an exquisite, bitter fruit is youth." He thanked Andre for the cool water and food, and left without saying anything else.

Andre had been in Ahn's thoughts also, though he'd surmised the reasons why the Frenchman had ceased his visits, for he was kept informed of all news and activities within the province, and he'd heard of Che Lan's death and the family's ostracism of Andre.

He'd heard other things, too, disturbing information from Saigon and Hue that made his own position more perilous daily.

The French were now in complete control of the Mekong Delta. The support Tu Duc had hoped to muster never materialized and the southern part of his kingdom was lost with almost no struggle. Those who had fought, men such as Che Lan, had done so not for their emperor, but for independence. The smoldering resentment against a corrupt mandarinate and centuries of abuse and exploitation were now fanned by Tu Duc's inability to resist the French.

In Hue there was the odor of dying dynasty. The unmistakable stench of decay and ruin wafted through the air and seemed to hang like a cloud above the palace. Corruption and decadence increased as those at court felt the first warmth under the imperial pyre.

For the first time, people openly began to speak of deposing Tu Duc. Ahn never participated in such talk, but he knew of the secret societies that had been formed to fight both the French and Tu Duc.

Ahn knew that eventually Tu Duc would have to turn to the French to save his throne, ceding his power and authority, allowing his country to become a colony in exchange for French help in overpowering internal dissent and all his enemies, real and imagined, of which he knew he would find himself in the forefront.

This is where Ahn thought that he could use Andre, so two mornings after Chien's visit, Andre was stunned to see Prince Ahn himself dismount from a black stallion.

Andre ran to greet him with a mixture of happiness and trepidation. This was the first time he'd been alone in the prince's company and he felt awkward, dirty, and sweaty before the immaculate, regal prince.

Andre thrust out his hand, but seeing how dirty it was, he was about to withdraw it, when Ahn took it, not even noticing the mud that rubbed off on his own hand.

"I have nothing to offer you," Andre said apologetically. "Only water. Or tea."

Not a man given to small talk, Ahn said, "I didn't come for food or drink. I came to discuss an important matter with you."

Ahn dropped on the ground in a sitting position. "I prefer to discuss business under the scrutiny of the sun."

Andre immediately dropped down facing him.

Without any preliminaries, Ahn said, "Now you need my help. However, in the future you may be able to help me and my family. I'm here to discuss our situations and explain how we can be of assistance to one another. I'm here to talk man to man, not as prince to subject, not as Vietnamese to Frenchman."

He held out his hand, palm up, and instinctively Andre knew that he was to place his hand palm down on it. Their eyes met, penetrated all barriers; then they withdrew their hands.

Ahn explained as simply as he could the political situation and the delicate position he was in with regard to his cousin, and he told him that he believed that in all likelihood the French would soon become dominant in the country. He said that since this was inevitable, he wanted Andre to have influence, and he admitted that his reasons were self-serving.

Then he outlined to Andre how he planned to accomplish his goals. For two hours they discussed strategy under the sun, weighing gambits and risks, until they settled upon a course of action.

When they finished, they shook hands once more.

Ahn mounted his horse and rode off, and Andre went back to the fields.

Two days later, having told his family only that he would be gone for some time, Ahn went with an armed escort to arrest Andre; then, under guard, Ahn brought him to Hue.

10

WHEN AHN AND HIS GUARDS rode into the imperial grounds with their shackled prisoner, the effect was sensational, and when they stripped him and chained him to the pillory, the courtyard overflowed with the curious, though no one mocked or cast stones, because they were too awed and amazed.

The guards, under orders not to maltreat the prisoner, stood fiercely vigilant over their charge, snarling at those who came close to view this golden-haired, golden-skinned creature who, even from a distance, smelled of meat and other strange odors.

The news fanned throughout the palace, and Tu Duc was immediately informed. Forgetting himself momentarily, he rushed to a window and looked out with incredulity. The incident could not have occurred at a worse moment: the French envoy from Paris was just concluding his negotiations and the sight of a Frenchman chained and held up to public ridicule would undo all that had been accomplished in the past months of delicate diplomacy.

Tu Duc was appalled, for such an action was an outrageous breach of manners and civility; then he was furious, more so than he had ever been, for this action was a personal embarrassment and humiliation.

In another wing of the palace, Maurice Vallot, the Count of Etinne, personal envoy of Emperor Napoleon, was preparing for what he hoped was the last meeting with the Vietnamese, when a military aide rushed in with the news. Vallot was tired, but grateful this tedious business was almost over, and he was chatting amiably with his valet when the aide told him that a Frenchman had been stripped and shackled in the courtyard and was to be publicly executed.

Vallot, a consummate diplomat and survivor of decades of the political pitfalls of republics and monarchies, a shrewd but generous and genteel man of seventy years, was not able to hide his shock at the announcement, and he too rushed to the window to see the spectacle. Such an incident had to be a calculated insult, and never once in all his years, even in dealing with the English, had he encountered such a thing. He thought he'd come to an understanding with the Vietnamese.

Napoleon was not inclined to military intervention in Vietnam, and in resisting the vehement urgings of the military, had sent Vallot to avoid armed hostility with them and arrange suitable accommodations between the two thrones that would create a facade of independence and integrity for Tu Duc, while providing France with significant military advantage and economic gain.

The French admiralty, believing it was essential to extend military power over the entire country, the initial piece of a vast empire in Asia which would rival England's, had long been acting independently from Paris. But the French admirals were becoming too greedy and militant, and Vallot had been sent to quell them and establish a channel of communication directly between Hue and Paris.

Vallot thought he'd been successful, but now there was this outrage in the emperor's courtyard. Vallot sent an aide to cancel the final meeting and to demand an immediate audience with Tu Duc.

Ahn, knowing of the negotiation between Tu Duc and the French, had calculated that his actions would drive a wedge between them and force both parties to protect Andre in order to save face.

When Ahn was shown in to Tu Duc's presence, the emperor could barely contain himself. In the two years since Ahn had last seen his cousin, Tu Duc had changed noticeably. The Emperor had grown fat and puffy and his regal bearing had degenerated to nervousness and impatience; he looked mean and small and harassed, and there was no majesty left.

Ahn made obeisances, but Tu Duc cut him short. "Have you any idea what you've done? You've humiliated me."

Ahn affected astonishment. "I? I've brought a criminal to you for punishment. I could have executed him myself, but because he's a foreigner, I thought it best that you handle the matter."

Tu Duc seethed with suspicion and fury. "Who is he and what has he done?"

"I have no idea. He's a foreigner."

For the first time in Ahn's memory, the emperor lashed out in anger. "What has he done that you've made a spectacle of him for all the French to see? What is his crime that I can justify such an insult to the French ambassador?"

Ahn explained patiently. "The man must be guilty of some great crime, otherwise he wouldn't have fled from his own people. He settled without permission in Ban Me Thuot. I consider him a dangerous influence. He's learned our language, purchased land, and worked it successfully. It will only be a matter of time before he starts to corrupt our people. I don't want a Frenchman in the province. If I allow one to settle, others will follow, and it will not be long before Ban Me Thuot becomes another Saigon." Then, calculating his insult, he said, "Or Hue."

Tu Duc flared furiously; he stood and pointed his finger at Ahn. "For that I should have you shackled in the courtyard. If I ever hear another disrespectful remark from you, cousin, I'll have you executed. Don't ever question my policies or judgment. Don't even intimate such a thing."

He clapped his hands sharply and his guards rushed in. He ordered his chamberlain to release the Frenchman instantly and turn him over to the French envoy with deep apologies, stating that a full explanation would be given by Tu Duc himself. Then he directed the guards to escort Ahn to a royal apartment to "safeguard" his presence, meaning that he was to see no one and go nowhere.

Ahn bowed perfunctorily, feigning having been slurred and dishonored, and he turned his back on the emperor and walked out of the throne room, leaving the guards to scramble backward to keep up with him.

He was pleased with his performance, but knew everything now depended on Andre's wits and luck. It was entirely out of his own hands, a matter of the French among themselves, and about them he didn't have a clue. Father Bergere always talked about French logic and reason, but it was a logic and reason which escaped his comprehension, and seemed to have a great deal to do with emotions and sentiment. They were rather like women in their thinking, Ahn believed, though that, he felt, was not an altogether bad thing, especially if one was seeking mercy and understanding.

There was a brief confrontation in the courtyard between Ahn's soldiers and the imperial guards before it was made clear that it was the emperor's decree that the prisoner be released.

The crowd was quickly and harshly dispersed, all under the watchful eyes of the French; then Andre was unshackled and handed robes by the emperor's chamberlain himself, then deferentially led into the palace and escorted to the apartments of the French delegation.

Vallot's aide accepted charge of Andre, stating that the count was disturbed by what he'd seen, and eager to hear the emperor's explanation of the unfortunate affair.

As soon as the chamberlain departed, the aide plied Andre with questions—who was he, where had he come from, what had happened?—but immediately Count Vallot entered the antechamber.

"Stop pestering the boy, Charles. You're as bad as the savages. Go fetch some water and nourishment for him. Can't you spot a godsend when you see one?"

Vallot approached Andre genially, but was carefully appraising him. "Actually, you don't look too bad. We may have to rough you up a bit to extract full advantage out of you." He laughed and clapped Andre about the shoulders. "Obviously Too Doo is mortified at what's happened. Let's not let him off so easily. Come, lad, let's have a chat."

Vallot led Andre into his private chambers, introduced himself, inquired solicitously about his condition, and was immediately disposed favorably by the young man's bearing and manner.

A shrewd, observant man, Vallot sensed that he was not faced with a simple matter, or one that was what it appeared to be. Years of diplomacy and intrigue put him on his guard, though his manner evinced affability and patient concern.

By the youth's carriage and deportment he guessed Andre was academy-trained, but not an officer, therefore a deserter, and he was about to begin a circuitous dialogue that would trap Andre into such an admission when the youth took him by surprise.

"Your Excellency, my name is Andre Lafabre. I am a deserter from the French Navy and I place myself in your hands, not for mercy, for I neither ask nor deserve that, but for whatever punishment justice deems."

"Well," said Vallot. He brought his fingers together and tapped them in quiet calculation, all the while studying the ramrod-straight youth before him.

Andre, whose innocence, directness, and earnestness never failed to impress older men and bring out their protective instincts, now stirred the compassion and magnanimity of the elderly count, a sire and grandsire many times over, and Vallot eased into bemused fatherliness.

"Honest and direct, is that what you're going to be? That may take me a moment to adjust to, unaccustomed as I am to anything forthright in this damnable business. But then, I forget how breathtakingly frank youth can be. A deserter, are you? Should I have you shot?''

Andre didn't answer, merely stared straight ahead, awaiting his punishment.

There was a knock at the door and the aide entered with a tray of food and drink, which he set before Vallot. ''Get the boy something to wear, Charles; it's unseemly for a Frenchman to be dressed in bedclothes. Never mind, just give him your jacket and trousers.''

While the exchange was being conducted, Vallot picked over the tray. ''Bring some more of these, whatever they are,'' he said, holding up a Chinese dim sung, ''and a bottle of champagne.

''Better,'' he said to Andre as he struggled to fasten the much-too-small uniform. ''Even an ill-fitting French uniform looks better than those winding sheets these people drape themselves in.''

He popped another dumpling in his mouth. ''No, I'm not going to have you shot. You may have done a great service to your country by having deserted; you're much more valuable here than where you were before. And there's certainly no need for Too Doo to know you're a criminal.''

He gestured for Andre to sit, and he pushed the tray toward him. ''Now, tell me who you are and what brings you here.''

Andre sat forward on the chair and spoke in respectful, soldierly precision, realizing that he'd made a good impression and that if he played his hand carefully, the count might overlook everything in his past in order to use him against the Vietnamese.

''I was born in Paris,'' he began. ''My father was killed in the Crimea while serving with the Duke of Parnasse.''

Vallot's eyes lifted slightly at the name.

''My mother, unable to support herself, applied to the duke for a position in his household and became a chambermaid. Later, the duke secured an appointment for me at the Ecole Militaire, out of gratitude for my father's sacrifice, he said.''

''Philippe did this? Extraordinary! I've never known him to do anything for anyone.'' Vallot poured champagne and lifted the glass to gauge its clarity. ''You know, Parnasse was supposed to come on this mission. I'm too old for this nonsense, almost perished on shipboard. I'm only here at the special urging of our emperor.'' He inclined his head, but, Andre noted, neither in reverence nor in respect.

''Yes, Parnasse should be here, but his wife took a severe turn for the worse, and has perhaps died.''

Andre forgot himself and jumped up. "Catherine!"

Vallot's eyes widened in amazement at the outburst; then they hooded over slyly and he eased back in his chair, his hands folding across his ample stomach, a content look spreading over his face. "Ah," he said.

Andre recovered immediately and sat down, recognizing his monumental blunder. "The duchess was very kind to me," he said weakly.

"Yes. Doubtless. A kind woman to many, I've heard."

"She is unwell?" Andre inquired cautiously.

"The duchess was not well for some time, and weakened during her pregnancy. Since the birth of the child, she has hovered near death. The duke has not left his wife's side; he resigned from government service and spends his days with her and the child at their château."

Andre was dumbfounded. Parnasse was alive. Catherine was ill . . . perhaps had died. There was a child. Whose? And he was not a murderer. His flight from France had been unnecessary.

All this was beyond his ability to absorb, and he simply sat staring at the count, whose eyes were on him with the same elation they would have bestowed on a forty-eight-carat gem.

"You were at the Ecole," Vallot prompted.

"Yes," Andre said absently.

"And then . . . you weren't."

"Yes."

Vallot waited patiently. Finally Andre regained his composure, seeming to come from a deep trance. "I dropped out of the Ecole and left France," he said at last.

"Were you a fugitive? Are you wanted by the police?"

"No, Excellency," Andre said, now with honesty. "I left France for other reasons."

The old count smiled. "Matters of the heart," he suggested.

Andre blushed genuinely, and the count sighed in satisfaction. The world was as it should be after all, he thought; this nonsense about diplomacy and emperors was all charade and illusion, a shadow play, of no consequence or import compared with the enduring tissue of love and youth and matters of the heart. Oh, and the intrigue, he thought. The scandal would be exquisite.

The old man felt warmed, and basked in contentment. How rich and good and complex, yet simple, was life. He felt young again. All this wretched business was gone in a sudden vision he had of ruffles and petticoats; he could smell the perfume and he almost felt the soft flesh of thighs.

"And it would not be advisable or appropriate for you to return to France, is that right?" he asked.

"No, Excellency."

The count poured more champagne and lifted his glass to Andre. "To you, my boy." He took a deep drink and raised his glass again. "To all of us," he added happily, still thinking of thighs. "Now, about this small matter of desertion from our Imperial Navy."

Andre told him exactly what had happened, leaving out nothing until he came to his arrival in Ban Me Thuot. He made no mention of his reception at Prince Ahn's and said nothing of their conspiracy. He said only that he had honestly received his land from Che Lan's father, worked his fields, then was arrested by the prince and brought in chains to Hue.

The bottle was empty and evening beginning to fall when he finally finished his story.

The count sat for many minutes in contemplation. The situation was so ripe for advantage and exploitation that he knew he'd have to give it careful thought in order to reap its full benefit. This youth could be of tremendous use, he realized. And it was such a lovely story, he thought, his mind still swathed in ruffles and lace.

"What is it exactly that you desire?" he asked at last.

"I want to return to my fields in Ban Me Thuot."

"That is all?"

"Yes, Excellency."

Vallot stood, indicating that the interview was over. "We'll present your case to the emperor in the morning, but I don't think you need worry. My aide will see you to comfortable lodgings. Good evening."

As soon as he was shown to his room, Andre dropped into his bed, too exhausted even to think about what he'd learned, and immediately fell into deep slumber.

That night Ahn was summoned to the emperor's rooms, though this meeting had none of the intimacy of their last. Tu Duc was barely polite, and offered him nothing to eat or drink.

At close quarters and in the privacy of his chambers, Tu Duc's face and manner revealed the ravages of the past years. Gone was his calm equanimity; now he seemed nervous and his eyes darted suspiciously. His once thin and exquisite fingers had become bloated, whitish from the choked circulation of the now too small rings, and his hands were puffy and never at rest.

The ease and majesty of his presence—the assurance of power—was now completely lost in his fear of ursurpation. Ahn saw that his cousin was beyond help or reach, an unhappy, dangerous man assailed and cornered, a monarch willing to sacrifice anything to maintain the facade of dominion. He saw too that he'd made a mistake in deserting his cousin; he should have stayed and helped Tu Duc, but now it was too late.

The emperor sat stonily across from him, and Ahn could feel his anger and tension. "Tomorrow you'll apologize to the French for what you've done."

Ahn's eyes flashed. "Certainly not. You can have the French sitting on the throne with you if you want, but I won't have one in my province."

Ahn knew he was playing at the outside limit of safety, gambling that Tu Duc was not yet sure enough of himself or of French support to risk turning on him, and that his fear of Ahn's popularity offered him temporary immunity.

Tu Duc quivered with rage; his lips drew tightly in fury and he was about to lash out when Ahn pressed quickly, his hand reaching out to touch the emperor's arm. "Cousin, Tu Duc, listen. I mean you no harm or insult. You are my emperor and lord, and I prostrate myself before you, but listen to me. Can't you see what's happening?"

Tu Duc looked down at the hand on his arm, but the fervor in Ahn's voice softened him, and he untensed slightly.

"Before, there were no French here. Your father and our grandfather, and the great Gia Long wouldn't even receive them, yet now they're all over our land, and you're thinking of apologizing to them. They have taken the southern part of the kingdom and are pushing for more, and instead of fighting them, you apologize. Soon they'll be here in Hue, not as emissaries but as rulers. And others will come, a succession of oppressors, one dog after another. Look at China."

Tu Duc turned his head to shield himself from harsh blows, the words of truth striking at his heart.

"Don't apologize. Don't accommodate. Be strong. Don't be afraid of our people. Lead them. I beg you, cousin, save us. I beg you in the name of my children, in the name of our country, in the name of our ancestors—save us from dishonor and oppression."

Tu Duc could not bring his face to Ahn, but he spoke a single whispered plea. "How?"

"Trust your people. Lead them. Show courage and resist the French. United, we'll never be conquered. Already there are secret societies throughout the land. They're not directed against you but against the foreigner, yet they're afraid you'll accommodate the French, so they'll turn against you first."

Ahn tugged gently on Tu Duc's arm until the emperor finally turned to him. "Cousin, our people will fight the French, with or without you. If they find you'll not lead them, they'll cast you, all us Nguyens, out. There'll be civil war. First we'll be consumed, then the foreigners, though it may take a hundred years. Resist, cousin. Spare your people and our children generations of bloodshed. These French will not save your throne, they'll only grant you terror-filled time; they'll take away your gold crown and place upon your head one of crushing guilt."

Ahn took both hands of the emperor, and the two men faced one another, inches apart. "I'm not your enemy, nor are your people. Your enemies are behind the throne, your courtiers and sychophants, your corrupt mandarins, those who care nothing about you or our country, who would sacrifice you and our honor for a single minute near the flame of power, from whatever source it comes."

Ahn dropped the emperor's hands and said gently, "There is nothing wrong in being afraid, nothing wrong in failure, nothing wrong in death." He stood. "But dishonor and betrayal . . . oh, cousin, that is hell."

Ahn bowed, and for the first time in his life, backed respectfully from the presence of the emperor.

For many minutes Tu Duc stared after him; then he bowed his head in despair. It was all true, everything he'd been told—words brought to his ears that had been the swirling howls of his ancestors' cries in his dreams—and yet . . . and yet what could he do? Fight? With what—lances and junkets against artillery and battleships?

He had but one weapon—time. Yes, terror-filled and guilt-ridden, and every minute of it was hell, but it was time, and precious, because as long as it lasted, there was still hope.

From behind hidden screens Lady Deng and the lord chamberlain watched the emperor fall back heavyhearted against his chair, then saw him slowly struggle up and leave the room.

"This prince is a dangerous man," said the lord chamberlain. "He would have made a good emperor."

"Yes," said Lady Deng coldly. "He was good at everything he did."

"But we have no choice," said the lord chamberlain.

"No," she said. "None."

* * *

Ahn was escorted back to his apartment and the door locked behind him.

He had no delusions about the effect of his words on the emperor or on his status. He was a prisoner, marked for execution, with little time left, even if he did get out of the palace alive.

He went to the open screen and looked out on the shimmering gardens. Overpowering sadness came over him as he saw the stillness and beauty. All was lost, but he was not thinking of himself or his life; instead he had a vision of the gardens in desolation, the palace become rubble, his country laid waste. He saw that so clearly, and he grieved because he could do nothing. He put his hand on the screen for support, so deeply and keenly did he feel what would happen.

Then he smiled faintly, for he was not a man for self-pity, or melancholy, and besides, the garden was still there, beauty and stillness were yet for the eye and ear to behold, life and happiness were today, and he still had happy memories. Though the palace was doomed, he could still hear within its walls the laughter and happy cries of his own youth.

Death and desolation were not to be feared, for they were unavoidable and therefore acceptable. Indeed, there was nothing to be unhappy about, no reason for despair. What would be, would be. What was, was. Of course, he thought, and took a deep breath, the darkness became the dawn, stillness became the morning, beauty became decay, then rebirth.

He turned from the screen, resigned and calm, and was making his way to bed when he heard a key in the door.

He watched serenely as it opened slowly, but instead of the armed assassins he expected, Lady Deng entered.

When he saw her heavy body trying surreptitiously to sneak past the door, he laughed outright.

She'd grown even stouter since he'd seen her two years ago, and though trying to camouflage herself with stays and the tightest ao dai he'd ever seen, there was no hiding her fatness. Perhaps in an attempt to draw attention from her fleshiness, her makeup was even more garish, so the total effect she created was of startling grotesqueness. In her features and face there lingered nothing of the seductive, sensual woman of twenty years ago; what stood in the doorway was a vulgar caricature.

"I wasn't expecting you," he said, regretting his laughter. "Come in."

Almost shyly she closed the door and moved a few steps toward him; then, realizing her appearance and its contrast to the stately, still-handsome man before her, she stopped, resentful and belligerent.

"Whom were you expecting?" she demanded.

"No one as welcome as you," he said graciously.

Disarmed and pleased, she went to him, so close that he saw how ravaged and dissipated she was, far older-appearing than her fifty years, and he had to restrain himself from backing away. There was no mistaking her intent. Her mouth was moist and her eyes dilating with desire. "I've never forgotten your lovemaking." Her hand went to his chest. "You were wonderful."

He backed away slightly. "Thank you. I enjoyed being with you then."

She pressed closer, sweaty and with hot breath. "But no more?"

He disengaged and moved across the room. "Don't force me to be rude, my Lady. Have you forgotten the murdered child?"

"Ah," she said. "Well, as a matter of fact, I had." Her eyes narrowed on him cruelly. "So much has happened over the years; it's hard to keep track of little details."

"I'm sure you've been very busy." He went to his dresser. "Would you leave, please."

"You will not make love to me?"

His back to her, he picked up his shaving kit. "No, my lady, I will not."

Knowing her so well, he watched her in his shaving mirror, even after she turned to go. He saw her reach into a sleeve, whirl around, and rush him, but he had plenty of time to step aside and grab her wrist, twisting until the stiletto dropped to the floor.

"Oh, Lihn," he said. "You had better hire assassins—you're too old and fat now to be a murderess. Or a whore. Go hire some boys to mount you."

He pushed her away. "Get out. The time hasn't come when you can murder a prince in the palace. I could have you put to death for this."

She was composed when she reached the door. "There isn't anything you can have done here; you're powerless. And soon you'll be among your ancestors, and no one here will remember you."

The door closed behind her and the key turned.

He put the stiletto in his shaving kit, then prepared for bed.

In the morning, Andre was fitted in a dark suit, instructed on how to behave, and sent in with Count Vallot to the throne room.

The French emissary made a formal but restrained presentation to the emperor, then introduced Andre, who also bowed moderately.

Tu Duc acknowledged them, though less politely than Vallot had expected. Vallot felt the tension and anxiety in the room, despite the outward calm, and noted immediately a presence he'd not seen before, an extremely striking and tall Vietnamese whose harsh gaze he'd felt from the moment he'd entered the room. He guessed this to be the emperor's cousin, the remarkable Prince Ahn he'd heard so much about.

Vallot was familiar with the gossip and intrigue of the Vietnamese court, and knew well Tu Duc's dislike and fear of his cousin, but he knew the prince was powerful in his own right, perhaps the only person who could stand up to the emperor, or, more importantly, influence his policy. Vallot was sure this emperor's sudden coldness was the doing of the prince.

All this complicated matters, thought Vallot, but he pressed on smoothly, ignoring the prince, who stood only a few feet from the throne.

"I have brought this young man with me so that he might hear firsthand, though I doubt understand, the explanation for the recent outrageous treatment he's received, which both he and I shall have to relay to his patron, the Duke of Parnasse, an intimate of our Imperial Highness, and one of his closest advisers."

As the translator rendered this into Vietnamese for Tu Duc, Ahn said sneeringly in perfect French, "What was the duke's 'ward' hiding in my province for?"

Very good, thought Vallot, who appreciated a worthy opponent; at last someone to engage his intellect and abilities. He turned to Ahn with all the considerable disdain he'd mastered over the years, then looked to Andre. "Is *this* the great warrior whose men brought you here in shackles?"

The translator struggled frantically to render this all to Tu Duc, but finally the emperor clapped his hands in exasperation, and there was complete silence. Then he directed the translation. When it was completed, he spoke to Vallot, then sat back as his words were translated.

"His Majesty wishes to introduce his cousin, His Highness Prince Nguyen Ahn Le. His Majesty will countenance no disrespect to the royal family, nor will he countenance discord in his presence. His Majesty finds the subject before him of little importance and no interest. There has been a misunderstanding. His Majesty regrets it and has graciously deemed the youth to be compensated for the misunderstanding. Then he wishes never to hear of this matter again. What is it the youth desires for compensation?"

Vallot knew when to push, to drive that inch more, but he knew too when a firm line had been drawn. He bowed to the emperor. "Your Majesty's generosity is magnanimous. This youth merely wishes to return to his rightful property, for which he has paid through labor. He asks nothing else."

Ahn looked scornfully at Vallot. "This charade is insulting. What business does he have here? Why is he in Vietnam? Is there some reason he can't return to France? I will not have this intruder in my province."

Vallot looked to Tu Duc, expecting him to rebuke the prince, but when the emperor said nothing, Vallot realized Ahn's power, and saw that Tu Duc was impressed with his cousin's challenge to the French. Such an example could be disastrous, Vallot realized. He saw that the situation was slipping out of control. He hadn't anticipated this, but knew enough not to make a stand over something inconsequential.

"Your Majesty, this youth is the lawful owner of property in Ban Me Thuot. He has violated no law and committed no crime. He wishes to return to his land, from which he was dragged in chains. You graciously offered to compensate him for the misunderstanding by granting him his wish. His wish is merely to return to his land. His wish is for you to enforce the law and protect him in a rightful cause."

And knowing all about lines, feints, and withdrawals, Vallot drew his own line. "And so it is the formal request of my government."

Tu Duc's answer was simple. "He may return to his land." Then the emperor stood, and without looking at anyone, left the throne room as all heads remained bowed.

Ahn didn't glance toward Vallot or Andre, and followed after Tu Duc. He asked for a private audience and, to his surprise, was shown in immediately to the royal apartment.

The two men eyed one another warily, not knowing what to expect, or how the other would react.

Ahn bowed perfunctorily. "I will accede to your decree."

"Of course you will," Tu Duc said curtly. "Moreover, I direct you to grant him more land. You wronged him; I want you to compensate him."

"I'd be humiliated."

"Generosity is not humiliation," said Tu Duc, "and I'm not trying to humble you. You spoke honestly and wisely last night, and I pondered your words, but I must follow my own judgment.

You are lord of Darlac, but my dominion is larger, and I must do what is best for the country, not a single part."

Their gazes locked for a long moment; then Ahn nodded. "I promised you loyalty and obedience and that I'd do nothing to make you regret your generosity to me. I'll do as you say."

He withdrew, extremely pleased; it couldn't have gone better, he thought. Now all he had to do was make sure no one ever learned of the conspiracy.

That evening Andre was Count Vallot's guest for dinner. As Vallot had spent the day in final negotiations with the Vietnamese, he'd had no opportunity to discuss with Andre what had transpired at court.

The two dined alone and Vallot was relaxed and unusually familiar with his young guest, growing expansive with wine.

"Dear God, I'll be glad to leave this damnable place. Dealing with these people is like trying to carve soup."

"Thank you for what you did for me," said Andre. "You've been very kind."

"Well," mused the old count, "it didn't go as well as I'd planned, but I hadn't foreseen the interference of that prince." Vallot studied his wine in the candlelight. "Now, there's a formidable man. I rather liked him. Thank God men such as that never reach thrones."

So that Andre wouldn't misunderstand, Vallot lifted his glass to him, then drank deeply. "To our own unformidable Imperial Majesty."

He raised his glass again. "And to my safe return home. All I need now is for the Prussians to sink my ship."

Andre couldn't contain his eagerness. "Do you think there'll be war?"

"Any day now," said Vallot dryly.

"And we shall destroy the Huns?"

The count's face was perfectly bland as he finished the glass. "Of course."

Andre was stunned. Vallot didn't believe in a French victory any more than Parnasse had. What was this? he wondered. Why a war if these wise and powerful men knew France was going to be defeated? Was this simply a means to topple an empire and be rid of the lesser Bonaparte? Or was it because old men had nothing to lose, perhaps even something to gain in the deaths of young men?

It was too confusing to Andre. The world was too subtle and complex for him; he couldn't keep straight these machinations and he marveled that men such as Vallot were able to pick their way through the mazes.

He hoped he could trust Ahn. He believed him just and honorable, but he realized he hadn't guessed right about anything or anyone yet in his life.

Vallot poured wine for them both. "My advice to you, young man, since you haven't asked it, is to return to this Ban Me place and work hard and make yourself rich and not offend that prince, though I doubt he'll last long, and simply bide your time. There's going to be quiet for a while; our affair with the Prussians is going to take our minds off this place, but in a few years we'll return. That's when you'll come in. Guide yourself carefully through these next few years, and . . ." He raised his glass to Andre. "Who knows what heights you might attain." His eyes sparkled. "I shall follow your career with great interest."

"Thank you very much, sir. I'm greatly in your debt. I hesitate to ask another favor, but . . ."

Vallot waved the request aside. "Of course I'll call upon your mother and reassure her of your health and welfare. And I'll send word to you of the condition of the Duchess of Parnasse, and extend to her your concerned salutations, if, God willing, she's able to receive them."

Vallot did his best to suppress a smile and remain serious; the youth was so earnest, he thought, so scrupulous. Such a dunderhead.

During the evening, Vallot waxed eloquently about France and urged Andre to reconsider his decision. How could anyone live among savages? he asked. Or why would they want to, even on God's behalf?—surely that was asking too much; it was almost too much to be asked to go to England, and that absolutely was the limit.

Were it not for the women, Vallot said, his eyes losing their opaqueness, becoming startlingly bright, there would be no point to this part of the world at all. Porcelain, jade, silk—fine things indeed, and hats off to Marco Polo—but the women . . . it was the women who made it all worthwhile. Here was a different creature altogether, the essence of femininity, the distilled perfume of womanhood. French women, European women . . . glorious creatures indeed, but an Oriental woman—and here Vallot practically shivered in delight—here they were untouched by God, pure unto themselves, and all the better for it, and damn the missionaries for the ruin they were about to bring.

"It's true," Vallot said, "you can't serve both man and God, and a woman touched by God is ruined for man.

"This you'll discover," he went on, "if you haven't already. And if you haven't, tonight should be a special occasion for you indeed."

Andre looked at him without understanding.

"I felt badly about how things went today; I think you were entitled to more than you received. The emperor also realizes that you were slighted by his cousin, so I made discreet inquiries about possible entertainments and diversions for you while you were still a guest here in the palace. I've been told these have been arranged, with the emperor's compliments."

Andre had such a vacant look on his face that Vallot wasn't sure he understood, and added in explanation, "There will be amusements for you in your room tonight. Unless you'd prefer not, of course."

At that Andre came alive. "No. I mean, yes, I would. Like them, I mean." He blushed, then laughed.

"I rather thought you would. Why, at your age, I . . . Well, let's not go into that."

Andre quickly finished his wine, and despite a show of casualness, Vallot could sense his impatience and eagerness. The youth was fairly squirming in his seat.

"I shan't keep you," Vallot said. "We can talk before my departure tomorrow." He stood and held out his hand. "Good evening, sir."

Andre thanked him again, and fairly flew back to his apartment. He hadn't been with a woman since Saigon, and the mere thought of what had been promised, perhaps concubines of the emperor himself, left him weak with desire and anticipation.

He was disappointed to find no one in his rooms, and he was beginning to wonder if this was some cruel joke, when there came a soft tapping at his door.

He tried to keep his voice steady, but it betrayed him, and at his somewhat choked words in Vietnamese, he heard giggling outside the door, and the tapping was repeated.

When he opened it on three exquisitely beautiful and delicate girls of perhaps seventeen, his face broke into such a grin that they all covered their faces to hide their mirth.

They came in quickly, and he closed the door behind them.

He didn't know exactly what was arranged or what to expect, but they immediately made it all clear. They closed about him so rapidly that he had no chance to say a word, and when their hands fluttered over him like the wings of bees, he had no desire to say anything.

No doubt they were being polite, he thought, but they seemed inordinately fascinated by his body, especially his hair and skin. Their girlish giggling gave way to professional ministrations, and within minutes they had removed all his clothing and led him to the bed.

At first he was content to let them tend him, and he gave himself over to the pleasure of their hands and mouths on him, gently nipping and tugging at his flesh, but the erotic sensation became so overpowering that he could not remain still, and writhing under their touch, he reached out for one, then another, and the third, pulling them onto him, groping under their silk garments, his hands and mouth seeking contact with their flesh, and soon they had removed all their clothes, and the four were on the bed naked, a tangle of bodies, searching, seeking, gratifying one another.

The women were expert, with him and each other, arranging him on the bed on his back so that all three of them were able to bring him simultaneous pleasure while he was able to smother himself with their flesh, his hands and mouth going from one to another, but each time he felt he could not hold off release another second, they sensed it and withdrew, keeping him on the edge of climax for so long that he was in agony.

His abandon was so great that he didn't notice when one slipped from the bed, or even when the second left, for he had mounted the third and she thrust up with such wildness and power that he was lost completely to her. Yet, again just as he was about to explode, she pulled away.

She jumped quickly from the bed, escaping his grasps, and when he turned around, he saw her slipping out the door. Standing only a few feet away, eyes lustrous with sex, her body heaving with desire, was a hideously made-up fat old woman.

Andre was so startled that he couldn't move, but when the woman came toward him, he pulled back instinctively on the bed, bringing a sheet around him, caught in a mixture of shock, embarrassment, anger, and frustration.

The woman's eyes appeared to burn through the coverings with a devouring, lurid look. Andre thought she was going to attack him, and he brought himself to a crouch.

"Who are you?" he demanded in French. Then, even angrier, he switched to Vietnamese. "Get out of here."

At that Lady Deng laughed. The carnality in her eyes was replaced by an amused, extraordinarily crafty look. She sat on the edge of the bed and patted the mattress.

"I have heard about the French, and I wondered how they made love, though perhaps not all are as vibrant as you." She tugged playfully at the sheet he held about himself. "Nor so handsome, nor equipped."

Andre had by now regained some composure, and though he had never heard of Lady Deng or of her power, he realized he was dealing with someone of great authority and influence, and that everything which had preceded had been carefully orchestrated.

"Who are you, and what do you want?"

"Your Vietnamese is very good," she said, "but it lacks the musical play; no doubt you will acquire it, but for the bedroom I think you should speak French—you are more comfortable and accomplished in that language, and it is a language perfectly suited for bedrooms."

Andre was amazed at how well she spoke French; her intonations were exactly right and she spoke it without the usual tentativeness or stiffness one uses in a foreign language. Her French was far better than the court translator's, and much superior to Ahn's.

"I'm here to help you," she said.

"I don't think I need any," he said.

Her eyes widened in a mock leer. "You were doing very well indeed."

Andre grinned, disarmed by her and enjoying her vulgarity, and realizing too that anger and indignation were somewhat out of place in his position. From Catherine he had learned the pleasure of frank sexuality with a woman, but this woman was even more direct, and because of her age and because he didn't find her threatening, he fell easily into a game with her.

"You should have joined us," he said.

She was amused. "That you could not have handled. Besides, I never share."

She moved onto the bed and pulled the sheet from him. Though repelled by her, he made no effort to draw away. In her grotesque way, he found her fascinating, so deviant and vile that there was a perverse appeal about her—the strange and powerful lure of degradation.

Her hand went to his reawakening penis and she stroked it back to full erection, and moving closer to him, she used both hands around his genitals, caressing and titillating him as no one had before. They sat facing one another, she fully clothed, and their eyes searched the other's, and he was hypnotized by her erotic, hungry look as her hands and fingers massaged and explored him.

She eased him back and he lay still as she tended him with all the expertise of her years and practice.

The sensation of her mouth and hands was too overpowering to resist and he closed his eyes, concentrating on touch, blocking her image from his mind.

Harder to block out were her sounds, but they were so guttural and eager that they too became exciting, and finally when she moved astride him, he was so consumed by the need for release that he was beyond caring, and he merely clamped his eyes shut.

She had planned this so carefully and with such desire that she was not about to let it end quickly, and employing every trick at her command and exercising her remarkable muscular control, she brought him again and again to the brink of climax, riding him and handling him like a racehorse. She savored him deeply, grinding down on him so hard that he couldn't move, yet from within herself pulling him in and up even more fully, then releasing him and easing out to the tip, then down so slowly that she shuddered under her own orgasms and could barely maintain her dominance.

Finally when he could not stand it any longer, she thrust wildly down on him and brought him to such a climax that he could not move from under her, and he lay still, eyes closed, breathing irregularly.

He didn't even open his eyes when she moved off him, though he should have, if only to see the smug and contemptuous look on her face.

So this was a Frenchman, she thought; certainly nothing remarkable, even allowing for his youth, and as she left, she was thinking of Ahn.

In the morning, Andre was mortified at what had happened, and disgusted with himself. The mere thought of the woman on him made him shudder, and he cursed his own weakness. He wanted to get away from the palace as soon as possible, and fortunately an opportunity presented itself.

Count Vallot summoned him to say good-bye, for he was leaving by ship that afternoon. He gently teased Andre about the previous night, though of course he knew nothing of Lady Deng, and Andre blushed dutifully.

"Since that prince dragged you here, it's only proper that he make arrangements for your return," said Vallot. "I've learned that he's leaving today also. The emperor has kept him a virtual prisoner, and he's not welcome back. I've seen to it that you'll go back with him in his party."

Andre thanked him, and for all he had done before, and the count bade him farewell and good luck.

In early afternoon Andre was escorted to the inner courtyard. The lord chamberlain and all the state ministers were present for the formal departure of Prince Ahn, and Andre was ignored in the crowd.

Ahn walked briskly from the palace, serene but formidable, and received the obeisances of the crowd; then he haughtily motioned Andre to him.

Almost instinctively Andre started; then he stopped and merely stared at Ahn. For a full minute the two faced one another, and no one in the crowd moved or made a noise.

Finally Ahn stepped forward and addressed Andre for all to hear. "It would give me pleasure if you would share my carriage on the journey."

And Andre replied in the same cold, loud tone, "Thank you for your gracious offer. I accept."

He followed Ahn to the carriage, waited for him to enter, then sat across from him as directed.

As the door closed, there was a commotion in the courtyard, and both Ahn and Andre turned to see Lady Deng coming imperially from the palace.

Ahn was so surprised at her approach that he didn't notice Andre gasp and grab onto the seat for support as she made her way directly to the carriage. Ahn turned to her but didn't lean down, so she had to speak up toward him; yet her voice and manner were surprisingly warm.

"I came to say good-bye, Ahn. I think we'll not meet again."

Ahn smiled. "I thought you'd come to ask for your dagger back."

She waved her hand and said airily, "They are easy to come by. As are boys to mount me; some I don't even have to pay."

Not once did she acknowledge Andre's presence, and now she held out her hand to Ahn and said with wistful tenderness, a hard, aging woman taking leave of the last thread of youth and love, "I'll only remember the happy times; they'll be a small jewel I'll carry near my heart."

He patted her hand, forgiving everything, for what is the point of bitter fruit? "Perhaps in another life you'll be a princess in the Palace of the Moon, and I shall visit you."

"Plan to stay awhile," she said with her old lust and vigor, and then she turned and went back into the palace.

The carriage moved off, out of the courtyard and gates of the walled citadel, and Ahn stared straight ahead, looking beyond Andre, to the ruin and death he knew were not far away, and it was a long time before he came from his trance and took note of Andre's presence.

"It went very well," he said at last.

"Yes," said Andre. "Exactly as you planned. Everyone seems to think you should be emperor."

The carriage was passing over the bridge on the Perfume River. Ahn watched the frenzy of activity, skiffs and sampans darting across the surface like water beetles, and on the banks, men labored like ants under crushing weights of goods: the only dignity he saw was of impervious water buffaloes cooling themselves in the water. "No," he mused, "I could do no more than Tu Duc; it's all lost."

"Can't you fight? Like the rebels in Saigon?"

The sun was blinding, but Ahn didn't pull the curtains. He wanted to see everything, and in the hateful and contemptuous looks of those who viewed the royal carriage, there was the answer to the other's question.

He shook his head in resignation. "The dynasty will have to fall and all the mandarins be purged, for if a foundation is flawed, it's only a matter of time before the towers topple; sometimes it's best to start over again rather than attempt to buttress and correct the flaws. But that's our problem. Your problem, the problem with your people, is that you'll try to lay your foundation in quicksand, and no matter how much you add on or shore up, the effort is doomed. Yet perhaps it's a good thing that your people have come. They can teach us what is bad about ourselves, and good, and someday we may become strong again."

"What will happen?" Andre asked.

Ahn smiled. "You must talk to Master Chien for answers to questions such as that. I think he'd tell you that it makes no difference what happens, for it has nothing to do with the harmony of the soul."

"I don't think I'm ready yet to believe that."

"Then you too shall continue to build on quicksand; hope is like any other appetite—insatiable."

They rode in silence for some time; then Andre asked with studied casualness, "Who was that woman?"

"Lady Deng? The woman who came to the carriage? I should have thought that Count Vallot would have told you. She rules the country, among other things."

Andre started noticeably.

"That's an exaggeration; of course, Tu Duc rules absolutely, but her influence is very great."

"Is she a good person?" The question was so simple and innocent that Ahn laughed. "I think there again you must ask Master Chien such things."

"You know her quite well," Andre said with hesitation. "She seemed sad to see you go."

"We've known each other for a long time," Ahn said simply. "But I'm not the person to ask concerning her; now that she's assumed the role of my executioner, I'm somewhat prejudiced."

Ahn pulled the stiletto from his robe and handed it to Andre. "If you're going to live in proximity to me, there are some things you should know for your own protection. My cousin and I have never been close, and now those near the throne are turning him against me. I have powerful enemies. The most powerful is Lady Deng."

"Why does she hate you?"

He shook his head slightly. "It happened a long time ago—before I was married, when I lived at court."

Andre tried to conceal his emotions. He couldn't tell Ahn about what had happened, and yet she might tell him. Had she done this for gain or blackmail? Obviously she'd used him, but for what purpose?

Disgust, shame, anger swirled within him. Was he always going to be just a pawn for others, a simple, expendable piece in a game he didn't understand—moved about and used, sacrificed by others more clever than he? Was Ahn using him unfairly too? Could Andre trust his word? And what would the prince do if he found out Andre had been so easily seduced and manipulated by his most powerful enemy? Should he be honest and admit it now?

He couldn't. And the thought of the previous night, that awful woman riding him, made him cringe inwardly.

Ahn rested back and closed his eyes. "I'll be very glad to see my family. The older I get, the more dependent I am upon them. And you must spend more time with us. We'd all like that; everyone is very fond of you."

Andre flinched at the words. How could he face them after this? And what if it ever became known?

He realized suddenly that he was thinking solely of Gia Minh's reaction.

She'd never forgive such a thing. Not that it made any difference, he knew, for she showed no interest in him whatsoever.

But after all, he thought, wasn't that understandable? He was weak and insignificant, a pawn. And the more he thought, about all that had happened, all the stupid mistakes and blunders he'd made—he hadn't even been able to kill Parnasse—his homelessness, where he was, his future, he fell deeper and deeper into despair.

And now he'd just betrayed Ahn, and perhaps ruined himself with his own weakness.

The sun beat down with furious intensity, and in the distance he saw the mountains and rain forest, an emerald world, translucent and mysterious, where he did not belong. For the first time since he was a child, he wanted to cry; he wanted to go home. He wanted to see his mother and great-grandmother.

From between sheathed lids, Ahn saw his torment, and he guessed accurately most of its cause. The boy is homesick, he thought; but more, he's caught in what he doesn't understand, and never will—the profound sadness of a good man in an indifferent world, the dilemma of life . . . hope. Hope, Ahn thought, that damnable thing, the source of all sorrow—the hope that something matters.

Chien had taught him that the Buddha was wrong: it wasn't desire at the root of suffering, but hope. Desire was petty, a yapping dog, but hope—there was the demon which flailed the soul, the inferno which fired the passions and consumed all. Hope—the ultimate deceit, the illusion, the sword upon which all men throw themselves, and the final cruelty, for without the illusion and deceit, without hope, man cannot live.

Ahn studied the youth with sympathy and curiosity. A Vietnamese would never feel so keenly the unhappy reality of life; he would merely accept it, and no matter what he felt, he would never show it. Ahn never would; besides, all things were foreordained and unavoidable, so what point was there in worrying or railing?

Yet he was touched by the display of emotion, the visible pain on Andre's face, and he realized suddenly that he liked this youth very much, and he almost involuntarily reached out to comfort him, as he would have one of his own children. And immediately he thought of Gia Minh.

His nostrils flared. For some reason this sad youth made him angry at his oldest daughter. Stupid girl, he thought.

Well . . . His eyes narrowed even further, but then they untensed and he merely closed them at the impossibility of what he had momentarily given thought to. He had no hope whatsoever in deceiving a woman; the very idea was ludicrous. He settled deeply in the carriage and attempted sleep.

Then his eyes opened slightly, and he was concentrating very hard. And yet, he thought, perhaps if . . .

11

AHN DELAYED HIS RETURN UNTIL an hour when he felt sure everyone would be asleep, but Xuan had left word to be awakened no matter what time he arrived, and was dressed and waiting when he entered the bedroom, creeping in so as not to disturb her, surprised to see her waiting expectantly, but very happy, and he kissed her tenderly.

"I was worried," she said. Then she looked up from where she'd nestled her head against his chest. "And I feel like such a stupid woman to say such a thing."

He brought her head back against his chest and smoothed over her hair with the palm of his hand; then he traced down the strands of gray with soft fingers and pulled her tightly against him. "There was no need to worry this time."

She raised her head, and their eyes met, and without a word she knew the danger was soon to come.

They sat on the edge of the bed and he told her what had happened at court, their success, but also of the serious deterioration of Tu Duc and of his enmity for Ahn.

Xuan sat with her hands in her lap, staring at the floor. "Will he send assassins?" she asked when Ahn had finished.

"Not now."

"But later?"

Ahn shrugged.

She sighed and put her hand into his. "There's nothing we can do?"

"No. Nothing."

She saw even more clearly than he the ruin ahead; it was all foreordained, a matter of waiting. Yet, as with him, there was no fear in her vision. His acceptance came from a Buddhistic stoicism, a belief in the completeness of the universe, the insignificance of self, while hers was a reflection of Catholic faith, a belief in greater good and future salvation.

"Perhaps it's well we had no son," she said, for she was thinking of the strife which lay ahead, and glad that she wouldn't have to sacrifice a son for that.

Ahn closed his eyes and said with crushing grief, betraying his sorrow and unhappiness for the first time in her memory, "Oh, I wish I could spare our children. I'd do anything for that."

She patted his hand. "They'll be fine," she said. "Women manage much better than men. We're much stronger."

"Yes, I know. But they must marry soon—that's the best protection. I want Gia Minh to marry the Frenchman."

"I think," said Xuan, "Gia Minh will marry whom she loves, Ahn."

"She may not have that luxury."

"Then she'll marry whom she chooses; don't let her think you're arranging it. She's too much like you to be made to do something she doesn't want."

"Don't you like him? Don't you think he'd make a good husband?"

"I think he's a very nice young man," said Xuan noncommittally.

So Ahn began his careful orchestration to bring Andre and Gia Minh together.

Andre resumed his visits, appearing every Sunday morning for mass, staying the day to talk and visit, then having dinner with the family in the evening. But the visits were as before, and Gia Minh paid no attention whatsoever.

After a month without a sign of progress, Ahn sought to enlist Father Bergere in his plan.

One evening, sitting together in the gazebo, mist from the rain forest winding toward them like smoke, Ahn asked him if he ever gave thought to returning to France.

The priest shook his head. "The France I left is gone, and it never meant much to me in any case. I was raised by nuns and grew up in the church. My life has been my religion. There's nothing in France for me." He sat back, a wistful smile of recollection on his face. "Oh, I miss some things." He turned to Ahn. "You know what I miss most? The smell of bread. You can't imagine how wonderful that is."

"But you like it here," Ahn asked.

"Yes."

"Do you think Andre can learn to live here? Could he give up his country as you have?"

"Do you mean, should he marry Gia Minh?"

Ahn laughed. "Am I so transparent?"

"You are." The priest was thoughtful for a moment, motionless as an Oriental sage, even having taken up the sitting position of one—legs slightly apart, hands stretched out on his knees. "There's too much passion in him," he said at last.

"Is passion such a bad thing, Master Bergere?"

"For Vietnam, yes. He's young and impetuous, and I don't think he's ready yet to give up his past life; I think France will call him back."

"Maybe France will come here; it already seems to be happening. Do you think he's a good man, fit for my daughter?"

The priest hesitated. "He's a good man, yes. Fit for your daughter? I'm not very good at that sort of thing: I think only they can decide that."

Ahn's face set firmly. "I want them to marry. A new culture is going to be formed here, and they must be a part of it." He patted the priest's hand. "I want your help, Master Bergere. You know the dangers ahead as well as I do."

Ahn confronted Chien about his thought the following day when they were walking through the gardens.

"What do you think about Gia Minh marrying the Frenchman?" Ahn asked.

Chien took the question as if he'd been asked about the heat. "No doubt the foreigner deserves it, but it would be a spiteful thing to do to him. You have wretched daughters, Lord Ahn."

"I know," he said. "I wonder where I failed."

"In having daughters in the first place. No doubt it's a punishment for some grievous transgression in a previous life."

"Well, they must marry; it's the best protection. The French will soon be upon us like a plague."

"The boy is eager enough."

"Is he?" Ahn looked at Chien for reassurance. "Are you sure?"

"When he looks at your daughter, he has the same transfixed look you used to carry on your face at court."

"That wasn't love."

Chien smiled. "I know. But it'll do. You lived in a poppy field and made your way druglike through the petals; all this poor boy has is a single thorny rose, yet it's the same narcotic which draws his tongue from his mouth. The rest will follow . . . or lead, as is the case with youths."

* * *

But still nothing happened. Andre came and went and seemed to make no impression on Gia Minh, and all contrivances to place them alone and together failed. She remained aloof and elusive, and he became less sure of himself, more awkward and tongue-tied, and Ahn watched with growing anger the frustration of his plans.

One evening after a particularly unsuccessful visit, Ahn threw himself down in a chair in the bedroom and watched, without seeing, his wife undress.

He gnashed his teeth as Xuan let down her hair.

"Idiot boy. Idiot girl."

Xuan smiled into the mirror, her brush working smoothly through the hair which reached to the middle of her back.

"Why won't she have anything to do with him? Why is she being so perverse?"

"She's only playing with him, Ahn. She's much taken with him."

"How can you tell? I don't think she likes him a bit."

"This is all just ritual. Women do play with men, you know."

"You never did."

"I had no opportunity. And is it terrible? I think it's a lovely game, sweet and innocent; it gives them exquisite life."

"I think it's shocking and scandalous. She's tormenting that boy, and he's too simple to fend for himself."

Xuan turned to him and raised her brush in warning. "Careful, dear husband, Nguyen prince, lord of Darlac—your dominion may be great, but it can't rule your daughter's heart. Have patience."

Ahn stood, his eyes eager, his mind filled with new plans. "Patience I have. It's time I don't have." He strode out the room to fetch Chien and Father Bergere. He had a new plan; he'd master his daughter yet.

The following Sunday, Andre didn't appear, nor the next, nor for a month, and no one except the younger sisters mentioned it.

"I don't know," said Xuan to them when they wanted to know why he no longer came. Ahn dismissed the matter contemptuously: "Maybe he got tired of the company of silly girls and old men." Chien and Father Bergere both professed ignorance of the cause, though it seemed to the girls that they were withholding some mysterious information.

Gia Minh continued to affect indifference, even when one evening at dinner Ahn lashed out at his youngest daughter and forbade her to mention Andre's name again.

A few days later the girls came upon Chien and Father Bergere engaged in heated argument, but the men stopped as soon as they saw the girls.

Obviously something wonderfully terrible had happened or was afoot, and the girls made it their sole enterprise to discover what it was.

An overheard conversation between the priest and Chien made it all clear. The three daughters managed to be passing near Father Bergere's rooms just after Chien had entered one evening.

"Don't bother," they heard the priest say by way of greeting. "The matter's closed. I won't discuss it."

They heard Chien settling in a chair, his silk robes rustling the hardwood floors. "It's a small thing," he said reasonably.

"The holy sacrament is not a small thing. I will not perform such a marriage. It's an abomination."

The girls edged closer to the door, tantalized, their eyes wide, their mouths slightly open.

They could hear Chien fumbling in his robes, and, exasperated, they listened to the inevitable munched apple. At last he said, "Ahn desires this marriage very much. It's the only way he can diffuse the power of the Trihns and ruin their alliance with the emperor."

They had never heard Father Bergere so angry; he stomped back and forth before the door so furiously that they pulled away, but his voice was so loud they had no trouble hearing.

"For this you want me to prostitute my religion? I don't care who desires such a sacrilege or for what reason, I won't even listen to it."

The only sound was the masticated apple. The girls could barely contain themselves; they wanted to rush in and throttle the story out of both men.

"Well," went on Chien at last, "if you won't perform the marriage, it'll be done in Hue, or Saigon if necessary."

"I don't care if it's done in Rome by the Holy Father himself, I won't do it. I will not marry that wretched boy to a group of concubines."

There was an audible gasp from the corridor, and the girls pressed closer to the door.

"The boy should have his ears boxed. I can't believe such depravity. And a Frenchman! I knew from the beginning he was no good, as soon as I heard about his life in Paris. I've never understood why Ahn has received him here."

Chien spoke so softly now that the girls almost tumbled over themselves trying to hear. They pictured him in his chair, eyes sleepy, his words and ideas coming from such a lofty region that by the time they reached the listener they seemed weary from the journey. "What is this preoccupation Westerners have with sex, as though this rubbing of bodies, this movement of organ and tissue has some meaning or significance? So the youth will spend his seed in varied fields—what does it matter?"

"It matters a great deal," said Father Bergere firmly, though not prissily. "I'm not about to sit here and discuss sex, ethics, and morals with you. I'm merely telling you that I won't marry Andre to that Trihn girl. I'm aware that marriages are performed for gain and property, but I myself won't perform one. I will not conduct a ceremony between a fallen French Catholic and a pagan Vietnamese one, a ceremony in which the only thing considered holy would be profit and property, a ceremony in which part of the dowry would be a harem, compensation for the age and ugliness of the bride."

"What if the bishop directed you to perform the marriage?"

"That would not happen."

"But if—"

Father Bergere spoke with finality. "I will not speculate on such a thing. Good night, Master Chien."

The girls scurried off, and as soon as they reached Ke's room, they burst into excited babble.

So that's why Andre had ceased his visits—he was to marry Ngue Hua Trihn, the unspeakably old, ugly, fat daughter of Phram Trihn, after Ahn the most wealthy and powerful man in the province, a close ally of the emperor. Andre had much to gain from such a marriage obviously—wealth and property, and a harem besides. And of course Phram Trihn could marry off his daughter only by promising such things. It was all loathsomely believable. How disgusting, they thought. But why would their father promote such a marriage? The reason had to be political; their father planned that the marriage would bring discredit and ruin to Trihn. As well it should, they reasoned.

It was insidious, they thought, disgusting, and they analyzed every aspect of it for hours, and they wondered about the rumors of Paris. What had Andre done? Of course this was why their father forbade the mention of his name.

Well, they'd known all along, of course, they told one another; it was there for anyone to see, from the first moment when Andre had kissed their mother's hand. They hadn't been taken in by him; what could anyone expect from someone so handsome, and a fugitive besides. Indeed, a fugitive from what? And all this time he'd visited with his shy, polite manners—all a deception, all merely a pretense to . . . They shivered with the thrill of what their imaginations conjured, and they went to bed fairly quivering with excitement, so close had they come to pillage and plunder and rape.

Except Gia Minh, who did not go to bed, but stole out of the house, saddled a horse, and rode directly to Andre's. Though she'd never been to his property, she of course knew where it was, and by the time she neared his land, she was more angry than she'd been in her life.

She rode furiously, with no thought as to what she'd say or do once she confronted him, only compelled by anger and outrage. Not for a moment did she doubt what she'd heard. Men were terrible—that she knew—capable of awful crimes and deceptions, but he'd deceived *her*. She had thought he liked her, had thought his puppy behavior real. Worst of all, and the thought of this made her even more furious, she'd liked him; he was the only man she could possibly—and she hit the horse a terrific whack—love.

She didn't see the walled jungle as she rode through the night, or the moon above, nor did she hear anything except the thundering hooves of the horse, and when she reached the open fields of his land, she saw no peace or tranquillity, no Eden of darkly silhouetted palms whose broad leaves sent rippling shadows across the earth.

She rode up the path to his hut and found him standing in front, squinting to see who had rent the night. He looked concerned and anxious, and when he saw it was she, he ran to the horse to steady it, and only then, his hand on her horse, his eyes apprehensive, his body entirely naked, did she realize she had no idea what she was doing here.

"Are you all right?" he asked. "Is something wrong? Is there trouble? Your family . . . is there—?"

"Get your hands off my horse," she ordered. "Of course nothing's wrong."

He backed off slightly, confused, and then too, he remembered his nakedness. "I . . . ah . . . excuse me," he said, and ran into the hut, returning in less than a moment, barefoot and shirtless, drawing the strings of his trousers.

"Are you alone?" she demanded.

"Alone?" He looked about, puzzled. "Of course. Who else would be here?"

"Who knows?" she said haughtily. "One of the concubines, or a troop of them. How dare you?"

He was completely bewildered. For a moment he simply

stared at her; then he went to her, stroked the horse soothingly, and said with concern, "Lady Minh, are you all right?"

She eyed him evilly; then suddenly she realized that she'd been tricked. There was no Trihn woman and no concubines—he was exactly as he appeared, simple and guileless, and she'd been deceived. That was obvious in the anxious eyes which looked up at her, and now she was even madder than before.

She slapped her hand down where he held the horse's bridle. "Outrageous." Then she hit him on the head, and he covered himself to ward off the blows.

"How dare you?" she yelled at him, her hand raining down on him until he grabbed her wrist. She pulled away, but he held tightly and finally forced her from the horse. She struggled, but his grip was so strong that her efforts were futile.

"Lady Minh, what's wrong with you? What are you talking about?"

"As if you don't know."

"I don't. I don't know why you're here."

She ceased struggling to study him. His face was intent on her, and there was no doubt in her mind that he was sincere. She had been deceived by those two old men, made a perfect fool of, and she was furious. "No, I suppose you don't know," she said scornfully. "You're too simple to understand anything."

He let loose of her hand and tried not to show the wound she'd just inflicted. He bowed slightly and turned back to his hut. "Forgive me, I must get up early; perhaps some other time I'll be able to let you insult me. I hope your family is not worried about your whereabouts. Good night, my lady."

With that he went up the stairs and disappeared inside, closing the screen gently but firmly on her.

She stood a moment staring after him; then she went up the stairs and slid open the screen.

He stood over his pallet and was about to shuck his trousers when the moonlight flooded the room and he turned to see her in the entrance.

"I was very rude," she said. "Forgive me."

"Of course."

"I was tricked."

He straightened but made no movement toward her. "I'm sorry. That's always painful. I know; I've been tricked often."

She stood stiffly in the entry, and to avoid his gaze, she looked about the single-room hut. In one corner was his pallet; the only other furniture was a small table and two chairs he'd made himself. There were a fireplace and hearth, a kettle and pans, some cooking utensils, stacked wood, and a disheveled corner which seemed to be his work area for carpentry; there was nothing else.

"Why haven't you come to visit us?" she asked without looking at him.

"I was told my presence was an aggravation to you."

"Who said this?"

When he said nothing and she knew he'd never tell her, she laughed, not bitterly, but in appreciation. "They did a good job; I can't believe they tricked me like that. My own father, too." Then she said softly, "No, Andre, your presence doesn't aggravate me."

He stood stock-still, though when he heard her voice his name, he shivered. It was the first time she'd said it.

"Why were you so rude to me?" he asked.

"I . . . I wasn't rude."

"You were never polite. You were so cold. You made me feel like I . . . like I was stupid and . . ."

She lowered her head. "It's because I . . . I didn't know how to act. I didn't want you to think . . . I mean, I wanted you to . . ." She looked up finally and met his eyes. "I was afraid."

"You?" He laughed. "I was afraid of you. I thought you didn't like me, that you couldn't stand me. I did everything I could, talked to you . . . tried to, anyway. You're the only reason I used to visit, but you were never even nice."

"I didn't know how to be," she said simply. "I was too shy."

She was framed in the entrance; moonlight streamed over her body like cascading water, and he was mesmerized. Far behind her he could see the outline of jungle, and from it he could hear the restless night murmurs. Everything seemed to swell suddenly, as though the world was on the edge of bursting open, and finally he moved, crossed directly to her. "I love you," he said. "I loved you from the moment I saw you."

She looked up at him, her face shining like a beautiful jade goddess's, and he was overcome with joy and desire. He grabbed her, not tenderly, and kissed her, covering her mouth with his, so hungrily that he hurt her, frightened her, and she pulled away.

So heated was he that he had to restrain himself from grabbing her back to him. "I'm sorry," he said, stepping away.

She watched his struggle, and lost her fear of him. She'd never witnessed passion before, had no inkling what a man could feel, and finding suddenly that this man was so powerfully moved by her, she was profoundly touched, and realized that it was passion which had brought her here, and passion in herself which she'd begun to feel in his bruising lips and crushing arms.

Now the moonlight reflected off his body, shimmering gold in the quiet hut, and she could see beads of perspiration, like morning dew, on his chest and shoulders, and though he had lowered his head in shame, when he stole a glance at her, there was burning intensity in his eyes, so powerful and desirous that she took a step toward him, her hand reaching out tentatively to his chest.

Her fingers traced lightly from his shoulder to his abdomen, the faintest touch, as though testing the reality of flesh, and in her eyes he saw that she had never touched a man before, or been kissed, and he stood completely still as she came to him and raised her face to his, lifting up on tiptoes to reach his mouth with her lips. Then he lowered his face and kissed her softly, so lightly and tenderly that this time she became demanding, and sought him, arms going around him, pulling him tight, her mouth seeking and searching his.

When his hands went to her, she didn't resist. He quickly unbuttoned her ao dai and slipped it from her shoulders, letting it drop to the ground. She wore nothing underneath, and she shivered when his hands smoothed over her body. His lips dropped from her mouth to her breasts, kissing and teasing the nipples until they rose in hard peaks, and she began to move gently against him when his hands probed the soft skin of her thighs, moved across her stomach and into the curling hair, his fingers dipping lower, touching sensuously.

His mouth moved back to hers, his tongue forcing it open, searching at the same moment his finger entered her, and she thrust her mouth and hips against him simultaneously, wanting more, and as she clung to him, ready, eager, he suddenly broke away.

"No," he said, and turned. "Not like this."

She reached down and pulled on her ao dai; then she went to him and put her arms around his waist and kissed his back.

"Oh, God," he said. "I want you so badly." He brought her hands from his waist to his groin, rubbing him so she could feel him, and she was amazed at the size and hardness, and understood she was not ready, and this was not the time.

He turned to her, took her hands in his, and asked solemnly, "Can you marry me?"

"Can?" she repeated curiously.

"Is it allowed? Will they let you marry me?"

She smiled. "Allow? They?"

"All right, then, will you marry me?"

There it was, she thought. Of course she would marry him; there could be no one else, she'd known that all along. And yet . . . and yet could she really—this man she knew nothing about, this strange man from another land? And where would they live, and how, and their children . . . ?

"Is there anyone else, in your country?" she asked.

"No," he whispered. "There never was anyone like you."

"Then I will marry you," she said.

"But . . ." He was thinking about the obstacles. Where indeed would they live—this hut? And how? And what would happen in this country, and how could she, a princess, live with him, and what would her father say, and the future—it seemed so dark and alien and unknown.

"I know," she said, and put her finger to his lips, for she knew what he was thinking, but after all, what did it matter where they lived, or how? She didn't care about such things, any more than her mother, Xuan, had, and the future she saw was not dark and terrifying, but of cosmic brightness, for she had found what she had not been sure she'd ever find, found what she had not known truly existed—love, someone to love, someone to love her.

"We must have plans," he said. "Should I ask your father tomorrow?"

"No," she said, "that won't be necessary." She had scores to settle. "I'll arrange everything."

Andre saw that he was a pawn again, caught in a struggle beyond him, a match this time between Gia Minh and her father and the others, but this time, he thought, how wonderful it was to be a pawn.

He kissed her happily. "Just tell me what to do."

"Everything will be fine," she said, and she loved the look on his face—it wasn't a puppy look at all, she realized—strong and incredibly sensual, yet so open and unassuming, expressive, a look totally foreign, one which could never be Vietnamese. She pulled him down by the neck so she could cover his face with kisses, and his arms went around her, pulling her close, and his mouth found hers. His tongue worked into her mouth and his hands pulled her hips to him and he forced his groin against her, grinding slowly, and she moved excitedly against the swelling.

His fingers began to unbutton her gown, and he whispered into her ear, "Stay with me tonight."

She pulled away. His eyes were so sexual, so hungry; she considered it seriously, wanting to give herself to him, wanting his body, wanting him in her, but no, she decided—she would wait, the anticipation would make it even more wonderful.

She broke from his grasp, and when he moved to her, she pushed him away gently. "You're dangerous," she said. "The stories of Paris must be true."

He stopped cold. "What stories?"

She laughed softly. "I don't know. I never want to know them. I don't care about anything that happened before."

She kissed him quickly and ran out. "I'll send word to you."

He watched her ride out of sight, merge with the darkness, swallowed by the jungle, gone so rapidly and completely that for a moment he doubted she'd been with him. Could this really have happened, he wondered, his unhappy life transformed that fast, more than what he dreamed fulfilled in mere moments?

It was so. He knew that in the joy he felt, in the beat of his heart and the throbbing in his loins. He wanted to shout his happiness, run, leap, fight, vent all the vibrancy within, and suddenly he raised his head and yelled to the sky, shouted to the moon—not words, just the inexpressible joy of his being.

Gia Minh said nothing upon her return, and appeared as indifferent as before to the charade performed for her benefit. More hints, and finally blatant references were made to the upcoming marriage of Andre to the Trihn woman, and still she failed to respond, though her sisters were riled to a state approaching apoplexy. Only Xuan seemed untouched by it all and never mentioned the matter, nor let anyone discuss it with her.

Finally, one evening at dinner, after numerous innuendos and intimations about Andre designed to get a rise out of her, Gia Minh casually asked her mother if she could have her wedding dress.

"It was my mother's," said Xuan. "Our wedding was rather hasty; there was no time to make an elaborate gown."

Gia Minh met her mother's inquisitive eyes, and conveyed everything in the most perceptible of smiles. "That will suit us perfectly; it'll be a most appropriate dress."

"Who is 'us'?" demanded Ke.

"What do *you* need a wedding gown for?" sniffed Su. "You'll have sooner need for burial robes."

Ahn, Chien, and Father Bergere exchanged quick glances.

Ahn, never good at the games women play, leaned forward and asked impatiently, "What are you talking about?"

Gia Minh dabbed her lips with a napkin. "I've decided to become a concubine. Since Andre's already getting such a dowry in the Trihn marriage, this won't cost you a thing, Father. Everyone will be happy: you'll be rid of me, my sisters can marry whatever oxen ask them, Andre will have yet another woman, and I'll be near the man I love."

The ensuing uproar was complete. Gia Minh smiled at her mother, and the two women continued to eat placidly, ignoring the bedlam at the table.

Finally Ahn clapped his hands so loudly that he gained silence from the others, but before he could say anything, Gia Minh turned on the three men.

"You dreadful frauds." She pointed her finger at Chien and Father Bergere. "Shameful, meddlesome old men. Andre and I decided two weeks ago to get married."

Ke shrieked in outrage and Su fairly swooned at the table.

"You silly girls," said Gia Minh. "There's to be no marriage with the Trihn woman; that was all a trick. And those stories about Andre were just lies. And you, Father—how could you plan such a hoax?"

She stood up. "I may not invite any of you to the wedding." With that she left the room.

There was complete silence as everyone watched her leave; then everyone burst out at once, but Ahn jumped up, leaving them all to stare after him as he ran out of the room.

They thought he was chasing after his daughter, but instead he went to the stable, saddled a horse, and rode directly to Andre's.

It was still light by the time he reached the hut. Andre had come outside at the sound of the approaching horse, hopeful that it was Gia Minh.

When he saw it was Ahn, who did not look pleased, he said nervously, "Good evening, Excellency."

Ahn made no pretense of greeting or politeness. "Are you going to marry my daughter?"

Andre stammered a moment, then braced himself, his eyes steady on Ahn. "Yes, sir, I am."

"It's the custom in this country to ask permission of the bride's father. Don't you think it would have been courteous to come to me?"

"Yes, sir, but . . ." He was going to place the blame on Gia Minh; then he stopped, and his voice took on an edge of belligerence. "I hope you have no objection."

"And if I did?"

"Then I'd be very unhappy, because you've been kind and

generous to me, and I'd never want to displease you, but I love your daughter, and I will marry her."

The two men locked eyes for a long moment; then Ahn broke into laughter and slapped Andre around the shoulders. "That damn girl. Of course I have no objection; I'm delighted. I thought it would never happen. I've been prepared to give you half the province to take her off my hands."

He ran to the horse, took a bottle of rice wine from a saddlebag, pulled the cork, and raised the bottle high. "To you, and long life, and a hundred children, and happiness and long life to each of them." Then he took a deep drink.

Andre was astonished, as much by Ahn's exuberance as anything else. The prince, lord of Darlac, suddenly seemed like an untamed, rebellious boy eager to romp, not the cousin of the emperor, a father-in-law to be feared.

Andre accepted the bottle but was too intimidated to relax, and after drinking, he handed it back stiffly.

Ahn studied him curiously, then said, somewhat in surprise, "You'll be my son. My heir." He stepped closer to the youth, scrutinizing his face as though searching for something; then, just as his daughter had, he reached out a finger to touch his face. Andre stood perfectly still, and when Ahn stepped back, Andre smiled, but Ahn turned his gaze away, across the fields to the horizon and growing darkness.

The jungle seemed to merge with the night, earth and sky becoming one, and Ahn took a deep breath, closing his eyes and lifting his head to listen to the harmony of the night, broken only by the discordant, shrieking cries of the cockatoo.

Andre waited respectfully while Ahn drank in the night. Finally Ahn opened his eyes, shifting his gaze from the jungle to the youth, a quizzical, slightly disturbed look crossing his features.

"You're going to have to be strong," he said at last. Then he looked again to the jungle, seemingly drawn to it, pulled by some mysterious force, and he said, "Come, I'm going to teach you about the jungle. The only ones who'll survive here are those who'll master the jungle and the night."

Together they rode for an hour, to where Andre had never been, to the edge of a dense wall of bamboo trees, where they dismounted and Ahn set loose the horse.

Ahn stripped off his robe and made Andre strip; then the two men entered the thick underbrush, each carrying a saddlebag.

As soon as they stepped through the wall, they were in a different world, absolutely dark and at first terrifying, and suddenly Ahn was gone, slipping quickly and easily through the bramble.

Andre followed blindly, crashing through the growth, his flesh stung and cut, and he could only barely keep up. Finally, just as he thought he could go no farther, they came to a small clearing and Ahn dropped his saddlebag, then sat down.

Andre collapsed beside him and drank greedily from one of the bottles in his saddlebag. He was breathing heavily, and as he wiped the sweat from his body, he saw that he was bleeding from a hundred cuts, and already bugs were alighting on him.

He watched Ahn pull leaves from a bush and rub them over his body, and when he did the same, not only was there soothing relief from the cuts, the insects disappeared.

That was the first thing he learned, but in the next weeks he learned a thousand other things—what to eat and what to avoid, how to move and stalk, where danger lay and what to listen for; he learned to use the jungle, make it work for him, rather than to work against it, and at the end of two weeks he felt comfortable: the jungle was not terrifying; he liked it.

And he had found the man who would be his father, and at long last he became a son. They shared and helped each other, bared themselves and told one another by words and otherwise all there was in each. They grew angry and raised their fists, and laughed, and in the end formed a deep and strong love for each other.

Ahn told Andre about his country, about the ten thousand things of which Chien always spoke—infinity; and at night, listening to the swarming life about them, the calls and cries of a thousand creatures, they talked of their fears and hopes, their dreams and disappointments.

One night, when they had penetrated to the innermost jungle, to where there was no brush and the treetops formed a continuous roof where no ray of sunlight reached, where only pale mushrooms, lichens, and liverworts survived, they revealed their final secrets. Dangling down from the trees like ships' rigging were aerial roots and vines, a thick web-world where one could envision giant spiders, and it seemed to Andre as though they had reached the inner sanctum of the world, and only here was the jungle silent.

In this quiet Andre spoke of Catherine and he told Ahn of that night in the palace with Lady Deng, and he told Ahn that he was afraid he was not strong enough, or smart enough, or good enough to survive.

"I'm afraid something will happen to you," Andre said.

"Something is going to happen to me, and everything will fall to you. And you will be strong enough. You must be."

Andre moved so close to him that their faces almost touched, and his eyes went deeper into Ahn's soul than anyone had ever penetrated. "That's what you're afraid of, isn't it? That I'm not strong enough, that it's hopeless, that everything's lost."

Ahn finally lowered his gaze. "Yes," he whispered.

Andre shut his eyes at the pain, but then he opened them immediately and glanced up. He could feel the spiders lurking above, watching, waiting.

Suddenly the eerie web began to move; it came to macabre life, swaying and twisting under the force of a gathering storm, and it seemed as if snakes were writhing in the sky.

Andre stood and turned his back on the scene. "I'll make my children strong enough," he said simply.

Then he went to find shelter, and Ahn followed him.

When they returned, their manner was such that no one said a word to them about their absence. Even Gia Minh held her tongue.

Ahn announced that the marriage would be performed immediately, and for once did not bow to his wife's wishes. Xuan wanted a grand ceremony, with all the pomp her own had lacked, but Ahn said there was no time, for once word got out, the emperor would do everything he could to stop it.

"Marriages are such hasty affairs in this family," Xuan said sadly, but Ahn explained that Tu Duc would realize he'd been tricked and see a dangerous threat in it. "It's the first alliance between French and Vietnamese, and he'll seek to prevent it."

Such was the case. Tu Duc flew into a rage when his spies brought word of the imminent marriage of Prince Ahn's daughter to the young Frenchman in Ban Me Thuot. He saw immediately the conspiracy which had deceived everyone, and his wrath was such that he finally gave in to those who wanted Ahn's death.

Lady Deng brought the news to the lord chamberlain. "The emperor agrees that it's time to end the difficulties in Ban Me Thuot."

Lord Chamberlain Phan Huy Du, who'd so cleverly undermined his predecessor, Huynh Bo Linh, now with Lady Deng had Tu Duc's complete confidence. Du was particularly deceptive in manner and appearance; he was very fat and amiable, never haughty, and he gave the impression of being the most pliant and trusting of men, a ruse which hid an extraordinarily suspicious and cruel nature.

"Had His Majesty listened to us before, we wouldn't have this problem now. This marriage could be a disaster for us."

Lady Deng was not so troubled. She settled her stout body on a settee across from Du; they looked like Halloween pumpkins, one grinning, the other leering. "A minor inconvenience," she said. "The French boy will pose no threat."

"He seems not so harmless; he deceived all of us."

"That was Ahn's doing. Believe me, the boy can be managed." Her eyes arched carnally.

Du laughed admiringly. "Him too? You are remarkable, my dear."

"I am; he was not."

"Your demands make for a harsh judgment. Tell me, my dear, is it true what they say about foreigners?"

"It's true that this one was built very well; one could hardly ask for finer equipment. But the craft . . . that was lacking."

Du inclined his head in mock sympathy. "What a disappointment for you. For your sensitivities, I know a small, exquisitively carved piece of ivory is preferable to the whole tusk."

"Indeed," she said demurely. "Though best of all would be the exquisitively carved tusk." Du laughed appreciatively.

"So it's too late to prevent the marriage?" He brought his pudgy fingers together and sat in immobile concentration. "But that may be to our advantage. In fact, I think we can turn this to our purpose."

When she heard his plan, Lady Deng was impressed, and bowed to acknowledge the fact. "You're remarkable, my dear. If you could make love like you scheme, we'd all be at your mercy."

"To each according to his tastes; that's what makes us so formidable together. Now, should you or I inform His Majesty of his plans?"

"Better you. I must make myself ready for the journey."

To Ahn's great surprise, a messenger came from Hue informing him that the emperor would arrive within the week; His Imperial Majesty had heard that Prince Ahn's daughter wished to be married. The emperor had graciously decided to journey to Ban Me Thuot to personally hear the request, rather than have it submitted by petition to him in Hue, as is the custom for the marriage of any member of the royal family.

Ahn saw through the scheme immediately.

As soon as he received word, he called his family together and said the wedding had to be performed as soon as possible. Tu Duc's visit was merely a pretext for stopping it.

Xuan was unhappy, for she wanted pageantry, and Gia Minh too had hoped for a special ceremony, but they saw that Ahn was right, and so it was decided that the wedding would be on the third day.

Ceremony meant nothing to Andre, and he was delighted that the wedding was to come so quickly. For him the hardest part was the prenuptial talk and confession before Father Bergere; he dreaded having to confront the priest with his past sins.

On the day before the wedding, at the appointed hour, Andre presented himself in the chapel. This was his first visit to the house in months, and he was ill-at-ease; he had not spoken to Gia Minh since the night she'd come to his hut, nor had he seen Ahn—all information about the wedding had been conveyed by a scribe.

Andre entered the chapel hesitantly. Father Bergere, kneeling at the altar, rose to greet him, and though the priest spoke in a normal voice, Andre could not help but whisper.

"We have no secrets here from our Lord; nor will the sound of our voices offend his ears," said Father Bergere. He shook Andre's hand warmly. "I haven't congratulated you; I'm very happy for you both." Then he briefly went over the ceremony. Andre said that he had no rings, but the priest said that would be no problem, and as for the best man, Father Bergere saw no difficulty in having Chien serve.

"Now," said the priest, "let me hear your confession."

Andre flushed deep red, but Father Bergere was all business; he forced Andre to his knees at the altar.

"Do you believe in the divinity of our Savior?"

"Yes, Father."

"Do you believe in the Holy Mother Church?"

"I do, Father."

"Do you believe in the forgiveness of sin and the resurrection of the body?"

"Yes, Father."

"Would you briefly catalog your mortal sins and other transgressions for which you humbly ask forgiveness of God."

Andre began an involved litany which covered nearly all the weaknesses of the heart and flesh, but having heard so many times such faults, Father Bergere knelt stoically, eyes closed, nodding rotely. Even the revelation about Lady Deng brought only the faintest flicker to his eyebrows. When Andre at last ran down, the priest granted him absolution and gave him a rather light penance to say at the altar.

"Thank you, Father," said Andre as he left.

The priest nodded. "Be a good husband and a good father, that's what matters most."

"I'll try, Father."

Father Bergere smiled kindly. "Someone such as you, my son, must do better than that. You're like Candide, but don't count on a happy ending; here is no El Dorado, and God is not a philosopher."

Not understanding a bit, Andre bowed respectfully and left.

As though he'd been waiting for him, Chien met him in the corridor. He took Andre's chin in his huge hand and peered intently into his eyes. "Have you been saved? You don't look any different."

Andre grinned. "Perhaps I've been saved all this time you've known me."

"I never doubted it a minute," said Chien.

"No, I don't think you have," Andre replied. "I have a great deal to thank you for. I know my marriage owes a lot to you. I'm very happy," he added needlessly, his face bursting with pleasure. "Will you come visit us often? I want you to be my teacher, and our children's teacher."

"Children already? You Westerners are always in such a hurry." He grew expansive, opening his hands. "I must teach you about the blade of grass."

"I thought that was from the teaching of Lao-tzu, not Confucius."

"Ah, you've been studying. Well, there was no Lao-tzu; he was a mythical figure, a hermit in one of the Confucius stories. People hostile to Confucius used to tell stories about his encounters with hermits and how they made fun of him; from these stories came a collection of wise sayings; these eventually were attributed to a Lao-tzu and called the Tao Te Ching. The sayings, though abstract, are nevertheless enlightening."

"And there really was a Confucius?"

"Oh, yes. His life and teachings are better documented than those of your Christ, though he lived five hundred years earlier. Unsurprisingly, they both said pretty much the same things. Wisdom is not very diverse."

"Did he have any good advice for a man about to be married?"

Chien broke into a great smile. "Everyone has that kind of advice, but I'll distill it all for you."

He assumed the standing position of a sage, right hand raised.

"We are obligated to do what is right and moral; it is our duty, and what is right and moral is knowable. The order and harmony of the world depend on each person performing his duty; there is the duty of common humanity to his fellowman; the duty of a man to help his friends; the marital duty; the filial duty to parents; the duty of loyalty to a lord. The precedence of duty is upward."

Andre listened politely, though it sounded vague, something one might expect to hear from an old Chinese or read in a fortune cookie.

But then Chien reached out a finger and gently tapped Andre on the forehead. Then he tapped him on the chest over his heart. Finally he tapped him on the crotch. "Remember the order and their respective nearness to the sky. Or remember that the pull of gravity is stronger nearer the ground, and reflect then on what it is which will keep you earthbound."

He was about to turn away when his face blanked in his mock-sage way and he brought his hands together. "But young men are not meant to soar; they are better equipped to plow the fields. How else shall the earth be tilled and richness renewed?"

Andre smiled as the older man walked off, his once-powerful and firm step giving way slightly to the hint of a waddling shuffle.

In their bedroom that night, Ahn and Xuan were quiet and removed, each thinking of their own wedding and the years in between. Every now and then one would steal a glance to the other, but the image conjured up such complex thoughts, the glance would be hastily diverted.

Xuan saw suddenly that they were more than mirrors for one another; they were far more revealing than one-dimensional glass which reflected mere deeds and actions, each's effect on the other. In his flesh before her there was both memory and oracle, what had passed before, and what was to come, and not just his past and future, but her own.

She brushed her hair before the mirror and watched him sitting in a chair, staring absently at the wall.

"Have you talked with the boy?"

Ahn turned to her, but it took a moment for her words to register. "Talked about what?"

"He has no father. Perhaps there are things he needs to know."

"That won't be necessary," he said, and returned his gaze to the wall, then brought it back to his wife. "Have you talked with Gia Minh?"

Xuan pulled the brush through her hair. "That won't be necessary."

Ahn's eyes shot open. "What do you mean?"

She laughed at his expression. "Some things are best left unsaid. No one told me a thing, and everything was fine. He looks like a gentle boy."

Ahn did not like the conversation; indeed, the thought of his daughter's sexuality was profoundly disturbing to him, and he ended the contemplation of it by going out into the garden.

The following morning was all preparation for the wedding, and that afternoon Andre appeared promptly as instructed, though his Western dress was found inappropriate and Ahn had him quickly fitted in one of his own robes.

Father Bergere's ceremony was as brief and simple as the one he'd performed for Ahn and Xuan many years ago.

In Xuan's wedding gown, unadorned and somewhat faded, Gia Minh looked so much like her mother that Ahn was moved to a most unusual public act: he took Xuan's hand in his own; then he leaned over to kiss her. But she was crying silently; tears flowed from her eyes, and he pulled her closer so that her head rested on his shoulder.

It was a subdued ceremony, for everyone experienced ambiguous feelings about the striking couple at the altar—joy and happiness, to be sure, yet an undercurrent of disquiet and foreboding flowed throughout the chapel. Only at the end, after the couple kissed and Father Bergere gave his blessing, was there any relief from somberness.

There was complete silence at the end of the ceremony; then Chien clapped, and remembering Tu Duc's behavior at their own wedding, Ahn and Xuan both laughed; then they all converged happily on the couple, bestowing congratulations and best wishes.

After a long reception and formal dinner, it was not until late evening before Andre and Gia Minh were able to leave. Though Ahn had offered them a special wing of the palace, or to send them wherever they wished, Andre declined, saying they would spend their wedding night in the hut.

Gia Minh was pleased, for the hut was where she wanted her marriage consummated, nowhere else, and she snuggled next to Andre as the carriage drove them through the warm, starlit night.

They stood outside for several minutes watching the coach disappear; then Andre pulled her to him and kissed her. She responded eagerly.

They lingered outside for only a few minutes because their desire for one another was so great.

Andre had lectured himself over and over to be gentle and considerate, to go slowly, but his passion was beyond his control. Yet she didn't want tenderness and restraint, for every night since she'd come to him she'd dreamed of this.

Her own desire and erotic fantasies had surprised her; she didn't know a woman could, or should, feel this way. She wanted to be in bed with this man, wanted his body, wanted him to possess her.

But who was there to talk with about desire? Not her mother, not her silly sisters, certainly not her father. Yet it was right what she felt, she knew it. Something this powerful and loving had to be right and good.

What could be improper between a man and woman who felt so much, so strongly for one another?

Now, finally with him, she didn't feel shy, and she gave over to what she felt, and as his hands went to her, his lips finding hers, she was ready, and he was amazed at the intensity of her response.

All his sexual experience before this had been part of the darker, furtive side of sex, the exquisite pleasure of the forbidden, and therefore he hadn't expected that the sexual response of a wife could equal that of a mistress or a whore. He hadn't foreseen that Gia Minh could be as passionate as the women he'd paid for.

At first the surprise shocked his sensibilities. Was it proper that a wife, a good woman, should hunger for his body? That her moans and cries should be so eager? But then, almost immediately, he realized how right it was, and how fortunate he was, that what passed between them was the pleasure and desire and fulfillment that had been his mother's and father's, the passion his great-grandmother had spoken of with reverence.

They made love with frenzied intensity. He entered her roughly and the pain made her cry out, but she immediately pulled him deeper, her fingers digging into him, at the same time thrusting up wildly until pleasure obliterated pain, and her cries of satisfaction brought him to the most powerful explosion he'd ever experienced, and he continued thrusting into her long after his release, remaining hard, rolling over and lifting her up and down on him until her movements came on their own, and she drove down on him with powerful, quick, deep strokes beyond her control, and continued after he had arched up in a powerful thrust and cried out. When she finally slowed her movements, she was out of breath and slipped off him in exhaustion, nestling in his arms, hearing her own quick breathing, and listening to his rapid heartbeat.

They hardly slept that night; within an hour her hand explored his body. His hardness and strength fascinated and aroused her; she squeezed him with both hands, so hard that he moaned, then thrust his hips up into her grasp, and she moved down on the bed to see, and as he worked up and down, she bent forward and took him in her mouth, squeezing the base with her hands. She loved the power she felt over him, and when he came in her mouth, she liked the taste of him, and then he raised up and kissed her on the mouth, tasting himself, and he forced her back and he ministered to her, and brought her to greater heights of pleasure.

And then they talked, and she told him all that she felt and that she loved him and his body and wanted no secrets between them, and he said yes to her, to his life, to whatever might happen in the future, and he thought: Thank you, God.

In the morning, lying naked and entwined, they were awakened by the squawking outrage of women, and they heard Chien barking at them, sending them scattering like chickens in the yard.

Chien clambered up the stairs, and before Andre and Gia Minh could cover themselves, he barged into the hut.

Gia Minh scrambled to pull a blanket over herself, and Andre sat up to cover her.

"What is this?" he asked.

Chien's eyes gleamed. "It's the custom for women to gather outside in the morning to make sure the marriage was consummated. They've been waiting for hours for news. What shall I report to them so they can return to their homes to badger their husbands?"

"That explains the women," said Andre. "What brings you?"

Chien inclined his head. "The same concern."

Andre laughed. "And what did you bring us in case we'd had a problem—medicaments? potions? a talisman? a mandrake?"

Gia Minh sat up beside her husband. The blanket fell away, and she put her arms around Andre and stroked his chest with her hair, all the while looking at Chien insolently. "Rest assured, then, Master Chien, there were no problems, though I was not aware of the physiological deficiency of the male that requires a period of rest after each exertion."

Andre bent to bite her neck. "Not a very long period of rest."

Chien smiled happily: the world was in proper order; there was balance and harmony—a man and woman were in love. "I am glad for you," he said. "But the reason for my visit was to tell you that your father learned this morning that the emperor and his entourage will arrive tomorrow."

"Tomorrow?" Andre was incredulous. "What'll he do when he learns about the marriage?"

Chien opened his hands. "What can he do when he sees such happiness and is asked to bless it?"

Of course there was nothing he could do—not publicly express his outrage and anger, nor even acknowledge the slight for not having been consulted about the marriage.

Because of the haste, Tu Duc had traveled with the barest entourage, accompanied merely by his lord chamberlain, Lady Deng, several ranking mandarins, plus attendants and scribes and guards, and the new French consul, the Comte d'Lyon, Edmond Abrial, recently arrived from Paris and intent upon solidifying and advancing the French gains.

The lord chamberlain, Phan Huy Du, and the French consul were placed in comfortable lodgings, but Lady Deng was consigned to a small apartment near the servants' quarters. The journey had exhausted her, and her cramped and noisy room offered her little rest; therefore she was unable to summon enough strength except to be a minor irritant.

Though Tu Duc had had many reports on Ahn's palace, he was not prepared for the luxury and tranquillity he saw; he was greatly displeased and more jealous than ever.

Count Abrial, seeing this, and seeing the stability of Ahn's rule, realized immediately the prince's danger and saw his threat to French interests. While pleased at the marriage of a Frenchman to a member of the royal family, he did not like to see the emperor upset, and he did not want this prince's position strengthened. Andre made a very favorable impression on him: here was a naive, obviously malleable young man who could be of considerable use, once out of the influence of Prince Ahn.

Ahn and Tu Duc had only one encounter, a barely civil discussion when Tu Duc accepted Ahn's invitation to see the garden.

From the palace everyone watched the two cousins stroll at arm's distance. Though the same age, they made a startling contast. Ahn's step was firm; he stood rigid and alert, a confident man of authority and self-possession, while Tu Duc's steps were slow and short, and he was stooped, seemingly weighed down by power, hounded by events.

"You lied and deceived me," Tu Duc said.

"My daughter and the Frenchman fell in love. I had no control over that. The modern world is more impetuous than the one we were raised in, my lord."

Tu Duc dismissed his words. "It was a clever stroke, though it will cost you dearly."

"You're a fool, my lord, to place your faith in the French before your subjects and countrymen. I'll willingly serve you. Will the French?"

"I'm not here to discuss my policy with you. We have nothing more to say to one another," and with that Tu Duc turned away and returned to the palace.

Andre and Gia Minh were oblivious of the intrigue, caught up entirely with themselves, so much so, and so obviously in love, that Tu Duc was genuine in his blessing, and his gift of horses and jewelry was far more generous than anyone expected.

Yet he cut his visit short and left after only two days, pointedly before a celebration in his honor planned by Ahn, to which he had invited everyone of importance in the province.

The emperor's farewell was ominously curt, though the lord chamberlain fawned, and Count Abrial could not have been more courteous. Yet Ahn knew they were all united to see his downfall, and that as soon as they returned to Hue they would set in motion the plans for his destruction.

On the day of Tu Duc's departure, the entire household gathered in the courtyard to watch the carriages drive away. Before Ahn and Xuan, making little pretense of interest, were Andre and Gia Minh, and beside them, giggling at the lovers, were Su and Ke, and off to the side were Chien and Father Bergere.

Ahn slipped his hand around his wife's waist and pulled her to him. She rested her head on his chest contentedly, and he looked over it to take in the tranquil domestic scene. He was very happy suddenly, and he had no regrets. He had done the best he could.

Xuan looked up at him, then to her family. "I wish—" she started to say, but he put a finger to her lips.

"Wishing cheats the moment," he said, and he kissed her forehead.

12

FATHER BERGERE ALWAYS SPOKE OF the time following Andre's and Gia Minh's wedding as a blessed gift, and so it seemed to be.

The first part of 1871 was happy and prosperous and it seemed that they all lived within a magical, protective cocoon which sealed them from the adversities and strife of the outside world.

As the Comte d'Etinne had predicted, there was a war, and France did lose, and because of the defeat there was a temporary end to the French drive in Vietnam.

Andre learned with shock that the Prussian Army had effortlessly cut through France.

Both sides had been spoiling for war, and numerous pretexts were used to bring about the hostilities, and finally on July 19, 1870, France had declared war. Three weeks later, the Prussians had pushed the French forces back to Chalons-sur-Marne and begun their assault on Paris. On September 1, at Sedan, one hundred thousand French soldiers and the Emperor Napoleon III were captured.

On the news of the defeat at Sedan, a bloodless revolution was staged in Paris, the emperor overthrown, and the mob, under Leon Gambetta, proclaimed a new republic.

Despite the hopelessness of the struggle, Paris held out against the Prussians, suffering months of famine, until the end of January 1871.

Bismarck signed the armistice, and the newly elected national assembly accepted the peace agreement on the first of March. The formal agreement, the Treaty of Frankfurt, was ratified in six weeks, and in it France agreed to pay a staggering indemnity within three months. In addition, Alsace and a large part of Lorraine were ceded to the German Empire of Wilhelm I.

The defeat was a humiliation for France, and sowed the seeds for the next war. Revenge was the hallmark of French foreign policy from the day of the defeat onward, and the Prussians, stunned also by their military triumph, entered a new phase of imperialism.

The Duke of Parnasse, among others, had expected French defeat, and felt it not an extravagant price to pay for the removal of Napoleon, but the Prussian victory had been too swift, and too complete, and the political chaos which followed was devastating. France entered a period of political paralysis, and the country wavered for years between republic and monarchy. Events in France overshadowed any concern abroad.

Using his wife's illness as an excuse, Parnasse stayed completely out of the limelight, and was untouched by the debacle. Realizing also the hazards of committing himself too soon, he remained out of the political fray long after the war.

Three factions vied for power, but Parnasse studiously avoided siding with any.

Had he played his hand only slightly better, with only a modicum of intelligence, the legitimist pretender, the grandson of the Bourbon Charles X, the Comte de Chambord, would have succeeded to the throne. His chief rival was the grandson of the Orleanist King Louis Philippe, the young Comte de Paris. The third faction, the least popular, and ruling solely by default, were the supporters of the republic.

A royalist, Parnasse of course would have preferred a monarchy, but he found the Comte de Chambord so intractable, so out of touch, so stupid, that he knew this man could never become king. The Comte de Paris was more acceptable, but Parnasse did not want another Orleanist on the throne, and he knew that the Bourbons would never accede to such a rule. So, secretly, Parnasse threw his lot in the end with the republicans, and enhanced his own position immeasurably—for a prince among peasants has far greater standing than a prince among princes.

Himself retired from politics, the elderly Comte d'Etinne kept Andre informed of what was happening. Andre remained, belatedly, abreast of events in France through the clever and acid letters of the count, and he learned also that his own mother was not well, but that Catherine had recovered completely.

Despite the relief from French interference, Tu Duc was unable to master the difficulties facing his country. He could not advance the economy, nor check the corruption of the mandarins, who seemingly now toiled to extract the last possible coin from the people.

For the first time in memory it became possible to buy a position in the mandarinate, and this as much as anything undermined and sullied Tu Duc's rule.

Try as he did, he could not consolidate his position, and he was unable to take direct action against Ahn, though Father Bergere continued to make disturbing reports of the emperor's intrigues.

Most devastating to Tu Duc were the secret societies, of vastly different political framework, but united in their opposition to the corrupt and ineffectual throne. The societies were everywhere throughout the country, and their activity quickly passed from that of plans and talk to that of terror and aggression.

Only in Ban Me Thuot was there stability, and no evidence of other world disturbances. The societies were there, but as there was no grievance of which to complain, they were organized only as eventualities. Ahn himself remained respected and powerful.

Ahn listened to Andre's explanations of the war in Europe, but it made no sense to him. Yet he was happy for the respite it gave his own country and he wished it might last forever, because he was caught desperately in the power struggle and knew sooner or later he would have to choose a side.

As it was, he was already drawn into the fray—forced to defend the policies of the emperor, yet at the same time shielding those rebellious to Tu Duc. Nothing was simple anymore, and each decision brought him down on one side or another. To decide a case submitted to him for arbitration was no longer a simple objective matter; he was now seen as favoring one side, a supporter of the emperor over another, or vice versa.

His outward manner was calm and did not reveal the stress he was under, yet inwardly he was torn and disturbed, for he knew he couldn't maintain the balance for long, and knew too that before he did choose a side, the other would seek to eliminate him. Even if he chose to rule through fear, ally himself with Hue, and rely on military power, Tu Duc would soon turn on him.

His position was hopeless, and in these days he turned more and more to Chien for counsel and company, and he became philosophical. "There truly is such a thing as fate," he said one day as they walked together through the garden.

"Indeed, my lord, everything is fated. One can arrange the pebbles on the beach in a myriad of ways, but whatever the design, the tide still rushes in."

"Yet doesn't the design matter before the tide levels it?"

"Not to the sea, my lord. Nor to the beach; nor the sun; nor the moon."

"I think," said Ahn, "that even so it matters; it matters to him who made the design."

Chien, who himself tired easily these days, sat on a bench and smiled at the no-longer-young man. "Indeed, my lord, for how we live matters more than that we live."

Ahn dropped beside him. They were silent a moment, each thinking fairly much the same thoughts; then Ahn said, "Teach me about death, Master Chien."

The garden had made him think of death: he found the patterns and control disturbing; the order reminded him of mortality—limited, temporary, unnatural, a vain conceit; he preferred the jungle and forest now.

For Chien, the garden had the opposite effect; he liked the order: it was harmony; it reminded him of permanence and eternity, immortality. The unruly jungle and forest made him think of mortality. "Perhaps you should speak to Father Bergere of death; death is his realm, not mine."

"It's too late for me to listen to Father Bergere. Perhaps if I'd been raised a Catholic, I could understand it. But now it all seems so insignificant—all that mythology about angels and saints, all that nonsense of heaven and hell, and sitting at the right hand of one of the gods, singing hymns."

Chien said nothing for a moment, but when he did speak, his words came without ridicule or contempt—they were soft and understanding. "It is a religion, I think, for those who haven't come to terms with life. Christianity seems not so much concerned with life as it is with death; death is at the core of that religion."

He stopped to make sure that Ahn understood him. "Now, this is not necessarily bad—it is merely a matter of emphasis. You see, there isn't much one can say about life—what the Jesus person said is hardly different from what Confucius said. The guide for a good life is very short and simple—and basically uninteresting and tedious; and besides, impossible to follow. Therefore, the different religions emphasize death, and the Christian death is the most elaborate, complex, and fascinating of all. You see, the Jesus death is all mystery and miracle, and through his triumph over death, Christians think they too shall triumph. It's a harmless conceit."

"What do you think we shall find in death, Master Chien?"

He smiled faintly. "I think you'll rediscover the time before your birth—the same thoughts, the same memories."

"Do you think about death, Master Chien?"

For several minutes Chien was silent. "No more, my lord," he said at last. He raised his eyes toward the horizon and his words came from a great depth within, never voiced before. "The masters taught me that death does not matter, that only how we live matters, and I believed it, and never gave thought to my own death. But then my wife and child died, and I found that death mattered very much. You remember I left after their deaths. I went to grapple with death, to reconcile with it, and I sought and pondered and wrestled and wailed, just like one of Father Bergere's Old Testament prophets."

He brought his hands to his knees and looked out somewhat sadly on the garden, for the pain of loss was still there. "Alas, I had no success. I learned that death was as the masters had said it was—nothing: nothing to fear, nothing terrible or frightening; it was absolutely nothing—without significance, without anything to follow, without any meaning. As life has no meaning, no significance, how can death be otherwise? No wishing, no hope can invest it with meaning, as nothing can be done to avoid it. Life is a leaf flickering, a petal falling, the wind stirring, and that is what death is."

"No salvation as the Christians believe? No reincarnation as the Buddhists teach?"

"I think not, my lord. My wife was returned to where she came from; my stillborn child never made the leap to life, but remained where she was, in the unfathomable unexistence, where we all came from, and to where we shall all return. We will all die, my lord."

"Yes." Ahn looked to the evening sky, a huge caldron of colors, to the fullness of the earth which stretched to the limit of his vision, and he said with deep regret, "But I don't want to."

And there the word was—"want"—the damnable word, the root of all suffering, desire, and together they both laughed, for it was want and desire of course from which they never escaped, and Chien rose with difficulty, putting his hand on Ahn. "Neither do I, my lord. The Buddha must have been a very passionless man. And shortsighted."

"Yes," agreed Ahn. "I think desire is not such a bad thing," and he was thinking of his wife and children, for he knew he would have suffered anything for them, and that to him they were worth any suffering.

Yet Ahn's children were fairly much oblivious of him and his concerns, so filled were they with their own lives, his two youngest daughters caught in the exquisite tortures of budding courtships, and Gia Minh with no thought except for her husband.

Andre himself had become a wealthy man, but though Ahn had bestowed on him considerable property and Gia Minh had brought a huge dowry, he still worked his own fields every day. Gia Minh went with him, an unheard-of thing for a titled woman, but she enjoyed the labor, and enjoyed most of all being with her husband, yet her time in the fields was short, for she became pregnant in the third month of her marriage.

Andre learned of this one night when he reached over for her in bed, but she pulled away. That had never happened before; he lay still a moment, then asked gently, "What is wrong?"

"I'm going to have a baby." She said it simply, conveying no emotion whatsoever in her voice.

Andre jumped up and lit a candle by the bedside; then he brought it to see his wife's face. "Are you not happy? Why didn't you tell me?" His own joy was obvious and he grabbed her hand. "Don't you want a baby?"

She lay serenely, her hands folded across her stomach. "Of course I do. I didn't know if you would."

As happened often with him, he wanted to say so much, was filled with so many thoughts and emotions, but he couldn't articulate them, and was rendered silent by his inability, yet she knew this about him, and could see in his face his great happiness.

"But . . ." he started, thinking: Why would she think I wouldn't be happy, and when will the baby come, and when did she know, and how? His mind swirled with thoughts and feelings, but he said no more, simply grabbed her happily, hugging her, then pulled away, afraid his weight and power might harm her.

"When?" he asked.

"In June."

He hugged her carefully, then lay beside her. "Of course I want the baby. Why would you . . . ? I mean, I want . . . ?" He sat up, unable to contain his happiness. "A baby! Do you think it'll be . . . ?" Then he laughed and hit the mattress with his hand. "I can't believe it. I don't care what it is. Do you?"

"I think a boy would be better," she said somewhat seriously, but he would have none of her somberness, and he jumped out of bed. "We have to tell your father. And Chien. And Father Bergere."

He was struggling into his trousers when she stopped him. "No. I don't want anyone to know. Yet."

"Why?" He went to her on the bed and sat in some confusion. Why was she acting this way? Why wasn't she happier?

"I just don't want anyone to know."

"Not even your mother?" He put his hand on her arm to comfort her, for he saw that she was nervous and uncertain. "I think you should tell your mother, Gia Minh."

"I will, soon. I just want to be alone with it awhile. I have to get used to the idea."

He leaned to kiss her, but she turned away. "We cannot sleep together until after the baby is born."

He raised his face. "Oh. Is that right?"

"Yes," she said. "It's too dangerous."

He nodded, not knowing a thing about babies, and very little of women, and thinking that sex probably was not safe, for theirs was a very physical sex, but he was not disturbed, not this night, not thinking of his child-to-be, and he lay quietly beside her, pulled tightly into himself to give her all the room on the bed, and though he wanted to talk, or hear her talk of their child and the future, he was content to contemplate it himself, and he fell asleep dreaming of a son.

Instead of the joy he expected to share with her, Gia Minh remained tense and nervous, even irritable, and finally he stopped mentioning the child because it seemed to annoy her. He didn't understand why she was acting this way and he wanted desperately to talk with someone. Finally he persuaded her to tell her mother, and the following day they made their first visit in six weeks to her parents.

Though anxious and unhappy by their long absence, Ahn and Xuan greeted them warmly and didn't mention their disappointment, nor did they seem to take note of the young couple's nervous and distraught manner.

Only later, talking together in Ahn's study, Gia Minh and her mother in Xuan's bedroom, did Ahn confront Andre directly. The youth could not relax, crossed and recrossed his legs, rubbed his arms, and cracked his knuckles, and answered Ahn's polite questions with distracted monosyllables.

Ahn had observed Andre's and Gia Minh's strange aloofness from one another, and now, knowing that he should never interfere, but unable as always to restrain himself, he faced Andre directly. "I want to know what's wrong."

Then, realizing his presumption, he sought to soften his approach. "Is there a problem between you and Gia Minh? She's a very strong-willed girl, I know."

Andre backed away slightly. "No, it's not that. Nothing like . . ."

"Well?" he demanded.

"I . . ." Finally he caught his breath and plunged forward. "We're going to have a baby."

Across Ahn's normally studied composure flashed a myriad of emotions—joy, fear, concern, surprise—all clashing, but finally happiness emerged triumphant, and he grabbed Andre's hand. "That's wonderful. A baby. You'll be a father. I'll be a grandfather. A grandfather!" He laughed. "No, I'm too young. But why are you so unhappy? Don't you want a child?" He clutched Andre's hand in sudden anxiety. "Is there a problem? Is Gia Minh all right?"

"Yes, fine. There's no problem. And of course we want the baby. It's just that Gia Minh's troubled. She's afraid."

"Afraid? Of what?" He dismissed the concern and slapped Andre on the back. "A baby! That's . . ." He started to rush out. "I have to tell . . ." Then he stopped, realizing it was not his place to announce such a thing. "Does Xuan know?"

"Gia Minh's talking with her now."

Ahn found it hard to control himself, and he paced the room. "This is wonderful news. You have to tell Master Chien and Father Bergere. We have to celebrate."

Andre shook his head. "Gia Minh doesn't want it like that. She'd be unhappy if I spoke of it. She didn't even want you to know."

"I'm her father," he said indignantly. "You're her husband. Babies don't belong to women," and unable to contain himself any longer, he ran to the door and sent a scribe to get Chien and Father Bergere.

He had such a pleased, triumphant look on his face that Andre laughed. One would have thought he was the expectant father. He ran again to the door and sent a servant for wine and ceremonial tea.

When Chien and Father Bergere arrived, Ahn was going to have Andre make the announcement, but he couldn't restrain himself. "You'll never guess," he said.

"A baby," said Chien.

Ahn looked shocked. "Why, yes. How did you know?"

Father Bergere laughed and shook Andre's hand. "Well, what else could it be with a blushing husband standing here?"

"But we must keep it a secret," said Andre. "Gia Minh mustn't know we've told you."

"Well," said Father Bergere, "we're good at keeping secrets."

"But we must celebrate," said Ahn, and when the wine and tea arrived, he proposed the first of many toasts.

The afternoon grew long and dark as the four men talked and

reminisced, and they were such good friends they were able to talk about Chien's wife and the sorrow of his loss, and Ahn spoke of the births of each of his own children."

"Will you be the godfather?" Andre asked Chien.

"Heathens can't be godfathers," said Father Bergere.

"But I've always been a Catholic," said Chien. "I was baptized the same time Ahn was."

"Oh. Well, in that case, it'll be fine," said the priest.

They all laughed and told Andre the stories of long ago when Ahn and Xuan were married, and the talk turned mildly raucous when Chien spoke of the early years at court. Then, turning to Andre, he said, "One thing you'll have to be careful of is this stupid superstition Vietnamese women have about copulation while pregnant."

Father Bergere coughed delicately, but was ignored. Ahn was frankly interested. "What superstition? I never heard of one."

"It's an old peasants' superstition, that intercourse would damage the baby, as if it were going to be harpooned in its walled chamber."

"Really," said Father Bergere.

"It's true, you know that," said Chien. "You deal with Catholic peasants often enough; tell us how many men have come to you in the confessional for such a problem."

"Yes, well . . . I have encountered the situation."

"I never heard of such a thing," said Ahn.

"You didn't marry a peasant," pointed out Chien. "But I did, and what a row we had about it. She wanted me to move out of the house."

Ahn said evenly, "Well, Gia Minh is no peasant, so we have no need to pursue this." The idea of sex and his daughter still made Ahn uncomfortable, yet when the three men looked to Andre, whose face was flushed and bowed, they all perceived immediately what was happening.

"No!" said Ahn.

Father Bergere discreetly looked away, but Chien opened his hands. "I told you, you have dreadful daughters. It's all there in their upbringing."

"Where did she get such a stupid idea?" Ahn demanded; then without waiting, he jumped up. "How long has this been going on?"

"I . . . I mean . . . she . . ." Andre stammered.

"Outrageous!" shouted Ahn, and he stormed out of the room.

"Dear Lord," said Father Bergere.

* * *

Xuan was holding her weeping daughter's head in her lap, softly stroking the hair, her own thoughts so richly complex that if one could have captured the look on her face it would have been a portrait of the full range of a woman's scope. There was such tenderness, direct and personal for the child whose head she caressed, but so ethereal and other-worldly that it encompassed every life of every child who ever lived. The look held the complete breadth of human sorrow and joy, a look of such sweep and understanding that it made a snigger of the Gioconda's smile.

Gia Minh had spoken of her fears, not of the child's birth, but of the life it would have and the world it would grow up in.

"It is not a time to have children," she said to her mother.

"There is no time such as that," Xuan said. "No child would ever be born if there was a requirement it be born in a time of peace and tranquillity, or that it be loved and fed, or that it be happy and healthy; there are no guarantees, my daughter. There were none for you at your birth. But look how well it turned out."

"I'm afraid."

"The child must never know that. I've been afraid every minute of your life; from before your life I feared for you. That's the parents' duty—so the child need not worry. Now every day you will worry, but every day will bring joy, as every day of your life has brought me joy."

"But will it? What if something happens?"

"Then you will have had the joy of what came before, and the memories forever. Trust God for his decisions."

"But what about the child? It'll become an heir to the throne—a French-Vietnamese child. Won't he be in great danger?"

Xuan had already thought of that, and she had no answer. "Perhaps the child will be a girl," she said. "Maybe you'll be blessed as I was."

It was then that Ahn burst into the room, but seeing his sobbing daughter, he forgot his mission and was overcome with concern. In pity and protection he rushed to Xuan's side. "What's wrong?"

He dropped to his knees. "Gia Minh, what's wrong?" He put his arms around her, and she burst into tears.

Ahn looked up in helplessness to his wife; his face was so bewildered and stricken that Xuan had to smile, and she patted his head too.

"We're going to be grandparents, honored husband."

"I know that. But why's she crying? I should be crying."

"She's afraid, my dear."

"Of what?"

Xuan laughed. "Of being a woman, a mother. It's not a simple thing, you silly man. We don't get to knock down doors and burst in on everyone whenever we wish."

Ahn hugged his daughter tightly. "Don't cry. Don't be afraid," but he was so lacking in his understanding of what she was feeling that even he realized his impotence and felt his awkwardness.

Gia Minh recovered quickly, unwilling to display weakness before her father. "I'm not afraid for myself," she said, drying her eyes.

"The baby will be fine," he said. "We have very healthy babies in this family. Don't we, Xuan?" He looked to his wife for support.

"She's not worried about that, Ahn. She's worried about the child being an heir to the throne, about how Tu Duc and the court might react to such a child."

"Oh," he said, and stood. The thought hadn't occurred to him, but he brushed the problem aside. Men didn't see babies as threats—even Tu Duc wouldn't give a thought to that. "We'll think about that later; it's not a concern for now."

Then, unsettled by the thought, however, he remembered what had brought him in the first place, and seeing that his daughter was not in real distress, he said sternly, "What is this nonsense that you won't sleep with your husband?"

Gia Minh's eyes flashed. "What business is this of yours? Did he come to you?"

"Of course he didn't come to me. Who would admit to having such a stupid wife?" Exasperated, he turned to Xuan. "Xuan, tell your daughter she is to sleep with her husband."

Xuan looked angrily at Ahn, but she turned to Gia Minh. "Is there a problem with you and Andre?"

Gia Minh shook her head.

"She believes in a silly superstition that a pregnant woman can't sleep with her husband. She—"

Xuan pushed him out of the room. "Go back to your drinking. You are an indelicate man—which is redundant. Leave us alone."

Chastened, Ahn left, feeling somewhat foolish and inept, but still a little indignant at the foolishness of a woman who wouldn't sleep with her husband.

"Now, what is this?" said Xuan to her daughter. "Has someone told you such a thing?"

"Is it not true?"

Xuan smiled. "It is not true. Life is not so fragile as that." She said gently, "I think you have disserved your husband. Or is it perhaps that you don't want to sleep with him? Is there some difficulty?" She grabbed Gia Minh's hands and held them tightly. "I've never talked about such things with you; perhaps I disserved you. Is Andre good to you?"

Gia Minh bowed her head. "He is very good to me, Mother. There is no problem. I just thought . . ."

Xuan patted her hand. "Well, there's no need to talk about it anymore."

In this way the difficulty between Andre and Gia Minh was overcome, and the entire family became intimately part of the pregnancy and birth.

The child was a boy, a sturdy infant with black hair and eyes, yet with definite features of the European father.

The delivery had been more difficult and complicated than expected, Gia Minh's cervix even more narrow than supposed, and the doctor told them she could bear no others, but the rejoicing was so great for this child, what mattered any others?

Andre said he wanted to name the child Che Lan, for the man who had brought him to Ban Me Thuot, and he hoped this infant son would be as strong and dedicated as the man for whom he was named.

At the christening, to which the entire village had been invited, Andre was surprised when the elderly parents of Che Lan appeared. He hadn't seen them since his friend's death, and he wasn't sure what to expect, but they bowed courteously and thanked him for the great honor he'd done them by naming his own son after theirs, and they made a present of an intricately embroidered animal that had been Che Lan's toy when he was a child. With this gift Andre finally felt that he was accepted, and belonged, bonded by his son to his new country; he felt for the first time that Vietnam was his home.

Yet he had little time to grow accustomed to this feeling before he received word through the Count d'Etinne that his mother was dying, and he had to make arrangements to return to France.

He didn't want to leave his wife and child, and of course he couldn't take them on such a journey, but he knew he had to return. Everyone understood; Ahn promised to have his lands taken care of, and Gia Minh and the child moved into the palace.

The trip would take months, and there was the possibility that his mother would be long dead by the time he arrived—the news of her illness was already ten weeks old. He was happy here, and wanted nothing more now than to spend time with his wife and infant. Who knew what he would find in France? Yet he had to go, if for no other reason than to make arrangements for his great-grandmother.

When Andre asked Father Bergere if he wanted to return with him, the priest declined, saying that he didn't care to see what had happened. France, Europe, was a world to which he no longer belonged, and which no longer interested him, he said.

Chien, however, said he would journey with him as far as Saigon. He had heard reports of this budding harbor city and wanted to see firsthand the decadence it was rumored the French had brought.

So with sorrow and tears the two set off, though it was more curiosity and impatience which steered Chien.

Ahn had provided them with a carriage and guards and they arrived in only five days, entering a city much changed since Andre had been part of the garrison. In only a few years the entire tenor had been transformed. It was no longer an Oriental city; now there was a European cast to it, and already all the new construction was more French than Vietnamese. French soldiers were everywhere; shops and cafés dotted all the tree-lined streets that were being widened to resemble the boulevards of Paris.

Andre himself was much stared at, but now the looks were deferential, for it was obvious he was a man of wealth and position, part of the French vanguard taking over the country.

Chien, stately in his white robes, imperial in his bearing, also drew looks of respect and deference, and together the two made a remarkable sight.

Luck was with Andre, for a ship was leaving within three days for France, and he had no difficulty booking passage, a first-class cabin with more room for his trunk than he'd had for himself as a seaman on the voyage over.

On the first night they dined elegantly in their hotel, but Chien could not contain himself and suggested point-blank to Andre that they go to the finest brothel in the city, one restricted to only the French and their special guests.

Andre tried to decline, but Chien pressed him relentlessly. "I'll never get to a French brothel unless you take me. Surely you can do that for an old man who has dedicated his life to serving others and bringing whatever slight happiness he could to them."

Andre laughed. "You are every bit the lecher I've heard about."

"Why is healthy manliness in the young labeled lechery in the old?"

"Because it's unseemly."

"I'm not asking you to watch, I'm merely asking you to bring me. It's shameful enough that I have to have an introduction to get in." He sat regally in his chair and glowered at Andre. "Why is it that the French have to have their own brothels? Is there something special about your activity or movements? Something the rest of us shouldn't witness or know about? Why is it—?"

"All right, all right, I'll take you, but don't expect me to go upstairs."

Chien said loftily, "I don't care where you go once I get in. Just spare me sanctimony; hypocrisy I can bear, sanctimony I can't."

Andre sent word through the hotel to the brothel of their requirements that night, and they were greeted extravagantly upon their arrival. Even Chien, who had been raised in the splendor of the Chinese and Vietnamese courts, was impressed. Here was opulence and luxury he'd not seen before, a silken, cushioned purple den so stunningly wicked in promise, so salacious and depraved in appearance, with the most garish and obscene pictures and statuary, that it took Chien's breath away, and even Andre succumbed to the atmosphere.

"Father Bergere would love it," whispered Chien. "It's everything that hell should be. And more," he said, admiring the vagina-shaped pillows.

"Maybe you should come with me to France, then."

He shook his head. "It would kill me outright."

"Well, have a good time," Andre said. "Should I wait for you down here, or can you manage to get back to the hotel by yourself?"

Chien stared at him, not severely, then sat down and patted the seat beside him. Andre sat down, and Chien spoke in a kindly, faraway voice. "I'm glad you brought me here; it shows me a side of Westerners I hadn't surmised. I thought you people took everything seriously, but at least here there is some grand understanding, some levity. My contact with the French has been limited to those priests, and to you, such a somber young man; I hadn't known there existed this other side."

"I don't think it's representative," Andre said dryly.

"Unfortunately, you're probably right, but it shows a slice of humanity I hadn't otherwise encountered." He made a fist and held it out to Andre. "What is this?"

"A fist."

"And this?" he said, opening his palm.

"Nothing." Then, seeing Chien frown slightly, he said, "An open hand."

Chien sighed. "You are so literal. So is Father Bergere. I think you must all be." He closed his hand into a fist, then opened it, then repeated the action several times rapidly."

Andre was perplexed. "What do you want me to say? What am I supposed to see?"

"You do not make a good pupil. I must start work on your son immediately before you ruin his mind with exactness and boundaries." He took a breath and explained, "I am holding out my hand to you—clenched and unclenched, but the same hand, differing only in form. Clenched, I can do little with it—strike, pound, beat. But open, I can do many things—shape, caress, stroke, grab, clutch, write, paint, twist, and so on. The same hand. Does it follow that the mind is similarly constrained or free? It does. It is form that matters; not the hand or the mind, but what one does with them."

Andre was not impressed. "I find this a peculiar place for a lesson, and I'm afraid it's lost on me."

"Just so," said Chien. "Then you sit here and contemplate your hand while I go upstairs," and he stood up and went to one of the girls sitting across the room who'd been watching the strange exchange between these two strange men.

Andre sat for a moment, feeling somewhat foolish, then inadvertently he glanced at his hand. It was in a fist. He quickly unclenched it, and when he raised his eyes he met those of the other girl. She smiled invitingly, expectantly, and he stood up and went to her. She took his hand, and without saying a word, led him upstairs, just in time for Chien to glance back and smile as he disappeared into one of the rooms.

They spent two days and nights in the brothel, and when they left, Andre was not remorseful in the slightest—he hadn't once thought of his problems, his mother, or leaving his wife and child, and now he felt invigorated and more able to deal with what confronted him. Most of all, it had been nice to lie with a woman again, for at the end of Gia Minh's pregnancy and the time since delivery, they had not been able to sleep together.

Chien too seemed a new man; his walk was brisker and he stood straighter.

"There's nothing like a woman to make a new man of you," said Andre.

"Or to make a new man old," said Chien. "Like the hand, it depends on what form the woman takes."

At the harbor, just before Andre boarded the ship, he asked Chien very seriously to reconsider. "Are you sure you don't want to go?"

He shook his head. "Some things are better not seen; dragons, I am sure, are more wondrous in the mind than in the sea. Reality merely robs imagination of its marvel. Old men have little left to imagine; I'll keep what little of the lovely child remains alive inside me."

They embraced, shook hands formally, wished each other well, and Andre boarded the ship.

13

ANDRE'S PASSAGE TO FRANCE WAS so uneventful and boring that he frequently wished that he was a member of the crew and had something to do. He had never had so much time on his hands, time without demands or commitments, and for a while was bored beyond belief and looked enviously on the sailors who scurried over the ship with their host of duties.

The few other passengers offered him little relief from the tedium; they were merchants or bureaucrats and he found their talk so dull and uninformed that he withdrew further into himself. With the officers he discussed and replanned the Franco-Prussian War, and talked about the disturbing growth of the British Empire throughout Asia. But mostly he spent his time alone, and finally grew accustomed again to solitude like he'd had before he married, and found pleasure in leisure and quiet contemplation.

Once again he fell in love with the sea and stared for hours at its tranquil, ever-changing surface, or its turbulent, roiling expanse, and at night he would stand at the rail looking out at the indigo vastness on whose iridescent waters shone a silver pathway to the moon.

He grew so accustomed and happy with the sea that he took no interest in the several ports the ship visited, finding them nothing but pathetic little stabs at civilization, ugly, obscene markers, graffiti scrawled on majestic coasts.

Yet he could not escape the excitement that swept the ship as it approached Mediterranean waters and sightings were made of other European ships. When they reached French waters he was as happy as any sailor, and he found himself longing with equal fervor to be in his homeland, and finally he saw that he was, first and foremost, above all things, a Frenchman, and shouted with everyone else when the coast of France was sighted.

In Marseille there was no evidence of the recent lost war; port cities are like the sea itself, impervious to the follies of men; commerce and exchange go on no matter who wins the wars, and it's only different uniforms staggering down streets, or bloodied in bars, or lying in crumpled heaps in hasty discard by battered beds.

Only when he left Marseille, on the journey north to Paris, did he see the ravages of war and the human witness in poverty and despair to the most recent of his countrymen's follies. In addition to the deprivation and starvation he saw along the way, there was evidence everywhere of the political chaos which gripped the country—marauding bands of the different factions, and villages flying different flags of loyalty, the most common of which were the fleur-de-lis ones of those supporting the Bourbon pretender.

But Paris itself showed little sign of the defeat. It was like a port city; indeed it was a harbor, the fulcrum of all activity, a bursting, bustling hive of commerce and intrigue which had no time to dwell upon what was, so intent were all to determine what and who would be.

Andre was absorbed so rapidly, assimilated so quickly, that he could not believe that he had been gone nearly five years; it seemed like he had just returned from a long weekend, for everything was as he remembered it, all the sights and smells, the same activities, the streets filled as before, the hawkers peddling as before.

He had no idea what he would find at home, but as nothing else had changed, he somewhat expected to walk into an unchanged life, and his excitement, and trepidation, grew at the thought of seeing his mother.

When the carriage stopped in front of the building, he paid the driver, then stood for several minutes taking in the street scene and gathering his courage. The street was as he'd left it; there was only a change of features within the shabby clothes, but the dirt and litter seemed the same, and there were the same sounds, and the same smells.

He mounted the stairs slowly, becoming more anxious with each step, and when he reached the door to their rooms, he found it ajar.

At first he saw no one, and thought the place deserted, for there was no furniture, but straining in the darkness, he saw a feeble, crouched figure in a corner. He went in cautiously, and the figure pressed tighter in the corner. When he stepped nearer, he saw his great-grandmother raise her hand to ward off a blow.

Her eyes were wild in fear, and she whimpered between terrified sobs.

There was no recognition in her eyes, only madness and terror.

"Grandmother . . ." he said in disbelief, and held out his hand to her, yet at his voice, and the movement of his hand, she shrank back further.

He dropped down on his knees, and said again, "Grandmother, it's me, Andre. It's all right. Don't be afraid," but there was no sign of understanding from her.

He moved closer, and he put out his hand to her arm, so emaciated and frail that he nearly recoiled from the touch.

"Grandmother, it's Andre, I've come to take care of you."

She still didn't seem to recognize him, but she allowed him to take her by the arm and lead her out of the corner.

In the room there were only a chair and a pallet for her bed. He sat her on the chair and made a fire in the hearth from the scattered twigs and chips of wood. For a long time he crouched at her side, rubbing and stroking her arm and talking to her soothingly, and when she fell asleep, he carried her to the pallet, and he slept beside her that night on the hard floor.

In the morning she was still so disoriented that she didn't know him, but she wasn't so afraid. Mostly she ignored him and set about sweeping the room.

"Where is my mother?" he asked. "Where's Denise?"

At the name her face flickered in memory, then blanked, and she went on sweeping.

He went to her, took away the broom, picked her up and carried her back to the chair. In his arms, she seemed to remember him, of being carried many times before, and a joyful smile came to her lips, but it was gone in a moment.

"Where did everything go?" he asked, pointing about the barren room.

She followed his sweeping hand, but gave no sign of understanding.

"How do you eat?" he asked. "Where do you get food?"

Again he was confronted by a wall of incomprehension.

In a moment the door opened. A middle-aged woman entered, but cried out when she saw him. She dropped the plate she'd carried in and ran back to the door, but his voice stopped her.

"Wait. Who are you? Don't be afraid. I'm her great-grandson."

The woman squinted from the doorway, then returned cautiously.

"Who are you?" he asked again.

She told him that she was a neighbor who checked daily on the old woman and brought her food.

"What happened to my mother?" he asked.

The woman looked away. "She died two months ago." Then she told him how there had been no one to care for the old woman after Denise died, and how those in the neighborhood saw to it that at least she had food.

"How long has she been this way?" he asked, meaning her madness.

The woman shook her head sadly. "She's very old. She hasn't known anything for a long time."

Andre thanked her for all she'd done, learned the details of his mother's last days—she had simply wasted away, expired of disease and exhaustion—and said that he would see now to the old woman's welfare.

That night, alone with the old woman, mad and terrified, whimpering at every sound, a hounded, pathetic creature who crouched in corners, he wept both for her and for his mother, but then he came to terms with himself for her death, and he put it away as best he could.

He changed the old woman, bathed her, fed her lovingly, and took her outside, though the light was so painful to her eyes that she covered them from the sun. Yet only in a matter of days she responded and he was amazed that she had flashes of lucidity.

At breakfast, when he handed her a cup of warm milk, she looked at him curiously, the first spark of recognition in her eyes, and she said, "Where's Denise?"

"At work, Grandmother."

She said nothing else, but he felt her eyes on him throughout the day as though her mind was struggling to remember who he was, and finally, late in the afternoon, she said tentatively, "Alain?"

He dropped beside her and took her hand. "It's Andre, Grandmother."

She whispered the name, testing its sound. "Andre?"

"Alain was my father. He died in the war, Grandmother."

"They all died in the war," she said. "They were all so stupid."

He laughed. "Yes, Grandmother. But I didn't go to a war."

She didn't say anything more, looked away and ignored him the rest of the day, yet the next morning, the very first thing, she asked him where he'd been.

"I was in the Ecole Militaire," he said.

"I know that," she snapped. "Then you ran away."

"I was in Vietnam."

The word struck another memory in her and she made a slight sound of recognition. "Yes," she said. "I remember, somebody came and said so." She thought on that a moment; then he watched her eyes cloud, and she slipped away again.

He noticed that in early mornings the old woman's mind was the most lucid, or after a nap in the afternoons, and with each passing day she grew both physically stronger and more mentally alert, and though she was ninety-eight years old there were many things she could still do for herself.

Andre decided to appeal for assistance to Maurice Vallot, the Comte d'Etinne. Perhaps he knew of a place where his great-grandmother could be cared for; he couldn't remain much longer in France, and of course he couldn't bring the old woman back with him.

So one morning he left the house and took a carriage to the fashionable apartment of the count, near the Arc de Triomphe.

The count, now retired, and with a great deal of time on his hands, was delighted to see him and greeted him exuberantly. He wanted to know all about Vietnam and Tu Duc, and all about Andre and his family, and it was hours before Andre could broach the subject of a suitable place for his great-grandmother.

"I think I know the place for her," the count said. "I've looked at it as a refuge for myself, since I'll be needing a place on my own in the not-far-distant future—unless my children solve my problem by pitching me in the Seine. I'll take you there; I might as well get to know the staff."

"You've been very kind," said Andre.

"Now you must do me a favor. I'm having a dinner party on Friday. You must attend. There will be some guests who'll be very interested in your firsthand knowledge of Vietnam. I think you'll find it an amusing evening."

Andre accepted gratefully and made an appointment with the count to accompany him the following day to the home where he'd place his great-grandmother.

That night Andre tried gently to prepare the old woman for the move. Her mind was remarkably clear; she was progressing every day and at times she seemed only slightly more infirm than she had been when he left.

"I'm going to have to return to Vietnam," he said to her as they sat before the fire, for though it was early September, she was chilled and needed the warmth.

"Why do you want to go back to that heathen place?" she asked.

"I have a wife there."

"A wife?" she repeated.

He still wasn't sure that she knew exactly who he was, for she constantly confused him with his father. "Yes, a wife. Her name is Gia Minh."

Grandmother was not impressed. "What color is she?"

"What do you mean, what color is she? She's the same color we are, just a little darker. And she's a Catholic."

The idea of a Catholic Vietnamese did not seem to please her; it was as though she was not expecting to share heaven with foreigners.

"But I forget," he said. "You're not a Catholic anymore. Or have you changed your mind again?"

"I'm not sure. But I don't think it matters much. I was born in anarchy, and it seems that I'm going to die in anarchy, and I suppose there'll even be anarchy in heaven. The only consolation, if indeed there is a heaven, is that I won't know anybody there. Especially if it's going to be filled with colored people."

"I have a son too," Andre said.

"I know," she said.

"How did you know?"

"I've known for years. How did you find out?"

"What are you talking about?" he asked, thinking her mind was slipping in and out of generations again. "My son is only a few months old, and I never mentioned him to you."

"Oh," she said, her mind precise on the moment, not a bit befuddled, "you have a colored one too? He'll make a nice match for the bastard one you have."

"What are you talking about?"

"I'm talking about that Parnasse bastard child. The mother came often to inquire about you while she was carrying the child. She was not unkind to us, but after the child was born, she ceased coming, though she did send a servant around from time to time to see if we'd heard from you."

"Catherine . . ."

"Exactly," said his great-grandmother. "You are all alike. The reason I confuse you and your father and grandfather and great-grandfather is that there's not a whit of difference among you. But there may be hope for your sons, since we haven't had a bastard or a colored one before. I'm almost sorry I won't be around to see what happens to them."

The following day he made the final arrangements to have his great-grandmother placed in the nursing home, and on the next he moved her in. To his surprise, she neither resisted nor resented the idea; on the contrary, she seemed pleased with her new accommodations.

"Why should I mind being waited on?" she asked him. "I've waited almost a hundred years for it. I couldn't wait much longer—it's come just in time."

"I'll come see you often," he said, hugging her gently.

She shook her head, not sadly, for she was arranging flowers on her bedstand, and he wasn't sure if she was dissatisfied with the arrangement or refuting his statement.

"Well," he said, knowing too that he'd never see her again, "I must go."

"Have you arranged for when I die?" she asked. "I want to be buried . . ."

"Yes, Grandmother," he said. As a child she'd brought him often to the cemetery and pointed out her plot—near, but not too close, to where her husband and son lay; she said she needed a little room.

"Come give me a kiss, then go," she said.

He did, holding on, not wanting to let go, for it would be forever, but she was more accustomed than he to final departures, and forever was but a short step for her, and she pulled away, giving him a light peck on the cheek. "Good-bye," she said, and turned back to her flowers.

The following night at the Count of Etinne's, Andre knew as soon as he entered the room that Catherine was there; he knew it by every sense in his body, and his eyes found hers as a needle finds north.

The count introduced him around, savoring Catherine for last.

"My lady, allow me to present a special guest of mine."

"We've met. Good evening, Mr. Lafabre. You're looking quite well."

Andre bowed. "You are more beautiful than ever," which was not altogether true, for in addition to having put on a little weight, her face had hardened, and her mouth now looked frankly mean. Her eyes had lost their kittenishness, were now hungry eyes of a large jungle cat, a dark absorbing green, and her hair had been dyed a demanding henna. "And the duke, how is he?"

"Fine," she answered, "better than when you last saw him."

"Upright at least," said the count, who'd heard the story from Catherine. "Actually," he said to Andre, "the duke is about ready to make his comeback. He's cleverly and carefully kept out of the limelight, letting the jackals devour themselves. I understand that he's ready to cast his lot with the republicans—not a dangerous gamble these days—though his decision is going to be a great disappointment to his cousin, the Bourbon pretender.

"Philippe is not scrupulous in his attention to the details of blood," said Catherine, her mouth fixing in not-so-faint contempt.

Was she talking about the illegitimate child? As always, Andre could not follow the intrigue and innuendos.

Others joined them, and it was soon that the count steered the conversation to Vietnam and invited Andre to give his views. As there were several ministers in attendance, and high-ranking functionaries from the colonial office, and numerous senior military officers, there was lively interest and discussion of the government's policies toward Vietnam, and Andre's opinions and observations were listened to attentively.

Yet all the while he spoke, he felt Catherine's eyes on him, and his own mind was only partially on Vietnam, and not at all on his wife and child there.

Andre gave his view that Vietnam should and could not be colonized, that all efforts to subdue and subjugate these people would be futile. This was vehemently refuted by those from the colonial office and the military, but supported by the Count of Etinne, and also by a young man, only a few years older than Andre, who had recently returned from several years in the United States and who'd had a leading part in the overthrow of the empire.

This firebrand, for he was somewhat wild in appearance and manner, was so interested in Andre's views that he never introduced himself, and it was only much later in the evening that Andre learned his name and first heard of Georges Clemenceau. He kept pressing Andre to meet with him, but Andre had his mind on other matters, and Catherine's gaze was so intense on him that he found his eyes searching for hers every few minutes.

"But, sir," said one of the men from the colonial office, "if we do not colonize Vietnam, it will only be a matter of time before others do. We must do so before the English settle there. Look what they've done to India."

"Quite right," said a general. "The Vietnamese have no army; their military is not even a paper tiger. We could run through the country in two months' time."

"Besides," said a man from the Foreign Office, "we have a duty to civilize these people—do you suppose they would be better off without Christian views and French ideas?"

"Indeed," said another. "Look at Africa and South America—we've brought civilization to these places. Why, we should try again with America, that being our only failure so far," he said to appreciative laughter.

"Don't disparage America," said Clemenceau. "I've just spent three years there as a journalist—we have much to learn from them; at least they aren't presumptuous enough to believe they can best decide how others should live."

"Give them time," said a diplomat, "they're young. They're not old enough to appreciate the joys of involvements and mistresses—they're still playing with themselves."

The talk then gave way to gossip and personalities, and Andre heard all the sordid details of all the sordid people who vied for power, and later, in smaller groups, he learned the sordid details of the lives of the sordid people in other groups across the room, and most of all he heard of Catherine, of her many affairs, of her child whose father was obviously not the duke's, a man whose sexual tastes were no longer a secret.

Finally, late in the evening, Andre found himself alone with her. Her aura was as sexual as before, but now he found it slightly repellent; it was too similar to Lady Deng's—too covetous, too demanding, yet he could not help being drawn to it, her breath hot on him, her body pressed lightly against his. And she knew her power over him; she playfully, out of sight of the others, let her hand drop into his groin, and he jumped as if shot.

"Come to the château," she said. "Philippe is here in Paris; he knows nothing of your return. We can be alone," and her hand dropped again, but this time he was ready, and didn't move as she stroked him sensually. "He'll find out soon enough about you, but why waste the time we have? Besides, there's someone I want you to meet."

"The child?"

"Yes."

"All right. When?"

She clutched him tightly. "Tonight if it were possible . . . but instead, tomorrow."

As soon as he saw the child, he knew it was his—it was himself as a child, only with jet-black hair, a beautiful child with perfect features, marred only by a rather cruel, ungiving mouth, and that unpleasantness was enhanced by a pouting, demanding manner.

"Louis, this is an old friend of your father's and mother's. Can you say hello to Mr. Lafabre?"

Apparently that was too much for him, and when Andre

dropped down on one knee to greet him, the child curled a lip and walked away.

They were in the entrance foyer, a spacious marble vestibule, and Andre felt foolish, on one knee, watching a five-year-old child dismiss him contemptuously.

"Don't mind him," said Catherine, "he takes after Philippe. He's an odious little boy." Then, without regard to the servant at the door or the nurse standing on the staircase, she put her hands around Andre's neck and brought his face down to hers, eagerly seeking his mouth.

Andre responded hesitantly, and out of an open eye he saw the child watching.

"God, let's go to bed. Now," she said, and grabbed his hand, and without letting him say or do anything, she pulled him to the stairway, brushing past the nurse, literally yanking him behind her.

"At least let me bathe," he said, for he felt dirty and sweaty from the horseback ride, and tired too because he'd ridden for the past four hours.

"Don't be so fastidious. I'm not; I love sweat."

She could not keep her hands off him, and barely waited for the maid to leave the room before she threw herself on him, moaning and whimpering even before his hands went to her.

"Oh, God, it's been so long. Oh, Andre, hold me. Yes, hurt me, take me now, I don't want to wait."

Her hands clawed at him, ripped his shirt buttons, and pulled on his trousers, not even bothering to take off her own clothes, simply throwing up her skirts and mashing herself against him, trying to work onto his quickly responding organ.

"Yes, yes," she said, thrusting against him, and she put her arms around his neck and drove herself onto him.

He had never seen such passion; never before had she been like this, and her demands and cries, his own long-denied need, overcame him, and without moving her from him, he carried her to the bed and threw her down, thrusting so deeply and powerfully that her screams of pleasure hurt his ears and filled the house.

When he climaxed, she did not let him go, but continued to work against him, urging him back to life with short cries and moans, and then talk that he'd never heard from a woman before. "Fill me," she said, "work me, deeper. Yes, more," and she pulled him deeper and gripped his hips so tightly, drawing him so far into her, that once again he exploded inside, and yet still she wouldn't loosen her grip on him, but finally he pulled away, yet she clutched his hand and brought it to her, her mouth locked to his, her thighs a vise against his hand.

When at last she reached her final orgasm, she hung on to him and smothered him with kisses.

"God, I missed you so much. I thought I'd never see you again. You're all I dreamed of. I wanted you so often. I hungered for you at night; I'd go crazy wanting you. You don't know what you did to me. I loved your body, loved what we did together, but then you were gone, and all I had was Philippe."

She said his name with such disgust that Andre flinched at the vehemence. "And the things he did to me after you were gone . . . and then when he learned I was pregnant . . . oh, it was awful, Andre, carrying your child, and him knowing it. He hates the child, but he can't let on to anyone that it isn't his."

"And you, do you like the child?"

"Strangely, the child is like Philippe, takes after him as if Philippe were his father. Like him? No, I don't like Louis. I don't like him at all, especially after what he did to me. He almost killed me. And look . . ." She raised her clothing and showed him the cesarean scars. "They butchered me for him, and Philippe said he wished I had died, that the scars were my punishment for you. He's an awful child, spoiled and mean."

Her anger and fervor took hold of her, and quickly turned to passion. She stroked him lovingly, then went to her knees over him, and took him in her mouth, savoring the taste of both their juices; then, when he was fully erect again, she lowered herself onto him, and rode him so long and hard that he was sore and exhausted when she finally rolled off him.

At dinner he asked if the child could eat with them, but the child's behavior was so surly and vile that Catherine had him taken away. Louis shrieked and had to be carried out, kicking and pummeling his nurse.

"The boy needs manners," Andre said tactfully.

"He needs to be thrashed. And he is, frequently, but it does no good."

Andre wanted to suggest love, but he knew that Catherine was not the type to dote on a child. However, he found in the next two days that her feelings for her child were hardly even maternal. She treated the child as a nuisance, a barely tolerable presence in her house, though she rarely saw the boy and never spoke a civil word to him.

For his part, Louis was sullen and obnoxious, and no matter

what Andre did—the games he attempted to play, the love he sought to bestow—the child remained aloof and contemptuous.

Andre knew that Catherine's own childhood had been one of neglect and solitude, and Parnasse's had been even worse, so of course they themselves were unable to respond to the needs of this child, but he saw that he could not leave the boy—his own son, after all—to languish in this palatial orphanage.

He learned that, so deeply resenting the child, Parnasse could not refrain from inflicting cruelties on him—withholding affection, leveling ridicule, administering beatings—yet the child worshiped Parnasse, so desperate was he for love and attention.

Louis was merely an object in the house, one to be hurt and maltreated by Parnasse, and one to be ignored and avoided by Catherine. Andre decided after only two days that he would take the boy with him. Louis was his son, and he knew he could better provide for him, despite the wealth and position the boy was heir to here.

He knew that Catherine would not miss him; she was so absorbed in her own life, so intent upon satisfying her own needs, that the child would be scarcely missed.

It was the change in Catherine which determined Andre's actions, for he thought carefully about taking the child from his mother, and weighed heavily the life the child might have in Vietnam, yet despite these considerations, he decided to take the boy.

Catherine had changed: there was nothing playful or girlish in her manner any longer; she was coarse and demanding, a selfish woman who even resented the attention Andre gave to their child. Yet as covetous as she was about Andre, she was not interested in him—she asked little about his life in Vietnam, and showed no concern for his problems. When he told her that he was married, she brushed it aside, and assumed that his relationship with an Oriental woman was merely one of expediency, and now to be forgotten since he had returned to France. She didn't even ask about his plans, for it did not occur to her that he would return to Vietnam.

She had become totally self-centered and he found her company no longer pleasing. She was vain and spiteful, and he was sorry for her, because she had meant something to him before, but she was now like a crazed fly, maddened by the array of the banquet table and by the refuse of the dump.

Sexually she was gluttonous, virtually insatiable, and she cared little for his needs or feelings. Andre had never felt used before, but now he felt himself nothing more than an instrument to fulfill her cravings, and when her hands and mouth went to him, he experienced no love or tenderness, just the wanton demands of a greedy woman.

After only two more days he could no longer bear staying at the château; he would not have minded riding over the estate or spending quiet time alone, but Catherine would not let him be; she demanded constant attention, and there was the incessant conflict with the child, who now saw Andre as a threat.

Louis turned hateful to both Andre and Catherine, became a shrieking monster whom even the nurse could not restrain, and his behavior brought out the worst in Catherine, who in turn became equally childlike and vicious.

Andre had strangely ambivalent feelings for his son, and he sensed a dark core in the being of this child. He himself knew little of children, could only look back to his own childhood for guidance, yet what he remembered was warm and happy, not dank and troubled as was the aura of this child. Yet it was his son, as much so as the infant in Vietnam, perhaps even more so, for already in the few months he'd had with his baby, he sensed an elusive nature to that child, an almost ethereal quality that was in essence Vietnamese, and which would always keep the child somewhat distant from himself; there would always be a part of Che Lan which would be strictly of his mother's side.

There was nothing ethereal about Louis, nor anything mysterious. He was obviously intelligent, and extremely quick, with an amazing perceptivity for others' feelings and emotions, and in his incipient ability to manipulate, Andre saw Catherine in him. From her also he got his dark features and sharp lines, almost too severe, but his face, its good, powerful cast, came from Andre, as did the boy's already developing musculature. His nature, however, seemed entirely his own.

The difficulty, of course, was going to be in getting the child out of the house; since the child didn't like or trust him and was almost too clever to be tricked, Andre knew he would have to take him in the middle of the night. That way he would have several hours' head start before Louis was missed.

Catherine wouldn't guess his destination, but Parnasse surely would, but by then he would be in Marseille and, with any luck, have booked a passage back to Vietnam.

That night Andre made sure that both Catherine and the nurse had more than a few glasses of wine, urging the nurse on, inviting her to talk of her charge and suggesting that she deserved at least one night's relaxation.

He was unusually attentive to Catherine, kept her wineglass

constantly filled, and in bed he brought her to such heights of pleasure that she finally fell into sated, exhausted sleep.

Earlier he'd prepared a horse and packed provisions, so at one A.M. all he had to do was get the child out of the house without waking anyone. That proved easier than he'd anticipated, for he hadn't counted on the deep slumber of a child; Louis woke, but soothing words and a soft hand put him asleep again, nestling in Andre's arms, scrunching into him for warmth and comfort.

What he hadn't counted on was the difficulty in riding with a sleepy child. His pace was so slow that he knew they'd be caught long before they reached Marseille on horseback. Finally he decided to risk a carriage ride, telling the child they were on their way to see his father, who had sent for the boy in order to show him a wonderful sailing ship. In expectation of that, the child was relatively well-behaved, but by the time they reached the port city, Louis had perceived that something was amiss, and he took advantage of Andre's nervous and tentative behavior, though everyone they met saw the two as father and son and bestowed smiles and help on them.

A ship was not leaving for Vietnam for over a week, and Andre could not risk waiting that long, so they left immediately for Genoa, hoping to catch the same ship when it stopped there, but as it turned out, probably for the best, there was no cabin available, and Andre had to book passage on a ship bound to Barcelona, where he then found a Spanish vessel going to the Orient.

Louis, torn from his home, and knowing now that he was not being taken to his father, alternated between sobbing and tantrums, but as travelers are accustomed to the obstreperous behavior of children, no one found his behavior amiss. Moreover, the physical resemblance between the two was so striking that no one would have thought the child not Andre's. Besides, who listens to a child? So all his cries and accusations were lightly turned aside.

Finally, leaving Barcelona, Andre told Louis who he was.

"You aren't. You aren't my father. I hate you," the child screamed, and could not be comforted, and no matter what Andre did, he could not change the boy's opinion.

"I want to go home. Take me home," he shrieked over and over, and nothing Andre told him about the wonderful land where they were going consoled him. Nor was the promise of a brother comforting to him. "I hate him too," said Louis, and Andre saw that the boy meant it.

Long after it was too late, Andre began to wonder if he hadn't made a mistake, if maybe this child did belong where he was, and that perhaps he was bringing disaster back with him.

Even asleep there was nothing peaceful or innocent about the child; he slept fitfully, moving constantly, and making strange sounds, as if he menaced sleep itself. Awake, the child was unrelenting, his black piercing eyes constantly calculating and assessing, but then, mysteriously, just as the ship passed the tip of Vung Tau, he transformed. He even smiled, and his nature became almost sweet. He clung to Andre, vulnerable and ingenuous, and Andre could not help but respond, yet deep down he wondered if this was but a pose.

Then he thought: No, he's only five years old, taken from his mother and home.

But then, looking down at the child at the railing, his eyes intent on the coast, he could almost feel hate emanating from the boy.

14

THOUGH PARIS HAD APPEARED MUCH the same after five years, Saigon had radically changed after only six months. It was now a city of bursting commerce, with a port busier than ever, from which a river of people seemed to flow off the ships, a flood of mercenaries and opportunists hoping to advance themselves and the expanding French Empire.

Andre wasted no time in the city; he hired a carriage and horses and left the following morning for Ban Me Thuot.

The southern part of Tu Duc's kingdom seemed to be faring better without him than it had under him; the signs of prosperity were evident as the provinces began to feed the hungry mouth of Saigon. Morever, the French had brought political stability and the French Army maintained tight order within the borders of Cochin China.

Leaving French territory, Andre saw less prosperity, and the evidence of political unrest was unavoidable. The carriage driver spoke of bandits in the mountainous areas of Phuoc Bihn and Quang Duc and refused to pass through this shorter route near the Cambodian border, and instead took the longer, safer passage that led through the jungle of Dalat, a stupendously beautiful emerald world where the emperor had a game preserve, and where in more tranquil times the royal family often journeyed for sport.

Louis seemed to enjoy the trip and was fascinated by the jungle. The colors and sounds delighted him and he wanted to stop to hunt tigers, but he was pacified by watching the gibbons swinging over the carriage, seeming to chase it on an aerial road. The boy was like a changed being; he was pliant and agreeable, but he shrank from every Vietnamese he saw and hung tightly to Andre both from fear and from dislike.

At times Louis was so precocious, his actions and manner so sophisticated, that Andre had difficulty remembering he was with a five-year-old child. But then he himself was only twenty-three, and had no experience with children; he might more realistically have been Louis's older brother rather than his father.

Though the jungle intrigued him, Louis would not hear of the new home he was being brought to, nor of the people. The only one who seemed to interest him was the powerful prince.

"Is he more powerful and stronger than my father?" Louis asked, clinging to his belief in the Duke of Parnasse.

"I'm your father," Andre said.

"My father is a duke. You're nobody."

When the carriage finally drew up in front of the palace in the middle of the afternoon, Andre bounded out, but he couldn't coax Louis from inside.

The door flew open and out rushed Su and Ke. They threw themselves on Andre, joyful and weeping, and in a moment Gia Minh appeared with their son.

Andre's eyes welled when he saw his wife, and he made no effort to hide his tears. He opened his arms for them and they came into his embrace. He hugged her tightly, gratefully, closing his eyes, so happy to be back that he wanted to remain in this embrace forever.

But before he had a chance to speak or take his son in his arms, Father Bergere and Chien came out of the door, almost pushing each other in their eagerness to get to him. He had never seen such haste before in the two men and he smiled happily as they came to him, their faces beaming, much more pleased to see him than he'd expected.

Behind them suddenly appeared Xuan, and as soon as he saw her his face fell and he forgot the two men shaking his hands. She was dressed entirely in black, and though her face was composed and serene, he saw etched sorrow, and he knew what had happened.

He left the others and went to her, holding out his hand to help her down the steps. He wanted to put his arms around her, but she was too regal for that. Her sorrow she could bear, her presence said, all sorrow, and she needed no comfort from others.

"We're happy you've returned," she said, her voice a public greeting, a formal welcome. "We've had difficult times since you've been away."

Andre wanted to drop down in front of her, yet she was treating him like a new lord, her manner that of royalty greeting royalty, and suddenly he realized that he indeed was a lord now—Ahn's heir.

"My husband was killed two months after you left, murdered on that spot there," and she pointed to where the carriage had stopped. "A band of outlaws posing as emissaries of the emperor killed him, struck him down with knives and swords. Six men. Since then we've had no peace, and my petitions to the emperor have not been answered. We are glad you're back, sad as this return must be."

Andre could find no words. The others watched him, awaiting a reaction, but he only stood dumbly.

Then Louis stuck his head out of the carriage. Frightened by all the people and noise, and deserted by Andre, he cried out, "Daddy."

Startled, for Louis had never called him that before, but also having forgotten the child, Andre went to him and took him in his arms.

"This is my son," he said. "His name is Louis."

Andre spoke the words to Gia Minh, his eyes steady on her.

As Su and Ke murmured to themselves, and Father Bergere's mouth opened, Gia Minh gave Che Lan to his nurse and went to Andre and the boy.

"This is my wife, Louis. I told you about her. If you like, she'll be your new mother. She'll love you and care for you always."

Gia Minh opened her arms. "Welcome, Louis. I'm very glad you've come to us. Would you let me hold you? You're such a big boy, I may not be strong enough. Can I try?"

Louis hesitated only a second; then he went to her, and she pressed him to her shoulder, and she smiled at her husband.

When he learned the details of Ahn's death, Andre found them as simple and spare as Xuan had first related them. He'd had no warning, no prior indication. Soldiers wearing uniforms of the palace guard presented themselves in the courtyard, claiming they had a message to deliver to the prince.

Ahn was returning from a stroll in the garden and he chose to meet them outside. There, in front of the palace, with only a scribe to witness, they drew swords and knives and struck him down. He died immediately.

"But who did it?" asked Andre.

"Tu Duc," said Father Bergere with disgust. "The palace uniforms were a subtle touch, making the imperial connection so obvious that no one would believe the clumsiness."

"Who else would gain from his death?" asked Gia Minh.

"But maybe it wasn't he," said Xuan sadly. "I just can't see him ordering it; he's not a cruel man, he never was, and in his own way, he liked Ahn. Perhaps it was ordered by those close to the throne."

The image of Lady Deng flashed in Andre's mind and he remembered what Ahn had said about her, calling her his "executioner."

"It is well you weren't here," said Chien. "They probably would have killed you also."

"Me. Why me?"

"You are his heir. You might seek revenge, rally those loyal to Ahn, form a bond with the French in Saigon—you could be a very dangerous man to Tu Duc. You're not safe. Nor is your son. Sons."

Xuan described to him the treatment the family had received since Ahn's death. While expressing shock and grief through his chief mandarin, Tu Duc had immediately ceased all rents and tributes from being paid to her. With the primary source of income gone, the family's power and position were seriously undermined. Moreover, all administration in the province had been placed in the hands of the mandarinate, and a special favorite of Tu Duc had been sent from Hue to oversee it.

In addition, word had apparently been spread of the emperor's disfavor of the family, for Xuan now found herself ostracized; no one called, and no one expressed sympathy. She had become a pariah again, and so had her family.

"I don't know what's going to happen to us," she said. "We are defenseless."

"I wanted to go to Hue and confront Tu Duc personally," said Gia Minh. "Even if he wouldn't do anything for us, I wanted to tell him what I thought of him. I wanted to spit on him," she said hotly.

"We counseled prudence," said Chien, raising his eyes.

"Well," said Andre, "maybe she should go to Hue. I have to go."

"Do you think it's wise?" Xuan asked.

"We'll be safe. Ahn was right, the French will soon take power, and I am, after all, one of them."

That night, having settled Louis in his own room and allayed his fears, even singing him a French children's song that he remembered from his own childhood, Andre lay in bed watching Gia Minh undress.

"Are you angry with me?" he asked.

"Because of the boy? Of course not."

"I didn't know about him before."

"Was his mother so bad you had to take her son from her?"

"Yes. Once she wasn't, but now she doesn't care anything for him, or anyone."

"You made love to her again?"

"Yes."

"Thank you for not lying."

"I'll never lie to you."

"Then I'll be careful what I ask you in the future."

She stood at the bedside, still as stone, her face expressionless, her long black hair cascading over her shoulders onto her silk gown.

He was afraid to touch her, not knowing how she would react, or even if she wanted him any longer.

"She was the first woman I knew," he said. "I thought she meant something to me, but she doesn't."

"I don't want to know," she said, and got into bed with him. "All I want to know is if you still want me."

He needed no words to answer.

Before going to Hue, Andre had to settle several small matters of the estate, though this was not difficult, as Ahn had arranged almost everything. He learned that the family was far better off than he'd supposed and would be able to maintain their manner of living even without the rents and tributes.

In Paris Andre had learned of the almost insatiable demand of the industrialized nations for rubber, and though he barely understood Goodyear's vulcanization process that had revolutionized the rubber industry in America, he knew that the vast rubber plantations which the family owned would become of inestimable value, and his first action on the part of the family was to purchase all the other plantations in the surrounding area. This he knew would give him leverage with the French.

The major problem was going to be Louis. The child perceived immediately how important his father was—but power and position were something the child had observed and learned well in France—and also he realized that he himself was in a favored, untouchable position. The girls, Su and Ke, doted on him, as did Gia Minh in her attempt to win him over, and so did Father Bergere. Only the old Chinese proved a menace to him, and he simply learned to avoid his presence. The woman he was to call "Grandmother" was a different matter; Louis sensed her formidable nature, and also that she did not like him, so he exercised great care around her also. But to the servants and his nurse he was insufferable.

On the day of departure, Father Bergere again expressed his concern for Gia Minh's accompanying Andre, but Andre said that despite his own standing with the French, it was she who was the second cousin of Tu Duc, the daughter of a prince, the great-granddaughter of Minh Mang. "They can hardly ignore her," he said.

Indeed they could not, and their arrival made a stunning impact, this attractive, sure young French-and-Vietnamese couple, the first mixed marriage seen at court.

Andre knew that how they carried themselves would determine how they were received, so he coached Gia Minh, who in fact needed little of it, on how to bear herself. "Remember who you are," he said to her. "Remember who your father was. Imagine that he's watching."

"Don't worry," she said. "I learned long ago about these people. All I need to remember is that they killed my father."

"Don't let that ruin what we've come for. We're here for Che Lan and Louis, and for all the others, not for revenge."

Though their appearance caused confusion among those near the throne, both Lady Deng and the lord chamberlain counseled that the couple had to be afforded courtesy and respect; after all, how dangerous could the couple be, these twenty-year-olds, they asked, without experience in politics and intrigue? They would be easy to destroy anytime, said the lord chamberlain; first let's see if we can use them.

Realizing where his power and protection lay, Andre presented himself first, without Gia Minh, to the French envoy, and was stunned by the extraordinarily courteous, almost deferential reception. Had he realized the difficult position the envoy, Raymond Auboyer, was in, he would have understood how advantageous his own position was.

The French situation in Hue was more confused than ever, and Auboyer saw Andre as a way out of his dilemma, caught as he was between the edict of caution he had from Paris and the pressures of military invasion he was under from the admiralty in Saigon.

Auboyer's duty was to maintain cordial relations with Tu Duc's court and to stay the hand of the militarists in Saigon, but the Paris government, plagued as it was by its own weaknesses, could hardly direct and implement a policy from six thousand miles away.

The military governor of Cochin China, Admiral Dupre, knew that Tu Duc's power and authority were so weak that France could easily expand her influence to Tonkin, the northern provinces surrounding Hanoi; indeed, over the entire Red River Valley and the Gulf of Tonkin.

Dupre's assessent was in fact correct, for Tu Duc had been wholly unable to master the social, political, and economic problems of the north, and was again faced with rebellion from his own people.

Because of the corrupt mandarinate and near-total confusion in the north, Tu Duc had been forced to take into his pay one of the rampaging Chinese pirate gangs. His own shattered military could not maintain order or repel the hated Chinese, so he'd had to ally himself with them. He knew of course that his own people would hardly fight now against the French to maintain the present system. Before, he'd had to make concessions to the French to maintain his own power in the north; now the French themselves threatened to take over.

Dupre and the Saigon admirals believed that seizing Tonkin was in the vital interests of French fortunes in the Far East, and their view was supported by the traders and merchants.

Yet there was a minority in Saigon who favored a gradual economic takeover, believing that a peaceful conquest would be in the better long-term interests of France. It was this view that had the support of the Paris government, and was the difficult task of Auboyer to implement, and for this reason he was so delighted to receive Andre—a Frenchman well-established in Vietnam, living peacefully, with ties to the royal family, and obviously very wealthy. Auboyer was most eager to advance the fortunes of this young man, for he saw Andre as the bridgehead of a peaceful French takeover in Vietnam.

Auboyer was a skilled diplomat, comfortably and reassuringly soft in appearance, whose manner was that of a finger posed permanently to test the winds, unobtrusive and tractable. Hue had been a difficult assignment for him, for the winds changed so quickly, and he was never sure which gale would dominate. He was no more confused by the labyrinthine intrigue than anyone else, but he was no more able to master events or influence direction, either.

He was aware of the murder of Prince Ahn and this young man's relation to him, but he felt that Andre could be a great influence in future policy, and he was, after all, French. Moreover, as Andre quickly and cleverly established, he was not without powerful allies in Paris—he very soon worked into the conversation his trip home and his ties to the Duke of Parnasse and the Count of Etinne, though Auboyer seemed more impressed by the dropped name of Clemenceau.

"I'm concerned for my family," Andre explained. "I am, by marriage and the laws of this country, legal heir to all that Prince Ahn bequeathed, yet I find that the emperor has done everything to minimize my inheritance. Surely I don't need to express how unfair this is. Were I Vietnamese, there would be no question of my inheritance. I appeal to you, as a Frenchman, to protect my interests. If I am to be subject to the illegal whims of the throne, then I couldn't possibly enter into any business or economic dealings with my countrymen—how can I sell rubber, for instance, to a French firm, if there is no guarantee that it wouldn't be confiscated? I am here to ask that you represent my interests."

"Of course," said Auboyer. "Your interests are in all of our best interests. I think the emperor will be receptive to accommodating you. After all, what choice does he have?"

He had no other choice, for once Andre had the official backing of the French authorities, Tu Duc couldn't risk offending him. Realizing Andre's position was for the moment invulnerable, Tu Duc sought to ingratiate himself and tie his own unsteady fortunes in Darlac to this young couple. Andre and Gia Minh certainly posed no threat to him, so he had nothing to lose by accommodation and kindness.

When they entered the throne room to present their respects, Tu Duc stepped down and took Gia Minh's hand. She dropped to her knees before him, but he helped her up, though he seemed sapped of strength, and unwell.

"I won't deceive you," he said. "Your father and I were not friends, yet he was a man I respected above all others and I valued his life. A rose is well served by its thorns, as is an emperor by wise counsel—despite its prickliness." His voice was not strong, and his hands shook.

To Andre, kneeling two paces behind his wife, as form dictated, Tu Duc extended his hand to raise him up. "I am sorry for the circumstances which bring you here, but I'm happy to welcome you. I greet you in friendship, and in the hope of a long and cordial relationship."

Both Andre and Gia Minh were disarmed, and though they didn't understand the reasons for the emperor's friendliness, they believed it genuine. He looked too infirm and hounded to be deceiving.

He said to Gia Minh, "Please convey to your mother my deep sorrow. I don't want to sound hypocritical: the differences your father and I had were well known, but my esteem for him was real, and we did not disagree on anything fundamental, only on means. We knew each other all our lives; we were children together in this palace and played at the feet of your great-grandfather. I regret your father's death very much, not just for the loss of a good and wise man, but also because of its strong reminder of my own mortality."

To their surprise, Tu Duc reinstated the rents and tributes, and made Xuan considerably more than a figurehead by giving her veto power over all administrative decisions in the province, an unheard-of honor for a woman.

Very pleased with what they'd accomplished in Hue—far more, and more easily than they'd expected—they decided to leave as soon as possible, declining all social events as inappropriate during the period of mourning for Ahn.

Once the court saw how well Andre and Gia Minh had been received by the emperor, and how the French envoy had pressed their claim, there was an outpouring of expressions of grief for Ahn's death, and best wishes for them. Everyone was kind and solicitous.

Only Lady Deng made no overture. On the contrary, and confirming in Gia Minh's mind her complicity in Ahn's death, she went out of her way to be rude, though the two of them made it a point to avoid her. But on the final day she appeared in their apartment just prior to their departure.

Andre didn't want to receive her, and was afraid she was going to mention their night together, but Gia Minh wanted the confrontation.

The young couple stood together holding hands, as children might before a wicked witch.

"What a lovely sight," said Lady Deng, easing her squat body into a chair. "I'm so happy the marriage has worked out so well. It's been very profitable for you, hasn't it, Andre?"

He recoiled at her use of his name, but she wet her full red lips and pressed on, "Well do I remember your first visit here to us."

She turned to Gia Minh, her eyes cruel as a boar's. "You can't imagine the sensation he made, stripped and chained to the pillory. Every woman at court wanted to rush out and save him.

We'd never seen a naked Frenchman before. Unfortunately, I've learned since that he's not representative.''

She turned back to Andre. ''But you certainly made a fine first impression for your countrymen. I shouldn't inflate your ego, but there was a bitter fight that night for who would have the honor of attending you.'' And back again to Gia Minh, her head turning with the slow rhythm of an adder's: ''Your husband distinguished himself, a most accomplished man in lovemaking, as you surely know; not like your father, but then, he—''

Gia Minh said with regal boredom, ''This conversation is uninteresting. Forgive me, I don't share your fascination for sordidness. Please go.''

Lady Deng smiled, her eyes growing narrower. ''I was wrong before when I said there was no resemblance in you to your mother. There's quite a bit.''

''Go. There's nothing you could say that would interest me.''

''The safety of your child? You might ask your mother about my fondness for infants.''

Gia Minh's eyes flashed and she went to her, her anger so intense that Lady Deng drew back. ''Say nothing more. Don't mistake me for my mother—she's a far kinder and more gentle woman than I. If anything ever happens to my child, to anyone in my house, I'll rip your heart from your body and throw it to the pigs. You are an evil, ugly, disgusting creature living long past your time. Beware, old woman. Now get out of here before I have the guards drag you out.''

When she was gone, Andre could not meet his wife's eyes, and he was cowed before her anger. She literally trembled with fury, but finally when she turned to him she was composed.

''I'm not even going to ask you,'' she said, rearranging the pillows in the chair, erasing all evidence of the other woman. ''I don't want to know. I'm going to blot all this from my mind and won't ever think of it. She was trying to come between us. It didn't work.''

When they returned to Ban Me Thuot, they reported every detail of their trip to everyone, except the final meeting with Lady Deng, and everyone rejoiced in their success.

Andre and Gia Minh moved back to the palace, Xuan forcing them to take the rooms she and Ahn had had, saying they were an unhappy reminder of the past and that she preferred smaller, sparer accommodations. Xuan took three rooms in a remote wing of the palace and resumed the manner of living she'd had before her marriage.

Father Bergere and Chien also moved to a farther wing, as did

Su and Ke, all turning over the palace as much as possible to Andre and Gia Minh and their two children, though this was not the young couple's desire.

"You are lord now," said Xuan, "and must live like one. As Chien says, 'Form is everything'; if you live like a lord, you'll become one."

"I don't want to become one. I'm not a lord; I grew up in a single room and my mother was a scullery maid. I can't act like a lord. If I attempted it, I'd be laughable or become small and mean."

"That isn't so," said Father Bergere. "You can be a good and wise lord—there are such things, you know. Ahn was such a man. He came here when he was even younger than you are now, and look what he built. You too can do grand things."

"Yes," said Chien. "And you too will have the benefit of our marvelous counsel. That was the key to his success, you realize."

"I suspected it was," said Andre. "At least I shall be as wise as he in listening to you."

The seven of them—Andre and Gia Minh, Father Bergere and Chien, Xuan, Su, and Ke—were seated at the dinner table, with Andre presiding and Xuan at the other end.

Father Bergere raised his glass of wine. "A toast to us all—to peace and happiness."

"Do you really think we'll ever have peace?" asked Xuan.

"Yes, perhaps," said Father Bergere. "If we're not too careful about how we define it, or particular about the quality of it."

"Peace is like a peeled potato," said Chien. "Smooth, nourishing, and essentially boring; someone always has to tamper with it—believing it better fried or boiled."

"A potato is better fried or boiled," said Father Bergere. "That was a poor metaphor—you're straining, my dear Chinaman; a carrot would have been a better example."

"I don't know," said Andre from the head of the table, "if I'm going to be able to stand a lifetime of this kind of talk."

"Oh, you'll get used to them," said Ke. "Father never paid any attention to them."

And that made Andre think. He looked over the table at those before him, thought of his two sons asleep in their rooms, and he had difficulty believing so much had happened, or that he had come so far—such a long journey it was, he thought, from that spare room in Paris before the fire with his mother and great-grandmother; such a world away from the Ecole, *L'Orient*, the garrison, and finally the hut across the fields; and so many people.

He smiled happily, unconsciously, and everyone at the table knew exactly what was in his thoughts, his face was so open and readable.

Indeed, he wondered, oblivious of everyone watching his thoughts, could there really be happiness and peace—were they at the first step on a road of prosperity and fulfillment, or on the edge of a precipice, a nightmare of war and grief?

Ahn had believed they were on the precipice, and he had not believed Andre could save them. His features frowned, then became determined, and they all watched the soundless show. But he would—he had to—save them all, especially his children. Look what he'd accomplished so far: in such a short time he'd restored the family fortunes and made peace with both the emperor and the French. Think of what he could accomplish in the future.

What could conceivably go wrong? He was surrounded by everything a man could want, and he was wise enough to know it, and strong enough to fight to preserve it.

No, he almost said aloud, they were not on the precipice, but at the beginning of a long happy journey.

Then suddenly there appeared in his mind a scene he'd witnessed that very day. He'd looked out on the gardens from Ahn's study, now his, and he'd seen his two children.

It was a warm, sunny day and Che Lan had been placed on the cool grass to crawl about. The nurse sat on a bench not far away, and Louis was climbing a tree.

The scene was so peaceful and comforting that Andre could not take his eyes away.

The nurse's attention was drawn to squalling squirrels in a nearby tree, and so quickly that he almost missed it, Andre saw Louis throw a handful of acorns down on Che Lan.

The baby began to cry and the nurse immediately went to him. She looked about to see what might have caused his distress, and finding nothing, she placed him back on the grass and returned to her bench. Louis had a wickedly pleased look on his face, but it passed quickly and he called happily from the tree to the nurse and waved endearingly. She responded with a smile and a wave.

In a moment Louis was throwing acorns again.

Andre had watched, at first with annoyance, then with deeper feelings of unease, and finally he'd yelled out the window at Louis. The boy began to cry, then dropped from the tree and ran to the nurse and threw his arms around her. She bent to kiss him and held him close.

Remembering the scene, Andre shuddered; then he shook the

image away, and was suddenly aware of everyone's eyes on him.

He flushed, and there was a titter from the girls, but he saw that Father Bergere, Chien, and Xuan were all watching him with intense disquiet, as though they'd seen his thoughts.

Then, as if to comfirm it, her eyes understanding and serious, Xuan lifted her glass. ''To the love and well-being of your two sons,'' she said.

Andre drank gratefully, but to his surprise, the wine tasted bitter.

II

15

1883

THE EMPEROR TU DUC COULD find no peace. Earlier in the day he had been borne in his gilded carriage five miles south of the citadel to the site of the imperial tombs, his favorite place of relaxation.

He had visited the tomb of his father, the Emperor Thieu Tri, and had ponderously mounted the steps of the funerary temple to stand before the red-and-gold-lacquered altar dedicated to him. Then he had been brought to the compound where he himself would soon rest.

It stood within a dense pine forest and was surrounded by a high wall. A portico with three gates led to a large lake which had a small island in the middle. Alone, laboriously he had mounted a large staircase to the monumental gate which opened on a terrace decorated with porcelain vases. He had rested there for a while, so long that it disturbed his guards and they had silently followed after him. Watching uneasily, they'd seen him walk the path to the courtyard, where there was a brick pavilion. Beyond it was a small reflecting pool of water and a bronze gate. Behind that was the future tomb itself.

The emperor sat on a bench and contemplated unhappily. He knew he had almost no time left. His eyes focused on the gate and he tried to see beyond, seeking a tranquil eternity, but he couldn't capture it. His troubled thoughts hounded him. The enemy ships had been sighted, and it was only a matter of time now before the French would be in Hue itself.

The ships were off the coast of Tonkin and the siege of Hanoi would soon begin. Tu Duc knew the outcome before the first soldier was landed; his own forces would not even fight for their throne.

He was sitting on the bench before the huge banyan tree and

he wanted to weep, but emperors don't weep, and weeping doesn't stave off disaster. The end was at hand; all he had feared had come to pass, and there was nothing he could do.

He closed his eyes, but the maddening fears and thoughts which swirled in his mind weren't blocked out. He bent forward and touched his chest; it hurt, and he understood now how his own father had died, as much from a broken heart as from the seizure which claimed him. His own heart hurt, and he felt beaten and defeated, facing a cavernous ruin on whose precipice he and his kingdom tottered.

Suddenly the image of Ahn, dead now ten years, came to him, but there was nothing reproachful or accusing in the face; the eyes looked sad and understanding, almost beckoning, the figure strong and vibrant.

He wished Ahn were here to talk with him. Perhaps he'd understand. He'd been right all along, and had he followed Ahn's advice, there'd be no ships and soldiers poised to attack.

Tu Duc sighed in the knowledge of his error. He should have fought. Now it was too late.

The emperor was an old man, much older than his fifty-three years. His physiognomy was that of an eighty-year-old; he walked in a stoop, with shuffling-old-man steps, and there was no life in his eyes. He was wizened and thin, and he had no joys; each day for him was a year.

And yet only ten years ago he thought he'd saved his kingdom, for in 1873 the Le pretender had been crushed, Ahn was dead, and the French had withdrawn all their forces from the north.

In 1872, Jean Dupruis, running arms to the Chinese, had seized a portion of Hanoi with four hundred fifty men, and had appealed to the French in Saigon for support. But France was not interested in a military takeover of the north, and the Paris government, involved in its own chaos following the defeat of the Franco-Prussian War, had ordered a conciliation with Tu Duc.

The military governor of Cochin China, Admiral Dupre, had sent Francis Garnier, a young, passionate adventurer and profound believer in the expanding French Empire throughout Asia, to evict Dupruis. With Tu Duc's hesitant blessing, Garnier had entered Hanoi with a small army, but instead of confronting Dupruis, Garnier had joined forces with him and set out on a campaign of aggression and terror that culminated not only in the storming of the citadel of Hanoi but also the capture of the important town of Nam Dinh, and with it control of lower Tonkin and the Red River Delta. He proclaimed himself "The

Great French Mandarin," and though there was little support for Tu Duc in the north, Garnier's policies were so arrogant and cruel that the French lost all support from the populace. He himself was killed shortly thereafter and all the French forces were withdrawn, with apologies to Tu Duc, and promises of no further aggression.

The French had decided on another means of taking control of Vietnam—a peaceful economic takeover—and these forces of moderation guided French policy for the next decade.

Tu Duc had most feared military conquest and was relieved at the French restraint, though he soon came to learn that what he thought was restraint was an even more effective policy of aggression, for he chained himself economically to the foreigner and grew more and more dependent upon him.

While France was solidifying its position in the south and sending strangling economic tentacles north, a change in temperament swept France itself.

In January 1875, after years of irresolution and bickering between the two rivals to the throne, the Assembly voted by a majority of only one vote to establish the Third Republic. Though it got off to a hesitant start, the Republic became a functioning, democratic parliamentary regime by 1879. To no one's surprise, an early supporter of the Republic, the Duke of Parnasse, was appointed to a high position in the Foreign Ministry.

While the forces of republicanism emerged victorious in France, there was no similar demand for democracy outside her borders; on the contrary, French foreign policy became more aggressive and imperialistic out of greater demand for overseas markets for her expanding industries, and also as compensation for the still-remembered humiliation by the Prussians.

In a reversal of previous policy, Paris sought to acquire all of Vietnam and add as much as possible to her Asian empire. Paris no longer cared about conciliation with Tu Duc; now the government prodded the French military in Saigon to take action.

Tu Duc sensed this as early as 1880, yet there was nothing he could do, so he merely watched and waited for the end, and now in 1883 it had come. He had no time left, and nothing left to offer. The enemy ships were in the harbor, and he had no forces with which to resist them. The end that Ahn had foretold had come to pass; the time he'd bought was ash, and the hell he'd sought to avoid was before him.

And he was dying; he could see his death in the eyes of those who looked at him, no longer with fear or reverence, but with waiting, appraising eyes, and he could almost hear the murmuring intrigue, the whispering talk over his coffin. His poor son had no hope of succession; even Tu Duc saw that. There would be chaos—that was his legacy, defeat and ruin, and this knowledge struck at his heart as painfully as his past failures.

Had he been so bad as to deserve this? he wondered. Was defeat the inevitable result of compromise and conciliation? He'd only sought time; was that so wrong? He had not wanted to fight; he'd wanted to spare his country that. Now he saw there was something worse than fighting.

Ahn had been right. He should have fought; he never should have conceded that first inch, for that had led to the first step backward, and after that he had been pushed and shoved faster and further, and he had never been able to regain his balance. He had foolishly conceded principles, believing they gave him time, but the price had not been worth the purchase, and now there was the demand for what he'd bartered. He had bartered the future, and sold his children's freedom. Better to have fought and died, he knew now, too late; better his own death than his children's slavery. Now that he had no time left, he saw that the time he had gained meant nothing.

The pain of that awareness was crushing. His heart hurt and he could not breathe.

His eyes caught sight of the chrysanthemums, brilliant in full bloom, yet they mocked him.

The air was so heavy it smothered him.

He clutched at his chest and fell to the ground.

The tall, dark, sensually handsome youth watched the horse approach. He was standing in a copse off the road, his rifle trained on the rider, and he debated whether to shoot. He'd never killed anyone before, and the idea intrigued him. He gave no thought whatsoever to the life of the rider.

Louis Philippe Lafabre was sixteen years old, and killing was one of the few experiences he'd not had. Love was another, but that one didn't interest him.

Louis could tell by the uniform that the rider was an imperial guard, and it was only his interest in the urgent message the man was carrying that stayed his hand.

Perhaps it was war. About time, he thought. He hated the Vietnamese, all Vietnamese, though he could tolerate the two women, Xuan and Gia Minh. His stepbrother, Che Lan, he couldn't stand at all, and Che Lan didn't bother to hide his feelings either. Already Louis's thirteen-year-old brother was active in the secret societies which had grown more numerous and powerful. Andre had asked his younger son not to join, but it was the sole time Che Lan had disobeyed his father. "I have to fight," he'd said. "I'm Vietnamese."

Though half-French, Che Lan saw himself only as a Vietnamese; it was this in particular, the denying of his French blood, which Louis hated so much in him. The two youths had never gotten along, but as the years passed, their animosity grew deeper and more bitter.

Louis lowered his rifle and let the rider pass; next time he'd kill the man, he decided, taking pleasure in his power of life and death.

He disappeared back into the heavy growth of the jungle. He loved it here; it was his refuge, and he had no fears. He'd loved the jungle from the first day he'd seen it, and now knew it better than anyone else; even Che Lan couldn't track him. He'd spent his first night alone in the jungle when he was ten, terrifying Andre and Gia Minh, and thereafter would disappear for days on end, though his father had forbidden him to do it and in the beginning had beaten him severely for it. Now it was accepted, as everything he did was, for Andre had found that nothing deterred his elder son. Andre could not control Louis—no discipline or punishment worked, and certainly reason didn't.

For his part, Louis neither liked nor respected his father; he thought he was a weak, insignificant man, a fool for living in the country, married to a Vietnamese, with a Vietnamese son. Louis had but one goal—to return to France; he'd never forgiven his father for having taken him away and brought him here. He hated Vietnam, everything except the jungle, where he went to get away from everyone—those old women Chien and Father Bergere, his stepbrother, his father and stepmother and Xuan, all the servants, and the Vietnamese who came to petition his father for assistance—he hated them all.

Louis was a loner; he'd had no playmates, no friends, had never confided in anyone, and no one knew his thoughts. Many times his father had attempted to penetrate his hard, smooth shell, but every time, Louis had rebuffed him. They would ride together, or hunt, and Louis would be polite, but there was no camaraderie between father and son.

The previous year, shortly before Louis's fifteenth birthday, Gia Minh had asked Andre to talk with him because several mothers from the village had complained about him; they said he'd promised money to their daughters to sleep with him.

"Did they?" asked Andre.

"They said no, but what else could they say? They could never marry their daughters otherwise."

When Andre talked with Louis about it, the youth seemed bored and insolent. Louis slouched in a chair across from his father in the den, his eyes sexual and sleepy.

"It's time we had a talk," Andre began. "I didn't know you were ready for it, but from what I hear, I suppose you are."

Louis stretched in a lazy, animal manner. "Are you going to tell me about girls and sex?"

"No, I'm not going to tell you anything. Is there anything you want to know?"

He laughed.

"There have been complaints, Louis."

"Nobody complained at the time. I never forced anybody."

"Then you did sleep with them?"

"Which ones do you mean?"

"How many have there been? And when did you start?"

He stood up. "It isn't gentlemanly to talk about it, but I'll tell you this much: one of the maids taught me to masturbate when I was nine, and after that I never had to do much for myself. And I've never had to pull their legs apart to get in between them."

When Louis had gone, Andre felt a coldness ripple through him, and he realized that he didn't know his son at all.

Nor did anyone. Chien and Father Bergere taught him, but they didn't profess to understand him. The boy was extremely bright and quick, with a true gift for learning, but he seemed barely able to tolerate them—realizing they had something to offer him, and taking it, but returning nothing. He listened to Chien talk about moderation and harmony, but his contempt was hardly disguised, and he laughed outright when Father Bergere attempted to teach him the catechism.

In fact, everyone was afraid of Louis, both because they didn't understand him and because of a cruel streak that ran through him and surfaced with lightning speed. Even Che Lan, who tried not to be afraid of his brother, kept a cautious distance, and never crossed him when he knew Louis was angry.

The women were mystified by him. He'd been a beautiful child, an extraordinarily handsome youth everyone wanted to touch and pat, yet he never responded, or if he did, it was transparently calculated. He never gave of himself, ever, no matter how much was offered him or how kindly he was treated.

Once, slightly in his cups, as Andre fondly called it, for it took only one cup for the seventy-eight-year-old priest, Father

Bergere said that Louis was an evil child, a diabolical creature who would one day cause great suffering.

"Evil?" asked Chien. "You're becoming as mystical as a peasant woman the older you get. The boy isn't evil, he's criminal, and ought to be flogged. You've spoiled him," he said to Andre.

"I don't know," said Andre. "I don't think beatings would have helped. He was this way when I first saw him. I think he was born this way. Maybe it's his way of getting back for the way he was brought into the world."

"Well," said Chien, "he's going to have to learn about the rules, and where the lines have been drawn. Right now he thinks they're there merely to be broken and crossed."

"I've tried," said Father Bergere. "He laughs at me."

And he did, at all three men. Father Bergere was an old man now, not enfeebled, but very frail, and Louis dismissed him as a silly old woman and avoided him whenever he could, his only contact coming at mass, which he was forced to attend, and an occasional confession, where he lied and never disclosed his sins.

Master Chien was more formidable, both in appearance and manner, now, at seventy, hardly changed for two decades: he seemed to have slipped into middle age early, then remained exactly the same, so that now in old age he appeared robust and youthful. Louis distinctly disliked him. He knew Chien thought he'd been overindulged and should be disciplined, but also he felt as though Chien saw through him, anticipated his actions and thoughts, so he found Chien's company disconcerting.

With his father, Louis had a strange relationship; on one hand he despised him and hated him for having taken him away from France, but on the other hand he looked to him for support and encouragement, and sometimes he appeared as a normal child, needing and wanting affection and attention, yet not knowing how to return it. And though it was Andre he resented most, it was from his father he learned most, and most sought to please.

Andre was thirty-four years old, as strong and powerfully built as he'd been ten years ago. Sometimes he himself had difficulty believing there was any change in himself, for he felt no older, thought himself no older, and was no different in thought or behavior. Though he was the richest and most powerful man in the province, he had trouble at times taking himself seriously—he didn't even feel he was an adult at times, that he was only a slightly older cadet, a somewhat aged seaman, the youth only a day or so ago married to the beautiful Gia Minh, before whom he stammered and stuttered, and before whom he sometimes still did. And now suddenly to have this teenage boy, his own son, a youth with needs and desires, a youth needing guidance and direction—all that was too much. What did he at thirty-four know to tell a sixteen-year-old?

Nothing. Any more than he knew what to tell the Vietnamese men who came to him for advice and direction on how to thread their way through the shoals of the present political situation. He himself felt in such a precarious situation that he was unwilling to advise others. He wanted to keep the lowest possible profile, knowing that any of the different factions could turn against him. He had ties to all those jockeying for power, but he was careful never to side too overtly with any of them.

He maintained his business dealings with the French and kept a cordial relationship with the French political authorities, but he never sided with them against the throne, and was careful to keep a polite and respectful relationship with Tu Duc, never giving him the slightest reason for fear or suspicion. Moreover, he never discouraged the secret societies, and though he asked Che Lan not to join them, he made it clear this was because of his age, not because of Andre's political feelings.

So when the imperial messenger arrived, Andre wasn't pleased to receive him, knowing that the time had come when he could no longer maintain his neutrality.

As was the family custom, Andre informed everyone of the news at the dinner table, for the entire family gathered at meals, and this was the time for discussion and argument, a period as lively as it had been when Ahn ruled the table.

After Father Bergere's grace, Andre said simply, "The emperor is dying."

Louis broke off a piece of bread and stuffed it in his mouth. "Good," he said insolently.

"That's an awful thing to say," said Father Bergere, crossing himself.

Though his Vietnamese was flawless, Louis rarely condescended to speak it, and now he said languidly in French, "Why be a hypocrite about it? Everybody wants Tu Duc dead."

Xuan ignored him and spoke to Andre. "What will happen when he dies?"

"He's decreed his son is to succeed him, but there doesn't seem to be much hope for that."

"I'll bet it's like flies around a manure heap in Hue now," said Louis. "They want you there, don't they—that's why they sent the messenger?"

"Yes," said Andre, startled at his son's perception. "They want me to intercede with the French who're attacking Hanoi."

Louis's eyes betrayed eagerness. "The French are in Hanoi?"

"Not yet," said Andre, "but probably soon."

"Not for long, though," said Che Lan vehemently, his striking Eurasian features flaring angrily. "We'll throw them out and send them back where they came from."

Louis was contemptuous. "Who's 'we'? A platoon of French grenadiers could defeat the whole Vietnamese Army. Couldn't they, Father? Tell the truth, don't stick up for him as usual."

"It's not the Vietnamese Army the French have to worry about, Louis, it's the guerrillas, and I don't think the French will ever defeat them," said Andre.

"Of course they will. What good are a bunch of peasants in a fight?"

"Enough!" said Xuan. "I don't want to hear about war and fighting. Tell me about Tu Duc. What's wrong with him? He's not very old, eight years younger than I."

"They say it's his heart. Would you like to go with me to Hue?"

"No," she said. "He'd think I came to gloat, and that's not the case."

"One of the weaknesses of women," said Louis pompously, "is that they forgive too easily. How can you not gloat when he was responsible for your husband's death?"

"That's enough," said Andre.

"Well, it's true," said Louis.

"For you to speak of women," said Chien, spooning soup easily into his mouth, "is for a monkey to tell about the universe from having seen a single star."

"I've seen lots of stars," said Louis with a sneer.

"Just so," said Chien. "And you are the first monkey to attempt to teach astronomy."

"Would you like to go to Hue, Master Chien?"

Chien opened his hands. "That would be a journey to see a dead chrysanthemum whose petals have all fallen save the last. I'd rather remember the flower in its full bloom." He closed his hands, then inclined his head toward Louis. "But take the little monkey with you—then he can teach us all about gardening."

"I'd love to go," said Louis, dismissing Chien's jibe, his manner changing, becoming civil and respectful, a very proper young man suddenly. "Can I go, Father?"

"I also," said Che Lan.

"I don't want to go if he's going," Louis said.

"Stop it," said Gia Minh. "You'll both go. I went at your ages and learned a great deal. Maybe you'll learn something too."

The three rode without guards or servants, taking the shorter but more difficult route over the central highlands, crossing the Kontum Plateau, and journeying through Pleiku, Konrum, and Dak To, then down into Da Nang. Andre chose this route rather than the coastal road because although it was more arduous, it was safer, and he trusted the montagnards. The montagnards were powerful tribes, fiercely independent, whom the Vietnamese had never been able to assimilate, therefore had simply left alone to follow their own laws and customs.

The montagnards had not yet been drawn into the fray, and Andre correctly felt it would be safe to pass through their lands peacefully.

On occasion they were stopped in the mountainous terrain and queried as to their purpose, but mostly they themselves were the object of the curiosity—a Frenchman who spoke perfect Vietnamese, though of a strange dialect, and his two sons, who did not look alike and who obviously had different mothers, one of whom must have been Vietnamese.

When they reached Hue, it seemed as if they were entering a city under siege, and as soon as they were admitted to the sacred palace, they could feel the panic.

There was no decorum about this death, instead palpable nervousness; people looked afraid and suspicious.

Louis and Che Lan clung closely to Andre, overwhelmed by the sumptuousness of their surroundings, but also uneasy about the tension of the palace.

They were brought to lavish private quarters near the royal apartments, and there Andre waited to be summoned before the emperor.

Tu Duc, unresponsive to his doctors, had slipped further and his death was expected at any moment.

Talk of succession was on everyone's lips, with no one even bothering to show deference or respect to the dying emperor. But the talk of succession was dwarfed by the news from Hanoi. The French had captured the city and were pressing through the Red River Delta. Hanoi had fallen without struggle and there was little resistance anywhere; a dying monarch ruled a dying kingdom.

Tu Duc's frail thread on life represented the last strand of his country's independence, and with his passing ended not just an era, but a millennium of imperial power and rule.

Finally Andre was sent for. He brought Che Lan and Louis, and all together they were escorted to the royal apartment.

The lord chamberlain himself greeted Andre in the antechamber of the emperor's private apartment.

He forced everyone else from the room, impatiently but politely suffered introductions to the two youths, then turned to Andre. "The emperor wants to see you immediately."

"But why me?"

"He's confused in his mind," said the lord chamberlain. "Just listen to him and nod. We'll talk as soon as you see him. You must help us."

"There's nothing I can do."

"You're French. That will help."

Seeming to reaffirm this, Lady Deng swept into the room. She took note of the two youths standing respectfully off to one side, then went directly to Andre, almost pushing aside the lord chamberlain.

Like Chien, she seemed unchanged by the past decade—in fact she looked exactly as she had when Andre first came to the palace, so much so that he withdrew slightly, and had to remind himself that this woman had to be in her mid-sixties.

Seeing her, he knew this was Ahn's murderer, but she was so alive and intense, her presence so powerful that he couldn't concentrate on anything except her appearance.

She dominated the room immediately, not just with her outrageous attire and makeup, all scarlet and black, but with her vibrancy.

Che Lan and Louis looked at her with amazement.

She stood directly before Andre and put her hand at the base of his neck.

"I must go live in Ban Me Thuot," she purred. "No one there ever seems to age. You look just like the handsome boy who came here many years ago."

Her hand stroked up his neck to his face. "What is it there that does it? Not clean living, I hope—that would be too much to have to pay."

She laughed throatily, then moved across the room to Andre's openmouthed sons. "Are these yours? . . . Yes, this one is surely," she said as her hand stroked Louis's face, then dropped to his chest and shoulders and wantonly felt. "Were I only a little younger," she said, then turned to Che Lan. She studied him a moment but did not touch him. "I see Ahn in him," she said at last, and turned away.

"Go see the emperor," she said. "He doesn't have much time

left. I'll entertain your sons and see them to their rooms while you're gone. Come," she said to Louis and Che Lan, and without even looking to their father, they followed her.

The emperor's room was prepared for death; the curtains were drawn and there was light only from candles placed near the head of the bed. The smell of incense was heavy and mingled with the musty odor of dying chrysanthemums.

Andre had never been to the private quarters of the royal family, but in this death scene there was nothing imperial or magnificent; all the accoutrements and trappings of power seemed child's toys before the infinite. It was a starkly mortal scene of a mortal man dying, the scepter beside his bed a mocking, impotent jest, a make-believe brandishment of power now unable to ward off the inching end of life.

Andre was brought to the foot of the bed, but the emperor could not see him, nor did his voice carry so far, and with a slight movement of his hand he motioned Andre closer.

He had seen the emperor twice before, but it was not the man propped up in bed, steadied by attendants. The face was ancient and haggard, the eyes barely open, the voice hardly audible. The man was as close to death as anyone Andre had seen.

Andre looked to the lord chamberlain, not knowing what to do or say, but Tu Duc recognized him.

"The ships brought you, didn't they?"

Andre didn't understand. He bowed his head before the emperor.

"And now they are in the harbors. Just as they were for my father."

Tuc Duc closed his eyes, gripped with pain, and when he opened his eyes his breath was labored. "What do you want?" he demanded. He struggled up, against the attendants who tried to hold him down, but he shook them off and raised himself slightly and his voice was a whispered rasp. "What is it you want? You've taken everything. What more do you want from me?"

Then he sank back into the pillows and closed his eyes, resting until he regained steady breathing. Andre waited and looked to the lord chamberlain again. The man nodded slightly and brought a finger to his lips.

In a moment the emperor reopened his eyes. His gaze was clearer and sharper and it focused on Andre. "I helped you once when you were brought here in chains."

"Yes, my lord, and I have served you faithfully since."

"And I allowed you to marry . . ." He strained to remember

the name, but before Andre could prompt him, he said, ". . . Ahn's daughter. I gave you horses."

"Yes, my lord."

"Now you must help me."

Andre bowed. "I will do anything, my lord."

"Intercede with the French. Stop them from taking my land."

Andre glanced to the lord chamberlain and saw him making an affirmative motion with his head.

"Yes, my lord; I shall try."

The emperor reached out and grabbed Andre's wrist; it was a surprisingly strong grip, but his voice was even frailer and more desperate. "You must help. You must stop them," and then he seemed to drift away, his eyes clouding and his voice sounding confused. "What is it they want?" he asked. Then he closed his eyes and he was asleep.

Nguyen Van Tuong came to Andre's side and released the emperor's grip from his wrist; then the lord chamberlain led him out, and the two men sat in the emperor's drawing room.

Nguyen was in his late forties, a thin, ascetic-looking man who'd reached the highest levels of the mandarinate but who was now locked in a fierce power struggle. He was committed to placing the emperor's son on the throne and serving as his chief adviser, but there were so many factions vying for control, not the least of which was Lady Deng and her followers, that his only hope was to keep them all divided, for there was little enthusiasm for Tu Duc's vain, silly, and underage son.

"There is nothing I can do," said Andre. "I can't intercede with the French."

"I know that," said Nguyen. "We all know that, except the emperor. There is nothing left to be done, we're aware of that—let's say that most of us are aware of that. There are a few on the Council of Regents who think the French can still be resisted. These men are your enemies and you must be very careful about them."

Andre immediately thought of his sons. "Lady Deng?"

"No, she is not your enemy; she believes we must cooperate with the French. Your chief enemy is Ton That Thuyet. He wants to place his own successor on the throne and rule as regent. He wants to fight the French."

"But why does Tu Duc think I can help?"

Nguyen shook his head sadly. "The emperor's lost all touch with reality. He lives in a long-ago world; frequently he talks with his dead cousin Ahn. He will be dead in a matter of days."

"And what will happen?"

"His son will succeed him, but only for a short time. The emperor's will must be carried out, but it cannot last. The boy cannot rule. There will be another emperor within days. There are two major factions—those who believe we must work with the French and those who want to resist them. I see no alternative but to cooperate; Lady Deng also sees the inevitability of French rule. We believe the time long past when we have a choice; the throne cannot last without the support of the French."

Andre knew of the various intrigues and factions, though he had not known Lady Deng supported the French, but he was confused about his own role. "What does all of this have to do with me?"

"You're French. You can be our liaison to the French military in Hanoi and Saigon."

Andre shook his head doubtfully. "I don't think I can be of much help. I have nothing to do with French policy."

In Nguyen's pressing eagerness, Andre saw the desperation of the regents' position. "We merely want you to convey our willingness to cooperate. We want peace with France. I'll tell you frankly that we want peace at any price, but needless to say we want to make the best possible arrangement that we can. We trust you. You've lived among us for almost fifteen years. We consider you not just a friend, but one of us. Am I wrong? Do you want the French to rule us?"

"No, you are not wrong. I've always felt my country . . ." He smiled. ". . . France, had no business here. All right, I'll help you. I'll do whatever I can."

Nguyen reached out and touched his hand gratefully, then took a deep breath and eased back in his chair. "It's going to be a long and bitter struggle here. I don't know how many of us will survive it."

"What do you want me to do?"

"Leave here as quickly as possible. There may be a bloodbath as soon as Tu Duc dies; in any case, you wouldn't be safe. Return to Ban Me Thuot and wait until we call for you. Then we will ask you to help us with the French. Right now we must fight among ourselves."

The two men stood and shook hands; then Andre went to find his sons.

He wasn't sure what to expect when he entered his rooms, but he was surprised to find Lady Deng regaling his sons with court stories. They seemed enthralled by her, especially Louis, and they barely took note of his entrance.

"Leave us," she said imperially to the boys. "Wait in the next room. I have important business to discuss with your father."

They dutifully left and she patted the settee next to her, but Andre chose a chair not too close.

"You seem to have captivated them," he said.

She laughed throatily and held two fingers apart in small measurement. "There's only a little difference between men and boys." She increased the distance several inches. "A little larger difference among some of you."

He blushed, but laughed, flattered despite himself.

"Your sons look like they might take after you. Too bad I'll never know. Your older boy looks fascinating. We communicated a great deal with our eyes. He's not a virgin, you know."

"Was that the subject of your talk?"

She laughed. "Oh, no. I was most proper and matronly. I told them stories about their grandfather, and about our soon-to-be-departed emperor. Did you talk with Nguyen?"

"I did."

She became all business, dropping all coyness and game-playing. "I never trust anyone to get it right, mostly because they never do, so let me make sure you understand. As it turns out, as always seems to be the case, Ahn was wise beyond measure in building your position. You can be of great service to us—and by 'us' I mean those who want to save this country. We can't resist the French militarily. The struggle would be hopeless and the throne couldn't survive. Our only hope is to reach accord with the French and extract some measure of independence."

"Have you thought that perhaps the throne should not survive?"

She said tartly, "That wouldn't suit my purposes. Probably there'll come a time when both the French and the throne will be cast out, but that won't be soon. In fact, you had better caution your second son about that. He's too young to become involved in the societies."

"He told you about them?"

She held out her fingers again. "I always had a way, you know. Surely you remember? Yes, he was quite pleased to boast of his work. He's an 'apprentice messenger,' I think he called himself. In any case, we're going to have several emperors in rapid succession, but I think we'll maintain the stability of the throne. We want you to help us when matters here have settled. We'd like for you to be our go-between with the French."

"I've already said I'd help."

"Good. Now I'll tell you something you don't know. The emperor's son will be replaced by one of Tu Duc's younger brothers—this has all been arranged, and as far as Nguyen believes, Hiep Hoa will reign for a long time. But Hiep Hoa will not last, because as soon as the regents discover what cooperation with the French means, and how much power they've lost, they'll replace him with someone who will fight the French."

"How can you know this?"

For the first time since he'd known her, she looked tired, almost weary. "Do you know how long I've had access to these rooms? Thirty-six years. No one has seen as much as I. No one knows as much as I. I've survived because I know how small and petty and selfish men are; I understand fully your limits and depths. Even before the French come, I know what they'll do, and I know how these men here will react. They'll hate their loss of power; they won't be able to bear being slavish to the French, not these men, so they'll rebel. They'll place a rebel emperor on the throne."

"And you?"

"I'll go with them, of course."

"And then?"

"They'll be destroyed. And I'll be alone with the new emperor, because just before the French counterattack, I'll have made an alliance with them—that's when I'll need you again."

"And why should I help you?"

"Because I alone can foretell what is going to happen—it's unalterable. The game must be played out exactly as I've said it will, but in the end there'll be peace. To last our lifetimes, and your children's provided you steer your children correctly."

"You're playing a game far into the future," he said.

She said easily, no longer weary, or even very old. "Oh, I plan to be around. That's why I'll survive—these men here are concerned only with the immediate. Too bad Ahn isn't here; he would have understood all this."

"So you've come to me—"

"Because we can help one another. I know it's not to your liking, but an alliance with me will profit you in the long run."

"Must I trust you?"

She laughed. "That would be asking too much, I know. Just watch and see if what I've said doesn't come true. I've never been wrong, you know. Ask that fat old Chinaman if it isn't so."

And what she said was so.

The Emperor Tu Duc died only a few days after Andre and his sons returned to Ban Me Thuot, and he was succeeded by his son, but the hapless youth remained on the throne only two days, for on July 30, 1883, the Council of Regents replaced him with Tu Duc's younger brother, who took the name Hiep Hoa.

Andre was called back to Hue, returning alone, ignoring the pleas of his sons to accompany him.

He found the new emperor guileless and ineffectual, but he worked with Nguyen and others to effect the Treaty of Protectorate, though he could do little to offset the harsh terms through which independence for Vietnam was lost to the triumphant French military.

Lady Deng told him to leave before the treaty was signed because a stigma would be attached to all those who participated in its signing, and she herself was careful to be absent when the treaty was signed on August 25.

Andre cultivated numerous contacts with the French military authorities and came away from the negotiations in high regard and respect by all parties, and then, on Lady's Deng's advice, retired to Ban Me Thuot to await the upheavals. Her last piece of advice was for Andre to send his sons away to school in Saigon and work their way into the French administration in the south. She told him to do this as soon as possible because the reaction to the French would come much sooner than anyone expected and there would be massive resistance in the north.

Again what she said proved true, for Andre had only just packed Louis off to the university in Saigon, to his great delight, when the Emperor Hiep Hoa was forced by the regents to commit suicide, his atonement for the shame he'd brought upon the country for his surrender to the French.

The unsuspecting victim of the regents' intrigue was replaced by an adolescent nephew of Tu Duc, and the regents now pursued an anti-French policy, hoping to garner the support of the people against the invader, though Lady Deng was careful to maintain her distance from the ruling faction—she took ill and remained indisposed in her apartment for long periods. She said she was growing too old for intrigue, and was retiring from court life.

Andre tried to send Che Lan away also, but the youth would not hear of it, and said he'd run away before he was forced to attend French schools.

Finally Gia Minh and Xuan interceded for him and persuaded Andre to allow him to remain in Ban Me Thuot.

But Louis was ready to go, in fact could barely contain his eagerness. He seemed so ready to sever the ties with his family that it hurt Andre, but he supposed it merely the nature of youth, and remembered his own departure for the Ecole, and how unfeeling he was for what his mother and great-grandmother felt.

He went with Louis to Saigon, hoping the trip together might bring them closer, or at least afford him a chance to give his son advice, but he felt foolish in the role of counselor, and remembered that he himself at that age was not open to advice or wisdom from anyone older.

Louis seemed completely preoccupied during the trip and took faint notice of his father's presence; he listened politely to what his father said, but Andre could tell the words made no impact—yet still he had to say them.

"I was almost exactly your age," Andre said, "when I left my family and began what I thought was my career. It didn't work out as I planned."

"I know. Are you ever going to tell me the stories about my mother and the Duke of Parnasse?"

"Yes. But not now. Now I want to tell you other things."

"About girls?"

"Don't be annoying, Louis. Or trite. You're not the first boy to sleep with girls. Everything you do has been done before. You weren't an immaculate conception, or even a legitimate one, for that matter."

Louis flinched, visibly stung for the first time in Andre's memory, and Andre sought to soften the blow. "I'm sorry, and it surely made no difference."

"Easy for you to say," he said bitterly.

"Louis, I'm not at all sure I was legitimate either—people weren't so scrupulous in times past."

"At least your mother and father were married to one another."

"Does that really bother you?" Andre was surprised, for as moral a man as he was, it never occurred to him that Louis would feel shame about the origins of his birth.

"Oh, no!" Louis sneered. "I don't mind it at all—that I have no mother, that my father lives with a slant-eyed Vietnamese, that I was stolen from my real mother . . . oh, no, I never think about it, and I'm sure no one in Saigon will ever bring it up."

"I see," said Andre, and he couldn't think of anything else to say.

"So what were you going to tell me, if not about women or about my mother?"

"I was going to give you words of caution—the advice my great-grandmother gave me, advice I didn't think I needed, and almost too late discovered was worthwhile, but maybe I'll spare you all that." He put his hand on his son's arm. "Louis, I'm sorry about . . ." But he had to stop because he wasn't really sorry about anything that had happened between himself and Catherine, or anything since, and he didn't regret having taken Louis from his mother.

"It's all right." The youth turned his proud head away.

Andre had had no father; no man had ever held or comforted him, and now he was unable to reach out to his own son. He wanted to, wanted very much to hold his son, but he couldn't bring himself to do it, and his inability to articulate what he felt—understood by his wife—left him apart and mute before his own child.

The two sat stiffly separated. Andre stared straight ahead, then finally said, "My great-grandmother was a very wise woman and lived to be very old. She died when you were a child, not long after my own mother died. When I went away to school, she told me to be careful. She never said exactly what I was supposed to be careful of, but I later found out she was talking about my own self. I was very filled with myself when I was your age. I thought I was much better than I was. I also didn't understand how bad the world was. People are not very good, Louis. You haven't seen any of those people, but you'll find many of them in Saigon. They'll want to use you; they'll flatter you and trick you, and you won't mean anything to them. In the end you'll find the only ones who care about you are your family, those who love you, those you love."

Louis turned his face to him; his eyes were penetrating and utterly cold, his face chiseled smooth like that of a Grecian statue, and his voice was as hard as marble. "I'll be all right," he said. Unexpressed, but clearly conveyed, he also said: No one loves me, and I don't love anyone.

Andre recoiled slightly from the look, and he wanted to say: No, I do love you; you're my son—I made you, and I want to keep you safe and protect you, and I want you to be good and decent and happy, strong and honest. I want you to love and find love, and I don't want you to grow old or be hurt. I want . . . I want . . . I want everything for you. Yet he could say nothing, only lower his head, and he stared at his hands, which he held clamped in his lap.

They rode the rest of the way speaking only when necessary, and of inconsequential matters, and when they reached Saigon and parted at the university, it was with mutual relief.

16

Saigon, 1886

LOUIS WATCHED THE NAKED GIRL beside him knead the small heated smudge of opium paste and prepare the darkened ivory pipe. She worked quickly and expertly and when she inserted the needle into the bowl, releasing the opium, the bead bubbled gently as she inhaled it; then she passed the pipe to him. He drew deeply and stretched out on the bed, a sigh passing his lips, then sharply took in his breath as her mouth worked between his legs. He drew again on the pipe and stroked her hair as she ministered to him, pleasure rippling his mind and body.

Again he drew on the pipe, then put it aside and concentrated on the dual pleasures. He watched her tongue him, her eyes meeting his as she worked up and down his shaft.

When the door opened, he didn't move or bother to cover himself, only turned his gaze to the interruption. The girl started up, but he placed his hand on her head and forced her to continue, slowly moving his hips up and down into her mouth.

The youth in the doorway took in the scene, then smiled. "It's almost seven," he said.

Louis looked from him back to the girl. "So?"

"So if you don't make your class, you'll go on report."

Louis closed his eyes, both hands holding the girl's head between his legs, and his voice was sleepy. "I've been on report a hundred times, but this is my only nineteenth birthday. I'm taking the day off."

The other youth laughed. "How can you tell your birthday from any other day? You treat them all the same. Should I tell Billot you're sick?"

"He won't believe it; tell him the truth. Tell him to come watch if he wants." Then he pulled the girl up and kissed her on the mouth, then rolled her over and mounted her.

The door closed. He laughed and rolled off, and in a moment he drifted off into drugged sleep.

So they'd put him on report—he knew it made no difference; there wasn't anything anyone could do to him. They'd threatened expulsion many times, but they'd always backed off. After all, he was the best student at the university, and that was without even trying. Besides, he'd made himself indispensable to the consul general, because no other Frenchman in Saigon had his command of Vietnamese or understood the culture and society as he did. Already at nineteen he'd frequently interpreted at the highest levels of negotiations and was privy to a variety of diplomatic and military secrets. He was invaluable, and he knew it, and was careful to maintain a polite and respectful manner with his superiors—but not with his teachers or the officials at the university; about them he couldn't care less, and he abused his privileged position whenever he felt like it, which was often, and becoming even more frequent.

He no longer bothered to hide his disdain for his teachers and attended classes only when there was a test. He'd found, somewhat to his surprise, that he could get by at the university with what Chien and Father Bergere had already taught him, and that he could excel with only token effort. From Xuan his exposure to art and literature already exceeded what was offered in his classes. He found school boring and unnecessary and only a slight hindrance to his pursuit of pleasures.

He'd found the brothels his first week in Saigon, and now there was no house he wasn't well known in, from the most luxurious ones, catering to the wealthiest patrons, to the lowest on the riverfront, where only the soldiers and sailors went, and there was no pleasure or deviation he hadn't tried, and none he didn't enjoy.

His extraordinary looks and abundant wealth made him welcome everywhere, and where he went and what he did made him seem older than he was. His utter self-confidence and poised manner allowed him to pass for a man in his mid-twenties, and numerous officers' wives had learned to their shock that they'd been risking their marriages and reputations with an eighteen-year-old.

He'd returned only once to Ban Me Thuot, after his first year, and had impressed everyone with his seemingly newfound grace and charm. His father was very pleased with his accomplishments at the university and congratulated him on his work with the consul general. He was also happy to see that Louis was taking such good care of himself; his son had grown to his full height of six feet, two inches, and had filled out to a perfect physical specimen. The only thing that unnerved Andre was Louis's smoldering, restless eyes, which seemed to harbor an uneasy, preying spirit. Andre was also somewhat disturbed at the amount of money Louis seemed to need, but his son told him that it was necessary for his clothes, and also he was generous with many of his schoolmates whose fathers were not so well-off.

But Louis's money didn't go to less privileged friends; in fact he avoided the company of those who didn't have wealth. Louis's money went to the brothels and for opium, and then rather quickly to gambling debts. Gambling seemed the only skill or game he couldn't master, and no amount of playing or practice improved his ability or luck. But he'd been told not to worry—his credit was good, they said, all he had to do was sign his name.

Of course he wasn't stupid, he knew what he was signing, and knew exactly the extent of his debt. Twice he'd eradicated the debt by handing his debtors certain documents he'd been able to take from the consul general's offices, documents that had substantially aided investors and realtors who were able to profit from acquisitions the French government subsequently repurchased; he himself had been able to make some money this way, but that he turned back in gambling.

Now his debt was again substantial; in fact he'd signed away all his rights to his inheritance, but that didn't bother him because he didn't expect to come into any money for a very long time. After all, his father was healthy and only thirty-seven. Nevertheless, his creditor had begun to press him, something he'd never done before. The man said he himself was pressed and needed the money. Louis didn't believe him and had refused his demands for money. He figured he'd be able to pay off his debt with more stolen documents, so he wasn't worried. Maurice Jammes, who held all his notes of debt, was an odious ferretlike man whom Louis loved to ridicule—ridicule which Jammes suffered obsequiously. Louis despised him and felt he had nothing to fear from him; such a mousey little man couldn't possibly cause him any harm.

He woke to lips nibbling his and hands caressing his groin. His head turned on the pillow to the girl and he reached for her, but she pulled away, laughing in a birdlike twitter. He grabbed roughly for her, but she jumped out of bed.

"Come here," he said. "I need you."

"Someone wants to see you; he's downstairs."

"Who?"

She shrugged. "A little man, very ugly."

"Jammes? Tell him to go away. I'm busy." He jumped out of bed and ran to her. She shrilled happily and didn't resist as he clutched her from behind and brought her back on his hardness. What he liked best about this girl was her noises; she chirped and sang just like a bird, and even now, squirming back against him, she let out little cries and sighs.

She was on him, his much larger body bent over her, thrusting deeply, when the door opened and a small Frenchman of indeterminate age, but neither young nor old, poked his shaved head in; his eyes leered at the sight of the couple and his mouth parted, his tongue wetting his lips.

"It'll cost you to watch, Jammes," said Louis, pulling out almost to the tip, then slowly sinking into her again.

"I'll bet you would let me watch, too, for money."

"Oh, I would. Interested?"

Jammes came into the room and closed the door. "How much?" His eagerness could not be contained and his breath came heavier as he watched the copulation before his eyes.

Louis reached for him and brought him closer. He took the girl's hands and ran them over Jammes's crotch, working the buttons, and his own hands went into the short, fat man's shirt, palming his chest sensuously, all the while thrusting in and out of the girl and forcing her naked body against Jammes's. He took a hand and brought Jammes's head to the girl's; then he leaned over and touched theirs with his own face and whispered, "Half of what I owe you."

Jammes could hardly breathe; his excitement and desire were agonizing, but finally he pulled away. "I can't. You bastard."

Louis, still behind the girl, forced him against the wall. Her hands went into his trousers as she rubbed up and down his body; Louis leaned over her, stroking his face, bringing his mouth to Jammes's. Jammes opened his mouth, trying to take Louis's tongue, but Louis drew back. "Half."

"Bastard!" and he struggled away.

Louis laughed and withdrew from the girl. He kissed her passionately, then went nonchalantly to the bed and stretched out, naked and fully aroused. The girl went back to the bed too and snuggled against him.

"All right, I'll pay, but not half. Ten percent."

Louis pulled the covers over them. "Half. And that's a bargain."

Jammes sneered. "I'll make you do it for free. I've had enough of you. Yes, tonight you'll perform for me for free."

"Get out of here, scum."

"Listen to me, you prick, that's exactly what you'll do for me, for nothing. I'm calling in the notes, Lafabre, every penny's worth. I want the money tonight, all of it. And the interest paid will be your performance—for that you can have the documents back. Otherwise they're sent with a full disclosure to the consul general. The word for what you've done, by the way, is treason, and the laws and punishments are rather specific."

Louis jumped out of bed and grabbed him by the throat, throwing him back against the door. "I could kill you right now." With one hand he lifted the man off the floor.

Jammes struggled, but even with both hands he couldn't release Louis's grip. His eyes bulged and his tongue protruded, and finally Louis let him go. Jammes fell to his knees; he clutched at his throat and tried to catch his breath.

"You'll pay for that; oh, you'll pay," he hissed; then he screamed out and scrambled away, trying to dodge the stream of urine from Louis above him.

"Bastard! I'll destroy you for this."

Louis spat at him and went to the bed, stretching out again beside the girl.

Jammes quivered with rage, so angry he was crying. He pointed a finger at Louis. "Tonight! Tonight you'll pay me every penny—I don't care where you get it. If you don't, I'll have the documents delivered to the consul."

"You know I can't get the money by tonight. Go away."

Jammes regained himself slightly, but his voice seethed with fury. "You don't seem to understand, Lafabre—I don't care if you get the money or not. I'm turning the documents over,and do you know what else?" He stepped to the bed and snarled, "I'm giving your notes to Tsae, the Chinese."

For once Louis looked interested, though not concerned. "Tsae? Why?"

"Because I owe him, and if you don't pay me, then I can't pay him; therefore it's very simple: I simply turn over your notes to him—a transfer of assets. I'll let him worry about collecting from you. I doubt he'll be so patient and understanding though; he couldn't care less about documents in payment either, the Chinese aren't interested in French secrets, and I don't think he'll want to wait until you come into your inheritance to get paid. Now, do you understand, you stinking shit! I wish I could be there when they demand payment and you don't have it. God, I would pay for that—gladly half of what you owe. That beautiful face of yours—they'll slice it like the soft belly of a fish. And that cock of yours you're so proud of"—he laughed—"you can become Tsae's eunuch. He'd like that—that's one of the few things he doesn't have, a white eunuch; it'd give him great standing."

"All right, Jammes," Louis said easily, though unable to hide a trace of nervousness, "let's talk."

Jammes's teeth bared and his face scrunched ratlike. "You don't seem to understand, we have nothing to talk about. I must pay Tsae by morning, so you must pay me by tonight—payment in full, or I turn the notes over to him and send the documents to the consul."

Louis knew he wasn't joking—his bold and challenging manner was completely out of character for him; moreover, Louis realized he'd made a mistake in humiliating him. The man would take great pleasure in destroying him. Louis had no choice. To be in Tsae's debt was unthinkable; the Chinese overlord of Cholon would take great pleasure in making an example of a Frenchman; his ferocity and ruthlessness were without bounds, and everything that Jammes said could easily come true.

Louis sat up in bed, his hand absently rubbing his cheek in contemplation, his mind racing to gain himself time. "All right, I'll get you the money. But you know I can't get it by tonight. It's already almost three, isn't it? The banks will be closing."

Jammes shook his head. "I told you, there's nothing to talk about. It's tonight or nothing."

"Now, wait a minute—"

"Oh, I love to see you sweat, Lafabre. I despise you. You don't know what pleasure this gives me. I've waited for this—all those times you mocked me, all your little jokes, all those times you threw money aside and laughed at the rest of us scrambling to get it because we weren't born to it like you were. Oh, no, we couldn't just sign a piece of paper and get more money, but you . . . you thought you could have everything. And your women. I think I hated that the most, the way you treated them, that even more than the secrets you stole. And you call me disgusting! You call me scum. What do you think you are?"

Louis got out of bed. Jammes gave a little cry and ran to the door, but Louis had gone to a chair and begun putting on his clothes.

Jammes stood with his hand on the doorknob. "You'll get the money?"

Louis said matter-of-factly, "I'll get the money, but it'll take me a while."

"Where will you get it?"

"I have rich friends, you know that. Where should I meet you?"

Jammes pointed to the girl. "That depends. Do you want to take off ten percent? The offer's still good."

Louis shook his head. "I won't give you that satisfaction."

"All right, we'll do it in public, but only because I don't trust you. I'll meet you at La Maison—Madame Genouilly knows me very well; we can use one of her rooms. You know the place?"

"Of course. I'll need at least until eleven tonight."

"I'll be there at eleven. You can have the documents and your notes back when you pay me."

Louis finished with his trousers and motioned the girl to help him with his boots, ignoring Jammes, and not even bothering to look up when the door shut behind him.

Louis had no difficulty discovering where Jammes lived; the second inquiry gave him all the information he wanted. He learned that Jammes never ate at home, so that meant he would have to return to his home after he ate, usually at nine, in order to get the papers to take to La Maison, for he'd never risk carrying such documents and notes for any period of time. Since Jammes lived off a main street, where he could easily hail a petticab for the twenty-minute ride to Madame Genouilly, Louis guessed that he'd leave his quarters at approximately ten-thirty and walk the three blocks to the cab.

The area was poor residential, the higher-class Vietnamese having been forced out by lower-class French. The buildings were all single dwellings cramped together with labyrinthine alleys stretched back into the poorer sections. There was no lighting, and very infrequent security checks—a patrol from the garrison coming by in early evening, then again in early morning.

Almost exactly as he'd anticipated, Louis saw Jammes return to his house shortly after ten. He was waiting across the street, obscured by a chestnut tree, and as soon as Jammes entered the house, Louis walked toward the main street in order to double back and meet him on his way to catch a petticab. The main street was crowded, but there were only a few pedestrians on the side streets.

Louis started back toward Jammes's house from the main street, feigning too much to drink and stopping to rest against trees and fences until he saw Jammes a block ahead walking his way. Louis timed their meeting to when they both reached a dark alley.

Drunks on the street were a common sight, so Jammes was

unsuspecting when the darkly dressed man leaning against a fence suddenly straightened and lurched toward him.

When he recognized Louis, it was too late and the blade had already slipped into his abdomen and was slicing up to his heart. Louis's other hand was heavy on his shoulder, forcing down so that he couldn't lift up, and just as he was crying out, Louis's hand clamped over his mouth so that only the faintest gasp escaped his lips.

Jammes was dead before Louis removed the blade, an eight-inch stiletto he slipped into his boot as he bent under the weight of the slumping body. Then Louis straightened, and with one arm held around the shoulders, guided the corpse into the alley, giving the appearance of two drinking companions stumbling home. Louis propped the corpse against the wall, felt for the papers and wallet, withdrew them quickly, then let the body fall, and walked rapidly out of the alley. The act took less than two minutes, and no one observed it.

Walking back to the main street, Louis was exhilarated. So this is how it felt to kill. He'd always wondered. He loved it, even more than sex. He'd never felt so alive and powerful. He filled his lungs with night air and strode powerfully down the street.

But surely he felt remorse; he felt he had to, but no—and he almost laughed—no, he didn't, not at all. Jammes was a contemptible little creature whose life or death made no difference to anyone; no one would mourn or miss him, and the world would in no way be diminished by his loss. Jammes was nothing, and killing him was like squashing a bug.

The strong survive and the weak perish—that was the rule of the jungle. Those shoots that couldn't reach sunlight died; those creatures that couldn't run fast enough, or hide, or adapt, or kill—they fell victim. And so it was everywhere. Those years in Ban Me Thuot had prepared him for life; the jungle had taught him how to survive—not those old women Chien and Father Bergere, not his foolishly principled, idealistic father.

He hailed a petticab and gave one last thought to Jammes—disgusting, odious man; how dare he threaten or stand in his way?

When he got in the cab, the driver turned to await his bidding, and only then did Louis realize he had no destination in mind.

He gave the address of the brothel; he was greatly aroused sexually.

* * *

Louis walked confidently into the office of the resident superior of Cochin China, six months after the murder of Jammes.

Jean Raymond De Barthelemy, a rotund, agreeable middle-aged man of medium height, came from behind his desk and greeted him with a warm handshake.

"I'm delighted to see you again, Louis—may I use the familiar? Since we'll be working together intimately, I'd prefer to dispense with formalities. In private please call me Jean."

Louis returned a firm handshake, but affected modesty and respect. "Sir, I'd feel uncomfortable using your name; I was not brought up that way. It would be very awkward for me to use anything except a formal address."

"How civil," said De Barthelemy, pleased and impressed. "I was somewhat afraid I wouldn't get you, you know. I know how many offers you had upon graduation—your talents are highly esteemed in all quarters, and I must admit that government service doesn't pay what you might have received in private employment."

"Sir, money is not my primary interest."

"No, but then, you're not a pauper, are you?"

Louis smiled engagingly. "No, sir; my father has provided generously for me."

"Then you are incorruptible?"

Louis laughed. "I am not without weaknesses."

"You flatter yourself; your reputation in these 'weaknesses' is formidable." He wagged his finger at the tall, dark youth. "I forbid you to meet my daughter."

"You have a daughter, Excellency?"

De Barthelemy slapped him around the shoulders and steered him to a chair. "As if you didn't know."

The year was 1888, early fall, and Louis had just accepted the position of private secretary to De Barthelemy. He had graduated from the university with the highest honors, though not with the highest recommendations from the staff and faculty; nevertheless, his work as a translator and interpreter with the civil administration had been so distinguished that his "character flaws," as it was delicately put, were simply overlooked—though none of the military or government officials he'd worked with found him cold, calculating, or arrogant in the slightest; on the contrary, they found him hardworking, respectful, and scrupulously discreet.

A background check on him disclosed that in his younger student days he'd had a fondness for gambling, but no one had seen him even turn a card in a long while. True he had a great weakness for women, and wasn't particularly mindful of their marital status, but then, he was young, and attractive, and . . . well, that was in the nature of things, especially in the nature of young, attractive men.

In his favor, in addition to his remarkable looks and exceptional command of Vietnamese, were his impeccable manners, his charm and elegance, his respectfulness, and his very good humor. Everyone in a position above Louis, in a position which might be beneficial to him, found him captivating, as did all women.

The background report on him glowed, and De Barthelemy was most anxious to hire him, but he'd been afraid that the offers of several private firms would be too much for Louis to refuse, even though he knew that Louis came from a very wealthy family and money was not a problem for him. He counted, correctly, on the fascination of power, and it was this temptation he'd dangled in front of Louis, promising Louis that he'd be involved in the highest levels of diplomacy and negotiations and administration. This very much interested Louis, who aspired to be far more than a provincial land baron in Ban Me Thuot.

Andre had never expected Louis to return to the estate, and was in fact both pleased and proud of his son's appointment in Saigon. He'd always assumed that Che Lan would stay with the land while Louis worked with the colonial administration.

But Louis had plans well beyond the colonial administration—such a little pond, he thought. He wanted to return to France; his appointment as private secretary was merely a first but necessary step in that direction.

He had no interest whatsoever in remaining in Vietnam; his family meant nothing to him, and what was happening within the country was profoundly uninteresting to him. As far as he was concerned, Vietnam was a conquered, pacified feudal land of meager civilization.

It was true, he knew, that Vietnam wasn't completely pacified—his own brother's commitment to the secret societies dedicated to the overthrow of the French proved that, but for the most part France ruled a subdued territory.

After Tu Duc's brother Hiep Hoa was forced to commit suicide in November 1883, the anti-French faction on the Council of Regents replaced him with an adolescent nephew of Tu Duc, the emperor who signed the new treaty with France in June 1884. This treaty was slightly more favorable to Vietnam, for though it gave France complete control of Tonkin, making the north of Vietnam a virtual protectorate, it left Annam, central

Vietnam, with its capital at Hue, relatively free of French interference and control.

Almost as soon as the treaty was signed, the regents replaced the emperor with another boy, the twelve-year-old Emperor Nam Nghi. It was under this emperor that Ton That Thuyet and the anti-French faction staged a rebellion against French control in July 1885.

The forces loyal to the new emperor made a surprise attack on the French garrison in Hue, but were driven back, and the French launched a furious counterattack.

For the first time there was a full-fledged fight against the French; had it come twenty-five years earlier, had Tu Duc instead of a twelve-year-old boy led the people, the French might have been defeated, but now there was no hope against the vastly superior French forces.

Emperor Nam Nghi was forced to flee, and the French placed their own puppet on the throne, the Emperor Dong Khanh, a man who owed much to, and was heavily influenced by, Lady Deng, whose health rallied after the defeat of the anti-French regents.

But the placement of Dong Khanh on the throne and the flight of Nam Nghi had long-lasting repercussions. This was the first time a non-Vietnamese-made emperor sat on the throne. The people's loyalty was to the old emperor, and rebellion and resistance broke out everywhere in central Vietnam. The fighting was so intense that wise French observers realized that no amount of force would ever subdue the will of these people—at best, it might bring a temporary peace. But the military felt otherwise and launched a six-month campaign of terror against the Vietnamese resisters.

The former Emperor Nam Nghi led these resisters, and his force grew as it was joined by the members of the secret societies, those who previously had conspired against the throne.

But their resistance was proving futile—it simply came too late—and now, in the fall of 1888, the French military had scored victory after victory over the fugitive emperor's forces, and it was believed to be only a matter of time before the rebel emperor himself was captured.

Louis had not returned to Ban Me Thuot, so he didn't know the depth of feeling against the French in the country. Had he listened to his brother and his comrades, he would have realized that a military defeat of the rebels would be a hollow victory. Louis had nothing but contempt for his brother's involvement with the secret societies, and he saw them as no threat to French rule.

De Barthelemy was less inclined to dismiss the societies and believed that unless the Vietnamese people were won over, the French position would never be secure; his own dealings with the Vietnamese left him with a high regard for them, and he found his new private secretary's vociferous dislike of them somewhat curious. But he was in all other ways pleased with his youthful assistant.

Louis had never considered any other employment than this appointment, and he'd carefully cultivated his contacts within the colonial administration to make sure it was offered; he saw this position as a stepping-stone out of Vietnam, for all he dreamed about was to return to France. How could anyone choose Saigon over Paris? he wondered—though he knew nothing of Paris, only fabled stories.

For years he worked toward achieving this appointment, though careful never to let on to anyone, knowing well the perversity of the human heart, which so frequently finds satisfaction in denying the desires of other hearts. He'd been most cautious in all his affairs since the murder of Jammes, in which he was never remotely implicated, for which he never had a moment's regret. He'd never inquired about the murder, and expressed no interest in it, though he heard through others that the police had passed it off as an anti-French assault—not an uncommon occurrence. His only concession to the event was that he never again entered into debt, and never gambled again.

He even tried to curb his sexual involvements, limiting them to the brothels, but he was less successful in this—women would literally not leave him alone; he was too handsome, too charming and poised, and there was an irresistible aura of danger and sex about him—his eyes were hauntingly provocative and his movements those of a stalking jungle animal.

Even Madame De Barthelemy approved of him, though she was in no way tempted by him. She told her husband that he would make a marvelous diplomat, for he perfectly fulfilled Princess Zerbst's dictum for an ideal diplomat—Empress Catherine of Russia's mother had said that the best diplomat should be a handsome young man of exquisite complexion with a great capacity for liquor, without becoming intoxicated. Louis easily fulfilled those requirements.

De Barthelemy's eighteen-year-old daughter, Felise, also approved of him, though she would have been too shy and embarrassed to admit it to anyone. She'd met Louis on several occasions, and though Louis had been studiously correct in his behavior to her, she'd yet been able to meet his eyes. She'd heard the stories about him, but that only added to his appeal—and to her longing. She knew she was too plain and uninteresting to catch his attention, and were it not for her father, he'd most likely not even talk to her.

Indeed that was true, but after all, her father was the resident superior, and thus Louis was quite interested in her. She herself was nothing to him, but he couldn't resist striking against her father and her father's position. Besides, the game of seduction was too alluring, the challenge of the virgin too tempting. It was too much a part of his nature.

The capture of the rebel Emperor Nam Nghi in November 1888, and the dispersal of his forces shortly thereafter, gave a triumphant air to the Christmas celebrations in Saigon that year.

De Barthelemy hosted a huge party for the entire colonial administration, but because the weather was so unChristmas-like for these displaced Europeans, it took on more the tone of a victory celebration.

Everything was done to give the party a Christmas air, but after all, the weather remained near-tropical, and no amount of imagining or wishing could bring about snow or Christmas trees, and no one wanted to sip hot drinks in sweltering heat.

The reception and dinner-dance were formal, a glittering affair of bejeweled women and uniformed men all doing their best not to perspire, though only Louis, accustomed all his life to jungle heat, managed to maintain a cool and collected demeanor.

He came by himself and carefully avoided any lingering attachment with any of the women who fluttered about him. He stayed among the bachelors and talked politely and deferentially to the senior members of the administration, never approaching De Barthelemy or his family after having paid his initial respects.

Felise hardly took her eyes off him, and her mother's heart went out to the poor girl, who so obviously pined after the debonair young man, knowing that her daughter had spent days preparing for the event with the sole purpose of appealing to Louis, though Felise would have been mortified to know of her mother's understanding.

De Barthelemy himself was aware of his daughter's feelings, and had secretly hoped that Louis would pay her some attention. In the three months Louis had served under him, De Barthelemy had become more and more impressed with him. He'd never encountered a brighter, more respectful, more faithful aide, and many times he'd entertained the vision of marrying his daughter to this most agreeable, most well-positioned, most moneyed young man, certainly the most eligible bachelor in Saigon.

Because of her father's position, Felise was not unattended at the dance. Young men clamored to dance with her, and she would have drowned had she drunk all the punch brought to her, yet she couldn't keep her attention on any of those she was with, and her eyes continually strayed to Louis.

Unable to bear her daughter's anguish any longer, Madame De Barthelemy approached her husband. "For God's sake, for my sake, for your daughter's sake, Jean, go have Louis dance with Felise. She'll take to her bed until the next party unless he pays her some attention."

"And how do you propose I arrange that, my dear wife?"

"Go up and tell him to dance with her."

"That would be wholly indiscreet. I can't interfere in what the young man wants to do."

"Nonsense, that's precisely your obligation as a parent. If you don't do it, I'll take to my bed also. Now, go arrange something; you're so good at that," and she pushed him in Louis's direction.

But he couldn't let his daughter see them together, so De Barthelemy sent a waiter to tell Louis to meet him in the library.

When Louis knocked and entered, De Barthelemy was nervously striding up and down the room.

"Close the door, Louis."

Louis stood respectfully, knowing full well what was to transpire, having awaited the call for some time, well aware of Felise's interest.

"You haven't danced with a single woman, Louis. Why not?"

Louis lowered his head and affected embarrassment. "Sir, I . . ."

"Well?"

"I . . . I couldn't bring myself to ask, sir."

Feeling the assurance of fatherliness, De Barthelemy sat down in an oversized chair and directed Louis to sit across from him. The comfortable surroundings of his book-lined shelves and the twinkling candle warmth of the chandeliers made him expansive. "Come, come, Louis, what's the problem? You know, I forget sometimes how young you are, and how difficult it must be for you without your family. I suppose you have no one to go to with your feelings or problems, and I guess I haven't made it very easy for you to come to me. You seem such an assured individual . . . well, I never gave thought that you might need someone older to talk with. Now, out with it, what's wrong?"

"Well, sir, I want to dance very much, but I . . ." He

stammered nervously, then finally seemed to gather his courage and looked up at De Barthelemy. "I was afraid you'd take it wrong, sir."

"Take what wrong?"

"Sir, I wanted to ask your daughter."

De Barthelemy tried to hide his surprise and pleasure. The young man was obviously, sincerely distraught. "My dear Louis, what in the world could I find wrong with that?"

Louis averted his glance. "I was afraid you'd question my motives. And I was afraid of your daughter's reaction."

De Barthelemy pulled his chair closer, and had to resist reaching over to give the youth a comforting pat. Young people always made such a muddle of things, he thought; there was his poor moon-eyed daughter, barely able to keep from falling over on the dance floor, her eyes glued on this young man, and here he was stammering away nonsense out of his own desire for her. Had he himself been that way? Of course he had, and he warmed at the memories of his own youth. So here he had a budding romance on his hands, and he hadn't even known it.

"You see, sir, I was afraid you'd think I was . . . well, ingratiating myself. I mean, look at all those men around her trying to gain her attention and impress her—not that it's because of you . . . I mean, her own charm is such that . . ." Louis stopped, bit his lip, and feigned acute embarrassment.

"Louis, I would never question your motives. I had no idea you were interested in Felise."

"Yes, that's the whole problem." He began to speak nervously, quickly. "I'm aware of my reputation . . . I mean, that I . . . that some of the women . . . that perhaps you wouldn't want me to present myself to your daughter, or that she would be repelled by me. You see, I've never . . . I mean, the women I've associated with . . . I mean, I've never been around a girl like your daughter—she's so innocent and pure." He laughed in self-awareness. "This all sounds so stupid, I know. It's just that I wouldn't know how to approach your daughter."

De Barthelemy did reach out. His hand patted Louis's arm. "How extraordinary. I never would have thought . . . but yes . . . I suppose you might feel this way. Though I hasten to add that your reputation is not . . ." He laughed outright. "Your reputation is perfectly scandalous, my dear boy. Well you should hesitate before my daughter. But I give you permission—no, I order you to present yourself to her. Now, not another word about this." He stood up. "We've been gone too long; my daughter is probably . . ." He thought better of indicating just how eager his daughter was; Louis's reputation was dreadful—he was devastating with women, and in this short exchange De Barthelemy saw how a woman could succumb to the boy's charm. Good thing the youth was so honorable, De Barthelemy thought, and held De Barthelemy and his family in such high regard.

When they returned separately to the ballroom, Louis waited only a few minutes before cutting in on a dance with Felise. The young man with her looked annoyed, and was not going to give up his partner, but Felise disengaged from him quickly and let Louis lead her away.

"I chivalrously decided to spare you further foot injury," he said, expertly moving her across the floor, his hands sure and forceful on her. "You've more than done your duty as hostess in indulging your admirers' awkwardness."

She was overwhelmed to have at last achieved being in his arms, but she was very nervous and shy. "I don't really think it was their fault; I mean, I haven't myself been—"

"You've been dancing with very clumsy men . . . boys."

"And what made you decide to save me so late in the evening?"

"I decided it was foolish to waste any more time. Pardon me, I'm not the retiring or stammering type, so let me speak forthrightly. I wasn't sure how you'd react to any overtures from me; I've wanted to approach you many times, but because of my position with your father, I thought it prudent not to, but tonight, seeing that you kept glancing in my direction, I thought that perhaps you wouldn't be averse to my asking you to dance. Was I wrong?"

No one had ever spoken to her like this. No man had ever been so bold. What a contrast, she thought, to the simpering talk from the others. She struggled to maintain her composure, though she couldn't betray her pleasure. "I'm very glad you asked me to dance, and I certainly had no idea you've had such difficulties in restraining yourself from approaching me. I knew you weren't the retiring or stammering type, but I didn't think you were reticent, either."

He smiled and pressed daringly against her. "Oh, I'm not."

She realized immediately that she was way out of her depth with him, couldn't begin to play the coquette, but that was all right, for she knew she wasn't suited for such games. She was not an unattractive girl, but more plain than pretty, and a rather simple girl in all her manners. Her mother's sure eye appraised her as a "very nice girl," and that was exactly what she was—not distinguished in any way, but not a dull girl either, a girl perfectly suited to be the wife of a young colonial official who would not go too far, yet nevertheless lead a happy, comfortable life in the company of their numerous children; a girl not at all suited for Louis.

Though not suited for Louis, she was strongly attracted to him; her heart sang out its joy, too loudly for the whispering of her mind to be heard, warning her of the impossibilities, even dangers of such a match. How many are so wise as to be able to turn aside the charming attentions of others? Whose ego is so self-aware as to deny itself flattery? The heart is no mirror of reality, but a fathomless vessel for the balm of love, and it is no filter or judge for that love.

He said he was attracted to her. Could she deny that, would her heart allow such an abnegation? No, not at eighteen, not when she wanted it above all things to be true.

She didn't know what to say to him; she wanted to please him, desperately wanted him to find her interesting and amusing, but she was afraid to speak lest he find her silly and childish, but too she was afraid not to speak; she was afraid of silence, for in it he might find her dull and boring.

She was in extreme agony, wanting and not wanting to speak, but then he saved her, for he knew her discomfort. At the end of the dance he put his arm around her and steered her to the glass doors that led to the patio. "Let's go outside," he said.

She felt every eye on her, and she was pleased for it; she felt so protected and significant, for the first time in her life, desired and important in her own right, not just because of her father.

Outside, he led her past numerous couples engaged in quiet and intense talk, and brought her to a secluded, darkened corner of the terrace.

All she thought, with an exquisite mixture of terror and desire, was what would she do if he tried to kiss her, but surely he wouldn't—not with so many people about, not after just having danced with her once. But if he did, what could she do, she who'd never been kissed, who'd never even been alone with a boy, who knew nothing of such things except what she'd talked about daringly with her girlfriends, who themselves had never been kissed and knew nothing? Would she now at last have something real to tell? But shouldn't she resist, or run, or scream?

Yet before she was able to decide a thing, his face was close to hers, coming closer, and his hand gently lifted her face, and he kissed her full on the mouth, and it was well he held her so tightly, because she would have fallen off the terrace had he released her.

His mouth was so wonderful, and the sensation so blessed, that of course she didn't resist, only parted her lips to let his tongue, so strong yet soft, enter her mouth. He brought her closer, tighter against him, and she gasped slightly as she felt his hardness press into her; then suddenly he drew away from her. He took her hand and led her back across the terrace, and she was in despair—had she not kissed properly? Had she tasted awful? What had she done wrong?

She had to fight back tears when they reentered the ballroom, but mercifully he didn't abandon her, which was her great fear—that he might just leave her stranded in the middle of the room, a public announcement of her unsuitability and bad breath. Instead he brought her to the refreshment table, offered her punch, while he himself quickly downed a glass of champagne.

She was almost afraid to look at him. In addition to having found her utterly lacking in kissing, did he also now believe she was cheap? Could anything be worse? She hated herself, wanted to run out of the room and lock herself away forever so no one would ever find her. Yet she finally raised a timid glance to him. His green eyes held her, bored through her, and his voice was deep and sensuous. "I couldn't trust myself."

She shivered and slightly spilled her punch. So that was it—passion—and she almost cried out. There wasn't anything wrong with her; he desired her, he felt passion for her. Her heart leaped; joy and relief surged through her.

He bent his face toward her, but she pulled back quickly. He couldn't kiss her here; he wouldn't dare. But was he able to control himself? The idea that she caused such feelings in him made her love him and want to protect him from himself.

"Louis!" she said.

He straightened. "I can't help myself," he said.

"You must. People will see."

He took another glass of champagne as though to cool himself down. "Will you go riding with me?" he asked.

"Yes," she said quickly.

"But I didn't ask you when."

She brought her hand to her mouth and giggled. "I don't care when."

"Tomorrow?"

"Yes," she said, more happy than she had ever been in her life.

* * *

And so began their courtship—properly chaperoned and decorous in all ways, but under which was a smoldering fire, for Felise could not forget their first night on the terrace, and more than anything wanted it repeated, and she could tell by his looks that he felt the same way. She felt she was no longer a girl, had left her silly friends behind with that passionate kiss, and she was eager to see unleashed the full extent and power of his passion.

Her father and mother were delighted with the courtship, and their happiness and love for their daughter blinded their vision; why wouldn't Louis be in love with their daughter? She was charming, kind, an excellent hostess—she'd make a perfect wife for this young man with such an excellent future, and from such an excellent background. And Louis was such a gentleman; they were as captivated with him as she was.

Louis maintained an absolutely correct manner with De Barthelemy, never taking advantage of his relationship with his daughter to shirk his duties or miss a moment's work, and every day De Barthelemy's esteem for Louis grew.

Both father and mother held their breath for the engagement, wanting it as much as Felise, but never saying a word to their daughter, and certainly never cautioning her—surely that was unnecessary, they thought.

One Sunday afternoon after church, just before a planned picnic, the aunt who frequently accompanied them, and fulfilled scrupulously her duties as chaperon, took ill, and Felise persuaded her mother to let them go off alone—after all, they were only going to the edge of the estate, no one would see them unchaperoned, and obviously the couple could be trusted. Wasn't their daughter sensible, and Louis honorable?

The parents acquiesced and the young couple rode off.

They found a secluded clearing. Louis tethered the horses, and as soon as he turned around, he took Felise in his arms. She was so startled she didn't even have time to turn aside the shred of resistance she might have summoned, but fell easily into his embrace, and matched the hunger in his mouth with her own.

She didn't pull away, even when his hands went to her breasts, caressing the outside of her blouse, and when he pressed himself against her and she could feel what was happening to him.

He knew that she was ready for him, but he went slowly. He pulled away and laid a blanket on the ground; then he lay on it and motioned her beside him.

The clearing was surrounded by a thick growth of ferns, and

above them the golden rays of the sun filtered through low-hanging limbs and boughs, making light patterns dance off the forest floor.

He brought her against him, brushing his fingers through her hair and holding her tenderly for a long while; then he sat up and took off his shirt, his eyes never leaving hers, and when he lay back down and pulled her against him, he felt her shiver and snuggle closer. He lightly touched her lips with his fingertips and traced the soft lines of her face; then his lips met hers in a deep kiss. Her tongue met his as he probed inside her mouth; then her arms wrapped about his back as he pulled her over on top of him. His strong arms encircled her and pulled her tightly against his muscular chest, her breasts squeezing against him.

Then, somewhat to Louis's surprise, she thrust her pelvis down slightly on him, gently at first, then more boldly, until she ground her hips down onto his hardness.

This was going to be much easier than he'd expected, he thought, and the idea of his conquest filled him with more desire and lust than she herself did.

Slowly he moved her off him and unbuttoned her blouse, stretching her out on the blanket, his mouth and fingers teasing her flesh. Her nipples were hard and she began to sigh and moan softly as his mouth moved from her face to her breasts. Then, when he was sure there would be no turning back, he unfastened his trousers and slipped them off, taking her hand quickly and placing it around his erection. She shut her eyes tightly, yet yielded with her hand as his own slipped under her skirt, all the while his tongue licking and his teeth gently nipping. Finally she opened her eyes and watched the power her hand held over him.

She stroked up and down, excited by what she was able to do to and for him, and she eased her hips up when he sought to slip off her skirt and take off her undergarments.

His hand was sensually stroking between her legs, and when she parted them, his fingers found their way to her wet vaginal lips. She was ready for him, but he wanted more than that, he wanted her to need him, to beg him, and she did. Within minutes of teasing and probing, with gentle soft stroking of her clitoris, she was arching her back and pelvis up for him. He put his mouth full on her and drove his tongue in and out with the same motions of her hips.

She called his name and tried to guide him toward her, but he held back, his hand working faster on her until she cried out, an orgasm rocking her; then he quickly moved over her and thrust himself in, so quickly that the pain of entry and her broken hymen were lost in the spasms of pleasure sweeping her, and almost immediately she began to respond to his slow, deep thrusts. In another moment she was thrashing under him, bucking wildly, and reached orgasm after orgasm.

He was amazed at her responsiveness, had not expected it from someone so shy and retiring, and it filled him with a greater sense of power and dominance. He drove forcefully into her and finally shuddered in explosive release, yet continued to grind into her as she worked herself up and down on him.

When he pulled from her, he continued to kiss her gently, and his hands smoothed over her body, then drew her against him and held her lovingly.

"I love you," he said, and she sighed. "You were wonderful; you're beautiful," he said, and she believed it, holding him tightly, feeling their warmth.

They nestled together for a long while, dropping off to sleep; then they made love again, and she wondered how it could be better than the first time, but it was.

Then they ate the picnic lunch, and he could not keep his hands off her, stroking and loving her, and she thought she could never ever be happier or more fulfilled, and she loved him and cared about nothing else than being with him and satisfying him.

She was transformed, and everything in her manner spoke of what had happened, and her mother knew as soon as she saw her what had happened. Surely the engagement would come now, she thought, but when no announcement was forthcoming, she brought her concerns to her husband.

Their daughter was ruined, a disgrace, and their own name besmirched. Louis had made fools of them all; they were at the mercy of his discretion. The worst part was that Felise was unconcerned and unrepentant, happy to risk further ruin and humiliation just to be near him.

Of course De Barthelemy could do nothing against Louis; his daughter's reputation and his own good name hung in the balance. He saw Louis's deception and wiles, and realized he was at the youth's mercy.

But, for Louis, a most inopportune pregnancy resulted. Now he had no choice: the only honorable, the only acceptable thing to do was marry the girl. This had not been in his plans; women, he angrily realized, were not unlike gambling, and he'd foolishly overplayed his luck. Now he was going to be saddled with a wife.

Yet he was gracious, and the matter was handled in a civil manner. Felise was ecstatic, her parents overjoyed by relief, and

Louis resigned, for the time being—a bad turn of cards, an unfortunate roll, but only a minor nuisance, certainly nothing important.

The wedding was so abruptly announced and realized that of course everyone understood the circumstances, but they were such an attractive couple, his aura so powerfully sexual, that all would have been forgiven even if the hasty bride's father were not the resident superior, so who was going to be daring enough to waggle a finger or whisper disapprobation?

Louis's salary was increased, a large dowry settled, and the couple moved into a fine villa.

Louis wrote a quick letter to his father, announcing the marriage, and then completely cast the whole boring business of married life out of his mind.

17

LOUIS READ THE COMMUNIQUÉ WITH dismay: the newly appointed minister of colonial affairs, Philippe Vincent Tourney Bourbon de Parnasse, Duke of Parnasse, was scheduled to arrive in Hue in six weeks. The minister would receive and instruct the chief administrators of the French protectorate.

The Duke of Parnasse. And his wife—the message said the minister would be accompanied by his wife, the Duchess of Parnasse, and all arrangements were to be made with her comfort and amusement in mind.

Louis hit his desk triumphantly with the palm of his hand and jumped up. It was only at a time such as this that he wished he had someone to share his feelings with. He wanted to tell someone of his joy—he was going to see his mother, the Duchess of Parnasse. His mother! But there was no one to tell or share with, and as always, he retreated into himself, closing all feelings and plans within, wrapping himself in a cloak of studied control.

Louis sat back down at his desk, his mind dispassionate and methodical. His mother would help him; she'd get him out of here. He had only the vaguest memory of her—a beautiful, tempestuous woman filled with life and movement—yet it was a memory he'd held and cherished since he was five years old. She was beautiful and young in his memory, and he saw her now in his mind unchanged. The duke he could not remember at all, and in straining his memory, all he could picture was a rather heavy, dark presence, cold and forbidding.

Suddenly he did have a clear vision in his mind: he was in a beautiful palace, in a marble foyer, and a thousand candles burned. He was a child, standing off to the side. A young man, his own age now, was there, and a beautiful girl—his mother—

and she threw herself into the arms of the man, and they kissed. Then the man looked over the woman's shoulder to him. With a start, Louis realized that the young man was his father.

What a shock that was going to be for him, Louis thought. He'd never discussed his mother with Andre, and he wondered what his father felt for her now. Then he remembered the age difference; his father was only thirty-nine, but his mother would be almost fifty. And the duke—he would be almost sixty now.

Would the duke help him, or would he resent him still as his wife's illegitimate child? He'd have to feel his father out for that information, but he knew his mother would help him. How could she not want her own child back?

All this couldn't have come at a better time, for he didn't think he could bear his present position much longer; he was sick of the life he was trapped into.

He saw that he'd made a mistake in marrying Felise; she was totally useless to him, and worse, a boring nuisance. They'd been married six months, and he couldn't bear her any longer. She'd been morning sick the first two months of their marriage, and in all the time they'd lived together, he'd never heard her utter an interesting, clever, or amusing remark. Now she was seven months pregnant and he could hardly stand the sight of her.

Nor had he bothered to hide his feelings from her, or his adulteries. In fact, he took pleasure in reviling her and comparing her unfavorably with his other women.

She'd been devastated to learn of this side of him, and now was in deepest misery over his treatment of her, but she was too proud to go to anyone with her problems, especially her parents, so she bore it all in solitary suffering, watching him come back from the beds of others, and listening to him ridicule her condition. To her the most horrifying thing was to have learned that he cared absolutely nothing for the child she was carrying.

Yet no one else knew. De Barthelemy and his wife thought the couple the epitome of bliss and contentment, and Louis was careful when around others to show his wife nothing but devotion and consideration.

Louis read the communiqué again. What a godsend; not only was this his passage out of the country, but the way out of his marriage.

When Louis brought the message in to De Barthelemy, the resident superior was not pleased—he didn't want to journey to Hue, and he didn't want to see the Duke of Parnasse.

"What's he like?" Louis asked.

"A very cold man," De Barthelemy said. "Very disagreeable, but also very clever."

"Do you know him well?"

"No one knows him well. Boulanger thought he did, and we know what happened to him." De Barthelemy pointed a finger at Louis. "Now, there's an example, if ever there was one, of the dangers of women to a man's career. Or to the fate of a nation."

And Louis thought, yes, another reason he'd miscalculated by marrying Felise, though his blunder was nothing in comparison to Boulanger's.

General Georges Boulanger in his own way personified the ineptness and indirection of the Third Republic. He'd been a hero of the Crimea, North Africa, Indochina, and the Franco-Prussian War, and until very recently had been the most popular man in France. The people had turned to this war hero as an alternative to the corruption and stagnation of a government unresponsive to the growing urban class, and one unwilling to face the economic and social problems of the Industrial Revolution.

Boulanger retired from the army to go into politics and was elected to the Chamber of Deputies; then, just months ago, he'd won an election in Paris itself. On the night of his victory, large crowds surged in the streets demanding that Boulanger march to the Elysee Palace to seize power, but the general was more interested in spending the evening with his mistress, Madame de Bonnemains.

Thus, the coup d'etat never materialized, and several months later, Boulanger himself fled to Belgium when he heard that he was going to be arrested for treason.

Had it not been for the woman, Boulanger could easily have taken control of the government.

The lesson had not been lost on Louis, nor another man.

One of Boulanger's early supporters had been the Duke of Parnasse, but Parnasse had seen that this posturing general was not the resolute hero to take charge of a nation, and he'd withdrawn his support and aided in the fall of Boulanger. For his work, the grateful president of the republic and the relieved deputies had made Parnasse minister of colonial affairs.

And now Parnasse was coming to Vietnam—Indochina, as it was now being referred to.

"The man has an unerring instinct for survival," De Barthelemy said, speaking of Parnasse. "How many people could go from intimate of Louis Napoleon to confidant of Clemenceau? The man's totally without scruples or principles." He shrugged. "No doubt he'll make an excellent minister for the colonies."

"I look forward to meeting him," Louis said.

"Well, it can't be avoided, though I hate to take you away from Felise at such a time."

"I've thought about that, sir, and I've come up with a solution. I'm going to take her to Ban Me Thuot as soon as we can make arrangements. She'll be well cared for there; my family has been very eager for us to visit. And Ban Me Thuot is only slightly more than half the distance from here to Hue—in this case we'll both be that much closer to her should she need us. I myself haven't been home in a long time, so with your permission I'd like to travel with Felise and spend time at home before meeting you in Hue prior to the duke's arrival."

De Barthelemy thought the plan excellent, and he gave Louis a month off to spend with his family.

But Felise was not pleased to learn of this plan; she didn't want to travel, or go somewhere unfamiliar, and she was frankly afraid of Louis's family. She wanted to stay in Saigon and be near her mother.

Louis had returned home and announced the news curtly. "I don't care what you want," he said. "We're leaving the day after tomorrow."

Felise had spent her day like she did most, alone. Since Louis was not interested in socializing, she'd been cut off from most of her friends, and had nothing to do during the day except oversee the staff. She'd eaten all her meals alone, padded about the villa looking for something that might interest her; then, when Louis hadn't come home even for dinner, she'd gone to bed, and was propped up, pillows supporting her swollen belly, when he came in with the news.

"Louis, it's not good for me to travel. Can't I please stay here?"

"You're not going on horseback." He sneered. "Besides, there's nothing wrong with you—you're not the first woman to travel while pregnant: I believe there's a New Testament precedent, though you're certainly no Virgin Mary."

"Stop that!"

He started to undress. "Your precious mother won't be here to take care of you anyway, she'll be with your father in Hue. My family will look after you. Or is that what's bothering you—are you expecting savages?"

"No, Louis, of course not, it's just that . . . I didn't want to meet your family like this."

"Don't worry, they're used to it. At least yours will be legitimate."

"Ours, Louis."

"Yours. It has nothing to do with me—one lousy intercourse."

"Louis . . ."

"You wanted it, you begged me. Remember? Remember lying there, calling out my name, moaning," and he mockingly imitated her noises.

"Louis, please . . ." She put her hands over her ears.

"I didn't force you. I didn't rape you. You were begging for it, so don't call it 'our' child, it's yours. It didn't mean anything to me, nothing. It wasn't even any good. It never has been with you, not once—the worse dried-up old whore is better than you."

"Stop it!"

He was naked and came to her side of the bed and stood. "I get more pleasure from my own touch than from yours." He began to stroke himself into arousal. "And I'd rather touch myself than touch you."

She closed her eyes and turned her head.

"It's a lot better this way. I don't have to listen to your disgusting cries and moans; I don't have to touch you. I can enjoy myself. And I'd rather look at myself than you."

He went to the full-length mirror and masturbated in front of it, all the while heaping abuse and ridicule on her.

Andre sat alone in the garden, mystified at what to do with his second son. He didn't know either of his sons, it seemed. Louis might as well have belonged to another species; Andre didn't even pretend to fathom his thoughts and feelings, but Che Lan was no better.

No matter how he tried or what he did, he couldn't penetrate the wall his second son placed between them. Che Lan had never come to him for advice or help, even as a child, but now, at eighteen, he seemed to avoid his father altogether. Never once had he confided in Andre, or demonstrated anything more than what he might have for a distant relative; the youth even seemed closer to Master Chien and Father Bergere, and certainly more so to the women of the house.

Andre knew of course that it was because the boy wanted to deny his French heritage altogether.

Che Lan was polite to his father, and deep down Andre supposed the boy loved him, but it was so restrained, and the barrier between them so concrete, that just being in the presence of his son caused Andre sadness.

When Che Lan had been younger, Andre had done everything

to draw closer to him; he'd gone hunting and fishing with him, had taught him to ride, taught him the jungle, and Che Lan had responded, yet never with the warmth and intimacy that normally passes between father and son. There was always a distance he maintained.

Andre had watched with unhappiness and trepidation his sons growing up apart, not just from himself, but from one another. They had fought as children; then in adolescence their differences turned to frank hostility; now, as young men, they could not bear one another. He had one son who was French and another who was Vietnamese, and both felt estranged from their father.

He was happy that Louis had found such a good position with the French colonial administration, and he was pleased, though surprised, at his son's marriage. He would have liked to attend, but he hadn't been invited, had only received a short announcement of the event.

Yet now he was to meet his new daughter-in-law. Andre fished the letter out of his shirt pocket and read the brief note again, a cursory page informing him that Louis and his bride would be arriving within a week and that she would remain with the family while he traveled on to Hue on business.

Of course he'd be happy to see Louis, and he was eager to meet his wife, but Louis's visits were becoming more difficult, especially as Louis and Che Lan could no longer even maintain a facade of civility toward one another. They bickered constantly and fought over everything; recently it was only through Andre's intervention that they didn't come to blows. When they were younger it would not have been a fair match, for Louis was much larger, but in recent years Che Lan had made up in speed and agility what he lacked in size—not that he was small, for he drew from Andre's size and musculature but he was several inches shorter than Louis.

Che Lan's tragedy, to himself, was that he drew as much as he did from his father, for as much as he wanted to escape his Western heritage, there was physically no denying it; he was a perfect blend of both backgrounds, possessing the sharp, fine features of his mother's face, her black hair and eyes, but he had the broader cheeks and forehead of his father, and his father's body, not the lithe, more sinewy one of his Vietnamese forebears. He was a strong, powerfully built young man of keen intelligence and quick wit who looked neither French nor Vietnamese, but exactly what he was, a hybrid. And he despaired of that, for never once had he thought of himself as anything but Vietnamese.

In his mind he was one of his mother's people, and his thought was more like theirs than his father's; it was more shaded and layered, not direct and differentiated—it was not the brightness and exactness of sunrise, but more that of a muted and obscure dawn, the shadows and evasions of dusk rather than the finality and definition of sunset. He was a good pupil of Chien's, and the bane of Father Bergere.

But about one thing he was absolute and adamant—the necessity of casting out the French. Yet he failed to see that this meant his father, and by logical conclusion, he himself. By the French he meant the military and colonial administrators and the rapidly expanding landowning class—he didn't mean his father, and his friends were polite and gracious enough never to allude to him in their anti-French talk.

So far there had been only talk, though a few firebrands were now pushing for open resistance and armed confrontation. The problem was that there was no central direction to their movement, and no unity with the many other societies and leagues opposed to French rule.

No one wanted French rule, but there was no agreement on an alternative, some desiring a strong and independent monarchy, others speaking for a democracy, and still others, the most vocal of them all, advocating something they called the "rule of the proletariat," an idea they got from a book they spoke of enthusiastically—*The Communist Manifesto,* by Karl Marx.

The problem was that there had only been a tradition of emperor and mandarins, and no one could really visualize the country under any other rule—the alternatives seemed only idealistic talk—and certainly Che Lan, whose great-grandfathers were emperors, never gave a thought to any other kind of authority.

Che Lan himself was so prominent in the rising tide against the French primarily because of his direct line to the throne, though he was unaware that some wanted to exploit him for that very reason. He frequently met with other groups and movements and sought to bring them all together, but the differences seemed too vast: the Catholics and Buddhists mistrusted one another, the landowners and peasants squabbled over land reform, and no one could agree on exactly what type rule, and under whom, the government should have. Then there were the technical problems—where to get arms, how to organize and train, who was to lead, what type of strategy to follow.

At this point the resistance was completely disorganized and ineffectual, hardly more than a debating society, or rather many of them, but they were vocal enough to already be a matter of concern to the French and to the Vietnamese collaborating with them.

Several friends of the family had already spoken to Andre and warned him that his son was placing himself in a dangerous position, that he was rapidly gaining a reputation for being a dangerous rebel against whom the authorities would soon have to take action.

It was for this concern that Andre had summoned his son outside for a talk.

Andre sat on a bench under the shade of a banyan tree and watched Che Lan approach, a smile coming to his lips. In deference to him, the youth had dressed in an unadorned tan robe, shedding his usual black peasant garb, a particularly offensive outfit that Andre believed he wore solely to provoke his family, but which all were wise enough never to comment on, except Gia Minh's two married sisters, who squawked in aristocratic outrage every time they saw him.

"Yes, Father," he said when he approached Andre, and he waited respectfully until Andre gestured for him to sit on the bench beside him.

Andre had never overcome his basic inarticulateness, nor did he yet see himself as master of any situation. Though he was Che Lan's father, he somehow felt himself hardly older, and only slightly wiser, and certainly not the person to impart advice. There was about him no pretension or presumption, and he rarely took himself seriously. In fact, he sometimes had trouble viewing himself as a responsible adult and was amazed that others treated him as such and deferred to him. He always expected someone to break out laughing. Of course, no one ever did, though sometimes he thought he saw smiles on the lips of Chien and Father Bergere when he spoke of weighty matters. He was likewise always a little surprised when his orders were carried out and that what he directed came to pass, and even seemed to work.

Now, speaking to his son, he felt acutely self-conscious, even though he'd gone over all he was going to say with Gia Minh. He really wished it was she outside talking to Che Lan, for he felt her political eye was far sharper than his, and her tongue was certainly more articulate; besides, the boy related far better to his mother, and even his grandmother, Xuan.

Andre gave a thought to these two strong women and drew a deep breath to fortify himself.

"This is going to be very difficult," he began. "I'm going to tell you things you don't want to accept, things I . . . things I probably wouldn't accept either, if I were you. I'm very glad I'm not in your position, and I'm sorry you have to be in such a position."

Che Lan's voice was low and melodious, utterly confident, and absolutely firm. "Father, there's no point in your telling me not to fight the French."

"I'm French, dammit!"

Che Lan was unruffled. "You're not an exploiter. I'm talking about the French in Hue, and Saigon, and Hanoi."

Andre started in again patiently. "There's no separating us. Nor can you be blind to what you are. Whether you like it or not, you're half French, and if the French are thrown out, you're going to have to go too." He put his hand on his son's arm. "Che Lan, you are never going to be accepted as Vietnamese."

Che Lan stared at him stonily.

Andre sighed. "How are you going to fight the French? They have a huge army and navy here; they easily defeated the old emperor's forces."

"There are many ways to fight, Father."

"Do you mean a guerrilla war? They'll hunt you down one by one. How many of you are there?"

"Many. The whole country will rise up."

"Nonsense. Already people are clamoring to ingratiate themselves with the French and get themselves into high positions—these people will fight you even more viciously than the French will. Never, never underestimate the viciousness of cowards. And what will you fight with? And who will lead? Some of the societies and groups won't even talk to one another. There's no central resistance."

"Is that a reason not to resist tyranny?"

Andre smiled at his son. "No."

"Do you think what the French have done here is right?"

"No."

"Then why don't you fight? Why don't you speak out?"

"Because I promised your grandfather I'd protect his family. Your grandfather was a very good and wise man who—"

"Who was killed by those who didn't want Vietnam free. Tell me, do you think my grandfather would stand by now and let the French make a colony out of his country?"

"I don't know what he would do now," Andre said truthfully.

"Well, if Ahn was the man I heard he was, I can tell you that he'd be fighting the French now."

"But, Che Lan, there are ways and there are ways. You've chosen the one which can't help but lead to futility, or worse." He put his hand on his son's shoulder. "Che Lan, the French know about you, and the Vietnamese who are working with the French would love to turn you in as a rebel. If you are not very careful, you're going to . . . there won't be anything I can do for you."

Che Lan shook the hand away. "I don't want you to do anything for me. I'm not afraid."

"Won't you give careful thought to what you're doing and see how dangerous it is? Won't you consider fighting another way?"

"What other way?"

"From within. Join the administration, become part of it, and change it as you rise. You're in a remarkable position—you have relatives at court, I have close contacts among the French—you could easily have vast influence in no time at all."

"And I'd have to learn to deal with people like my stepbrother every day. No, thank you. I'd have to learn to be a sycophant. No, thank you. I'd have to kiss French asses. No, thank you."

He looked at his father with fierce determination. "Father, I've got to do what I have to do, you know that. I will not live as a slave to the French. I won't have my child be a slave."

He looked away quickly, flushing, and suddenly he wasn't the strident revolutionary, but the very embarrassed boy.

Despite all the seriousness of their talk, Andre laughed. "No! Has the revolutionary fallen in love?"

Che Lan tried to regain his fierceness, tried to stare down his father; then he grinned and lowered his head. "Yes."

Andre slapped his son around the shoulders. "Well, for heaven's sake, tell me about her. Who is she? Where did you meet her?"

"Her name is Ly Mien Con. You know her father, he's a merchant. We met at a political meeting."

"Her father lets her go to antigovernment meetings?" Andre couldn't hide his disapproval.

"She's not the type of girl a father could tell what to do."

"Oh." Andre smiled faintly. "One of those," and he was thinking of his own wife.

Suddenly Andre was filled with fatherly feelings. Che Lan had never before demonstrated any interest in girls, and now he felt solicitude and protectiveness for his younger son. In his mind he saw the boy stammering and foolish before her, as inept and helpless as any puppy.

"When are you going to bring her to us? We'd love to meet her. Why don't you invite her for dinner?"

"She doesn't want to meet you, either you or mother."

"Why not? We're not so frightening."

Che Lan's hands twisted in his lap and he couldn't bring his eyes to meet his father's. "Father, it was this I thought you called me out to talk about. I thought you knew."

Finally he brought his eyes to his father, and seeing the utterly puzzled look on his face, he gathered his courage and said quickly, "Ly is carrying my baby, and she'll marry me only if I leave here. She doesn't want to meet you because you're French, and she won't meet Mother because of her ties to the throne."

Andre was stunned, so stunned that his face still registered perplexity. Then he felt like a fool—treating his son like a child, lecturing him, not for a moment imagining . . .

"We're going to marry and live on a small piece of land farther out in the province."

"What? But you can't . . . I mean, your mother . . ."

"Father, I love Ly. We've been sleeping together for three months; we knew what we were doing, and the baby . . . well, we're ready for it. We've talked about our future; we know it isn't going to be easy. I'm sorry she feels the way she does about you and Mother; maybe she'll change her mind, but I can't make her. She's her own person. We're different people and we accept each other for what we are. I don't believe many of the things she does—I'm not a Marxist."

"A Marxist!"

"But she is. We can't live with you and Mother, and I can't stay here any longer—I know I can't work against the French and live here on a French plantation."

"Che Lan . . ."

"I have to live my own life, Father."

"But you don't have to leave us. And she . . . if she met us, I'm sure . . ."

"Yes, maybe, and I'm sure someday that will happen, but not now."

Andre bowed his head.

"It'll be all right, Father. It'll just take time."

"I never expected anything like this. I never thought about you getting married, or even . . ."

"Sleeping with girls? Did you think Louis had a monopoly on that?"

Louis! Dear God, Andre thought, he'd forgotten all about

him. He felt again for the letter in his pocket. "Your brother's coming in a few days. He's bringing his wife."

Che Lan grimaced.

"Spare us all that, please. It's going to be hard enough adjusting to what's happened without you two fighting. Can you be civil to one another for a few days?"

"*I'll* be civil."

"Thank you, that's all I ask." He took a deep breath, looked at his son, then shook his head, but with a faint smile on his face. "When are you leaving us to go out into the world? It's not an easy place, I assure you. I was your age when I first set out, though I didn't have the burden of a wife. I suppose there's no keeping you back, any more than there was hope in holding me back."

"I'll leave as soon as Father Bergere will marry us."

Andre's temper flared. "Why will she let Father Bergere marry you? He's French."

"Priests are different."

"So are fathers and mothers. And what's she marrying you for if she doesn't like your mother's blood or mine—does she suppose yours is different? More proletarian?"

"Father . . ."

"All right, all right. But you have to tell your mother—I won't. And your grandmother. And you can't leave here until Louis and his wife have come."

Che Lan nodded. "All right."

Andre waved his hand. "Now, go tell your mother; and let me sit here and absorb it all."

He watched his son walk away; then he exhaled deeply and looked up into the tree's gnarled limbs and full foliage. Suddenly he didn't feel like a young man anymore.

Che Lan tapped lightly on the door of his grandmother's sitting room and entered quietly when she bid him, so somberly that both Xuan and Gia Minh exchanged glances as he approached.

They were having tea, a daily ceremony, for Gia Minh visited her mother every afternoon at this time.

The room was almost harshly bright. Sunlight streamed in through open windows and reflected off highly polished wood floors; there was almost no decoration or furniture to mute the dazzle; it had the simplicity and purity of light itself, and the two women, dressed in white, added to the templelike aura.

Gia Minh took her son's hand and patted it when he came to her and bowed to his grandmother.

"How nice you look, Che Lan," said Gia Minh, smiling slightly at Xuan.

He nodded absently, and they waited. He was so much like his grandfather, Ahn, that they knew he wouldn't be able to hold back his thoughts for more than a moment; he might make some woefully transparent attempt at polite conversation, but then he'd barge into what was on his mind. It was of course the single-mindedness of youth, but also the boy was stunningly like Ahn, so much so that it frequently disconcerted Xuan, who felt at times as if she was with the man she'd married over forty years ago, a man who hadn't aged a moment.

"How are you feeling, Grandmother?" he asked politely, and before she could answer him, he turned to Gia Minh. "Mother, I have to talk to you."

The two women waited stoically, as they had for Ahn, but as they never did for Andre, for there was no outwaiting him; for Andre they simply had to anticipate and outguess.

"You know I love you very much."

She didn't even bother to nod, simply waited.

"Mother, I'm going to be married."

There was no expression on either woman's face.

"Her name is Ly Mien Con. She's pregnant with our baby."

He stopped for a second to search his mother's face for some hint of how she felt, but he could detect nothing in her utterly quiet features. When he looked to Xuan, he saw the same passive mask.

"We're going to be married and live away from here. I already talked with Father about it. I told him I had to live my own life. I told him I had to fight the French. I hope you understand that; I can't stand by and let the French take over our country."

Xuan brushed aside his last words. What nonsense all the politics was. "Is the girl all right? Does she have someone to take care of her? You should bring her to us."

"She won't come, Grandmother."

"She needn't be ashamed," said Gia Minh.

"It's not that, Mother. She's not ashamed; we don't feel that we've done wrong. She won't come because . . ."

"I see," said Gia Minh, understanding perfectly. "Do you love her very much?"

"I do."

"Well," she said, and could think of nothing else. She stood and embraced her son, and feeling his back muscles contract, she knew the pain he held inside. "You must tell her that she's always welcome here. Tell her that she has our love, and can have anything we have to offer whenever she wishes to accept it. Tell her—"

Che Lan broke away. He squeezed his eyes to keep back the tears; then he bowed quickly to his grandmother and escaped from the room.

Gia Minh watched long after he was gone, overpowering sadness sweeping her. Then she turned and there were tears streaming down her face. She went to the older woman and dropped down on her knees and placed her head on her lap. "Mother . . ." she said.

"Yes, I know," said Xuan, stroking her hair gently, "I know."

Che Lan regained his composure as he strode down the corridor, and by the time he reached Father Bergere's rooms, he was fully restored—purposeful and energetic.

He knocked loudly and heard a very soft voice inside bid him in.

Che Lan opened the door, but merely stuck his head in. "Am I disturbing you?"

The priest, gaunt and frail, was lying on his bed. He didn't bother to open his eyes. "Everything disturbs me. The still air itself buffets me about. Please come in and close the door—the draft will blow me out of the bed."

Father Bergere was eighty-four years old, and though he said he felt every moment of those years, and he was frail, he was surprisingly energetic, and his mind was not affected in the slightest.

He raised himself with some difficulty, straightened his cassock, then went to his table and sat down, motioning Che Lan across from him. His hands shook slightly, a palsy which embarrassed him, and he clutched them together in his lap.

"Perhaps you shouldn't have gotten up," Che Lan said. "It might be better if you'd hear me lying down."

"Oh, dear," the priest said. "One of *those* conversations. Well, actually, they're sort of like a wicked confession—I find them very invigorating. Well, let's have it." He inclined his head in a priestly manner, as he would in the confessional, and he half-closed his eyes.

"Can you marry sinners, Father?"

"There wouldn't be many marriages otherwise," the priest said dryly. "Are you planning on getting married?"

"Yes. Would you marry me?"

"Well, I suppose you have a bride in mind. Is she a Catholic?"

"Yes. Of a sort."

The priest sighed. "Aren't they all. I find marriages in this family very trying. What do you mean, 'of a sort'?"

"She's Catholic, but she's also a Marxist."

"And what, pray, is a Marxist?"

Che Lan frowned, showing every bit of his perplexed eighteen years. "I'm not altogether sure; it has to do with politics."

Father Bergere waved his hand in dismissal. "I'm not interested in a girl's politics. I'm interested in her soul. I don't suppose it's pure, is it?"

"Father, I—"

"Oh don't be such a prude," he sniffed. "I've been a priest for sixty years; if there's something in the world that I haven't heard about by this time, the shock would be the end of me. Besides, I learned long ago not to pay much mind to what bodies do—that bogus Chinese sage was right about that, at least."

"Well, she's pregnant, if that's what you mean."

Father Bergere nodded. "That's what I mean. And I take it that no angel whispered the news in her ear?"

"Father?"

"Oh, never mind. The men in this family are tiresomely predictable. Your poor parents. And hers too. When do you want to get married?"

"As soon as possible. But it must be a very small and quiet ceremony, just the two of us and you."

Father Bergere's eyes flickered with his first sign of interest. "Is it a secret?"

"No, but . . . we don't want anyone else there."

The priest studied him for a moment; then he spoke slowly with all the wisdom of his years. "I suppose this has to do with that Marxist thing, or politics of some kind, but, oh, dear boy, that's wrong. A wedding . . . a wedding is the affirmation of hope, it's a joyous thing—it's a sacred thing; it's a sacrament for a reason. You're asking God to bless a union, a shared life—you don't want it done in spite and denial. You want it witnessed, you want everyone to see your joy and take part in it; it's a time for renewal. Oh, my dear boy, you're only going to be married once. God will be there; don't hide Him, share Him. Long after this Marxist thing is gone and forgotten, you'll still be married, and you will have your family and the very unhappy memories of how you denied them a special part in your life."

He patted the youth's arm. "Now, you think about this. I'll marry you—before a multitude, or just the three of us hiding in a cave, whether she's as chaste as the Virgin, or as big as a hippopotamus, be you a wise man or a fool . . . but, my dear boy, I want a blessed event, a day of joy and sharing, a day of hope and happiness—for all of us."

Che Lan lowered his head. "I'll talk to her."

"You do that. And send her to me if that doesn't do any good." He struggled up. "Help me find my glasses. And where's my cane? I want to take a walk."

Che Lan handed the glasses to him, but the priest's hand shook too much for him to steady them, so Che Lan placed them for him; then he bent over and kissed the priest's forehead.

Father Bergere's hand fluttered up and he waved him away in pleased embarrassment. "Oh, go talk to that silly girl."

As Che Lan was striding away from Father Bergere's rooms, he turned into another corridor and collided with Chien, almost knocking the Chinaman to the floor.

"Master Chien! I was going to look for you."

The Chinaman braced himself against the wall. "Next time send a servant."

"Are you all right?" Che Lan asked, not a bit solicitously, for he could tell Chien was all right, and the man's robust manner and appearance were simply not such as to invite any concern. Chien was seventy-five, but people had to keep reminding themselves he was an old man; he could easily have passed for twenty years younger.

"May I talk with you?"

"Talk?" I thought you wanted to wrestle."

"I've just come from Father Bergere; now I need your advice."

"Doubtless you do, but I probably couldn't begin to unravel his nonsense; my advice is simply to forget what he told you."

Che Lan laughed. "Don't you two ever tire?" He steered the old man toward a sitting room. "I'm thinking of getting married, Master Chien."

Chien shuffled toward a chair and settled himself comfortably. "I believe you're past the stage of thinking about it. What is it you want to talk about?"

Che Lan closed the screens. "It's rather complicated." He took a seat across from Chien, a little pompously, and quite filled with himself.

Chien eyed him placidly, then reached into his robes and extracted a plum, one of his few concessions to age—plums and grapes, for matters of dentistry, having replaced apples, though to the despair of the girl who did his laundry.

"Ly Mien Con and I are going to be married; she is going to have my child. The problem is that she's a Marxist—do you know what that is?"

Chien's eyes were blank, awaiting enlightenment.

"She believes in a classless society. People such as father and grandfather, our whole family, have exploited others, the workers, and they must be overthrown. Eventually there will be equality and the state will wither away."

Che Lan waited for some sign from Chien, but when there was none, he plunged on. "The proletariat will rise up and overthrow the capitalistic and feudal societies. Bourgeois institutions such as religion and family will disappear in the classless society; there will be no rulers or exploiters. There will be social and economic utopia."

Che Lan stared expectantly at Chien, very pleased with his speech.

Chien stared at him a moment, then spat the plum pit onto the floor.

"Everyone will be equal," Che Lan said a little tentatively. "The history of the world is the struggle between classes and exploitation."

He waited a moment. "Don't you think so?"

Chien's face set severely. "The history of man is the struggle to get into the next higher class in order to exploit those below. No one wants to be equal—everyone wants to be better and have more. There will never be a classless society because there will always be a ruling class."

"But—"

Chien waved his hand imperiously. "I won't listen to foolishness from a child, especially one talking about something he doesn't begin to understand, and using words he doesn't comprehend—bourgeois, indeed. If you and that girl want to spend your time talking nonsense and making babies, that's your business, but don't come to me to listen to it. There's a reason age is revered—one of them is that old men know better than to listen to young men, and especially young girls."

Though he was speaking calmly and his manner was quite at ease, he betrayed his agitation by reaching into his robes and pulling out another plum, which he rolled in vexation in his palms. "I must tell you, though, that of all the things I have ever heard, what you have just said is the most mindless and stupid, and I'm not at all surprised that you heard it from a woman. You are talking against the basic law of nature—not just of man—the desire to dominate and master, the law of survival. Even as the trees in the forest rise toward the sun, and those which fall into the shadow of the taller ones die, so do men seek to rise to power and dominion over other men. So it will always be. Now, what is it you wish to talk about?"

Che Lan was now reluctant to go on, but at last he said, "Ly Mien doesn't want Father and Mother to attend the wedding. She says they're from the feudal order and . . ." He lowered his head under Chien's fierce gaze.

"To whom is your first and foremost duty?"

Che Lan had never seen Chien angry before. His voice was cold and demanding, his manner utterly impersonal.

"To my father. But I love—"

Chien cut him off. "The world is not ordered by love, but by duty. Love is fickle and foolish and subject to whim and emotion; duty is concrete and permanent. As everything has a name, everything has a place, and without this order there would be no harmony in the universe. Your duty is filial, and it is sacred, for upon it rests harmony, and without it is chaos and ruin. Shame on that girl who would turn a son against a father. And shame on you for even listening to such a thing."

"But, Master Chien—"

"How dare you turn against your father! That's the foremost evil in the world. Your father has done nothing to deserve this. Wicked boy! Foolish boy! Why are you listening to a woman talk politics, anyway? Better to listen to monkeys chatter about the moon. Ungrateful child!"

Che Lan jumped up. "All right, all right."

But Chien wouldn't let him go. "You've failed your first test as a man—turning to a woman against your own family. Unhappy child! The stain you bring on this family will never wash away."

Che Lan composed himself. He suffered the words, then said evenly, "You have made me realize my error, Master Chien. I beg your pardon."

But still Chien wouldn't relent. "I taught your grandfather and the Emperor Tu Duc. Even your father, who came from a country far away, listened to me. I am an old man and have seen many things and listened to all forms of nonsense and evil, but I have never seen or heard of a son turn against his father. When that happens, the world will come undone; dragons will rise out of the sea and devour the land."

Che Lan bowed his head, then withdrew.

Chien sat for a long minute; then he went outside. He saw Father Bergere at the end of the garden and he caught up with him just as the priest was about to walk into the bordering jungle.

"You must not go in there. When sons turn against fathers, the jungle is no longer a safe place to venture; the tiger would turn on the snake."

Father Bergere stared at the heavy growth; then he turned back and placed his hand on Chien's arm. "The boy talked to you too? Isn't that extraordinary? Imagine. I'm afraid it's the beginning of the end, my dear Chinaman. What did he call this thing? Marxism? Anything that would turn a boy against his family is a very dangerous thing."

"It was bound to happen," said Chien. "The emperor's lost the mandate from heaven; now he takes orders from the French. If the surface is disturbed, imagine the turmoil below. The order has been undone, my dear priest."

"Oh, I think the boy will come to his senses."

"Yes, he will. But the balance has already been upset; the harmony is undone. It began a long time ago—when the Westerner first came."

"Yes," said Father Bergere, stopping to look back toward the jungle. "We never should have come."

"But then," said Chien, patting his arm, "we never would have been saved for eternal life. What's a little disharmony compared to that?"

Father Bergere smiled, put his arm in Chien's, and the two old men made their way back.

Che Lan sat across the hut from Ly; he tried to concentrate on the speaker, but he couldn't take his eyes off her. She looked so intent and vibrant, raptly listening to the speaker, but he could tell from her expressive face that she was carefully weighing and considering his words.

Shamed by her attention and the lack of his own, he turned back to listen to the agitated man in the front of the cramped room, but it was no use—he was tired of talk and couldn't listen to any more of it.

For him it was all simple: you got arms and fought the French; he wasn't interested in the intricacies of the polemics. If the French were thrown out, the emperor could rule again. He listened to Ly and others debate a new order and argue the merits of democracy, but it made no impression on him: the first thing to do was to cast out the French; after that they could worry about what form of government should rule.

His eyes went back to her. This time she felt his gaze and

turned to frown at him, but he only smiled and continued to stare. He didn't understand how she could feel such passion for words and ideas, especially such vague ones. But she was a passionate woman, incredibly so, almost frighteningly so, and it was this he loved most about her. He had the example of strong women set for him by his mother and grandmother, but Ly was an even more dominant personality and he'd been immediately drawn to her.

The night they'd met, in a hut indistinguishable from this one, she'd addressed the gathered men—she was the only woman, a girl of eighteen—and he'd sat in amazement listening to her well-thought-out and articulated words. He'd fallen in love immediately, as much taken by her beauty as her intelligence.

She was not slight, and there was nothing delicate or fragile in her beauty. She was tall, with long black hair and a full figure, and her manner and appearance were confident and forceful. She was an intimidating woman, not at all deferential. In fact she had laughed at him the first night of their meeting and dismissed him as a child. He'd been stung, and stood apart watching her argue with the older men.

In the beginning she'd avoided him, and he knew it was as much because of his family as his inability to become interested in the political arguments, but gradually she became friendlier, and she realized that he simply was not a man for talk and ideas, but one for action.

As soon as she accepted him as he was, their relationship became physical. He'd been somewhat shocked when she initiated sex with him, but she told him that it was her right to do what she wanted with her body, and that women had too long been exploited by men. She said she enjoyed sex and asked him why it should be something solely for men. In this, as in so many other things, she opened his thought. She said she couldn't stand the feudal order in the country which bound women to men, and she hated her father for what he'd done to her mother. She said she'd never be subservient and dominated, be it to the French or any male. She wanted freedom, and not just as a Vietnamese, but as a woman.

She changed his views on almost everything, and showed him new ways to see. Yet he could accept her strength because of the strong, powerful women in his own family. But while he loved her deeply, he was still intimidated by her.

They had been sleeping together for three months, yet even so he wasn't completely confident of his position with her. Two weeks ago when she'd told him she was pregnant, she seemed neither worried about her condition nor concerned for the future, and she'd refused his offer to marry. He knew that she liked him, but he wasn't sure that she loved him, nor whether she'd ever marry him. But for him there was only her; he could never love another after her.

So now his dilemma was acute: he had to choose between his family and her. She'd made that very clear before; to her, his family represented everything that was wrong with and which plagued Vietnam.

He was staring so intently at her that he didn't realize the meeting had ended. He'd attended meetings such as this for years, and he was bored beyond endurance by them. They were always the same, furtive meetings in peasant huts, a litany against the French, endless debate as to what to do, and nothing ever resolved.

They met at the door going out, and he put his arm around her and kissed her fully on the mouth.

"I love you," he said.

"You didn't listen to two words tonight."

"I've heard them a thousand times—it's always the same, just talk; I'm tired of talking."

She reached inside his tunic and grabbed his skin. "So's everyone else; if you'd been listening, you'd have heard that we're finally ready for the next step."

"I didn't hear anything."

She stroked his chest sensuously. "I know."

He pulled her hands down. "Stop doing that. I can't think. What step?"

"We're getting weapons from Hue, rifles stolen from the army."

"But . . . I mean, when . . . I mean, what will we do with them?"

Her hands went back to his chest, then circled around his back and dropped down lower to reach for his hips. "We talked about that, too. Why do you even come to these meetings?"

"To see you." He guided her against the wall of the hut and pressed tightly against her, kissing her neck and ears. "Can we go somewhere?" he whispered.

"Yes," she said, and pressed back against him. "We have to talk."

He laughed and led her to the house. "We've had enough talk for one night."

* * *

They nestled in each other's arms, sated and happy from their lovemaking, he still inside her, his mouth nuzzling hers, their naked bodies bathed in the glow from the moonlight streaming through the open screens.

They had ridden directly to the hut Andre had built years ago, now deserted and in disrepair. Che Lan had played here as a child, and sought refuge in it as an adolescent, and brought Ly here for their lovemaking. It was their private place and they had fixed it up for their small needs—a bed, coverings, some candles.

She pulled away from him and sat up on the bed. "We have to talk about getting married."

He sat up too, fully awake and tense, for this was what he had dreaded.

"My family is very unhappy," she said.

"You told them about the baby?"

"Yes."

"I should have been there when you told them. I want them to know that I—"

"It was my business to tell them. But I didn't know how much it would hurt them. My mother cried, my father cried . . . even I cried, and you know how I feel about my father. Still, I couldn't hurt him this way. He can't help the way he is or how he thinks; he doesn't know any other way. He can't understand how I feel, and my poor mother, she can't understand anything. All they know is the past. I've hurt them enough as it is."

She looked at him directly, but for the first time he saw her vulnerable. "Will you marry me, Che Lan? I'll be a good wife for you, I promise."

He took her hands and brought them to his mouth to kiss. "I asked you to marry me as soon as you told me about the baby. I want to marry you now. I want to live with you forever. I ask only one thing of you. If you love me, you'll understand. I want you to meet my family. I want you to come to my house. I want to marry you with my family present. I can't hurt my family by turning from them, any more than you can hurt your family. My family can't help the way they are, either."

"Yes," she said. "I was wrong before; I saw that when I saw how much I hurt my parents."

"Thank you," he said, kissing her mouth and pulling her down against him.

The meeting was arranged and everyone was nervous and ill-at-ease, especially Andre, who feared a confrontation and unpleasantness, but everyone went so out of his way to be polite and gracious that there wasn't the slightest conflict.

Ly had expected simple, spoiled women, and was surprised to meet such well-informed, strong personalities. Gia Minh asked her directly about her involvement in the secret societies and professed great interest in the movement. Xuan asked numerous questions also, and Ly was completely disarmed by her kindness and solicitude.

Father Bergere and Chien she found endearing, though she had trouble taking men so old seriously.

But her biggest surprise was Andre; she'd expected a much older man, forbidding and arrogant. She liked him exceedingly, much against her expectation. He was kind and charming, and, she discovered, somewhat shy; he was a very attractive man, she thought.

They were in the sitting room, drinking tea and making polite conversation, when Father Bergere leaned forward in his chair and said to Ly, "Well, I just have to know—what is a Marxist?"

There was an almost audible gasp and shushing sound; then there was an uncomfortable shifting of bodies on seats, but Ly met Father Bergere's gaze directly. "A Marxist believes that the masses have been exploited by the landowners and ruler, and that the wealth should be redistributed. We believe in a classless society of equality in which everyone works according to his ability and receives according to his needs."

"What a marvelous idea," the old priest said, nodding his head and turning to everyone else for confirmation. "Don't you think so?" he asked Andre.

"Yes, I do," said Andre.

"I think it sounds just wonderful. Maybe I'll become a Marxist too," said Father Bergere.

When she had left, Che Lan couldn't contain his pride and pleasure. "Don't you like her?" he asked everyone.

And they, rather much to their surprise, had to admit that they did.

Hasty visits were planned between the two families, and the marriage was arranged for the following week, a delay Che Lan agreed to only upon the explicit request of Andre, who wanted Louis and his wife to attend.

Che Lan was not eager to have his stepbrother at his wedding, in fact had planned to avoid him entirely during his visit, but he'd acquiesced to his father's plea, though he told him a conflict probably couldn't be avoided, especially as Ly and Louis would most likely detest one another.

But Andre foresaw no difficulty. Probably Louis was a changed man since his own marriage, he said. Everything would be fine, he predicted.

Andre was very happy at the prospect of his older son's return, and his younger son's marriage. He didn't even mind the idea of being a grandfather, though the thought of it made him laugh. He wondered what his own great-grandmother would have said to his becoming a grandfather. But he quickly drove that from his mind, for it conjured up his youth and France, and he still found those memories painful. He didn't want to think about Catherine.

18

IN THE MIDDLE OF A stifling hot afternoon, a carriage drove up to the house in Ban Me Thuot and Louis jumped out. He had no time even to stretch his legs before his father came down the steps and embraced him, and behind him appeared the rest of the household, who'd been waiting in the living room ever since they'd received word that the carriage had reached the city.

"You look wonderful," said Andre, clasping his son, a gesture Louis bore with only faintly disguised distaste.

He nodded to the others but made no move to greet them more warmly, and they all stood awkwardly until Gia Minh said, "Well, let us meet your bride."

"Yes," said Andre, "for God's sake, get her out of that hot carriage and into the house."

Louis thrust his hand inside the carriage as though he were fetching an apple, and in a second Felise stepped out, obviously frightened and embarrassed, though she did her best to affect composure.

Everyone merely watched openmouthed as the very pregnant Felise stepped gingerly out of the carriage. She clutched her bonnet and attempted a smile, but it froze on her lips as she saw the stares of everyone before her.

Xuan recovered first and stepped forward, embracing the girl and kissing her cheeks in the French manner. "We're very pleased you came. Welcome to our house. I am Xuan."

Felise made a slight curtsy to the regal white-haired woman. "I know who you are. You are Princess Nguyen."

"No, I am Xuan, and this is my daughter Gia Minh."

Gia Minh stepped up, all graciousness and solicitude, and as direct as she had always been. "We had no idea you were pregnant. How lovely. But shame on you, Louis, for not telling us. And shame on you for having her travel in such a condition, though we're delighted to have you." She took Felise's hand, then instead hugged her in welcome. "This is my husband."

Felise put out her hand, quite amazed and taken with Andre's youthfulness—her own father was many, many years older—and Andre raised it to his lips. "I'm very happy you've come. We shall do our best to make you comfortable. Was your journey tolerable?"

Felise, relieved by the family's warm and gracious welcome, overcame her initial nervousness and fairly radiated happiness. "Oh, I'm very pleased to be here. I've been so looking forward to meeting Louis's family. And the trip was—"

"Can we go inside instead of jabbering here in the heat?" said Louis, rudely cutting her off.

"Well, not before I meet her," said Father Bergere, and he came tottering down the steps and almost fell into her, but Andre steadied him upright. "How are you, my dear? I'm Father Bergere. I'm very old and fragile, but do give me a careful kiss. It's only been in my advanced age that I've realized how much I enjoyed such harmlessness."

She leaned forward and kissed his cheek. He beamed happily. "And that dreadful Manchu there is Master Chien. I've dedicated my life to saving his soul, but I've lived in vain."

Chien came down the stairs somberly and bowed to her. "You honor us with your presence; there is much luck and happiness bestowed on the house which receives a mother with her child."

Felise took Andre's arm and was led into the house. "I *am* glad to be here," she said emphatically.

Louis's feelings for Felise became readily apparent to all in a short time; he treated her with contempt, alternately ignoring and ridiculing her, and made no attempt to hide his dislike for her.

No one could understand why; she seemed a lovely girl, and they were all taken by her simple decency and the joy she took in everything. No one said a word when Louis abused Felise, but they all cast their eyes down in embarrassment.

When they were alone together in the study after dinner, Andre tried to broach the subject with Louis. They had brandy and sat on rattan chairs across from one another.

"She really is a charming girl," Andre said. "And she seems quite devoted to you."

"Yes. You'll find her no trouble while I'm gone."

"You don't seem very excited about the child."

"I'm not very excited about the child."

"Well, you'd better get used to it. And the idea of having a wife also. That doesn't seem to please you much either."

"Oh? Does it show? More brandy? It's really not bad—far better than that swill Felise's father serves."

Andre gazed at his son thoughtfully. "Why did you marry, Louis?"

"Isn't it obvious? It was the honorable thing to do, wasn't it?"

Andre's finger ran unhappily around the rim of his glass. There were so many things he wanted to tell his son, but he knew it was all futile. Where had he gone wrong with Louis? he wondered. Or had it all been determined long before he took him away from France? And wasn't there anything he could do now? Can't you tell another how to be happy, and kind, and good? And can't another see what's right and meaningful?

"I suppose you should know this," Louis said, breaking into his thoughts. "I'm going to Hue to meet with the Duke of Parnasse. He's the minister for the colonies."

As hard as Andre tried, he couldn't hide his surprise. "Parnasse?"

"His wife's coming also. You remember her—my mother?"

Andre didn't give him the satisfaction of a response; instead he poured more brandy, then studied its color in the light. When he brought his gaze to Louis, it was completely noncommittal.

Louis met his gaze evenly. "I think it's time you told me about my mother now."

"All right," Andre said, settling into the chair, apparently at ease, "though there isn't much to know. Your mother and I were strongly attracted to one another once. She was married to Parnasse, but it wasn't a happy marriage. When I was invited to their château during a vacation period from the academy, I had an affair with your mother—that's when you were conceived. While I was there I learned that Parnasse had killed my father; he'd also made my mother his mistress. One night I thought I killed him—that's why I fled France. Only when I returned some years later did I learn that you'd been born. That, rather briefly, is the history."

"Why did Parnasse kill your father?"

"I don't know, though I can guess. Parnasse likes men; once he tried to bribe me."

Louis smiled appreciatively. "It all sounds like a sordid business."

"Part of it was, but not the part with your mother. I liked her very much. I suppose I was in love with her then; I was only nineteen. She had a great deal of life, and was very beautiful."

They stared silently at one another.

"Do you think they'll help me?" Louis asked at last.

"Help you what?"

"Get out of here. I hate this country. I want to go back to France. None of us belongs here, except that stupid stepbrother of mine."

"I think you should be very careful around them, Louis. I suppose your mother would help you, if she can. Parnasse? I don't know what he'd do. I understand that he wasn't kind to you as a child; he may still resent you."

"Well," Louis said, not a bit concerned, "we'll just have to see what happens. Is there anything you'd like me to convey to them for you?"

Andre ignored that. "Please be careful, Louis. Remember that Parnasse killed your grandfather. Don't trust him."

"I'll be careful," he said with assurance and self-satisfaction. Then he went to the brandy and poured more for himself. "And speaking of unpleasant things, where's my stepbrother?"

"I wondered when you were going to ask about him."

"He doesn't often come to my mind. Is he avoiding me? That would be nice, though much too considerate of him. Or is he at one of his tribal meetings, planning the overthrow of civilization?"

"I suspect he's working on the property I gave him."

Louis's eyes narrowed. "You gave him property?"

"Don't worry, you're getting a wedding gift of exactly the same value."

"What's the occasion for his gift?"

"Your brother's getting married in a few days. He too is doing the honorable thing, though I believe he's also motivated by love."

"Che Lan?" Louis laughed. "I didn't even know he was aware of women, he's so wrapped up in his ridiculous politics. Why, I may have to change my opinion of him."

"I don't think so—just be pleasant, that's all we ask. And try to be civil to her."

"I'm always civil to women—I like women."

"You might not like Ly. She's even more politicized than Che Lan; she's a Marxist."

Louis laughed outright. "A Marxist! Well, it serves that ass brother of mine right. You know, he's going to get himself in serious trouble pretty soon, not that I care, but if you do, you'd better have a talk with him."

Andre sighed. "I have; it's like talking to you."

"Then maybe what he needs is some time in jail—that ought to cool his fervor . . . hers too."

Andre looked at him uncertainly. "You'd never say anything to anyone, would you? He is your half-brother."

Louis stood, affecting great boredom. "He's nothing to me."

Back in his rooms, Felise had waited up for him. She was excited and happy and wanted to talk.

"Louis, I really like your family. They've all been very kind. I like them all. And Father Bergere and Chien are so—"

"Oh, shut up, Felise, I don't even want to listen to you. Your voice is whining even when you're not whining." He undressed and stroked himself to arousal. "I need you tonight. Just shut up and don't say anything. Serve some useful purpose for a change."

When Che Lan returned the next day from working on the hut where he and Ly were going to live, he and Louis greeted each other with cold correctness, exchanging insincere congratulations to one another.

Che Lan didn't expect to like Louis's wife, and was highly reserved when he met her, but she was so pleasant that he couldn't help but warm to her, yet he sensed in Felise's sad manner her unhappiness, and he correctly guessed it was Louis's doing. She seemed much too nice for him and not at all the person he would have expected his stepbrother to marry.

Louis, to everyone's surprise, got on well with Ly, and she, who'd been prepared by Che Lan to expect the worst, found him charming. He asked her about her politics and seemed to take a genuine interest in her views.

In private he castigated Felise for having no views, and he compared her unfavorably with Ly, calling her mindless and boring. She wept and felt alone and isolated, lost in the preparations for the marriage, and humiliated by her husband's treatment of her.

The wedding was a simple ceremony attended by only the two families, and after a brief celebration, the couple retired to their hut.

The following morning, before anyone else rose, and without saying good-bye to his wife, Louis departed for Hue.

The atmosphere of Hue had changed drastically since the last Vietnamese resistance had been overcome. The evidence of French authority was everywhere, with French troops present on all the streets.

At the palace the French maintained the facade of Vietnamese rule and limited their presence; there were no troops on the imperial grounds, and only a few French officials and clerks coordinated policy with the mandarinate. Outwardly the palace and palace life seemed unchanged from the days of independent rule, but Louis noted immediately the underlying changes, the deference and obsequious behavior of the Vietnamese to the French. There was no doubt at court as to who ruled the country.

For Parnasse's visit, the duke and duchess were lodged in the refurbished apartment where Xuan had once lived. Other senior officials were spread throughout the palace; De Barthelemy was given a large suite in the wing with Parnasse, and Louis had an adjoining room.

De Barthelemy was very pleased to see him and happy to hear of Felise's comfort. He told Louis that he'd arrived just in time, for the reception for the Parnasses was to be held the following night, and De Barthelemy's private meeting with the duke was for the morning after. Louis learned that Parnasse had arrived two days before but had sequestered himself in his apartment to recover from the long journey; he had not yet met with the emperor or the chief mandarins.

As soon as he was settled in his room, Louis sought out the one person at court who would tell him everything he needed to know.

Lady Deng lived in ostentatious splendor in the center of the palace, not far from the royal apartments. Though an old woman—seventy-one—she still exercised vast influence; she had sided with the winning forces and continued to advise the man she'd helped place on the throne, the French puppet, Emperor Dong Khanh.

She was delighted to receive Louis, flattered by his visit, and wanted to know all the news of Ban Me Thuot.

Age had at last mercifully softened her appearance; she was even fatter, and her once garish makeup and costuming now made her look somewhat dowdy and ridiculous. But there was nothing diminished or softened in her manner or thought.

She motioned to a settee, then sat beside him, her breath hot and her eyes leering.

"You're much handsomer than your father," she said. "He had such a cow expression on his face. Yours is wonderfully, sexually wicked. Your promise is undeniably appealing."

He laughed and didn't draw back in the slightest.

Her hand dropped to his knee and stroked softly. "You're one of my few regrets," she said. "I'd love to have you in my bed.

Alas, I have nothing left to entice you there with.'' She batted her eyes and drew her hands up to her chin in self-mockery. ''My beauty has faded. And as you French have taken all power, I can't even bribe you with that. What is it you come to me for?''

''Homage, my lady. And information.''

''And in return?''

''Even more useful information. I shall be able to help you considerably.''

She gestured about her luxuriously appointed room. ''My needs are simple. And my position secure.''

''I can make it invulnerable.''

She laughed. ''At my age, the only temptation would be time; would you bribe me with another day of life?''

''You look as though time is no pressing matter. Perhaps you should settle for safety. I can guarantee that. I think we two understand one another. Too bad we're separated by so many years—we would have made a wonderful partnership.''

She appraised him carefully, then smiled. ''We might not have survived one another.''

They bantered a bit, then settled down to an exchange of information. Though she knew more and had more to pass on, she was willing to do it because she saw in his cunning, self-assured nature a valuable ally for the future—he was unquestionably the most clever foreigner she'd encountered, and, to her appreciation, the most amoral.

He wanted to know exactly what the mandarins thought and if the regents could be trusted. She told him that despite their public denunciations of the rebels and the secret societies, they all maintained liaisons with the different factions. She herself had a vast network of informers and even knew of Che Lan's activities in Ban Me Thuot.

''We are siding with you, but you certainly don't have our loyalty. We're merely waiting, though my own view is that the throne will become so reviled for its submission that when the revolution comes, it will be the end of both the French and the monarchy.'' She smiled. ''But that will be long past my time, and yours, so we need not concern ourselves with that.''

''My concern is for the long-range interest of my country.''

''Nonsense. Anyway, there is no long-term future for your country in Vietnam; you already destroyed what little possibility there was for that. There was no support for the throne in the north; the French had a great opportunity to win the people's support, but you lost it. You thought that by killing enough people you'd end the resistance, but you only made the roots stronger and deeper."

Louis knew only vaguely of the repression in the north. In the south there was little need for that, as the area had long ago been pacified, and the central part of the country had been spared because of the limited French presence. Now he learned the extent of the terror in the north—of burned villages and mass shootings, and of the public executions of notables. She told him that now the French were hated even more than the throne had been and that there would be no end to the enmity.

"You know the people and the history," she said. "No matter how long it takes, the people will eventually rise up against you. You could prolong the arrival of that day by tempering your rule—but temperance doesn't seem to be in the nature of men's rule. If anything, I understand that the repressions are going to get worse. All you'll succeed in doing is uniting the people against you. The Vietnamese hate you; without your military the people would rise up and kill you all within twenty-four hours, and those here at court would be the first to turn against you. Over the years you will need an increasingly larger military to protect yourselves. Youth is idealistic and energetic, and ours will fight you until they win; you'll grow fat and lazy with your colony and will be cast out. Ask the Chinaman if I've ever been wrong."

"Oh, I know you're right," said Louis. "I've lived here long enough to know no Frenchman belongs here. But it's such a profitable country, France will never give it up."

"A more enlightened rule could see that that need not happen."

Louis well understood this; he had not been tutored in Oriental thought and history in vain. He knew that repressive French rule would be self-destructive in the long run, for though he despised his stepbrother and all Vietnamese, he respected their dedication and perseverance, and knew that the guerrillas would eventually defeat the French.

They talked for a long time, then dined together. Though wary of one another, they were too much alike not to appreciate the other's company, and they parted with mutual satisfaction.

Louis had never been as excited and nervous as he was before the reception for the Parnasses.

The gathering was not small; in addition to the chief colonial administrators, the ranking military officers were present, altogether over a hundred men. The only woman present was to be the duchess.

As Louis waited with the others for the arrival of the Parnasses, he had to forcibly restrain himself from drinking, knowing that giving in to that temptation to calm his nervousness would dull his thought and might lead to disaster.

The reception was held in one of the palace's larger ceremonial rooms and everything possible had been done to erase the Vietnamese flavor—French flags, the Parnasse crest, military banners, and uniformed waiters. The sea of frock coats and dress uniforms, the banquet table with its silver service and crystal, a quartet playing chamber music, made one forget he was in the heart of the walled citadel in Hue—it was a scene out of Paris.

At precisely five, the music stopped and an officer called the gathering to attention, announcing His Excellency the minister for the colonies, the Duke of Parnasse, and the duchess.

There was energetic applause, then a carefully orchestrated flow of senior officials and military men toward the duke and duchess, all told previously in what sequence they were to present themselves, and how long they were to remain in conversation.

Louis remained far back so he could observe. At first glance, Parnasse was an imposing man, tall, with aristocratic carriage, but closer examination was not flattering. His dissipation could not be hidden by the makeup he used, nor his fatness held in by the corset he wore. His attempt at youthful appearance merely accentuated his age.

In stark contrast was the duchess, far more youthful-looking than her fifty years. She was remarkably elegant and poised, small and thin. Her hair was white, but the effect made her look like a young woman trying to appear old, an effect enhanced by her vitally green eyes, and the small black beauty patch she wore on her cheek.

For a long time Louis stared transfixed at his mother; a riptide of emotions passed through him, emotions he'd never felt before. Against his will he was drawn to the woman before him, wanting suddenly to be alone with her, to approach her quietly and say the simple word "Mother."

Finally he was aware of a touch on his elbow and he realized it was his time to present himself to the couple, first to the duchess, then to Parnasse.

For the first time in his life, his stomach hurt him from anxiety, and he lost his cool demeanor.

He was only a few feet from her, the third away from presenting himself when her eyes, never completely at rest, moved down the line and met his.

They fixed on him instantly, and knew him immediately. He

was caught in her gaze, pinned by the incredible burst of recognition, amazement and joy in her look, and then, just as quickly, she turned away, back to the man before her, and he nearly stumbled, as if released from a powerful grip.

She took her time with those before him, betraying absolutely nothing; he was amazed at her composure and control, and when he reached her, he could only stare, completely forgetting the proper words of introduction.

"Why, Louis," she said, "how good to see you again—it's been such a long time. You look marvelous. Are you staying here at the palace?"

"Yes, madame, I . . ." he stammered.

"Well, we must get together, there's so much we have to talk about." Her eyes shone in triumph. "It's been so nice to see you again." She turned from him to the man behind, who was waiting to present himself.

For several seconds Louis merely stood there blocking the line; then he felt intense eyes on him, and when he looked about, he saw Parnasse staring at him. The duke quickly turned to the man he was with, as though embarrassed by being caught in such a forthright stare, but then he glanced back again to Louis, a searching, questioning look on his face.

Louis moved away from the duke, but Parnasse's eyes kept traveling to him. At first Louis felt nervous and intimidated, then he realized that despite the probing for recognition in the stare, Parnasse's gaze was both inviting and carnal, unquestionably so, and suddenly Louis gained confidence: here was his leverage. His father had been right—there was no denying that in Parnasse's eyes.

Louis waited long past his turn to present himself, until almost the end of the reception; then he made his way to the duke, who tried not to stare at him, but who couldn't avoid it.

Before Louis could present himself, Parnasse took his hand. "I know you. But that isn't possible, is it? Why do you look so familiar?"

"My name is Louis Philippe Lafabre, Excellency. You knew my father, Andre Lafabre, and my grandfather, Alain, who served with you in the Crimea."

Parnasse went white and stepped back, so noticeably affected that a military aide stepped forward to assist him. As practiced and controlled as Parnasse was, he couldn't hide his shock.

Louis searched his face to see what emotions would dominate: at first there was fear, then wariness, then anger and resentment, but then these gave way to a more calculated, probing gaze, and Louis returned an expression of veiled interest and invitation.

"How amazing," said Parnasse. "What are you doing here?"

"I'm secretary to Mr. De Barthelemy, Excellency."

"De Barthelemy . . . Oh, yes." Parnasse was obviously still startled and off balance, and realizing this, so as not to give Louis further advantage, he dismissed him. "I'm delighted to see you again, Louis. Perhaps we'll have an opportunity to chat before I leave."

Louis bowed and moved away, feeling Parnasse's eyes on his back. He mingled easily with the others in the room and affected a completely nonchalant manner. Every time he looked toward his mother, he found her surrounded by attentive men and deep in conversation. The several times he glanced toward the duke, he found Parnasse staring at him, and each time he gave the duke a calculatedly encouraging smile, nodding his head slightly, his eyes sensually inviting.

As the dinner was only for the senior administrators and officers, Louis was not invited, and he ate alone in his room, waiting to be summoned.

The call came even earlier than he'd expected; a military aide escorted him to the Parnasse suite, then discreetly disappeared.

The door was opened by Catherine; she beamed radiantly, then grabbed Louis to her, saying over and over, "Oh, my dear, my darling boy."

There were tears in her eyes when she disengaged and stood back to take him in.

"You look wonderful. What a shock it was to see you; I almost had heart failure. But I knew I'd find you, knew I'd see you again. But to have you there, suddenly standing in front of me . . ."

She clutched him again and let out a choked sob. "Oh, my lovely boy. Oh, Louis." Then she pulled him into the room and closed the door, wiping at her tears with a handkerchief. "This is the happiest moment in my life. You haven't said a word. Tell me how you are—no, don't talk, let me just look at you. And you are glad to see me, aren't you, I can tell in your eyes. Oh, I'm so happy. Dear God, I need a drink." Her hands trembled as she poured herself a brandy. She offered it to him but he shook his head, a genuinely happy look on his face.

"I couldn't stay at that dinner, couldn't make small talk when I knew you were here. I had to see you. And I'll never let you go. Do you remember me?"

"You are more beautiful than I remembered."

"Oh, Louis . . ." She put her arms around him. "But I'm not, of course," she said, still pleased. "I'm old. But do you remember me, really? You were only a child. Oh, the things we could have done together; the plans I had for you. Oh, God, when he took you . . . but Philippe was glad. He'd hated you, and didn't want you back. There was nothing I could do. I wanted you so badly."

She went for another brandy, nervous and giggling. "And you know, I never drink," She laughed. "It's just that . . . well, you just can't know what it's like to have your child back. I feel like a girl again. I'm so happy. Well, I'm just babbling on; you must think me a perfect fool. Well, let me see you. Turn around. Goodness, you are handsome, handsomer even than Andre was. Well," she said, finishing the brandy, "let's not get into that.

"Now, tell me about yourself. I want to hear everything from the beginning. No, start from the end. What are you doing here? What do you do? Are you married? How is . . . yes, how is Andre?"

So he told her, tracing back briefly as far as he could remember. He was amazed how comfortable he felt with her, and how much he liked her. She was beautiful and warm, and for the first time he felt as though he belonged with someone.

She listened to him raptly, sitting beside him, stroking his face and every now and then hugging him, testing his presence, making sure he was real.

"Well, you're coming back with me," she said when he finished. "You're leaving this ghastly place and returning to France. Surely you don't want to stay here among these savages?"

"No, but there are problems," he said. "What about the duke?"

She waved her hand in contemptuous dismissal.

"And Felise. I know this sounds awful, but I don't want to take her with me."

Catherine frowned, slightly perplexed. "But she's your wife. She's going to have your child."

He shrugged helplessly. "I married her because I had no choice; she was pregnant. It was all very stupid and childish; I should have known better. But I don't love her, and I couldn't bear to live with her."

"All right, then, we'll get an annulment; that'll be no problem in France—we have the influence. And certainly De Barthelemy won't cause difficulties; he won't jeopardize his career over such a thing."

"But about the duke—will he permit me to return? How will he feel about me?"

"Philippe and I came to an understanding long ago. We have

much to talk about, Louis; I hope you won't be shocked—though you don't strike me as the naive or prudish type."

Her hand caressed his cheek. "I don't think you take much after your father. I believe you're my child. Did Andre tell you much—about me and Philippe?"

"He never spoke of either of you when I was growing up. We talked slightly before I came here, but he didn't say much. He told me a few things, but he was rather discreet. He never said anything derogatory about you."

"That was nice of him, but I wouldn't have expected anything else from him. He was a very good man—is. I'm sure he hasn't changed."

"He hasn't."

"What did he tell you about Philippe?"

"He told me I should be very careful of him. He was not very flattering about the duke."

"Well," she said tartly, "there's no beating around the bush, a swine is a swine."

"Why have you put up with him?"

"Ah, my dear,I was not born a duchess, I had to marry a duke; one can't be too choosy about them. Besides, as I said, we've come to an understanding; we've not interfered with one another's private lives. We have separate interests."

"I see. But will the duke tolerate me?"

Her eyebrows arched. "Don't be modest, Louis." She studied him carefully a long moment, then said levelly, "I think you should have a talk with Philippe. You might be able to come to some understanding; there's a possibility he might legitimize you—would you like to be the Duke of Parnasse someday?"

Louis smiled. "I would very much. If I hadn't been taken from France, that would be my due, wouldn't it?"

"Yes. The entire inheritance, everything. Now you have to win it back."

"It comes with a price, doesn't it?"

Her eyes were steady on him—calculating and knowing. "It does. You must decide for yourself if the cost is too great, or well worth it. Do you understand me?"

"Perfectly. Is there no other way?"

"I'm afraid not. However," she said, and patted his arm, "take comfort in the awareness that I too paid quite a price for my position."

"Has it been worth it?"

She didn't hesitate. "Yes. All things of value come with a price; I've been well satisfied with my purchase."

He nodded in understanding; then they talked awhile longer, but he left before Parnasse's return, for she told him it would not be good if he found them together.

The following morning Louis went with De Barthelemy to his private meeting with Parnasse.

The duke was excessively polite to Louis and kept glancing at him while De Barthelemy briefed him on the stable and untroubled region around Saigon. His eyes conveyed his interest, and he was almost blatant in his manner of encouraging him, asking his comments and advice on everything De Barthelemy told him.

What he didn't understand, he said, was why French rule was so smooth in the south, and so difficult in the north.

Louis gave him a short and lucid history of the two regions, telling him that the French in Vietnam were dealing with two different peoples and personalities. The northerner was far more aggressive and warlike, and had in fact centuries ago defeated the southerner and absorbed his independent kingdom of Champa. The southerner was more pacific and agreeable, and by nature more willing to accept foreign domination. The southerner also, he said, was no match for the northerner in fighting ability.

Parnasse was very impressed with his discourse and asked him if he thought the north would ever submit to French rule.

Never, Louis told him. Then he was able to steer the talk to the dangers of the French policy of repression, and worked in all the information and gossip he'd learned from Lady Deng. He expressed his own view that the country could never be colonized successfully, but that the more repressive the measures were, the more problems and resistance the French would encounter.

Parnasse listened intently, obviously impressed, and De Barthelemy was pleased with the way his assistant and son-in-law handled himself.

When they left, De Barthelemy congratulated Louis. "He was quite taken with you. I wouldn't be surprised if he offered you a position with him in Paris. Felise will be very proud of you and the impression you made—as I am."

As Louis expected, the call from Parnasse came in late evening, following a reception given by the emperor. Parnasse excused himself early, complaining of fatigue, and had sent an aide to summon Louis to his apartment.

Louis was shown into the study.

Parnasse came from his desk and shook hands. He reeked of cologne and was heavily made-up, his cheeks rouged, and he wore lipstick. The effect was grotesque, doubly so because

Parnasse wore a long smoking robe that was opened at the collar to reveal his flabby white skin.

Louis immediately detected his nervousness and vulnerabliity, despite Parnasse's bravado manner. He knew the hold he had over Parnasse. He was expert at this type of game, and everything in his own manner was sexual and sensual. His movements were lynx-like, and when he stood before Parnasse, much closer than form dictated, he shook his hand in an almost caressing manner, his eyes and mouth in a sleepy erotic smile; then he moved back slowly.

"Well, Louis," said Parnasse, not controlling his eagerness at all, "how good of you to come. I was afraid you might be otherwise engaged this evening. I wanted to compliment you privately for your presentation this morning. You are, without question, the most impressive and promising young man in our administration here, and you seem to know and understand far more than even our senior officials. Please sit down," and he motioned to the sofa. "Would you join me in a brandy?" Then suddenly he remembered Andre. It was almost too much for Parnasse, this youth who seemed to understand, and appeared willing—the son and grandson of men he'd desired so much. "Or do you not like brandy? Would you care for something else?"

"Brandy would be fine, Excellency."

Parnasse brought it to him, his hand shaking slightly; then he sat down on the sofa beside him.

"To you, Excellency," said Louis, raising his glass.

"To us," said Parnasse daringly, his breathing unsteady, but his eyes meaningful on Louis's.

Louis smiled and accepted the toast. "To us."

Parnasse downed his drink to give him courage. "You've talked to Catherine?"

"Yes, I have."

"Then we all understand one another?"

"Yes," said Louis.

"What terms do you require?" asked Parnasse, his hand falling on Louis's thigh.

"I want to be legitimized as your son." He put a hand behind Parnasse's neck and softly caressed. "That way I could live with you without there being any talk."

Parnasse shuddered at the touch, the realization of more than forty years' desire.

"I've had the papers drawn up. Catherine oversaw it; everything is neat and tidy."

"You understand about my wife?"

"Yes. We don't want her in the way, do we?"

Louis stroked the back of his neck. "No."

Parnasse moved his bloated white face toward Louis. "You are the handsomest of them all," he whispered.

Louis didn't close his eyes, nor did he have need of blocking anything from his mind; he was utterly in control and dispassionate. His hand pressed on Parnasse's neck and drew him closer; then he opened his mouth to receive the older man's.

That night, every fantasy and desire of Parnasse's was fulfilled, and by morning he was completely under Louis' spell.

Louis slipped from the duke's bed and was gone by the time he awoke, the papers safely in his possession.

He reported his success to Catherine; then neither spoke of the matter again; instead, they laid plans for their departure. Catherine said she'd work out the details with Parnasse—all Louis had to do was be ready to sail in two weeks' time. It was decided that Parnasse would inform De Barthelemy that he was bringing Louis back with him, but no mention would be made of the break with Felise—that would be handled once they all returned to France.

That very day Parnasse informed De Barthelemy that he had transferred Louis to his staff and had provided him with quarters closer to his own. De Barthelemy was surprised, and a little put off by Louis's suddenly cold manner to him, but he had no choice other than to accept the situation and congratulate Louis.

Louis immediately made himself indispensable to Parnasse, serving as translator when he met with the emperor and mandarins, and providing Parnasse with unusually sharp and astute observations of personalities and situations. To his great pleasure, Parnasse soon realized that he'd gotten far more than an extraordinarily handsome bed partner.

Despite his infatuation, Parnasse maintained a public manner of total discretion, and only one person realized what was happening. That, of course, was Lady Deng, but her eye looked for such things—and naturally found them.

During one negotiation session between Parnasse and the Vietnamese, she congratulated Louis on his promotion, her eyes and mouth expressing her complete understanding.

"The duke seems so much happier now than when he first came," she said. "I hope his happiness is not too demanding for you."

Louis had smiled. "It's not."

"No, I suppose not. I too served an old man once. They are grateful for so very little."

So as not to jeopardize anything, Catherine remained in the background; she knew that she would have her time with Louis later on. And she had such great plans for him.

Louis's mind too was filled with plans. This was just the beginning. France would open unlimited opportunity for him. There would be wealth and position, an open invitation to every circle of importance. What a small price he had to pay, he thought. Besides, it wouldn't last long—the duke was not a well man. He probably wouldn't live very long at all, Louis guessed—let him enjoy his happiness while he could.

And the duke was happy, more so than he'd been in his entire life. He even deceived himself into believing that Louis cared for him. He hungered for it so badly that he believed that anyone as passionate and attentive as Louis had to be in earnest. He could hardly bear it even when Louis announced that he had to return to Ban Me Thuot to straighten out his affairs prior to departing for France, though Louis promised that he'd be back within ten days. He fretted that Louis would change his mind, and he tortured himself with jealousy over Felise, and Louis was careful not to completely reassure him.

When Louis left, both he and Catherine were triumphant, and filled with dreams of the future.

The last person he saw before leaving court was Lady Deng. She had guessed that Louis would be returning to France with Parnasse and would soon, on his own, become an important man in colonial affairs. She wanted to solidify her relationship with him.

"Please give my best regards to your father," she said. "Also, bear some advice and wisdom to your brother from me."

"Che Lan? What do you know about him?" Louis was careful not to disclose his true feelings for his stepbrother.

"As a favor to your family, I'll pass on some information."

"The world is run by favors and favors returned, isn't it?"

"How well you understand things," she purred. "Tell your brother that the French know that the stolen rifles are in Ban Me Thuot, and for the time being he must be careful to dissociate himself from any overt activity. He too might have a promising future—but only if he is cautious."

"Thank you," said Louis. "I certainly wouldn't want any misfortune to come to him."

Then, completely satisfied, Louis left for Ban Me Thuot.

19

FIVE LONG WOODEN CRATES LAY on the floor of the hut; Che Lan couldn't contain his eagerness any longer, and broke one open, pulling out a new magazine-loaded Lebel rifle, only that year adopted by the French Army. Stacked to one side were boxes of ammunition, all stolen from the French garrison in Hue. The sixty rifles and ammunition had been brought here because no one else would risk having them in his possession.

Che Lan handled the rifle admiringly, running his fingers down the gleaming metal barrel and raising and lowering the polished wood stock into his shoulder. It was a beautiful rifle and would give them great advantage over forces still using the slower hand-loaded ones. If, he thought, he could ever get anybody to use them, for the arrival of the weapons had made everyone even more nervous and cautious. The others were all good at talk, but now that they possessed weapons, they had very little to say.

He went to the open screen and aimed toward the jungle. The day was cold and rainy, the beginning of the monsoon season, and though it was early afternoon, it was dark and forbidding.

Watching from across the room, Ly was suddenly troubled by the sight of her husband with the rifle. She knew he was completely lost to it, and to his dreams of fighting the French.

He aimed steadily toward the trees, then pulled the trigger. When it clicked, Ly shuddered involuntarily.

"I don't like it," she said, her hand instinctively going to her abdomen.

He lowered the rifle and faced her, his face flushed with excitement. "The talk has to end. Now it's time for action."

"But this—"

"It's the only way. Do you want our child a slave to the French?"

He went to her and kissed her forehead, feeling very protective and powerful, clutching the rifle in his hand.

"Please put it away," she said "Hide all of it."

"Women are going to have to use the rifles too; it's not going to be just a man's fight."

He held out the rifle to her. She stared at it but wouldn't take it.

"I thought you'd be stronger," he said

Finally she accepted it. It lay heavily in her hands, a cold piece of metal and wood; an awful thing, she thought. She gave it back immediately and rubbed her hands on her arms to rid herself of the touch; then, cleansed, she brought her hands again to her belly and caressed it.She felt immensely sad. "Please put it away," she said again to her husband.

He nodded, though reluctant to do it. He loosened the floorboards and struggled getting all the crates and boxes into the hiding place that he'd used ever since he was a child. No one would find them here, he knew.

Louis reined in his horse a short distance from the house and stared at the almost magical sight of the palace rising out of the mist and rain; he was mesmerized by it, the dark gray day enveloping the jungle, light sheets of rain carried by the wind against the palace, whose tall, steep roof rose majestically over the evergreen mantle of the rain forest. This he would miss, he knew—scenes such as this, days such as this—and he would miss the monsoon as much as the sun, for he loved its dark, terrifying power.

He pulled off his hood and lifted his head to let the rain wash his face and neck; the coolness made him shiver and feel even more alive. Nothing in the world could be this wonderful, he thought, the clean rain, the pure air of the jungle, its lush, heavy smell, the intense movement and sound, an almost bursting vibrancy. This he would miss above all, and even now, after three days' journey from Hue on horseback, he felt renewed and invigorated; he wanted to strip off his clothes and merge with this primeval life.

But instead he dug into the horse's side and rode toward the house.

After he dried off and warmed himself, he went to see his father in his study.

"We didn't expect you back for at least another week," Andre said. "Was there a problem?" He had not looked forward to his son's return.

"Not at all; quite the opposite, as a matter of fact. I have a lot to tell you."

Andre was wary of his son's manner; he'd never seen him so self-assured and intense—Louis's eyes fairly gleamed. "Have you seen Felise yet?"

"Felise? Why would I want to see her? She's all right, isn't she?"

"Yes, your wife is fine, Louis." Andre stressed "wife," but it made no impression on him.

Louis dropped into a chair and stretched out his legs. "That feels good," he said. "Every muscle aches; I dread the ride back."

"You're returning to Hue?"

"Would you get me a drink? I'm too sore to get it myself. Yes, I'm returning almost immediately, as soon as I tie up some loose ends here."

Andre brought his son brandy, then sat across from him.

"Aren't you drinking?" asked Louis, raising the snifter to his lips.

Andre shook his head and waited. The two gazed at one another; then Louis plunged in directly.

"I liked my mother. She's still very beautiful. She asked about you."

Andre said nothing, and his eyes revealed no more than polite interest.

"She's a remarkable woman," Louis continued. "I don't see why you left her."

"She was married," said Andre simply.

"That didn't prevent you from sleeping with her. You could have fought for her."

"For someone so pragmatic, you're sounding very romantic," said Andre with a slight smile. "Your mother was married to a duke; I was a nineteen-year-old cadet. She was not about to leave him for me."

"Well, it would have been nice to have had a family," Louis said somewhat petulantly.

"You had a family here; you still do. And now you have your own, a wife, and soon a child."

"No. That's what we have to talk about. I'm leaving here forever—I'm going to France."

"Felise can't possibly travel in her condition, and it would be a year before the baby could be brought on such a trip."

"Felise isn't coming, and I'm not sending for her. The marriage is going to be annulled." He stretched out even farther, his long legs reaching halfway to his father, and he finished his brandy, his eyes steady and sure on Andre.

"What do you mean? You can't have your marriage annulled."

"I can't, but the Duke of Parnasse can arrange it; he's got the influence."

"Parnasse? What does he have to do with this?"

Louis sat up straight and brought his legs together. He looked directly at his father. "Now we're at the heart of it. You're not going to be my father any longer—the Duke of Parnasse is. He's going to legitimize me and make me his heir. Someday, and not too far in the future, I'll be the Duke of Parnasse."

Andre betrayed no emotion; he sat serenely, his hands on the arms of the chair. "And how is he going to legitimize my son as his own?"

"I was born a Parnasse, Father—don't you remember? I was taken away from my real parents when I was very young. Now I'm returning to them. But don't take it personally, it's strictly a business move."

"I see. And what has this cost you?"

Louis held his gaze. "Nothing that I can't live with," he said evenly.

Andre's eyes flashed, and though he tried to control his anger, it slipped out. "That's disgusting. I'm ashamed of you."

"I can live with that too," Louis said calmly. "Father, I can live with almost anything to become a duke."

"Oh, Louis, Louis. No; don't do it, it isn't worth it. I gave up a career because of that very proposition, and your grandfather gave up his life. Don't make it all in vain. Nothing is worth dishonor, Louis. My God, think of what you're doing. How can you live with yourself?"

Louis shrugged. "I told you, it's a business arrangement."

"But, dear God, your wife. Your child." Andre leaned forward, almost pleading with his son.

"It's all arranged. I've been made his personal secretary and I'll be leaving with him when he returns to France next week."

"Does Catherine know?"

"Oh, yes. She worked out the details; in fact, it was her suggestion. She's much more realistic than you."

"Jesus," said Andre, and he closed his eyes.

"It's not so bad, Father. Don't take it so hard. In fact, it's all rather ironic. Look at what you and your father suffered at the hands of the duke—and now I'll become the duke."

Andre shook his head. "I don't want to hear about it, Louis. All I ask you is that you think of your wife and child. Don't do this to Felise; she doesn't deserve it, and I don't think she's strong enough to bear it. Go to Parnasse if you must, but don't annul your marriage; don't do this to her."

"Father, I don't love her. I married her because she was pregnant. I—"

"You say that as though her pregnancy was her own doing. You made her pregnant."

"I made a mistake, I admit that. But what is so terrible about trying to correct it now? Why should we be miserable the rest of our lives? Why drag out a marriage like this?"

Andre was incredulous, his amazement even greater than his anger. "Have you no thought or care for her or the child? Can't you see what this would do to her? She'd be ruined, Louis; you'd destroy her life. I don't care if you don't love her, just don't annul the marriage. Let her go to France with you—at least there people understand about marriages of convenience. You could have your own life, but at least she'd have her honor, and the child would have parents."

"No," said Louis simply. He straightened himself, preparing to leave. "I'm making a break from this place, a complete and final one; I don't want any reminders, and I certainly don't want any unnecessary baggage."

Andre stood first. "Then go. We'll all be better off without you. You aren't my son any longer; you do belong with Parnasse."

But as soon as he said the words and saw Louis going toward the door, he was overcome with regret and guilt, and he stopped him.

"Louis!"

He turned toward his father, his face dispassionate, not even interested in the final words.

Andre moved to him. "I didn't mean that." His voice was almost a whisper, and he was having difficulty controlling himself. He wanted to pull Louis to him, hug him and hold him, erase all the past, wipe out all the wrong and sorrow—but it was a stranger standing before him. "You are my son, Louis, and nothing can change that, and I . . . I love you. I love you more than my life." He had to brush at his eyes, but he was unashamed of his tears. "I shouldn't have taken you . . . or maybe I should have done things differently . . . I don't know. I don't know now what was right or wrong. I'm just sorry it turned out the way it did. Forgive me for making you unhappy in your life. You don't belong here, I see that now." He put his hand on his son's arm and looked deeply into his eyes. "I hope you find happiness wherever you seek it."

Louis turned away coldly. "Don't worry, I shall."

* * *

When Louis came into their rooms, Felise was surprised, for she hadn't expected him for at least another week. As always when he returned, her initial reaction was mixed—happiness and trepidation; she was glad to see him, but fearful of how he would treat her.

She had just risen from her afternoon nap, though she really hadn't slept, had just lain on the bed and drifted in and out of consciousness, thinking of the child and picturing herself with it—soft visions of play and love. She had moved her chair before the window and had sat in contemplation of the somber scene which captured her own feelings.

It was late afternoon, and dark, and far in the distance she could hear the long, rolling thunderclaps of a storm; the sound seemed to ride the hills toward her, just over the tops of the dense trees. The jungle seemed so forbidding to her, an eerie world of danger and cruelty, and as much as she liked it here, she could not overcome her fear and dislike of the land itself. Only yesterday she'd gone for a walk with Father Bergere, the two of them as slow as turtles, but she'd come back vowing never to venture out again. He'd pointed out several vipers hanging from trees, which she'd thought had been branches, and they even saw a cobra. He told her never to come out alone, for it took a long time to learn what to look for.

He told her that while the area swarmed with poisonous snakes, they would never attack unless provoked, except for the king cobra, the largest poisonous adder, which had been known to pursue men—but this snake was very rare. Far more common were the lesser cobras and vipers, and though they would make every attempt to avoid people, they'd strike if they were surprised or felt threatened.

So frightened had she been that she couldn't enjoy the rest of the jungle sights he'd pointed out, the brilliant geckos and lizards, the gorgeously plumed birds, and the foliage.

She would not go out there again; she would watch the beauty from her window. Besides, she liked it in the house; she had never been treated more kindly. Xuan and Gia Minh each visited her at least twice a day and inquired about her comfort and needs, and at least once during the day Father Bergere or Chien would stop by for a talk. They insisted she take her meals with them and went out of their way to include her in conversation. In just the short time she'd been with the family, she felt completely at ease and comfortable. Even Andre—for he'd insisted she call him that—couldn't have been more gracious and solicitous. She was grateful in particular for his kindness, and found it difficult at times to remember that he was Louis's father.

She rose quickly from the chair when Louis entered the room, and stood nervously, waiting to see how he would treat her.

She always felt shy and deficient before him, and there was nothing intimate in their relationship, just occasional sex, which he'd made degrading for her.

He tossed his jacket on a chair, then sat on the bed to take off his boots. "How are you feeling?" he asked.

Just that simple inquiry warmed her; she could not recall a recent time when he'd asked how she was. She went tentatively toward him. "I'm fine, thank you. But you must be exhausted; did you ride all the way? I didn't think you'd be back for a week. Is everything all right?"

He didn't answer, concentrated on his boots, and to fill the vacuum, she chattered on, telling him how kindly she'd been treated and what she'd been doing.

When he got his boots off, he stripped off the rest of his clothes and lay back on the bed, luxuriating in the softness, and his tiredness that at last could be indulged.

She sat on the bed beside him, almost afraid to touch him, afraid of rejection, but desperately wanting his closeness, any sign of care and need. His eyes were closed and she simply looked at him; then her hand went to his leg, stroking hesitantly at first, until she was sure he would not recoil from her, then more sensually. He began to respond to her touch, and she moved onto the bed beside him. He rolled toward her, his hands going to her blouse, and she whispered, "Please be careful."

He used her quickly, but not roughly, then fell asleep immediately. She roused him to help him under the covers, then lay with him for some time, grateful for his almost-tenderness, and happy with the hope that perhaps everything would be all right. Lying beside him, she felt the baby moving inside her, and she put her hand on her husband, and she was content.

At dinner that evening, no one had seen her so happy and radiant, and when she returned to their rooms, she found that he hadn't stirred. She nestled beside him, and slept that night with peaceful dreams.

In the morning he had breakfast sent to their rooms. His manner had changed completely, and from the first moment she was fearful of him; he was cold and dispassionate.

They were sitting across from one another at a small table, and he quickly downed a cup of coffee.

"I want to have a sensible talk with you, Felise—no hysterics, no nonsense. Just see if for once you can't summon the sense to discuss something intelligently."

"It isn't necessary to talk this way, Louis," she said softly.

He put both his hands on the table and looked deeply into her eyes. "I'm going to leave you, Felise. You know I don't love you. I married you because of your father. There, it's out. But surely you knew this."

She clutched at her side, but she wasn't sure if the pain had come from the baby or from his words. "No, Louis, I didn't know that. I thought you cared for me."

"I do care for you; I just don't love you. I don't want to hurt you now, that isn't my intent at all, but I must speak honestly—I don't want there to be any illusions. Please let me get this out. I thought marrying you would help my career, but I realized my mistake immediately."

She closed her eyes, the words falling like blows, words she knew to be true, words she'd been afraid to face.

"I'm leaving for France next week, Felise. When I was in Hue, I met my mother, the Duchess of Parnasse. When I was a child, my father took me from her. Now I'm returning. The duke is going to legitimize me as his son. It's all been arranged, and they'll arrange an annulment for us."

She was truly shocked. "An annulment? Louis, what are you talking about, we have a child."

He shook his head. "You have a child."

"It's our child," she said angrily.

He shrugged. "I don't want the child, Felise; I don't want any part of it. It's your child."

"How can you say that? What's wrong with you? We made this baby. It's alive inside me—feel it."

"Felise, calm yourself. Please get it into your head that the baby doesn't mean a thing to me. I'll take responsibility for it, of course; the child will be well taken care of, but I won't be tied to it—it's not going to be the basis of my life, or the continuation of my unhappiness. I want out of this marriage, and I'm going to get out with an annulment."

She jumped up, tears and anger fighting for control. "I won't let you do it."

"It's not a matter of that; there's nothing that you can do about it, Felise—oh, you could complicate it slightly, I suppose, make it extremely unpleasant, but I'm sure you don't want that. You wouldn't want me to have to explain how I married you out of pity, or was coerced by your father, who was shamed by his pregnant daughter who'd been sleeping with half the garrison in

Saigon. Of course, our marriage was never consummated—I merely did the gentlemanly thing by attempting to legitimize your bastard child."

She looked at him with incredulity, searching his face for some sign that he was not serious, that this was some awful joke, some new torment, but no, everything in his manner told her that he was in earnest. "You really would do this, wouldn't you, Louis?"

"Indeed I would, if necessary. But you won't let it come to that; your father will convince you of the wisdom of a quiet, amicable settlement. Everything will work out nicely."

"But what about the child? You must care something for it."

"Felise, please get it into your head—the baby means absolutely nothing to me."

"But what's to become of us?" The full horror of it began to strike her. What would she do—deserted by her husband, annulled, wiped out as if she hadn't existed, disgraced and discarded? What would she do with her child, a fatherless bastard child? Where would she live? Who would support her? She'd become a charity case of her family, a disgrace who had to be hidden away. Dear God, and the child. What would become of it?

"Louis, don't do this," she pleaded.

"You'll be all right," he said. "You'll find another husband. Some young man in the colonial office will—"

She put her hands to her ears and closed her eyes, trying to drive it all away.

"My family will take care of you. You could even leave the child here with them and return to Saigon. You could tell everyone the baby died. No one would know the difference."

"Oh, my God, Louis," she cried, shaking her head.

"The baby would be well cared for here."

"Oh, dear Jesus," she moaned.

"You'll find someone else. There's no need—"

She flew at him, her hands going to his face, but he easily deflected her hand and pushed her down on the bed. She struggled against him, but he held her down until she was exhausted and collapsed.

"You'll be all right," he said. "It's not as bad as it seems. Please try to think about it rationally."

He stood over her a moment, then left the room.

She lay utterly drained and stunned. For a long while she didn't move; then she began to cry, softly at first, then deep wrenching sobs. She doubled over in pain and grief, holding her belly, and then she remembered the night before, his hands on her, his body on hers, and she began to twist in agony, and then she screamed, a loud, piercing cry, and she screamed over and over, and her hands beat the bed.

She lay exhausted, her gaze unseeing out the window, and then she focused on the faraway trees of the jungle, and she knew what she would do.

Louis saddled his horse and went out riding, his last ride over the land where he'd grown up. In his mind, the matter with Felise had been resolved. He knew how he'd hurt her, but he believed she'd get over it. She'd be hysterical for a while, but she was too simple to sustain any emotion or thought for long; she'd quickly fix on something else—she'd make plans and busy herself with them. She was such a cow, he thought. Then he drove her completely from his thoughts.

For two hours he rode through the morning mist and drizzle, down all the back roads that led into the province's interior. Several times he stopped to savor the serene beauty, but as the morning wore on, the storm came closer, sweeping across the country from the Bay of Cam Ranh and Nha Trang, gaining force over the central highlands, and raging down now from the plateau of Darlac. It was going to be a fearsome storm, he knew, and he headed back toward Ban Me Thuot before its full force unleashed.

He was only a few miles from Che Lan's hut when he decided he'd stop in—not to see his stepbrother, but to see for the final time where he too had played as a child. The hut had been his secret place also, and he'd spent many solitary hours there. Curiosity also drove him; he wanted to see how Che Lan and Ly lived.

But they weren't there. He walked out into the fields to find them, but they weren't there either—out agitating, he thought contemptuously, and went back to the hut. He didn't like what they'd done to it; it no longer resembled his childhood fort. Now it was a well-kept, nicely fixed dwelling, comfortable and domestic, not at all what he'd expected. He thought they'd be living in squalor, but instead it was clean and tidy, and very traditional—there was nothing French or Western in evidence.

He was about to leave in disgust—it was so homey and Vietnamese, so contrived—when he noticed packing straw and metal banding in a corner; it was the metal banding which caught his attention, for it was so out of place in the rustic room, so foreign. So French, he thought, and immediately made the connection to the stolen rifles Lady Deng had mentioned. Surely

Che Lan wouldn't be so stupid as to have the rifles here, he thought. But yes, he would, he decided; that would be in keeping with his arrogance and conceit and shortsightedness—not even seeing the irony, or hypocrisy, of despising the French, hating everything about them, yet taking their weapons and using their technology. That's what he hated most about his stepbrother, and thinking about it now rekindled his animosity for him.

Stupid, Louis thought, leaving evidence about like this, so sure no one would think to look here. They're hidden under the floorboards, Louis said to himself, their storehouse, hiding place, secret haven from childhood. The damn fool. The first place anyone would look.

It took him only seconds to find the loose boards, and he needed to pry up but one to see he'd been right.

Louis was angry; it was one thing to talk insurrection—he'd let his brother mouth all the banalities—but taking up arms was another matter; stealing weapons was something altogether different. He'd have to put a stop to this, and talking to his stepbrother wouldn't get him anywhere. All right, Louis thought, if he wants to play grown-up games, let him take the consequences. Besides, it'd be better to find out what happens to rebels this way, rather than taking a bullet in the brain or being executed. He'd actually be doing Che Lan a favor by turning him in—would be saving his life, in fact.

He saddled his horse and rode directly to the authorities in Ban Me Thuot.

No one saw Felise leave the house; she slipped out a side entrance and cut through the garden toward the bordering jungle. Though it was cold and the wind drove the rain in gathering force, she wore no cover or coat, and her arms were bare.

She was resolute and in full control of herself; the hysterics were over; she'd made up her mind. She couldn't live with the humiliation that would fall on her, and she wouldn't let her child grow up with that mortification. She had nothing to live for.

The decision had come easy. She wasn't afraid of death; she was afraid to live. She had been such a foolish woman, she thought, such an abject fool; she deserved to die. There was no point in going on—for what, to live a life of being pitied and mocked? A silly, simpering existence, dependent upon others? No, to die was much better than that.

But she feared the means. She was terrified of the jungle, and she shivered, not at the cold but at what lay before her. It would be an awful death, she knew, but so fitting.

The jungle forest was a wall around the palace, a stark barrier from where one stepped from cultivation and order into a dangerous green labyrinth, an enveloping, devouring growth that would quickly overrun the palace itself if allowed to go unchecked.

She stood only a moment at the barrier, then plunged in.

To her surprise, it was quiet; no wind or rain penetrated, and it was not cold. Here, at the edge, the jungle was nearly as dense as in its heart; a thick mat of fronds and ferns covered the floor, and the aerial roots of Aaron's rod and climbing figs hung from the trees and brushed at her face.

The silence was so soothing and peaceful that she shed some of her fear. It was like a church in here, she thought, hushed and dark, the light muted by the foliage as if it were filtered by the stained glass of a cathedral. It was an almost holy place, she thought.

She walked on, deeper into the jungle, her hand reaching up to the branches, not a bit afraid, merely waiting for one of the branches to strike.

It was beautiful, she saw, just as Father Bergere had tried to tell her, and she noticed for the first time the exotic flowers, the brilliant funnel-shaped blossoms of the Chinese athea, pink and blue bursts of rhododendron, orchids, tropical roses, all interwoven among shimmering eucalyptus and silver oak.

About her was an unearthly peacefulness, a tranquillity she'd never experienced. She didn't want to go on; she wanted to stay in the midst of this green realm of serenity. She stopped; here maybe she could think. She hadn't known there was so much peace and beauty in the world. She'd been wrong; the jungle wasn't threatening, not here anyway; it was a sanctuary, shielding her not just from the storm beyond, but from the inner demons which pursued her.

She reached down and pulled a frond; its intricate, delicate pattern made her think of lace, and that made her think of her grandmother, and she saw her in her mind, bent over with her needles, nearly blind, making a christening veil for the baby. She wanted to see her grandmother again. And her mother.

She started to weep quietly. She wanted someone to hold her, to understand. Her mother would. So would her father. She wasn't alone. Yes, she'd been foolish, and made a dreadful mistake, but it wasn't the end of the world. She still had her family, and they would love her and the baby. And she would love the baby.

She'd been simple and weak, and Louis had hurt her terribly, but that was no reason to give up everything. She'd be all right, she'd get over this, and she'd make a life for herself and her child.

There was beauty here, and love in the world, and she'd been foolish not to see it. She'd been about to make a terrible mistake. How simple she'd been, she saw now; she'd be stronger—she'd face everything and go on. She'd bring her child into the world and love it and care for it and show it beauty and the wonders of the world, and she'd never think back on all this. She'd forget Louis; he was cruel and evil, but she wouldn't let him ruin her. He cared nothing for her; all right, she'd face that. It hurt, but that was no reason to give up everything. No reason to give up her child.

She'd have the baby. They'd care for her here, and when she was strong again, she'd take the baby home. She'd face everything squarely. She'd raise her child, and teach it right and kindness, and she'd accept whatever happened to her.

She placed the frond carefully on the jungle floor and turned to go back, resolute again, and slightly exasperated at her own foolishness.

After no more than fifty yards, she stopped; was this the way she'd come? She hadn't been paying attention, and it all looked the same. She continued on a short way, then stopped again. This wasn't right, she thought, and she started back, but she'd walked only a few minutes when she stopped again in confusion. She turned about slowly and realized that she had no idea which way she'd come, or which way was the direction back. She stood completely still in the jungle and listened. Suddenly the silence wasn't tranquil, but menacing; the stillness not peaceful, but forbidding. And it was cold. She shivered and rubbed her arms. Drops of moisture fell on her; she felt wet and clammy.

She had to get out of here; it'd be dark soon and she'd never find her way. She'd heard the jungle at night; it was a terrifying place, filled with shrieks and howls of prey and predator.

But she couldn't be too far from the house, she hadn't walked too long, had she? How long ago had she entered the jungle? She couldn't remember. Had it been an hour, two? Or only a few minutes? She was completely disoriented; not only was there no direction in the jungle, but no time either.

She couldn't stay here; no one even knew she'd come out here—they'd never find her. But which way should she go? She might only be going deeper into the jungle.

Dear God, she thought, what can I do? She couldn't stay and she couldn't go on.

She was terribly cold. And she was afraid. It was so quiet that maybe if she yelled someone would hear her. She called out, screamed as loudly as she could, but the noise was lost immediately, muffled by the foliage, and then she realized that no one could hear her over the storm anyway.

She had to get out. She plunged into a thicket and ran, but branches and thorns tore at her clothes and face, and her arms bled. She forgot herself and screamed again, then ran on blindly.

She cried hysterically. Suddenly the jungle wasn't quiet any longer. There were noises all about her, and nothing was still—everything moved, and things crawled all about her. Birds screamed. She was terrified; her hand touched something slimy; she recoiled and shrieked again and again; then she fell. Bugs were on her, everywhere, her arms and neck, on her face. She tried to crawl away but her clothes were caught; she pulled, ripping her dress, and she collapsed, sobbing.

Then she heard it, an awful hissing.

She knew immediately what the sound was. She'd stumbled into a snake's liar, the vibrations of her frantic movement, not her screams, having startled and frightened the creature.

She tried to raise up, but the hissing grew louder and more intense.

Then she saw it; it was huge, at least seven feet, reared up, waist-high, its tonguc quivering like a flame, no more than three yards in front of her.

She looked in horror at the spread hood, its malignant black eyes, the seething red tongue whipping in front of its metallic-silver head, and she jumped up screaming.

She tried to break away, but as soon as she moved, the cobra sprang, sinking its teeth into her arm, drawing back quickly, then striking again; then it disappeared.

She looked at her arm. An oily greenish fluid, the venom, oozed out of deep slashes and mingled with blood. The pain was excruciating; then immediately the area around the bites grew numb and began to swell.

She screamed, long, piercing cries of horror; then she ran, wildly crashing through the underbrush.

Within moments hands restrained her, fought to hold her still, but she struggled to get free, and wouldn't stop screaming.

In another moment Andre was with her; he held her tightly, pressing her to him, trying to smother her cries and terror. She didn't recognize him, had already slipped into shock, and fought to get away.

Andre tried to soothe her, stroked her head, and attempted to steady her violent shaking.

Her maid had seen her leave the house and go into the jungle. Knowing her unhappiness since her husband had returned, having heard her cries and sobs, the maid went directly to Xuan and told her that Felise was gone.

Alarmed, having heard from Gia Minh that Louis was leaving her, Xuan feared for Felise and immediately went for Andre. As soon as he was told, he sent all the servants into the jungle to look for her, and went in himself.

They had searched for her for over an hour when they heard her screams.

As Andre held her, a servant noticed her arm and pointed it out to him. He examined the wound and knew immediately what had happened. Her forearm had swollen enormously; only a cobra's bite could do that so quickly, or make such deep slashes. He steadied her face and looked into her eyes, and he knew that it was too late.

Still, he took his knife and cut deeply into the wound so it would bleed freely; then he ripped his own shirt and tied a tourniquet just below her elbow.

Together with the servants he carried her back, telling one of them to race ahead to have Gia Minh and Xuan send for a doctor.

Felise had stopped struggling, lay almost inert, the paralysis working its way through her system, and the men ran with her through the jungle. Almost as soon as they left its cover and broke into the open fields that stretched toward the house, the full force of the storm struck. A torrent of rain beat down on them and the wind came at them at gale force. They struggled with their burden and could barely make headway against the raging force. They stumbled and fell, but driven by Andre, they finally reached the house.

Gia Minh and Xuan ran from the house to meet them.

"What happened?" shouted Gia Minh over the storm. "Will she be all right? What was she doing out there?"

"Cobra." Andre shook his head wildly. "She won't make it, it's too late."

Xuan was the most calm. She directed that Felise be brought into the kitchen, quickly examined the wound, and then looked into her eyes. She crossed herself. "The baby. We have to save the baby."

"A doctor. Did you send for the doctor?"

Chien bent over Felise, who had begun to twist and writhe on the pallet bed they'd made for her. Her breath was coming in deep gasps and she was beginning to choke. Her arm had swollen monstrously. "There's no time for a doctor," Chien said.

"Dear God," said Gia Minh. "Andre, you'll have to bring the baby out."

For the first time in their lives, she saw fear in his face. "I can't," he said. "I can't do that."

Father Bergere knelt beside Felise. He steadied her head, looked into her dilating eyes, saw the bluish hue of her skin from asphyxiation, then made the sign of the cross over her. "She's dying," he said. "You must save the baby. You cannot let the child die."

"But, my God, I don't know what to do. I can't cut into her."

Xuan directed the servants to bring towels and tubs of water, boiling and cold; then she went to Felise and ripped open her dress and cut away her undergarments with a knife.

Andre was amazed at her calmness, and that of Chien and Father Bergere. They seemed utterly in control of themselves, but his own hands shook so badly that he knew he couldn't even hold a knife.

"You must cut here," Xuan said, drawing a long line across her belly. "Cut hard, but not too deep. First you'll cut into the flesh and tissue of the abdomen."

"I can't do this," Andre said, shaking his head, then turning away from Felise's agony. Her hands reached up to clutch her throat. Her eyes bulged and then she strained up, her breath coming in wrenching gasps.

"Then," said Xuan, drawing on his arm, forcing him to look, "after you've cut through the peritoneum, which lines the abdomen and isn't too tough, you'll come to the uterus. You must cut hard into that, but if you go too deep, the knife will strike the baby. Cut just enough to go through. Then you must reach in with your hands and pull out the baby. It'll be inside the placenta, which you must cut away. Finally, when the baby is free, you must tie the umbilical cord, then cut it."

Andre's eyes were wide in fear and uncertainty. He looked to the others staring at him, then about the room, which flickered in light and shadows from the gas lamps, and from outside he could hear the crashing storm.

Xuan tugged on his arm, drawing back his attention. "The baby will be all right, but you must hurry. When she dies, there will be no more blood or oxygen going to the baby and it will die too. You have only a few minutes, Andre. Think only of the child."

Xuan had Felise carried to the long kitchen table and directed where the servants should hold her. The tubs of water were on the floor beside the table, and there was a large stack of towels nearby..

There was no question now but that Felise was in her last moments. Her breath was so labored and desperate that it seemed impossible that she could draw another.

Andre accepted the knife Xuan held out to him, tested its feel; then he put it down and sent a servant for his straight razor.

Father Bergere began the final rites, anointing the body and feet, chanting the ancient Latin supplications.

When the servant returned with the razor, Andre handed it to Xuan.

"You bring the baby out," he said. "It would be better for the child. I am not so lucky."

"You are stronger," she said, trying to return the knife.

"No," he said. "You are the strongest. Better that life should flow through your hands."

They gazed at one another; then Xuan plunged the blade into the hot water and told the servants to hold Felise still. Gia Minh held her head, caressing the cheeks, softly whispering unheard words into her ear.

Xuan made the sign of the cross, drew a deep breath, then made a cut.

There was a gasp from Felise, and her body recoiled, but the venom had so paralyzed her, and she was fighting so hard for breath, that she seemed oblivious of the pain.

Xuan wiped sweat from her forehead and brought the razor down again, slicing through tissue; then the uterus bulged up, released from the tight confines of the skin. There was surprisingly little blood, so tautly drawn had been the skin, but as soon as Xuan cut into the uterus, blood and fluid spilled out. She cut quickly through the muscle, though it was tougher and more sinewy than she'd expected, and she could hardly see her incision for all the blood.

She closed her eyes for a second, seeming to draw even greater strength and resolution from within herself; then she dropped the razor and reached into the cavity to pull out the baby. Her hands were drenched in blood and they groped within the slick, pulpy tissue, but then she felt the baby; her hands were on it, and she pulled out the entire mass from the uterus.

No one had even noticed that Felise had ceased breathing and her body had gone totally slack.

Xuan's mouth set more firmly, a small determined woman fighting for the life of a child. She gripped the razor again and sliced at the placenta, a pulpy mass of tissue and blood, and finally she extracted the baby.

"Dear God," cried Andre at the bloody, motionless form. "It's dead."

Xuan tied the umbilical cord with twine, then cut the cord. The child lay still in her hands. There was no sign of life.

Instinctively she turned it upside down and slapped it. There was no response, so she slapped it again harder.

"Oh, God," cried Gia Minh, overcome not so much by the brutal horror of the scene as by anger. The child must live. She grabbed the infant from her mother. She held it by the feet and plunged it into the tub of cold water. She brought it out, then plunged it in again, and when she yanked it out the second time, the baby sucked in, filling its lungs. Then it screamed.

There was a chorus of joyous cries. Andre was so relieved that he hugged Gia Minh so hard that he almost crushed her with his happiness.

Xuan wrapped the shrieking child in tight blankets and comforted it in her arms, the cries unrelenting, but each one sounding stronger and healthier.

She held out the child to Andre. He seemed unsure of himself and stood awkwardly.

"It's your child," she said. "It has your blood."

He looked at the tiny figure and saw that she was right; its features were broad and strong, and its head glistened with a downy coat of blond hair.

"Thank you," he said, taking the infant in his huge hands.

The baby stopped crying instantly, so abruptly that he smiled; then he cradled it next to him. "I didn't even notice if it's a boy or girl," he said.

"A boy," said Xuan.

Father Bergere closed Felise's eyes and relaxed the facial muscles; then they wrapped the body in a sheet and moved it to a back room.

Only after the baby was washed and clothed did anyone think to ask where Louis was. The mere mention of his name set everyone's spirits down.

As if by agreement, no one spoke of Felise, nor of what had prompted her to walk out into the jungle, though all knew what it was.

While the women cared for the baby, Andre went outside. The storm had not abated, but now it seemed less fearsome, almost cleansing, and he stood in the garden letting the rain wash over him.

He was not a religious man, and even now, after this almost miraculous birth, his feelings and thoughts were too torn for him to direct any thanks to God, yet nevertheless he felt some force beyond him at work.

Now there was a child. What was to become of it, and who would care for it? And how would he be able to tell Felise's parents about their daughter?

There seemed to be no end to the sorrow in this country. Perhaps Louis was right to be leaving, he thought.

But where was his son? he wondered. Of all times to be gone . . . But he knew that Louis would not be touched by what had happened.

Andre was exhausted, but he knew he couldn't sleep. In his mind was a kaleidoscope of images: Felise dying, the blood, the motionless infant. He needed to be alone, but not to think.

He went into the house and began to drink in his study, as much and as quickly as possible, to ward off concentration.

Gia Minh had never seen him with too much to drink, but she understood his need, and said good night quietly, kissing him lovingly.

He drank himself to sleep, but was awakened shortly before dawn by a servant who'd kept watch nearby and told him that Louis had returned.

"Have him come here," Andre directed, then straightened himself up.

In a moment Louis entered, smooth and sure, and only moderately curious that his father would call for him at this hour.

Seeing his son sobered Andre immediately. "Where have you been, Louis?"

Louis raised his eyes, was about to answer that it was none of his business, that he was a grown man who didn't have to account to anyone, when he perceived that something must be amiss. "I had business in town; then I got caught in the storm. I decided to visit some old friends. Please come to the point, Father. What's wrong?"

"Felise is dead."

Andre searched Louis's face; the only emotion that registered was surprise. There was no sign of grief.

"She went out into the jungle, for reasons which you can probably understand. She was bitten by a cobra. She died early last evening."

Louis averted his gaze from his father because he knew he couldn't hide his true feelings. He hadn't wished Felise's death—such a thing had never even occurred to him—but now that she was dead, he saw how much easier everything was. He wasn't happy that she was dead, but it certainly suited his plans nicely, far too much so for him to feign grief. It was all very accommodating of Felise, he thought, one of the few timely things she'd ever done.

He didn't even make an effort to deceive Andre; he said nothing.

"We were able to save the baby, Louis. You have a son."

Louis couldn't contain his surprise. "The baby lived?"

Andre watched him with mounting anger and contempt. "Yes, he's very healthy. That rather complicates things for you, doesn't it?"

Louis recovered quickly, but he realized the delicacy of his position. He couldn't legally disown his child, annul his son. "I don't want the child, Father."

"I didn't think you would. But neither do I think you'd make a fit father."

"Would you take him?"

Andre stared at his son with profound sorrow. "You really would give up your child? He means nothing to you? Louis, go look at him. You'll change your mind when you—"

"Father, let's not kid ourselves. You know I'm not going to take the child with me to Paris, and I'm certainly not going to stay here. I'd like for you to raise him. If you won't, I'll go to the De Barthelemys; they'd love to have Felise's child."

"We'd be happy to raise him here."

"Then it's agreed?"

Andre stood, exhausted and with heavy heart. He was losing one son, and gaining another, but the loss was painful beyond words. "All right, Louis, it's agreed. Would you like to go look at your son?"

Louis stood and stretched. "No. This way you can tell the child he lost both his parents the same night."

They separated at the door, going to their rooms, but Andre stopped in the corridor and turned. "One final thing. Is there any name you want to call him?"

Louis shook his head, and didn't even stop. "Call him whatever you wish."

20

BREAKFAST WAS SOLEMN AND SUBDUED, Felise's death casting a heavy pall over everything. Even the birth of a healthy baby couldn't lighten anyone's spirits.

Louis had washed his hands of the whole matter, in fact had already gone out that morning by the time the others sat down for breakfast. He wouldn't take part in the funeral plans, and had no desires or wishes concerning any of the arrangements. He was leaving the following morning, so he wouldn't even be attending the funeral.

Andre wanted to consult with Felise's family about the funeral, but of course there was no time for that in this heat and humidity.

Among themselves they decided to have a simple closed service the following afternoon. Felise would be buried in the family cemetery, close to Ahn.

They were discussing the final arrangements when Ly suddenly burst into the room.

She was nearly hysterical and out of breath, disheveled and wild-eyed, and she ran to Andre, grabbing his arms as he jumped up. "They've taken him," she cried. "Soldiers. Early this morning they came for him. They knew just where to look."

Andre tried to calm her, but she shook her head frantically. "Someone told on him."

He held her so tightly that she couldn't move. She struggled a moment, then gave up and began to cry.

Xuan and Gia Minh were at her side. Gia Minh stroked her hair. "Tell us what happened. We'll be able to do something. Just calm yourself."

She dropped down into a chair, so distraught that she could barely speak, but when she looked into the strong faces, already deeply etched in sorrow, she composed herself and drew a deep breath.

"They came before dawn, many soldiers, and they burst into the house. They made us stand there naked, and they laughed at us. Then they began to hit Che Lan." She shuddered. "Then they kept asking him about the rifles. He wouldn't tell them anything, so they kept hitting him. But then they went right to where they were hidden, as though they'd known all along. When they found them, they beat him even more; then they took him away. They said they're going to shoot him."

She jumped up and grabbed Andre. "Stop them! They'll kill him."

Andre sat her down and crouched beside her. "Who took him? French or Vietnamese soldiers?"

"Vietnamese."

"Where did they take him?"

She shook her head. "I don't know. They just said they were going to shoot him. Please. Hurry!"

Andre held her steady. "Tell me about the rifles."

For a moment she wouldn't look at him; then she hid her face in her hands. "They're French rifles, stolen from the army. They brought them here, and Che Lan hid them. But nobody knew where they were. How did they find them?"

Andre turned to Gia Minh. "They'll take him to Hue and turn him over to the French. I'll go immediately."

Gia Minh's face was stricken. "What will they do to him?"

"I don't know," he said.

"They'll make an example of him," Ly said. "They'll kill him. Oh, my God," and she began to weep.

"I'll take Louis with me," Andre said. "He'll be able to help."

"Would he, though?" asked Xuan.

Andre's face set severely. "He will."

He sent a servant to find Louis, then went to his room to pack for the journey.

His manner was calm, but he was torn by grief. Would he have to plead to Parnasse to save his son's life, at the same time he was losing his first son to him?

How could he face Parnasse now? But he would. He'd get on his knees to save his son. He'd beg if he had to. Dear God, he thought, why are you doing this to me?

A servant came in to tell him that Louis couldn't be found. His horse wasn't gone, so perhaps he had merely taken a morning stroll.

Damn him, Andre thought. He couldn't leave without Louis. Then Andre stopped. How did they know where the rifles were?

. . . No, Louis was cruel, but he wouldn't do that. Besides, how would he know where they were? There must have been an informer in the group. The French had spies everywhere. You couldn't trust anyone. He'd told Che Lan. The fool. Damn him, too.

After breakfast, Father Bergere stood on the veranda and tried to gain some peace from the tranquil morning, but his thoughts were disturbed and unhappy. Though he had sat at countless deathbeds and seen every manner of sorrow and travail, he'd been profoundly upset by Felise's death. In his mind he envisioned the pain and grief that must have driven her into the jungle, then the terror of her death. She seemed like such a sweet girl, he thought, so undeserving of what had happened to her.

Louis had driven her to that—of this there was no doubt in his mind; he was an evil person. He'd been an evil child, cruel and vicious, and now he'd grown into an evil man.

Father Bergere was not a mystic; his thought was cool and linear, and age had not softened it. Louis had come to them as a wicked child, and thus he'd remained. The reasons for this, Father Bergere didn't know, and couldn't guess. We are all born in original sin, the priest believed; perhaps this child was cursed with a greater burden, one from which he was never strong enough to free himself. Father Bergere had tried to like Louis, had tutored him and taught him the catechism, had tried to instill in him right from wrong, but Louis had taken from him only what could advance him, and had left behind the heavy weights of principles and morals.

Now there was a parentless child. But the boy would be all right, he knew, for it would be raised in love and tenderness. If only he himself were not so old . . . But he was a very old man, and so was Chien, and this child would be raised without them. When he'd held the infant the night before, he'd had such a strange feeling of mortality—the two of them on the opposite thresholds of existence. He could almost feel the life slipping through his own fingers into the body of the child.

It wasn't a sad feeling at all, and he wasn't afraid of death. He saw in the child the wonderful continuity of life, and in his own passing he saw the rounded sphere of God's plan. He and the child were the two terminals of existence, and it filled him with wonder to behold it, but then when he thought of what passed between, human life, he was filled with unhappiness—all the sorrows and disappointments, all the pains and griefs that this child would experience.

The world was a terrible place, and life a long journey through unhappiness and sorrow to death and decay. Yes, he had made it, and his life had been rich and full, but it was not a journey he wished upon others; after all, he'd had his God, and that was his comfort—he'd been spared so much of the sadness which accompanies most men on their journeys. He had not had to bear what Andre suffered.

He was eighty-four years old and the world was more a mystery to him now than ever before; or rather, the design of God was now more a mystery to him. He saw no sure hand guiding the affairs of men, and certainly not a benevolent one. His faith was unshaken, and it was this alone, faith, which gave him courage, and gave meaning to life. What he marveled at was the faith of others who had suffered so much—he himself had never been sorely tried in his faith. His doubts had all been intellectual, clever forays of the devil into his mind and thought, but nothing substantial—not the loss of a child, the death of a lover, a gratuitous affliction or impairment bestowed by God.

His own faith was intact; yet he wondered sometimes how he would have responded had his faith been truly challenged. How faithful to God would he be now if he were Andre, a man about to lose both of his sons?

But surely God wouldn't allow that to happen. Yet deep down he knew that indeed God would. It was all mystery, and there were no explanations. He'd given up any attempt to explain away the world long ago. When he'd been young he'd scoffed at the older priests who'd passed off explanations with the platitude that "only God knows," but now he saw that that was the only answer. Perhaps there was a plan or a design, but it was beyond his comprehension or vision. Things happened, good and bad, mostly bad, and he didn't understand any of it. He could accept the evil of men, but it was the evil of God, His cruelty, or at best, His indifference, which Father Bergere couldn't understand, and at last gave up on, declaring unknowable, a mystery over which his faith got him, to which prayer was the only answer.

When he was assailed with doubts and difficulties, he prayed. Today he would pray, he decided.

The rain had stopped and a beautiful mist hovered over the land; he especially liked days such as this, and how many more would he see? Not many, he knew. He wouldn't be able to go out much longer. Even now, every day was a struggle and the slightest exertion tired him. No doubt his body would fail him completely soon. Perhaps he'd end in drooling madness—he knew he couldn't count on God to spare him that mortification.

He stepped from the veranda and crossed into the garden. He knew what he wanted to do—he wanted to see the grotto; it might be his last opportunity.

When he reached the wall of the jungle, he stopped a moment and thought of Felise, and strangely he had a vision of himself in infirmity and madness, a helpless, pathetic, insentient old man, mouth agape, sightless. He shivered. The bite of a snake was far preferable to that. Death was often better than life. This is what Felise must have decided. He couldn't fault her for that, and he didn't think God would punish her. How could he punish those not strong enough to bear the cruelties and sorrows he himself placed before them?

It was his religion which was so harsh, Father Bergere had long ago decided, not God. His religion had been devised by men, and he couldn't hold God responsible for their foolishness. Nothing that man touched went unstained—so it was with His church. You made your way through the world the best you could, Father Bergere believed, and you made your own peace with God. In the end you stood alone before Him, and He was just and merciful. Of that Father Bergere had no doubt, and no fear.

He went to the path that led through the jungle, a threadbare trail almost overgrown, which ended at the grotto, a large cave at the base of a huge overhanging cliff. A small crystalline stream ran through the bottom of a wide ravine and fed the emerald pool around which jagged rocks formed the entrance to the cave. It was his favorite place to go, a shrine in the jungle, but he hadn't been there in a long while; it was always something he was going to do, something he'd continuously put off because it took so long and was so difficult to reach—but today he would go.

He raised his hand to brush aside the dangling vines, and stepped into the enveloping jungle.

From the veranda, Andre frowned at the sight of the old man disappearing into the dense foliage. The priest was too old to be going out alone, he thought, but he couldn't tell him that. No doubt he was just going for a short stroll; it'd be all right, he thought, and turned away, scanning the horizon for any sign of Louis.

Andre was anxious to depart; he wanted to reach Hue before the soldiers arrived there with Che Lan, but he couldn't leave without Louis. Louis would have to inercede with Parnasse—it was the only way to save him. Louis wouldn't want to, but he would—of that Andre had no doubt. But where was he? He'd left the house hours ago. Andre knew his son's love of the jungle, how he could spend whole days and nights out in it; even as a child he'd had no fear of it. Andre would wait another hour or so for him; then he'd have to go in search of him. He could be anywhere, but his favorite place, where he'd found him many times as a child, was the grotto.

Father Bergere almost turned back several times; it was much farther than he'd remembered, and he had to stop every ten minutes or so to rest. But, he reasoned, if it was so beautiful here, think what it must be like there, so he pressed on at his slow pace, losing himself in the awesome serenity—the call of a bird bringing back decades of memories, a twisted vine reminding him of another jungle path, another journey of long ago, a felled tree making him think of the impermanence of all things. The walls of the jungle and its canopied top closed him in and provided a gloominess as dense and as hushed as that of a Gothic cathedral. He was utterly at peace.

But after nearly two hours he was exhausted and wished he hadn't come; he worried that he wouldn't be able to make it back. And like a fool, he thought, he hadn't brought anything to eat; he didn't relish eating berries for nourishment. And he was thirsty. How much farther could it be? he wondered.

He stumbled several times and caught himself moving off the path. That would be fatal, and he pinched himself alert. He must be careful; he could walk right into a snake, or grab at one from a vine.

The terrain grew steeper and more difficult, but he knew he was near now. He would come to the ravine soon.

That was the most treacherous part, and he inched his way down the path, carefully clinging to the vines of climbing plants. At the bottom of the ravine he came to the stream and picked his way along on the water-smoothed stones. Above him moisture dripped from the trees; everything was damp and glistening green.

He followed the stream as it ribboned through the jungle. The ravine narrowed, and then suddenly he had come to the end and the grotto was before him.

Stretching in front and above him was a sheer cliff, but at the base was a large pool, and beyond the grotto in the rock, a cave that extended deep into the cliff. Around the outside of the cave, circling the pool, were huge stones, and beyond them were the densely overgrown slopes of the ravine.

He had come to the end of the path, but it was more like the end of the world, or its heart, utterly peaceful, utterly beautiful.

He sighed in relief and worked his way as quickly as he could to the pool and raised himself with much difficulty onto one of the stones. Exhausted, he sat down to rest.

Each time in the past when he'd come, he'd startled animals that were drinking at the pool. Once he'd come upon a troop of gibbons, and they'd departed in irritated surprise, and always before he'd been met with the shrill cries and trills of birds, but this time there were no movement and no sound around the grotto.

Yet, as tired as he was, and as peaceful as the surroundings were, Father Bergere couldn't gain a measure of tranquillity. He felt tension and disquiet. There was something wrong in the air; and some long-ago memory surfaced in his thought, something troubling, even frightening, but it was indistinct, just a faint echo in his mind.

He shifted and tried to get comfortable on the rock; he was so tired. Then he felt eyes on him and he knew suddenly that he wasn't alone. He roused himself and looked about, and there on a rock in front of the grotto, barefoot and bare-chested, sitting with his arms around his knees, his eyes sleepy, but not kind, was Louis.

Father Bergere was taken aback, but he quickly composed himself and took in the strange sight. Louis looked like a young god in front of his secret temple, a primeval deity from the forest or jungle sitting on his haunches in sinister repose. In spite of the almost heathen aura conjured in the scene, the priest found it mysteriously, compellingly beautiful.

"You look like you belong here," the priest said.

"I do," said Louis, his voice soft and alluring.

"I forgot how you used to come here as a boy, just like a little pagan."

Louis smiled without warmth; his eyes hooded, and he rested his head on his knees.

"Your father's is looking for you. He wants you to go with him to Hue. Che Lan's been arrested."

Louis made no response and showed no interest.

"But you knew that, didn't you?"

The faintest smiled crossed Louis's lips.

"Of course. That's how they knew where to look for the rifles, wasn't it? You informed on him."

Louis didn't raise his head, but his voice was slightly amused. "For someone as old and senile as you, that's pretty clever."

"My God, what an evil creature you are. But you've always

been that way. You were a wicked child, and now you're a wicked man."

"What a quaint term—'wicked.' Do you really believe in such a thing?"

"Indeed I do, Louis. I'm not senile, but I am old enough to have seen most of the evil in this world—now I've seen a man turn on his brother. But, dear God, why? What made you do that?"

He said simply, "I don't like him."

Father Bergere stared at him in disbelief. "You would have your brother killed because you don't like him?"

Louis shrugged his shoulders. "I don't care what happens to him. To any of you."

"You can't be that insensitive. Your father means something to you, surely."

"Haven't you heard? He's not my father any longer—I have a new one, a duke. Someday I'll be a duke, and I don't give a damn what happens here. I'm leaving tomorrow. I'll never see any of you again, and I'll never give any of you another thought."

He stretched languorously on the rock and closed his eyes, blocking out the priest, lost in his own world, a lordly animal in his lair.

"What do you mean, you have a new father? What kind of humorless joke is that?"

Louis didn't open his eyes. "You wouldn't understand it. Suffice it that I'm returning to France with my mother and her husband."

"You're renouncing your own father?"

Louis laughed. "You use such formal words for such trivial things. But have it your way. Yes, I'm renouncing my father. Yet look at it this way—how generous I am to give up my inheritance to my stepbrother."

"Whom you just turned over to the soldiers. Who may be executed."

"Your outrage is very tiring. How do you manage to summon such energy at your age? Why don't you just recede into oblivion like you're supposed to?"

Father Bergere was outraged, and deeply insulted; he'd never encountered such disrespect, and Louis had never dared behave this way before. Then he realized that Louis was baiting him, and he overcame his anger, admonishing himself for having fallen so easily into his trap, and for having so quickly lost his equilibrium.

"I forgot how clever and obnoxious you can be," the priest

said. "And what a liar you are. I can remember your faked angelic manner in the confessional, your wholly dishonest repentance. What I never understood was your stupidity."

Louis opened an eye on him, flashing warning anger.

"Yes, stupidity. You thought I was deceived. Your act was so transparent, so inept."

Louis closed his eye. "You weren't worth my best effort."

"But why the attempt to deceive God?"

Louis laughed. "What God?"

Father Bergere crossed himself. "That's blasphemy."

"Blasphemy isn't as offensive as nonsense. Keep your God to yourself, you stupid priest. Don't insult me as well as bore me."

Father Bergere was incredulous. "You don't believe in God? You would risk eternal damnation for such egotism and arrogance?"

"Spare me this. There is no eternity, and no damnation. There's the world as we have it, and the little time allotted us—and I certainly don't plan to waste any of it on religious babble. I plan to enjoy the time I have—and the pleasures are all worldly ones."

Father Bergere looked at him with a certain fear, as though he were confronting some sort of demon.

"Oh, come now, Father. Don't be so surprised, or afraid. You're looking at me as though I were the devil."

"The devil possesses you," he whispered.

"What a superstitious old woman you are. I outgrew all religious tripe when I was eight years old. There's no devil, my dear priest, any more than there's a God. I'm no serpent, priest; I'm a rational man who possesses free will; I do what I choose to do. You'd love to believe otherwise, though, wouldn't you, seeing yourself—the sainted defender of God's truth—pitted against the devil? A dialogue here in the jungle, where you meet the tempter? Can't you face the simple truth that someone might not believe your drivel?"

"Oh, Louis, Louis," the priest said. "Don't. Don't turn on God. Don't condemn your immortal soul to the fires of hell."

Louis shook his head in disgust. "Do you know what hell is? It's a wasted life—it's being poor and insignificant. Hell is boredom, priest; it's prayers and abnegation, it's doing nothing, and being nobody. I want to revel in life, to touch, and taste, and feel everything. I want riches, and women, and power. And when I die, I want to die sated, having missed nothing, having no regrets. So don't talk to me about your idiot God, or about my father, or stepbrother—they mean nothing to me. And neither did Felise. Or that baby."

"My God, how did you come to this?" Father Bergere had listened to him with disbelief that approached horror, but it quickly turned to pity. "You poor child," he said.

"Don't you dare affect that manner with me."

"Oh, Louis, you're lost."

Louis sat up and glared at the priest, stung by his pity and condescension, truly angry. "Lost? You simpering old maid, you don't know anything." His eyes glinted evilly and he leaned forward toward the priest. "How would you like to save me? Would you hear my confession?"

"Don't make a mockery of the sacraments. I couldn't hear your confession unless you were sincere."

"Oh, I'm sincere, just not penitent. Where would you like me to begin? Come on, Father, hear my confession. You said I was dishonest before; well, I'll tell you the truth this time—I'll tell you everything."

Father Bergere felt suddenly uneasy; there was something driven and destructive about Louis now, as if he'd slipped into his own world, one beyond the reach of normal men. His whole person seemed transformed, animal and cruel; his body glistened, and his eyes burned malevolently. He didn't sit, but seemed to crouch on the stone, waiting to spring.

"What would you hear, priest? Do you want to hear about me and the duke? Or would you rather hear stories about Saigon? Brothel stories? Sailor stories? Or is that too tame?"

"Louis, stop it! I won't be a party to this."

"How about Felise? Would you like to hear some intimate stories about her? Yes, let me confess my sins and abuses against my dear wife."

He leaped from the stone, startling the priest, and stood beside him, pressing his face into his. Father Bergere had never seen eyes as these—they were possessed, and he was frightened. The old man tried to move away, but there was nowhere to go; he was held by the eyes and the lustrous, moisture-beaded skin.

"I'm glad she's dead." Louis fairly hissed the words between his teeth."

"You killed her. Just as if you'd plunged a knife into her."

"She wasn't the first, you know."

Father Bergere drew back his head, horrified and afraid, but Louis leaned his face closer.

"In Saigon. I killed a man, with a knife." He brought his hand sharply into the old man's side. "Just like that."

Father Bergere cried out at the pain, but it only excited Louis more. He brought his hand up again, catching the priest just below the rib cage.

Father Bergere bent forward, clutching his side. "Stop it, you're hurting me, Louis."

Louis's eyes were ice. "You don't matter, priest. But now you know too much."

Father Bergere tried to move away. "Louis, stop it. What's the matter with you? I'm going to tell your father on you."

Louis laughed. "You simpering fool, you make me ill. I hate weakness."

Father Bergere was incredulous. "What's wrong with you, Louis? You're not well. You're sick."

"Stop that!" Louis looked at the priest with intense anger. "Don't you say that."

"It's true, there's something wrong with you."

Louis's eyes flashed furiously.

"All the time, we thought you were just spoiled, but it wasn't that at all. You couldn't help yourself, you were sick. You should be put away. You can't go back to France, you need help. I'm not going to let you go, I'm going to see to it that you get help."

Father Bergere started to climb from the rock, frailly lowering himself, but Louis was enraged and pushed him into the pool.

"God damn you," he yelled at the priest.

The water was only waist-deep, but the old man had difficulty raising himself. He staggered up, then fell back.

"You bastard," screamed Louis, and jumped in beside him. "How dare you say anything like that to me? I could kill you for that."

Father Bergere struggled up. "Yes, like you did Felise, and the other man. Like you're going to have your brother killed. You're diseased, Louis, like a stricken animal. You've got to be stopped."

He raised his hand to make the sign of the cross over him, but Louis struck his hand away furiously. "Don't do that! God damn you, don't do that."

Louis was no longer in control of himself. The priest's words had cut through him like a knife, and the wound blinded him.

"I hate you. I hate all of you. You've never liked me, none of you."

He was almost crying. "Nobody's ever liked me. I didn't want to come here. And you have no right to say these things to me. I've never had anything I wanted. I didn't want a wife. I didn't want a child. I want my mother."

Father Bergere looked at him with amazement and fear. He backed away. "You're insane."

Louis rushed him. "Don't say that. Take it back," He grabbed the old man by the throat and choked him. "Take it back."

With all his might, the priest broke away. He shook his head, unbelieving of what was happening before him. "May God have pity on you, Louis."

He backed away, but slipped. He saw Louis's hands coming down on him, and suddenly he remembered the dream he'd had so long ago.

The last thing he saw before Louis submerged his head was an extraordinarily handsome youth, golden-skinned, eyes mad and cruel, stnding above him. He felt hands close around his throat, and his head pressed under the water.

Father Bergere struggled feebly, his arms flailing like the broken wings of a bird. He sank to his knees, his hands vainly trying to loosen the vise-like grip around his neck.

It was exactly like the dream, but he couldn't wake.

Hands tore at Louis's arms. He was lifted out of the water and thrown aside.

Stumbling up, he saw his father standing furiously over the priest.

"You bastard," Andre screamed, trying to raise the old man, whose arms were outstretched and whose face floated down in the water.

Louis threw himself at his father, knocking him backward. He jumped on him, his hands beating down on his head; then they found his throat and he squeezed.

Andre lay on his back, submerged, his son straddling him. The pressure around his neck was crippling. He couldn't breathe.

He was able to turn over and bring himself to his knees, but the hands strangled him, and Louis jumped on his back, pressing him with his full weight.

In a final, desperate burst of strength, Andre rose powerfully out of the water, bringing his arms back, his elbows catching Louis in the sides so forcefully that he cried out and loosened his grip.

Louis was thrown backward, off his father, and he landed, arms outstretched, against the rocks.

There was a dull crunching sound. Louis opened his mouth in surprise; his eyes widened in fear. He raised his head slightly, then sank back, motionless.

Andre struggled to regain his breath. His hands worked at his throat; then he waded toward Louis.

Louis's eyes were open. Blood trickled from his slack mouth.

Andre reached down in horror and tried to raise him. The body was limp and crumpled in his arms.

"Oh, my God," Andre cried, and dropped to his knees. He held his son by the shoulders, but the head rolled back, the neck broken.

"No! God, no!" he screamed.

Suddenly there was a roar from the trees, and shrill cries filled the air. A thousand birds beat their wings and lifted into flight. The entire jungle was rent by their thunder; then, just as suddenly, it was quiet, and Andre was alone, sunk on his knees, his lifeless son in his arms.

He cradled him to his chest, his hand stroking his head, and he began to cry. "Oh, Louis. Oh, God. My son." He was racked by sobs, and he buried his face in his son's neck.

Then he raised his head. "No! No!" he screamed. "It isn't so. Please!"

He grabbed Louis's face and shouted into it, "Don't die! Don't! Please, please!" He shook the face, but it moved so lifelessly in his hands that he pulled away in dread.

The jungle was completely quiet and still.

Andre gently laid his son back on the rocks and went to Father Bergere, floating facedown in the water. He picked up the old man effortlessly and carried him to the bank.

He sat between the two corpses and cried until he could cry no more.

When he felt he was drained of his tears, he slung Louis's body over his shoulders and began his way back.

The corpse grew unbearably heavy, but Andre didn't falter, and he tried not to think of his son, yet images flashed through his mind of Louis as a child and of their times together, and finally, just before leaving the jungle, Andre dropped down. He held Louis in his arms, cradling his head to his chest.

"I'm sorry," he whispered, filled with grief and remorse. If only he hadn't taken him from France, he thought. If only he'd left him with Catherine. And now he'd have to tell her. And how could he save his other son from Parnasse's fury?

He was exhausted by the time he returned, and the corpse had started to stiffen in rigor mortis.

Gia Minh, Xuan, and Chien met him silently on the veranda.

"Father Bergere's dead too. Louis killed him."

Gia Minh let out a cry. Xuan crossed herself, and Chien lowered his head.

"Why?" asked Gia Minh.

"I don't know. I came on him drowning the priest. We fought; he fell against the rocks."

They looked at Louis, lying grotesquely stiff; then, without another word, they turned away and went inside. Andre sent servants to bring back Father Bergere, and he went into his study to be alone.

He was sitting at his desk when Gia Minh came in and went to him. He buried his face in her side, and she stroked his head in comfort. "I loved him," he cried. "I don't think I can bear it. Why did I come here?" But the answer was in her strong grasp as she clutched him to her.

Later he went to Xuan in her rooms. They stood and held hands, her eyes soft and loving on him. "You'll never get over it," she said. "I think of Ahn every day of my life; it's a wound which never heals, a pain which never goes away."

"I came to tell you how sorry I am about Father Bergere."

"We were friends for almost fifty years," she said. "He was a very kind and good man." Then she smiled gently. "Don't be sorry for him. I don't think he's unhappy where he is."

He found Chien late that night sitting on the veranda staring toward the jungle. They sat together side by side for a long time without saying a word. The night was cool and stars had finally broken through the cloudy sky.

"I'm going to miss that old priest," said Chien at last. "I was getting rather fond of him. He made me feel not so old." Then he looked over to Andre. "There are many sorrows in this world, but you've now suffered the greatest. Nothing can touch a man like the death of his child. There is no comfort from that; and the loss of a wicked child is just as great as that of a good one."

"How does one live with such sorrow, Master Chien?"

The old man spoke slowly, and from far away, his eyes never leaving the dark jungle. "Life and death form the whole, like the yin and yang, but they are not equal parts. Life is such a tiny thing, such a short span. We forget its insignificance. How does one live with sorrow? Life is sorrow; it's growing old and seeing ones we love die; it's dying ourselves. There is no avoiding this. One can accept it and live in harmony with the nature of things; or one can fight it and spend one's life in futile struggle."

"But one can't help but struggle, Master Chien."

"Of course," he said with a smile, repeating his life's teaching. "How we live is more important than that we live. Each day is a struggle to overcome vanity and foolishness. But what is done, is done, child; to howl at yesterday's sorrow is to bay at the moon."

"I don't think I could bear it if something happened to Che Lan too."

Chien reached over and patted his knee. "Now you are baying at the moon yet to rise."

Andre bowed his head. "Yes, you're right. I'll do what I can to save him; I'll beg if I have to."

"Indeed," said Chien. "Sometimes it's not best to be the blade of grass."

"But it's taught that the frailest blade can withstand the strongest gale."

"And so it can. But even the strongest blade can be trampled underfoot by an elephant. Or be eaten by a dog. Go save the son you do have; lock away in your heart the one you lost."

Andre didn't wait for the funerals for Felise, Louis, and Father Bergere. He left immediately for Hue, and when he reached the Imperial Palace, he asked first to see De Barthelemy.

From his manner, De Barthelemy knew immediately that his daughter was dead. Andre withheld nothing from him, and expressed his deep sorrow and regret for the part his son had played. Then he told him about Louis's death.

When Andre finished the story, De Barthelemy asked what he could do for him. Though overcome with grief for the loss of his daughter, he asked if there was any way he could help Andre. "We don't need words," he said. "What words can adequately express such a loss? We're united in tragedy. And in a grandchild. Can I help you?"

Andre told him about Che Lan and De Barthelemy promised he'd intercede on his behalf. Though Hue was not in his jurisdiction, he was sure the governor of Annam, which comprised Hue, would listen favorably to his request.

Andre expressed his fear that Parnasse would interfere, but De Barthelemy said it wouldn't be necessary to involve him, and he cautioned him not to let Parnasse know about Louis's death.

"I'm sure that I can get the French military authorities to drop their charges against your son, but there's nothing I can do about the Vietnamese." He asked Andre if there was someone he knew who might persuade the Vietnamese to drop the charges also.

Andre said there was; he thought immediately of Lady Deng.

The two men talked for a while longer, about their children briefly, and common interests; then Andre thanked him for his help and promised that he'd bring the grandchild to Saigon for them to see.

Lady Deng was very pleased to receive Andre and ushered

him into her sumptuous quarters, where she had him sit beside her on the settee.

"Ban Me Thuot must be as airless as a mummy's tomb," she said. "No one ever ages there. In six years I see only three more lines in your face. And not an ounce of flesh more." She rubbed his still flat stomach and wantonly grabbed his sides. "Nothing even to hold on to."

"You look good too," he lied.

She laughed and leaned her face into his. "Want to take me to bed? It would serve you right for such an outrageous falsehood." She patted his cheek. "Stick to the truth; that was always your strength—it was so refreshing, and unexpected. Now, what brings you to this poor old neglected woman? Not curiosity, I hope, a museum visit."

"I need your help. Only you can help me. My son is in prison."

"Louis? No, no, of course not him. The other one. What's his name?"

"Che Lan."

"Yes, the would-be rebel. I've been following his activities. What happened to him?"

"He was arrested. He had rifles which were stolen from the French."

She was exasperated. "But I told Louis to warn him about that."

"You knew? You told Louis?"

She smiled in her wicked way. "I may be old, but I try to keep a hand in." She cupped his crotch lightly with her hand.

Despite himself, he laughed. "You must have been truly wonderful when you were young."

"That is not a nice thing to say to a lady," she said in pretended pout. "It implies I am no longer wonderful. Your son Louis would not make that mistake. Yes, I told him about the rifles, and he said he'd warn Che Lan."

"I see," he said. So it was true, he thought. Louis did inform on him.

Watching his face, she guessed immediately what had happened. "Perhaps I should not have told him; I didn't know there was trouble between them. He's a remarkable person who'd turn his brother in."

"He's dead," Andre said simply.

She searched his face for a clue to what had happened, knowing he'd never tell her. "That will be sad news for the duke," she said at last, her eyes revealing to Andre that she knew everything.

For a long minute they sat staring at one another. Finally she nodded. "I'll help you. Partly because his arrest was my doing. But also because I happen to sympathize with what he's doing. The French are much worse than I thought. They're really greedy, small people." She added distastefully, "They're not very clean, either. In fact, they remind me a great deal of the Chinese—except they're not nearly so manly. I don't mean that to insult you; I exempt you from all of that."

She stood up. He stood also and followed her toward the garden.

"If I were a young girl," she said, "I think I'd be doing exactly what your son is doing. And his wife; I heard about her also."

She took his arm and led him outside. "Yes, I'll help. But first let's have a talk. I want to hear about everybody—your stepmother, that fat old Chinaman, the priest. You know, I remember them all so well, even though it's been more than forty years since they left court." She shook her head in happy memory. "Those years were the best."

She stopped in the middle of the garden and looked about herself sadly. "Now it's very boring—hardly worth my talents at all. Court is now like a wooden stage play; not even that, more like a puppet show. The French control everything. There's no life here anymore—no grandeur, no sweep. And the intrigue is so petty and trivial. I'm thinking of retiring from court life."

"What would you do? Where would you go?"

"I may become a provincial lady."

He laughed at the idea.

"I mean it. A dear man, not young—he's nearly sixty, one of our more corrupt generals—has asked me to marry him. He's retiring and wants me to set up his home with him in Quang Ngai. Of course he's marrying me for my money, but we get along quite well and should be able to amuse ourselves till one of us passes on. I'm seriously considering his offer."

"I don't think they're ready for you yet in the provinces."

She laughed. "Oh, I've mellowed. See, I haven't even attempted to seduce you." Her startlingly carnal look returned. "To give you an opportunity to better your last performance."

When he flushed, she patted his cheek. "I'll never let you forget that. But come," she said, going back toward the palace, "let's see about your son."

* * *

The first beating had broken his left arm; the second had crushed his right foot; the third was a clubbing that left his entire body bruised, bleeding, and swollen.

He lay crumpled on the floor of his cell, lying in his own vomit, unable to raise himself.

"You're going to die unless you cooperate," they'd told him. "Each time we come, we're going to make it worse for you. The next time might be your eye."

The French interrogater had held up a truncheon. "Or we can rupture you with this—that's a particularly painful experience. Or we can cut you with this," he said, pressing a knife into his groin. "All we want are names. Tell us who gave you the rifles. Tell us who else is involved."

They'd beaten him repeatedly on the journey to Hue. He'd been shackled and thrown sideways over a horse, and humiliated in every possible way, but the torture had only begun when he'd been thrown into the garrison prison in Hue. All about him in other cells he could hear the cries and moans of other prisoners, heard their beatings and tortures until his own became so bad that he lost all awareness of what was happening around him.

He'd not been fed, and was given only drops of water. They treated him like an animal—called him monkey and tied a rope around his neck, dragging and pulling him around the cell, kicking and taunting him until he'd lose consciousness. He knew they were going to kill him whether he talked or not, so he was determined he wouldn't inform; he'd suffer anything rather than give in to them.

At night he tried not to fall asleep because he was so afraid of the rats; he could see their red eyes in the corners of the cell, and several times they'd scurried over him and he'd seen their bared teeth.

He couldn't stand because of his crushed foot, and he couldn't raise himself because of his arm; he had to lie on the wet ground on his right side. Now when he heard footsteps coming toward him he curled tighter, ducking his head, involuntarily bringing his broken arm up to shield his eyes.

"Get up!" A boot came down on his head, grinding on his ear; then he was kicked sharply in the small of the back.

He cried out and stretched backward. Immediately he was grabbed by the arms and lifted up.

He screamed when they pulled on his broken arm, and then again when they brought him to his feet and made up stand. He tried to shift his weight to his good foot, but they struck him in his right side so hard that all his weight shifted to his left leg.

The pain was excruciating and he tried to sink down, but arms held him up, yet not enough to ease the pain in his foot.

"We're not going to waste any more time with you," his interrogator said. "Either you tell us what we want to know, or you die now."

He pressed a razor blade against his neck and drew it down sharply to his chest, then lower, slicing all the way to his groin.

Che Lan drew in his breath at the incredible pain, and he could feel the blood pouring from the slash.

"Which is it going to be? This?" He pressed the blade against Che Lan's eye. "Or this?" He cupped his scrotum and drew the blade lightly across the testicles and up the shaft. "Or will you talk? Tell me quickly."

Through swollen, puffy lips, he was barely able to spit; instead the saliva merely dribbled from his mouth.

Furious, the interrogator kicked him savagely in the groin, then struck at his head as he collapsed, slipping mercifully into unconsciousness. He had thought for sure that the threats would work; now he saw that he indeed might have to kill the youth.

Che Lan had no idea how long he'd lain on the cold, wet ground, but he woke to the cell door being opened. He was so weak, and hurt so badly, that he didn't think he could last through another beating; he knew he couldn't stand any more pain.

Andre dropped down beside him and raised his head gently. Che Lan couldn't see him, but he knew the hands. He began to cry; then he fell unconscious again.

At the palace, Che Lan's wounds were treated, though the surgeon said he'd be lame the rest of his life. His arm and the cuts would heal, but it would be months before he regained his strength.

"It could have been worse," Andre said. "It still might, if you continue what you've been doing."

Che Lan could barely see out of his bruised eyes, and every word was painful through his swollen, cut lips, yet he managed to look at his father, and his voice was strong. "They'll never catch me again; I'll never be a French prisoner again. I'd just like to know how they found me out."

Andre said softly, "Louis told them."

"That bastard."

"He's dead, Che Lan." Then Andre told him all that had happened, about Felise, and Father Bergere, and the baby.

When he finished, Che Lan turned away, filled with grief for

Father Bergere and Felise, but when he turned back to look at Andre, his eyes were cold. "He didn't mean anything to me. I hated him. But I'm sorry for you, Father."

Andre lowered his head. "I don't think I could bear it if something happened to you too. Promise me you'll stop fighting the French. Please, Che Lan."

Che Lan reached over and took Andre's hand. "No, Father, I can't do that. I'm going to fight them the rest of my life. You know I have to."

Andre couldn't look at his son. He squeezed his hand; then he had to leave the room.

Andre waited until Che Lan was strong enough to make the journey back to Ban Me Thuot before he went to see Catherine, the day before her departure also.

It had been eighteen years since they'd last seen one another, and when Andre made the request for an appointment with the duchess, he wasn't sure she'd receive him. But the positive response came back immediately, in part however because Catherine had grown concerned about Louis's failure to return.

Andre dreaded the meeting; he didn't want to see Catherine again, wanted all reminder of that past put behind him, and he dreaded telling her about Louis.

She received him in the drawing room, having carefully arranged herself on a chaise, stretched regally, her manner insouciant, a not altogether successful attempt at boredom.

She was nervous and fidgeted with her hair and makeup until the moment he was shown in.

He stopped in the doorway to view her; then he smiled faintly, gathering courage from the realization of the trouble she'd gone to in order to impress him.

"Louis was right," he said. "You are beautiful."

Though she attempted a haughty, superior air, she couldn't hide her nervous agitation. Indeed, time had not changed Andre that much; he was still the strong-looking, vibrant lover of many years past.

She softened immediately. "You look wonderful, Andre. Please sit down. Can I get you something?"

"Thank you, no. I can stay but a moment; I'm on my way home."

"Surely you can spare me a little time."

"I don't think you'll want my presence after what I have to tell you."

Her eyes narrowed on him suspiciously; she'd already lost her child to him once. "What do you mean?"

"Louis is dead, Catherine." He said it evenly, without emotion.

She looked at him unbelievingly; then, when she realized he was serious, she brought her hands to her mouth to stifle a cry.

He told her everything, sparing her no detail. "I'm sorry," he said when he finished. "He was my son and I loved him, but he was an evil person."

Catherine was dry-eyed, her voice cold and accusing. "First you took my child away, then you killed him."

"It was an accident, Catherine. I never meant him any harm; I would have given my life for him."

He could see her inner struggle for composure, her crushing pain, and he wanted to go to her, to hold her and comfort her, to share her sorrow for their lost son; he wanted to break through the barrier which separated them, but he couldn't, and he knew she wouldn't receive him.

At last she said, "Thank you for telling me. Please go now."

He turned and left the room, his last sight of her sitting like a stricken queen.

He was on his way back to Che Lan when he encountered the duke's entourage in the corridor. He recognized Parnasse immediately, a caricature of his former self—fat and bloated, his face as self-satisfied and cruel as a boar's.

And Parnasse recognized him, unable to hide his surprise, a comic confusion spread over his features. Had Andre come to reclaim Louis? Did he know about them? Anxiety replaced confusion, but then he summoned a supercilious manner, a contemptuous look of dismissal, and he strode on.

Andre returned to his rooms and made the final preparations for departure.

Word of Che Lan's safety had already been sent ahead, but the knowledge of his release didn't diminish the joyful reception of his return.

Though he tried to make light of his injuries and feigned discomfort at all the attention he received, he loved the doting concern of Ly, Gia Minh, and Xuan.

The ride back to Ban Me Thuot had depleted all his strength, and he was placed in a room in the palace and lavished with care and love.

Ly sat with him most of the day, talking and reading, and slapping at his good hand, which seemed bent solely on finding its way beneath her clothes.

"You're not strong enough," she admonished him, but at last he enticed her to lie with him. She gently kissed his wounds, unable to keep from crying, and they went slowly and easily, and there was no difficulty at all.

One day Xuan sat with him while she held the baby. Several times the child had been brought in to him, but he expressed no interest whatsoever in it, yet this time, as Xuan talked, mostly stories of the court life of long ago, his eyes kept traveling to the infant.

Without interrupting her speech, she brought Paul over to him and carefully nestled him in Che Lan's right arm.

He looked down on the incredibly small creature—he'd never held a child before—and his face registered fear and awe.

"You'd better get used to it," Xuan said. "You'll have your own child soon enough."

"What will happen to him?" he asked in an almost whisper, afraid his voice might disturb the child.

"He will grow up loved and cared for, just as you were."

He looked down on his brother's son, and despite all the hatred he'd felt for Louis, all the pain he'd suffered because of him, he couldn't help but feel immense tenderness for the infant.

The tiny feet kicked and the little hands grabbed at the air, and Che Lan smiled at the life cradled beside him.

"If he knows love, he'll be a loving child," said Xuan. "If he sees strength, he'll be a strong child. If he's shown kindness, he'll be kind. He'll be what he sees, Che Lan."

Understanding this, Che Lan leaned over and kissed the child.

Because it was too difficult for Andre, and to spare him, Gia Minh went through all of Louis's belongings, saving only a few things to keep for the child.

She glanced casually through his papers before burning them, and was about to toss a wax-sealed envelope into the fire when she changed her mind and opened it to read.

The document was signed and had the seal of the Duke of Parnasse, and it recognized Louis as his son and heir.

In disgust she put it back in the envelope and threw it into the fire, but then immediately she pulled it out.

That would be for Paul someday. It would be his decision—his passport out of Vietnam if he ever needed it, for who knew what lay in the future for that poor child in this sad country?

21

Dien Bien Phu: March 16, 1896

THE MOUNTAIN AIR WAS WET and cold. Che Lan shivered and pulled tighter into himself, so exhausted that only the coldness kept him awake; more than anything he wanted to curl up and fall asleep, to close his eyes for a few moments, but he knew that if he gave in for only an instant, he'd sleep through the night.

But maybe, maybe if he rested for just a minute . . . He leaned his head back against the tree and closed his eyes. Then he jerked forward instantly, his mind filling with the memory of a soldier's slit throat, the body resting back against a tree in just the position he was in.

He shivered and his hand rubbed his neck, and he was fully awake again. He'd seen too many dead men to make such a stupid mistake.

Then he thought he heard something in the ravine, and he strained forward to listen.

The night was completely dark; there was no moon and he couldn't make out anything in the jungle. Yet it wasn't still; the jungle was disquietingly alive, not just from the wind and light rain, but with the all too familiar sounds of enemy movement—the brush of cloth, the press of a boot, a whisper, the silence of all other life as the predator moves through the night—a charged, breathless quiet almost screaming danger.

He leaned forward and closed his eyes, concentrating. There was someone out there; he knew it. But it couldn't be; they couldn't have tracked them here.

He listened so intensely that his head began to throb, but he heard nothing more; he eased up slightly.

There were not many of them left, and no more places to flee, so if the French had found them, they'd have to make their final stand here, though there was no doubt how it would end.

They were fewer than eighty men and they'd suffered defeat after defeat, pursued relentlessly by the French, forced from one hiding place to another, until at last they'd had to take refuge in the mountains just beyond Dien Bien Phu. They'd trekked tortuously through the mountainous jungle, single file through heavy brush, carrying their wounded and a few supplies, until they'd come to what they thought was safety in the isolated, rugged terrain of Dien Bien Phu, not far from the Laotian border. If the French had pursued them here, then it was the end.

He snapped forward. Someone was coming up the ravine. But when he listened again, there was no further sound. He knew how exhaustion played tricks on a man, and fear too, and the jungle itself; in a moment he eased back against the tree—maybe it was all in his mind, for he wasn't sure that he could trust his own senses any longer.

But what if they had been tracked? How could he accept that it had all been for nothing—all the suffering and hardship, all the dead? He couldn't, for none of his ardor was diminished—only his idealism, and the belief in victory.

How different from what he'd felt when he'd joined the rebellion six years ago; then he knew, absolutely believed, that they'd triumph over the French. He was barely twenty then, soft and young. Now he was twenty-six, and there was nothing soft about him at all, and he felt as old as he was tired; victory was a dead dream, and the rebellion dying embers.

Yet it hadn't been in vain, for defeat wasn't the worst thing, nor was death—to have fought and lost was better than to have acquiesced. But dear God did it hurt to lose, to have the French triumph. And it would hurt every day for the rest of his life, every day he looked on his children or into his wife's eyes, every time he saw a Frenchman . . . every time he looked into a mirror.

Yet he'd do it again, would fight every battle again, suffer every pain and hardship. His only regret was having been too young, only fourteen, in 1884, when the regent Ton That Thuyet had fled with the child emperor Nam Nghi. Then the entire country had been set afire by the emperor's flight, and by the elevation of his docile younger brother, Dong Khanh, to the throne. A massive force rose up from all sectors of the population, but the most effective one was in the north, where the mandarin Phan Dinh Phung led his guerrillas.

But the rebellion had been doomed from the beginning, and the fugitive emperor captured in 1888, betrayed by his own followers, and sent into exile. Yet the resistance continued under Phan, an elderly, ailing, scholarly man, though he was unable to forge a national movement; the many groups opposed to the French remained isolated and disorganized, suspicious of one another, and unable to overcome their differences. Moreover, with the exile of the young emperor, many who had resisted the French turned loyal to the new puppet emperor, and because he was an obedient servant of the French, followed his example. Cooperation with the French became socially acceptable, and profitable.

Che Lan had joined the resistance anyway. He left home in 1891, despite his father's pleas. After his marriage and the birth of his son, and because of being tortured by the French, he found it impossible to remain in Ban Me Thuot.

Ly didn't try to stop him, or hold the infant over him to keep him from going. She said she understood, and she did, but she wept bitterly, fearing she'd never see him again.

It didn't take him long to see the futility of the cause, but he fought nonetheless. Besides being hopelessly outnumbered, he saw that the movement would fail for a more fundamental reason: Phan Dinh Phung's Can Vuong movement had no program for reform and change; Phan and the other leaders were Confucian scholars, traditionalists by nature, appealing to old loyalties and beliefs, yet the monarchy had been discredited, and it was clear that the old methods and policies wouldn't work against the challenge of the Westerners. What was needed was reform, new social and political policies, but they couldn't come from these men.

When he first arrived, he found the others suspicious of him because of his French blood—his father had been right, he wasn't trusted, but because of this he threw himself with fervor into the movement, taking foolhardy risks, often frightening the others with his daring and courage. Often dressed in a stolen French uniform and speaking flawless French, he'd bluffed his way into the French lines, past Vietnamese conscripts fighting for them, then opened the lines for his own men to break through.

He quickly gained a reputation among the rebels, but also with the French, who placed a high reward on his head. He rose in the ranks of the rebels despite his youth and French blood, and soon became a lieutenant of Phan's. He mastered the art of guerrilla warfare, striking unexpectedly, withdrawing immediately, and kept the French forces off guard and on the defensive.

The only real advantage the rebels had over the French was that the French forces were filled with Vietnamese conscripts, many of whom secretly sympathized with the rebels. But in the long run, the rebels were no match for the better-trained, better-equipped French Army, and by 1894 the rebels had been chased into the mountains, and defections were now epidemic.

For the last two months they'd fled the French, but they'd only been able to stay a day or two ahead of them. In the beginning Che Lan had been able to lead harassing raids on them, but now his forces were too weak. Worse, Phan was seriously ill; if the old man remained on the run, he'd die soon. In a last desperate attempt to save the movement and the old man, Che Lan had broken off with a small band, trying to decoy the French. If they were caught, it was the end.

He cradled the rifle in his lap and ran his hand down the metal barrel to the wooden stock; as always, excitement and anticipation ran through him, an almost sexual charge, and his belly tightened, and he was fully awake. But the feeling depressed and saddened him and he placed the rifle in his lap again. He didn't want to kill anymore; he didn't want to fight anymore, either. He wanted to go home; he wanted to see his wife and children. He wanted to lie in bed with Ly and hold her, to fall asleep in her arms, to be comforted and soothed. He wanted to laugh. He wanted to make love, not softly, not tenderly, but to drive out all of this, to purge himself.

And he wanted to play with his children. Trinh was six, and the twins—boy and girl—were nearly three; he hadn't seen them in two years, the last time he'd been home.

He had almost no recollection of his younger children; they'd been conceived when he went home the first time, and he didn't even know about them until his last return. But Trinh had remembered him, as had Paul, and they'd hung on to him the entire time he'd been home, running into his room the first thing every morning to make sure he was still there, and not going to sleep at night until he came in to tuck them in. They followed him about during the day, content merely to be in his presence, playing by themselves, but always aware of his nearness.

It was for them, his children, that he was fighting, he told himself, for whom he'd suffer anything. His children would be free someday, and all the foreigners would be gone. This was all he lived for, and someday he'd triumph—he knew it.

The image of his children came to him and his mind fixed lovingly on the two older boys. They were like brothers, so completely different from how he and Louis had been. Yet too they were so unalike. Paul was quieter, more sensitive, Trinh more rambunctious and physical, the one who led. Che Lan had been pleased at this, for despite his fondness for the little blond-haired boy, he never could rid himself of a slight distance from him because of the memory of Louis. He was happy that his own son seemed more sure of himself and active.

He'd returned home the last time during the winter monsoon, but when the weather turned fine he grew restless, his eyes fixing in a faraway stare at the jungle, and the mountains beyond, and Ly knew he would soon be going.

His father again tried to dissuade him. "Your children need you," he said.

"My children need to be free," he'd answered. "I have to fight for them."

They didn't understand, of course, when he told them that he had to go away; they couldn't understand "far away" or "a long time," and couldn't comprehend danger or death, and for weeks after he was gone the two boys went into his room in the mornings to see if he'd come back during the night, and for months afterward they asked when their father was coming home. Now he was only a faint memory to them.

But they were so alive to him.

He closed his eyes and saw them in his mind, could almost feel them crawling over him, squealing with happiness.

Then the sounds came again, much closer this time. He sat bolt upright, clutching the rifle tightly in his hands.

They were camped on a ridge in a mountainous jungle, and this night there were four listening posts spread out from the main body. Though he was one of the leaders, Che Lan had volunteered for the night watch in order to let another sleep.

He strained forward and could distinctly hear movement; the ravine seemed alive, and he could clearly hear voices. For a second he debated: should he fire a warning and alert the others, or try to get back to the main camp and wake them? If he got back and woke the others, they could ready an ambush, but valuable time would be lost, time in which they could be fleeing. Did they want to make their stand here, or escape to fight somewhere else?

Should it perhaps end here at Dien Bien Phu, or should they run? He said the name slowly to himself—Dien Bien Phu. Then he decided: let it be here. This shall be the place.

He rose to a crouch and was about to slip away to warn the others when there was a burst of rifle fire from behind him.

He heard the cries of attack, and the entire ridge erupted with rifle fire.

They were surrounded, and the assault had come from the other sides. The French had ringed the ridge and set up the ambush from the ravine, hoping to drive the rebels into it, killing them as they ran down the slope to get away from the main attacking force.

Che Lan could hear cries and screams. His comrades were being killed in the camp; the French had penetrated through the other listening posts and had caught them by surprise.

There was a tremendous barrage of rifle fire, the noise drowning out the screams of the wounded. No one was getting away.

Che Lan dropped down in the brush. He couldn't go to the others—he'd be killed along with them—and he couldn't get away down the ravine. He was trapped.

The rifle fire began to abate; there were scattered shots, then a sudden burst, then quiet for a moment, then random fire again. Voices called from the top of the ridge to the men in the ravine. An officer ordered them to move up, sweeping the ridge to flush out whoever might be hiding. The rebel camp had been taken, he gloated.

Che Lan heard the men below him start up the ravine, slowly probing their way toward him.

He pressed close to the ground and tried to check the fear racing through him. From behind he heard shouts, and cries for mercy, but then came bursts of fire, and he knew the captured and wounded were being executed, and he knew he'd be shot too if he were taken prisoner.

The men were moving up the ridge slowly, carefully checking the brush, only twenty feet apart. There was no possibility that he wouldn't be discovered. For the first time he could remember, he was truly afraid.

They were so close he could hear them talking; then he saw them clearly. The men to his left and right were French, but the one directly in front of him was Vietnamese. If he continued on his path, he'd walk right over him.

A command in French from farther down the line stopped the advance. The Vietnamese soldier was less than ten feet away, so close that Che Lan could easily make out his features. He was very young, no more than eighteen; his eyes darted nervously, and from the way he clutched his rifle rigidly in front of him, Che Lan knew he was inexperienced and afraid.

Most likely he was a conscript, poorly treated, homesick, forced against his will to track down his own countrymen.

Then the youth's eyes found him; shock spread over his face, and he seemed to jump backward, but he didn't take his gaze from Che Lan's. Their eyes locked on one another.

Che Lan showed no fear, and there was nothing pleading in his look. The soldier turned his head slightly, as though to call to the others, but he kept his gaze on Che Lan and he didn't raise his rifle. For another full minute they stared at one another.

Again the soldier turned his head slightly, and his mouth opened to call out, but he changed his mind and his jaw set firmly.

The command came to move forward. In a line with the others, the youth moved toward Che Lan, and when he came to him, he stepped around and passed on.

Che Lan felt such relief that he leaned forward and placed his head on his kness. He was drained, and took deep breaths to steady himself. For several minutes he sat motionless, exhausted and thankful; then he felt an exhilaration of relief, and he began his way down the ravine.

It had not ended, he vowed. Dien Bien Phu was just the beginning.

22

Ban Me Thuot: June 24, 1896

XUAN SAT ON A BENCH IN the courtyard and watched the children play in the grass before her, fighting intermittently, tumbling over, running to her every few minutes for a reassuring pat.

Trinh and Paul were in the garden, climbing trees and swinging from branches. She could hear their cries of happiness and glee, and every now and then a stern admonishment from Chien, who was with them.

The day was beautiful and calm, so peaceful that were it not for the children she'd be lulled to sleep. It was not a day for pensive thoughts, yet she couldn't look upon the children without being reminded of Che Lan. The twins knew nothing of their father, and it was rare now that the older boys asked about him.

Two months ago the family had heard about the defeat of the rebels and the death of Phan Dinh Phung. Those rebels who hadn't been caught by the French had drifted back to their homes, and they'd waited for Che Lan, hoping that any day he'd return, but the weeks, and now months, had dragged on.

At first no one believed any harm could have come to him—surely he'd appear some morning—yet after two months their fears pressed so heavily that they no longer spoke of him.

Xuan wondered for whom it was the worst—Gia Minh, Ly, or Andre? How many times had she seen each of them standing before windows scanning the horizon? How many times did her eyes catch the fear in theirs?

She could hardly bear to look at Andre, who still bore the anguish of Louis's death, but the suffering was no less in Gia Minh's face, and Ly, despite her effort to conceal it, often had to hide her face from her children.

Xuan wanted to comfort them all; she had so much love and

compassion in her that she felt she could easily accommodate every misery and misfortune in the world.

She wanted to tell them not to grieve, no matter what happened. She wanted to tell them of the peace that she'd found, the acceptance of all things which sustained her life and gave her contentment. She couldn't understand God's will, but she'd learned to accept it without questioning or challenging.

Her faith gave her strength and dwarfed everything else in her life. She cared not a thing about politics, and no longer even made a pretense of interest in what was happening in the country. After Tu Duc's death, it all seemed so alien to her, a tawdry stage play with insignificant players and an incomprehensible plot.

What did any of it matter, she thought, all the intrigue and hatred and fighting, all the arguments over government and economics, all the societies, when there was family to love, children to love, God to worship?

It didn't matter to her what happened with the country; one form of government seemed no better than another, one ruler no more enlightened than another. Of course she knew that men had to worry about such things, but she wished it were not so; she wished they could be content with love, could find pleasure in the simple unadorned things, did not always have to stamp their own vain mortality on things, and she thought suddenly of Ahn's rock garden.

She could sit here forever in this garden, she thought; she could love these children, and comfort them, and be content the rest of her life. She could feel the warmth of the sun, and contemplate the beauty of the garden, and never move from this bench. If only others could do the same, she thought. When they had all this—and she was thinking of the children, and the sun, and the garden—why would they want to take up arms, or build a wall, or arrange rocks in a garden?

Poor Ahn, she thought, but there was no sadness in her recollection, only love and warmth. Still, he'd be unhappy today to see what had happened. He'd be like Che Lan, and she'd be like Ly, worrying every moment of his absence.

Her heart went out to them all. She felt as though she stood at a great distance, her advanced age making her a removed observer. She was seventy-five and quite frail, and at times she thought she had only the most tenuous tie to life, even less than Chien's, whose great age nevertheless did not place him at such a distance from the everyday.

Of course she worried and fretted over them all, and how

could she tell Gia Minh not to worry about her son, or not herself grieve at the pain Andre felt for Che Lan? Yet she knew what they didn't, that time mutes sorrow, and age assuages grief. No day went by that she didn't think of Ahn, but the pain was gone long ago. Her memory was not that of jutted cliffs and rugged rocks, but of an untroubled expanse of water, a smooth surface over which her mind passed easily.

She couldn't tell anyone how she felt, for there were no words to express it, but the others were able to draw great strength and peace from her simply through a look or a touch of the hand. The children sensed it most, and they loved her above all others in the house.

Even Andre sought out her presence. He would never discuss his problems, but seemed to find solace just sitting with her. She knew how troubled he was, not just by the loss of Louis, and his concern for Che Lan, but by the difficult position he was in with the French and Vietnamese, caught between them, and trusted by neither.

The French distrusted him because of his family ties to the throne and because of his son's association with the rebellion. He wasn't one of them, and they resented his stature and wealth; he'd grown immensely rich from the rubber trade, and was one of the largest landowners in the country. On the other hand, the Vietnamese trusted him less and less as French power increased and resentment and hatred of them grew.

Andre knew how delicate his position was, and he tried to stay out of politics entirely. Che Lan's involvement with the rebels had caused him serious difficulties with the French, and he knew that he couldn't save his son if he fell into their hands. At the same time, he sympathized with Che Lan and the rebels, but he knew too how futile their struggle was. Always hanging over him was the memory of Ahn, and Ahn's fear that he wouldn't be strong enough to save the family.

Xuan was aware of the danger of Andre's position, and it worried her, because she knew the cruelty men were capable of, and her greatest fear was that someone would seek vengeance on the family for Che Lan's activities.

But this day, sitting in the sun, the children before her, she had no premonitions. Watching the children play, she thought of her own children, and warm memories of her youth and love for Ahn passed over her. There was nothing unsettling in her reverie; even unhappy times she saw with the disinterest of a tarot reader turning over cards on a table.

She was staring at the trees across the fields when she suddenly saw soldiers emerge, six of them, moving quickly and with purpose. Their hurry and determination seemed so out of place in the languid day that her attention fixed more closely on them.

Soldiers were no longer an uncommon sight, and before the collapse of the rebel movement, patrols had often stopped to search for Che Lan, thinking he'd return to see his family, but the soldiers had always been deferential and courteous.

But she could see that this patrol was different; they were moving too fast, and there was something in their manner which sounded warnings in her.

The children didn't see them and continued their play, but when she looked toward the garden, she saw that Chien had also observed the soldiers. He called the boys out of the tree and brought them to his side, his hand resting on their shoulders for protection, but also to restrain them from running to meet the soldiers.

Xuan looked toward the house for a servant so she could send him for Andre, but then she remembered Andre and Gia Minh had gone into Ban Me Thuot, and had taken Ly with them.

Alarmed at the steady advance, she stood and went to the children. She took their hands and started with them toward the house, but immediately the soldiers broke into a run toward them, their bayonets flashing in the sun.

Xuan stopped, knowing that she'd never reach the house. She gathered the startled children behind her and faced the soldiers defiantly.

The two boys tried to pull away from Chien, wanting to run to the soldiers, but he rebuked them sharply, and stepped back with them toward the jungle.

The soldiers bore down on Xuan and raised their rifles.

Chien grabbed the boys roughly and turned them away.

"Run," he said. "Run into the jungle and hide. The soldiers will kill you if they catch you. Hurry. Run. Don't leave one another, and don't come out until someone you know comes for you." He pushed them away. "Hurry. Don't stop."

With her arms holding the children behind her, Xuan wasn't even able to ward off the first blow from the rifle. The stock caught her in the side and threw her to the ground. She tried to raise herself to protect the children, but she had no breath in her and she lay helpless.

The children began to cry, but the soldiers turned on them so quickly that no one from the house heard them.

A soldier bayoneted the little girl, the long blade passing

completely through her; then he stabbed the boy. Another soldier ran his bayonet through Xuan.

They died instantly, and only seconds had elapsed since the soldiers had arrived.

The other soldiers looked around and saw the two small boys fleeing, and they saw Chien shuffling toward them, his hands raised above him, outstretched, his white robes flowing, an angered prophet descending upon them.

Immediately the soldiers gave chase to the boys. Paul and Trinh looked over their shoulders and saw them closing in; Paul gave a frightened cry but ran on beside Trinh as fast as he could.

Two of the soldiers outdistanced the others and ran headlong toward Chien. He stood his ground and made no effort to get out of their way, instead tried to block their path.

They came upon him from both sides. One hit him with his rifle butt, catching him on the shoulder, knocking him backward forcefully. The other stabbed with his bayonet, but the blade slashed through his robes harmlessly. Chien fell to the ground. The soldier stabbed again; this time the blade cut easily through the flesh of his abdomen.

Trinh and Paul saw Chien fall, and the soldier stab him; they both began to cry, but they didn't stop running and reached the jungle wall as the soldiers started after them again.

They slipped through it quickly and ran hand in hand through the dense underbrush. The denser foliage and entangling vines were above them and didn't impede their flight.

When the soldiers reached the jungle border, they were confronted by a massive, almost impenetrable green barrier. They thought they'd seen where the children entered, but standing before the jungle wall, they looked to one another in doubt.

They waited until all six were present; then they spread out and started through. Immediately they were absorbed by the wild growth and could barely see one another, though they were only ten feet apart.

Their harsh penetration raised a cacophony of outrage from the birds and insects. They waited until the noise died down; then, far ahead of them they heard the unmistakable sounds of someone trying to run through the underbrush.

They quickly followed the sounds, but they themselves made so much noise that they had to stop every few feet to make sure they were still on the right track.

They fought the vines and brush, but their progress was so slow that the noise from the children's flight grew fainter, then stopped altogether.

The soldiers came together. Their orders were to kill the children, and they couldn't go back and tell their superiors that two of them had been able to elude six men. They discussed it for a moment among themselves; all of them knew the jungle, all had grown up in it, and they all knew how to stalk. The children were hiding, but the men knew that they wouldn't be able to remain still. If the soldiers kept moving closer, they'd come upon them; then, like rabbits, the children would break and run, and they'd have them.

The soldiers spread out again and started moving forward, their eyes searching the underbrush, their bayonets probing the thick growth.

Paul and Trinh huddled together and heard the soldiers approaching. They were terrified, and tears streamed down their faces. They'd stumbled into a narrow cleft in the underbrush, a small partially underground breach in the jungle floor, and they'd crawled inside. They scrunched down as far as they could go, but the crevice wasn't large enough to hide them completely.

Their eyes were wild with fear; they'd seen what the soldiers had done, and they'd heard the stories of how the soldiers had murdered Ahn.

The sounds of the soldiers moving through the jungle came closer, and they could hear the bayonets slashing in the brush. As they drew nearer, Paul started up from the hiding place, but Trinh grabbed him and held him from bolting. Paul began to whimper from fear; then he followed Trinh's example and put his hands in front of his mouth.

They could clearly hear footsteps, and the soldiers talking to one another. The steps stopped and they could see the boots, muddied black; then they saw the blade of a bayonet, dried red, and they closed their eyes tightly; but in a moment the steps moved on, and when they opened their eyes, the soldiers had passed beyond them.

The children didn't move, hardly breathed for fear the soldiers would come back. They lay almost paralyzed as the afternoon wore on, and they didn't speak to one another.

It grew darker, and still they didn't move. The jungle began to stir as night set in; everywhere about them was alive with noise and movement. They moved even closer together, their eyes open wide in fear.

They were asleep in each other's arms when they woke to the sounds of someone crashing through the brush toward them. They jerked up and threw themselves together, then tried to burrow deeper into the hole, whimpering as the noise came closer.

Then they heard Andre calling their names.

Overcome with joy, they jumped up and shouted, "Grandfather! Grandfather, here we are," and they were crying when he grabbed them to him, and he buried his face into their necks, and he was sobbing too.

He was certain they'd been killed.

When they'd returned from Ban Me Thuot in early evening, they'd found the bodies exactly as the soldiers had left them. He'd seen them first, from a distance, and he tried to prevent Gia Minh and Ly from approaching on horseback, but as soon as they saw the forms sprawled on the ground they'd urged their horses on.

Andre reached them first, and one look told him everything.

As soon as Ly saw her children, she began to scream, and Andre couldn't restrain her from throwing herself on them. Gia Minh crossed herself and closed her eyes, then went to Ly to comfort her, but Ly was hysterical, clutching the corpses to her, smothering them with kisses. She held the children to her and rocked with them, her face upturned to the sky, her eyes unseeing, her mind crushed with grief.

Gia Minh left her side to sit beside her mother. She stroked Xuan's head, then took it into her lap and stared too with unseeing eyes at the rising moon.

Andre left them and drew his revolver from a saddlebag, then he cautiously approached the house. The screens were open, and there was every sign that the house had been rapidly deserted. He found no servants, but no sign that the house had been disturbed.

He called his grandsons' names, almost afraid to raise his voice, not wanting to hear the silence that he knew was going to be the response.

He knew what had happened, could picture the terror in his mind, and knew who had sent the soldiers, and why. It was because of Che Lan, retaliation for his challenge to the French. The French had done this, had hired mercenaries, and their message was that no one was safe in challenging French authority.

Standing alone in the silent house, he was nearly crazed with anger, but then his terror for the two children overcame him. In his mind he could hear their screams, and feel their fear, and see them killed.

He ran from the house.

Ly rushed up to him. "Trinh! Where is he? Dear God, where is my son?"

He held her to him. "I don't know. There's no one in the house." Then, over her shoulder he saw Chien's crumpled body lying in the garden.

"Oh God," he said, and ran.

He knew he was going to find the other bodies, and he looked nearby for them before he went to Chien, but Gia Minh called out to him, "He's alive. Come quickly."

Andre dropped down on his knees beside the old man and raised his head. He heard faint breathing, but he was unconscious, and so weak that Andre was afraid he wouldn't live long enough to tell them what had happened.

He sent Ly for water while he unfastened Chien's robes and searched for wounds. Finding only the one on the stomach, a deep but clean incision that had bled little, he felt for broken bones, knowing how fatal they could be to a man of Chien's age. Satisfying himself that there were none, he told Gia Minh that if the blade hadn't cut into an organ, the old man might be all right.

When Ly returned, they wet his face and lips, but he didn't respond.

"We have to get him inside," Andre said, and the three struggled with him into the house.

Andre sent Ly for a doctor and to notify the police, mostly to keep her busy and to get her away from the house, because he felt that as soon as he went out into the garden, he'd find the other two bodies.

Chien's breathing became stronger but he didn't regain consciousness.

Gia Minh and Andre had yet to speak of what had happened, but there was no need for words.

"I'm going out to look," he said, and she understood what he expected to find.

He searched for an hour, calling out their names, and each time there was no response, and each time, inside the house, Gia Minh closed her eyes in pain.

When he returned he was so distraught and disheveled that Gia Minh left Chien and went to her husband. "Maybe they're alive," she said. "Maybe they were kidnapped."

He shook his head. "They wouldn't let them live." Finally expressing it, he began to weep. "Oh, God," he cried. "How could anyone do this?" He hid his face in his hands and sobbed.

Gia Minh stood stoically beside him. Her father had been killed, and now her mother. Her grandchildren lay murdered on the ground outside, and her son was probably dead also. Yet she didn't cry. Her face was strong and resolute, though her grief was almost more than she could bear.

Chien stirred on the bed. His eyes opened, then closed again in pain. His tongue moved over his lips and he tried to speak. They gave him water and he drank thirstily.

Andre went on his knees beside the bed. "Chien. Can you hear me?"

Chien grimaced in an attempt to speak. His hands went to his abdomen.

"Where are the other boys, Chien? What happened to Paul and Trinh?"

"The jungle," he whispered. He tried to rise, but fell back in exhaustion and pain. "In the jungle. Hiding."

Andre ran from the room and out of the house, and he crashed through the jungle wall, shouting their names, calling until he thought his lungs would burst, running through the dense growth, heedless of the branches and vines which cut his body, and finally when he heard them calling him, he cried out in joy and relief, and when he grabbed them to him, he thought he'd crush them.

Two weeks passed, but none of the heavy sorrow lifted from the house.

Andre seemed drained of all exuberance and vitality; he went through the motions of managing his affairs, but even his movements were such that he seemed to walk under a great weight. He couldn't sleep, and now worked late into the night, though much of his time was spent in sad reverie.

He had little interest anymore in his estate; he didn't care about rubber, or rice, or money. What was the point now that he had lost his sons?—for he was sure now that Che Lan was dead too.

His wife couldn't comfort him; he slipped away from her, and now he thought more and more of his own youth, and what had brought him to this unhappy country. For the first time since he'd been in Vietnam, he thought longingly of France. It would have been better had he never come here, he thought.

He was at his desk, with plans and accounting papers before him, but he really wasn't seeing them, and it was nearly midnight, long after everyone else in the house had gone to bed.

Suddenly the screen slid open. He jumped up, startled, and reached for his revolver.

The figure before him was so gaunt and worn that at first he didn't recognize his son, and when he finally did, he was too stunned to move.

Che Lan stood hesitantly, framed by the night and garden, looking beaten and unwell. "Father . . ." he said.

"My God," said Andre, and he rushed to his son and threw his arms around him.

Having come this far, Che Lan appeared unable to go farther, and he collapsed in his father's arms.

Andre half-carried him to a chair, then knelt beside him, his hands testing the reality of his presence. "Are you all right? Are you wounded? Oh, my God, Che Lan, are you hurt?"

Che Lan summoned a faint smile. "I'm fine." He sank back in the cushions and closed his eyes. "I thought I'd never get here."

Andre went for brandy and brought it back for him. "I was so worried. After you didn't come home and we didn't hear anything . . . I mean, I thought that . . ." He grabbed his shoulder. "Oh, God. I feel just like a silly woman." He wiped at his eyes. "I may cry."

He put his hands around his son's neck, and he was crying.

"Where have you been? Why didn't you send word you were all right? After Dien Bien Phu, I thought you were dead. My God, your mother! We have to tell Gia Minh."

Che Lan restrained him. "Not yet. Or Ly. We have to talk first."

Then Andre remembered the events of the past two weeks, and he looked suddenly as though he'd been hit by a hammer. "Yes," he said, his joy instantly gone.

Che Lan noted the change and sensed something wrong. "Is everything all right?"

"Where were you?" Andre countered, trying to lead away from the subject.

"With the montagnards. I knew the French would be looking for me, so I fled and stayed with them." He studied his father's face, and saw that he hadn't been listening. "Father, what's wrong?" He stood up. "Something happened. Tell me."

Andre put his hand on his shoulder and forced him back in his chair.

"Tell me." He struggled up against Andre's arms. "Ly! My children! What is it?"

Andre could barely meet his eyes, but he forced himself to look into his son's face, and he held his shoulder tightly. "The twins are dead. And Xuan. Soldiers came two weeks ago. But Ly and Trinh are all right."

Che Lan's face broke into a look of horror. "My babies!" he cried, his voice an agonized howl. "My babies." He closed his eyes from the pain that was physical; then his eyes opened in fury. "Who? Who killed them?"

Gone were his exhaustion and weakness. He grabbed Andre and shouted in his face. "Who killed my children?"

"Mercenaries. From the French."

"Oh, my God," Che Lan cried. He sought about for something on which to settle his rage. His hands twisted uncontrollably; then he clutched them to his sides and bent over, thinking he was going to be sick. "Oh, God., Father."

Andre put his arms about him, and Che Lan buried his face in his father's chest and began to sob, all that he had suffered and stored within him pouring out in a torrent.

"It's all right, it's all right," Andre said, holding him tightly, wanting to shield him from all sorrow and pain, his own grief for his son's pain crushing.

Finally Che Lan gained control of himself. Drained, he sat down to listen to what had happened.

"It was because of me," he said, lowering his head when Andre finished.

Andre said nothing, and averted his eyes, unable to witness the pain of that horrible truth.

"How can I live with that?" he asked. "I killed my own children."

"No," said Andre. "Never think that. You didn't harm your children. Others did. There's no blood on your hands; you can't blame yourself. What was done, was done by others. There's no provocation for murdering children and an old woman."

Che Lan closed his eyes and rocked slowly, gripped by guilt and remorse. When he looked up, his eyes were filled with tears. "What can I do, Father?"

"Do nothing," said Andre, understanding the dimension of his son's question.

"But I can't," he said, and now his heart steeled, and coldness spread through his being. "I have to avenge their deaths."

"And what will become of Trinh? And Ly? Or your mother? The soldiers will come again."

"But I can't let it go."

"Think of your wife and son, Che Lan. There's nothing you can do without risking their lives."

"But how can I let the deaths go unavenged? How could I live as a man with my children killed like that? Would you have me become a willing servant of the French? Let my son grow up that way? I can't, Father." He jumped up, seized by rage. "I won't let it go. I won't! I fought the French for years; I was beaten and humiliated in their prison. My children were killed by them. I'll never let it go. Never! I'd rather die."

"But, Che Lan . . ." Andre started, then stopped, for what could he say? What would he himself do?

Che Lan's fury was gone, replaced by an almost sad resignation. "I told you long ago that I'd fight the French as long as I lived. I never thought it would involve my family, but now that it has, I have no choice. I can't submit. There's still a resistance. I'll join up with it, and it'll grow and become stronger, and someday . . . someday, Father, we'll win."

"You can never return here again if you take up arms against the French now."

"I know that."

"Oh, Che Lan," Andre said, overwhelmed with sorrow. "Don't do this. Think of what you're giving up. Your son needs you. Your wife needs you." He went to him and put his arm on his shoulder. "I need you. I couldn't bear to lose another son."

"Maybe it won't come to that, Father."

Andre closed his eyes.

"Don't you understand, Father? Some things are more important than life."

"That's what your grandfather would have said."

"Was he wrong?"

"No," Andre whispered. Then he remembered what he'd told Ahn in the jungle so many years ago, that he would make his children strong enough. And so it had happened. "Ahn would be very proud of you. As I am. It's just that . . ." But there were no words to describe his sorrow and unhappiness. "I don't want to lose you," he said at last.

Che Lan put his arms around his father, and the two men embraced.

"I think it's best that you don't tell Ly or Mother that I came back."

"I can't do that, Che Lan. Why don't you go see them?"

He shook his head. "I couldn't, I couldn't say good-bye to them."

"Then stay awhile. Don't go tonight."

"That would only make it harder."

"But you can't go like this. You can't just walk out of our

lives. You have a wife and child. You're my son. You can't just disappear into the night."

Che Lan gripped Andre's shoulder. "Father, I can't stay here. I love Ly, you know that—more than my own life. I love Trinh. I love you and Mother. But that isn't enough. Being free is more important."

He stepped back. "I'm going to go now, Father." He smiled faintly. "I don't think this is the end. Do you?"

Andre's heart was so heavy he could barely speak. "Dear God, I hope not."

They embraced, and then Che Lan was gone, and Andre was staring at a half-moon over the jungle canopy.

He stepped outside, wanting to call back his son, but there was no sign of him; the night had swallowed him completely.

He felt a hundred years old. How could he laugh again, or look upon anything with any joy? And then he thought: Oh, God, why did I come here? But that was so long ago, and so innocent, so beyond his control. And once he came, how could he have ever left? He'd been trapped, as if in quicksand, and there was no way out; the seeds had been sown, and now came the bitter harvest.

23

Ban Me Thuot: April 1906

CHIEN SAT IN THE GAZEBO AND dozed peacefully. It was mid-afternoon; he was sated from the noon meal, content to drift in and out of mild sleep, soothed by the gentle breeze which carried the smell of jasmine and lilac. The heat was not oppressive; it was late April, and the days were clement.

Soft light and the scent of flowers waxed through the lattice-work of the gazebo, a delicate structure of red cedar that resembled an airy pagoda in the middle of the gardens, and to which all the pebble paths led like spokes of an old wheel, the hub of which was the gazebo itself.

Wisteria wove in and out of the lattice, and the green leaves rustled gently in the spring breeze.

He sat perfectly still—from a distance, seemingly part of the natural order. Only close up, seeing his great age, his skin mottled and wrinkled, did his mortality contrast so starkly with the timeless perfection and beauty of nature; then his appearance became a cruel reminder of man's frailty and infirmity. But despite his heavy and dull body, his mind was at one with his surroundings; his thought was not active, but passively serene, and he was possessed of an other-worldly calm.

Ten years ago, when the soldiers had come, Chien thought he was going to die from the wound in his stomach; he performed the last rites and rituals, and settled in his bed to pass peacefully from this life, even though the doctors told him the wound was not severe and he hadn't suffered any broken bones from the fall.

He lay in bed three days, allowing no intrusions, and never once speaking. On the fourth day, sore and stiff, he got out of bed and went into the kitchen; then he went about his business as if nothing had happened.

Some years later he felt death camped at his side. A bout of influenza left him so weak and debilitated that he knew he would never rise from his bed. Again he made the preparations for death, and again, completely at peace, he prepared to die. But death struck his tent and left the old man alone in his room, his hands folded, stretched serenely in his bed, his eyes wide open, feeling well and healthy and ravenous.

A month ago, a summer cold confined him to bed. He was ninety-three years old and he didn't respond to the doctor's medications or to any of the home remedies brought by a host of concerned neighbors and friends.

The cold turned to pneumonia, and again he prepared himself to die. He examined his life and made peace with himself, and one night, feeling weak, and unsure he could draw breath till morning, he bade farewell to everyone in the house, then fell into a deep sleep.

He passed in and out of consciousness for three days, but on the fourth, the fever broke and he had no difficulty breathing. Again he found himself open-eyed and well on his deathbed.

Though pleased to be alive, he was somewhat exasperated, and he vowed never to waste another moment in preparing for death.

"You're never going to die," said Andre after this last siege.

"Just as well," he'd answered. "It seems a great deal of trouble; besides, I'm sure death isn't very interesting."

"What do you expect to find there?" Andre had asked.

But as a good Confucian, Chien couldn't be drawn into conversation about life after death; the subject held no interest for him. He had waved his hand in dismissal. "As the Master taught, 'You can't know about death before you know about life.' I don't yet know about life. I know only about the broad brush strokes, not the intricate details; I see the faint outlines, not the art."

But he seemed so wise, so very old and knowledgeable, that people came from everywhere to listen to and to draw from him. The boys, Paul and Trinh, were awed by his age, and rendered him respect and attention that bordered on amazement, for as old as he was, his mind was sharp and lucid, and his tongue quick and pointed.

"How is it that you have lived so long?" he was frequently asked, and he would invariably answer in the words of Confucius: "Man's lifespan depends upon his uprightness." To Andre and the boys his eyes would twinkle when he said this, and dropping his sage manner, he once told them what he really thought was responsible for his longevity—"luck and good bowels."

Because he was part of a dying caste, a Confucian scholar, and a legitimate one at that, having studied in Peking, people pilgrimaged to hear him discourse and tell the stories of the days before the French.

Nowadays the ancient Chinese texts weren't studied as before, and their value was deemphasized. Now everyone studied French, and in the schools a new system of writing was being taught in place of the Chinese characters—the Jesuits had introduced the phonetic spelling of Vietnamese.

More than anything, Chien despaired of this, for he believed foremost in language, and the proper names for all things. He said that the worst harm that had fallen upon the country was the corruption of the language, for in quoting Confucius, he said: "If the designations are not correct, language will not be clear. If language is not clear, duties will not be carried out." And it was upon duty, he taught—certainly not on anything so foolish as love—that the entire structure of society rested.

In his own mind he saw that Vietnam was doomed; the soul of the people had been corrupted. As the emperor had lost the mandate from heaven, so had the people lost their basic nature—the proper duties were not being performed, even the rituals of ancestor worship ignored.

"It's the new order," Andre told him, but Chien had shaken his head. "It's not order at all; it's not even new—it's what there was before there was order."

But though he saw doom for Vietnam, his age displaced him from care or worry; despite what went on about him, he himself would perform the rituals. He saw his duty now as to impart the ancient wisdom to the two boys, and to live himself according to the teaching set forth in the *Analects* of Confucius. He took an interest in everything that went on about him; he inquired about Andre's businesses, and discussed politics with Ly; he debated religion with Gia Minh, and challenged the boys on every new idea they brought to him. His eagerness to learn was as great as ever, but nothing he heard altered a thing he believed.

He believed in tradition, and what he taught the boys was exactly what he'd taught their father and their grandfather, and what he himself had learned eight decades ago. He taught them Chinese, ethics, music, and he discussed with them anything which came into their eager minds.

One day they wanted to know about girls, though they'd discussed the matter at length between themselves. Joshing one another, and with a very false sense of bravado, they approached Chien on the subject.

His eyes looked blank. He hesitated. He seemed to be recalling something lost long ago in his memory. "Are there still girls in the world?" he asked in mock surprise.

"Are you that old?" Trinh asked.

Chien laughed. "No," he said. "That's called death. But I didn't realize you were that old." They were fourteen then.

"Your goal is manhood at its best, isn't that right?"

They nodded.

"And you are seeking to be perfect gentlemen."

Again they nodded.

"The Master taught that there are three things which the perfect gentleman avoids. The first is sexual intercourse while still too young, before the blood and breath have settled down. The second is fighting after the man has grown up and his blood and breath are strong. The third is further acquisitions after he has grown old and his blood and breath have thinned."

He tapped them both rather severely. "For you to worry about sex at your age is as bad as for me to covet money at my age. Neither would do us any good."

That had certainly not settled their blood or breath, but it did stop them from pursuing the subject with him, and he'd heard no more about it from them in two years.

Now, from under hooded lids, he saw them sneaking toward him, converging on the gazebo from different directions. He always saw them, but he never let on, and allowed them to jump out at him, always appearing unstartled and utterly serene, as though gently awakening or coming peacefully from some faraway meditation. His composure always amazed them, and they thought indeed that he possessed complete inner peace.

But, he now thought, they really shouldn't do this anymore. One of these days he wouldn't see them, and he'd have a heart attack. He closed his eyes, parted his lips in gentle repose, and braced himself.

The two youths edged closer, then crouched to spring at the old man.

Though closer than most brothers, they were as unalike physically as they were temperamentally.

Paul was tall and strapping, just like Louis, and his extraordinarily refined good looks were those of his father, but he was very blond, like his mother and Andre, and his disposition was mild and pleasant like theirs.

Chien saw a great deal of Andre in the youth, and little of Louis, and this pleased him, for Paul seemed to have gotten the best of them both; he had Andre's nature, his affability and kindness, and he had Louis's quickness and penetrating mind. Paul loved books and ideas, and he was a far better student than Trinh in all regards; even his Vietnamese was better, and his Chinese certainly was. If only Paul hadn't looked like a Greek statue, Chien could have taken him more seriously as a Confucian scholar, for his manners were already that of a mandarin—he was deliberate in speech, wise in thought, and slow and graceful in movement. Everything about him bespoke an older, more civilized, more gracious nature, a court scholar, but alas, one was confronted with a very blond, very handsome, very Western-appearing youth. And when he smiled, which was often, his face broke into ingenuous pleasure, and there was Andre all over again, and nothing of the mandarin.

Yet in Paul's own mind there was no confusion about himself; he was Vietnamese. He even had trouble with French, and spoke it less well than he did both Vietnamese and Chinese. It really never occurred to him that he was French, and certainly not a colonial. He was every bit as Vietnamese as his cousin Trinh was, and it never entered his mind that Trinh was anything less than one hundred percent Vietnamese.

It certainly never entered Trinh's mind; he made no allowance whatsoever that he had a quarter French blood, or that his father was half-French. He saw his father as one of the foremost patriots of Vietnam, and it was his sole desire to follow in his footsteps.

He was a great deal like his father, but Chien saw in him more of the boy's great-grandfather, Ahn, a vitality and impetuosity that rendered it impossible for him to master scholarship or meditation. His was a restless spirit; he was a youth of action and drive, with a quick mind and a fast temper. It was not easy for him to sit still—the contemplation of a chrysanthemum would have driven him to distraction—and now at the age of sixteen he had to be restrained almost forcibly from running off to join with his father and the other rebels.

What kept him home was the strong counsel of Andre and Gia Minh, the pleas of his mother, Ly, and his devotion to his family, especially Paul. The family was very close, and the elders lavished attention and warmth on the two youths. Andre in particular devoted himself to them, more than he had to his own sons, and he was not so old that he couldn't have passed for their father rather than their grandfather; even now at fifty-six he was remarkably fit and youthful.

The boys loved Andre, and were devoted to one another as brothers, but it was Che Lan who stirred their imaginations and fired their dreams. He was both real and myth, and they talked about him and his exploits with never-ending eagerness.

Che Lan's visits were infrequent and unpredictable; sometimes he stayed only a few days, other times nearly a month. He was wanted and pursued by both the French and the Vietnamese, but Ban Me Thuot was a relatively safe haven, for there was little French presence, and much sympathy for the rebels.

Ten years ago, on that night when his son had left the house, Andre had truly believed that a dreadful fate awaited Che Lan, and that the entire country would be pitched into bloody strife.

For months he was in the deepest melancholy, believing that each day would bring news of his son's capture or death. But the season changed and life went on, and there were details to tend to, and another season came. There were problems and joys, vexations and rewards, and more seasons passed; there was a flow of news about the rebels, and Che Lan himself, yet nothing major seemed to change.

Finally he came home. Andre and Gia Minh were ecstatic with relief and happiness, and Ly's joy knew no bounds, yet it was immediately apparent that he was even more dedicated to the cause of independence, and nothing could dissuade him from leaving again. Over the years, the course of Che Lan's life and its brief intersections with theirs came to be accepted, and the family fell into the complacency about French rule that the country at large exhibited.

After the rebel defeat in 1896, the rebellion had gone into a dormant period, with most of those who hadn't been caught and executed returning to their villages to take up their lives. It seemed to many Vietnamese that French rule was no worse than, and in many cases better than, the former rule of the Nguyens. Village life continued unchanged, and most people never even saw a Frenchman—the spirit world of the ancestors was more real than the foreigners from France.

Nevertheless, French rule was real, and not benign. Vietnam, along with Laos and Cambodia, had become part of French Indochina. The grand scheme of an Oriental empire, a huge colony to rival Britain's, had at last come about, and in Vietnam itself the French wasted no time in extracting profits from its new acquisition.

To do this, the French began massive public works and development programs using peasant labor—paving roads, laying railways, pushing canals and construction projects throughout the country, all paid for by increasingly brutal taxation. Profits from rubber, textiles, the spice trade, mineral desposits, all gained through cheap forced labor, filled the coffers in France.

There was only one center of resistance after the rebel defeat, far in the north of Tonkin, where the bandit-rebel Hoang Hoa De Tram conducted raids against the French.

De Tram was a coarse man of no formal education, and his resistance to the French was as much opportunistic as it was political. But Che Lan didn't care; even had his children not been murdered by French mercenaries, he never could have accepted a French-ruled Vietnam. But after the deaths of the twins, his hatred ran so deep that he lived for only one goal—the defeat of the foreigner. He cared only about fighting the French, and if it was done by a man whose motive was greed and power, so be it.

When Che Lan first returned to Ban Me Thuot and told his father about his activities, Andre had been shocked. De Tram was a common criminal, Andre said.

"I don't care," Che Lan had answered. "He's fighting the French; it's their goods we're stealing, and the people are behind us."

Gone was the idealistic youth, and in his place there was now a cold, murderous young man, a son whom Andre hardly knew.

Ly was frightened by him. "I didn't marry you for this, or bear children to raise them fatherless," she said. "I want a husband, a man at my side, not one to steal into my bed at nights and flee before morning."

"It was you who first hated the French," he'd answered. "You were the one who always talked at the meetings—it was you who had all the fine ideas of resistance and freedom."

"That was before I had children and lost them. Before I found out how cruel and stupid it all was. Before my husband became a murderer and a criminal. How could the French be any worse than those who ruled before? The people deserve what they've gotten, and I can live with it, if only I can live in peace with my child."

"I'd rather die," he said.

He didn't return for eighteen months, but when he came back the raw edge of his hatred was gone, and so was his commitment to De Tram. He didn't want to be a bandit anymore; he wanted something meaningful to fight for. Besides, he was nearly thirty years old.

He reconciled with Ly, and poured out his heart to her. "I don't know what to do," he said. "I can't live here; I can't accept how things are. Can't you see that I have to go on fighting?"

"Yes," she said. "I understand. It's just not how I saw our lives. I want us to be a family. I want us to raise our son in peace and happiness. That's more important to me than who rules the country. Before, I cared about such things. No longer. I'd rather live with you and Trinh under the French than not have you here, or to lose my son too. But I understand how it's different for a man."

When he came back the following year he was brimming over with idealism and plans. The year was 1902 and he'd met with Phan Boi Chau, who'd left the Can Vuong before the collapse and spent the next years in his village, where he'd achieved renown as a scholar. In 1900, however, Phan was ready to take up the struggle against the French again.

Phan's strategy was simple—to unite the diverse factions of the resisters, to find support with the royal family, to obtain foreign aid, and to cast out the French once and for all.

During the next three years Chẹ Lan returned often to Ban Me Thuot, each time more confident and passionate about the future. He told the family in 1903 of the formation of the Modernization Society, the united alliance against the French, and how they'd enlisted the support of Prince Cuong De, a direct descendant of the great Gia Long's eldest son. Soon the entire country would rise up against the French, he said.

His son believed him, and his enthusiasm and passion passed to Trinh, and to Paul.

Andre listened to all that Che Lan said, but he never commented; he knew it was all futile. He wanted his son to succeed, but he knew he couldn't. He had made his son strong—Ahn could not have hoped for more—but it would make no difference; a free and independent Vietnam was not to be, not in his life, not in his son's life, he knew.

Gia Minh knew also, but she gave no hint of it to Che Lan. She listened raptly to his stories, to his plans and dreams, and she pretended it was all to happen just as he believed.

Caught in the middle was Ly, who wanted her husband back, and desperately feared that her son would follow in his footsteps. She didn't believe in the cause her husband was devoted to, but she was wise enough not to discourage him or castigate him. She didn't want her son to have to choose between them, because she knew it would only drive him away.

And Trinh was straining to go; each time Che Lan returned,

Trinh's passion was fueled even more, and his desire to join his father grew even stronger.

He could see the men of his country on the verge of striking out for freedom and independence, and he wanted to be among them. He dreamed of fighting with his father and the Modernization Society, of casting out the French, and establishing Prince Cuong De on the throne.

Now he lived only for his father's return, and to plead with him to be taken along. He could barely face his studies, and had to force himself to learn what he thought was outdated and foolish. He felt that he was on the edge of manhood, but knew that manhood was a journey beyond Ban Me Thuot.

But there was still the youth in him, and he delighted in the game he and Paul played on Chien.

Seeing the old man sitting serenely in the gazebo, they had split up at the edge of the garden to circle around him.

They crept slealthily toward him, then on signal crouched in the bushes, let out a murderous yell, and flung themselves onto the latticework of the gazebo and leaped inside.

Chien opened his eyes slowly, placidly, as though his mind were disengaging from the farthest horizons of thought, and he gave them a soft smile.

They dropped down on the bench beside him, disappointed again in their inability to startle him.

"What were you thinking about, Master Chien?" Paul asked, his eyes respectful, almost reverential.

"One doesn't so much think at my age as he remembers." He smoothed his linen robe and folded his hands in his lap. "I was remembering when I was your age, in China, before I came to Vietnam. Oh, my," he said, surprised suddenly at the thought. "That was over seventy-five years ago."

His eyesight was no longer good, and he turned his gaze to the not-far-away jungle that was only a mask of green to him. "My mind is like a vast desert now, yet sometimes coming out of the shimmering haze are mirages of memory. I think I was just sitting here contemplating the peacefulness, and perhaps it was a bird's call which brought me back. Or maybe the smell of jasmine. But there I was again, a young man."

"Are you sorry you came?" Paul asked.

"Oh, no."

The idea captured Trinh's interest, and he turned to the old man. "Was it hard for you to leave your country?"

"No, but only because I thought I was returning. Had I known I wasn't . . . then perhaps I never would have left. You see, I believed then that as Confucius taught, 'China without a recognized leader is preferable to foreigners with all their leaders.' "

"Do you still believe that?"

Chien smiled. "Unlike you who are too young to challenge what is taught, I'm old enough to know what to challenge and what to disbelieve. Now I know that people are good or bad regardless of borders. Boundaries don't confine goodness, nor bar wickedness. Princes can be good or evil wherever they are found. The perfect gentleman is not defined by territory, and manhood at its best knows no borders."

He leaned forward, the master scholar once again, and he tapped Trinh on the arm, recapturing his interest, which seemed to have wandered to the jungle beyond. "And what makes for true manhood," he asked sharply.

"Reciprocity," Trinh answered quickly. "Not doing to others what you don't want done to yourself."

Paul sniggered and cast him a superior look. "That's the answer for the Right Way."

Trinh would have jabbed him in the sides had Chien not been between them.

" 'True manhood consists of realizing your true self. It is upholding the moral order and the rituals,' " said Paul with satisfaction.

Trinh gave him a withering glance and quoted back smugly, " 'The perfect gentleman reaches complete understanding of the main issues; the petty man reaches complete understanding of the small details.' "

"Enough," said Chien tiredly. "What brings you out here to rent harmony and peace, and bore an old man?"

"We were talking about government," said Trinh with grand pomposity.

Chien closed his eyes. "You are sixteen years old and talking about government? That's as pointless and whimsical as an ninety-three-year-old man talking about sex."

At the word, both youths blushed, but Trinh caught himself quickly and put on a bravado act. "We were talking about government, but I was thinking about sex."

"As usual, you have it backward—talk about sex, but think about government."

"Let's talk about sex, then," Trinh said impertinently.

Chien stroked his robe and settled back as though to regain his sleep. "What would be the point? All you know is what you've been practicing on yourself. We don't need the details."

Paul laughed uproariously and pushed Trinh. Trinh crimsoned and pointed his finger at Paul. "You're worse than I am."

"Enough," said Chien. "I forget how tiresome you both can be until I've spent a moment with you. Run off and leave me in peace."

"No," begged Paul. "You have to talk to Trinh. He wants to leave. He wants to go off and join his father. I told him he's not ready yet; he has to study more."

"Study what?" asked Trinh contemptuously. "What's the point in learning anything when your country's been taken over by enemies? We have to fight. Just like my father is. It would be dishonorable not to fight. You yourself taught us, Master Chien, that 'When a state is following the Right Way, one enters its pay. If one enters the pay of a state which is not following the Right Way, it is shameful.' "

"We aren't old enough," Paul said. "They wouldn't want us."

"There are lots of things we can do. How old do you have to be to shoot a rifle?"

"The same age as to be felled by one," said Chien. Then he went on more gently. "The time will come when you will join the others, but now you would be more hindrance than help. Surely you aspire to be more than a simple soldier. Your grandfather is a wise and good man who has studied and learned much, and your great-grandfather was a great prince. You must honor his memory by learning all that you can. You have just begun your journey to manhood; it is a straight path, but not an easy one, and there are many enticing side roads. Be diligent in the pursuit of knowledge, for that is the weapon you must armor yourself with. You want to join the world of men and fight your country's enemies? Then first become a man. Have your comrades accept you as an equal, not as a boy. Bring them something more than passion. Someday you both may do grand things, but the time is nowhere near yet."

As he talked, a man came out of the jungle.

Paul jumped up from the bench, the never forgotten image of the soldiers leaping to his mind. His face clouded and he strained to see.

Trinh turned to look also, and immediately he stood, protectively stepping in front of Chien. Then, squinting into the sun, he recognized the figure, and shouting for joy, ran from the gazebo.

In a second, Paul raced after him. Chien bent forward to see, but all he could discern was a blur of movement.

Halfway to the man, Trinh yelled out, "Father!" and sprinted across the fields, throwing himself into the outstretched arms. Trinh was almost as large as Che Lan, but Che Lan picked him up and swung him around. Then Paul was on him, hugging him around the neck, and immediately they shouted questions at him, wanting to know where he'd been, what he'd done, and how long he was staying.

Che Lan ran to get away from their badgering; the boys pursued him happily, chasing him across the fields, but Che Lan easily outdistanced them, despite his age and the slight limp from favoring his bad leg. He was thirty-six, yet looked ten years younger, remarkably lean and conditioned, and when he reached the gazebo, his breathing was hardly labored.

He entered respectfully, and bowed to the old man. "Good day, Master Chien. Are you as well as you look?"

"I feel as though I could run footraces with boys. Do I look that I could? Or do I look my age?"

"You look like you always have."

"So do you. Probably you'll still be running footraces at my age too. Some people never act their age."

Che Lan laughed. "And some people never change. Will you forever be admonishing me?"

"Probably, since you never seem to learn anything. Is the revolution over? Is that why you've returned?"

The boys burst into the gazebo, but in deference to Chien, they quieted, and waited patiently.

"No," said Che Lan, "the revolution's not over; it's not even begun. I came home to see my family."

"How long are you staying?" asked Paul.

Trinh stood before him. "I'm leaving with you this time." His look was almost belligerent.

Che Lan smiled and tousled his hair; then he held out his arm for the old man. "Come, let's go to the house. I want to see everybody."

They walked slowly, and all the way Che Lan fended off Paul's and Trinh's questions.

From the house, Gia Minh saw them approaching, and her heart caught when she recognized her son, and for the first time she saw how much he looked like her father, Ahn.

She looked about, thinking to call to Andre and Ly, but then she changed her mind and returned her gaze to her son, wanting to cherish quietly this view of him, as though for this brief moment she alone possessed him.

She felt as though she'd hardly been a mother, for those years of his childhood had been so turbulent—Andre in France, then returned with Louis, Ahn's murder, and the hard years afterward. Then she'd been replaced by another woman so soon—he seemed still a boy when he married, but she'd lost him even before then; he'd talked nothing but freedom and independence since he'd heard the stories of his grandfather and knew the history of his country.

At first that hadn't perturbed her, for her father's passions ran through her also, and she knew that had she been a man, she'd act no differently from Che Lan. Yet so much had happened over the years; the sorrows and joys, the everyday affairs of life had filtered her view so that the cause of country was muted.

Other things matter more—love and happiness, the peace and comfort of a man and woman together, children, sunsets, and the glow of starry nights. Now she wanted all that for her son, wanted him to share in the fullness of the heart which she felt.

More than ever now she felt like a mother, but now she wasn't needed for that. Here, coming toward her across the fields, was her son, yet he wasn't returning to her, but to his wife and own child.

What a strange sight they made moving toward her, she thought; her man-child, and beside him his man-child, and beside him another man-child, all with dreams, and desires, and ambitions, all with the folly of hope. And soon they would all go off in different directions to different futures. They would all leave her.

Melancholy swept her. She was not well and suspected she had not long to live. She felt immensely tired and drained lately; each morning she had to struggle out of bed. So many things beyond her understanding had happened to her body: no one had forewarned her of menopause—she supposed at first that this overwhelming tiredness was just another phase of age, but then she'd begun to bleed slightly, and now she felt definite discomfort. But she kept it all to herself.

And poor Andre, she thought. He was too good, too kind, and it seemed unfair that he should have to age too. He was growing somewhat thick around the middle, and his face was creased deeply from the sun; he didn't stand as straight as before, and his hair was gray, and his eyes often revealed the sadnesses of the past.

He desperately wanted Che Lan to return and stay, to take over the management of the estate, and was hurt by the realization that Che Lan cared nothing about it. Now his greatest fear was that he'd lose his two grandsons also.

And seeing Trinh cling to his father, Gia Minh knew that this couldn't be delayed much longer. What saddened her just as much was the knowledge that Paul would go too, for what would become of him? He was so out of place, and the poor boy didn't even know it.

Looking out at them, she felt as though she possessed a far-seeing eye, that she stood at a distance from their lives and could view them with other-worldly detachment. In that gaze she saw that they were all caught in an immense wheel of events beyond their ability to control. She was almost glad she wouldn't live to witness it. She'd seen enough. Her last visit to Hue had confirmed for her that the Vietnam she'd known and grown up with was irrevocably lost. She kept distant but cordial ties to her relations at court, but saw life there so pathetic, so false and out of touch that she knew the monarchy would never rise again: it was a charade for the players alone—the audience had left.

The foreseeable future lay with the French, her husband's people, though he was not of them; it lay with their ships and weapons and commerce, and her poor son had no hope in the fight against them.

Yet she gazed proudly at him moving toward her; he looked strong, healthy, as though he alone could wrest the destiny of his country away from the French, but it was only illusion, and this almost made her weep, for she wanted so much for it to come to pass; it was, after all, her blood in him, and Ahn's, and that of emperors before him, yet she knew it was not to be.

Nevertheless, she would maintain the illusion, and bolster it in Trinh. And it would go to his children, and then perhaps someday . . .

She wiped her eyes and went to greet her son.

"And then what?" asked Trinh of his father.

Che Lan waited a moment for effect. "Then we all went to Japan."

"Japan! You were in Japan?" But Trinh's question was lost in the excitement from the others. Even Andre couldn't hide his surprise and interest.

"Japan . . ." he said to himself, the word echoing in his ears like the gong of a temple bell. He had always wanted to travel there; it was an exotic mystery surpassing even that of China, a land of geisha and samurai, a land of fierceness and beauty, now the most powerful country in the East. Last year Japan had humiliated Russia in a war, the first time a Western nation had been defeated by an Oriental power, proving not just the supremacy of Japan, but destroying forever the myth of the invulnerable

Westerner, and providing other Asian peoples with the idea and hope that they too could defeat the Westerner.

They were all seated around the dinner table listening to Che Lan's tales of what had happened to him since his last return.

As form dictated, he'd first paid his respects to his mother and father. Their welcome had been unrestrained, especially Andre's, but Che Lan attributed this to his father's age, and he noted with some melancholy how Andre was growing old. But finally he'd been able to take leave of his parents and break away from Trinh and Paul to be alone with Ly.

As always when reunited, they first demonstrated an awkward formality toward one another, inquiring with excessive politeness about each other's health and activities. They could feel the warmth of the other's passion, and see love and need in the other's face, but they remained apart, as shy as schoolchildren, until at last she reached out for him, welcoming his body back to hers.

They made love hungrily, trying to repossess the time they'd lost; then they talked and filled in the details of their separate lives.

When they appeared from their rooms in late afternoon, an aura of strength and love surrounding them, the boys held back, embarrassed, as though a wall of adulthood, the impenetrable mystery of a man and woman together, stood between them, and it was a while before Che Lan was able to ease their discomfort and again draw out their enthusiasm.

But by dinner they were all comfortable with one another and the talk centered around Che Lan's activities.

"Why did you go to Japan?" Gia Minh asked. To her, Japan was as remote as the moon, and more hostile.

"Because Phan Boi Chau and the others in the Modernization Society think that we can't defeat the French without Japanese assistance."

There was a barrage of questions about Japan and the people, but Che Lan ignored them, wanting to give a clear narrative, as much to order his own thoughts as to explain what had happened and what he'd seen.

"Last year there was the first dissension among us all. A man named Phan Chu Trinh—he's two years younger than I am—started a reform movement. He thinks we can work with the French."

"Never," said Trinh hotly.

Che Lan hushed him. "He doesn't believe in violence; he

thinks Vietnam can be changed into a democracy if we cooperate with the French."

"That's what I've been saying for years," said Andre. "The only way to save Vietnam is by working with the French. You'll never defeat them militarily." He pointed his finger at Che Lan. "And the Japanese won't help you."

Che Lan shrugged. "Chau thinks they will, but I'm not so sure. On the other hand, I don't trust the French, either."

"We have to do it ourselves," said Trinh. He was so carried away that he stood up, his hand raised defiantly.

The others stared at him calmly, indulgently, and feeling somewhat ridiculous, he sat back down, but not completely cowed. "Isn't that right, Master Chien?"

The old man smiled, seeing more and more of Ahn in the youth, and very pleased by it. "If I were building my nest, I think I'd be careful about asking the weasel or the wolf for help."

"Yes," said Che Lan, "that's how I'm beginning to feel, too. But right now the split is between those with Chau, who want Japanese help, and those with Trinh, who want to work with the French."

"Well, tell us about Japan," said Gia Minh impatiently. "What is it like? How did you get there? What did you see? Stop this nonsense about Chau and Trinh and tell me about Japan."

Che Lan settled back in his chair, refusing the rice wine his father offered him. "We left early last year from Haiphong and stopped in Hong Kong."

"Hong Kong," murmured Chien. The others turned to him, and Gia Minh frowned at the salacious look on his face.

"We were there only a short time," went on Che Lan hurriedly, "just long enough to make a few contacts and to observe British colonial rule. I know you hate the English, Father, but their administration seems more enlightened than the French here."

"About Japan," prompted Gia Minh, wholly uninterested in the politics.

"We had to wait a little while until the Russo-Japanese War ended, but finally we left from Shanghai for Yokohama."

"Shanghai," murmured Chien, but he caught Gia Minh's sharp glance and his face blanked into a stoic mask.

"When we reached Japan, the weather was unbearably hot and humid, and it rained every day in July. The fall is nice, but the winter is very cold. I've never been so cold. And there was snow."

"Snow?" queried Paul. "What's that?"

"It's white, like feathers falling out of the sky, but very cold."

"It sounds lovely," said Ly.

"It was, but it's so cold; then it melts, and there's an awful mess. I think we're much better off without it."

"And the people?" asked Gia Minh.

"Very strange," he said. "I don't think you'd like them, Mother. The men are very harsh; they strut and shout and stomp about all the time."

"Were it not for the snow, I might think I was here," she said sweetly.

"No. There it's all bluster and for show. Your ears hurt after a while, and you get tired of watching the men trying to out-strut one another. They're not very genteel, except when they drink tea, but they make that such a tedious business; it goes on forever, and the tea tastes terrible besides. It's green."

Chien stuck out his tongue. "Green?"

"And their food isn't very interesting either. Mostly they eat raw fish. It's all rather primitive."

"And the women?" Ly asked.

"I never noticed any," he said, smiling.

"I'm sure not, but what did you hear about them from the others?"

"That they have broad faces and wide noses and too much flesh. I heard that they giggle a great deal, and cover their mouths when they talk, and always avert their eyes before a man."

"It sounds like a ridiculous place," said Gia Minh.

"Well," he said, "women there are certainly kept in an inferior position. It's not like here, where they can have property and position, and cause all manner of mischief and grief."

"That rather makes up for the green tea," said Chien. "But tell me about their emperor."

"I'll tell you this much: they don't have a problem there with loyalty; they have a form of emperor worship. Actually Japan is still feudal; they have warlords and a warrior class—it's not possible that a foreigner could take over Japan, the people would never abandon their emperor; they'd fight to their deaths."

"That's what we need here," said Trinh.

Chien shook his head. "The emperor has lost the mandate from heaven; he isn't worth dying for."

"Yes," agreed Che Lan. "We have no emperor, and nothing or no one to put in his stead. I'm beginning to think we ought to do away with the monarchy."

Gia Minh was shocked. "My father, your grandfather Ahn, was a royal prince. My great-grandfather was the Emperor Minh Mang, the best and wisest ruler Vietnam has had. How can you deny your own blood?"

"Those days are past, Mother. The monarchy is weak and corrupt and has no support."

"Then what kind of government do you propose?" she asked.

He shook his head. "I don't know. A democracy won't work because we're not ready for it; we're a country of small farms and peasants, and the people aren't even literate. What we need is a strong samurai class to rule the country, like the Japanese used to have, a military cadre willing to sacrifice anything for freedom and independence. Only people such as these could throw out the French; what we need are ruthless, single-minded fighters."

"But you still haven't told me what form of government it would be," said Gia Minh.

"That's exactly it," he answered. "I don't know."

"Don't you remember the old meetings," asked Ly, "when we used to talk about Karl Marx and the rule of the proletariat?"

He laughed. "You know why I went to those meetings. I never heard a thing for looking at you." He turned to the two youths. "I was only a little older than you. Every week there were secret meetings, and it would be nothing except talk and talk, and the only reason I'd go was to see Ly, and she did more talking than anyone else. Your mother was quite a revolutionary in her time, Trinh."

"I still have the pamphlets," she said. "Perhaps you ought to read them now, Che Lan, especially *The Communist Manifesto*."

"Let me read it," said Trinh.

"Me too," said Paul."

Andre looked disconcerted, and he tried to change the subject. "Are you going back to Japan?"

"Probably, but only because Chau is so optimistic about getting their help. Already he's convinced them to allow us to open a school there, and their military academy has agreed to accept some of our students."

Trinh's eyes lit, and he opened his mouth to speak, but Che Lan pointed at him. "But you're not going."

"Why? It's time I did something. I can't stay here any longer."

"I know, but I don't want you going to Japan. In the long run, the Japanese will turn against us. I want you to go to Hanoi."

"Hanoi!" said Andre in alarm. "That's too far, and too dangerous. He should go to Saigon to study."

"No place is safe, Father, but a good school is going to be opening soon in Hanoi. It's going to teach Western ideas, and I want Trinh to go to it."

"Western ideas!" Chien stuck out his tongue again. "Green tea. I thought the problem was the Westerner. What do you need his ideas for?"

"Because times are changing, and we're going to have to change with them, or remain a backward colonial country."

"But I don't want to go to school," said Trinh. "I want to fight. I want to go with you."

"No. I want you to study and learn. We're not ready to fight, because we don't know what we're fighting for. It's not enough to want the French out—we have to have something to replace them with. That's what I want you to find. Maybe it's the monarchy, maybe democracy, or maybe it's communism—I don't know. But until we find something, until we can all rally behind it, we'll never get rid of the French."

"What about me?" asked Paul. "Can I go too?"

They all turned to him. He sat intently, his sharp blond features fixed on Che Lan, his blue eyes penetrating, and suddenly they all saw the impossibility of his position.

"We'll go together," said Trinh eagerly. "Won't we, Father?"

"Is that so?" asked Paul, not taking his eyes from Che Lan.

There was a long pause, and everyone except Che Lan averted his gaze from Paul, knowing that the awful moment of truth had finally come.

"No," said Che Lan gently but firmly. "You cannot go."

"Why?"

"Because you are not Vietnamese."

"But—"

Che Lan cut him off. "No. You're French. You'd never be accepted."

"I'm not French! I was born here. I'm as much Vietnamese as Trinh."

"Paul," said Che Lan, genuinely grieved, "I know how you feel, and I'm very sorry, but the time has come for you to face the facts of your heritage. I wish it made no difference that your blood is completely French, but it does; surely you can see that. You'd spend all your time trying to prove yourself, and yet you never could—they'll see your blond hair and your blue eyes, and they'll see a Frenchman, and they'll never accept you as one of themselves. I know from experience; some people still don't accept me, and never will, and there's nothing I can do about it because the simple fact remains that my father is French."

"It's true," said Andre. "I've lived here for thirty-five years, and could live here for another one hundred, yet I'd always be the foreigner."

"I *have* lived here for nearly a hundred," said Chien, "but I might as well have come this afternoon for all the good it would do me to turn into a Vietnamese."

"But I was born here," Paul tried to explain, almost pleading. "I feel Vietnamese, I . . . I am Vietnamese. Aren't I, Trinh?"

Their eyes met, and locked for a long minute; then Trinh lowered his gaze to the table.

Paul looked as though he'd been struck physically. He jumped up and was about to run out of the room, his eyes brimming, when Che Lan commanded him to sit down. He obeyed, but had to keep his head down for fear the others would see his tears.

"You know," said Andre evenly, "for years I've listened to everyone say terrible things about the French, and I've never said a word. You all seem to forget that I'm French, and that it's hurt to hear these things. Don't you think it's bothered me when my son has tried to deny the French part of himself—my part? And now my grandson disavows it. Of course I realize some of the terrible things the French have done, but they've done some good things too. Before the French came, Vietnam was a primitive, backward nation ruled by a corrupt mandarinate. Since the French have come, roads and railways have been built, industry and shipping started, education and medicine spread. Vietnam is finally entering the modern world, and they wouldn't have without the French."

"But look at the cost," said Che Lan. "And it certainly wasn't done out of kindness."

"I know that, and I don't believe that France should make a colony out of Vietnam; all I'm saying is that not everything the French have done is wrong. They've laid a foundation that wouldn't be here otherwise. Now is the time to build on that foundation—together. I think it's stupid and childish for everyone to deny the French contribution, just as it's stupid and childish for you to deny your own blood. Perhaps my mistake was in not telling you about your French ancestry, in not forcing you to face it. Maybe then you'd be proud of what you are, rather than ashamed; maybe then you'd stop trying to deny what can't be denied."

His manner was more cold and stern than any of them could remember. "I think that rather than attempting to escape the truth, you should all be more honest and courageous and face facts as they are. There's nothing wrong with being French, and I don't want to hear any more nonsense about it in my house."

"Your grandfather's right," said Che Lan to Paul. "It took me a long time to accept it, but I did. I learned years ago that while I might try to forget I was part French, others never would—that's why I'll never be a leader in the movement: the others simply can't overlook my French blood. But that's all right because it's given me a better, more objective perspective about things; I'm not blinded by prejudice or dogma. I can see that Chau is making a mistake by denying any cooperation with the French, yet trying to establish it with the Japanese. But I can see also that Phan Chu Trinh is wrong by excluding violence and armed resistance and counting entirely on French help. The answer lies in between, and that's going to be the contribution of both of you boys."

Paul looked up at his uncle. He idolized Che Lan, and now, hearing there was a role for himself, he hung eagerly on every word.

"You're in a unique position, Paul. You're entirely French, but you think and act like a Vietnamese; you understand them, and know how they feel. You can do something that none of the rest of us can do: you can change how the French feel; you can make them see things differently. You can work on the other side."

"I don't understand."

"A long time ago, Father wanted me to go to Saigon and study, then join the French administration. But it wouldn't have worked because I was half-Vietnamese; the French would never have accepted me. But you're different and wouldn't meet the obstacles I would have. You could easily become part of the French administration. With your background and advantages, you could probably someday become governor. Think of what you could do and change."

"But I don't want to go to Saigon. I don't want to be an administrator."

"What do you want to do?" asked Andre.

The future had never really occurred to him; he'd been perfectly content with the present. He and Trinh had talked, of course, but only in vague and general terms—fighting the French, joining the rebels—so there was no clear idea in his mind of a life beyond the walls of the house. He frowned, trying to summon some vision of what he might want to do.

"He's too young to be thinking of a future or a career," Gia Minh said. "And so's Trinh. They're only boys."

"They're sixteen years old," said Che Lan, "ready to go off to school. They can decide there what kind of careers they want, but the time has come to send them off—Trinh to Hanoi, Paul to Saigon. Between them they can accomplish remarkable things."

He became excited at the idea, and his enthusiasm spilled out. "Why, between you, working on both sides, you could change the whole course of history for Vietnam. There's never been an opportunity like this. You can shape a new country. You could do what Ahn couldn't do, or myself, or anybody. You could both become leaders of the two sides, and work together."

He looked at them solemnly. "You could save us. You could spare bloodshed to generations—to your children and your ancestors. You could unite this country."

He turned to his mother and father. "They could do it, they have it in them. And they have the right blood. Maybe everything has happened as it has so that this could come about."

For a moment, staring at the two youths, Andre was carried away also. Perhaps everything had led to this, the direct line from Ahn to Trinh, and from himself to Paul. Why couldn't it happen? It would be the fulfillment of Ahn's dream, and the realization of his own promise to him; they were strong; they could do it.

But then, they looked so young, so innocent, so bewildered, that he wondered how it could ever be. What chance did they have in the labyrinth that was Vietnam? For a moment he thought of Tu Duc and Ahn, and Lady Deng, dead now many years, retired and forgotten by the time she died peacefully in Hue at a very advanced age; and he thought of Parnasse and Catherine. And he thought of Louis. What hope did Paul and Trinh have in a world populated by people like that?

Then he changed his mind again. They were young; it would work out. "I think it's a wonderful idea," he said. "Everything Che Lan says is true. Is it all agreed?"

"It is," said Che Lan for both boys. He poured rice wine for them all, even the youths; then he raised his cup. "To a free and independent Vietnam. And to Paul and Trinh to bring it about."

They all drank deeply, finishing the last drop, but in a second, both boys clutched their throats and began to cough and sputter.

The others laughed, and when they recovered, Paul and Trinh joined in sheepishly.

"That doesn't bode well for future liberators," said Chien.

"You'll see," said Trinh. "Together we're going to make a new Vietnam."

Chien smiled gently. "I rather liked the old one, when there was peace in the kingdom. But in any case, if you want me to see this new one you're going to make, you'd better hurry."

Andre looked at his family, focusing on his two grandsons, now about the same age as he'd been when he headed off to the Ecole Militaire nearly forty years ago. Nothing had turned out as he'd expected, and he wondered what the next forty years might bring. That would be 1946; he'd be long dead, he knew, and Che Lan would be an old man, perhaps dead himself—and the boys? And Vietnam? Surely it would be a free and independent nation by then. And his grandsons would have shared in that victory, fighting together. Look at the bond between them; nothing could sever that.

Warmed by the prospect of such a happy and secure future, he took Gia Minh's hand and brought it to his lips. It would all be fine, he thought, and he was so confident that he didn't even notice the overwhelming sadness in his wife's eyes.

24

March 1909

"HEY, PAUL, SOME SLANT-EYE downstairs wants to see you."

Paul cringed at the words shouted up the stairwell. He was in his dormitory room studying, and he quickly laid aside his book to go down to see who it was, because Vietnamese were not allowed in the living quarters of the students, or, for that matter, hardly any place where the French colonials were.

Paul was in his second year of school in Saigon, and he liked it less every day. He found the curriculum easy enough, for like his father before him, he'd been so well tutored at home that his courses were unchallenging, but it was the atmosphere of the school, the other students, and the attitudes of both them and the faculty that he hated and which made life so difficult for him.

He didn't like the dormitory, either. It was his first exposure to Western architecture and life, and he found it jarring, though it was a simple two-story stucco building of neoclassical design, almost Spartan in purity and line—light and clean, but too militaristic for him, rising and asserting rather than blending like the Jade Palace in which he had grown up. It typified for him all that was wrong with France and Western life—it was not a part of the natural order, but an effort to impose a harsh and artificial order on the world. Like the city—an imposition on the land, whose boulevards and block buildings, lights and noise, did not flow or merge—the dormitory was cold and lifeless, alien to this land.

Paul knew he didn't fit in, and in return there was an undercurrent of resentment and distrust of him. He wasn't liked, and the other students considered him a traitor to his class. No one else among them would have had a Vietnamese visitor, yet Paul had had many, until he'd arranged to meet them elsewhere so as to spare them the embarrassment and humiliation of being insulted and made to wait outside his dormitory. He'd cautioned all his Vietnamese friends not to come, so he was mystified as to who might be downstairs.

Closing the door to his room, he caught the contemptuous looks of several other students who'd come out onto the landing to see what was happening.

For the most part, the others were sons of wealthy colonials and ranking bureaucrats, overly indulged, and mostly spoiled, not gifted enough or interested enough to return to France for their studies. They were here for lack of anywhere else to go, for some not-too-strenuous studying, some social polishing, to meet others like themselves who would one day run the affairs of Vietnam, and to have a good time. Having a good time comprised most of their efforts, and consisted of women, drinking, opium, and gambling.

Paul, who'd led a sheltered life in Ban Me Thuot, at first had been shocked and unprepared. Intellectually and temperamentally he wasn't suited for license and dissipation, and he was offended by the contemptuous attitude the others had toward the Vietnamese. Yet in the beginning, to be amiable, and also too shy to resist, he'd joined in with the others in their pursuits; but drinking gave him terrible headaches and made him sick the entire next day, and opium made him feel stupid and lethargic, and it never gave him the release and pleasure that his own discipline and thought did, and gambling he simply found boring and unstimulating. Women posed a different problem.

Paul was a romantic. He had been raised by Vietnamese women, and he transferred the affection and idealism he had for Gia Minh and Ly to the brothel girls he went to. He was so inexperienced and naive that he believed the pretense of the girls; he thought he meant something to them, and believed their attentions and ministrations were sincere, and he never knew they were laughing behind his back, though they thought he was handsome enough, and nice enough, and were grateful that he found no interest in abusing them like the other young men did.

He couldn't help himself, he grew infatuated with every girl he slept with. He truly liked women, and there was no artifice or cunning in his manner toward them; he assumed that their behavior to him was just as genuine.

He nodded curtly to the others on the landing, then went downstairs.

"Trinh!" he shouted when he saw his cousin, and he reached out to embrace him, but Trinh pulled back, uncomfortable and on guard.

"What are you doing here? I thought you were in Hanoi. Come in."

Trinh shook his head.

"It's all right, you can come in."

He sneered. "I don't want to come in." His gaze was mocking, but when he saw Paul's happiness in seeing him, he softened. "Can't we go somewhere else?"

Paul understood. "Let me get a jacket."

He bounded up the stairs, ignoring the looks from the others, and in a moment the two were on a main street, headed toward the center of the city. Several times Paul tried to put his arm around Trinh's shoulders as he'd done so often in the past, but each time Trinh rebuffed him.

"What's the matter with you?" Paul asked.

"We can't touch one another. This isn't Ban Me Thuot. You're French, I'm Vietnamese. People will think . . . They won't know we're cousins."

As it was, the two received inquiring and unfriendly looks from everyone they passed, French and Vietnamese.

"Well, why are you here?" demanded Paul. "Is everything all right at home?"

"Everybody's fine."

"Even Chien?"

Just a little blinder and more forgetful. He keeps thinking I'm Father, or Ahn."

Paul stopped and tugged on Trinh's arm. "Hey, I'm sorry about what happened at the dormitory."

"Don't be. I was expecting it. I run into it all the time in Hanoi. The French closed the Free School, you know. They said it was subversive." He laughed. "It was. But it's just gone underground—same professors, same students; it's just more dangerous now."

"I'm sorry."

Trinh led him away, for they were beginning to draw frowns from the passersby. "We've come to expect that sort of thing too."

Paul let the "we" pass.

They came to the café. Trinh hesitated at the door of the obviously French establishment, but Paul led the way in and took a table even before the maître d' had an opportunity to direct them—or slight them—as Paul feared he might because of Trinh.

The café might have been transported directly from Paris: bentwood chairs surrounded bright metal tables, each bearing a crisp linen tablecloth and a vase of flowers. Waiters wore white jackets and moved with languid haughtiness from the tables to the ornate bar, where a vast array of liquors and aperitifs were displayed. Overhead, bamboo fans stroked the air with a rhythmic clacking, and the movement was reflected in the tall mirrors that surrounded the walls. The already intense brightness was heightened by the polished parquet floors, yet the atmosphere was subdued and intimate, and the obviously well-to-do clientele, mostly French, engaged in brisk, animated conversations.

Trinh found the setting unnerving, and he stirred uncomfortably in his chair, his face registering disapproval and contempt.

Paul could feel the distance between them. Though they hadn't seen each other in eighteen months, it seemed much longer to Paul, and the person across from him was vastly changed from the one he'd known before. Trinh seemed much older and more mature, also restless and on edge.

"God, I hate Saigon," Trinh said. "It's like an old whore, flopped on her back, legs spread. You don't see decadence like this in Hanoi."

"Decadence?" asked Paul, glancing about the fairly modest surroundings.

"All the softness, all the cafés and diversions. All the women. Hanoi hasn't prostituted itself to the French like Saigon has."

Paul could see that his cousin really had changed. Gone were the playfulness and humor, and he wasn't happy to see the transformation.

"I suppose you're down here a lot. Have you got a mistress?"

"No," Paul said softfly.

"You just go to whorehouses?"

"Sometimes. Aren't there whorehouses in Hanoi?"

"Of course. Wherever there's exploitation and repression, you'll find them."

Paul smiled. His cousin was beginning to sound like a pamphlet. "So what do you do for sex? Still playing with yourself?"

"I have a woman," Trinh said in a worldly, bored voice. "We're living together. We're thinking of having a child."

"A child! Are you married?"

"That's a bourgeois convention. Kim and I aren't interested in such nonsense."

Paul searched his face. Was this the youth he'd grown up with, joked and laughed with only a short while ago, hidden with in the jungle from the soldiers, loved?

Just then a group of Frenchmen entered, rudely and imperiously demanding a table that was already occupied by several Vietnamese. To avoid a scene, the Vietnamese quickly moved, and the Frenchmen sat down, making loud and disparaging remarks.

Trinh's face hardened into hatred. He stood up and looked down on Paul. "Let's get out of here. I can't stand being around the French."

He said it in French loud enough for the men to hear. They turned, but when they saw Paul, they looked confused, and only watched as the two youths passed by.

When they were on the street, Paul put his hand on Trinh to stop him. "You're going to get yourself into a lot of trouble if you're not careful."

"It's just that I hate the French so much."

"Trinh, I'm French. So's Grandfather."

Trinh stared at him a moment, then smiled. "Okay, okay. C'mon, let's go someplace to drink."

They found a Vietnamese bar on the next block; it seemed almost primitive in comparison to the one they'd just left. Here were no linen and mirrors. The interior was dark and shabby, with wooden chairs and tables that wobbled. There were no fans, and the only noise was that of several older men slapping tiles on a Mah-Jongg board. The owner approached politely; he looked tired and harassed and his age showed by the crinkled skin at the base of his throat, exposed by the open-collared shirt. He smiled pleasantly at Trinh, and stiffly at Paul. No bottles were displayed, so they ordered beer, and it was brought uncooled and without glasses.

Neither was an accomplished drinker, and the alcohol soon went to their heads, but it took the edge off their feelings, and Trinh grew warmer the more he had to drink.

"I'll bet you don't have many friends, do you, Paul?"

"No. I get on better with the Vietnamese, but they hold back too."

"Poor Paul. What are you going to do?"

"I don't know. I don't see how I'm going to work my way into the colonial administration when I can't stand it. Besides, they won't want someone with my views. I don't see myself going anywhere. Che Lan seemed to think I was going to have a magic passage, but it's not that way at all."

"I know. Father thought I was going to have an easy time of it too. He didn't count on the school being closed down, or the way the French have turned on the rebels. They don't even give them a chance anymore. When they catch them, they kill them."

"That's why you should be more careful."

Trinh finished a beer and ordered another. "Don't worry

about me. Hey, I've forgotten to tell you why I came. Grandmother wants you to go home. She wouldn't tell me why. She even made me promise not to tell Father and Grandfather I was coming for you."

"But I have classes. I have . . ." Then he stopped. If Gia Minh wanted him, he'd go, and there was no question that he'd hesitate for any reason, and both he and Trinh knew it. "I'll leave tomorrow. Are you ready to go?"

"I'm not going with you," Trinh said. He concentrated on his beer. "I have some business here."

Paul laughed. "Messages to deliver. Bombs to make?" He couldn't take his cousin seriously as a revolutionary.

"We have lots of sympathizers here. I have to make contact with them."

"What does Che Lan think of your activities? And your girlfriend?"

A disappointed look spread over Trinh's face. "Father's changed. He's back in Ban Me Thuot now. He dropped out of the movement just before the disaster in Hanoi last year, though that was a good thing—they'd have caught and killed him otherwise."

"Was that the poisoning? We don't hear much down here; they try to hush up problems."

"That was it. Phan Boi Chau wanted to strike against the French, but Father said they weren't strong enough yet. They had a falling-out when Chau went to De Tram and asked him to join in. Father said De Tram couldn't be trusted—he remembered De Tram from when he was a bandit. Anyway, the plan was to poison the French troops in the garrison. The Vietnamese troops were then supposed to revolt, and De Tram's forces would attack the city. Hanoi would fall, and uprisings would start all over Vietnam. Father said it'd never work, so he left. In any case, the whole thing misfired—the poisoning didn't occur, De Tram didn't attack, and most of the rebel leaders were captured. Thirteen were executed, but Phan Boi Chau got back to Japan. Except now the French have persuaded the Japanese to expel all Vietnamese."

"Che Lan said the Japanese couldn't be trusted. He was right about that, too."

"Yes. So Chau and Cuong De had to leave and the schools were closed. The prince went to Europe, and Chau went to Thailand."

"What happened to Phan Chu Trinh? Is he leading the rebellion now?"

"No. He was arrested last year."

"So that's the end of it?"

"It's not the end, but things don't look so good right now. Father's very unhappy; it's hurt him a lot. He's helping Grandfather with the estate, but he doesn't like it. He doesn't care about rubber trees or rice. He's like a caged tiger. But it won't be for long. He'll find his way back into the rebellion; it's just that now he doesn't know what to do."

Paul looked directly at his cousin. "What are you doing?"

Trinh shrugged and poured more beer for them both. "Just biding my time."

"I don't believe you. Don't you trust me anymore? Don't you remember the jungle?"

Trinh lowered his eyes. That was the indestructible bond between them, that day in the jungle in each other's arms, hiding from the soldiers.

"All right," he said. "Some of us are doing something. Since the French closed the schools and killed so many leaders, we've had to go underground. We're trying to bring together the different groups around the country. Some of us are stockpiling weapons, and a few are part of a guerrilla faction that's . . . trying to unbalance the French."

"You mean murder them. Is that what you're doing?" He saw that his cousin was fully capable of that. "Are you killing people?"

Trinh ignored him, his face completely masked, despite all he'd had to drink. "You know, I'm a communist."

Paul's head was fuddled from all he'd had to drink. He tried to remember exactly what a communist was, but he couldn't draw a clear picture of what his cousin was supposed to be. "I read about that once," he said, "but forgot."

"Mother gave us that pamphlet a long time ago. *The Communist Manifesto*. Remember?"

Paul spilled a little beer. "Oh, yes. But I can't remember what it said, just that is was really boring."

"It was about the exploitation of the proletariat and the redistribution of wealth."

"Christ," Paul said, pouring more beer. "Spare me that shit."

"We're going to win someday," Trinh said. "I mean it, Paul. You better learn about it. It's the future for this country." Though he'd drunk a great deal, his manner was completely controlled; his eyes were hard and defiant, and his words were a sworn promise.

Paul didn't like his cousin this way; there was something cold and cruel about him, something in him which would turn him against anyone, even Paul himself. He downed the rest of his beer and wiped the foam on his mouth with his arm. "So tell me about your girlfriend."

"We share the same ideology," Trinh said.

"Jesus! Do you love her?"

Trinh frowned at the word; then he grinned. "Only you would talk about love. I keep forgetting about you; you're as bad as a woman. You got it from all those dumb novels you used to read. I like her, okay? We function well together."

"Function?" He had a sudden vision of them with wheels, on a track.

"Intellectually. And physically." He waited a moment, his face composed and inexpressive; then he said, "We fuck a lot."

Paul laughed. Trinh was grinning, and for the first time they felt the barriers were down between them.

"Where'd you meet her?"

"At the school."

"There're girls at your school?"

"Of course. Women are going to be part of the revolution too."

Paul held up his hand to stop what he knew was going to be another diatribe. "Just tell me about the fucking."

"No one there believes in the old bourgeois morality."

"You mean everybody's doing it?"

Trinh broke into a great smile. "Right."

"Maybe I ought to learn more about this communism thing," Paul said.

"What about you? Haven't you found anyone?"

"Sure. But I have to pay for them. And I have a bad habit of falling in love with them."

"Prostitutes?"

Paul grinned. "It's just redistribution of wealth."

They talked and drank on, and for a time it was like it had been before. They spoke of Ban Me Thuot and their youth, and told stories of Andre and Chien and the others.

When they were leaving, Paul put his arm around Trinh, and this time Trinh didn't recoil. They stumbled outside, laughing, oblivious of the others on the street.

"Let's go back," Paul said, then immediately remembered that it would be impossible for Trinh to stay in the dormitory.

Quietly, unobtrusively, the two separated, seemed to sober, and they walked side by side.

"Thanks anyway," said Trinh, sparing Paul the embarrassment of having to withdraw the offer, "but I have a place to stay. I told them I'd be in, and they'd worry if I didn't show up."

They let it go at that, but the gulf was between them again.

"When will I see you?" Paul asked.

"Come visit me in Hanoi."

"Maybe we ought to meet on neutral ground at home."

They seemed reluctant to say good-bye, perhaps sensing what lay in the future, and for a few moments they remained at a corner, trying to prolong their time together, but at last they shook hands. Trinh turned away first, and in a moment was gone.

Paul stood alone for a while longer, then, depressed, started back. He knew that things would be very different between them from now on.

"How well you look," said Gia Minh, embracing him at the door. "You've grown even more. And you're blonder. Or have I just forgotten how golden you were?"

He squeezed her to him, felt her frailty, and wanted to say in return how well she looked, but she was obviously unwell.

"Was it a good trip? You must be exhausted." She brought him inside and sent servants for refreshments.

It was early afternoon on a spring day. Paul had journeyed three days, but the sight of the house and his grandmother erased his tiredness; he felt at home and safe.

"Where's Grandfather?"

"In the fields, with Che Lan. Your uncle's come back, you know."

"Yes, Trinh told me. We had a good visit together."

"Did you?" Her wise eyes appraised him. "I found him somewhat changed." She smiled. "But you seem unchanged. Which means you must still be unhappy in Saigon. Are things no better there for you?"

"The same," he said, and changing the subject, "Where's Aunt Ly, and Master Chien?"

"Ly is visiting friends, but she'll be back later. Master Chien is sleeping. He's beginning to show his age, I'm afraid. But then, so am I."

It wasn't age she was showing, but something more insidious. She looked drawn and frail, her skin an unhealthy pallor. Even her hair, once so full and lustrous, now seemed dull and thinned. Her eyes were sunken, and though they shone yet with bright intelligence and warmth, they only heightened the disintegration of her body, a gauntness that made her seem so wan that the animation she now demonstrated was obviously forced and artificial.

''Are you all right, Grandmother?'' he asked her.

''I'm tired,'' she said. I was sixty years old last month. That set me back a bit.''

He looked at her with concern. ''You don't look good,'' he said honestly. ''Are you ill?''

''I may have a touch of something,'' she said lightly. ''I've lost my appetite; but don't you think it's done wonders for my figure? I'm as thin as when I married. You only remember me as plump as a pear, but when I was young . . . well, your grandfather found me quite pleasing.''

''He always has. It was shameful the way he never could keep his hands off you. Trinh and I used to laugh about that.''

She smiled happily, and seemed to forget him for a moment, thinking of Andre. ''He's a very affectionate man.'' Then she said sternly, remembering his presence, ''Your grandfather is a very good man.''

He smiled. ''I know, Grandmother.''

She took his hand and patted it softly. ''And you, have you found a girl?''

''No.''

''A handsome boy like you? There must be girls chasing you all over Saigon.''

He laughed. ''I don't think you have a very good picture of Saigon, Grandmother.''

''Well, aren't there parties, and teas? Surely there are all kinds of social activities, and there must be many lovely young ladies there.''

''Ah, it's a little more casual than that, Grandmother; but I haven't met anyone.''

''Well, actually, I was asking for a reason, and I'm not unhappy that you haven't found anyone yet.''

Once again, as so often in the past, her simple and kind manner had disarmed him, making him forget what a clever and shrewd woman she was. He'd forgotten that she always had an ulterior purpose. She was by far the smartest person in the family, he thought; probably even smarter than Chien. Andre seemed like a lumbering bull compared with her, and Che Lan was too quick-tempered, and Ly didn't have her penetrating eye.

Paul saw Gia Minh as a figure from the past, one who belonged to the era of throne and court life; he could see her in his mind, dressed ceremonially, passing through the fabled rooms of the Imperial Palace, talking conspiratorially, intriguing for power and dynasty.

"Thank you for coming so quickly," she said. "I wasn't expecting you for another day or so."

"Is everything all right?" he asked.

"Yes, fine," she reassured him, "but I needed to talk with you as soon as possible. First, though, you must eat. You must be famished."

He let her dote on him, and they both loved it. He had always loved her above all others, perhaps because he sensed that he held a special place in her heart. And he did, partly because she saw him as such an outcast, a misplaced orphan, a crippled bird unable to get back into its nest; but also because she saw so much of Andre in him. This is how he must have been—a very good and kind boy, warm and loving. So it had been she who'd tucked him in at night and comforted against all the ills and monsters of childhood, against disease and dark, and thunderstorms, and it was to her he'd gone even in adolescence when he needed someone to be with. She was his refuge from the men and their physicality; she, with a soft pat or stroke, settled his soul and righted his being.

After he ate, she settled across from him and assumed a businesslike manner.

"I'm glad no one else is here. I have to talk to you alone," she said. "I want you to go with me to meet your grandmother."

Paul looked confused. "But you're my—"

"No. I want you to meet your father's mother."

The stories of his father were so vague and seldom told that he had difficulty summoning a clear picture of him. About his father's mother he knew almost nothing, only that she was a woman his grandfather had known in France before he came to Vietnam; it was not a subject anyone discussed.

"Your grandmother is the Duchess of Parnasse—the dowager duchess; her husband died some time ago."

Gia Minh spoke matter-of-factly, betraying no emotion about her husband's lover of long ago. "I don't know what your grandfather's told you . . ."

"Nothing. No one's ever said anything about her, and hardly anything about my father and mother."

"That's because they're painful memories, Paul. But I'll tell you about your grandmother because Andre might not want to talk to you about her. A long time ago, when your grandfather was your age, he had an affair with the wife of the Duke of

Parnasse. She was older than Andre, and they had a great attraction for one another, but then the duke discovered the affair and Andre had to flee France."

"Why would he—?"

"There's more to it than that, but he can tell you the rest. Later, after Andre came here and we married . . ." She stopped, unable to pass over that so lightly. "We were very much in love, Paul. He was such a handsome, vital man. I remember when I first saw him, and when he kissed my mother's hand." She smiled to herself, the scene playing in her mind as if it were yesterday. "I thought I would faint. Oh, you have no idea what a silly girl I was."

Gia Minh hardly ever spoke of the past, and now, seeing her lost to it, Paul could tell how unwell she was. She looked haunted, an almost-shadow with the most tenuous hold on life.

"After Che Lan was born, Andre learned that his mother was dying, and he returned to France. There he discovered that the duchess had borne a son of his. He returned to Vietnam with that child—your father, of course. Nearly twenty years ago, the duke and duchess came to Vietnam; he was the minister for the colonies, and your father was a very ambitious and successful young administrator. He decided to return to France with the duke and duchess."

"Was he going to take Mother and me with him?"

"I'm not sure what his plans were, but then there was the accident in which your father was killed."

Paul had always felt there was more to his father's death than the story of the accidental fall, but he never pressed about it, for it was obviously a source of great unhappiness to his grandfather.

"The duchess returned to France after Louis's death, but she's come back. She knows about you, and wants to meet you. I want you to go with me to Hue to see her."

Paul studied Gia Minh carefully. "Why?" he asked at last. "Do you want me to leave with her? Do you want me to go to France?"

She didn't say anything.

"Are you trying to send me away, Grandmother?"

She handed him an envelope; he opened it carefully and extracted a yellowed sheet of paper. He read it quickly, then more carefully, but when he looked up at Gia Minh, he was still puzzled.

"It says the Duke of Parnasse acknowledges my father as his son. What does that mean? How could he say my father was his son?"

"Andre kidnapped Louis when he was a little boy. According to the official documents, your father was born the son of the Duke of Parnasse. There was no hint of scandal. As far as everyone was concerned, the duke was Louis's father. That paper merely reaffirms it, and makes Louis his heir. His only heir."

"Then that means I . . ." He stopped, unable to express it.

"It means you're the legitimate heir. It means, I suppose, that you would become the Duke of Parnasse." She said calmly, "I think that you would be a very rich and powerful man in France."

Paul sat dumbfounded.

"That's why I want you to go see your grandmother." She reached out and took his hand. "You should be aware of the possibilities before you."

"But I'd never leave Vietnam, or you, or Grandfather, or anyone here. I don't care about being the Duke of Parnasse. There isn't any royalty anymore; it'd just be a title."

"That may be so," she said, "and I know how you feel about us, but I think the time's come for you to think realistically about your future. You should consider whether you really belong here, whether you might not be better off in France."

"Grandmother. How can you say that?"

Her manner was firm, and there was no longer any suggestion of frailty. She seemed exactly what she was, a determined, strong, immensely intelligent woman. "What do you plan to do, Paul?"

He faltered, both at the directness of the question and at her tone. "I . . . I'm not sure."

"Do you want to come back here and help your grandfather manage this estate? Do you want to oversee rice paddies? Do you want to negotiate the sale of rubber?"

He lowered his head. "No."

"Do you want to be a colonial administrator?"

He shook his head. "I couldn't do that," he said softly.

"Then what are you going to do?"

He twisted on the chair in agitation. "I don't know."

It was unnecessary for her to say anything more. Until now he'd been able to avoid facing it, but here in the silence before her, the dilemma was clear and inescapable.

"I think we should go tomorrow," she said.

"Tomorrow?" he whispered. "Does Grandfather know?"

She shook her head. "I'll tell him tonight." Then she closed her eyes against the pain she was going to inflict on him. Andre didn't deserve this, she thought. He'd been fleeing the Parnasses for forty years, yet here the woman was again, prepared to take his grandson from him. And here was she, his wife, going to deliver him up.

Just then Chien entered the room, bent and shuffling, using a cane. He appeared ancient, so infirm that Paul jumped up to help him.

Gia Minh held him back and said loudly, "Good afternoon, Master Chien. Did you have a good rest?"

"Excellent," he said, his voice surprisingly strong. "I'm completely refreshed; I feel only ninety."

Paul bowed to the old man, but he realized that Chien couldn't see him.

"Please join us for tea," Gia Minh said, again very loudly. "Paul has come back to visit us."

"Who?" Chien squinted and doddered closer. When he was close enough to see, he appraised him a moment, then sat down precariously, and Paul was certain the old man didn't know who he was.

Gia Minh poured tea for him, only a half-cup, for his hand shook badly and he would have spilled more.

"One doesn't need to pretend at my age," Chien said. "I don't have the faintest idea who you are."

"Andre's grandson. Louis's boy," said Gia Minh.

"Oh, yes," said Chien. "Where have you been?"

"In Saigon, Master Chien."

Tea spilled over his lips and dripped onto his robe. "Now I remember." His eyes lit in recognition. "Do you still recall the teachings of Confucius?"

"Of course, Master Chien."

Chien turned to Gia Minh. "He was the best student I had. Better than you, and much better than your husband."

"Andre?"

"No, no, not him. Ahn. And certainly better than what's-his-name . . . you know, the terrible one."

"Che Lan?"

Chien snorted. "He doesn't even count; he never thought about anything except what lay between that girl's thighs. I mean the other awful one."

"Trinh."

"Dreadful student," said Chien in disgust. "There was a mistake at birth; this one should have been born Vietnamese, and the other one French."

Gia Minh looked to Paul and smiled. The old man's mind was still good, but imprecise to time and person. Sometimes he was hopelessly fuddled, but in early morning, or after a nap, he was generally good.

Gia Minh blotted his lips and chin, which he didn't seem to notice or mind, and she poured him more tea. "We were talking about that very subject, Master Chien. I'm glad you're here to help us."

"One can't do much about the way one's born; that's rather beyond help or hurt."

"My feeling exactly," she said smoothly. "One can't change how he's born. Do you think a Frenchman can become a Vietnamese?"

"Ah," said Chien in understanding. "So that's what we're talking about; the same old thing with this boy." He turned to Paul. "Surely you remember what the Master said: 'If an urn lacks the characteristics of an urn, how can we call it an urn?' "

"There are no tall, blond, blue-eyed Vietnamese," Gia Minh said needlessly. "But you know, Master Chien, Paul may become a duke. Do you think one should ignore that opportunity?"

"A duke," Chien marveled.

"Not a real duke," said Paul. "Not like the Duke of Chou."

"But a duke nonetheless," said Gia Minh. "Don't you think Paul should return to France and claim the title?"

"I think," said Chien, "that to become a duke, one should even go to America."

"They don't have dukes there," said Paul.

Chien's mouth turned down in disdain, as if the deficiency of dukes explained the barbarism of that strange land.

Suddenly he sat straighter, and a look of penetrating sharpness came to him. He turned to Gia Minh. "Are there no cookies?"

"I beg your pardon." She handed him a plate and he picked over it carefully.

He gummed one noisily, then turned his attention to Paul. "You never should have come."

"Sir?"

"No," he said, shaking his head, lost in thought, "it wasn't your fault. We shouldn't have let you stay. The priest was right after all."

Paul looked to Gia Minh questioningly. She made a slight motion with her finger for him to remain quiet.

Then Paul realized that the old man had jumbled him in his mind with Andre.

"I had a dream once," said Chien, placing his hands in his lap, his eyes open but unseeing. "It was a long time ago, but I redreamed it only the other day. It was a terrible dream. Everything was waste and ruin, as if a fire had consumed the land."

His eyes opened and there was nothing confused in his gaze. "The dream had to do with you, Paul." The old man leaned forward, his look keen and hard. "Go to France; become a duke or a peasant, but leave Vietnam. Here there will only be tragedy—for you and for everyone and everything you touch."

Paul looked as if he'd been slapped.

Chien stood without difficulty, bowed slightly to them both, put all the cookies in his robes, and shuffled out of the room.

25

For the better part of the morning, Gia Minh had tried to conceal her extreme pain and discomfort, but it was no longer possible, and now when the carriage was jarred and jostled on the uneven road, she moaned softly and grimaced.

Across from her, Paul was so intent upon the landscape they passed through that he didn't notice Gia Minh's distress.

The journey to Hue had been shortened considerably by the improved roads the French had built, and everywhere along the roadway was evidence of French engineering, but the human toll was evident also: peasants toiled under back-breaking weights in the intense heat, and armed French soldiers stood over Vietnamese labor gangs. Yet the progress was undeniable, as was the increased cultivation of the fields.

"It's much different from before, isn't it, Grandmother?"

She gripped the carriage armrest. "Very," she said. "When I first went to Hue—it was with my father and Master Chien, over forty years ago—this was all jungle." She smiled despite the pain. "They were bringing me to find a husband. They kept parading these ridiculous boys before me, and the palace swarmed with eunuchs."

"Eunuchs. Really? They still had them then?" The idea of eunuchs conjured up for him a vision of an ancient and decadent court, a fabled time long past.

"I'm sure eunuchs are still about. I understand they live forever, spared as they are the stresses the rest of you are plagued by."

"I don't think that's a longevity to be desired," Paul said, trying to suppress a grin.

"And what would you know about that? You're supposed to be the diligent student."

"I am."

"Nonsense. You're just like your grandfather. He was quite devastating when he was young. Well, he still is, of course, but then he possessed a remarkable innocence. It was so appealing. You have it too, though I suppose it's all a sham."

He laughed. "Was Grandfather's a sham?"

"No," she admitted.

He turned from the window, no longer interested in the scenery. "Tell me about court. What will it be like?"

"I'm afraid to imagine. I can hardly keep track of the emperors; it seems they change with the seasons. The French deposed Tran Thai less than two years ago. They said he was insane; that never seemed grounds to get rid of a monarch before, so I suppose it was merely a pretext to put someone more pliant on the throne. Now a nine-year-old boy rules. Duy Tan. You can't get more pliant than that. No, I can't tell you what you're going to see. All I know is that it's nothing my father would want to see."

"Prince Ahn? What was it like in his time?"

Gia Minh tried to settle more comfortably. Talking took her mind off her pain, and the memories were pleasant, so she was happy to tell the stories of Ahn and Tu Duc.

Paul listened raptly until the carriage came to an abrupt halt, nearly throwing Gia Minh to the floor.

"Bandits!" said Gia Minh, bracing herself. She was stuffing her purse between the cushions when the door was thrown open.

"Get out," a voice shouted in French.

"Who's in there?" another voice asked.

"An old slope-head. Hurry up, get out of there, you."

Paul guided Gia Minh back on the seat and stepped out alone. Before him were six French soldiers, obviously surprised to see him.

"What is it you want?" he asked them.

Though young, Paul cut a figure of authority and position, and the leader of the group sought to make amends. "It's just a security check, sir. We're searching for contraband."

"And is that how you do it, abusing women?"

"We didn't know it was your carriage," one said lamely.

"It's not. It's my grandmother's. Please apologize to her."

They looked to one another, as though debating whether they could humble themselves to a Vietnamese, but seeing Paul's manner, and the richness of the carriage, the leader stepped forward.

"I beg your pardon, madam," he said to Gia Minh. "Please forgive my rudeness."

Gia Minh nodded curtly, and the soldier turned to Paul. "There have been problems with rebels in the area. We were just following orders."

"I'm sure your orders weren't to insult women and degrade Vietnamese."

"Sir, I was out of line. I regret it. May I ask your destination and business? Those are my orders."

"We're traveling to Hue. We have business at court. My grandmother is related to the royal family."

"Very good, sir. I'm sorry to have troubled you." The soldier motioned to the driver that it was all right to continue on; then the soldiers quickly moved off the road and disappeared into the treeline.

Paul got back in the carriage but couldn't look at Gia Minh. He was embarrassed for her and for himself. They rode in silence for many minutes; then she asked, "What would have happened if you hadn't been with me?"

"I don't know," he mumbled shamefacedly.

"What if it'd been Ly and she'd been alone? She's much younger and prettier than I."

He shook his head, unwilling to accept even the idea of that. "No. They wouldn't have done anything. They're soldiers."

Her voice was cold and firm. "Paul, soldiers murdered my father. They murdered my mother. They murdered my grandchildren. You were there; you saw it. They would just as easily rape my daughter. Can't you see what is happening in this country? It's only going to get worse. And Che Lan will go back to the rebels. And Trinh will fight with them. And his children will. They'll all fight the French."

She leaned forward and forced him to look at her. Her eyes were angry and resolute. "And if I could, I'd fight them too."

She held his gaze for a long time; then she eased back, though her eyes didn't soften. "That's why you must leave."

"But maybe I can do something," he said. "Maybe Grandfather's right; perhaps I can change things."

She shook her head. "You could stop the soldiers this time. But the day will come when you can't. The day will come when no one can stop the blood. And no one will be able to save the women or spare the children."

They arrived at the palace in late afternoon as the fading day's light seemed to drip like molten gold from the eaves of the steep tiled roof.

The palace was more impressive than Paul had imagined it

would be. The monarchy had been so long impotent that he'd half-expected a dilapidated, perhaps even hollow structure, but certainly not the magnificence before him. The palace was surrounded by six miles of walls, ring upon ring, leading into the "Great Within." Battlements and pagoda roofs towered over the walls, and within were courtyards, gardens, and temples.

The carriage passed through the gates of the guarded walls and came to stop in a massive courtyard. Attendants appeared instantly, and without giving him an opportunity to savor his surroundings, led him inside to their apartments, large airy rooms with screens that opened onto gardens. He was even more impressed when Gia Minh told him that they were in a remote wing of the palace, far from the royal apartments and throne room.

She told him that she was exhausted and apologized for not showing him the rest of the palace, but she suggested that he explore it on his own. He was free to go where he wished, except for certain private or sacred places, but he'd have no trouble finding his way because attendants would go with him.

While Gia Minh rested before dinner, Paul set out through the corridors, trailed discreetly by two elderly men (he wondered if they were eunuchs) who twice politely cautioned him from entering certain passageways.

He passed a number of richly robed men and women, but he drew no looks of curiosity or interest. The palace was quiet and subdued, possessed of a monastic calm, as lifeless as the people were, without animation. The gardens were perfectly kept and beautiful, but he found them depressing, and after an hour he returned to his room, pensive and melancholy. He felt as though he'd walked through a ghost palace. Even the air seemed musty and heavy.

"It's not a very cheerful place," he said to Gia Minh when they were dining alone.

"When I first came here with my father, the palace was bursting with life and activity. It was a very exciting place, though I thought it foolish at the time; I suppose now it's become a mausoleum."

"The French did it," he said.

"No. It bled to death from a self-inflicted wound. The men were not brave enough. They left the fighting to their descendants."

"And why wouldn't you have me fight?" he asked quietly. "Why would you send me away?"

"Because, my dear Paul, you are the enemy. You can't help here; no foreigner can. You must all get out, or be driven out."

Though she spoke kindly, and her eyes were warm on him, he

felt the impenetrable distance she'd set between them, something he'd never felt before, and he knew she had cut him loose from her. She was speaking to him now not as a grandson, a child she'd raised, but as a foreigner, an implacable foe.

"But I don't want to leave, Grandmother."

"You can't remain," she said simply.

"But—"

She shook her head. "You must all go. You have no right here. This is our country."

What she said was so cold and impersonal that it hurt him; yet, searching her face, he saw only kindness and love.

"I don't understand," he said.

"That's because you're not one of us. You aren't Vietnamese, Paul, and there will be no peace until you're all gone. My father's ancestors knew that, the Emperor Minh Mang knew it, my father knew it, I know it, Che Lan knows it, Trinh knows it. And it will come about; someday you will all be gone."

She reached across and patted his face gently. "You will never be happy here. Master Chien is right: there is only tragedy for you here. I love you too much to let it happen."

He bowed his head and finished his meal in silence.

Paul had a restless sleep and woke tired and unsettled in early morning. He lay in bed for some time, trying to recall exactly what it was that had disturbed his sleep, but nothing concrete came to his mind, just the overall impression of disquiet and foreboding. He felt as though he'd been unable to breathe properly, that the air was too laden with murky and unhappy memories, stirred and agitated by troubled spirits moving dolorously throughout the palace.

He breakfasted by himself, then went for a walk, slipping out through the back screen to avoid the attendants.

Though it was not even eight o'clock, the sun was already high and intense, and the morning humid. He heard no birds, as if they too lacked the energy to bestir themselves in this place. The palace was as quiet and lifeless as the night before.

He had toured the entire citadel, a prototype of the Great Within at Peking. The rampart-encircled square had been started by Gia Long over a hundred years ago and had been sumptuously added to by succeeding emperors.

Entering the Ngo Mon, or Noon Gate, he had paused before the Five Phoenix building that towered above the gate, where the emperors made ceremonial appearances. Then he had crossed the Bridge of Golden Waters to enter the huge esplanade in front of the Palace of Perfect Peace, dazzling gold and red in the early-morning sunshine. He walked the tree-lined paths beyond lotus pools and balustraded flower gardens, then went into the royal gardens which Father Bergere had trooped every morning over sixty years ago.

He sat on a bench to savor the richness of the flowering blossoms; peonies of myriad colors defied the somber, sad atmosphere of the palace, and seemed to possess a power and aliveness which mocked the temporal intrusion of the foreigner. Here was elemental nature, a harmony and tranquillity impervious to the human charade of politics and diplomacy.

For the first time Paul felt the truth of Gia Minh's words: he didn't belong here, not in this garden, not in this country. Though born and raised here, he felt alien; he had no kinship with the spirits here—they were not his ancestors, and he was no descendant of this land. He was not a part of this place, but an intruder, a misplaced piece in the scenery.

He loved the garden's serenity and thought the palace beautiful, just as he loved the jungle in Ban Me Thuot, but he saw clearly now that he was an observer of this harmony, not a part of it.

It was indeed his skin and hair which didn't meld with what lay about him, but it was more, something indefinable, some essence of himself which kept him separate from the harmony. It came over him as a simple realization—he didn't belong here.

When he returned to Gia Minh, he was going to tell her what he felt, but he found her so distracted that he put it off.

Gia Minh was worriedly before the mirror, fretting over her appearance. She was dressed in a simple but elegant ao dai, and her hair was carefully coiffed, but there was no disguising her frailty and illness.

Paul saw at once that she was nervous.

"You look very nice," he said.

"Do I?" She studied the mirror for reassurance, then laughed deprecatingly. "What a vanity. Though I suppose she's just as nervous as I—two old women trying to hide the ravages."

"A matter of honor," he said smilingly.

"Andre's honor as much as our own," she said, but he didn't understand.

"Do you want me to go with you?" he asked.

"Yes. I want to talk with her first; then I want you to see her."

He nodded. She took his hand and patted it. "I love you very much, Paul."

"I know," he said.

"Come," she said, but she stopped a last time before the mirror.

* * *

They were brought to a central wing of the palace, and liveried attendants showed them into the vestibule of a luxurious apartment decorated in French style.

In less than a moment another attendant came out to announce them, but Gia Minh directed Paul to remain seated while she went in alone.

She felt tightening anxiety in her stomach, though it wasn't evident in her demeanor as she entered the salon.

Standing across the room before an open screen which framed the garden was a striking woman, tall and erect, bejeweled, and with sculptured white hair. Her facial features were not at all softened by age, and her figure was that of a young woman. She looked carefully posed, but she couldn't hide her surprise when she saw Gia Minh.

Catherine had been so concerned with her own appearance, so disturbed by her own age and decline, that it hadn't occurred to her that Andre's wife would likewise have become an old woman. Catherine was still so self-centered that what happened to others escaped her notice or interest. She had expected that Gia Minh would be a beautiful, young, exotic woman, but someone she could overwhelm with her position and manner. She had not expected a tired, obviously unwell elderly woman.

Nor had she expected a woman whose features were so obviously intelligent, and whose gaze was so penetrating and knowing. Catherine thought she detected amusement on the other woman's face, and she quickly stepped away from the screen and went toward her.

''How do you do,'' she said, extending her hand, somewhat surprised when Gia Minh shook it, rather than using it to curtsy. She saw that the other woman was going to treat her as an equal, something Catherine, a duchess of extraordinary wealth, was not accustomed to, especially here in Vietnam, where she'd been treated with such obsequiousness.

They appraised one another quickly.

The woman was more regal and imposing than Gia Minh had anticipated; she had a little trouble imagining her with Andre. Andre was dear and sweet, a kind and good man, but what would this woman have seen in him? Yet, she realized, what had passed between them had occurred over forty years ago, and the image of Andre forty years ago came vividly to her. Yes, she thought, this woman would have been greatly attracted to Andre, and wouldn't have hesitated pursuing what she wanted. Here was a strong, willful woman. Louis's mother.

Catherine had even more difficulty imagining Andre with this woman, partly because Gia Minh looked so ill, but also because she looked too intelligent, not the vapid little creature she'd guessed for him. She knew Gia Minh was the daughter of a prince and great-granddaughter of an emperor, and she couldn't picture her with the handsome but essentially simple youth who had been Andre.

"Thank you very much for coming to see me," said Catherine, her speech polished and slow. "I was surprised when I learned you would be bringing"—she hesitated a second over the word, then plunged on—"my grandson. That was very kind and considerate of you. Won't you sit down?"

She directed Gia Minh to a settee and sat close to her. "May I get you something?"

"Thank you, no."

"Are you sure?" Catherine inquired, genuinely concerned about Gia Minh. She was not a cruel woman, or unfeeling, despite the rare opportunities she'd had to demonstrate her warmth, and now, seeing the other woman so obviously sick, she was moved by compassion.

"You are not well," she said.

"No," said Gia Minh, "I'm not." There was no point in trying to hide it.

"Is there anything I can do? I can inquire about doctors. There must be some fine physicians here."

Gia Minh smiled faintly. "You are kind, but it would be unnecessary."

Catherine reached out and pressed her arm. "I'm very sorry. Is there nothing that can be done?"

"No, the doctors say there is nothing."

Catherine suppressed a shudder, the memory of her husband's death still vivid in her mind; he had wasted to almost nothing by the end, and his last months were agonizing. In Gia Minh's face she could see the disease's same course, the pallor of ebbing life, as if it were being sucked out through the eyes.

Gia Minh wanted no pity. She sat very straight and met the other woman's eyes, bringing up the matter directly. "But Andre is very well. He's changed little over the years."

"I'm glad," said Catherine, put somewhat off balance by the directness. "I . . ." She couldn't say "loved," for she wasn't sure she had ever loved him. "I . . . knew him only when he was very young. I suppose you know the story."

"He's never mentioned anything. But I always knew that he felt a great deal for you."

"He was such a handsome man," said Catherine. "And so nice." She smiled. "It was all my fault; but I don't regret it a bit. Why did you come?" she asked suddenly.

"Because I want Paul to return to France with you."

"Yet you raised him."

"And I love him. I love him so much that I can bear to have him leave."

"And the boy, how does he feel about it?"

"He doesn't want to leave, but he's beginning to realize that he can't stay."

"And Andre? How does he feel about it?"

"We haven't discussed it. He knows why I'm here, and it'll hurt him more than anything to lose Paul, but he won't stand in the way. I think he knows that it's for the best."

"I don't understand," said Catherine. "Why do you feel Paul should go?"

"Because he's French, and the French don't belong here," she said simply. "There will be fighting all the days and years they're here. I don't want him to have to fight all his life. You see, he's different from other men—he wouldn't like that."

"Will he go with me?" Catherine asked anxiously.

"You'll have to talk with him."

"I'll do anything for him. He's my only heir, you know; he'll have everything."

Gia Minh handed her the envelope she'd found in Louis's papers.

Catherine recognized her husband's seal and handwriting, and she read the page twice before looking up. "I wondered what happened to this. I knew Louis had it. He would have become Duke of Parnasse."

"And Paul?"

"Yes. An empty title, I'm afraid; but still, he'll become duke."

Gia Minh stood. "Then I leave to let you talk with him."

Catherine was surprised at her abruptness, and reluctant to terminate the conversation. "Must you go?"

"I have little time," said Gia Minh. "I must arrange things as quickly as I can. I'm happy to see that Paul will be well cared for."

They shook hands. "Please give my regards to Andre," Catherine said. "Has he been happy here?"

Gia Minh considered the question carefully. "He's not had an easy life here. There have been many sorrows. It probably would have been best had he not come."

She smiled. "You see, I love him enough that I can say that; I love him so much that I could have borne his not coming to me."

Catherine watched the door close behind her; then she bowed her head. She wished she could have said such a thing, but there had never been anyone in her life.

Paul stood up when Gia Minh came out. He looked worried, but she reassured him. "She's very nice; I think you'll like her."

He sat alone for several minutes, growing more anxious, and with no idea what to expect.

When the large double doors opened, he jumped up, expecting a servant to lead him in, but instead, an extraordinary woman appeared, the most graceful, elegant person he'd ever beheld. No queen could be as beautiful or stately, he thought. He was not even aware of age; her figure and features were exquisite, and she didn't so much move as float toward him, as a cloud might. She was dressed all in white, with the faintest light blue floral design on her floor-length gown. Her carriage was perfect, and on her lips was the most warm and dazzling smile. With her she brought a marvelous scent, airy waves of summer flowers.

He was overwhelmed, unable to talk or bow.

For her part, when she saw him she almost stopped in mid-step. It was as if she'd walked into the past. Here before her was Andre; she had to overcome her amazement and force herself to continue on, but the closer she got, the greater the resemblance became, down to the startled, shy, and innocent look on his face.

He stood perfectly still, unable to move, and she swept to him, bathing him in perfume, and she pressed her cheeks to his, her hands holding his.

"My dear," she said, her voice musical and sensual, each word slowly and softly articulated, "I am so happy to see you. You are perfection, a vision out of my dreams. Are you real?" Her hands lightly squeezed his shoulders, and she again pressed close to him; then she stepped back to see him.

He could still say nothing. At last he bowed and began to stammer a greeting, but she laughed lightly—it was Andre all over again—and she slipped her arm around him and led him toward the open doors.

"I forbid you to call me 'Grandmother,' " she said laughingly. "You would make me feel decrepit."

"Madame," he said, finally summoning presence enough to speak, "surely you could not be my grandmother."

Indeed she didn't look old enough to be so, despite the fact that she was seventy years old.

"Yet I am," she said triumphantly, "and I would have known you anywhere. You look exactly like Andre did. You are nineteen? Exactly his age when we became lovers."

He tried not to betray any sign of surprise or unworldliness at her directness, but she sensed it immediately. "Oh, my dear, it was the most passionate and lovely romance. And look what it brought." She opened her hands in a proud gesture to him.

He laughed.

She brought him to the settee and sat down beside him, never relinquishing his hands. "Let us get to know one another. I want to hear all about you."

Her eyes dazzled him. They rested on him with such rapture and interest that he forgot his shyness. She possessed the same amazing power she'd always had over men, and he couldn't help but succumb to her charm and grace. Her way was to flatter men with her entire concentration on them, but in this case, there was nothing artificial in it. She couldn't take her eyes off him; he reminded her so much of Andre, of her own youth and happiness, but at the same time, there was something freshly compelling about Paul himself, and she realized what it was: she liked him, and there were almost no others about whom she could say that.

"I hardly know what to say, madame; my life hasn't been very eventful; I can't imagine a thing that's happened to me that would interest you."

"I want to hear all about you," she said. "I want to know how you feel and what you think. I want to know about your life—what you do, what you like. I want to hear everything."

She became very serious, and brought his hands into hers. "You are all I have, Paul. My husband died two years ago, though he was dead for me a half-century ago, and my only child—your father—was taken from me nearly forty years ago. I thought I had him back once; in this very palace, nineteen years ago, I thought he was mine again. Then Andre killed him."

"What?" Paul jerked his hands away; his face was incredulous.

She grabbed his hands back quickly. "I thought you knew. Oh, dear God, I never would have said that if I knew . . ."

He jumped up. "He killed my father! Grandfather? Why?" He looked stricken.

She'd guessed he hadn't known about Louis, and continued masterfully, "Paul, that was nineteen years ago. I don't hold it against Andre; I know how much he's suffered. I know how much it hurt him when he learned your father was returning to France with me."

"But why did he kill him?"

"I never should have mentioned this; this is a matter between you and Andre. Besides"—she lowered her head—"it hurts me too much."

"But—"

She shook her head. "Please."

Seeing her distraught, he sat down to comfort her, his own anger swept away in the compassion he felt.

"Now there's only you," she whispered. "I'm an old woman, and I have no one else."

He put his arm around her.

"I was so happy when I learned I would see you. I wanted you with me so much all these years. I wanted to come so many times, but the thought of this place"—she shivered—"and the memory of your father . . . I just couldn't. But then finally I knew I had to."

She looked up, her eyes wet with tears, and she stroked his face. "You are everything I hoped you would be—more than I dared hope. Oh, Paul, I'm so happy." She clutched him tightly. "I don't want to lose you. I couldn't bear that, not you too. Come with me," she pleaded. "Let me show you Paris. Let me show you the world, Paul. Don't leave me alone. Can't you see what you mean to me?"

"But . . . I . . ."

She stood, becoming animated, her eyes filling with life and excitement. She gestured to the open screen on the garden, but her wave took in all that lay beyond. "Do you know what's out there? Oh, Paul, let me show you. The life! The wonder of it all."

She laughed, a girlish laugh of happiness and conspiracy. "Paris! Do you know, there are automobiles there now. Imagine! Electric lights. Telephones. There's movement and music, theater, balls. And color—dresses and pretty girls." She reached for his hands. "Oh, the girls, Paul. They'll be mad about you. Parties and dinners. The Bois de Boulogne, the Tuileries. Cafés and boulevards."

He laughed, caught in her gaiety; her enthusiasm was infectious.

"I'll take you everywhere, show you everything. We'll travel—Rome, Florence, London. Oh, Paul, it'll be wonderful."

She sat down, serious again. "You shall be rich. All that I have shall be yours—the apartment in Paris, the château. I'm a very wealthy woman, Paul. That's why the duke married me, but he died a rich man. You'll have what was his too, and his title. You'll become Duke of Parnasse."

Her eyes sparkled. "You have no idea the doors and hearts a title opens. Do you know, I still get marriage proposals? Men no older than you don't seem able to restrain themselves from professing their devotion."

"Of that I have no doubt, madame."

She smiled radiantly. "You'll be devastating, Paul. The other young men are so pale and sickly-looking, so worn and jaded. What a delight you'll be. Say you'll come."

"Well . . . I . . ."

"Don't break my heart. You must come." She squeezed his hand tightly and looked pleadingly into his eyes.

"But here I . . . I mean . . ."

"It needn't be forever. Just a visit. Come for only a year, just to see."

"A visit." He jumped at the idea. "Yes. I'd like that."

She didn't press him, trusting that once he got to France, once he saw Paris and life there, he'd never want to leave. "That would be wonderful," she said.

"But I must finish my studies here first. There are things I must do first."

She hid her disappointment, knowing that she could lose her advantage by pressing too hard. "I understand. It will give me time to prepare for you also. When can you come?"

"I'll finish school in eighteen months."

"So long? I shall be a relic by then. How can I wait so long for you?" She held up her hand. "But I shall. The anticipation will be exquisite; it will give me something to live for." She pressed her cheeks to his. "It will be all I live for."

He remained with her the rest of the day and dined with her that evening, falling more and more under her enchantment. He'd never known women such as this existed, and he was utterly captivated. There was a strength and femininity, a frankness and directness about her completely different from that of the Vietnamese—here was something exciting, even daring, and he was drawn irresistibly to it. She made him laugh; she challenged his thought; she flattered him; she gently mocked him. She made him feel interesting and masculine, powerful and clever, and when the time came for him to leave, he could barely pull himself away.

"Can I see you tomorrow?" he asked, as a suitor might.

"You never need ask such a thing. I live only for you from now on."

In the morning he breakfasted with Gia Minh and was struck by the vast difference between the two women, but also, very clear now, was Gia Minh's illness.

"Grandmother, what's wrong?"

"I didn't sleep well," she said. "The air here is so heavy and sad."

"No, Grandmother, it's not that."

But she wouldn't discuss it with him. "I'll be fine when I get home. Maybe I'll even go to Dalat for a rest cure. Maybe I'll make your grandfather go with me; he needs a rest too."

At the mention of his name, Paul's face hardened. "Grandmother, will you tell me the truth if I ask you something important?"

"Of course."

"Did Grandfather kill my father?"

Gia Minh was taken off guard; she'd never expected such a question. "Did she tell you that?"

"She thought I knew; it was just a passing comment. Did he kill my father?"

Gia Minh looked away. She didn't say anything for a long time, turning over in her mind all that she could or should tell him. At last she brought her eyes to him. Her face was firmly set, neither kind nor unkind, and she spoke to him in a manner that deprived him of any sense of anger or outrage. "Perhaps we erred in not telling you the truth about your father. We sought to be kind and to spare you unhappiness; that may not have been the wisest course. Yes, your grandfather killed your father. He had every justification for doing it. Louis was not my son, so I won't speak against him. I want your grandfather to tell you what happened. But until you hear the story, I don't want you to think anything bad of Andre."

"All right. I'll put it away until he tells me what happened. She doesn't blame him either, or at least she's forgiven him." He paused a moment, then plunged on, unable to hide his enthusiasm. "I liked her very much, Grandmother. She wants me to go to Paris to visit her. I told her I would, after I finished my studies. She made it sound very exciting."

Gia Minh smiled. "I'm sure that it is. If I were young, I'd want to go too. I don't think I'd even wait to finish school."

"I'm not ready to go yet," he said. "I have some things left to do."

"Well, I'm glad at least that you've decided to visit."

"Did you like her?" he asked impulsively, then realized the inappropriateness of the question.

"I think you'll be in very competent hands," she said.

"How long will we be here?" he asked, changing the subject.

"You can stay as long as you wish, but I must go tomorrow."

He couldn't hide his disappointment. "Tomorrow?"

"You needn't go back with me."

"Of course I will," he said, catching himself, and pretending it made no difference. He would have liked to spend more time with Catherine, but he knew he couldn't let Gia Minh travel back by herself, especially now that he knew what kind of treatment she might be subject to.

So it was decided that Catherine would return for him in eighteen months. She'd arrange everything for him in Paris, and he'd complete his studies in Saigon. He told her there was no need for her to come back for him, but she was insistent. She wasn't going to take any chances that he'd change his mind or that something would come up to prevent him from going.

Their farewell was not sad, but filled with promise and expectation. She wanted to leave him with a picture of strength and vivacity, so instead of tears or sorrow, she made him laugh. She kissed him on both cheeks, then brought up his hands and kissed them.

"Good-bye, Grandmother," he said, and she smiled in triumph as he turned away.

When they returned to Ban Me Thuot, Gia Minh was so weak and in such pain that she went directly to bed. Even Andre, who'd tried so desperately to ignore her decline over the past several years, could no longer avoid it.

After the others had left, he stood quietly beside her, his hands twisting helplessly.

She was exhausted, tired even beyond pain, but she reached over and took his hands, patting them gently. "I'll be better after I rest."

He wanted to ask what was wrong, but he was afraid to know. He looked frightened and dropped to his knees beside her. "I couldn't stand it if anything happened to you," he whispered.

She flinched as a spasm of pain gripped her. Her hand clutched him tightly; then she relaxed. "I'll be better in a day or so."

He bowed his head. "Yes." He started to stand, but she held him. He didn't want to hear about Hue, didn't want to know anything, and wanted to escapc before she could tell him.

"I liked her," Gia Minh said. "She's still a very beautiful woman."

Andre couldn't raise his head.

"Paul is going to visit her when he finishes school. It's arranged; she's going to return to get him. He wants to go. Let him, Andre; don't make it hard for him. Promise me."

He forced himself to look at her. "All right," he said, knowing that he was going to lose the boy.

"You must talk to him about Louis. He knows what happened. She thought he knew. It's time he learned about his father."

He closed his eyes. He had hoped he'd never have to face that, but here it was before him.

He waited until she fell asleep, then left the room.

That night Andre called Paul to his study. Dreading the talk, he braced himself with several drinks, but the alcohol only heightened his nervousness. He paced in agitation, and almost lost his resolve when Paul entered the room, a wary, faintly hard look on his face, confronting him with a reserve Andre had never seen before.

"Would you care for a drink, Paul?"

"No, thank you, sir."

Andre motioned him to a seat. "I was hoping I'd never have to tell you this story," he began.

"About killing my father," Paul asked coldly.

"About killing my son," said Andre evenly. "But I want to tell you the whole story, about Catherine, about why I came to Vietnam, and about your father."

Andre spoke as dispassionately as he could, and it was very late when he came to the part about Louis and the murder of Father Bergere, and his fight with his son.

"I didn't mean to kill him. He fell against the rocks; it was an accident."

Paul said nothing. Andre searched his face for a clue as to what he felt, but it was an impenetrable mask.

"I suppose I never should have brought him with me," he said at last. "I should have left him with Catherine and Parnasse. But then he'd never have married your mother, and you would never . . ."

Paul stood up. "Is there anything else I should know?"

Andre shook his head.

"Good night," said Paul, turning and leaving him alone.

Andre sat alone for a long time, finishing another drink. He'd lost Paul, he knew; perhaps the boy had understood about Louis, but it couldn't help but change how he felt about his grandfather. He'd go to Catherine now. Oh, God, how he'd dread to lose him, but maybe it was the right thing—the youth didn't belong here.

He poured another drink, not wanting to go to bed. He shivered suddenly at the thought of Gia Minh and tried to drive her illness from his mind. He couldn't face the thought that anything might happen to her. And now he would lose Paul. And he knew that Che Lan would leave him too; he could see how much his son yearned to return to the fight against the French.

He downed the drink quickly. He'd be alone. Was this what it was all to come to? He'd lived for this, to end like this? Suddenly the memory of Catherine came to him. He went for another drink, but changed his mind and went to the open screen. He was drinking too much, he knew; he was not the man he used to be, not as strong, not as wise, not as good. He didn't like growing old, and now he understood what his grandmother had meant when she'd rolled his flesh between her fingers. He pulled on the skin of his arm, then released it immediately; it was soft and fleshy, like the decaying pulp of rotting fruit.

Oh, God, he thought, I want to be young again. Then he almost laughed. And I suppose the dead would like not to be dead. And what is the hope of that?

Standing on the patio, he couldn't see the jungle; it was a black wall at the end of his sight, but he could hear it. Tonight it was shrill and unsettled, seething and moving in the darkness. Tonight it was alien and forbidding, and he didn't like it. He wished he were far away. Suddenly he envied Paul; he'd like to go to France too. He'd like to see Catherine.

The jungle was insistent; shrieking filled the night, driving away his thoughts of Catherine. He stared out into the blackness; then he felt suddenly cold. He had the most awful sensation that Louis was out there, restlessly, murderously stalking the night.

He closed the screen behind him and went for another drink.

In the morning Paul woke much earlier than usual. He had packed the night before. All he needed to do was dress quickly and grab a few things from the kitchen to take with him. He'd be several hours gone before anyone noticed his departure. He had to leave; he couldn't remain in the house another day. He needed time to be alone; too much had happened.

He felt no anger for Andre; his father was such a vague figure for him that he couldn't summon any emotion for him, and as much as he'd fantasized about his mother, she too was only a dream figure for him, so the stories about them and their deaths had no more reality than that of a fairy tale.

Yet as Andre had known, everything for Paul had changed. He felt cut off, alien, a superfluous figure in the drama of their lives. He'd been a fool to think that he was one of them, that he belonged. He was a misfit, a pathetic figure everyone felt sorry for. Well, he wouldn't live like that, he wouldn't be anyone's object of pity.

He packed some meat and provisions and was preparing to go out the kitchen to the stables when Che Lan came in on him.

It was not yet dawn and Che Lan had to strain in the darkness to make him out. He'd coiled instantly upon coming across someone unsuspectingly, and Paul had drawn back in fright. Che Lan's eyes flashed in the dark, his entire body radiating danger, and Paul saw how formidable and fearsome he was. Che Lan's brute power had always intimidated him, and the stories about him had only made it worse—he knew his uncle had killed many men.

Che Lan untensed when he recognized him, and nodded at what Paul was carrying. "Early for a picnic, isn't it?"

"I'm leaving."

Che Lan grunted and went to the table to see what the servants had set out.

Paul had expected some comment, perhaps even an effort to stop him, but Che Lan ignored him completely.

Che Lan was an almost mythical figure for Paul; he revered him, and had been jealous of Trinh for having him as his father. Though Che Lan had been good to him, there had always been a distance between them, and try as Paul had, he felt he'd never been able to work his way close to his uncle's heart.

Now he stood alone with him in the dark cool morning, and he wanted to talk, but he didn't know how to begin, or even what to say.

Che Lan sensed this, and when he looked up at Paul, he smiled. "I remember many mornings leaving like this, before everyone was up. I couldn't stand to say good-bye. I guess when I leave the next time it'll be like this too."

"Those used to be the worst mornings in our lives—waking up and finding you gone. That used to hurt a lot."

"It's going to hurt your grandmother and grandfather the same way when they wake up and find you gone."

"They'll understand."

"Understanding never lessens pain, Paul. Why are you leaving?"

He shrugged. "To go back to school. It's not working out like you hoped it would, though."

"Nothing is."

"I'm going to go to France, you know."

''Yes, Mother told me. I think it's a good thing.''

Paul looked at him, eager for approval. ''Do you really?''

''Sure. A great opportunity. I'd like to send Trinh too, but he wouldn't go, of course.''

''Then you think I don't belong here either.''

''I think a person should take his opportunities where he finds them,'' he said noncommittally. ''You know, when I was your age, I thought that everything was an either/or situation, that everything was irrevocable, with no time to waste or to make a mistake. I've learned that it isn't like that at all. There's plenty of time, and lots of alternatives. You have time to experiment. Don't be so serious about things. Go to France; if you don't like it, come back. What's there to lose?''

Paul smiled. ''You make it sound simple.''

''It is.'' He laughed. ''After all, it doesn't sound like a terrible situation you'll be stepping into—money, title, women. It's pretty hard for me to sympathize with your plight. You'll be in Paris, and I'll be here in the shit of the rice paddies. Why am I comforting you? Fuck you.''

Paul grinned. ''I guess you're right. Anyway, it's not for a while yet.''

He was ready to leave, but hesitated. ''Can I ask you one thing before I go? I want to know about my father. I want to know what he was like. All my life, no one ever spoke of him. Now I want the truth.''

Che Lan's eyes hardened. Paul could feel his anger. Finally he said evenly, ''I don't like to talk about him.''

''I have a right to know. Was he as bad as Grandfather says?''

Che Lan took a deep breath, then let it out slowly. ''I'm sure your grandfather didn't tell you half the things your father did, and you don't want to know them. One of the greatest sources of happiness in this family was that you turned out to be nothing like him.''

Che Lan moved so close to Paul that their faces nearly touched. ''Louis and I were only three years apart, grew up together just like you and Trinh did. I hated him; he was the worst person I've ever known. I have nothing good to say about him, so I don't want to talk about him. Let the bastard rot undisturbed. Forget him. He murdered your mother and would have left you—you meant nothing to him; he didn't even want you.''

Paul bore the words stoically, and nodded when Che Lan finished. ''I guess I'd better go. Will you say good-bye to everyone for me?''

Che Lan shook his head. "Learn to say your own good-byes. Or learn to get up earlier. And stop feeling sorry for yourself."

"I don't," said Paul, stung.

Che Lan smiled and clapped him around the shoulders, leading him to the door. "You're going to have to get harder, Paul."

Then he tousled the youth's hair and pushed him away. "No, don't. Stay as you are. Someone ought to stay untouched in this fucking world."

26

January 1911

ANDRE LOOKED DOWN ON HIS wife and fought back tears. Gia Minh lay wasted and motionless on her bed, the only sign of life her labored breathing. She was asleep now, her only release from pain, but he knew she'd soon be seized again by the full agony of the disease.

He couldn't bear to see her in such pain; in the early stages she'd been able to control it, but in the past several days she'd slipped out of consciousness, and cried out from the torment. He'd tried to find a place where he couldn't hear her cries, but they'd followed him wherever he went. At last he'd gone back to the room and sat beside her, holding her hand as she moaned and cried. Even when she screamed, he remained with her, each cry piercing him as though it were a knife. He sat with her until the cries subsided into moans and whimpers and she'd dropped into fitful sleep; then he'd leave to get his own rest, but his own sleep was twisted and tormented.

For two weeks she'd been in the final, agonizing throes of the disease, grown now so emaciated and weak that she hadn't been able to feed herself, and her skin was pulled so tightly on her body that he could see the skeletal form. She'd lost all control over her bowels and no longer recognized him, though she seemed eased when he held her hand or stroked her face.

He'd watched the disease sap her of life, but for a year they'd never spoken of it, pretending she was merely tired. But at last it had to be faced, and he'd wept when she told him what he already knew. He'd dropped to his knees and buried his head in her lap. "Oh, God," he'd cried. "No. Please."

She'd patted and comforted him. "It's all right," she'd said.

She'd known for a long time that she was dying and had come to a sad resignation about it. She wasn't afraid, and as the disease wore on, wasting her and bringing such terrible pain, she'd come to accept it with something almost approaching welcome.

Before she was unable to get out of bed, during the last weeks of summer, she had spent long hours in the garden. Sometimes she woke before dawn and would be outside before the sun rose over the jungle, seeming to escape up from the confines of a thick green web, showering the darkness with light. She'd listen to the jungle's symphony of life and she'd forget her pain, but then it'd come back as the sun rose higher and the heat became smothering.

At dusk too she'd go out alone into the garden. The sun would drop lower on the horizon, but it seemed more that the jungle rose to grasp it, the trees and shadows reaching up to swallow the sun, an ominous beginning for the dark night. And the noises of the jungle changed, becoming charged with shrill anxiety, and the low murmuring that was like a heartbeat was stilled, and in its stead came sharp cries of danger and unrest. Then too she forgot her pain as she watched the transformation, and she imagined that it was her own life merging with the night.

During the last weeks she and Andre spent most of their time together, not speaking, just holding hands, but at times Andre couldn't bear the sorrow he felt, and he'd raise his hands to cover his eyes, shielding his tears, and she'd comfort him, but there was nothing more that she could say than, "It's all right"; softly, "It's all right."

He was overcome with grief and couldn't hide it from her.

Though overwhelmed by the awesomeness of her own death and the fearsome mystery that lay beyond, she felt immense sadness for Andre. Poor man, she thought, what would become of him? She felt as though she were deserting him, leaving him alone and vulnerable.

"I want you to remarry," she'd said to him one day, strolling in the garden, but he'd looked so stricken that she'd dropped the matter immediately. One time she asked if perhaps he might return to France, but he'd merely shaken his head.

Just before she was unable to leave her bed, on the last day they had together in the garden, she reached for his hand and said, "I've loved you always. I loved you from the day I first saw you. Do you remember that day?"

He was not able to fight back his tears. "Of course, and you led us into the salon, and I sat there too shy even to look at you."

"You've made me very happy," she said. "Always." She tightened her grip on his arm. "Don't let me hurt too much."

He turned to her, fear coming into his eyes. "What do you mean?"

"When the times comes, don't let me suffer."

"Gia Minh . . ." he whispered. "Don't."

She shook her head. "Promise me that, Andre. Don't let me hurt too much."

That was what she feared, not death, but becoming helpless and insentient.

He closed his eyes at the thought. She was asking what his great-grandmother had asked forty years ago. He hadn't been able to do it then, and he knew he couldn't now.

But that was before he'd seen what ravages the disease had brought, had listened to her screams and cries, her begging for death, her grotesque helplessness.

He stared down at her now, hearing her whimpers and moans even in sleep, and knew she had only an hour before the agony struck again and her mind and body were ripped by searing pain.

He'd loved her all their days together and was bewildered at this cruel end. She didn't deserve this; no one did. She'd been kind and good and suffered enough in this life; it wasn't right that her death should be so hard too.

Andre dropped down on his knees beside the bed. "Oh, God," he said, and rested his cheek on her hand. He didn't want her to die; more than anything in his life or this world, he didn't want to lose her. But he knew she couldn't be saved; there wasn't going to be a miracle. She would get worse, slip further, suffer even more pain and humiliation, and she would die: this woman he had loved for forty years, the only woman he had loved.

How could he live without her? he wondered. He didn't want to. She meant more to him than anything else, certainly his own life, even his son. That was a different love—harder, more demanding—going straight to his heart, but to a different chamber. The softer part of his being, his vulnerability—his essence—that was his love for her.

He wanted to talk to her one last time, hold her, lie with her, but she was hardly recognizable as the woman he'd loved; the cancer mocked her, had made a ghastly, grisly joke of her life and vitality. What lay on the bed was not Gia Minh, but a helpless, hopeless shell that could only suffer pain.

He would not let it go on; he would do that much for her—the only thing left he could do.

But he couldn't think about it. He stood, kissed her on the lips, then eased the pillow from behind her head and placed it over her face. Dear God, he said, please don't let her struggle. When he pressed down, there was no resistance and he held the pillow over her face until long after she was dead.

He was afraid to lift it off, fearing horror or accusation in her eyes, but when he finally did, her eyes were closed, her face had eased, and she looked peaceful and at rest.

Then he dropped to his knees and prayed, not for her soul, for he knew she did not need his prayers, but for his own, and then he cried unashamedly, and at last collapsed exhausted in the chair beside her bed.

A servant found him in the morning. A glance told her that Gia Minh was dead, but also that something was wrong with Andre. He was awake, but unmoving and unseeing. He sat completely still, his hands holding the pillow, his gaze fixed on the floor.

The servant ran to Ly's room to tell her what had happened.

Ly threw a robe around herself and went immediately. She felt Gia Minh's cold hand, the flesh already stiffening, and seeing the pillow in Andre's hands, she guessed what had happened. She sent the servant out of the room, took the pillow from his hands and placed it back under Gia Minh's head, then helped Andre to his feet and led him to his own room. He didn't resist, and when she eased him onto the bed, he closed his eyes and immediately fell asleep.

Andre slept the entire day. She didn't disturb him, oversaw all the arrangements for the funeral, and the following morning carried his breakfast in to him, but he appeared hardly changed from how she'd seen him sitting in the chair beside Gia Minh's bed. She urged him to eat, and tried to engage him in conversation, but he didn't touch the food, and made no responses.

She cursed Che Lan for not being here; he'd left months ago to rejoin the rebels, and she'd heard nothing from him. She always knew he would be leaving again, but she'd been surprised at the abruptness of his departure: one morning he simply announced that he was leaving. There'd been no warning, and she'd detected nothing in his manner which would have indicated his actions. He simply left, though this time she'd not been silent about it. "You're too old for such foolishness," she'd said to him. "You're forty years old. Leave this nonsense to young men. Or is that what's bothering you? That you can't stand to see your son taking your place in the fight?"

Trinh had long been active in the underground movement in

Hanoi, a rebel actively sought by the French authorities. "Am I to suffer silently the loss of both my husband and my son? Am I to wait here for word of your capture or death, going about my business, pretending I understand or that it doesn't bother me? It's futile and stupid, and you're too old."

"You're probably right," he'd said, "but futility, stupidity, and old age aren't reason enough."

She'd urged him to stay on at least until Gia Minh died, but he was deaf to that appeal also.

Now she needed him, for she didn't know how to deal with Andre, and the entire burden of the estate and its management fell to her.

She had run the household for a long time, nearly a year before Gia Minh's death, and she'd assumed the care of Chien, but she had only the sketchiest understanding of how the estate was managed. Andre spoke little of business and there never seemed to be any difficulties or crises, but this, she knew, was a tribute to his acumen, not a reflection of the ease of the business.

Almost immediately she found out how right she was, for even before the funeral, decisions were brought to her to place before Andre regarding rubber negotiations and problems about labor difficulties. But Andre would not listen; rather, he would listen, but show no interest or even acknowledge that he understood.

She thought that this would pass soon after the funeral, but it didn't, and he sank deeper and deeper into torpor, and the requests for decisions were pressed more and more urgently.

Andre almost never spoke, and he seemed oblivious of what was happening about him. He ate little, cared nothing for his appearance, and would not even have shaved or bathed had Ly not forced him to. She felt alarm when he began to leave his room at night, and would sit in the room where Gia Minh had died. Several nights she found him sitting by the bed, the pillow again in his hands. She led him back to his room, and at last took to locking the door of Gia Minh's room.

He began to look haggard and old, a frail, unwell, elderly man losing his mind.

No matter how hard she tried, or what she did, she couldn't interest him in the affairs of the estate, and he gave her no counsel. At last she made a few tentative decisions on her own, relaying them as coming from Andre, and when there were no dire consequences, she made a few more, and things ran smoothly, and no one questioned the directions that she said came from Andre. She placed herself between him and the various foremen of the different enterprises, and no one knew that the orders and decisions were not coming from him, but gradually she began deciding things as soon as they were presented to her, without making the pretense of consulting him, and her directions were carried out unhesitantly.

She increased the wages of all those who worked on the estate, so significantly that other landowners complained, but her answer was to raise the allotment of rice each worker was given. She made loans no one else would have made, and her dealings with even the lowest worker were marked by courtesy and respect.

Andre had always enjoyed a reputation for fairness and honesty, but now when people spoke of him and the estate they did so with as close to warmth and affection as one could in reference to a great landowner. There was talk of course that Ly was behind it all, for there was no hiding things from the servants, but it made no difference.

Ly found that she fell easily into the role that had once belonged to Xuan, and even Ahn before his death. There was a constant stream of petitioners, and soon she was arbitrating between parties in disputes, and giving advice on finance and family. She found she thrived on this activity. Before, she had always been in the background, a shadow to Gia Minh, the outsider, the daughter-in-law.

She made her mistakes, to be sure, erring always on the side of generosity, the heart being more susceptible to deception than the mind—yet the loss was negligible, and she learned from the mistakes. Soon no one could claim to best her in any transaction, though by the same token no one ever claimed to have been cheated by her.

She managed all the affairs of the estate and the household, yet still she found time to care for Andre and Chien, spending time with each every day, though she found the time with Chien more pleasurable, for he had great periods of lucidity when his faculties seemed hardly diminished, but Andre remained totally removed and mostly mute.

She found herself so occupied and satisfied that she began to feel guilt and remorse that she didn't miss her husband and son more than she did. She missed them, of course, but they had their own interests and activities that had always been apart from her, and now she had her own. She liked work and responsibility, and found that she was as good at managing things as any man, better in fact. And what she was doing was important, she felt; she could see the results in the fields, and in the gratitude of those who worked for her. She believed that what she was doing was every bit as important as what Che Lan and Trinh were doing; she was prospering, and helping others prosper.

Six months quickly passed. It was Tet, the new year, and she had just made sizable gifts to all who worked for her, and was settling down to spend the holiday quietly when Che Lan suddenly appeared.

He arrived one midafternoon, the house nearly deserted of servants, who'd been let off, and he found her in Andre's study, seated at his desk, going over documents and figures.

He stood in the doorway, waiting for her to run to him as she had so often in the past upon his return, but instead she merely stood up and waited for him to come to her. He did, and took her in his arms, kissing her passionately, and she responded, but somehow he felt a difference in her, and he stepped back to look at her.

"You look good," he said at last.

"And so do you, husband. Arms and revolution suit you very well. You look much better than when you left here. You look younger and refreshed. War is such a rejuvenating thing, marriage and home such a debilitating thing."

"Don't mock me, wife," he said, and took her again in his arms, but she pulled away.

"There are some things I must tell you, Che Lan."

"About Mother?" He'd guessed her death, knew when he'd left he'd never see her again.

"Six months ago. Your father's needed you." It was a mild reproach, for she knew how much he loved both his parents, but also how he couldn't help himself; he would fight till the end of his days, she knew.

"Is he all right?" He turned, as if to go to his father, but she restrained him. "It's good you've come back."

Then she told him all that had happened, though she didn't tell him how she had found Andre with the pillow and what she suspected.

"And he just sits all day? He doesn't do anything?"

"He loved her very much, Che Lan; more even than we knew. She was all that he had."

"He has me. And Trinh and Paul. And you."

"You left him. Trinh left. Paul is going to France. I'm just the daughter-in-law. He's given up."

"But I had to go. He understands that."

"Yes, he understands, but that doesn't change anything; he feels all alone."

"Well, it'll be all right now. I'll take care of him." He took her in his arms and held her tightly. "It's been very hard for you. I'm sorry. Thank you for all you've done."

"Where's Trinh?" she asked. "I haven't heard a thing from him."

"I don't know," he said. "I suppose he's in Hanoi."

"Weren't you there too?"

"No. I've been in Thailand."

She made a slight sound of disgust. "Japan, China, Thailand. Why don't you just stay here where you belong? That's all such foolishness, Che Lan; nothing's going to come of it. You're chasing everywhere when what needs attending is right here. You and the others spend all your time talking revolution and making futile plans when you should be here working with the farmers and peasants, helping them, being at their side. You're not going to accomplish anything from Thailand, any more than you did in Japan."

"I know that, but I had to find Phan Boi Chau. He's still our only hope, and he can't come back here. The French would kill him as soon as they got hold of him."

"And you?"

"No. I can move about. I have to be careful, but I'm the only one who can travel freely."

"And what now? Where are you going next?" she asked tiredly.

"I'll stay here."

"For a while."

He lowered his head. "For a while." When he looked up, it was with shyness, and she took pity on him.

"Then let's make the best of the time we have," she said. She put her arms around him. "I've missed you very much."

He clutched her tightly, breathed her in, and rocked with her gently, his head nestled in her hair.

"Come," she said, and led him to their room.

They made love hungrily, almost illicitly, he felt, for it was as if she were a different person. She led him, was as aggressive as he was, and for the first time he felt he was experiencing the full sexual power of a woman. Before, he had sometimes felt as though he were using her, was not altogether sure of her response, but now he felt as though he'd entered into a full and mutual sexual relationship.

"I should have come back sooner," he said, stretching comfortably on the bed. Then he reached for her again. "But at least we can make up for all the lost time."

She pushed him away. "Not in one afternoon. Go see your father."

He put it off as long as he could, but finally he went to Andre's room and knocked on the door.

There was no answer. He tapped again. "Father. It's Che Lan."

He heard steps; then the door opened on his father, and he had to check the shock he felt on seeing him.

Andre had aged twenty years; he looked a gaunt, unwell old man. Andre smiled faintly, a self-conscious smile, knowing how unkempt and haggard he looked, but still happy to see his son.

Che Lan stepped into the room and drew his father into an embrace, his arms encircling him, feeling the thin and unmuscular limbs. When he stepped away to look at him, Andre bowed his head and stood motionless, his hands at his sides. He made a pitiable sight, and Che Lan felt immense sorrow for him.

"Father," he whispered. Then he went to him and took him in his arms. "It'll be all right now."

"I loved her so much," Andre said, his voice choking, and he clutched onto his son tightly.

"I know; but it doesn't do any good to grieve like this, Father. She wouldn't want this."

"I don't know what to do," he said.

"We'll talk about it later," said Che Lan. "Let's go to dinner. The first thing you need to do is eat. A bath wouldn't hurt you, either; or a shave." He tugged on his arm. "Come on, let's go eat something."

The dinner made for a strange setting, Andre shy and embarrassed, Chien passing in and out of comprehension, and Che Lan and Ly solicitous for them both, but at the same time absorbed with each other.

Andre ate more than he had since Gia Minh's death, and he tried conversation, but it was as though he were speaking an unfamiliar language.

Chien seemed not to notice the change in him, but he was aware that Che Lan's appearance at the table was something new. Che Lan explained to the old man that he'd been in Thailand working with the revolutionaries.

Chien listened with great interest and appreciation, even more intently than Andre did.

"I love the stories," said Chien when Che Lan finished. "At my age, life is like a play, and I am a very appreciative audience. I find it all entertaining and amusing; it isn't even necessary that

I understand all that's going on—the costumes and actions are enough. People come and go, like walking on and off the stage, and sometimes I can't remember who is who, or what happened before, but it's all most enjoyable. And what's best is that I can hear the same thing over and over again and not get bored. That's the nice part of being addled."

"You're not addled, Master Chien," said Ly, fondly stroking his arm.

"Well, forgetful, then. You see," he said, pointing to Che Lan, "this boy just told me that he went to Thailand, but for the life of me I can't remember why, though I remember it was a fascinating story. But now I'll be quite happy to listen to it again."

He sucked contentedly on soft fruit. "At least it's nice finally to have someone here who tells stories." He pointed at Andre. "That man hasn't said anything in years. He's very boring."

Even Andre laughed. "I haven't been well, Master Chien; but I'll be fine from now on."

They had to coax him, but gradually he did take part in the talk. Ly asked his advice on several estate matters, though of course she didn't need it, but from his answers it was apparent that his interest in his affairs was returning.

When Che Lan spoke of the situation in China, he also showed interest.

"The revolution will come soon there," said Che Lan. "Sun Yat-sen is a great man. I think he'll overthrow the monarchy in a year or so. Then he'll help us."

Chien was appalled. "A revolution? In China?"

"Tz'u Hsi, the old dowager empress, is dead, Master Chien. A five-year-old boy is emperor. The mandate of heaven is lost."

"I remember Tz'u Hsi," said Chien. "What a wonderfully wicked woman. If there'd been an empress like that here, there'd have been no problems. She was much more of a man than Tu Duc."

"The time for emperors and empresses is gone, Master Chien," said Che Lan gently.

"Nonsense. Who else could rule?"

"In China there's going to be a republic."

"A what?"

"A republic. The people choose their ruler; they'll have elections."

"Waste of time," said Chien. "Dreadful mistake. They'll choose the wrong ruler. People can't be trusted to do the right thing. A republic? That's an awful idea."

"That's what we're going to have here someday, Master Chien."

"Terrible," he said. "Even Tu Duc would be better."

Andre shook his head sadly. "Ahn would not be happy to hear his grandson say such a thing, Che Lan."

"From what I've heard about him, Father, you may be wrong; he might have been the first to see that the days of monarchy are over. And they are. It took me a long time to come to that, but the monarchy must go. We're going to need help from China to throw out the French, but they won't give it to maintain emperors. Even Phan Boi Chau sees that now. Besides, we couldn't enlist young followers to support a monarchy. Trinh and those like him would never fight for an emperor."

Chien, who'd nodded off, raised his head suddenly in recognition. "I know him. Terrible student. Worst I ever had. Where is he?"

"In Hanoi. He's just like his father," said Ly.

"Who's his father?" asked Chien.

"I am," said Che Lan.

"Oh, yes, now I remember. Another terrible student. Runs in the family. I wasted my time with all of you. I should have abandoned you all to that priest. Except for what's-his-name, the French one."

"Paul," suggested Andre.

"Yes. Whatever happened to him?"

"He's in Saigon, finishing his studies," said Ly. "He'll be coming home shortly. But then he's going to France."

"I love it," said Chien, nodding off again. "Better than a play."

The next morning Andre was up early, dressed and shaved and finished with breakfast before the others awakened. He was gone the entire day, checking the fields and consulting with the foremen, and when he returned in the evening he had nothing but praise for Ly.

The following day he went over the books and accounts with her. She expected him to resume where he'd left off, but to her great surprise he asked her to continue managing the affairs of the estate.

"You're doing as well as I ever did," he said. "In fact, you've made some improvements I never would have thought of. The workers seem more content than ever, and they're working harder. Besides, I'm over sixty years old; it's time I turned all this over to someone—though I have to admit I never thought it'd be to a woman. I'd always hoped it'd be to Che Lan, but he obviously has no interest in land or business. Nor does Trinh, it seems. Maybe his wife will, though, when he marries; then it can be passed from you to her. There is, after all, a tradition of strong women in this family. I don't just mean Xuan and Gia Minh, either; my great-grandmother was a remarkable woman too.''

He smiled in a way she hadn't seen, in a way, she realized, that had captivated Gia Minh so many years ago—a totally genuine, disarming, and boyish grin. ''But I've come to see that all women are remarkable.''

''That's probably what he needs,'' said Che Lan when Ly told him how much better Andre was, and what he'd said about women. ''A woman would be good for him.''

But he didn't know quite how to bring that up to his father; there had always been a distance between them—not for lack of love, but from formality and shyness. Both felt that they talked around one another, never quite with one another.

A few days later Andre and Che Lan were stopped in a grove, resting their horses, after riding over to the rubber plantation.

''Ly's done a remarkable job,'' said Andre. ''There really isn't much for me to do anymore.''

''Think of where that puts me,'' said Che Lan. ''There certainly isn't need for three of us trying to run things. I feel like a woman around here. I should be going pretty soon.''

''Stay. I'll turn everything over to you both; it would take two to handle all this.''

Che Lan lay flat on his back and stared up at the trees. ''First off, I'm not interested in any of this. Second, what would you do?''

Andre was braced against a tree trunk, his arms around his knees. ''I've been thinking about that. There really is a lot I can do.''

Che Lan propped himself on an elbow and looked at his father. ''What do you mean?''

''Offering my services to the colonial administration. I probably know more about this area and the people than any other Frenchman. I could do a lot of good.''

Che Lan's eyes narrowed. ''You're not serious?''

''I am. Why wouldn't I be?''

Che Lan sat up; his voice was cold. ''Because what's wrong with this country *is* the French administration. The only good you could do would be to help get rid of it, not join it. I'd hate to end up fighting my own father.''

Andre didn't pursue the matter; he didn't want to risk confrontation with his son now, though he saw that there was going to be difficulty in the future. French rule had been good for the country, Andre thought. There were problems, to be sure, but certain policies could be modified. In any case, administration now was far better than it had been in imperial times. Affairs were nowhere near as bad as Ahn had feared they'd be under the French, and probably a time of self-rule would come. It was time for Vietnam to be led into the modern world, but certainly they weren't going to do it on their own, he felt.

"Well, it's just something I was toying with," he said. "It wasn't anything immediate. The only pressing thing I have to do is send Paul off to France."

Che Lan was not mollified, and his eyes were still suspicious on his father. "Yes. Paul should go to France."

"Maybe he'll be back."

"I hope not," said Che Lan.

"He's your nephew; he was raised like your son."

"He's my brother's son; he's French. He doesn't belong here. I'd hate to have to fight him too. I don't want Trinh and me to have to fight you and Paul."

"It would never come to that," said Andre.

Che Lan stood and went for his horse. "I hope not, Father. That'd be the final tragedy, fathers and sons fighting, brothers fighting."

Andre got his horse and led it out of the grove, side by side with Che Lan. Across from them in the fields, a peasant toiled under the burning sun with his water buffalo. The animal moved with stately grace and slowness, impervious to the man beside him, and the heat. The man was dwarfed by the animal, and together they made a tableau of tranquillity and endurance.

"It's such a peaceful country," said Andre. "Nothing will happen."

The family was seated around the table for the last time. Paul, who'd returned from Saigon the week before, was leaving in the morning with Andre.

The past year had not been a happy one for Paul. He was leaving no friends, and few pleasant memories, and as time wore on, he looked more and more forward to going to France. Saigon depressed him; the city was becoming even more colonized, more corrupt and decadent, and the people seemed to welcome it. There was little resistance to French rule in the south, but Paul saw that he could never be a part of that rule.

The trip to France provided him with a grace period before he'd have to decide what to do with his life. He had no expectation of remaining in France; Vietnam was his home.

He'd somewhat dreaded his final trip to Ban Me Thuot. Ly wrote him that Andre hadn't been well since Gia Minh's death, and he knew that his farewell would cause him more pain. But much to his surprise, Andre looked extraordinarily well, more fit and vital than he'd seen him in years, and he seemed to have accepted Paul's decision to go.

"If you don't mind," he'd said to Paul, "I'd like to see you off."

"I'd like that, Grandfather. I didn't want to go back to Saigon alone."

"Perhaps you'll come back. I have a feeling that you will."

"I know I will."

When Trinh returned unexpectedly to say good-bye, Paul was touched and pleased beyond words, and in their final days together they put aside all their differences and never spoke about politics or the future.

On their final day together, they went out into the jungle to the spot where they'd hidden as children from the soldiers, and they came back subdued, but closer than they'd been in years.

"I'm going to miss you," said Paul. "I *have* missed you. I'm sorry for everything that's come between us. None of it mattered."

Trinh put his arm around his shoulder. "Maybe . . . maybe it'll turn out all right," but he didn't believe the words even as he said them, and it made him very sad, because he wanted them to be true.

"When I come back, you'll probably have a wife and children. You'll be a settled old farmer."

"Well, maybe the wife-and-child part, but not the farmer. I almost brought Kim with me. I wanted everyone to meet her, but this isn't the right time. You'll meet her when you come back. Maybe you'll bring a wife with you. You'll come back a duke, bringing a duchess."

Paul laughed. "Che Lan would sink the boat."

Trinh smiled. "I might help him."

But at dinner that night, Trinh announced that he was going with Paul and Andre in the morning.

"Now where?" asked Chien, who was having difficulty keeping track of all the activity and people in the house. "I've never seen so much coming and going. I couldn't keep up with it all even if I wasn't gaga."

"Paul's going to France," said Ly, "and Andre and Trinh are going with him to Saigon to see him off."

"Saigon," the old man murmured. "I was there once. With your father," he said to Ly.

"Who?" asked Trinh.

"Ahn. We had a very good time."

"I'll bet." Paul laughed.

"We went together once too, Master Chien," said Andre.

"We know about that," said Ly. "We heard about the pillows."

"Oh, my, yes," said Chien. "How could I have forgotten? I wonder if they're still there?"

"Doubtless," said Ly. "Some things never change."

"Well, I suppose I should go to see it once again before I die," the old man said.

They smiled, knowing he'd forget, even if it were feasible for him to make such a journey.

But in the morning he was ready to go; he'd packed his bag, an old, battered valise, and dragged it out with him to breakfast. He looked remarkably robust and smiled happily at everyone when he sat down.

"I dreamed about the pillows," he said. "I think I had an erection. But it's been so long, I couldn't remember for sure if that was what it was. Maybe it was just a cramp."

Paul and Trinh sniggered into their plates.

"Dear God," said Ly.

"Master Chien, you can't go," said Andre.

The old man looked so wounded that Andre immediately regretted his words. He said soothingly in explanation, "It's a very long journey."

"We're not walking, are we?" Chien asked.

"No, of course not, but it'd be a very tiring trip for you."

"I'll be fine," he said, settling to his breakfast. "I love trips."

"But—" began Andre.

Chien raised his hand to end further discussion. "This will be my last journey. I don't care if I don't get beyond the outer gate; I'd rather die on a journey than in my bed, especially since nothing interesting happens in my bed anymore." He plopped fruit in his mouth and smacked loudly. "But you know, I think I had an erection this morning."

"Dear God," said Ly. "Take him with you."

"Yes," said Paul. "He should go. Please, Grandfather."

Andre looked to Che Lan for help, but his son only shrugged. "Oh, all right." Then, more gallantly, he said to the old man,

"We'd be honored to have you accompany us, Master Chien. Did you pack everything you need?"

He looked surprised. "What do I need at my age?"

Ly went to the valise and opened it. It contained a spare pair of slippers. "Perhaps just a little more than this," she said, and took the suitcase back to his room to pack it.

27

THE TRIP DID WONDERS FOR Chien; no one had seen him so well and alert in years. He slept and talked and ate the entire way, and he made them all laugh with his stories of Ahn and Lady Deng and Father Bergere and court life long ago.

But the trip was much slower with the old man along; they couldn't travel nearly so fast, and had to stop frequently for him to relieve himself, and it was a laborious job to help him in and out of the carriage, and they had to stop earlier in the evening for lodging, and start later in the morning. In all, they arrived three days later than they'd planned, on the day the ship was scheduled to leave.

They drove through the bustling streets directly to the harbor.

The day was unusually hot and humid, even for July, and the cramped, noisy city only intensified it.

Chien strained to see, but his eyes were too weak to make out anything except blurred shapes, so he settled back and was content to let the others describe the city to him, and the port scene when they arrived at the harbor. The five-thousand-ton passenger freighter *Admiral Latouche-Treville*, triumphantly white and majestic, dwarfed everything else in the harbor. A huge French tricolor flapped haughtily from its stern. On the upper deck, red-white-and-blue awnings marked the first-class cabins, and white-uniformed stewards moved purposefully along the decks making the final preparations for sail.

"It's beautiful, isn't it?" asked Paul.

"It's certainly different from what I sailed on," said Andre.

Even Trinh was impressed, though he tried not to show it.

Chien shook his head, marveling. It was big enough that he could see it clearly. "How is it that such a thing doesn't sink?" he asked.

"Ballast," said Trinh, then he looked meaningfully to Paul. "And a little hole would send it straight to the bottom of the ocean."

The carriage was halted at the entrance to the ship's berth and allowed to go no farther.

"Would you mind waiting for me?" said Andre. "I'd like to have a few minutes with your grandmother alone. Perhaps you could get Master Chien something cool to drink."

He got out of the carriage and made his way to the gangplank.

Paul watched him thread his way through the dockside activity. "I'd love to be there for that meeting," he said.

"I want to see the ship," said Chien, and started out of the carriage.

"You stay with him," said Trinh. "I'll go find something to drink."

Paul helped the old man out of the carriage and led him toward the ship. He saw Andre going up the gangplank, and he looked for Catherine on deck, but couldn't see her.

She was in the ship's salon, which she'd had reserved for her use, thinking that perhaps Andre would come with Paul, and she didn't want to meet him in her stateroom; she needed more room, a larger stage. Cramped quarters made her nervous.

The last three days had been torture for her; she was afraid something had happened, that her hopes and expectations would be dashed, just as they'd been with Louis. She'd become nearly frantic this last day, and had already ordered that her things be unloaded if Paul didn't show up by sailing time. She wasn't going to return alone; she wasn't going to let Andre thwart her again.

When word was sent to her that Andre had arrived, she flew to the porthole to see if Paul was with him. When she saw him leading an ancient Chinese toward the ship, she clutched her hand to her heart and caught her breath. Then she sent for Andre.

She tried vainly to strike the right pose. She hadn't seen him in twenty years, on the day he brought her the news of Louis's death, and before that she hadn't seen him in nearly another twenty years, when he took her child from her. Her memories of him were when they were young; they were passionate, happy memories.

Catherine was seventy-one, and there'd been no joy or happiness in her life in a long time, no real, unfettered joy since her days with him so many years ago. Her life had been like the furniture and decoration in her apartments and château—heavy and baroque, gilded and cold. Her life was staged and trivial, endless diversions which didn't divert, amusements which didn't amuse, lovers who didn't love.

She didn't feel old, felt that the girl she'd always been was trapped within the wrinkled, sagging flesh, a prisoner of some cruel trick, and she hated her body now for what it had done, what it had become, its betrayal.

Yet she looked remarkably well, considerably younger than she was, a most regal-looking woman, but now, waiting for Andre, she couldn't hide her nervousness and anxiety. What would he think of her after all these years?

A knock came firmly and without hesitation, and when she said "Come in," he entered briskly, so seemingly at ease that she might have thought he'd only stepped out of the room a short while ago, or that he'd just left her, returning to fetch something he'd forgotten.

And yet he had changed; the leanness was gone, the vibrancy muted. His face showed wear and sadness, and the eyes revealed many sorrows. But she smiled on seeing him, comforted somewhat by the graying hair and mildly thickened body, for there was still so much in his carriage and presence that reminded her of the youth she'd loved.

"Why, you've gotten old too, Andre. I was afraid you might not have changed."

He laughed good-naturedly and kissed her hand. "You're still a beautiful woman, Catherine."

She was pleased, and motioned for him to sit on the sofa beside her. "I was getting worried. I thought perhaps you were going to prevent Paul from coming."

"I promised my wife I'd bring him."

"Is she . . .?"

"She died seven months ago."

Catherine took his hand. "I'm very sorry, Andre. She seemed like a very fine woman, and I know she loved you very much."

"I was very happy with her. I . . ." But he couldn't go on; there weren't words for what he felt.

"I never found anyone, you know." She smiled. "It wasn't for lack of trying, but I never found anyone after you. Yet we certainly weren't meant for one another, were we? I often wonder about my life now. Even with all I've had, it's not been very happy. My fault, of course. That's why I'm so grateful to you for bringing Paul to me."

She pressed his hand. "I want to thank you for letting him

come. You see, I don't have anyone. You don't know how happy this makes me."

"Then I'm very glad."

"But why did you come? I didn't expect that."

"I wanted to see you again. I've never forgotten you."

She brushed at her eyes. "My God, I haven't cried in forty years. I was afraid I never meant anything to you."

"Oh, I fought it, but it never did any good."

She grabbed his hands suddenly. "Why don't *you* come? I mean it, leave this wretched place and come back to France."

He laughed. "If I listen to you, you'll seduce me away just like you did Paul."

"Well, why not? Come back for just a visit. You'd be amazed at all that's changed."

"No doubt I would. And perhaps I shall later on; I've given it some thought. Do you think there's going to be a war?"

"Of course there'll be a war. Men always have wars. They love wars. Just like you used to love that silly uniform. There'll be a terrible war."

"I want you to keep Paul out of it."

"Of course I shall. I'm not going to lose him to the army or the Huns after all I've gone through."

"It seems to run in my family's blood. My father, and all his forefathers, fought in wars. My grandmother said we were very stupid."

"I have no doubt. But you needn't worry about him. Besides, he doesn't strike me as the type who'd charge off into battle."

"Did I?"

"God, yes. And you were thrilling in that uniform. I remember the day I came to visit you at the Ecole. I couldn't keep my hands off you." She laughed at the memory. "And you were so shy. And so aroused."

He blushed, as he always had with her. "Perhaps I will come to visit you in Paris."

"You'd better hurry," she said. "Soon I'll be in Pere Lachaise beside Philippe. Though I'm thinking of having him moved. I can't bear the thought of spending eternity next to him."

"He died several years ago, didn't he?"

"Four years ago. At first I thought his end fittingly awful, but I've come to forgive him."

They lost all track of time and place. They sat side by side, absorbed with one another, rediscovering how great their attraction for one another was.

While they talked, a most remarkable meeting was about to take place.

Chien had walked the entire length of the pier to see the ship. Paul had tried to urge the old man back to the carriage, but he was tired of being confined.

The sun was unmercifully hot and the old man leaned more and more on Paul's arm, until finally he stopped and couldn't go on.

Paul knew he couldn't get him back by himself, but he saw no sign of Trinh.

Chien's breathing became labored and he had difficulty standing. Paul was growing alarmed when suddenly he caught sight of a Vietnamese deckhand from the ship coming toward them.

Without saying anything, the youth helped move Chien to the shade cast by the ship's bow and eased him onto a pallet; then he ran off and in a moment returned with water.

Chien drank eagerly and his breath became more regular.

"It's too hot for such an old man," said the youth, admonishing Paul in Vietnamese, though not expecting the Frenchman to understand his words.

"He's a very stubborn old man," said Paul. "He's never listened to anyone in his whole life. Thank you very much for helping."

The Vietnamese youth eyed Paul curiously; he'd never heard a Frenchman speak such good Vietnamese, and had never heard a polite word from one.

Paul propped Chien comfortably on the pallet and gave him more water. The old man seemed dazed, but he'd be all right.

"My name is Paul Lafabre," he said, extending his hand. "I'm going to France on this ship. Are you one of the crew?"

"Yes," said the Vietnamese. "I'm a cook, but they have me loading cargo."

Paul eyed him carefully. The youth was slight, but not frail, thin and angular, with remarkably intense eyes and a shrewd, intelligent face. "You don't look like a cook," he said.

"I'm not. That's just what I'm paid to do. My name is Nguyen Sinh Cuong; I'm going to France too. Then I'm going to return here and help free my country."

He sounded so much like Trinh that Paul almost laughed, but the youth spoke without defiance, as though he were relating a simple, unalterable fact.

Chien roused himself and tried to stand, but they restrained him.

"You should rest, Master Chien. Would you care for more water? You have this gentleman to thank for it."

Chien scrutinized the youth before him, so closely that Paul was about to apologize for the old man's rudeness, but then Chien asked suddenly in Chinese, "What name will you be called?"

In Chinese, the youth answered, "Ho Chi Minh, honorable Grandfather."

" 'He who enlightens,' " translated Paul.

Surprised, the youth turned to him. "You speak Chinese too?"

"He was my best pupil," said Chien.

Just then Trinh ran up to them. "Are you all right, Master Chien?" he asked, out of breath, handing him a bottle of water.

"Late as always," said Chien. "Terrible student. If I drink any more water I'll have to piss into the ocean, and one shouldn't pollute the sea. Ho Chi Minh here has already saved my life."

"Who?"

"See?" said Chien. "Terrible student. Never learned any Chinese. All he ever wanted to do was sleep with that girl." He turned to Trinh. "But I have to tell you, she turned out very nice."

"You're talking about my father and mother," said Trinh wearily.

Paul introduced Trinh to Nguyen Sinh Cuong, and sudden recognition spread over Nguyen's face. "I understand now. I know about your family. We all know about the great Prince Ahn. And your father, too, but he was wrong to support the monarchy."

"I know," said Trinh, "but he's changed his mind."

"It's too late. The French aren't going to be defeated for a long time—until I return."

"Oh," said Trinh coolly. "Are we going to have to wait for you?"

"Yes," he said matter-of-factly. He bowed to Chien and extended his hand to Paul. "I hope you have a good journey."

"Thank you. I hope we meet again."

"I'm sure we shall."

Chien studied them both thoughtfully, then said unhappily, "I'm afraid you will."

Nguyen nodded curtly to Trinh, then walked off.

"What a presumptuous, obnoxious ass," said Trinh as he watched the figure disappear. "Who was he?"

"Who he said he was," answered Chien. "Now, help me back. I need to relieve myself."

Andre and Catherine had come out on deck. "I have to say good-bye," Andre said. "I must find lodgings for the old man."

"Will you promise to visit me in Paris?"

"I'll think about it seriously. I promise that much."

"It's not too late for us, Andre. We could manage a few happy years."

He took her hand and kissed it.

She laughed. "Remember when you almost knocked me down?"

"You were the first woman I kissed."

"Wouldn't it be nice if I were someday to be the last?" She pressed his cheeks with her own. "Good-bye, my dear Andre."

He bowed, then went down the gangplank and caught up with the others before they reached the carriage. "Thank you for being so patient. We had a very good visit. I think you're making the right decision, Paul. You're going to have a wonderful time in Paris."

"It won't be forever; I'll be back soon."

"Maybe I'll go see you there. She's very persuasive." He smiled. "She always was. Would you like to meet her, Trinh?"

Trinh saw her at the railing, an elegant white-haired woman, ramrod straight, looking very willful. He turned away. "No, thank you."

"I should be going," said Paul. He directed the coachman to bring his luggage to the ship; then he embraced Chien.

"How do I say good-bye?" he asked.

"Is it forever?"

Paul held the old man tightly. "Yes. I certainly love you. Thank you for teaching me, and helping me, and for saving me that day in the jungle, and . . . for everything." He pulled away, and wiped at his eyes.

"I was going to be brave and hard about all this." He clasped Trinh. "Be careful, brother," he said.

"Come back," whispered Trinh. "We'll still fight together someday."

Paul broke away. "I'd better go before I change my mind. I didn't know it was going to be so hard to say good-bye."

Andre put his arm around his shoulder and walked him toward the ship. "I wish I had some wise words for you, but I don't. Just be a good man, Paul. That'll be enough; it'll see you through."

They embraced; then Paul said hoarsely, "Good-bye, Grandfather," and he went up the gangplank.

Andre watched him disappear into the ship, then reappear on deck beside Catherine. They hugged one another; then they waved down on him. He raised his hand.

They went inside, and he stood alone on the pier, but then Chien was at his side.

"Well, Master Chien, it's ending like it began. The ship brought me forty years ago, and now its taking away my grandson. Nothing's changed."

"Oh, no," said the old man. "Everything's changed." He opened his hands to the air about him. "The dragons are gone. And there are no more gods. And no more emperors."

Andre smiled. "What does that have to do with me?"

Chien's blurred gaze took in the harbor scene. He shook his head somewhat sadly. "You and your ships brought us this world without dragons and gods and emperors. You brought us a world only of men."

"Is that so bad?" asked Andre, but he knew the answer even before Chien spoke it.

The old man stood still, silent, and almost elemental, Andre thought. At last he said, "I liked it better when there were dragons."

He raised his head slightly, and Andre was sure that he could see perfectly. His voice and manner were strong, his eyes clear and prophetic. "But dragons are immortal," he said. "They'll return."

Then he put his hand on Andre's arm for support and began to shuffle away.

About the Author

A grauduate of Duke University, Michael Peterson attended the University of North Carolina Law School, after which he received a job in Washington, D.C. working on defense contracts for the government. As a federal employee, Mr. Peterson spent much time in Vietnam, and in 1968 he joined the Marines—only to be shipped back to Vietnam as a soldier. Upon returning to the United States, Mr. Peterson enrolled in Duke University on the G.I. bill to study English and writing. He lives in West Germany with his wife and two children.